S0-BIA-677

The Pearl Brooch

The Celtic Brooch Series, Book 9

Katherine Lowry Logan

COPYRIGHT PAGE

All rights reserved. No part of this book may be used or reproduced in any manner whatsoever without written permission of the author, except in the case of brief quotations embedded in critical articles or reviews.

This is a work of fiction. Names, characters, places, and incidents are the product of the author's imagination, or are used fictitiously, and any resemblance to actual persons living or dead, business establishments, events, or locales is entirely coincidental.

An original work by Katherine Lowry Logan. *The Pearl Brooch* copyright © 2019 by Katherine Lowry Logan

Print Edition

Website: www.katherinellogan.com

Editor: Faith Freewoman
Virtual Assistant and Story Development Consultant: Annette Glahn
Studio pictured on the cover: Studio d'Arte Toscanella, Owner and Artist Lukas Brändli #firenze
Willow Oak illustration—pencil on paper—by Lukas Brändli
Cover Design by Damonza
Interior design by BB eBooks

THE CELTIC BROOCH SERIES

CAST OF CHARACTERS

Alphabetical Order

1. Bonnard, Marguerite: Sophia's French maid and companion, seamstress

2. David, Jacques-Louis: French painter, supporter of French Revolution

3. Digby, Seamus (present-time): deceased grandfather of Sophia Orsini, solicitor in Edinburgh, Scotland (first mentioned in *The Sapphire Brooch*)

4. Digby, Seamus (1700s): solicitor in Richmond, Representative in Virginia House of Delegates, ancestor of the mysterious Mr. Digby

5. Fraser, Blane Allen: son of JL and Kevin Fraser, grandson of Elliott Fraser and Meredith Montgomery, grandson of Pops O'Grady, brother of Austin O'Grady and Lawrence

6. Fraser, Elliott: Chairman of the Board of the MacKlenna Corporation, husband of Meredith Montgomery, father of James Cullen Fraser and Kevin Allen Fraser, grandfather of Blane and Lawrence, former equine vet (first appeared in *The Ruby Brooch*)

7. Fraser, James Cullen: son of Meredith Montgomery and Elliott Fraser (first appeared in *The Last MacKlenna*)

8. Fraser, Jenny "JL" Lynn: former NYPD detective, VP of Development and Operations MacKlenna Corporation, wife of Kevin Allen Fraser, mother of Austin O'Grady, mother of Blane and Lawrence Fraser, sister of Connor, Patrick "Rick", Shane, and Jeff O'Grady, daughter of Retired Deputy Chief Lawrence "Pops" O'Grady (first appeared in *The Broken Brooch*)

9. Fraser, Kevin: husband of JL O'Grady, CFO for MacKlenna Corporation, biological son of Elliott Fraser, brother of James

Cullen Fraser, father of Blane and Lawrence (first appeared in *The Last MacKlenna*)

10. Fraser, Lawrence "Lance" Paul: newborn son of JL and Kevin Fraser, grandson of Elliott Fraser and Meredith Montgomery, grandson of Lawrence "Pops" O'Grady, brother of Austin and Blane

11. Grant, Amber: wife of Daniel Grant, mother of Heather, stepmother of Noah, sister of Olivia Kelly O'Grady, daughter of Matthew and Elizabeth Kelly, mining lawyer, amateur paleontologist, gourmet cook (first appeared in *The Amber Brooch*)

12. Grant, Daniel: husband of Amber Kelly Grant, father of Noah and Heather, former Pinkerton agent, former Union cavalry officer, member of President Lincoln's security detail during the Civil War (first appeared in *The Amber Brooch*)

13. Grant, Noah: son of Daniel and Amber Grant (first appeared in *The Amber Brooch*)

14. Hemings, Sally: Thomas Jefferson's enslaved maid, half-sister of his late wife

15. Jefferson, Martha "Patsy": Thomas Jefferson's older daughter

16. Jefferson, Maria "Polly": Thomas Jefferson's younger daughter

17. Jefferson, Thomas: Ambassador to France, Secretary of State, sage of Monticello

18. Kelly, Elizabeth: mother of Amber and Olivia, grandmother of Noah and Heather Grant, grandmother of Elizabeth "Betsy" O'Grady, lawyer (first appeared in *The Amber Brooch*)

19. Kelly, Matthew "Matt": father of Amber and Olivia, grandfather of Noah and Heather Grant, grandmother of Elizabeth "Betsy" O'Grady lawyer (first appeared in *The Amber Brooch*)

20. Lafayette, Marquis de: French aristocrat and military officer who fought in the American Revolutionary War and in the French Revolution

21. MacKlenna, James Thomas: land owner, Representative in Virginia House of Delegates, father of James Thomas Sean MacKlenna (first mentioned in *The Ruby Brooch*)

22. Mallory, Amy: wife of Jack Mallory, mother of Patrick (adopted) and Margaret Ann, former Olympian, ESPN baseball analyst (first mentioned in *The Broken Brooch*)

23. Mallory, Carlton Jackson "Jack": husband of Amy Spalding Mallory, father of Patrick (adopted) and Margaret Ann, brother of Charlotte Mallory, New York Times best-selling author (first appeared in *The Sapphire Brooch*)

24. Mallory, Charlotte: surgeon, wife of Braham McCabe and mother of Lincoln, Kitherina, and Amelia Rose, sister of Jack Mallory (first appeared in *The Sapphire Brooch*)

25. Mallory, General: Jack's ancestor

26. Mallory, Mrs: wife of General Mallory

27. Mallory, Patrick: adopted son of Jack and Amy Mallory (first appeared in *The Diamond Brooch* as Patrick Wilson)

28. McBain, David: veteran, author, President of MacKlenna Corporation, husband of Kenzie McBain, father of Henry, Robbie, Laurie Wallis, Alicyn, and Rebecca (first appeared in *The Last MacKlenna*)

29. McBain, Kenzie: veteran, West Point graduate, MacKlenna Corporation attorney, wife of David McBain, mother of Henry, Robbie, Laurie Wallis, Alicyn, and Rebecca (first appeared in *The Emerald Brooch*)

30. McBain, Henry and Robbie: twin sons of David and Kenzie McBain (first appeared in *The Broken Brooch*)

31. McCabe, Braham: former Union cavalry officer, lawyer, senator, husband of Charlotte Mallory and father of Lincoln, Kitherina, and Amelia Rose, Jack Mallory's brother-in-law, Kit MacKlenna Montgomery's first cousin (first appeared in *The Ruby Brooch*)

32. McCabe, Lincoln: son of Braham McCabe and Charlotte Mallory (first appeared in *The Sapphire Brooch*)

33. Montgomery, Cullen: lawyer, author, founder of Montgomery Winery, husband of Kit MacKlenna Montgomery (first appeared in *The Ruby Brooch*)

34. Montgomery, Kit MacKlenna: founder of Montgomery Winery, wife of Cullen Montgomery, goddaughter of Elliott Fraser, guardian of Emily Duffy (first appeared in *The Ruby Brooch*)

35. Montgomery, Meredith: owner of Montgomery Winery, wife of Elliott Fraser and mother of James Cullen Fraser, grandmother of Blane and Lawrence Fraser, breast cancer survivor (first appeared in *The Last MacKlenna*)

36. Moretti, Gabriele "Gabe": General manager at Montgomery Winery in Tuscany (first appeared in *The Diamond Brooch*)

37. O'Grady, Austin: son of JL O'Grady Fraser, brother of Blane and Lawrence Fraser, drafted by the Cavaliers (first appeared in *The Broken Brooch*)

38. O'Grady, Connor: former NYPD detective, Vice President of Global Security for MacKlenna Corporation, husband of Olivia Kelly O'Grady, father of Elizabeth "Betsy", brother of JL Fraser, Shane, Rick, and Jeff O'Grady, son of Retired Deputy Chief Lawrence "Pops" O'Grady (first appeared in *The Broken Brooch*)

39. O'Grady, Jeffrey "Jeff": former NYPD detective, lawyer for MacKlenna Corporation, husband of Julie O'Grady, brother of JL, Shane, Patrick, and Connor O'Grady, son of Retired Deputy Chief Lawrence "Pops" O'Grady (first appeared in *The Broken Brooch*)

40. O'Grady, Julie: wife of Jeffrey O'Grady (first mentioned in *The Broken Brooch*)

41. O'Grady, Olivia Allison: wife of Connor O'Grady, mother of Elizabeth "Betsy", older sister of Amber Kelly Grant, daughter of Matthew and Elizabeth Kelly, Realtor, lawyer (first mentioned in *The Diamond Brooch*)

42. O'Grady, Patrick "Rick": Marine, former NYPD detective, brother of JL, Connor, Shane, and Jeff, marketing director of Montgomery Winery, son of Retired Deputy Chief Lawrence "Pops" O'Grady (first appeared in *The Broken Brooch*)

43. O'Grady, Shane: Director of Global Security for MacKlenna Corporation, brother of JL, Connor, and Jeff O'Grady, son of Retired Deputy Chief Lawrence "Pops" O'Grady (first appeared in *The Broken Brooch*)

44. Orsini, Sophia Frances: painter, art instructor, granddaughter of Seamus Digby

45. Parrino, Peter "Pete" Francis: former NYPD detective, VP of Global Security for MacKlenna Corporation, JL O'Grady's former NYPD partner (first appeared in *The Broken Brooch*)

46. Monsieur Petit: Jefferson's butler in Paris

47. Ricci, Isabella: granddaughter of Maria Ricci (first appeared in *The Diamond Brooch*)

48. Ricci, Maria: companion of Lawrence "Pops" O'Grady (first appeared in *The Diamond Brooch*)

49. Short, William: Thomas Jefferson's secretary

50. Watin, Léopold: 18th century French painter and color merchant

1

Florence, Italy—Sophia

ARTIST SOPHIA ORSINI'S reproduction of the *Mona Lisa* had the same enigmatic smile that made the original oil the most famous painting in the world. But was the *Mona Lisa* special because people believed her to be, or was there some other quality that made her fame inevitable?

As of six years ago, Sophia no longer wondered. There was no other artist in the world who could have rendered a work of art so skillfully and with such controlled majesty as the original Renaissance Man, Leonardo da Vinci. He was a man born with infinite grace, talent, beauty, and intelligence, and the most lovable and generous man Sophia had ever met.

With one exception—Pete Parrino.

Their annulment when she was seventeen left her full of regrets, and even after twenty years she was still berating herself for not fighting for him, and heartbroken because he didn't fight for her.

Two emotions about the same thing—lost love.

Now, twirling a paintbrush back and forth between finger and thumb, she critically evaluated her painting's texture and brushwork. Did she get it right this time? While she was mentally comparing her first attempt at recreating a masterpiece with this painting, her phone rang. She glanced at the caller ID and gave a resigned laugh.

Setting her palette aside, she answered the call. *"Pronto."*

"You don't have time to laugh. You should be finishing my painting," her client Ivan Bianchi said.

"I am," she said. "I have a couple more things to do, then I'll put her aside to dry while I'm on holiday."

"She can dry at my house as easily as she can dry at the studio."

"If you want to risk smudging the portrait, come pick her up."

His heavy sigh came through the phone. "I'm out of town and won't be back until you return."

"Two weeks from tomorrow, Ivan. I'll be here, tanned and rested. But even then, the painting won't be completely dry."

"I'll be careful. *Ciao a presto.*"

She laughed again and hung up.

This was the fourth painting Ivan had commissioned. Their business relationship got off to a rocky start because he couldn't keep his hands to himself, but he finally got the message she didn't mix business with pleasure, and he wanted the painting more than he wanted Sophia. After that he kept his hands in his pockets and only pulled them out to pay her. And he paid well.

The techniques she learned from Leonardo, and the other Old Masters, improved the quality of her paintings to such an extent that her work routinely sold in the six-figure range. This painting was no exception. Combining her talent with a strong business model, she reached thriving artist status four years ago and was now at full sustainability.

Ivan's commission had come at an opportune time, and the down payment was financing her upcoming holiday. Her annual adventures weren't cheap. Not only did they require months of planning and extensive research, but also a significant cash outlay. While she'd budgeted for the trip, the fabrics and embellishments for her dress were more expensive than other period-correct ensembles she made in the past. And the wholesaler where she previously bought her gemstones and pearls was out of business, forcing her to pay full price for white South Sea pearls. The plan was to sell the pearls to pay her living expenses in Paris. The diamonds were for emergencies.

There was one last thing she needed to do with her *Mona Lisa* before leaving it on the easel to dry in her climate-controlled studio.

She tipped the brush in the black paint on her palette and signed her John Hancock—S.F. Orsini—at the bottom right-hand corner. Once she was finished with a painting, she always signed it. It was her way of saying, "This piece is complete, don't rework it."

And this one was complete, finally.

On the back of the portrait, she added the date, location, and Ivan's name on the bottom left-hand corner.

The timer beeped, and she glanced at the clock on the wall. It was five o'clock. She went to lock the studio's front door and lower the automatic security gate, but before she could turn the lock, she was startled by the appearance of two of her pre-teen art students, sisters Emma and Greta Russo.

"What a wonderful surprise," Sophia said. "What brings you two out on a hot Friday afternoon?"

The giddy girls bounced on the balls of their feet. Even in class, keeping them still was a challenge. "Miss Sophia, we couldn't let you leave town without bringing you a bag of *ciambelle*," Emma said.

"We thought you'd want some snacks while you're traveling," Greta said.

Sophia gave both girls a big hug. "I love your nonna's *ciambelle*. What a treat." She peeked inside the bag. "Yum. I might eat them all tonight."

"You have to save them for the train…or plane," Greta said, obviously fishing for information.

"Or maybe you're driving," Emma added.

Sophia put her finger to her lips. "I never give any hints about my holiday." Nobody would believe her anyway.

They giggled. "We know. We were just hoping something would slip out."

Emma craned her neck to see inside the studio. "Did you finish her? Can we see?"

"Yes, I finished. And yes, you can see." Sophia stood aside, holding the door, and let the budding artists in to view what she had created.

Emma and Greta stood in front of the painting, mouths agape. "She's exquisite," Emma said.

"Will we ever be able to paint like this?" Greta asked.

Sophia sat on her stool. The girls wouldn't dare touch the painting, but Sophia was overprotective, and until she released the portrait to Ivan, she would continue to be. "If you practice, practice—"

"And practice," Emma said. "We're going to sketch every day while you're gone."

"When I get back, you'll have to come over and show me your work so I don't have to wait until class starts in September. Now give me a hug. I've got a ton of stuff to do before I leave."

They hugged her, and she ushered them to the door. "Have fun, Miss Sophia, and don't eat the *ciambelle* until you're on your holiday," Emma said.

Sophia waved goodbye. Five seconds later, the girls were distracted by their phones. Which was why Sophia required all electronic devices to be turned off during class. But she had the best students. They were talented and creative, and she loved them all. Of course she loved kids, whether they were her students or not.

When Emma and Greta disappeared around the corner, Sophia checked the sidewalk in both directions to make sure no one else was coming to surprise her. The coast was clear. She locked the door, flipped the BUSINESS OPEN sign to CLOSED, and lowered the automatic security gate. When she heard the lock click, she sashayed into the back room to turn on the alarm, dropping a few bars.

"Loveable artist walking Florence / Rappin' to the paint in a Paris state of mind / Stressful, adventure, old, like a Time / Beyond the walls of travel, life is defined / A long ago jewelry is quite the foolery / Yea, yaz / In a Paris state of mind."

Her rapping wasn't any better than her singing, but nobody could hear her.

The alarm-activated light came on, and the LCD screen blinked.

The cameras cycled through the system, showing views of the front of the building, the studio, the storeroom, all the rooms in the apartment, the third-floor storage, and the backyard. It might be an unpretentious studio on the cobblestoned Via Toscanella, but her building had a state-of-the-art security system. The windows and doors were now secured, and the IR break beam in the walk-in safe was activated. A handheld remote allowed her to deactivate a single door to allow entry in the event of an emergency or an after-hours visitor. Her jewelry and paintings couldn't be any safer if they were stored in the Accademia Gallery. Well, maybe that was an exaggeration, but close enough.

Her studio was now officially closed, locked, and alarmed for the next two weeks.

She mounted the stairs to the apartment, where she toed off her shoes and left them on the top step. The building's northern exposure had sold her on the location for a studio, but the frescoed walls in the upstairs living room sealed the deal. She'd remodeled the kitchen in what she called a sleek Tuscan style, and turned three bedrooms into two master suites plus a small room for her sewing machine and desktop computer.

The door to that room stood ajar, with fabric remnants scattered on the floor along with a pillow and blanket. She had fallen asleep while adding the finishing touches to her blue-green wool and silk reversible traveling dress, made from a flame-retardant and stain-resistant fabric. A white blouse to wear under the waistcoat was folded over the ironing board, and a large felt hat trimmed with teal moiré ribbon, an antique silver buckle, and an ostrich feather plume sat atop her sewing mannequin's narrow shoulders.

Instead of confronting the mess, she went to the kitchen, looking forward to finishing the Florentine steak and roasted vegetables she had for lunch. The waiter at the restaurant down the street had kindly boxed up the leftovers. But when she looked in the refrigerator, the box wasn't there.

"Dang. I left it at the restaurant." What was she going to eat now? The *ciambelle*? While she was looking in her empty refrigerator, her phone rang. The call was from Lukas, owner of the Osteria Toscanella.

"*Pronto.*"

"Sophia, dear. It's your dinnertime and you forgot your leftovers. I'm bringing you something to eat. Open the back door."

"You don't need to do that. I can eat something out of the freezer."

"You hate frozen food. Besides, I want to see your *Mona Lisa* before Ivan carries her away."

"I'll buzz the door open." She waited a couple of minutes before unlocking the door with the remote. Then she opened a bottle of wine and poured two glasses. A light blinked on the remote, indicating the back door opened. When she didn't hear Lukas on the steps, she went to the apartment door. "Are you coming up?"

"In a minute."

She knew what that meant. He was looking at the painting. She carried the glasses of wine down to meet him.

He was standing in front of the *Mona Lisa*. "This is extraordinary." He kissed Sophia's cheeks and exchanged the carryout box for a glass of wine.

"Coming from another artist, that means the world to me."

"This is much better than your first attempt." He sipped his wine. "If you painted in the eighteenth century, they would consider you one of the Old Masters."

"I'd much rather copy them than be a contemporary, but thank you."

"I'm surprised Ivan's not here to pick it up."

She sat on her stool and placed the carryout box on the worktable. "If he was in town, he would be."

Lukas's attention moved from the painting to Sophia. "You look tired. I know July is a hard month for you."

"It gets a little easier every year."

He put an arm around her and hugged her to his side. He was her gentle giant—handsome, thoughtful, and twenty years older. To change the subject, she said, "Thanks for dinner. If I'd been forced to eat frozen food, I might have thrown up. I get so anxious before leaving on a holiday."

"If I was going off to meet a married lover, I'd be anxious too."

She spit out wine in a peal of laughter. The red wine hit the paint-splattered floor and blended right in. "Where in the world did that come from?"

Lukas grabbed paper towels and wiped up the wine. "It's the same two weeks every year. You never say where you're going, or even how you're getting there. It has to be a married lover."

"Oh, Lukas…" This time she burst out in a fit of good-natured laughter and slipped off the stool, somehow managing not to fall on her butt or spill the rest of her wine. When she finally got herself under control, she wiped her eyes and safely sipped again. "You can't imagine how wrong you are. Besides, you'll always be the second love of my life."

And there it was, just like that, the knot of pain in her chest. While it had become smaller over time, it never disappeared. It was a chronic illness—a permanent condition she managed to control in the privacy of her brain.

And the laughter stopped.

Lukas threw the paper towels into the trash. "Go to America and find him. This has gone on way too long. Every summer from the middle of June to the middle of July you go through this."

"I can't. I don't want to know he's happily married with kids who look like him and a wife pregnant with another one."

"If you're not going to America to look for him, then whatever you do, be careful out there."

"I will." She changed the subject. "What about your mom? You haven't mentioned her lately. Is she doing better?"

He shook his head. "If she doesn't improve, I'll have to go to Naples for a few months and let my partner manage the restaurant."

"Stefano will do a good job. If there's anything I can do, just ask."

"You can be careful and not take any risks." He finished his wine, set the glass on the work table, and glanced up at the clock.

"I've got to go. There's a large group of Americans doing a food and wine tour, and I'm providing the main course."

"That's such good advertising for the restaurant. I hope they'll all come back for another meal." She walked him to the rear door and he kissed her cheeks again.

"I worry so much about you. Be extra-careful this year. Weird things have been happening to people I know, and I don't want you to be one of them."

She placed her hands on his muscular back and pushed him toward the door. "Go, before I change my mind and cancel my trip to stay home and read. How boring would that be?"

"It might be boring, but it would be safer." He stopped and turned around, taking her hands in his. "I have two tickets next month for a performance of *The Nullafacente* at the Teatro Niccolini. Will you join me?"

"If you're here, I'd love to go. It's been ages since I've seen a good play, but if you leave town, give the tickets to Stefano."

"I'll do that. I read a quote about the play in an advertisement. The director said, 'This work is a lie, but lying, sometimes, if observed well, brings us closer to the truth.'"

"Hmm. I'll have to think about that one." She opened the door. "*Ciao caro.* I'll see you in two weeks, or whenever…" She locked the door behind him. Lukas was such a good friend, but his worrying stressed her out. She'd have to remember to light a candle for his mother.

When she returned to the kitchen with the boxed dinner, she set the table with her grandmother's china. Dining at home or in a restaurant, according to Nonna, was a culinary delight that should never be rushed or distracted by phones or TVs.

After dinner, she carried her second glass of wine into the sewing room and pulled a chair up to the desk. The utility bills for her grandfather's old law office in Edinburgh needed to be paid for another six months. Sophia visited there once after her grandmother died, just to see the place, which was located a block off the Royal Mile. The two-room office was strewn with books and files and looked like a lawyer left work one day and never returned. And that's exactly what had happened when her grandfather dropped dead from a heart attack. If she could find a buyer, she'd sell it.

After paying the utility bills online, she responded to an email from a potential client, who would have to wait until she returned to discuss the project. Then she sent her accountant notice that she was going out of town. Her CPA had a copy of her will, a set of keys, and security codes to the building. If after six months, Sophia didn't return, the CPA had instructions to put all assets into a trust for one year. If she didn't return after that year, the instructions were to liquidate all assets pursuant to the terms of her will.

With business out of the way, she unlocked the safe under the desk. Inside were velvet pouches holding her collection of diamonds and pearls, along with a small jewelry box, a gift from her grandmother. Folded into the box's lid was a fragile letter written by James MacKlenna following the death of his father in 1625. She didn't open the letter. She already knew the contents by heart.

Sewn into the box's velvet lining were embroidered designs of four Celtic brooches, identical except for the gemstones in the center of each brooch. The first brooch had a sapphire, the second an emerald, the third a diamond. There was no sapphire, emerald, or diamond in the box, but there was an antique pearl brooch.

On her deathbed, Nonna had pressed the brooch into Sophia's hand and made her promise to guard it well. Now that Sophia understood its secrets, she was determined to do as Nonna had asked, and as James MacKlenna had instructed. If the Keeper referred to in the letter had already returned, and the sapphire, emerald, and diamond brooches had found their way to him, then so would her pearl.

Sophia turned her brooch over in her hand. It was already warm, as if it knew she would soon call upon its magic. Her first time-slip was an accident. As soon as she sounded out the Gaelic words in the inscription on the pearl, the fog had carried her back in time to Florence in the year 1504. She spent two days living in absolute terror until she bumped into Leonardo da Vinci chasing butterflies.

Was she scared now? Of course, but being scared wasn't going to stop her from going back to Paris in the year 1786. She knew everything about the Court of King Louis XVI and Queen Marie Antoinette. And she'd studied the life and work of the queen's official portraitist, Élisabeth Vigée Le Brun, the artist she intended to commission.

Sophia set the brooch back inside the jewelry box and returned it to the safe. The apartment was so well-protected she could have left the brooch on the windowsill, but she was pragmatic, and never tempted fate. She laughed at the ridiculous thought.

If slipping through time wasn't tempting fate, then, good grief what was?

She straightened up the sewing room and organized the few clothes she was taking with her. Satisfied that she'd done everything she could for the night, she climbed into bed and began to visualize what she would do when she woke up: Tai Chi, dress, say the magic words, arrive in Paris, trade a pearl or two for a few thousand livres, make living arrangements, and…

Her eyelids drifted shut.

When the alarm sounded the next morning, Sophia popped out of bed. Her right knee had been bothering her recently, but it wasn't bad enough to skip her daily Tai Chi practice, although she did cut her two-hour workout down to an hour.

Later she stood in front of the full-length mirror, adjusting her ostrich plume hat atop a curly wig with blonde ringlets framing her face to her shoulders, then mixing with her natural hair to cascade down her back. A quick turn this way and that, and she smiled. It truly was a gorgeous ensemble.

Satisfied with her appearance, she opened the safe again and removed the brooch and pouches of diamonds and pearls. She added an antique gold and platinum necklace and earbobs with pearls and gemstones to a separate pouch. A girl always needed extra jewelry, especially if she scored an audience with the king or queen.

The jewelry pouches were tucked into one of the deep pockets sewn into her skirt, along with a small velvet bag filled with a toothbrush, dental floss, antibiotics, pain relievers, and water purifying tablets. An extra chemise and a Tai Chi outfit for morning workouts were folded into teeny-tiny squares and added to the skirt's other hidden pocket.

She picked up the pearl brooch and almost dropped it. The pearl seemed hotter than usual. She tossed the brooch back and forth between her hands. It was more fired up than she was at the idea of going through the fog—always a frightening experience. No matter how often she jumped aboard the twisting, turning roller-coaster and traveled at warp speed with dips and banked turns, she always wanted off, but nothing could stop the magic.

With the tip of her fingernail, she opened the large pearl in the center of the brooch. Without the slightest hesitation, she recited the inscription engraved there: *"Chan ann le tìm no àite a bhios sinn a' tomhais an' gaol ach 's ann le neart anama."*

The air filled with the heavy fragrance of damp earth, and a thick veil of fog arose from the floor, flowing across the room, swirling and creeping up the walls. The atmospheric conditions were identical every time it appeared, and the effect was just as disorienting.

"Take me to Paris in the year 1786." As the fog settled over her, she closed her eyes and visualized the *Place de la Concorde* as it would have been, not as it looked today.

Within seconds she was strapped in and zipping along at full throttle, unable to prepare for the massive hang time in the middle of a loop, followed by a stop inside a tunnel that almost made her believe something had gone wrong before she was catapulted backward, climbing up into a massive loop again. The G force was so intense, she almost blacked out. That was the worst part. But it was quickly over, and she rolled to a gentle stop.

When she stepped out of the fog, she found herself surrounded by hundreds of farmers and laborers, timeworn and weary, who were yelling and shaking pitchforks in the air.

She shoved the brooch deep into her pocket and hid beneath the leafy branches of a chestnut tree while scanning the scene around her. Although the buildings, clothing, and streets all resembled the eighteenth-century paintings of Paris she'd seen, nothing in her research mentioned riots in 1786.

Nearby, a man stood atop a table waving a pistol. "Citizens, there's no time to lose. The dismissal of Necker is the death knell of a Saint Bartholomew for patriots! This very night, the Swiss and German battalions will emerge from the Champ de Mars to massacre us all. Only one recourse is left…to take arms."

Necker? Take arms? My God. What year is this?

2

Lexington, KY—Kevin

THE WEATHER FORECAST throughout the Southeast threatened hotter-than-hell temperatures. It was an unusual heat wave, even for Kentucky.

The newscaster claimed it was the last day. No one believed it. Eight o'clock in the morning, and you could already feel it in the air, an unfamiliar weight curling down on Kevin Fraser's vineyards at MacKlenna Farm. If the heat wave continued, they'd start worrying about retaining acidity in the grapes. The acidity would dip as sugar accumulated, and make the backbone of his fresh grapes shapeless, lacking in promise, and ultimately flawed.

But for the next two days he'd hold off worrying so he could enjoy the family get-together at Mallory Plantation in Richmond, Virginia.

Since his dad had the corporate jet in California, Kevin and his wife JL were flying his Cessna to Richmond. He was a private pilot with over fifteen hundred hours of flight time under his belt. He never took any chances, especially with his family on board, and never violated the FAA's bottle-to-throttle eight-hour abstention from alcohol rule. In fact, he obeyed all the rules all the time, without exception. He'd come close a time or two, but that was before he married JL, before she had their son Blane, and long before she got pregnant again.

He logged onto a flight-related blog to read the chatter. He'd listened to the local newscaster, but when he was flying he didn't rely solely on weather reports delivered in a studio by a newscaster with capped teeth and helmet hair standing in front of a green screen. He wanted to hear from pilots with firsthand information. As expected, nearly all the messages recently posted confirmed it was a perfect day to fly.

At Blue Grass Airport, Kevin filed a flight plan and went through the preflight check. It was so damn hot, his shirt was drenched, and the heat wilted everything green in the landscape and shimmered up from the tarmac.

JL came out of the hangar in her own petite, six-month pregnant atmosphere. You could still see the young girl in her walk. The one thing, even after a decade as a cop, she couldn't make over—her ballerina stroll, distinguished by her upright carriage, extended neck, and carefully turned-out feet. He'd seen teenage pictures of her with her telltale accessories: bottled water, Capezio labels, and a leotard-stuffed shoulder bag with slipper ribbons dangling. If they ever had a daughter, he could imagine her looking just like her mom.

JL was tapping on her phone with the long cord of her headphones fluttering in her wake. It was no wonder her headphones never lasted more than a year. And with wireless earbuds, she always lost either the left one or the right one.

"Sorry, I had to potty."

"Figured," he said, helping her up into the copilot's seat. She accidentally jabbed him in the chest with a small, pointy elbow, and he tangled his fingers in the cord, tugging the headphones halfway off her head.

"Are you trying to tear up my Beats?" She pulled them off the rest of the way and shoved the headphones with the cord bunched up into her flight bag.

"I don't have to, love. You do a fine job of it all by yourself." He rubbed his chest and made a mental note to add a new pair of headphones to his for-JL Christmas list.

After removing the chocks from the wheels, he climbed up into the cockpit, where JL was plugging in her aviation headset. Surprisingly, she treated them with more respect. A wide, proud grin replaced the sad, basset-hound look she had been wearing since waking up without a good-morning hug from their four-year-old.

"What's up?" he asked.

She flashed her phone. "Elliott just sent this picture of Blane stomping through the California vineyards."

Kevin enlarged the picture. "Look at him. He's copying Elliott's arrogant stance."

"Seriously? He's copying you. You stand the same way. You're both Elliott's clones. I hope little Lawrence"—she patted her belly—"copies Pops instead. His stance isn't arrogant."

"You're right about that. He carries himself as the mean ol' son of a bitch he was as Assistant Deputy Chief Lawrence O'Grady. I don't want people afraid of my kids."

"What? You'd rather people think they're assholes?"

"Dad and I aren't assholes."

"Well, at least *you* aren't."

To show her what a good guy he truly was, he clamped his hand over the back of her head and kissed her like his life depended on it. The kiss was hungry, hard, and over far too soon. God, he loved her. He reached over her and made sure the door was shut properly. "Buckle up, sweetheart."

She kissed him back with even more fervor, and he growled against her lips.

"I was hoping you wouldn't notice the belt." She pulled it under her belly and over her hips and adjusted the shoulder strap so it fit snugly between her breasts. When the tongue clicked into the buckle, she glanced up at him. "Satisfied?"

"Not in the least, babe. And you look sexy as hell in those skimpy white shorts." He loved the way her clothes hugged this and molded to that. The shorts and halter top looked damn good on her, but he loved her best with nothing on at all, riding him, her heavy breasts in his hands.

"You have no idea how uncomfortable this is."

He gave her an arch look. "The sexy shorts?"

She rolled her eyes. "The seat belt." An uncharacteristic dent appeared between her sleek eyebrows, which were a little darker than her brown hair these days, since her hair had turned almost bronze from walking in the Tuscan sun during May and June.

"I don't want you bouncing out of your seat if we hit turbulence. And don't try to unhook it when I'm not looking."

He turned his attention to the aircraft. After a call to flight service for his clearance, he taxied to the runway. But before the plane lifted off, he removed a laminated card from his pocket and tucked it into the corner of the instrument panel—his lucky charm. It was a quote attributed to Leonardo da Vinci: *"Once you have tasted flight, you will forever walk the earth with your eyes turned skyward, for there you have been, and there you will always long to return."*

Kevin could have written it. Other than when he was wrapped in JL's arms or hugging his son, there was no place he'd rather be, especially on glorious days like this.

The plane soared off the runway. He banked the aircraft and headed east toward Virginia and into an ocean of air. The Cessna, with its decks and rudder, its port and starboard, its logs and small library of aeronautical charts, flew toward a state whose history could be charted back to Jamestown, Thomas Jefferson's Monticello, and the fall of Richmond.

The flight was uneventful, and JL was asleep before the plane even left Blue Grass Airport's airspace. Not surprising, since she was up and down all night with heartburn. Being pregnant was harder on her this time, and she frequently swore this was the last one. He didn't believe it. She wanted a daughter, and so did he.

Now, as the plane descended on approach to the runway at Chesterfield County Airport in Richmond, she woke up, stretching. "That was a short flight."

"You missed some incredible views of the Shenandoah Valley."

"I've seen them all before. I'd rather arrive rested than awe-inspired."

"Now there's the cynic I love."

"What can I say?" She held up her hands. "Beneath all my carefully crafted cynicism, I'm really a romantic at heart."

He laughed, then turned his attention to landing the aircraft. For a perfect landing you had to fly a perfect pattern on approach. Airspeed was king. He didn't want to be too slow or too fast. He notified the tower. "Chesterfield traffic, 32 Alpha Charlie is turning left base, runway five, full stop at Chesterfield."

He was a bit high and needed to get down. But he decided not to add any more flaps, bringing the power back instead. He kept the nose down, nailing his airspeed. Ninety on downwind, eighty on base, seventy on final, slowing to sixty. It was a stabilized approach all the way to the ground.

Just before reaching the threshold, a sudden downburst of wind rocked the aircraft and the wheels hit the ground hard. JL screamed, grabbed the edge of the seat with one hand, the door with the other.

The plane bounced back into the air a few feet, and when it came down again the left gear collapsed, so the Cessna touched down only on the rear and right front wheels. The plane swerved and the left wing tipped toward the ground.

Kevin was hit with a surge of adrenaline. He could recover from this, but he could do nothing to reassure JL except bring the plane to a stop without killing them.

The plane skidded off the runway into an open field, and the wing dug into the grass and whipped the plane into a sharper left turn which he was powerless to correct. He muttered a string of obscenities, then stood on the brakes. They were useless. The impact must have severed the hydraulic line.

Operating on training and reflexes, he kept the plane from flipping over as it plowed through a chain-link fence and uprooted a post, which then slammed against the windshield and created a star break, obscuring his vision.

JL screamed again.

The plane hit a tree, the nose crumpled, and the tail tipped up before slamming back on the ground, hitting them with a double whammy, snapping Kevin's teeth together so hard he bit his tongue.

He tasted blood. His brain was rattled. But the plane had stopped, and it wasn't engulfed in flames.

They'd survived.

He found the master switch and killed the electrical power.

Then he looked over at his bride. A lump in his throat cut off his breath.

JL's white shorts were spotted with blood.

3

Paris (1789)—Sophia

T HE COLONNADES AND shops emptied as the mob, stinking of sweat and rotting teeth, raced into the streets with pitchforks and pruning hooks raised high in the air, yelling, *"Vive le roi. Vive Monsieur Necker, Vive le tiers état! Liberté."*

Long live liberty. Long live the third estate.

Sophia didn't have time for political demonstrations. She was on a tight schedule. If she didn't find Vigée Le Brun's studio and commission her portrait today, there wouldn't be enough time for the artist to complete the painting.

Her plan was to start her search at the Louvre. Any artist with an atelier there would know where to find Le Brun. But to get to the Louvre, Sophia had the daunting task of navigating through the throng of revolutionaries. She knew the rules of walking through crowds: stand straight, square her shoulders, and set her elbows at a defensive angle.

Sophia asked a woman pinning a cockade to her brown wool dress, *"Qu'est-ce que se passe, Madame?"*

"Le roi a embauché des étrangers pour détruire nos récoltes," the woman said.

The king hired foreigners to destroy our crops? That made absolutely no sense to Sophia.

"Nous devons nous défendre."

"Où va tout le monde?" Sophia asked.

The woman pointed. *"À l'Hôtel National des Invalides."*

"Quelle est la date aujourd'hui?" Sophia asked, but the woman looked at her oddly, then disappeared into the crush of rioters. Maybe she didn't know the date. All Sophia wanted was confirmation the year was 1786.

While she tried to figure out what was going on, hundreds of Parisians spilled out of narrow side streets, as if the gates of hell had been lifted and the hordes set loose. A fitful breeze exacerbated the stink of so many unwashed people in one place.

She was jostled, pushed, and compressed into a sea of filth and anger.

Going home and starting the adventure over would be the smart thing to do.

She reached into her pocket, surreptitiously pulled out the brooch, and lifted the pearl on its hinge. She turned slightly and adjusted her sleeve to hide it from those around her. Then she whispered the incantation, *"Chan ann le tìm no àite a bhios sinn a' tomhais an' gaol ach 's ann le neart anama."*

Nothing happened.

She said it again, a louder whisper this time, but still nothing. She rubbed the brooch, trying to warm the pearl. But there was no fog and no roller-coaster ride through the time warp. She gave it a third try. When nothing happened, fear reduced life to slow motion. It was a sure sign of insanity when she tried to do the same thing over and over but expected a different result.

The brooch was not going to take her home yet.

Shots rang out, and men yelled, *"Prendre les armes."*

White gunpower smoke burned her eyes. Good God. Weren't thousands of pitchforks and other makeshift weapons dangerous enough without bringing out the guns?

An unstoppable force with a destination in mind swept her along in the middle of the insanity. When the Hôtel National des Invalides came into view and thousands of peasants rushed the hospital to take possession of the guns stored there, a single overriding truth became obvious:

The mob was preparing to storm the Bastille. She didn't have to wonder about the date now. It was July 14, 1789.

Her fingers clenched around the brooch, something solid to keep her grounded. The stone had never been an unreliable partner before. It had always taken her to the exact place and time she commanded, and two weeks later returned her home.

Now, it was off by three years, and had abandoned her in the middle of a revolution for two frigging weeks. But it had brought her here and would take her home again. *Keep that in mind and stick to the plan.* The start of a revolution caused only a minor course adjustment. Vigée Le Brun was still in Paris. Sophia could still get her portrait painted.

All she had to do was escape thousands of enraged revolutionaries.

She shuffled forward. If she didn't keep moving, she'd be knocked down, run over, stomped on, and wouldn't survive the next hour, much less two weeks. There had to be a way to break free of the sardine-like mob packed shoulder to shoulder in the narrow street.

The city stank worse than sixteenth-century Florence. Open gutters clotted with waste ran along the middle of the streets. Even if she could, she didn't dare look down to see where she was stepping.

If the mob was on its way to the Bastille, then people were going to die. Just because she wasn't from this time didn't mean she was exempt from becoming a casualty of Bastille Day.

Time didn't stand still or move rapidly, either. It just existed in paralyzing madness. The horde swept her forward in an endless wave of anger and threats.

The rumor buzzing through the rabble said there was a trove of two hundred fifty barrels of gunpowder stored in the cellar of the Bastille. Sophia didn't know if it was true, but the mob certainly seemed to believe it. Should a spark reach the gunpowder, the

Bastille would be leveled, possibly killing everyone inside and out, including Sophia, stuck somewhere in the middle of the teeming horde.

The Bastille was razed around Bastille Day. But did it blow up, or was it demolished?

Another rumor reached her that Governor de Launay was surrendering. She didn't know who he was, but the idea of surrender was a positive sign. Then came another one—Monsieur de Corny had asked for a parlay. Again, a good step forward. No one wanted to shed French blood, but the revolutionaries were demanding the gunpowder, and the forces inside the Bastille were refusing to give it to them.

Parlay, please!

Then news reached them that the drawbridge to the first courtyard was breached. That excited the mob further, and the horde pushed forward. Then the second courtyard was taken as well, and the mob smelled victory.

As Sophia neared the second courtyard, Bastille defenders were taking positions on the roof, their muskets aimed at the throng.

A man shouted from the roof, "Withdraw or be fired upon."

Somebody near Sophia yelled, "He won't fire."

Sophia yelled, "They will. Get back!" Her voice was muffled by the crowd surging forward. People were going to be killed.

I've got to get out of here. Now.

But no matter where she turned, she couldn't find an opening.

The fortress had stood on the east side of Paris for four hundred years. And, today of all days, the crazed mob intended to raze it.

The order to fire was given, and the men on the roof fired their muskets. The heavy lead balls shredded the flesh, organs, and bones of the rioters. Screaming and moaning, they fell to the courtyard's paving stones, wounded and dying.

Shaking, Sophia ducked, as did others. The white smoke blinded her. The chaos was disorienting. The courtyard reverberated with the sounds of more gunshots and men barking orders. The barrage of gunfire momentarily shocked the mob, but the rioters gathered their forces and charged forward again, discharging their weapons at men on the roof, some hitting their targets. The second charge was met with another blistering volley of musket fire. This time the crowd fled farther back, leaving the second courtyard littered with corpses.

Sophia huddled with a group of women. Now would be the time to escape, but she would be noticed if she ran in the opposite direction, making her an easy mark.

How was she going to get out of this nightmare? When the rebel artillery moved forward to set up and take aim at the final draw-bridge, it created a small opening in the crowd.

This might be her chance.

She angled her way toward an open gate leading to a different section of the courtyard and a pathway out of the Bastille. Should she take it?

She who hesitates is lost. I know. I know, but...

The rebel artillery cannon fired. Rolling vibrations shuddered up through the rocky ground. The third courtyard was breached, the rebels charged forward, and their screams reached a deafening pitch.

She bolted, hurrying through the second courtyard and away from the battle. A strong wind carrying thick white smoke and the charcoal smell of gunpowder swirled around her. The drawbridge was only a few yards away.

Two men carrying cannonballs stepped out of nowhere, both wearing coarse trousers and jackets that hung loose on their skeleton-like frames. Their stares were unnerving. Using her peripheral vision, Sophia hunted for other avenues of escape. Forward was the only way out.

The man on the right straightened with arrogant confidence and pointed at Sophia. "There's de Launay's daughter trying to escape."

Sophia had a flashback to when she was attacked in Florence. She would *not* allow it to happen to her again.

Both men dropped the lead balls and advanced on her. Her instinct said to run. Her training said, *Prepare to fight.*

She balanced on both feet. "You've got the wrong girl. I'm not anybody's daughter."

She angled her body toward the men to present a narrower tar-get. The position was front-weighted, with the forward leg more bent than the back leg, preventing her from being pulled forward. *Damn skirts.*

Her moves confused the men, and they stopped. But one of them, the most insolent of the two, leered suggestively and elbowed his crony, nodding toward her.

"Come on," she said, bravely tempting them. She was tired of all this crap.

Then *wham.*

She was grabbed from behind, knocking off her hat and smash-ing the feather as the two men in front rushed forward.

Great. Three against one.

She pushed against the man holding her and kicked out, adding more force to compensate for the weight of her skirts. Amid a blur of blue, she slammed a foot into the crotch of one of the men. He dropped and rolled, groaning.

The other man had the reflexes of a rattlesnake. He yanked her skirts and twisted them around her legs, preventing her from kicking again. Then, out of pure meanness, he slapped her. If her clothes hadn't been so restrictive, her elbow would be smashing up against his nose with a sickening crunch.

With one man crushing her in his iron grip and the other lugging her legs, they rushed back to the rebels, yelling, "We found de Launay's daughter trying to escape."

Her emotions were scattered into twisting layers of fear, help-lessness, and outrage, but they quickly organized themselves into a steely determination to survive. "I'm not de Launay's daughter," she yelled in French. "You've got the wrong girl."

A brute of a man dragged a filthy mattress out of a room facing the courtyard. "Bring her here. We'll use her to get her father to surrender."

Hail Mary, full of grace, the Lord is with thee.

Several terrifying possibilities for how they intended to persuade de Launay came to mind. "I'm not his daughter."

Blessed art thou amongst women...

A lump lodged in her throat, threatening to cut off her air. *Stay calm.* Fear would only impair her judgment. And right now she needed all her senses razor-sharp and focused.

...and blessed is the fruit of thy womb, Jesus.

They threw her onto the mattress. She landed hard enough to bite the inside of her lip, and she tasted the tang of iron.

The taste of blood spiked her fighting spirit. With her legs free, she rolled off the other side. The man in the loose jacket raised his foot to kick her, and before she had even a split second to prepare, his boot crashed squarely into her sternum, expelling every bit of air from her lungs and sending a shock wave of pain through her. She sailed backward and rolled.

Holy Mary, Mother of God...

The weight of a man's foot on her back squashed her, pressing her face into the mattress, which smelled of sweat and body odor. Before she could even try to take a breath, he removed his foot and his powerful hands flipped her over, twisting her painfully and leaving her totally immobilized.

Another man appeared carrying a flaming branch. His muscular body strained the seams of his dirty black coat. He yelled, "De Launay! Open the gate or we'll burn your daughter." The makeshift torch was mere inches from the stuffing poking out of the torn mattress ticking.

...pray for us sinners now and at the hour of our death.

"Burn her. Burn her. Burn her," the bloodthirsty crowd chanted.

Pain lessened as air once again filled her lungs, but panic threatened to override every bit of her training. Her eyes never left the torch. If he dropped it, she wouldn't go up in flames all at once, since everything she wore was flame-retardant, but she could be badly burned.

She kept her eyes on the fire. The man's arm held steady above the mattress. If he let go, she'd roll toward the man who just kicked her, lift her skirts, and take out his legs with an explosive kick that would probably doom her, but she would not go quietly into the night. Not her. She'd take someone with her. And the man who kicked her was at the top of her list of candidates, followed by the jerk who slapped her.

A prison official ran to the edge of the roof to see what was happening. The earsplitting crack of a gun discharged behind her, and the man tumbled off the roof, landing only a few feet away, the cracking of his bones echoing the gunshot.

Nauseated, she was unable to pull her eyes away from the murdered man. This was madness, but staying calm was still her best defense.

Minute by minute, though, it was becoming increasingly more difficult to hold onto calm or sanity. The caustic smoke from the discharged weapon stuck in her throat and made her cough.

A man in tan breeches scrambled through the throng of rioters, yelling, "Stop this. It's disgusting."

He yanked the torch away from the man and doused it in a nearby barrel, where it sizzled and went out. Then he threw it on the ground. "We're not murderers." He looked down at Sophia, his eyes wide with anger.

She lay there preparing emotionally for a last fight. Her head was spinning, her chest was throbbing, and she was scared, for sure, but hopeful. Hope scared her most of all. If she lost it, she'd have nothing. In a wobbly voice, she said, "I'm not his daughter."

"Tais-toi," he said sharply, before squatting to pick her up as easily as deadlifting dumbbells. Then he whirled on the mob and roared. "We are not murderers."

The rioters instantly showered him with a volley of threats and insults. "Put her down or we'll burn you both."

They continued to shout and sneer, but they didn't attack him. Sophia curled into his arms, tucking in her skirts and making herself as small a target as possible while he wove his way through the crowd. The weight of her pockets assured her that her assets were still safe deep inside her skirt.

A man with a pitchfork pointed the tines at her rescuer, who shoved the peasant aside. "There's been enough killing. She's not de Launay's daughter."

No one else opposed her rescuer. He plowed through the crowd, passing the dead and wounded sprawled in the courtyard. Sickened, she looked away, but the images of their mutilated bodies were already seared on her brain. Ten years from now she'd still be able to sketch the scene exactly as it looked right then.

She hid her face in the cloth of her rescuer's dark blue jacket and mumbled the incantation.

"What'd you say?"

"It's a Gaelic saying about love." She glanced up at his dark eyes and wispy, curly hair. Despite the scar on his cheek, he had an open, trusting face. "I can walk now."

"Are you sure? They were rough with you."

She nodded. "I'm sure."

He gently set her on her feet, but she leaned against him for a moment until she got her balance. Her gut hurt, her back hurt, but nothing was broken, thank God.

"We have a way to go," he said.

She made a snap judgement while keeping a wary eye on the street. His appearance and kindness warranted her trust. "Where are we going?" If it was away from the Bastille, she didn't really care.

He glanced over his shoulder. "No one is following us, so I'll take you to my shop. You can clean up there, and then I'll see you safely home."

"Thank you for what you did. You took a terrible risk. They could have turned on you." She lifted her skirts above her ankles and sidestepped a nasty-looking stream of dirty water mixed with offal running down the middle of the street. Her nose twitched from the distinctive smell of hops from the breweries as well as the sickening stench from the tanneries.

"What they are doing is wrong," he said. "They're good people, but desperate. That's not who they are. They're hungry and angry, so they'll do things they wouldn't normally do."

"Then we should hurry in case they change their minds and

come after us to finish what they started."

The Bastille was behind them now. The din of the angry voices subsided, but the cannon and musket fire rattled the windows in the buildings they passed. On her left the flying buttresses of the apse of Notre-Dame Cathedral were visible. So they were walking toward the Louvre, which was where she wanted to go.

They turned into a rabbit warren of narrow medieval streets and a maze of shadowy alleys she wouldn't dare walk through at night, or even unaccompanied during the day. It was a place where criminals escaped through back passages and secret openings. The odors were both sweet and sour—sweet from the flower stalls lining the banks and sour from the sewers that dumped filth and disease into the Seine.

She stayed close to her courageous rescuer, sensing a gentle, quiet spirit resided in his soul. "Has there ever been a city with as many intricate passageways and blind alleys as Paris?"

"There's no other city like Paris," he said. "Its hundreds of streets are narrow, crowded, and full of stalls where Parisians hawk their wares. This street is usually so crowded a carriage can't get through."

They were north of the cathedral now. Dangling shop signs extended out over the street. If she didn't watch where she was going, she could easily hit her head. A bookstore advertised copies of *The Life and Opinions of Tristram Shandy, Gentleman* by Laurence Sterne. Above the shops, upper floors were built out over the streets, blocking the sunlight.

"The streets are so dark," she said.

"Only the first floor is taxed, so homes have larger upper floors. And it's better to stay very alert. Garbage and chamber pots are emptied directly into the streets."

"So we have to watch our feet to keep from stepping in human excrement while looking up to dodge flying garbage and the contents of chamber pots."

"And don't forget the animals roaming the streets, especially the wild boars."

Next to the bookstore was a glovemaker's shop, the door slightly ajar. A heavily pregnant woman leaned against a counter speaking to a customer. On the other side of the street was a dressmaker's shop where a seamstress was cutting fabric laid out on a table, a small child standing on a stool watching her. A jeweler's swinging sign creaked in the breeze. Under it, a man sat behind a worktable with a loupe held up to his eye.

Should she stop and trade a pearl or two? No, not yet. She didn't want her escort to know she carried valuables in her pockets.

"Why aren't these people out protesting? Can't they hear the screaming and gunshots?"

"They don't want to get involved," the man said.

"But you did."

"Politics is a curse I can't avoid." He stopped in front of a door painted a grayish-green with a handle covered with grimy finger-prints.

The hairs on the back of her neck stood on end. There was no dangling shop sign.

He had a kind face and even kinder eyes, but still… Would he bother to rescue her only to lure her to another kind of horror? If she kept her wits, she could handle a one-on-one unwanted encounter. The pleasant aromas—fresh-baked bread and coffee—wafting out into the street from a nearby shop also softened her unease.

He unlocked the door and pushed it open for her to enter. The space was filled with light from two large windows and the acrid smell of paint. She had entered an eighteenth-century atelier. Her alerted senses relaxed, as did the tightness in her neck and shoulders.

She moved slowly through his studio, her skirts swishing as she glided along one side and then the other. Ancient, styled urns, plaster models of female nudes, and swathes of fabric in varied, intense shades of green and blue cluttered the room.

Then she turned to a large painting resting on an easel, and what she saw there nearly overwhelmed her. It was the six-by-eight-foot *Portrait of Antoine-Laurent Lavoisier and His Wife.*

As Sophia approached the portrait, her heart thumped wildly. She'd seen the painting at the Metropolitan Museum of Art in New York. It was considered one of the most important portraits of the eighteenth century. The subject, Monsieur Lavoisier, was known as the founder of chemistry. It was brilliant.

She looked at her host, her jaw dropped. "You're Jacques-Louis David."

He smiled and bowed. "I'm honored you've heard of me."

"Not only heard of you, but I've seen several of your paintings. You're a brilliant painter, a premier artist, with a preference for the kind of strong light and shade used by followers of Caravaggio."

He poured water from a pitcher into a basin and handed it to her along with a linen towel. "You can wash away the dirt."

She saw her reflection and gasped. "Oh, my. I'm quite a sight." She removed the wig and shook out her natural hair. "If I devote a day to repairing this, I might be able to wear it again."

"I know a wigmaker who would repair it for you, and he wouldn't charge as much if I tell him I'm painting you."

In her planning, she'd considered the possibility Jacques-Louis David might be in Paris, but doubted her tight schedule would give her time to visit his atelier. "You want to paint me? Now *I'm* honored." She dipped a corner of the towel into the cool water and patted it against her mouth, cheeks, and forehead. "Of course I will sit for you. How could I not?"

Jacques-Louis David was not only one of the foremost painters of his time, but he was also an active politician. His intervention on her behalf made sense now.

She turned back to the painting.

"What do you think of it?" he asked.

"You're asking my opinion? Well, the dominant colors—red, black, blue, and white enhance the painting." She pointed her finger at Monsieur Lavoisier. "The black suit he's wearing takes on a luster from the whites and reds surrounding it, and the instruments here," she pointed again, "have a shimmering quality. The flask has the brilliance of the finest glass…" Then she pointed at the test tubes on the table. "They have a flat, dense look of thick glass. It's brilliant. Each instrument has its own distinct texture, and reflections play off their surfaces with a marvelous lightness."

He circled his hand, a signal to continue. She wasn't intentionally stroking his ego. He was extraordinarily talented, but if he wanted praise, after what he had done for her at the Bastille, he deserved all the heartfelt flattery she could dole out.

"You expressed your respect and affection for the Lavoisiers through an air of"—she lifted her hands in praise—"superior simplicity. This painting will be adored for centuries. You've created a masterpiece. But why isn't it on public display?"

"I finished it in December, but it wasn't permitted a public display at the Paris Salon for fear that an image of Lavoisier might provoke anti-aristocratic aggression from viewers." Jacques reached for her hands and studied them closely, rubbing his thumb over the callus on her middle finger. "Only a painter could see what you've described."

"I paint. But you, Monsieur David, are the master painter."

"You know my name, but what is yours? I know you're not de Launay's daughter."

"Sophia Orsini."

A look of surprise and delight blossomed over his features. "Orsini? I've heard of your family, Madonna. A very powerful one in Rome."

Leonardo had often called her Madonna as did Lukas, a polite form of address for a woman in Italian-speaking areas. "I'm in the Gravina line." In her time, the last existing line of Orsinis. "I've been in Florence studying painting, but I'm from America."

He picked up a few strands of her hair and held them in a beam of sunlight. "Your hair has the earthy, sun-brushed hue of wheat, and reminds me of the bounties of harvest time. I would paint you just as you are now."

He found a green ribbon and tied it around her hair, letting the curls drape over her shoulder. "I spent several years in Tuscany, and what I remember most is the sun beating down on cobblestones and reflecting off the faded yellow, blue, and green buildings, breezes rustling through the olive trees. The air rich and fragrant. Hills thickly covered with forests disappearing into the blue, hazy sky. Then, far off in the distance, are mountaintops sprinkled with snow."

She'd finished washing her face while he painted an extraordinary word picture, bringing Tuscany very much alive. "It takes a painter and poet to see what you've described."

"To achieve their goal, masterpieces must charm but also penetrate the soul, and make a deep impression on the part of the mind that's close to reality… The artist must have studied all the motives of mankind, and he must know nature thoroughly. In short, he must be a philosopher."

She wasn't a philosopher, but she was looking at one.

"How did you get involved in the events of the day?"

"Bad luck," she said. "I only just arrived in Paris for a visit. I hadn't even arranged for lodging before I was caught up in the mob. If you hadn't stepped forward, I'm afraid to think what would have happened to me."

"I don't know what they would have done to you, Madonna, but I knew I couldn't stand by and let it happen."

A man burst into the studio. "Jacques. *Mon Dieu,* you're here. They're taking de Launay to the Hôtel de Ville. They're planning to kill him." The man rushed to the back of the studio, opened a door, and disappeared. He returned almost instantly, strapping a sword belt and scabbard to his waist. "Hurry."

Jacques turned back to Sophia. "I must go. I'll take you to the American ambassador. You'll be safe there."

"We don't have much time. I have a hackney waiting," the man said.

Sophia and Jacques followed the man outside and climbed into the carriage. "What happened?" Jacques asked. "Did you see the governor taken prisoner?"

"When the Bastille was being ransacked, de Launay tried to blow up the gunpowder. If he'd succeeded, everyone inside and outside the Bastille would have been killed. Instead, they captured him. Second Lieutenant Elie and Pierre-Augustin Hulin are escorting de Launay to the Hôtel de Ville for the Revolutionary Committee to decide his fate. As bloodthirsty as the mob is, he might not make it there."

"They won't kill the governor," Jacques said.

"They're in a killing mood. One of the Bastille's defending soldiers stopped de Launay from blowing up the powder, but the mob was so crazed they didn't realize the soldier just saved their lives. They cut off his hands and hung him from a lamppost. If they get hold of de Launay, they'll do the same or worse."

The man's report churned her stomach. To keep from throwing up, she breathed deeply through her nose and exhaled through her mouth.

The man gave Sophia a cursory look, making her stomach even worse, while he addressed Jacques. "I heard you rescued a woman from the Bastille."

"Word travels fast in Paris," she said. "I wasn't in the Bastille. I mean, not as a prisoner. I was singled out. The mob believed I was de Launay's daughter."

"I've seen the governor's daughter." The man peered over Jacques's shoulder at her, the ghost of a smile on his face. "You couldn't be mistaken for her. Jacques couldn't even make her desirable on his canvas. But you, mademoiselle... your painting would be an immediate sensation at the Paris Salon."

"That's very kind of you to say." She held out her hand. "I'm Sophia Orsini."

He kissed the back of her fingers. "Léopold Watin at your service."

"Léopold's an excellent varnish maker and color merchant," Jacques said.

"No offense," she said, "but there's no longer an emphasis on the craftsmanship aspect of painting since painters stopped making their own paints."

"None taken," Watin said. "Although it isn't the case with

Jacques. He understands his materials and applies paint correctly."

"Because you're always standing at my elbow, whispering in my ear," Jacques said.

Watin responded to Jacques's comment in such excited French that she couldn't follow what he was saying. Even when they talked more slowly, the noise from the carriages rattling over the cobble-stones and vendors hawking their wares from wooden stalls made it difficult to hear the men's conversation.

She rested against the side of the enclosed carriage and gripped the door handle, her knuckles turning white. The river water was stirred by the air, and a breeze coming off the Seine carried the odor of gunpowder and the stink of the streets.

She gave herself over to her thoughts. What could she have done differently? And why had the brooch brought her to Paris at such an explosive time? What happened to her at the Bastille came back in a flood of terrifying memories, and she had to breathe deeply to restore her inner calm. Without the benefit of her Tai Chi training, the outcome today might have been quite different.

The carriage, caught in a tangle of traffic, rolled along slowly, squeezing past stalls encroaching into the narrow street, every one of them piled high with wares and produce. Watin stuck his head out the window. "We're almost there, but a cart is stopped sideways and impeding the flow of traffic. We'll have to walk the rest of the way." He rapped on the wall of the carriage. "We'll get out here." The carriage lurched to a stop, and Watin alighted with a sprightly hop. Jacques followed, then helped her down.

Guns were fired in the distance, but not in the direction of the Bastille. "Where's the gunfire coming from?"

"City Hall," Watin said. "We have to hurry."

She didn't want to go the Hôtel de Ville and be subjected to more violence, but she couldn't leave the safety of her companions.

The crowd was as thick, hot, and angry as it had been at the Bastille. There was a stink in the air as powerful as a physical blow. And it wasn't unwashed bodies or gunpowder. It was the rot of death.

Watin grasped her hand firmly and led the way through the crowd, inching closer to the front of the Hôtel de Ville and the entrance to City Hall. "Stay close." He didn't have to remind her, or Jacques either. He followed closely behind, hovering at her shoulder.

"What are they saying? I can't hear them," she said.

"They're debating how to kill de Launay."

She squeezed Watin's hand. "Haven't they had enough blood today?"

"It'll take more than killing to fill their empty bellies. I've got to stop this," Jacques said.

"You can't go out there," Watin said. "You deprived them of killing the woman they thought was de Launay's daughter. If you try to save him, they won't let you walk away this time."

She looked at the gaunt, angry faces of the men and women standing closest to her, all wearing red and blue cockades. If they knew the revolution would continue for the next ten years, would they be so eager to stand here today demanding justice?

Watin pointed. "The governor is being escorted to the front of City Hall. If he makes it through the front door it will be a miracle."

"There's de Launay," a man yelled. "The Revolutionary Committee will decide his fate."

The crowd shook their rakes and swords in the air, screaming.

"No. They won't do anything," another man yelled. "*We* need to decide his fate."

A man close by yelled, "Drag him behind a horse over the cobblestones. Make him suffer."

She turned away from the man, afraid he'd remember her from the Bastille. *Don't be ridiculous.* There were thousands gathered there. No one would remember her.

But if anyone did recognize her, they'd want to kill her too, and Jacques wouldn't be able to save her again. Needing a disguise, she untied her hair and let it fall over her shoulders and down her back. It wasn't much, but it was all she had. She shrank behind Watin, once again hiding in plain sight.

"Why do they dislike him so much?" she asked.

"He's a proud, stupid despot," Watin said. "The prisoners and soldiers hate him. If he'd been willing to compromise like the officers at the Invalides, he could have avoided this."

De Launay's eyes darted from one side of the mob to the other, and she felt sorry for him. He must have realized it was futile to fight, and his only hope was to avoid a lingering death. Showing a frantic burst of energy, he shouted, "Let me die." Then to hasten his own death, he kicked a man squarely in the genitals with his heavy riding boot. It was a brutal kick, and the victim screamed and writhed on the ground.

"Kill him. Kill him," the crowd chanted.

Sophia flashed back to the angry mob screaming for her death. The horror of what almost happened and the sickening reality playing out within feet of her was overwhelming.

"This isn't right." Jacques made a move to intervene, but Watin stopped him.

"Stay out of it."

The mob attacked de Launay viciously, piercing his body with pitchforks and bayonets.

She jerked back and slapped her hands over her face. "Oh, God. Oh, God. Why?"

De Launay, horribly wounded, toppled into the gutter, still alive, anguished moans pouring out of him, but it wasn't enough for the mob. Several men fired their pistols into his twisting body.

She was sickened by the sight. When a man attacked de Launay's neck with a saw, her stomach cramped. "I *have* to get out of here."

The crowd surged forward to watch the decapitation, separating her from Watin and Jacques. The harder the mob pushed, the wider the separation, until she could no longer see them. The crazed mob formed a circle around the beheading. Frantically looking around, she spied an opening in the crowd, allowing her to escape for the second time.

But where was she going? And she hadn't said goodbye to Jacques and Léopold.

She couldn't wait around to find them. She had to get as far away as possible.

She was about a mile from the Palais Royal. She could go back there and decide what to do. Maybe one of the shop owners could give her a lead on where to sell her pearls or find a place to stay. The farther from the Hôtel de Ville, the quieter the city, and the safer she felt.

When she reached the Palais Royal, she kept going, passing the Tuileries Palace and the Place Louis XV, walking briskly down the Champs-Élysées, her footfalls echoing back from the rows of trees lining both sides of the wide dirt avenue.

There were a few people hurrying by in carriages and on foot, and an old, snorting horse pulling a cart with creaking wheels, but compared to where she'd been, she could have been on the other side of the moon.

The ache in her side forced her to stop and rest.

A stiff breeze picked up, rustling the branches and sighing through the grass. It would be easy to believe she had imagined the horrors she just witnessed, except she was dirty, her boots were covered with muck, and while she could probably reclaim her wig from Jacques's studio, she'd permanently lost her hat.

She leaned against a wrought iron fence at the rue de Berri guarding the entrance to a mansion. The residence's façade glowed in the afternoon sunshine while the sun blinked back from leaded, paned windows.

Ahead of her stood a massive gate, one of dozens in the wall circling Paris, placed there to collect taxes from farmers when they came to town to sell their produce. Some portions of the Wall of the Farmers General still existed in the twenty-first century, like the rotunda of the Parc Monceau.

The city gates opened, and a man on horseback and wearing a dark green coat trotted through. A tricorn hat sat atop sandy-colored hair. His broad shoulders and strong arms exerted expert control over the stallion beneath him.

He continued on through the second gate leading to the mansion, where he swung down from the saddle with athletic grace. He handed the reins to a servant dressed in livery, and they spoke briefly, although she was too far away to hear what was said. The horse nickered and pressed his big face against the servant's shoulder.

The man—tall, slender, square-shouldered, with a long face and high nose—was familiar to her. She pressed her nose against the fence for a better view, and wrapped her fingers around the bars, hoping he would turn her way. He cocked his chin slightly, and his eyes, deeply carved below bushy eyebrows gazed at her.

Oh merda! Thomas Jefferson.

He was more handsome than in any painting she'd ever seen of him, and she had an uncanny ability to remember details of art she'd seen in person. He was also handsomer than the bust by the greatest sculptor of Jefferson's time, Jean-Antoine Houdon, considered to be the definitive image of Jefferson. The bust portrayed him as an intellectual and idealistic statesman with his strong brow above a knowing half-smile. Gazing into his face—a living, breathing face—her memory collided with reality.

They homed in on each other for a moment in shocked silence.

The power and intelligence flashing in the widening of his eyes consumed all thoughts of Houdon's bust and being in the wrong place at the wrong time. Her only interest right now was painting him exactly as he looked at this moment. His eyes, and the passion gleaming there, were permanently imprinted on her brain.

"Excusez-moi monsieur." She waved, hurrying through the wide-open gate. Jefferson removed his tricorn and tucked it under his arm. Unaware of the yard's hazards, she stepped in a pothole—too deep and too narrow to step out of unharmed. She wrenched her knee and face-planted against his rock-solid chest, shrieking.

Jefferson tossed his hat aside and grabbed one of her pinwheeling arms. *"Oh, mon Dieu."* He adjusted his grip and prevented what would have been a very nasty fall. Then he swooped her up into his arms. It all happened in a split second, long enough for another surge of adrenaline to explode through her and temporarily block the pain of her knee injury.

He smelled of leather and outdoors, sunshine and possibility. Her senses rose up with primitive sharpness, and she tried to count the rapidly increasing beats of her heart—seventy, eighty-five, a hundred or more. He seemed to take up the whole of the outside, as if he absorbed all of Paris, leaving only his solid arms and broad chest.

All sorts of things passed through her brain, including *where could she find a sheet of paper and pencil?*

Then excruciating knee pain reminded her she'd been dumped in the middle of the French Revolution, thanks to the *maledetto* brooch, and no good could possibly come of that.

4

Paris (1789)—Sophia

A LEATHER-SCENTED SILENCE rolled over her, warming the air, and Sophia breathed it in deeply. If only she could breathe out the knee pain in equal measure, she would enjoy the moment.

Thomas Jefferson hadn't simply swallowed her world, he'd become it. And in the bright sunlight, his intense, deep-set blue eyes gazing down at her changed from blue to gray and back again.

"Est-tu blessée?"

His accent, a combination of colonial-era British with a bit of Scots thrown in, was mesmerizing. In response to his question, she could only shake her head. Slowly, her heart rate returned to its usual pace, and her nerves settled down and smoothed away their jagged edges.

Jefferson carried her up several steps to what appeared to be the residence's main entrance, while the heat radiating from him further soothed her shattered nerves. He ducked below the lintel before pausing momentarily in a vestibule. A patch of new sunlight shone through the transom onto his red hair, and she nearly wept, not from throbbing knee pain, but solely because she didn't have a paintbrush in hand.

Her brain snapped pictures of him instead. *Click. Click. Click.*

She had to paint him. Right now. She nibbled the corner of her lower lip as she mentally fit him into a frame, zeroing in on his most prominent features—angular nose, pointed chin, long neck, freckled complexion, and reddish hair turning sandy as it grayed. But his grayish blue eyes were his most arresting feature.

The reception hall led into a circular salon and smelled of lilies and polish. She was about to tell him to set her down anywhere when she noticed the domed ceiling with an oval painting of a white, winged horse pulling a chariot. She leaned back against his shoulder and gazed appreciatively at the extraordinary artwork. It had to be an allegorical painting of the one on the ceiling of the Apollo Salon at Versailles by Charles de La Fosse.

The painting at Versailles, along with the room's stuccos, recently underwent restoration, as she learned from an art blogger who posted regularly on the project. Jefferson's ceiling might have been done by Jean-Simon Berthélemy, who'd been commissioned to paint the ceilings in the Palais du Louvre and other palaces. This could be one of his. The room was rich with the ambiance of a museum.

She pushed aside her study of art and returned to her study of Jefferson, preparing to paint him exactly as he looked at this moment—curious yet concerned. But even with those emotions flickering over his face, the intelligent man she knew him to be was evident in the set of his jaw and the way he carried his height with natural grace. His arms weren't quivering from the strain of carrying her up the stairs, and the taut skin on his face had a ruddy hue that would likely disappear when his heart rate, elevated from a brisk horseback ride and carrying her, returned to normal.

A black ribbon held his thick, full hair just below his collar, and her fingers itched to untie it, to let his hair fall free. Her mind went immediately to working out a composition, drawing imaginary straight lines, laying out her painting on canvas, constructing the armature to support his portrait. She wanted to paint him as he was at this crucial time in his life, when cascading events in his public and private lives led to him living vibrantly in France while fretting constantly about America.

Her shoulders, the small of her back, and her knee were all

shooting warning pains up and down her body, but she somehow managed a smile, her cheeks warming slightly. "I sprained my knee. It hurts, but I've gone through worse today."

He let out a bark of laughter, and the sound was richer than she could have imagined. "You speak English." Not waiting for a response, he carried her to a sofa with a serpentine high back and gently set her down.

The blue-silk upholstery was cool and soft beneath her.

"I'm Sophia Orsini from New York City. I've been living in Florence for the past few years." Now the obfuscation would start, as it always did when she traveled back in time. She had trained herself to react quickly, to be creative in her responses, but to always keep her story as close to the truth as possible.

Her knee needed icing. Did they even have ice in 1789? "I was traveling with a companion, but we were separated when a mob confiscated our carriage and raced toward the Hôtel des Invalides to steal muskets." This was the sixth time she'd used some variation of the missing companion and stolen carriage and luggage story, and so far it had always worked.

He rested one hand on his hip, the other he raked through his hair to the ribbon in a masculine gesture she adored—silly as it sounded. In the room's natural light, tiny lines fanning from the outer corners of his eyes were visible.

"I'm sorry for your misfortune," he said. "I'll see what I can do, but first I'll send word to a physician to call on you immediately. He can give you laudanum for pain."

"That's not necessary. I'm sure all available physicians are at the Bastille, but if you have any ice, it will help with the swelling."

"I'm not familiar with the use of ice on injuries."

"Ice reduces swelling and inflammation, and eases pain by numbing the affected area. It works on migraines, too. Cold constricts blood vessels and helps reduce the neurotransmission of pain to the brain. Instead of registering pain, it registers, 'Oh, that's cold.'" *Okay, maybe neurotransmission was a bit too much.*

He gave her an odd, disbelieving look.

"Trust me, it works."

"I'll try it on my next migraine." Jefferson called with a slightly raised voice, "Mr. Petit."

A man dressed as a butler appeared in the salon immediately, as if he'd been standing close by waiting for a call.

"Bring a bucket of ice—" Jefferson said.

"Ice chips," Sophia said. "And a towel, please."

"A bucket of ice chips and a towel," Mr. Petit said. "What size chips do you require?"

Jefferson looked at her with a raised eyebrow. "Mr. Petit is my maître d'hôtel. What size ice chips should he bring?"

Her sternum was tender, but it didn't ache as much as her knee. Both places needed ice packs but, dressed as she was, it would be impossible to ice. "Small. Pebble size."

"And a towel?" Mr. Petit asked.

"I'll add ice chips to the towel and wrap it around my knee. The cold will reduce the swelling and pain."

After Mr. Petit left with his instructions, Jefferson said, "You mentioned a mob going to the Hôtel des Invalides to steal muskets. Did they get the weapons? And how long ago did this happen?" His voice sounded strange…far away, as if someone else was asking on his behalf.

"A few hours ago. But that's not the worst of it."

He moved to an open window facing the Champs-Élysées, as if from this distance he could see what was happening. The Bastille was almost four miles away, but even in the quiet countryside surrounding Jefferson's mansion, a low rumble could be heard over the occasional shouting of men standing guard at the nearby gate.

"Did you witness what happened at the Invalides?"

She dropped her eyes for a moment, not wanting to relive any of it, but she knew he needed a report. "I got caught up in an angry and aggressive mob. No matter how hard I tried, I couldn't get out.

"After they got the guns, they stormed the Bastille. The rioters shot the guards, and the guards shot the rioters. They finally breached the drawbridge into the third courtyard and gained control of the gunpowder. A bit later they escorted the governor to City Hall, but refused to hand him over to the States-General, and brutally murdered him." The mental images flashed in front of her mind's eye, and she shook them away before they could make her sick.

The hurried click of bootheels on the hardwood floor grew louder until a younger man, dressed more fashionably than Jefferson in a brown coat, embroidered waistcoat, and a linen shirt with decorative cuffs, entered the salon carrying Jefferson's hat. While he also cut a striking figure, he didn't have Jefferson's commanding presence. In fact, he was gawky.

"Mr. Jefferson…" The man's Southern voice was alarmed, and his gaze jumped between Jefferson and Sophia.

"If you're going to tell me Parisians stormed the Bastille, Mademoiselle Orsini has already informed me."

"I couldn't get close enough to see what was happening, but I heard the screams and cannon fire. I returned immediately to tell you."

"I need to see the situation with my own eyes so I can report accurately to Secretary Jay."

"You shouldn't…" She caught herself, knowing she saw the events of the day through a unique lens, from a future perspective, not a present-day one, and her words had to be measured carefully. "I mean…"

"Go on. I prefer finished sentences," Jefferson said.

"I won't presume to tell you what to do," she said, "but it's not safe out there. The king's dismissal of his finance minister, who is sympathetic to the people, caused this eruption. I saw the mob kill the Bastille's governor, and I heard rumors that the lieutenant governor was also killed, along with several guards. The rioters are now a heavily armed force."

Jefferson turned to face the man. "William, I need to find Lafayette."

"I'll find him," William said. "He's presiding over the National Constituent Assembly at the Church of Saint Louis." William acknowledged Sophia with a slight nod. "I'm William Short, Mr. Jefferson's secretary. Were you injured by the rabble?"

"I acquired a few bruises from being at the Bastille, but I hurt my knee when I stepped in a pothole in front of the house."

Mr. Petit returned with a small silver bucket and an armload of towels. "Oh, Mr. Petit, how kind. Thank you," she said.

"Is there anything else you require, mademoiselle?"

"A cup of hot tea with lemon, please. Willow bark, if you have any."

With a silent nod, he hurried out of the room.

Sophia made a move to lift her skirts to evaluate the injury and apply ice, but both men were watching her curiously. "I need to see how bad it is. Do you mind?"

"You need a physician," Jefferson said.

"I can treat this more effectively than any doctor." *At least any eighteenth-century physician.* If she'd been at home, she would have gone to see the orthopedist who treated her prior twists, sprains, and breaks.

Jefferson and William turned in unison to face the fireplace. Sophia untied the garter on the injured leg and rolled the stocking below her knee.

"On a scale of one to ten"—she said, more to herself than the two men who were waiting impatiently—"the pain is about an eight. I'm pretty sure it's an MCL sprain." She filled a towel with ice chips, then wrapped another towel on top of it to tie it securely around her knee.

She wiggled her toes inside her shoes and considered taking them off—her shoes, not her toes—in case the swelling continued down her leg to her foot. But it would have to wait. She arranged the icepack before making herself presentable again.

"I'll send for a physician to come when he can," Jefferson said.

"There's no need. He won't approve of what I'm doing, but for a sprain, I'm following proper protocol." Which probably didn't make any sense to him, but she didn't want a doctor trying to treat her injury. He might want to amputate. "If I keep it iced, compressed, and elevated, the swelling will go down in a few days."

"How long do you keep the ice on?"

"Ten minutes, remove for ten minutes, then reapply as often as possible for the first twenty-four to forty-eight hours."

Jefferson rubbed his wrist, probably remembering the dislocation of a few years earlier that, according to a political biography by Jon Meacham, would bother him for years. "But it could be broken."

"I've had broken bones before, and I know I don't have one now. My knee will hurt for a few days, but if I treat it right, it'll improve." She reached behind her for a pillow and slipped it under her leg, then leaned back in the sofa.

"How did you end up at the Bastille?" Mr. Short asked.

"I got stuck in the middle of the mob and couldn't get away. Wrong place, wrong time. It sounds silly when I think about it, but we were packed together so tightly that I could only move with the mob, not against it. When I did find a chance to get away, I was caught by a couple of angry men. Luckily, Monsieur David came to my rescue. He was going to bring me here to meet Mr. Jefferson, but we got separated at the Hôtel de Ville, so I came here on my own."

"I've met Mr. David on several occasions. He was wise to insist you come here. What about your companion? We need to find her?"

"There's no need. She was paid to travel with me to Paris, and her family is here. I'm sure she went to find them." Another lie that always worked, and she could see it working on the two men standing in front of her.

Jefferson tugged on the chain of his gold pocket watch and checked the time. "Patsy and Polly are at the Abbaye Royale de Panthémont." He closed and pocketed the watch. "I'll send word to my daughters to stay at their school until order is restored in the city."

It might take ten years.

"I'll get a message to Lafayette, then go to the Abbaye," William said. "You should stay. You'll have visitors throughout the evening." Then to Sophia he said, "Is there anything I can do for you while

I'm out?"

"Are you familiar with the queen's jewelers, Charles Boehmer and Paul Bassenge? I have jewels I need to sell to pay my expenses. And since my baggage was lost when our carriage was confiscated"—another recycled lie—"I need clothes, paint supplies, and money to book passage to America."

"You're a painter?" Jefferson asked.

"You're going to America?" William asked simultaneously.

"I am," she said to Jefferson. "I am," she said pointedly to William.

It was time to roll out a variation of her second most-used explanation for her presence. "I've been studying in…Tuscany, but my work there was done, so I came to…Paris to complete my studies before returning to…New York. After what I experienced today, I don't plan to stay any longer than it takes to arrange transportation."

"It must have been frightening to arrive here on a day such as this," Jefferson said.

She glanced at her hands and nervously chipped a bit of blue paint off her fingernail. In her real world, she never broke a promise, never fabricated, never told a bold-faced lie, and never exaggerated her talent. Honest to a fault. Except when it came to her holidays. Then she lied to everyone.

"If I'd known I'd be arriving on the eve of a revolution, I wouldn't have come. But what happened in Paris today will be seen as one of the most important events in world history."

"France is in transition," Jefferson said, "but not a revolution. The monarchy will withstand the turmoil."

You're wrong, Mr. Jefferson. You might praise it now, hesitate over it, but eventually you will recoil from it.

"I disagree," she said. "America is the torchbearer of liberty to the world. The political creed you penned will have implications around the globe. Why would the French peasants not want the same unalienable rights—life, liberty, and pursuit of happiness—you professed in the Declaration of Independence? And you've been the tip of the spear pointing General Lafayette in the right direction with his Declaration of the Rights of Man and Citizen."

"You are frighteningly well-informed, mademoiselle, and you sound like a politician. The general only presented a draft three days ago." Jefferson's whole demeanor changed, as if he'd been ordered to stand at attention—chin up, chest out, shoulders back, stomach in, eyes locked in a fixed position. "I've always believed enfranchised women might take it into their minds to run for office instead of focusing on their husbands, hearths, and children."

She managed a nervous laugh, and she would have been offended if she'd hadn't previously been subjected to fifteenth, sixteenth, seventeenth, nineteenth, and twentieth-century men espousing similar sexist views.

"I don't have a husband, hearth, or children. I'm not a politician, but I am opinionated. I have strong views about the role of women in our new democracy. But I'll strive to keep them to myself and focus instead on painting magnificent architecture like the Louvre and the Hôtel de Salm, and the gardens of le Jardin des Plantes and le Jardin du Roi."

To Jefferson, the mention of gardens and architecture was an at-ease command. He relaxed his shoulders. "The gardens are more appropriate endeavors for a woman. What else do you paint?"

"Whatever a patron commissions—buildings, landscapes, portraits."

"Is there anyone in Paris who will recommend you?"

"No one but me," she said. "If you want to know about my style of painting, I would say...I'm influenced by the Old Masters: Rubens, Rembrandt, Caravaggio, and a current English painter named Thomas Lawrence. Like him, I'm known for bold use of color and technical innovation."

"My dear friend Maria Cosway mentioned the young artist. She said he was considered an artistic prodigy."

Sophia was familiar with the artist's paintings and Cosway's affair with Jefferson. "Lawrence was also referred to as a chocolate box painter because his paintings are the kind of overly sentimental, sweet art that decorates—"

"Boxes of chocolate?" Jefferson smiled. "The next time I visit À la Mère de Famille, I'll ask for a painting on my box."

William cleared his throat in an obvious attempt to get Jefferson's attention. "Sir, I should go. Lafayette might travel to Versailles before I can get a message to him."

"I need to make arrangements for lodging. There are hundreds of expats in Paris. If you would introduce me to other Americans, I'm sure they could recommend temporary lodging."

"Expats?" Jefferson asked.

"Expatriates."

"Mademoiselle, since my negligence caused your accident, you'll stay here until you can walk again."

"Paris is very cosmopolitan, Mr. Jefferson, but a woman who isn't a member of your family living in your household wouldn't be prudent. I wouldn't want to sully your reputation, much less my own."

"Then I shall commission you to paint my garden. I've had other painters stay in my house. John Trumbull spent several months here. So it's not unheard of for me to provide accommodation to painters and other travelers from America."

"I've seen Mr. Trumbull's paintings," she said, mentally flipping through his portfolio. "Some of them aren't historically accurate, but history will forgive him for his inaccuracies."

There was a subtle flicker of shock in Jefferson's eyes. "Historical inaccuracies? Give me an example."

"If a painter is going to paint an event in the past, he needs to be sure the fixtures, furnishings, clothes, and hairstyles are correct. If I painted a scene from the early years of the Revolutionary War, I wouldn't clothe soldiers in uniforms they were only wearing at the end of the war. A hundred or even two hundred years from now, art critics will notice those mistakes."

"A hundred years from now, no one will know what uniforms were worn."

"You know what Caesar wore," she said. "Why would soldiers in the Revolutionary War be any different? Besides, don't you look at paintings now and find mistakes? Why would the future be any different?"

"I disagree." Jefferson locked his hands behind his back and paced in front of her. "It's my opinion, Mademoiselle Orsini, that every artist believes in three kinds of truth. Simple truth is the appearance of things. Ideal truth consists of selective combinations of parts. Perfect truth combines the simple and ideal, and is probably truer than truth itself. This theory allows painters the license to compete with literature as a liberal art."

"Are you saying there aren't inaccuracies in paintings, just selective combinations of parts to create an ideal truth?" she asked.

He smiled, and the color of his piercing gray eyes changed back to the enticing gray-blue, and he looked at her as if she was the center of a confusing universe, or, better yet, a bug in a jar, an object to study up close and at his leisure.

"I look forward to exploring the idea of ideal truth at length," he said. "First, though, we need to settle the matter of your lodging. I also have selfish reason for asking you to stay here at the legation. I have tried to shelter my daughters from French morals, but since Mrs. Adams left for London and then returned to America, they've had no other woman to model American manners and morals. It's not that our morals are better than the French, but they are better for us. And being around you will remind them of the difference as they prepare to return to Monticello."

Sophia had been a role model for many young female artists and could appreciate what he was asking of her. "Your offer is very generous, but I don't want to cause a scandal that would be far worse for your daughters."

"You are an unescorted American in Paris who injured herself due to my negligence. No one will think it inappropriate for you to stay here while you recover. And while you're recovering, you've agreed to paint my garden."

If she agreed to paint Jefferson's garden, it would mean she couldn't commission Vigée Le Brun to paint her portrait for her collection or sit for Jacques. But she would much rather paint than be painted. "You've just commissioned an American portraitist, President Jefferson." She realized her slip immediately. It wasn't the first and wouldn't be the last. She'd learned several holidays ago that when she misspoke, she only had to smile and act like she wasn't aware of what she'd said.

"Thank you for the promotion, Mademoiselle Orsini, but ambassador to France is a far greater challenge than I ever anticipated, and I have no desire to serve our young democracy in any other capacity."

"Whatever role you play in the future, sir, you'll do it quite well."

"There will be no other role. When I finish here, I'll retire to Monticello."

"Then I hope to have a few paintings of you and your garden completed so you can enjoy them in your retirement."

If she thought matching wits with him would be a challenging game, she'd better rethink and get over it. He was an intellectual, an endlessly curious man, and too perceptive to let her slips go by unchallenged.

She must be on guard. At all times. Because the consequences of revealing the future to him would far outlast her brief presence in his life.

5

Mallory Plantation, VA—Matt Kelly

MIDSUMMER VIRGINIA WEATHER was hotter than Hades. The recent squalls had raised the humidity level to match the temperature, something Matt Kelly hadn't experienced in a lifetime of living in Colorado. But after two years of living in the Commonwealth, he was slowly adjusting. It was on days like this, though, that he second-guessed his and Elizabeth's decision to relocate.

He was already wiping sweat off his face when he walked into the air-conditioned library at Mallory Plantation. When Charlotte Mallory and her husband, Braham McCabe, first mentioned building a state-of-the-art library and resource center on their property, Matt offered to move his extensive collection of books and maps from his ranch to the plantation.

Braham said he'd happily accept the donation if Matt and Elizabeth would live on the plantation. So they sold their ranch to their daughter, Olivia, and her husband, Connor, to house the next generation of Kellys/O'Gradys, and built a stately home on five acres of land they purchased from Braham and Charlotte.

Now they lived close to their other daughter, Amber, her husband, Daniel, and two wonderful children. Amber's health and the grandkids—Noah, age fourteen, and wee Heather, age two—were the reasons they gave up all they had built in Colorado and moved to the outskirts of Richmond. Noah was more than a step-grandchild. After only four years, they were almost inseparable.

His gaze shifted to the rows of bookcases packed with first edition classics and history books. Like the twenty thousand books Thomas Jefferson sold to the Library of Congress to form the nucleus of the library, Matt's collection formed the nucleus of the library at Mallory Plantation. And also, like Jefferson, Matt had shopped at every bookstore in every city in every country he ever visited, and turned over every book with his own hands. Jefferson's Holy Trinity were Francis Bacon, John Locke, and Isaac Newton. Matt's were Jefferson, Lincoln, Roosevelt, and, when he was asked for his Holy Trinity plus one, he included Churchill.

Over the past four years his role as historian, librarian, and world tour guide had evolved. He spent his days teaching and advising the MacKlenna Clan children while Elizabeth worked remotely in the MacKlenna Corporation legal department. The clan had one child in medical school, one finishing his second year at Harvard, and two others applying for early admission there. And the role model to beat all role models, Austin O'Grady, recently graduated on the Dean's List at the University of Kentucky, was drafted by the Cavaliers, and was playing in a summer league in Las Vegas.

Matt's most challenging students, by far, were the McBains's ten-year-old twin boys. If he ever made a mistake, they pointed it out. It was as if they stood over his shoulder when he wrote his lecture notes and knew exactly what he was going to say.

Matt had just finished reviewing his American Revolution lecture notes to be sure they were mistake-free, and he now had time to skim *The New York Times* before class started.

He logged into his account and quickly perused each section of the paper, planning to go back and read the articles later.

One article, however, caught his attention, and he stopped to read it. An Orsini painting of Thomas Jefferson sailing to America was recently discovered during a renovation of one of the oldest homes in Amagansett on the South Shore of Long Island.

Orsini, an eighteenth-century portraitist, painted like Donatello a century before the renowned painter bridged the gap between nineteenth century Impressionism and early twentieth century Cubism. Orsini, along with Charles Willson Peale, John Trumbull, and Gilbert Stuart were all well-known portraitists of the Founding Fathers.

To find an unknown Orsini painting was astounding. If the painting sold at auction, it could break seven figures, especially if it was proved to be another life painting.

Matt entered a tickler into his calendar to check on the status of the painting in five days. He could incorporate a study of Orsini's work into an art history lecture scheduled for next month. The kids would enjoy researching the provenance of the Jefferson painting. He finished writing the tickler just as Elizabeth rushed through the back door.

"Matt!"

He gathered up his notes and tapped the ends on the table to align the sheets into a neat pile, then attached a binder clip. "Over here."

Breathing heavily, she stopped at his desk and leaned over to catch her breath. "I ran over...here. Charlotte called... She needs us...at the hospital."

Matt's heart dropped to the pit of his stomach. He jumped to his feet, overturning his chair. "Why? What for? What's wrong?"

He mentally ran through the list of family members for possible illnesses. He hadn't heard of any sickness or accidents in the past twenty-four hours. But if Charlotte was calling and needed them, it was a serious matter. "Where is everyone?"

Elizabeth patted her chest as if the simple gesture would restore her normal breathing rhythm. "Amber has wee Heather in the big kitchen. Braham and Daniel have the older children in the garden."

"For their agronomy lesson. Right." Matt picked up his chair. "The kids are due here in an hour for a Revolutionary War lecture." He grabbed his phone and slid it into his pants pocket. "What about Jack and Amy?"

Elizabeth led the way to the door. "They're meeting with the event planner to go over last-minute details for the party this weekend. I volunteered to babysit Margaret Ann, but Amy didn't need me."

Matt held the door as they stepped out into the hot, humid air. It had to be at least ninety degrees with ninety percent humidity. They hurried to Elizabeth's white Mercedes, where Matt opened the passenger door and she slid in. "Did Charlotte give you any idea at all what was going on?"

"No, and in the four years I've known her, this is the first time I've ever heard fear in her voice."

Matt hurried around to the driver's door and climbed in. Before he started the vehicle, he said, "I should tell Braham I'm leaving."

"Charlotte didn't mention him. Either she already called him, or she'll call him once we get to the hospital. She probably didn't want to tell him while he's with the children."

"Good point." Matt steered the car toward the exit. If everyone on the plantation was okay, then what was the emergency? "Where's Elliott?"

Elizabeth stopped texting and looked up at Matt. "That's an odd question right now."

"Considering Elliott's health issues, it's really not."

"Well, the last I heard he was feeling fine. He took Blane to Montgomery Winery to spend the weekend helping Meredith get ready for the grand reopening."

"I'm not sure a four-year-old will be much help. He'll be more of a distraction."

Matt turned onto the highway and the vehicle picked up speed. "Since James Cullen went to Harvard, Blane has filled the hole James Cullen left behind. If Elliott and Meredith didn't have the four-year-old to spoil, they'd fly up to Cambridge every weekend."

"Why don't they Skype?"

"Meredith does, but Elliott wants to be able to hug his son when he sees him."

"Which would drive James Cullen crazy. He was ready to leave the nest," Elizabeth said.

Matt flipped on his blinker and passed a pickup truck hauling bales of hay. "He'll stay in Cambridge and go to grad school, law school, or med school. He won't be back to Lexington for several years."

"The family is so spread out now that James Cullen doesn't have to be in Lexington to be part of the family," Elizabeth said. "Look at Kevin's brother-in-law, Shane. He's lived in Australia for eight years, but he never misses a meeting, and is almost always at the castle or the ranch for the holidays."

"You're right," Matt said. "By the way, where are Kevin and JL? I heard they decided to come to the plantation for the weekend after all. Did Braham say anything to you?"

"Kevin's flying them up in his Cessna."

Hospital. Emergency. Kevin flying the Cessna.

It wasn't a stretch to connect the dots. The car swerved toward the side of the road. Elizabeth gripped the edge of the doorframe and pressed her right foot into the floorboard. "Matt!"

He righted the car and squeezed Elizabeth's hand. "Sorry! I think I know what's wrong."

6

Florence, Italy—Pete

PETE PARRINO FINISHED his dinner at the Osteria Toscanella and paid the check with his Amex since he hadn't been to the ATM to get euros yet. If he hadn't hired a car and driver through Blacklane, a European-based chauffeur company, he wouldn't have had cash to pay for a taxi.

The restaurant owner told him there was an ATM near the Gelateria Della Passera two blocks down the street.

Gabe Moretti, the general manager of Montgomery Winery in Tuscany, made the dinner reservations so they could catch up on the latest family news. At the last minute, a problem with a vendor came up that kept Gabe from leaving, so Pete had dinner alone.

Pete's trips to the winery were always too short to spend much time in Florence, which held special meaning for him. His grandparents emigrated from Tuscany to America shortly after World War II and opened an Italian restaurant in Little Italy. Pete's aunts, uncles, and cousins still operated the restaurant today. He'd grown up listening to stories of Tuscany told in Italian and fell in love with the country long before he ever visited.

He slung his computer bag over his shoulder and said goodbye to the owner of the restaurant. The summer evening was unusually cool, making it a perfect night to stroll down the cobblestone Via

Toscanella and grab a gelato before returning to the winery.

He slowed when he spotted a man with his hands cupped at the sides of his face, peering between the slats of a rolling steel security door. Because Pete was a former NYPD detective and current VP of global security for MacKlenna Corporation, his nefarious-doings antenna shot up. But the man, who was wearing a sleek, dark blue Kiton K50 suit and brown Barker ostrich shoes, didn't look like a run-of-the-mill burglar.

Pete sauntered up beside the man. "See anything interesting?"

The man whipped around, his face flushed, obviously embarrassed being caught. "*Mi hai spaventato.*"

"Sorry," Pete said, although he wasn't. He'd intentionally startled the man to watch his reaction. If he'd been scoping out the premises to break in, he wouldn't be doing it on a public street at dusk, when he could easily be seen.

The rolling steel door had solid panels at the top and bottom, as well as a grill over the plate glass window. The glass had stained wooden mullions dividing it into squares and rectangles.

Inside the studio, three panels of canvas fabric hung from a curtain rod above the transom, leaving four-inch gaps between each panel so gawkers could peer inside the studio. A narrow table with a red tablecloth stood between the window and the curtain panels displaying artfully arranged sculptures and small paintings on easels. Propped against the glass was a small sign with the store's website—www.StudioSFOrsini.com.

Orsini was a common name in Italy, but whenever he heard it he thought of Sophia. "Looks closed to me," Pete said. "Whose studio is this?"

"Sophia Orsini," the man said.

And there it was, just like that, the old knot of pain exploded in his chest—his chronic condition that had never healed, and tended to flare up at the oddest, most unexpected times—like now.

When Sophia's parents ripped them apart following her graduation from high school, they sent her to Italy to live with her grandmother. He tried to follow her, but their priest had stopped him and convinced him the Orsinis had done what they believed was best for their daughter.

"She's seventeen," the priest reminded him. "She's young, and not sure what she wants to do. You're a college student. You'll never be able to give her what she needs. You have to let her go."

So he did. Because life was different back then. But one thing never changed. When his heart threatened to stop beating from the pain and bitterness of his loss, he knew another heart beat for him, because Sophia had told him that hers always would.

"Sophia was supposed to return from her holiday yesterday," the man said. "This is the third time I've been here today," he continued. "I commissioned a painting she promised to deliver yesterday because I'm having an event at my house tonight and planned to show it off. But I can't reach her."

Somehow Pete managed to breathe through the obstruction in his chest. "Do you have her phone number?"

"I've called a dozen times. She doesn't answer. It's not like her," the man continued. "I have three other Orsini paintings, and they were all delivered on time."

The man reached between the slats and jiggled the door handle. Even if the door opened, there was no way to squeeze through the slats to get inside. While the man continued to peer in, Pete scanned the tan stucco building, spotting security cameras at both corners. The electrical wiring ran along the upper third of the studio, just as it did on the adjacent building. But the wiring to Sophia's building looked newer than the others.

"Is Ms. Orsini a successful artist?" Pete asked.

The man thumbed through text messages on his phone. "I commissioned this painting over a year ago, and it was months before she could even start on it. She finished it before she left on her holiday."

"That busy, huh?"

The art lover punched keys on his phone, writing a text message. "Ms. Orsini's paintings now sell between two and three hundred thousand euros. The first painting she did for me cost twenty-five thousand. That was five years ago. Now she's internationally renowned and exhibiting at top galleries around the world."

"Which increases the value of the first painting," Pete said.

The man raised his eyebrows. "Right, and the second, and the third. In another two years, only major art collectors will be able to afford her work."

"I noticed the security cameras on the corners of the building. Does she have valuable paintings inside?"

The man gave Pete a suspicious leer.

Pete shook off his cop look and extended his hand. "Pete Parrino. Retired NYPD detective."

The man shook Pete's hand. "Ivan Bianchi. I own a family-run winery in the Sienese area of the Chianti Classico."

"I work for one close by in the Chianti Colli Fiorentini."

"Which one?"

"Montgomery Winery."

"I'm familiar with them. The owners are trying to buy up all the neighboring vineyards."

Pete waved away the comment. "Just a rumor. Two's plenty."

Ivan tapped out a cigarette from a package of Marlboro reds and flicked a lighter. "Glad to hear it." He puffed before asking, "Are you familiar with Sophia's work?"

"No. I knew a Sophia Orsini many years ago in New York. The woman I knew would be late thirties, blonde, wavy hair, robin's-egg blue eyes, five-two, and has a little bump in her right earlobe."

"You sound like a detective." Ivan flicked the ash off his cigarette. "Your description fits Sophia, but I've never noticed anything unusual about her earlobe."

If you had kissed every inch of her, you would.

"She doesn't keep her work in the studio," Ivan continued. "Her paintings either sell or she exhibits them. If she's got a security system, it's for protection." He glanced up, squinting, and pointed when he spotted the cameras. "I've never noticed them before, or any inside the building." He looked down at his wristwatch. "I've got an appointment. I'll come back tomorrow."

Ivan turned to go, but Pete held him up with another question. "Do you know where she went?"

Ivan shook his head. "Earlier today I asked the owner of Osteria Toscanella if he'd seen her. If anyone knows where she went, he would, but he didn't know."

"Are they a couple?" The unexpected spike of jealousy after all these years surprised him. But it wasn't any of his business. He certainly hadn't lived a priestly life.

"He's a painter, too. If it's anything more…" Ivan drew on his cigarette. "That's their business."

"What's her mobile number?" Pete asked.

Ivan flipped open his phone folio and pulled out a business card. It was one of Sophia's. "You can have this. I've got all her information in my contacts."

Pete committed the number to memory before slipping the card in his shirt's chest pocket. "Have you been by her house to see if she's home and not answering her phone?"

Ivan pointed to the windows above the studio. "She owns the entire building. The first floor is her studio, her apartment is on the second, and the third floor is empty."

"Have you ever been upstairs?"

"Once. She had a painting she wanted me to see. I was surprised. Her studio is eclectic, with student art hanging on the walls, but her apartment has the feel of *plein air*."

"I don't speak French."

"Sorry. It means outside. The frescos on the walls give the apartment a garden ambience, like Monet's garden in Giverny. If you ever want inspiration, sit there for an hour. *L'ispirazione arriverà.*"

Pete's cop radar was sending signals. He'd spent too many years investigating disappearances and murders not to be alarmed. If she didn't return by morning, he would break into her apartment to look for clues to her whereabouts. "What does she paint?" he asked. "Modern art? Portraits? Landscapes? Lily ponds?"

"Whatever the collector wants. The painting she just finished for me is a copy of the *Mona Lisa*."

"An exact copy, or one with an Orsini twist to give it her own interpretation, a modernistic touch?"

"We had an argument over her interpretation. She wanted to paint the portrait using the vivid colors da Vinci would have used."

"Since I'm not an art aficionado, I have to ask. How would she know the original colors?"

"She researched the copy of the *Mona Lisa* in the Prado Museum in Madrid. It's believed that copy was painted by one of da Vinci's students about the same time da Vinci painted the original. The Prado painting has had a less eventful life, and the colors are still vivid. She wanted to use those colors, and I wanted the painting to resemble the painting in the Louvre."

"As the client, I guess you got your way."

Despite Ivan's distress, he laughed. "If you think that, you don't know her. She can be very persuasive, especially when it comes to art."

Pete's throat tightened, and even if he needed to respond he couldn't have found his voice. Sophia's persuasiveness had ultimately led to their downfall, but he never blamed her, only himself. He should have done what he knew to be right and said no to her, but he had loved her too much to deny her anything, even an elopement.

Ivan looked through the slats into the studio again and tapped his finger on the glass. "The painting is on the easel in the middle of the room, drying. You can only see the back of it."

Pete looked through the slats, too. "Was she trying to torture you? To be this close and not see the front." He straightened, hands on his hips, and tapped his fingers in a light tattoo. "Is there another window?"

"A large window on the side of the building lets in the light from the north, but it's too high to see inside from the street. The Old Masters painted only with northern light, and Sophia wants her students to paint under similar conditions. The lights in the studio are never on when someone is painting."

"Maybe one of her students knows where she is. Or maybe one of them can open the door for you."

"She doesn't teach during the summer." Ivan butted the cigarette against the cobblestone with his heel. "If I hear from Sophia, I'll mention you to her."

Pete produced a leather business card case and handed a card to Ivan. "Here's my contact information." Pete watched Ivan until he disappeared around the corner onto Via dello Sprone then glanced up at the cameras again. With his experience, he could easily breach her security system. Sophia's delayed return could be legitimate, but it didn't sit right with him. Why wait another day?

He walked down the side of the building along Via dei Velluti until he reached a wrought iron gate. He pushed it open and stepped into a private courtyard with large terra-cotta pottery planted with healthy lemon trees, red and white flowers, and ferns. He stuck a finger into each pot. Someone was watering the plants in Sophia's absence. The soil was moist, and it hadn't rained.

Then he saw a small business sign peeking out of the flowers— *Ragazza di fiore.*

A white Fiat 500 was parked in the driveway alongside a light blue motorbike. Memories of Sophia's white Volkswagen and red Schwinn bicycle returned to haunt him. Her parents bought the car when she turned sixteen, and, ignoring their prohibition against anyone riding with her, she often chauffeured him around.

God, that was a long time ago.

He made himself comfortable at a table under a pergola and booted up his laptop. It would be dark in about thirty minutes, when he intended to break into her apartment, but first he needed information about her security system. Several years ago David McBain, President of MacKlenna Corporation, had shared highly sensitive information about the software he created to allow a user to enter the dark web—a sub-world of illegal activity—and hack into someone's server and override security systems without leaving digital footprints. Once Pete hacked into her server, the door to her studio might as well swing wide open.

Forty-five minutes later the latch on the back door slid open with a click.

Pete packed up his computer and entered the building to find the alarm-deactivated light was on and the LCD screen was blank. Using only a penlight, he moved through a storage room packed with shelves of paint, stacks of panels and canvases, books on painting techniques, still life objects, and a Keurig coffee pot and a basket of pods.

In the studio, he stopped to gaze at the *Mona Lisa,* which was propped on an easel in the middle of the room. As he told Ivan, he wasn't an aficionado, but he knew what he liked. Although if he was asked what he liked about the painting other than the *Mona Lisa* smile, he couldn't say.

He scanned the walls of the studio, taking it all in, and then climbed the stairs to the second floor, almost tripping over a pair of paint-splattered shoes.

The frescos covering three walls in the living room were incredible. He had to agree with Ivan, and although he couldn't remember the French expression, he remembered the translation. He could almost smell the flowers in the garden.

He walked through each room, getting his bearings, then sat at her desk and booted up his laptop again. Using the proprietary software on his computer, he quickly logged into her email and found a travel folder with subfolders for the past five years. A folder for the current year said PARIS TRIP. Inside the folder he found an itinerary for a spring trip to Paris, emails scheduling a meeting with a researcher, and others arranging for a tour guide. There was no information about a summer trip. No plane, train, car rental, or hotel reservations.

He stretched out his legs, and his shins bumped a sharp edge under the desk. He looked underneath to see what it was and found a small safe with a combination lock.

He stood and stretched. Her vehicles were parked in the back. Had she gone with someone? A secret lover? Possible. But he didn't want to go there.

He went back through the apartment. If he believed she was on a holiday with a secret lover, then he should pack up his gear and get the hell out. He returned to the office but stopped in the doorway and looked back into the living room. Was he imagining a spatial difference, or was there a variation in the width of the room? He returned to the living room. No, he wasn't imagining it. There was almost a three-foot difference in the width of the living room compared to the kitchen, the bedrooms, and office. What the hell was going on?

He tapped the wall on the side of the room sharing a common wall with the adjoining building, and found it wasn't drywall or plaster. It was steel. His curiosity was already piqued, now even more so.

He searched every inch of the wall until he found a trigger cleverly hidden in a tree branch painted in the fresco. He pulled it, and a door slid open without a sound. Six lights came on. One above each of five paintings, all of Sophia, and one above an empty easel.

She was an astonishing beauty. Each painting captured her in a different light, even the one of her dressed in a clown's suit. Whoever the artists were, they were extraordinarily talented.

Using the penlight, he looked for the artists' names. The first one was signed by da Vinci. The clown's suit was signed by Picasso. The third by Donatello. The fourth by Rubens. The fifth by Degas.

Pete backed up until he bumped into the sofa. He sat slowly, taking it all in—Da Vinci, Picasso, Donatello, Rubens, Degas. He might not know much about art, but he recognized those names. They had to be forgeries. And if so, why go to so much trouble to hide them?

He stared while the minutes ticked by. After almost two decades on the police force not much shocked him, but this blew him away. He had to document what he found. Using his phone, he photographed the paintings from multiple angles. Satisfied he had all he needed, he closed the door to the secret room, returned to his computer bag, and removed a rare earth magnet.

The answers had to be in the small safe.

The rare earth magnet would open most commercial-grade electronic safes on the market. The manufacturer of Sophia's safe had a design flaw in the system—a nickel piece from China. He placed the magnet on the door and pulled the handle. It opened immediately.

Inside he found a small handgun and a jewelry box. He had hoped to find a file, a journal, letters, anything that would explain the paintings. Nothing. Out of curiosity, he opened the jewelry box.

And nearly dropped it.

"Holy shit!"

His phone rang, flashing Connor O'Grady's name and number. "Yo, buddy. What's up?" Pete asked.

"There's been an accident," Connor said, using the clipped, in-control cop voice he rarely used since retiring from the force. "You gotta come home."

The bottom that was already dropping out of Pete's world, collapsed completely. "I'm in Italy. What happened?"

"Kevin and JL were flying in Kevin's Cessna to Virginia. The tires blew out on landing. The plane went through a fence, hit a tree. But thankfully, they're okay."

JL was his former partner, and together they had gone through bad shit before, and they almost always walked away—although sometimes beat up and barely breathing. Pete gripped the chair before asking, "If they walked away, what's the emergency?"

"JL went into labor."

"She's only twenty-eight weeks. Do babies survive if they're born that early?"

"I don't know. Look, I've got to go help Olivia. Betsy just woke up from her nap and she's cranky. We should be in the air within ninety minutes."

"Are you renting a plane?"

"The Frasers are flying in from Napa with a stop in Denver to pick us up."

"Where's your dad?"

"Jeff and Julie are getting him to the hospital to be with JL. They should be there before we leave Denver. As soon as I learn anything, I'll let you know."

"I'm glad Blane was with his grandparents. If he'd been with

Kevin and JL—"

"He wasn't. So don't think about it. Look, I've got to go. Betsy's crying and giving Olivia a hard time."

"I'll be wheels up in an hour. The flight to Richmond will take about nine and half hours."

"Okay. I'll see you then," Connor said.

"Let me know if you get an update."

"Sure will, pal."

Pete dropped into the desk chair. Good God. JL and her unborn baby were in danger, and another brooch had shown up. No way in hell could he tell anyone in the family what he just discovered.

He studied the interior of the box. If the tapestry lining was to be believed, then the box once held four brooches: a sapphire, emerald, diamond, and pearl. Since the first three were already in the MacKlenna Clan's possession, Sophia was time-traveling with the pearl.

Also in the box was a fragile parchment written in what looked like Gaelic. He photographed the box and the parchment before returning them to the safe.

Prior to leaving the apartment, he took movies and photos of each room, every book lying on tables and in bookcases, all the paintings on the walls, and the contents of the closets. He also dumped out the trashcan next to the desk and photographed the trash. Then he did a fast check of the third floor.

It was empty.

Moving quickly, he returned to the first-floor storage room, where he moved supplies to make room for his laptop on a wide shelf, then logged back into the security system and rearmed it. He had forty-five seconds to leave the building before the alarm was triggered. After replacing what he'd moved, he was out of the building within fifteen seconds, and strolling along Via Toscanella within thirty.

Away from the building, he called his driver and told him to meet him at the far side of the Ponte Vecchio Bridge. His second call went to the pilot flying the jet he leased for this trip. His third call went to Gabe to let him know what was happening and that he couldn't return to the winery.

Within forty-five minutes of meeting his driver, he was on the plane, wheels up.

He spent the next hour reviewing photos of Sophia's apartment, the brooch box, and her art work. He should forward the photographs to David, but not until JL and her baby were out of danger. He knew JL well. She'd dealt with a teenage pregnancy, and instead of giving the baby up for adoption, she and her family raised him. And look at Austin now—heading to the Cavaliers.

But if JL lost a baby at twenty-eight weeks, she'd never recover. She was cynical, hard-edged, and difficult at times, but he'd never had a better friend.

If he told her about Sophia, JL would tell him to go find her. Matter of fact, JL told him twice a year to do exactly that—on every anniversary of their elopement and on Sophia's birthday. But he'd never been brave enough to follow JL's advice. He didn't want to discover she was happily married with a passel of kids who looked exactly like her.

When Sophia's parents had his and Sophia's marriage annulled and sent her to Italy to live, he quit college and joined the Marines. If Sophia had truly been in love with him, she would have fought harder to stay together. But her parents had wanted more for her than he could provide.

And now, twenty years later, their paths crossed again.

He studied the photographs of her portraits on his phone. She was more gorgeous today than she'd been at seventeen, and she'd been a knockout then. Was it even possible for her to have taken five trips back in time? He was a betting man, and he'd bet against it. It contradicted everything the family knew about the brooches. And if she managed it, then where was her soul mate?

The next picture he flipped to was the fragile parchment. Some of the words resembled ones he'd seen engraved on the stones, so it should shed light on the origin or purpose of the brooches.

Using the plane's Wi-Fi, he opened a Gaelic dictionary. David knew the language and could easily transcribe the letter, but Pete wasn't ready to confide in his boss or any of the O'Gradys—Pops, Connor, Shane, Rick, Jeff...or JL.

Although keeping news of Sophia from JL would be hard as hell. She'd been blessed or cursed with an overactive sixth sense, and she would know intuitively that something was on his mind.

Elliott Fraser was the same way. Pete would be surprised if Elliott didn't already sense another brooch had been discovered. Maybe it was part of being the Keeper, sensing the energy of activated gemstones.

But the life of Elliott's second grandson hung in the balance and would override all other emotions and sensations.

Pete turned his attention back to translating the parchment. When he got to the end, he came out of his seat, hitting the table and spilling his whisky. "Goddamn it!"

The flight attendant came to his assistance, and after mopping up the spill he tried to return to the photo of the parchment, but couldn't. He paced the interior of the midsized airplane, trying to connect the information in the letter with what he knew of the brooches.

His phone rang. It was Elliott. "Crap." He couldn't avoid talking to the chairman of the board of MacKlenna Corporation. "Parrino."

"What's your ETA?"

No hello, how are you?

"Seven hours. What about you?"

"Three," Elliott said.

"Do you have any news?" Pete asked.

"JL's stable and doesn't need emergency surgery right now, but she's had an abruption. If the placenta continues to peel away from the uterine wall, the blood flow to the baby will be disturbed and they'll have to do a C-section."

"What are the baby's chances of surviving at twenty-eight weeks?"

"Fair. Not great. Not good. Just fair."

"Jesus." Pete used another cloth napkin to soak up more of the whisky he spilled in his lap. "Kevin's got to be a mess. Have you talked to him?"

"Briefly. JL is in better emotional shape than he is."

"Connor told me what happened," Pete said.

"Kevin held it together, and probably saved their lives."

Pete sat back on the sofa. His eyes burned, thinking of the terror they'd experienced. He could have been returning to the States to attend their funerals. "I hope this doesn't cause Kevin's PTSD to flare up again, but I can understand if it does."

"The lad knows the triggers and has a great therapist. He'll be okay unless the baby doesn't make it. Then all bets are off."

"Charlotte will make sure JL has the best doctors and care. I'm glad they're in Richmond."

"If they save my grandson, the hospital will get a new wing. And I'll be sure they know it, starting as soon as I get there."

It wouldn't be the first hospital wing Elliott had endowed. There was a Fraser wing in a hospital in Napa, and a wing at the University of Kentucky Medical Center. "I'm sure the Director of Philanthropy is well aware of who JL is and will be standing at the door with a hand out as soon as you show up."

Elliott managed a chuckle. Then there was silence.

"Elliott. You still there?"

"Yeah. There's something else, Pete. I haven't mentioned this to David or Meredith."

Here it comes.

"There's a disturbance in the ether. When I've had this sensation before, we discovered a brooch was active. It's not one of ours."

"You just confirmed what I wanted to deny," Pete said. "A woman I knew twenty years ago has the pearl brooch. She's disappeared, and I don't know where she's gone."

"Can't do anything right now. She'll have to wait. Nothing is more important than my grandson."

7

Richmond, VA—JL

J L SAT BOLT upright in bed, flung her arms up to cover her head, and screamed. Strong arms wrapped around her as she struggled to catch her breath.

"JL, sweetheart. You're okay. Open your eyes. We're in the hospital. Open your eyes, JL."

Hospital? She slowly dragged her hands down her face, over her breasts to her belly. Why was she still wearing her seatbelt?

"Open your eyes," Kevin said again.

All she could see through the cracked windshield was the tree coming toward them.

"My baby." JL's voice sounded odd, smoky and raw.

"The baby's fine."

He was lying. Where was Pops? Her father would tell her the truth, just as he told her years ago when her mother died.

"Where's Pops?"

Kevin gently pushed her hair off her face and kissed her forehead. "He was here earlier, along with everyone else. When the doctor said you and the baby were out of immediate danger, I asked them to go home. Pops wanted to stay, but I told him he'd be a bigger help if he was at the plantation when Elliott and Meredith arrive with Blane."

Blane, my sweet baby boy.

She shivered. If he'd been on the plane…

But he was safe, and if what Kevin was telling her now was true, so was their baby. It was all too confusing. She slowly opened her eyes to see the love of her life with a bandage on his cheek and red bruises on the side of his face.

"The belt hurts my belly. Will you unhook it?"

"It has to stay on, babe. Look at the fetal heart monitor. See the top line? That's Lawrence's heartbeat, measured in increments of ten, with markings every thirty beats."

"Stop it! Don't be so technical. My brain is all jumbled."

Telltale signs of worry were on full display as he shoved his fingers through his hair. "Sorry. It's normal. He's doing okay."

She glanced around the room, noting pale yellow walls, landscape paintings, big, comfortable-looking chairs, and two oval braided rugs. The blinds hadn't been closed against the encroaching evening, the lights behind the bed were dimmed, and there was a steady click of heels in the hallway.

She wasn't sure of the time, but clearly visiting hours weren't over yet. There was no dinner tray with an uneaten meal sitting on her rolling over-the-bed tray, but there was a plastic pitcher with tiny drops of moisture on the sides, along with a plastic cup, the TV remote, a box of generic tissues, and a damp washcloth. Liquids but no food. Why?

Bad vibes sizzled like a live electrical wire dancing on the ground.

"I'm a hell of a detective, Kev. If everything is okay, why am I in this nice suite? There's a flat-screen TV, collectibles on glass shelves, refrigerator, birthing ball, rocking chair, and medical supplies hidden in wood-paneled cabinets."

"Wait a second. What makes you think medical supplies are in those cabinets?"

"Because the trash can next to it needs to be emptied, and there's another trash can next to the bed. Whatever the nurses got out of the cabinets, they dumped the trash in the nearest trashcan."

The way Kevin lounged over the bed railing, his body blocked most of the monitor sitting atop a wheeled cart behind him, and she couldn't see the display. "Scoot over so I can see." He barely moved an inch, so she snapped her fingers at him. She'd been hooked up to the fetal heart monitor before and knew the monitoring would detect changes in the fetal heart rate. When he didn't move, she became alarmed.

She knew firsthand what it was like to enter a dark alley without backup, knowing a perp was waiting in the shadows. She'd much rather face a son of a bitch with a gun than the truth Kevin was obviously keeping from her. A tiny toe beat a drum roll into the wall of her uterus, as if in sympathy, or maybe protest.

"Okay, tell me now. What's wrong?" she demanded.

Kevin didn't say anything, his expression fixed. Then he came right out with it. "You're in labor."

A lead weight landed on her chest, tanking the teeny-tiny bit of hope she'd been holding onto. "He can't be born now. He's only twenty-eight weeks. He won't have a chance."

"In a few days he'll be twenty-nine weeks. Every day he stays where he is will make him stronger." Kevin raked his fingers through her hair, twisting it behind her ear. "With a lioness for a mother, he's well protected."

"Sharp claws and all. So watch out. Better not keep anything from me, mister." She gripped his hand, growled against his palm, and nipped at his fingers. "The doctor can give me the drug to stop labor. Or have they done that already?"

He looked out the window into the darkening sky. After a moment he turned back and held her gaze. "You're a realist, JL. You'd kick me in the nuts if I kept something from you. So here it is… You have a placental abruption. That's why you're spotting. It often happens to pregnant women involved in accidents."

"Abruption? What exactly does that mean?"

"Part of the placenta has peeled away from the uterine wall."

JL wasn't the best person to have around in a medical crisis. She didn't handle them well. Not even kids' banged-up knees. But Kevin used to be an EMT, so she depended on him to take care of the sick and injured.

It wasn't that she couldn't be sweet and caring. She could. But sickness and injuries in other people scared the hell out of her. She knew her irrational fear stemmed from her mother's illness and death. But knowing the source didn't make it any easier to handle.

"Lawrence isn't in distress now, but the situation could change. Is that what you're saying?" The words barely made sense to her. Kevin stroked the side of her face with a shaking finger. She couldn't look at him. If she saw fear in his eyes, then she'd lose all hope. Her heart smashed against the wall of her chest and adrenaline hurtled through her veins.

"You've got a great medical team, babe. They're monitoring you and our little guy. You're a fighter. He's a fighter, a tough guy like your dad, so we picked a good name for him. While you were sleeping the NICU team stopped by to introduce themselves, and to let us know they'd be in the delivery room to take care of Lawrence as soon as he's born, whenever it happens."

"NICU?"

"Neonatal Intensive Care Unit."

She had personal experience with intensive care units, but a unit just for babies made her shiver. "What…what happens if the placenta keeps…" She could barely say the words. "What happens, you know, if the placenta keeps peeling away?"

"In pre-term cases, it's a bigger problem. There's no magic pill. All the doctors can do is wait and see. If the contractions and spotting get worse, they'll try to deliver the baby vaginally. If he goes into fetal distress, they'll do a C-section."

Her world imploded. If it was just her, she'd cope okay. But her body was supporting her baby's life. "It's because of my age. We should have gotten pregnant as soon as Blane had his first birthday. We shouldn't have waited so long."

"It's not your age. It's my fault. We should have flown in the big jet."

When he grimaced, she instantly gripped his hand. "It's not your fault, Kev. We've flown in your plane hundreds of times. There was no reason not to fly in it today. It was a freak accident. You saved our lives."

She turned so she could see him better. "I'll stay in bed. I'll be the best patient they've ever had. I'll eat what I need to eat. I'll get lots of sleep. I'll stay off the phone. If I follow the rules, it'll all be okay. I'll only listen to elevator music. No hard rock. When Blane comes up here, I'll stay in bed and read to him."

"You? Be agreeable?" The crow's-feet around his eyes crinkled as he teased her. "Blane can come up for visits. But you know how he is when he goes to the plantation. He barely remembers us. All he wants to do is play with the big kids and go to Uncle Matt's school."

A contraction tightened her uterus. She reclaimed her hand, rubbed her belly, and studied the monitor. When it was over, she raised the head of the bed, trying to get more comfortable.

"We need to call Austin," Kevin said. "He'll be pissed as hell if you don't tell him you're in the hospital."

"Summer league in Las Vegas starts tomorrow. If I tell him, it'll mess with his focus. I can't tell him yet."

"He's your son. And don't forget what happened when you didn't tell him about your divorce," Kevin said.

"I'll never forget. And I promised never to keep secrets from him again."

"What if he sees the crash on the news?"

"He's in Las Vegas," she said. "He won't see it on the news, and besides, this is different. Nobody's in danger. I'll call him tomorrow. If he can get through the first couple of days of league play, he'll be able to handle our news better." She glanced at the closed door and changed the subject. "Where's Charlotte?"

Kevin looked through the monitor printout rolling out of the machine, fan-folded it neatly, and stacked the paper in the corner of the top drawer of the cabinet. "Do you remember talking to her when the ambulance brought you in?"

JL rubbed her eyes, then closed the right one, then the left one, then squinted, trying to clear the distortion in her vision. "Vaguely."

The word came out slowly, sounding like she was under the influence.

"Charlotte called in her personal obstetrician. She wasn't on call, but she came in for you. There hasn't been a significant change in your condition since you arrived."

"I remember the crash, the EMTs. I think I was screaming."

"Not screaming. Just yelling at the EMTs. You could have a bullet in your gut and you wouldn't complain, but when you're pregnant you don't handle pain as well."

She closed her eyes, hoping she wouldn't see wavy lines when she opened them again. "When I was pregnant with Austin, I was seventeen, away from my family, and scared. When my water broke, I believed my baby was going to die. I lost it."

"I know, babe." He kissed her, and his lips were soft and warm and reassuring.

"Can I have something to eat? I'm starving."

"Probably not, but we can ask. This suite comes with the services of a private chef."

"Yeah right," she grumbled. "Which really means a designated cook in the cafeteria."

"There you are. I just knew underneath all that cynical bluster I'd find the woman I love."

"What cynical bluster?" She made a face. "I love you too, Kevin. And I hope Lance, aka Lawrence Paul Fraser, will look exactly like you." The baby stirred beneath her heart, stretching out a long limb, as if expressing his opinion about the name. She managed a smile.

He squinted at her. "Lance?"

"Yeah, but stop looking at me like that."

"Like how?" he asked.

"Like… I don't know. Like you're calculating sine, cosine, and tangent."

He clamped his teeth over his lower lip and his shoulders shook as he tried not to laugh. "I haven't done trig in decades. What made you think of that?"

She shrugged. "I heard Patrick and Lincoln FaceTiming with

Emily. They were doing trig homework. So if you're not doing trig in your head, then stop looking at me like I'm a bug in a petri dish."

"I promise I don't have trig or chemistry on my mind. I just haven't heard you call the baby Lance before, is all."

"Hmm," she said, squirming to get comfortable. "I must have been thinking about his name while I was asleep. But don't you think it'll be a while before he grows into it? Lance might fit him better at first."

"Whatever you want. I'll just call him laddie for the next few years."

She knuckle-punched his arm. "You will not. That's Elliott's name for the boys."

The door opened and a tall, lanky nurse wearing blue scrubs strolled in. "Hello, Mrs. Fraser." She stopped at the chalkboard, erased the nurse's name, and wrote Sherrin in block letters. "I'm Sherrin, your nurse. How're you feeling?"

The mid-thirties nurse's wire-rimmed glasses sat on a narrow nose. No engagement ring or wedding band. After years of sizing up people in an eyeblink, JL wasn't likely to stop anytime soon.

JL lied through her perfectly capped teeth, mumbling, "Not so bad."

Kevin moved away from the monitor, and Sherrin approached the bed, checked the IV connection, and adjusted the monitor belt around JL's belly. Satisfied nothing else needed adjusting, she unfolded the paper he'd just folded so neatly and studied several feet of the printout.

"They're still irregular. Is there anything you need?"

"A loaded cheeseburger would be nice. But I'll settle for a dish of chocolate ice cream for now."

Sherrin tsked. "You can have ice chips. How's that?" She smiled at Kevin. "The ice machine is in the lounge down the hall."

"Yum," JL said sarcastically. "Will you bring me two cups?"

He looked at her over the top of his reading glasses. "Two cups of ice chips. What will Trainer Ted say when he does your next weigh-in?"

JL waved him off. "Do you really think I care? I complain every time I enter his domain. He's evil incarnate. The next time he gets an offer to manage someone else's gym, he should take it. We'd all be happier."

"And fat and out of shape," Kevin said on his way out.

The nurse refolded the graph paper, made notes on it, tore it off the roll, and slipped it into one of two deep shirt pockets. "Dr. Winn just finished a delivery, so she should be in to see you shortly. Is there anything I can get to make you more comfortable?"

JL folded her arms atop her belly. "Have you seen Dr. Mallory?"

"There's a note in your chart saying she called thirty minutes ago to see how you're doing. She's keeping an eye on you."

"She's the original eye in the sky."

"How long have you known her?" Sherrin asked.

"A few years." JL had a hot flash and let the covers fall below her belly. She was always either hot or cold these days, and would be very happy when her body's temperature regulator returned to its usual efficiency.

While Sherrin typed notes into JL's record on the in-room computer station, Kevin came back with a pitcher of ice chips and two small cups. He stopped to read over the nurse's shoulder.

"Looks like Sherrin is putting an A-plus on your chart." He handed JL a cup and spooned in some chips from the pitcher.

Charlotte Mallory swished in behind him and stopped to read over the nurse's shoulder too. "Who got an A-plus?"

"Hi, Dr. Mallory." Sherrin hopped up so Charlotte could sit and read the notes.

The beautiful blonde spouse of Braham McCabe was now in her mid-fifties. Except for a few lines at the corners of her eyes, Charlotte hadn't changed a bit since JL met her in a Napa, California hangar following the conclusion of a murder-kidnapping-extortion case involving the entire MacKlenna Clan.

Charlotte was always calm. Always cool. Always in control. And JL loved her to the moon and back.

Charlotte logged off the computer, came over to the bed, and hugged JL. The warm familiarity of her signature apple-scented hair and clean scrubs was a boost to JL's psyche.

Charlotte was there and had the situation under control. Now everything would be all right.

"The contractions haven't changed. They're still irregular. How're you feeling?"

"Better now." JL chomped on the last of the ice chips, and Kevin refilled her cup before putting the pitcher in the small refrigerator. "Have you heard from Elliott? We haven't."

"We haven't heard from him in the last"—Kevin checked the time on his watch—"thirty minutes."

"They just landed," Charlotte said. "They're going to the house first."

JL dug her spoon in the ice chips. When she birthed Austin they let laboring patients have Jell-O. All these years later, they were trying to starve her. As soon as the ice hit the roof of her mouth, she slapped her palm to her forehead, hissing. "Brain freeze. Ouch."

"Here. Drink something warm." He handed her a bottle of water that had lost its chill a few hours earlier.

She set the ice chips aside and took a long pull on the plastic bottle. After a moment the brain freeze dissolved. "Call your dad and tell him not to come up here tonight. It's too late. I don't want him pacing and watching me like I'm going to steal the silver."

Kevin laughed, but there wasn't much humor in it. "What are you talking about?"

"Haven't you seen the way he looks at me when I eat food he doesn't think I should eat? Or work out a minute longer than Ted has on my schedule? I don't know how Meredith survived carrying James Cullen and having chemo at the same time. Elliott had to have been a royal pain in the ass."

"He's always a pain in the ass. But you *are* carrying his grandson," Kevin said. "And you've been through this before."

"No. Last time was different. Remember? I didn't let him in my room until after Blane was born. This time he'll want to monitor the situation. I don't want him here." JL grabbed Charlotte's hand. "You call him. He listens to you. Tell him…tell him…it's not good for his health? No, wait. Tell him this is a stressful situation and he might have a real stroke this time."

"You'll have to tell him," Charlotte said. "I won't run interference unless he's doing something detrimental to you or your baby's health. Elliott might be controlling and overbearing, but he'd never do anything to hurt you."

"Doesn't emotional harm count?" JL sipped from the water bottle again before capping it. "Well, at least if he has a stroke he'll already be in the hospital."

Sherrin checked the levels on JL's IVs and wrote something on her palm. "I heard Dr. Fraser rented the other suite on this floor."

JL spit out the water. "Nooo! Say it ain't so."

"I've heard he's a handsome Scot," Sherrin said.

JL dabbed at the wet sheet with a wad of tissues. "Kevin and Charlotte's husband are handsome Scots, too, and much younger and nicer. Don't let Elliott fool you. If he doesn't get his way, he'll cuss you out and blame you for whatever is wrong."

Sherrin's eyebrows met in the center of her forehead, and Kevin gave her a sympathetic smile. "Dad's not quite that bad. But if you see him, don't tell him your name."

"He'll hold the donation of a new labor hall over you so you'll do his bidding," JL said.

Sherrin covered the name tag pinned to her shirt. "He won't hear it from me." Then to JL she said, "If you need anything, honey, press your nurses' call button." She adjusted the position of the call button so it was within easy reach, then patted JL's hand and left the room.

JL tugged on Kevin's shirtsleeve to pull him down for a kiss. He kissed her lips, then the hollow where her neck and shoulder met, and her skin tingled with pleasure. "If Elliott and Meredith are taking Blane to the plantation, why don't you go meet them there? At least one of us can tell Blane good night."

Kevin cupped her cheek. His touch was steady and reassuring, and her nerves settled, as if they'd all been tucked into bed by a comforting hand. He kissed her again. "Blane will be so wound up he won't care. And if I leave now, by the time I drove out to the plantation, spent time with him, and drove back here, I'd be gone almost three hours. I'm not leaving you."

"There are scrubs in the closet, along with a personal hygiene kit. At least there were the last time I was in here as a patient," Charlotte said.

Kevin glanced around the room. "I haven't looked through all the drawers and closets, but if JL had been allowed out of bed, she would have done a complete inventory of the suite."

"True." JL finished the ice chips and handed Kevin the empty container. "Are you going home tonight?" she asked Charlotte.

"I have a patient in ICU, so I'm spending the night here to keep an eye on both him and you."

Holding the cup, Kevin pointed toward the sturdy, ready-for-use sofa upholstered in chocolate-colored fabric. "I'm going to pull out the sofa bed and get some sleep."

JL wiped her hands and face with the damp washcloth. "Has anybody heard from Pete?"

"Connor called while you were asleep, and said Pete is on his way." Kevin tossed the cup into the trashcan. "*Swish*. Fraser hits the three! Nothing but net."

"Good luck with that." JL looked down at the gentle mountain of her pregnancy, the protrusion from her once-lithe body, and for the thousandth time she prayed her baby would be born healthy. "Why's Pete coming back?"

"Because you're in the hospital."

"But he has work to do in Italy."

"It'll get done later. Besides, you're not his partner or his boss anymore. He can make his own decisions, and you wouldn't want it any other way."

She gave Kevin a skeptical eyebrow. "He'll always be my partner, and we'll always have each other's back."

"He surrendered the job on our wedding day."

"You can't surrender a job like that. It's a lifetime responsibility," JL said.

"And I accepted it, Jenny Lynn O'Grady Fraser."

She covered her ears. "Don't call me that. Sometimes children never match the name they're given at birth. Which is further evidence of why Lawrence should be called Lance."

"Lance it is. I won't argue," Kevin said.

"I think Pete's coming home for you," Charlotte said, "but he was already perturbed because the gathering was scheduled after his trip to Italy was put on the calendar. He hates to miss family gatherings," Charlotte said.

"Poor guy. He feels left out. Most of us are married and having babies. He needs to meet someone special."

"I fixed him up with a woman on staff last time he was here," Charlotte said. "They went to Monticello for a charity wine tasting and had a great time, but he never called her again."

"I'm afraid he's got Sophia on his mind this year. It would have been their twentieth wedding anniversary," JL said.

"Bless his heart." Charlotte's phone beeped, and she checked her messages. "I'm needed in the ICU. Then I'm going up to my office for a while. If you need me, call my cell."

JL reached out for a hug. "Thank you for everything. I can't imagine going through this without your support."

Kevin hugged Charlotte, too, and closed the door behind her. "I thought the Sophia business was supposed to be on the Q.T. I didn't think Pete wanted everyone to know."

JL rolled from side to side, searching for a comfortable position to ease the pains shooting down her lower back. "If he wanted to keep it a secret, he shouldn't have told Jack, who tells his sister everything. Ouch."

Alarm appeared on Kevin's face. "What's the matter?" He turned to watch the monitor.

"Nothing. Just my back. Amy told me last week that Jack's going to write a romance novel about Pete and Sophia." JL stopped to breathe through a contraction. When it was over, she continued, "If they won't get back together in real life, he's going to give them a happily ever after in print."

Kevin grimaced, but JL couldn't tell if it was about the idea of Jack writing a love story or what he saw on the monitor printout.

"What's wrong?" she asked.

"New York Times best-selling historical author Jack Mallory isn't going to write a romance novel. Trust me. He was just teasing Amy. If Pete and Sophia were ever going to get back together, it would have happened before now." Kevin unfolded more monitor sheets. "You hear stories of people finding a former boyfriend/girlfriend and living happily ever after, but it's mostly crap."

"Now who's the cynic?"

He refolded the paper and stacked it neatly. "What you don't hear about is how those couples hook up and then break up. You can't rekindle teenage love."

Suddenly, pain thundered around her back to her abdomen like an approaching freight train, slamming into her brain in a cataclysmic explosion. Fluid gushed out and soaked the bed. She grabbed the bedrails. "Water...broke." She kicked back the sheet and a cry mixed with pain and fear ripped through the interior of her lungs. "Blood!"

Kevin turned from the monitor just as she looked up to see the veins in his neck hammering while he looked down at her bloodspattered gown. He tried to relax his face so his fear wouldn't show, but JL could see it in his eyes, and knew without a doubt that this was bad.

"Jesus!" He reached over her, hit the nurses' call button, and slapped an oxygen mask on JL's face at the same time. Then he hurried to the door, yanked it open. "Fetal's down!"

"Can I help you?" the nurse asked through the intercom.

"Find Dr. Winn. Fetal's down! Stat!" Kevin roared from the doorway.

JL's brain flipped from panic to fear to terror, and she squeaked, "Call Charlotte."

He came back to the bed and shoved the over-the-bed tray out of the way. It clanged against the wall. "I'll text her 911. She'll come back immediately."

As people rushed into the room, everything started spinning. The contractions rocked off the scale. She groaned, and more warm blood gushed out between her legs.

In the dark recesses of her mind, JL was alone in a dark alley, blood seeping from a bullet wound above her hip. She was sweaty and cold all at the same time.

Kevin's voice sounded distant to her, and she became aware of the room seeming to shrink smaller and smaller. She was floating away, disembodied, apart from everything happening around her physical body thrashing in the bed.

I'm going to die...

8

Paris (1789)—Sophia

SOPHIA GAZED OUT a window in the salon overlooking the Champs-Élysées. A stiff breeze picked up, rustling the tree branches, sighing through the grass, masking the faraway sounds of angry Parisians.

Fingering the silk drapery with rococo flower motifs, she watched Mr. Short and Jefferson swing easily into a phaeton. Because of the way they interacted and their obvious fondness for each other, it was easy to understand why Jefferson called William his adopted son. They were related distantly through one of his late wife's half-sisters, but there was no resemblance other than their Southern accents.

She continued to gaze out the window long after the men drove through the gate, watching a robin waiting on an open perch. He flew off to catch an insect in flight, oblivious to the turmoil in the city.

Jefferson had been too curious after listening to her account of the events of the day to accept only one version. He decided to find Lafayette himself and get news of the actions of the Assembly, and then collect his daughters. Since Jefferson was attending to both tasks William had volunteered for, William agreed to visit the queen's jewelers to sell a few of Sophia's pearls.

She was left in the capable hands of Mr. Petit, who just now returned carrying a properly laid tea tray with a flowered porcelain teapot, matching clotted cream cup, a covered sugar bowl, cup and saucer, lemon, and a plate of mouthwatering pastries. Before she could settle in with a cup of tea, however, she needed sketching materials.

"Does Mr. Jefferson have chalk? I'd like to start sketching while he's away, but I need either chalk or pen and ink, plus several sheets of paper."

"In his cabinet, mademoiselle. If you'll come with me... Oh, you can't walk. If you tell me exactly what you require, I will bring them to you."

"I can't walk, but I can hobble. Is it far?"

"Down the hallway. Will a cane help?"

"It might."

Mr. Petit disappeared and returned a few minutes later to offer her an extravagant walking cane made with a Malacca shaft, a long brass ferrule, and a handle in ivory pique with gold and tortoise shell. She'd seen a similar one in a museum.

If she only had a limp, the cane would have been helpful, but having the use of only one leg, it wasn't very practical. After struggling through three torturous steps, Mr. Petit offered, "Lean on me, mademoiselle."

Together they made their way down the hall to a room at the corner of the house. Her back hurt, her stomach muscles were tender, and her knee throbbed. But pain had never stopped her before. If anything, pain was a motivator. Not that she sought it out, but when an injury tried to stop her, perseverance overcame the setback. But perhaps not this time...

"Please stop a minute," she said, biting back tears.

"Certainly mademoiselle. Let me get a chair," Mr. Petit said.

"No. I just need to be still for a moment." She should have let Mr. Petit collect the supplies. She couldn't stop now, though. She latched on to Mr. Petit again and continued hobbling until they finally reached the corner room, and the limits of her endurance and pain tolerance. She grabbed the doorframe.

"Is this Mr. Jefferson's office?"

"Yes, his cabinet."

"I thought you meant a cabinet with shelves holding supplies. I didn't realize it was an actual room."

The rectangular office had large windows to capture the full southern exposure. The light wasn't what she would choose for painting but for sketching it would work nicely. She studied the high walls, which were bulging with leatherbound tomes, with additional freestanding bookshelves jutting out like ribs.

An ingenious revolving bookstand with five open books on adjustable shelves allowed Jefferson to consult multiple works at one time. The room was a living, breathing space that captured her imagination, and she mentally sketched him standing there, spectacles balanced on his nose, reading from two books at once. The use of different books for props, maybe to add texture, would bring different points of interest to a composition.

"Do you think Mr. Jefferson would mind if I sit at his desk for a while?"

"I don't know, mademoiselle. Only Mr. Jefferson and Mr. Short have ever worked in this room."

"I won't make a mess, and I promise to be out before he returns."

Still holding onto Mr. Petit's arm, she hobbled over to a lectern and a revolving tabletop on the other side of the room. Even the leather chair, pulled up close, revolved for easy access.

She pointed to a contraption holding a pen. "What is this?"

"A polygraph," Mr. Petit said with a knowing grin. "The device holds two sheets of paper and two connected pens. When Mr. Jefferson writes, the other pen follows to make an exact copy."

"The original copy machine? Very impressive."

"He has written the inventor, Charles Willson Peale, to suggest improvements."

"The painter? Interesting." Her mind continued to sketch Jefferson here and there, reading books and composing his correspondence.

She let go of Mr. Petit's arm and hopped on one foot toward the desk. Mr. Petit opened a drawer and withdrew several sheets of paper and a box. "You'll find sticks of chalk in here. An array of quill pens and ink pots there. If you'll sit, I'll go get the tea service." He held the chair out for her. Bracing herself on the desk, she lowered to the chair.

While Mr. Petit went to reclaim the tea, she squirmed a bit in the swivel chair to get the feel of the leather seat, which was over-stretched from constant use.

She considered the man she intended to sketch. He was more physically impressive than his paintings and sculptures suggested. How could she tap into that? How could she show the idealist, the man who had a greater talent for envisioning what ought to be than the skill to lead others into the future he imagined? She wanted to paint the man who feared exposing his soul again to the pain.

A pain she could relate to.

Mr. Petit returned with the tea tray and set it down on the desk. "Would you like me to pour?"

"I can manage. Thank you."

"Is there anything else you require?"

"Not right now. If I do, is there a pull cord in here? I don't think I'll be able to come find you."

He pointed to a thick cord dangling from the ceiling. "It's here, mademoiselle."

After Mr. Petit left, she propped her legs on the leather-covered bench under the revolving desk. *Dang.* She forgot the pillow. Mr. Petit returned moments later with a pillow, ice bucket, and the rest of the towels. "I thought you might have need of these."

She almost cried. What a sweet man. "Thank you so much."

He gently lifted her injured leg and slipped the pillow beneath it. As soon as she had some privacy, she'd dig into her pocket and take a couple ibuprofen. Willow bark tea, nature's aspirin, would help, but right now she needed more than nature could provide.

Finally situated, she picked up the silver strainer and placed it over a cup as she poured, added a slice of lemon, and then nibbled on the pastries, very carefully, to avoid spilling crumbs on her drawings and Mr. Jefferson's desk.

She was pleasantly surprised with the contents of the box. The natural red chalk was a warm, vital color and would add liveliness to her drawings. Thinking about where she was—in Jefferson's cabinet—she hummed "The Room Where It Happens" from the musical *Hamilton: An American Musical.*

She'd been so enthralled with Hamilton's story that, after seeing the musical in London, she went on an audiobook spree starting with the Ron Chernow book that inspired the musical, followed by Jon Meacham's *Thomas Jefferson: The Art of Power,* James Thomas Flexner's *Washington: The Indispensable Man,* David McCullough's *John Adams,* Walter Stahr's *John Jay: Founding Father,* Paul Staiti's *Of Arms and Artists: The American Revolution through Painters' Eyes,* and finished with Walter Isaacson's *Benjamin Franklin: An American Life.* The audiobooks had kept her entertained at night while she made her reversible dress and undergarments, but by the time she finished Franklin's memoirs, she'd satisfied her curiosity and moved on to stories about eighteenth-century painters.

While she flipped mentally through the audiobooks she'd listen to about the Founding Fathers, she drew a sketch of the room without details, just positioning his contraptions, books, and furniture in the space. Then she experimented with placing Jefferson in the room, interacting with different props. Her favorite was of him standing at the revolving bookstand with his hand marking his place in one book while his finger flipped the corner of a page in another.

The light changing to amber and the daylilies visible from the window folding in on themselves were the only indication of time passing, but she kept working, too manic to stop.

She also sketched a few pictures of the mob storming the Bastille, and even drew a pair of crutches, complete with measurements based on a previous pair she'd used. Jefferson might know of a carpenter who could make them quickly.

Her hand couldn't keep up with the outpouring of ideas, as evidenced by the diminished stack of paper in the drawer. The next time Mr. Petit came in, she'd ask for more paper and directions to the water closet the house was rumored to have.

A gaggle of voices in the hallway distracted her for a moment, but she quickly went back to her sketch. It didn't concern her. She had exhausted her ideas for this room and only needed another few minutes to finish up. Tomorrow she would tackle the garden.

The annoying sound of someone clearing their throat forced her to look up, and what she saw standing in the doorway caused a sickening feeling in the pit of her stomach. The expression "hair on fire" must have originated with Jefferson.

A last ray of the waning sun beamed through the window directly onto his sandy-colored hair, setting it afire with sunset colors.

His fists were clenched at his sides, and tension hunched his shoulders. *Oops.* She had planned to be out long before he returned, but time got away from her.

Dozens of sketches were scattered on the desk, but most were on the floor, a habit she'd developed long ago—her controlled chaos of creativity.

He didn't say anything as he moved slowly into the room, stooping to pick up the closest drawings.

"Oh, hi…you're home."

Jefferson's ruddy complexion was even redder now. "Our agreement was that you would paint the garden."

"Well, I didn't make it there today." She returned pieces of chalk to the box and straightened the papers on the desk. "This is one of the most fascinating rooms I've ever been in. It's like a peek into your mind. It looks like you, feels like you, smells like you."

She could keep talking, but it wouldn't do any good. She doubted if anyone, especially a woman, had ever transgressed Jefferson's unwritten law—Thou shall not, under fear of severe discipline, meddle with the master's cabinet.

She returned the empty teacup to the tray and brushed away pastry crumbs scattered on the desk. "I was so enthralled that I had to get my ideas down on paper. I didn't intend to spend the afternoon here."

He picked up several more pieces of paper and thumbed through them. Not only was his face turning a brighter red, but his hair was too. He held up a handful of sketches, shaking them, mimicking the sound of fluttering wings. Then he held one sheet separate and apart from the others.

"What is this?"

Jefferson wasn't as angry as Sophia's father was when he discovered she and Pete had eloped, but close. She had refused to show fear then, and she refused to show fear now.

She was in the wrong, no doubt about it. Not only had she invaded Jefferson's space, but she had drawn a sketch he probably considered inappropriate.

"Why, pray tell, am I only half dressed?"

"Oh, that one... Well, you're looking only at what's not there, instead of what is." If she'd been able to walk, she would have gotten up and taken the sketch away from him. "Instead of focusing on you in the sketch, tell me what else you see."

"A grapery."

"Look closely. It's a place that provides physical and emotional protection. It's a vineyard or grapery at sunset. Can you smell the sensual flavors of the flowering vines, the earthy scent of soil after a thunderstorm, the sunburned grass?"

The same look of puzzlement he had earlier returned, but with more intensity. "You didn't answer my question."

"This isn't about what *I* see. It's about what *you* see."

"I see a man half dressed."

"Then I'm sorry for that, because I see much more. Thick, ropy muscles in your neck, shoulders, and arms, strained from hours of toiling in your vineyards. You wouldn't be working in the soil wearing a coat, embroidered waistcoat, and linen shirt. No, your collar would be open, your sleeves rolled to your elbows, shirttail partially untucked, hair unbound. It's an earthy, sensual experience.

"Look at the sketch. You have dirt in your hand, studying the life in the soil. A man wearing a coat with lace on the sleeves doesn't feel the soil, doesn't smell it, doesn't squeeze it between his fingers. And that, Mr. Jefferson, is why you're only half dressed."

"Sophia." The way he whispered her name, with his mix of accents, might have been the second most seductive sound she'd ever heard.

"Thomas," she said, matching the softness of his voice.

He sat in a chair next to his revolving bookshelf and leaned forward, elbows on his knees. "How do you know?"

"I'm not sure what you're asking."

"Your painter's eye saw a man others haven't seen. How'd you know?"

"I work with my hands, but I paint from my heart. I take in sensory information and push it out through my paintbrush. Anyone can make art, but not everyone can make you feel something when you view it." The conversation was straying in a direction she didn't want it to go, and tension was palpable in the room. Painting him might be the most difficult commission she'd ever undertake.

She changed the subject. "Did your daughters return with you?"

He nodded and slowly got to his feet again. "The girls have gone to their rooms to rest before dinner. We're having guests. I'll ask their chambermaid Sally to see if she can find something in Patsy's wardrobe to fit you."

"That's not necessary. I came prepared." Her jacket was slung over the back of his desk chair. She waved a sleeve. "My jacket and skirt are reversible. I have a necklace and earbobs for some bling and a rhinestone comb for my hair. After a bath I'll be respectable again." She glanced down at her hands. "My hands need a good scrubbing, too."

He wiped his finger down her cheek. "And your face."

"Having chalk on my cheeks is an occupational hazard."

"What is bling?"

"Whatever the queen wears—anything expensive and ostentatious."

"Is it French?"

She laughed and then converted it into a more tactful cough. "No, it's universal. One of those words that's the same in all languages."

He slipped her jacket off the chair. "Reversible clothes? I've never heard of such a thing." He held up the blue-green wool and silk jacket, then turned it inside out and examined the reversed side, which featured hand-painted flowers on silk and linen. "Two in one."

"Much like your polygraph."

His gaze shifted from the jacket to the polygraph and back to the jacket. "A very clever design, and practical for traveling."

"Thank you."

He gave her the same surprised look he had earlier when he discovered she spoke English. "You designed your traveling dress?"

"Designed and made it. I wouldn't do it again. I spent almost a year working out the patterns for both dresses and sewing them together, and I swear I ripped out twice as many seams as I sewed."

"You paint, sew—what else do you do?"

"I don't sing or play an instrument, but I make a mean pasta." When his confused expression leaned more toward embarrassment, she said, "Mean is an expression of awesomeness. I'm sure in your travels you've had a pasta dish with a Bolognese sauce or pesto or cherry tomatoes and mozzarella with cheese sprinkled on top."

"You mean macaroni."

"Macaroni, ravioli, spaghetti, tortellini. Pair a pasta dish with a medium weight Sangiovese wine, fresh focaccia bread, and a green salad…" She kissed her fingers. *"Delizioso."*

One eyebrow quirked up. *"Delizioso.* You speak Italian, French, English. Any others?"

"A few expressions in German. What about you?"

"I can read in several languages, but, I'm ashamed to say, I struggle with speaking French."

"If you can't hear how a word sounds, it's hard to know how to say it.

Êtes-vous d'accord? It means do you agree?"

"*Êtes-vous d'accord?*"

"Since you have an ear for music, foreign languages should be easy for you." She gazed up at him, and the slow, rhythmic thump of her heart surprised her. There was an attraction here that couldn't be denied.

Two weeks. It's all the time I have.

"Your auburn hair is striking. At sunset in the vineyards, with rays of the dying sun beaming through your hair…"

Flushing, she jerked her eyes away from his face. The vision of him in the vineyard was too erotic. Had her erotic feelings been expressed in this sketch, too?

"May I take another look?"

He handed the sketch to her, and she appraised her work. Women would drool if she painted this. While there was nothing overtly sexual in the sketch, it was there in the undertones. The combination of tense cords of tendons bunching in his neck, eyes lingering hungrily on an object only he could see, and long-fingered hands caressing a bunch of grapes in one, dirt in the other, would have every woman believing she was the object of his desire.

She made a move to crush the drawing in her hands, but he caught one of her hands in mid-flight. "This is one artist's depiction of a vintner. I'd like to keep it." He slipped the sketch to the bottom of the stack of drawings he had collected off the floor.

She had to say something to break the tension reverberating in the room. "I'm glad your hair isn't powdered and curled at the sides."

Talk about lame.

"I do observe the fashion required at the French Court and use powder and pomade then."

"Well, just so you know, I'd never paint you with powder and pomade. Two hundred years from now, a painting of you with hair *au naturel* will sell for a lot of money."

He picked up a strand of her hair and rubbed it between his fingers. "This is like corn silk." He brought it to his nose. "And smells like a crisp morning on a seaweed-strewn New England beach."

"Very visual. Very descriptive. Hair blowing in the breeze, waves lapping at bare feet. I can see you there. Very swashbuckling. It would be a magnificent *plein air* painting, too. But the vineyard is more you, I think."

William came to the door, glanced around the cabinet, then focused his attention on them. "What…happened here?"

Jefferson backed away from her and moved to the other side of the desk. "Mademoiselle Orsini has been sketching this afternoon." Jefferson handed the sketches to William. "She's especially pleased with the one of me in the vineyards."

William thumbed through the pages, and when he came to the drawing in question he straightened and said, "But you're dressed like a laborer."

"The mademoiselle's explanation is reasonable, although I would never agree to pose for such a painting." He reclaimed the offending sketch from William and slipped it into a leatherbound portfolio. The rest he returned to Sophia. Then he saw the ones she'd done of the events at the Bastille and the one of her crutches.

"Are these sketches of the Bastille accurate?"

"To the best of my memory."

"And this? What are these?"

"Crutches. Do you know a carpenter who could make them? I included the measurements, since he probably can't make them adjustable."

"What does this question mark represent?"

"The bottom tips need something soft so they won't scratch the floors, but won't be slippery, either. I'm not sure what's available."

"I've never seen this design before. Are you sure it will work?"

"Unfortunately, I've had a couple of injuries that required using them. They work quite well."

Jefferson showed the design to William. "This is brilliant, and so simple. My carpenter could easily make these."

While William studied the drawing over Jefferson's shoulder, she asked him, "Were you able to sell any of my jewels?"

He pulled a pouch out of his pocket. "There's a complete accounting in the bag, along with the proceeds and the rest of your pearls. Mademoiselle Rose Bertin, the queen's dressmaker, was visiting the jewelers, and I asked her to call on you tomorrow. She said she would bring a mantua maker and milliner."

"The queen's gowns cost thousands of livres apiece. I can't afford Mademoiselle Bertin. But I'll meet with her and the pattern maker. Maybe we can collaborate on something appropriate. Then I'll go to the market and purchase used gowns. I can remake them, add embellishments, and no one will know the difference."

She yawned. The day had finally caught up with her. "How much do you think a pair of crutches will cost? And I will add a bonus if they can be made in the next few hours."

"A few sols, I would think," William said.

"Less if my carpenter can make them," Jefferson said.

"Take what you think you'll need." William removed several coins and returned the pouch to her. "And I would like to pay for my lodging," she said.

Jefferson's chiseled features pinched in disapproval. "Certainly not."

According to Meacham's audiobook, money was always an issue with Jefferson. "I don't want to be a financial burden, and I don't want to use a bank. Money just sits in vaults growing restless and reproducing itself."

She withdrew a handful of bills out of the pouch and slipped them into his desk drawer, enough to cover her lodging. After all, she'd be going home with dozens of sketches of him. She could paint a few portraits and more than recoup the money.

"If merchants show up at my door demanding payment for your purchases, I'll use that money. Otherwise, it will remain right there."

"Don't be stubborn, Mr. Jefferson. It doesn't suit you. I've used your paper and chalk. I'm staying in your house, eating your food, drinking your tea, using your cabinet. Take the money, please." She slipped her jacket back on, but stockings and shoes were out of the question. "Now if you don't mind, I'd love to take a nap. If you'll tell me where to go, I'll hobble there."

He gave a deep, throaty laugh. "You're calling *me* stubborn? To see what a stubborn person looks like, you needn't look past your own straight-edged nose. You can't hobble upstairs."

"No, but I can sit down and climb up on my bottom."

He raised one eyebrow. "Not in my house!" He picked her up and started for the door.

Willian rushed in front of Jefferson. "Let me carry her, sir."

Jefferson brushed past him. "I carried her into the house. I can carry her up the stairs. If you want to be helpful, get her shoes, please."

"Sir, if you'll carry her to the stairs, I'll carry her up."

"I'm not a weakling," Jefferson said.

She bit back a smile, finding it rather endearing that they were arguing over who was going to carry her.

William grabbed her shoes, then matched Jefferson's stride as they hurried down the hall. "I'd never call you a weakling. If we arm wrestled, you'd beat me nine times out of ten. I'm merely worried you might reinjure your wrist."

"Don't be ridiculous. Her weight isn't on my wrist."

Sophia flashed a panicked look at William. He straightened his jacket, then blocked the first step of an ornately carved walnut staircase. "I'll take her from here, sir."

Arguing over her would have been flattering if it hadn't been over something she could do for herself, albeit with some difficulty. Where was Mr. Petit when she needed him?

Jefferson huffed a sigh of frustration. "Have it your way." Sophia was carefully transferred to William's waiting arms, and Jefferson preceded them up the grand staircase. When they reached the landing, he reclaimed her.

"I appreciate your gallantry," she said. "Both of you. Hopefully I'll have crutches to assist me by the time I have to go back down."

Mr. Petit appeared magically, as if summoned like a Genie from a bottle.

"The mademoiselle's room is prepared. I'll have a pitcher of hot water brought up."

"Thank you, Mr. Petit," she said. "Also, the ice has melted. Could you send up ice, too? I need to rewrap my knee."

Jefferson carried her into a bedroom, and a servant girl came in behind them, carrying a pitcher of steaming water, the ice bucket, and several towels folded over her arm.

"Sally, would you please help Mademoiselle Orsini? She hurt her knee and can't walk."

Sally set the pitcher on the washstand, smiled what could have been her best smile, and curved her best hip. "Yes, sir."

"I can manage just fine," Sophia said, yawning.

Sally held onto the doorknob, and if looks could growl… "If I'm to help the mademoiselle, you and Mr. Short need to leave us be."

Sophia fell back on the bed. Noticing details of a setting were second nature to her, and even though her eyelids would only stay open if propped up with toothpicks, she noted the position of a full-length mirror with a gilt frame standing next to a stunning marble-top commode with bronze doré pulls and key plates. A chair upholstered in blue silk stood between two open windows with pale blue silk draperies. A four-drawer chest was inlaid with delicate medallions of porcelain, and the trundle daybed she was lying on had the lower portion extended, and the coordinating cotton counterpane was thick and soft.

"Mr. Petit told me about the ice on your knee. It's probably melted now. Do you want me to wrap more ice in a dry towel?"

"That would be very nice, Sally." Sophia reached into her pocket and handed over a stocking. She had removed both and used one to wrap her knee. "I'm sure the wrap I made out of the other stocking is soaked through, so you can use this one."

While Sally unwrapped her knee, Sophia sat up and removed her jacket, blouse and stays, and unbuttoned her skirt.

When Sally finished wrapping a fresh ice pack around Sophia's knee, she asked, "Is it too tight?"

"It's perfect." Sophia yawned. "You must have done this before."

"No, ma'am. Mr. Petit showed me how to do it in case you needed help. I'm glad you did. It would have been a shame to waste such good learning. If master ever has a hurt knee, I'll know how to wrap ice around it."

"It has to be right after the injury. Starting an ice treatment days later won't work as well."

Sally nodded thoughtfully as she hung Sophia's clothes on pegs mounted to the wall next to the washstand. Sophia scooted out of her skirts and handed them to Sally to hang too, but before Sally hung them, she used the clothes brush to remove the mud at the bottom of the skirts.

"This fabric cleans up so fast. Never seen that happen before."

Sophia tried to listen but she was too tired, and within minutes fell into a deep sleep.

9

Paris (1789)—Sophia

A NIGHTMARE OF being burned alive woke Sophia, shaking and sweating profusely. Heat engulfed her in a world surrounded by chaos. A glaze of sleep encrusted her brain and held it captive in the gloomy darkness of her subconscious. A place she didn't want to dwell.

Instinctively, she flung her arms out as she struggled to punch through the crust toward safety. But where was that? She didn't even know if it was yesterday or tomorrow.

In that limbo moment she didn't know if she cared. But then, unexpectedly, the events since she arrived in Paris charged into her consciousness, hauling a horde of memories—*Storming the Bastille. French Revolution. Almost killed. Thomas Jefferson.*

She cracked her eyes open to find moonlit darkness with a single burning candle. She rolled over, forgetting about her knee. "Ouch!" she hissed. How could she forget her freaking injured knee? The intense, shooting pains melted the glaze of sleep.

She rolled onto her back again. The cover of sleep might be scary, but it was less painful than the reality of being awake. When she'd been carried into the room earlier, the hooded blue of dusk had fallen. That's how she thought of dusk when painting *en plein air*. Now the inky-colored sky had a full moon and a blaze of stars. How long had she been asleep? Without a watch, there was no way of knowing.

She pulled herself up, propping a couple of pillows behind her, her limbs stiff and ungainly. What should she do now? Stay in bed? Go back to sleep? Sleep wouldn't be possible without a couple of ibuprofens, which required getting out of bed. Besides, the icepack had melted and soaked the wrapping around her knee. She removed it and used another towel to dry her leg.

As much as she hated doing it, she hobbled over to where her skirt hung from a peg and dug into the pocket for her pouch of goodies. Dry-swallowing pills was never a good idea, especially ibuprofen, but she did it anyway. Then she dropped the wet towels into the wash bowl.

"Well, I'll be…" Leaning against the washstand were a pair of crutches. She snugged them under her arms and did another turn around the room. The sticks were solidly built, with both handgrips and shoulder rests padded and covered with soft leather. The carpenter had done an awesome job.

The first time she was a walking tripod, she hadn't figured out how to maneuver through the world and had a miserable experience. But after a broken foot, two twisted ankles, and now a bruised knee, she pretty much had the sticks figured out. Stairs and crutches were mortal enemies, though. She had her own strategies for going up and down, but not in an eighteenth-century dress.

She put the crutches back and returned to bed, accompanied by a rumbling stomach. Just a piece of fruit or bite of cheese would hold her until breakfast. She could pull the bell cord, but if the servants had all gone to bed, she didn't want anyone having to get up on her account. Save for a few creaks and pops and an occasional chirp, the house was silent, inside and out.

If she intended to go downstairs for food, she'd have to get dressed, as unappealing as it sounded. What were the chances that someone was still up? She opened her door and listened. No sounds came from the hall, the other bedrooms, or the salon below. Everyone must be in bed. Maybe she could get away with wearing her Tai Chi uniform.

After dressing, but before tackling the stairs, she centered herself and visualized climbing down one step at a time. Was going downstairs worth it? Her stomach chose that moment to growl, at which point she had to agree, it was. She set the crutches on the first step.

Each time a floorboard creaked she cringed, but kept going down the winding stairs, lit by limited circles of flickering brightness. Somewhere a door swung open, the creak echoing through the silence. When she didn't hear voices or footfalls, she continued, descending slowly to the first floor, where more candles cast weird shadows on the walls.

The door to Jefferson's cabinet stood open, and the soft yellow light of a single flickering candle flared from his office. The scratching of pen on paper enhanced the eerie ambience. *He must be writing his report to John Jay about the events of the day.* He was a prolific letter writer, signing each one—TH Jefferson.

TH. She let the initials play on her tongue. Did they all use initials? A. Hamilton, A. Burr, G. Washington. No, James Madison used his whole name.

She hobbled on her crutches toward the door, where she watched him move away from the desk to stand alone, a specter in the semidarkness, a motionless silhouette facing the window, the breeze whipping through his unbound hair. His shirt was open at the collar, sleeves rolled to the elbow, and the stark white of the fabric glowed in the lamplight.

He must have sensed her there, because without looking her way, he asked, "Was it your ordeal with the mob or the afternoon sketching that tired you?"

She was so taken with the *mise-en-scène*, with the man, with the moment—she couldn't speak. And when she finally did, her voice sounded raspy from sleep. "The ordeal." She crutched her way into the room without waiting for an invitation. The fresh, intoxicating scent of lavender and citrus filled the air, and she glanced around for its source until her eyes settled on him.

"I can paint all day and never get tired."

As he stepped back from the window, he slipped his index finger in the book in his hand and closed the pages over it. He gestured toward a large blue chair that earlier had books and papers stacked high on the seat. Then he appraised her in a long intense gaze: her hair draped loosely about her shoulders, her shirt, pants, and probably even the exact state of her circulation.

"What are you wearing?"

She raised her chin and crutched over to the chair. "Chinese shirt and trousers. I may not be appropriately dressed, but I am sufficiently covered."

His expression was one of utter disbelief. "I'm not so sure."

She held out her injured leg. "I've heard it said I have golden antelope legs, but if I were you, I wouldn't believe the rumors." She dropped it slowly. "Actually, in China women wear loose trousers."

He continued to stare, his eyes flashing some emotion bordering on more than disbelief. "Mademoiselle, you are not in China."

"True," she replied, her tone measured, "but I am hungry, and I couldn't descend the stairs in layers of skirts." She collected her crutches in one hand, sat, and propped them against the windowsill next to the chair. "You would expect me to take reasonable precautions while staying here. Right? If a crutch had caught on my hem, I would have tumbled to the bottom of the staircase."

"If you had tugged the bell pull in your bedroom to summon a servant, coming downstairs would have been unnecessary."

"Not in the middle of the night, especially when I'm capable of fending for myself."

"Fend for yourself?" His voice was so saturated with irony, she could have wrung it out of the air and mopped it up with a towel. "I don't believe it's possible, and I'm indebted to Mr. David for taking care of an American citizen under my protection."

Ah-ha. So he found out what happened at the Bastille.

"Monsieur David asked me to sit for him."

"I saw him earlier tonight and he mentioned the possibility." Jefferson sat in his desk chair, exchanged his finger in the book for a slip of paper, and placed the volume aside. "I was embarrassed to have to inform him that my negligence caused you further injury."

"Then I'm sure you wouldn't want him to hear how I tumbled down your stairs, too."

Just before he answered, he paused, and his eyes darkened, as if the weight of sudden realization brought about a chemical change in him. "Mademoiselle, do you always win an argument?"

She smiled demurely. "I try to, sir."

His face visibly relaxed. "I've come to accept situations in Paris that I would never accept at home. Your attire is unconventional but not unseemly."

"Coming from you, Mr. Ambassador, I consider that a compliment." With her leg hanging down, the throbbing intensified. She had to either prop it up on a stool or cry. As if reading her mind, he moved the bench from under his desk over to her and gently lifted her leg. She sucked air through her teeth.

"You need to see a doctor and get something for the pain."

"Not yet. The pain hasn't moved from an ouch to an ahh yet, but it will. The leg really doesn't like to be left dangling. It's better when I keep it raised."

"Is that why you woke up? Because of the pain?"

Sophia removed the pillow at her back and slipped it under her knee. "Some pain, but mostly hunger. Since I missed dinner, I was hoping to find a bone to gnaw on in the kitchen."

"I'm sure Mr. Petit can find something more filling than a bone." He reached for the pull cord.

"Please don't disturb him. If you'll point me in the right direction, I'm sure I can find a midnight snack on my own. I wish someone had awakened me so I could dine with everyone else."

"Sally went in to see about you. She said you were sleeping soundly."

"She also changed my ice pack."

Jefferson returned to his chair. "Mr. Petit watched you do it and was able to instruct Sally."

She wasn't sure when Mr. Petit watched her. There must be spy holes in the walls. "Sally told me she was pleased to know how to ice and wrap in case you have another injury."

"I dislocated my wrist a few years ago. It still hasn't healed properly." He rubbed his wrist, and his pained expression spoke to the intensity of the experience.

"You and Mr. Short mentioned your injury earlier. It should have been iced right away. It would have helped enormously with the pain and swelling."

"Next time I'll know about icing, and if I injure my leg, I'll know how to make a pair of crutches." He sat back in his chair and steepled his hands. "You're moving well with them."

She rubbed her hand along the padded handgrip of one of the crutches. "The swing-through gait is pretty easy, and I've had to use them before. You just have to remember to press down on the handgrips."

"I tried them out, although they were too short. It took me several tries to figure out how to use them."

"The wood is such a rich dark brown. Is it walnut?"

"I wanted to use the strongest wood available."

She cocked her head. "You made them?"

"I supervised the construction to be sure they were made correctly. However, I did make a minor design change."

Her mouth twitched with suppressed laughter. "Why am I not surprised?"

He narrowed his eyes. "If a design change would improve the operation of an apparatus, the change should be made. The crutches were too short for me, and the altered design will accommodate taller patients."

"I didn't want to complicate things, so I skipped that step," she said, "but you saw the need immediately. I'll take good care of this pair so you can give them to another houseguest." From the look on his face, her attempted joke didn't go over very well.

"Every time I see them, I'll remember my negligence caused your accident. I should have noticed the hole in the yard and had it filled. It's been done now."

"The knee was already bothering me this morning. Stepping in the hole only twisted an already weakened knee." She folded her hands in her lap and appraised the rest of the office to see what else he'd done since she left the room in disarray. The tea tray had been removed, most of the books were off the floor, and the shelves on the revolving bookstand were now empty and waiting to be cluttered again.

Mr. Petit appeared at the open door. "Mademoiselle, I heard your voice. I'm sure you're hungry. May I prepare your dinner now?"

"Thank you, Mr. Petit. Maybe some cheese and bread. Fruit if you have any."

"That won't do," Jefferson said. "She'll have the grilled pork cutlets with piquant sauce. There's broccoli and asparagus from the garden and a slice of watermelon." The way he said it sounded more like wah-a-tah-mill-i-an.

"If I eat all that, I'll never go back to sleep," she said. However, Monsieur Petit took his orders from Jefferson, not her. He left, she assumed, to prepare her dinner as instructed.

"I have an extensive library." Jefferson waved his hand to encompass the shelves of books. "I should be able to find a sufficiently dry and boring book to help put you to sleep after you eat."

"I noticed a book on gardening lying open on the floor this afternoon. I bet that one is dry and boring." She studied the leather bindings, wondering how many of these books were now, or would in the future, survive the Library of Congress fire? And if there was a boring gardening book, how many people had been inclined to read it? Probably a slew of Jeffersonophiles.

"Just curious. Why would you spend money on a boring book?"

"Even boring books have something to offer."

"A gardening book?" She laughed, wiggling her thumbs. "You'll notice mine aren't green."

"From algae growing on the outside of earthenware pots?" He gave her a killer smile that reached his eyes. "You might not have algae stains, but I'm sure you routinely have paint on your hands or chalk on your face."

She touched her face self-consciously, recalling how gently he'd rubbed chalk off her cheek. According to the biography she listened to, Jefferson enjoyed women of superior education and experience who also had artistic and musical talents. He considered them his intellectual equals. Did he see her as an educated, talented woman?

The short, wide pendulum of the Pillar Clock resting on the mantel ticked off irreplaceable seconds and minutes. The room was getting warm, even with a steady breeze from the windows. She reached for her crutches, and, creating an awkward segue asked, "Would you like to walk in the garden while I wait for my late supper?"

"A walk?" He knitted his brows to an inquisitive point. "You should rest."

She braced the crutches under her arms and replied, as calmly as she could, "I need air. Can we walk halfway around the garden?" What she really needed was space. A lot of it. "Besides, I want to see it in the moonlight. Then tomorrow when I go out to sketch, I won't have to imagine what it looks like at night."

"We can go as far as you'd like." He followed her out. "You manage the crutches well. I was confused by your measurements. But I finally realized the distance from under your arm to six inches beyond your shoe allows for the proper swinging motion. The design also requires upper body strength. You and my daughter Patsy are close in height, and she couldn't support herself. How is it that you can?"

"I practice an ancient form of Chinese exercise called Tai Chi. It promotes good health through meditation and movements, and it works the entire body to build strength and flexibility."

"Where'd you learn a Chinese exercise? Did you travel to China?"

She stopped in one of several circles of light in the hallway. "I learned from a Chinese master who was visiting Florence. It changed my life."

He nodded, and his expression said he was considering her answers, but had more questions. "I'd like to see it performed. Will you show me how it's done?"

"As soon as I can put weight on my leg, I'd be happy to. The philosophy of Tai Chi is simple yet profound. The core concept is, everything consists of two opposing forces that harmonize with each other to create a whole. Every left has a right, every up has a down. There's a yin-yang, white-black, exhale-inhale, release-store, expand-contract, give-receive, offense-defense. But what it does for me is sharpen my focus and increase my creativity."

"How long have you been doing it?"

She continued crutching her way toward the salon. "Five years. I wanted to feel empowered and able to protect myself. Now I spend the first two hours of every day doing the exercises and meditating. The training kept me calm and enabled me to survive what happened at the Bastille. I've never experienced such violence and anger."

"A form of meditation that strengthens and protects you. Now I'm even more curious."

"Tai Chi is the deadliest self-defense martial arts ever invented."

"Martial arts have developed independently in many different cultures throughout history. But I've never encountered anyone who practiced it, and certainly not a woman."

"Wait until you see a demonstration. It's compelling to watch, and very graceful."

They reached the circular salon, where Mr. Petit was instructing a servant carrying a tray with silverware and dishes.

"Mr. Petit, we'll be walking in the garden," Jefferson said.

"Would you like dinner there?" Mr. Petit asked.

Jefferson deferred to her. "Do you have a preference?"

"Dinner in the garden sounds delightful." She considered the hazards of mixing wine with using crutches and decided one glass wouldn't impact her balance. "A glass of red wine would be nice. Maybe a medium-bodied red like a Chianti. It would pair well with the grilled pork, don't you think?"

He pursed his lips. "One doesn't drink wine to wash down food.

One drinks cider or beer. Then one lingers after the meal with a fine bottle of wine and good conversation."

"But wine enhances the food's flavor on your tongue," she said. "The crispness in white wines brings out the light, delicate flavors of fish and chicken. Big, red wines with tannins like to marry with the fats in marbled meats and high-fat cheeses. The buttery taste of an oaked chardonnay marries well and enhances the flavors of foods with cream sauces. You're a foodie, Mr. Jefferson. Try it. You might like it."

"I'm a *what?*"

She couldn't tell if he was offended, shocked, or ready to laugh. "Didn't someone accuse you recently of being unfaithful to good, old-fashioned roast beef in favor of French cuisine?"

He smirked. "My nemesis Patrick Henry, an ignorant man who has probably never opened a book, was mistaken. My table has always been supplied with Southern staples—fried chicken, country ham, a variety of peas, beans, and greens."

"And wine," she added.

"What wine would you pair with fried chicken?" From the confident look in his eyes, he believed he would win the challenge.

She leaned on the shoulder rests. "Fried chicken is a fatty food, and champagne is an acidic beverage. The bubbly clears your palate for chicken, and chicken clears your palate for champagne. They are a perfect pairing. I know my wines, Mr. Jefferson."

"If you can tell me how to get vines to grow in Virginia, I'll believe it."

"It could be the plants. Take a European grape and cross-pollinate it with an American grape to create a hybrid. That'll combine the flavor of a European wine with the hardiness of an American wine." She shrugged. "Or it could be the climate. Wait two hundred years and climate change will make it warmer." She groaned. She couldn't continue to banter with him. "Speaking of warm, let's go outside where it's cooler."

To Mr. Petit he said, "Uncork a bottle of Chianti and bring two wine glasses."

"Do you want the wine after dinner?"

"The mademoiselle would like her wine with her meal," Jefferson said. "And since I've already dined, I'll have a glass with Mademoiselle Orsini's stimulating conversation."

"I'm sorry to be such a bother," Sophia said, "but if you have lemon, I'd like a glass of water with lemon slices."

"To wash your hands?" Mr. Petit asked.

"No, to drink. Thank you."

Jefferson led her through an oval-shaped drawing room and opened the French doors to the widest possible extent. He hovered, arms outstretched, ready to catch her as she climbed down the steps to the garden.

She inhaled the heavy night air. The moon was not quite full, but the sky was so clear, so cloudless, the whole planet appeared gilded in silver. Her one good leg nearly trembled at the magic and beauty of it all.

"Do you want to sit or walk?"

"Let's keep walking." Her knee throbbed, but she had asked for a walk in the garden. To sit down now would make her seem silly and indecisive.

He directed her toward a low hedge. "The path starts here."

They followed a serpentine path, wending their way through the garden. In the moonlight, it was enchanting. She didn't care where they went, and obviously he didn't either, so long as they remained linked by their pulsing thread. Lanterns lit the path as it wound its way to the top of a low rise. There she found statuary, a torch-lit pond, and a parterre with an ornamental arrangement of flower beds. Mr. Petit must have sent someone ahead to light the torches.

"What is climate change?" he asked.

Uh-oh. It took a moment to come up with an answer. "Well...let's see. Have you heard about the Ice Age?" She didn't know when evidence was first discovered, or how she would explain it if the term was unknown to him.

"I haven't heard that term either."

Double uh-oh. "Well, hmmm. I heard it in...Florence. This man claimed the earth was covered by ice millions of years ago."

"Who was the man?"

She continued hobbling along on the crutches, stalling. Finally, she said, "I was painting and not paying full attention. I'm sorry. I didn't catch his name."

"What else do you remember?"

Go slowly, and don't get specific. Remember, he doesn't miss a thing.

"He mentioned the glaciers in the Alps shrinking. I don't know how he knew that. I'm not a scientist, I'm a painter, but from what I heard, he believed the earth warmed, and the ice melted. I just figured if the earth warmed once, it could warm again. That's climate change. You should talk to Benjamin Franklin. Didn't he study the effects of deforestation on local climates?"

"He's also studied the Gulf Stream, but if I understand what you said, Virginia could get warmer and the vines could survive the winter."

"All you can do is track the outside temperature year after year and see if it changes significantly."

He frowned. Not a good look for him. "I'm looking for an alternative crop to Virginia's soil-leaching tobacco. I need to talk to this man. Do you think he's still in Florence?"

"He was very old. He's probably dead by now." Needing to change the subject, she asked, "Did you get more news about what happened at the Bastille?"

He clasped his hands behind him and lowered his head for a moment, as if gathering his thoughts or compartmentalizing them. "While you slept, after I gave instructions to my carpenter to make the crutches, I visited a friend, Madame de Corny, and received another firsthand account. It was as you reported. She also had news from Versailles."

Sophia hobbled around the torchlit pond, watching dragonflies skim the water's surface. Other winged insects buzzed and swarmed the scented air. She moved back from the water, leaned on the crutches, and waved away the bugs.

"What did she say?"

"The slaughter of the people, the beheading of the governor, and the lieutenant governor so concerned the King that, along with his two brothers, he went to the *États-Généraux,* promising to disperse the troops. He pledged reform to restore peace and happiness to his people."

Jefferson skirted the pond to meet her, and together they continued along the serpentine path with Sophia setting the pace. "I wrote Thomas Paine tonight and told him I have never seen a more dangerous scene of war than what I saw on the streets this afternoon."

"I predict the French Revolution will be longer and bloodier than America's."

"How often do your predictions come true?"

"I have about a ninety-nine percent accuracy rate." She wanted to kick herself in the butt. She couldn't give Jefferson hints of the future in a playful game of I Predict. He was too smart for her.

"Then I predict this is the one percent," he said.

"I can't pick which predictions to believe and which ones to ignore."

"I can," he said. "If this chopping off of heads is to become *à la mode,* then I'm apt to wake every morning wondering if mine is still sitting on my shoulders."

She laughed, although she shouldn't, but he had such a wonderful sense of humor. "Mr. Ambassador, I don't believe your life is in danger. At least not like it was during America's Revolution. If the war had been lost, you, Washington, Franklin, Adams, Hamilton, Henry, and the rest would have been hung as traitors, and your places in history would be only footnotes."

He led her to a bench on the path snugged in between two trees, and they sat together in the moonlight. There was an unease about him, and she sensed it had nothing to do with her and everything to do with the situation in France, and knowing he would soon leave the country.

"What's the king going to do? Is he concerned for his safety?" she asked.

"He seems to trust Lafayette, who is in command of the new National Guard. The king agreed to come to Paris to meet at City Hall."

"With all those armed citizens? He's very brave."

"The people love their king. I'm not sure about the queen, but they don't want to overthrow him. All they want is food and representation."

"Your sympathies are with the people, aren't they?" she asked.

He started to rise, then sank back on the bench with a perplexed frown. "I can't get involved in this. I have to stay neutral."

"Lafayette is your friend. He'll need your help to navigate France's revolution. You can't remain uninvolved."

"If you see that so clearly, so will others. I'll have to be even more circumspect."

"You'll manage fine," she said.

"How could you know?"

"You've already been through this. You're just coming at it from a different perspective. And the general was a key figure in securing America's liberty. He's a national hero in France. The Bastille has fallen, and Paris is on fire. Hundreds have died violently, and thousands of citizens are marching around armed with pistols. The only hope for peace rests on Lafayette's shoulders. He'll become a leader of the liberal aristocrats, and an outspoken advocate of religious tolerance and the abolition of the slave trade."

"I'm continually amazed at how well informed you are."

"People talk while I'm painting. I pay attention. And here's my second prediction of the evening...or morning. You and the general will both lead long, productive lives and die crotchety old men."

A long silence ensured before he teased, "Since I've just used up the one percent, it looks like I'll die a crotchety old man."

They both laughed, and after the laughter died they sat comfortably in silence until she asked, "Is the moon waning or waxing? I always get those confused."

"It's waning." He leaned back against a tree and glanced up. "There's a tale written by Ariosto in 1516 about a knight named

Orlando who fell in love with a pagan princess, but after she married someone else, he went mad and traveled around the world causing destruction."

"Until Saint John," she continued his tale, "carried him to the moon, where he went to the Valley of Lost Things and found his sanity."

"You've read it?"

"It's an Italian epic poem."

Mr. Petit cleared his throat. "Mr. Jefferson, dinner is served."

"Thank you, Mr. Petit." Jefferson stood and gathered her crutches. "Mademoiselle, your wine awaits."

They followed the path back to the entrance to the garden, and when they reached the point where they left the path, she gasped. What Mr. Petit had accomplished during their meandering conversation was nothing short of astounding.

Eight poles set in a circle, six feet apart, were wrapped with greenery and flowers. The poles were connected by swagged ropes, also wrapped with greenery. A chandelier lit with a dozen votive candles hung in the middle of each swag. The poles circled a table set intimately for two and covered with a white tablecloth. The scent of the thick, velvety-petaled roses permeated the air, and a candelabra with sputtering candles, china, and polished silverware completed the tableau. If she'd been planning a seductive scene to paint, she couldn't have done better.

It was magical, and would be burned into her memory for the rest of her life. Like Leonardo guiding her hand while she painted. Like Pete...

She couldn't go there. Some things were just too painful to pull out and dissect.

Her artist's eye placed Jefferson at the table pouring wine, the full sleeves of his white, lace-frilled shirt billowing in the night air, but it didn't work, and she mentally erased it. The scene was far too intimate, too revealing, for her to paint. Which disturbed her. Why was it not too intimate, too revealing to paint him in a vineyard?

She didn't have an answer.

Servants pulled upholstered chairs away from the table, and she and Jefferson took their seats. It seemed the household was awake at this hour anyway. She could have used the pull cord. But then she would have missed this romantic setting.

Mr. Petit adjusted a bench under the table and helped her settle her leg there, then left and returned with a pillow and bottle of wine. Jefferson examined the brass medallion hanging around the neck of the bottle. Satisfied, he poured a small portion into his glass and raised it, but instead of sipping from it, he offered the wine to her.

"For you, mademoiselle."

She tilted the glass slightly and looked at the wine against the white tablecloth. "It's a clear ruby red." She gently swirled the wine in the glass to release the flavors. The wine ran down the inside of the glass in pronounced legs. She buried her nose in the glass and inhaled the aromas. "Apple, blackberry, cherry. Cinnamon, pepper, nutmeg. A bit of violet and wild mushrooms."

She sipped and swished the wine around to coat her tongue and roof of her mouth, holding it for a few seconds to enable the aromas to percolate in her nasal passages. There was an explosion of taste. She swallowed and considered the aftertaste. "There's a juicy, zingy quality that makes it crisp and fresh, creating a velvety texture in my mouth. It's very good."

Jefferson nodded at Mr. Petit, and he and the other servants faded into the background. Jefferson's eyes never left her face, and when she emptied her glass, he refilled it.

"Mr. Franklin told me when I arrived here that French wines, food, and women had been a revelation, and now it was my turn."

When he raised his glass, his eyes glinted with either mischief or wine. She wasn't sure which. She slowly twirled the base of the goblet.

"Have you found Mr. Franklin's observations to be true?"

He didn't shy away from her question. "I've written extensively about French food and wines. But the women of the continent have surprised me with their sophistication, pleased me with their wit and charm, and confounded me with their political knowledge. American women who have spent time on the continent, such as yourself, Abigail Adams, and Angelica Schuyler Church are equally sophisticated and charming."

"Enlightened and educated women are sophisticated, charming, and witty, regardless of where they live. But I will agree France allows women, of all colors, freedoms they wouldn't find elsewhere."

"Of all colors?"

She wasn't going to discuss the central contradiction at the heart of America's founding. Jefferson was messy and contradictory. After listening to the Meacham book, Sophia knew Jefferson had included a passage attacking slavery in his draft of the Declaration of Independence, but the passage had initiated such an intense debate among the delegates gathered in Philadelphia that it was ultimately deleted.

"Yes," was all she could say. She cut into the grilled pork cutlets with piquant sauce and chewed, occupying her mouth so she wouldn't say more. She didn't come up for air until she'd eaten all the pork, broccoli, asparagus, and watermelon. At last, she set down her fork and wiped her mouth with the linen napkin.

"I didn't realize I was so hungry. Thank you for insisting I eat more than cheese and bread."

Lines around Jefferson's eyes deepened as he lounged in his chair, watching her and smiling. "You look like you've missed a few meals. While you're here, I'll set plenty of food in front of you."

She could take offense at his remark, but thinking back to the poor, starving women she'd seen earlier, she was on the skinny side. "I don't need more food. If I gain even a pound, I won't be able to wear my dress, and I'd have to wear these trousers all the time."

He sipped his wine, smiled. "I'm becoming rather fond of your trousers."

Okay. Change the subject.

She considered a toast she could make, and tipped her goblet toward his. "To Ambassador Jefferson: father, inventor, astronomer, violinist, architect, horticulturist, mathematician, and obsessive book collector. May you always have… / Walls for the winds / A roof for the rain / Tea beside the fire / Laughter to cheer you / Those you love near you / And all your heart might desire." She clinked her glass with his. *"Slainte."*

He contemplated the crystal goblet in his hand. "I've never cared for the English tradition passed on to the colonists to offer up toasts, but yours was not forced."

"It's an old Irish Blessing my grandmother taught me."

"She was Irish?"

"She was Italian and married a Scotsman." Sophia didn't want to talk about her family. It would be too easy to slip up and reveal more than she intended. She shivered. It was getting cool out.

"You're cold. We should go inside."

Within fifteen seconds, Mr. Petit appeared with a light shawl. "Would the mademoiselle like a *châle?*"

She smiled up at him. "You're so thoughtful. Thank you."

Jefferson accepted the light cotton shawl from Mr. Petit and spread it over her shoulders, brushing her neck softly with the backs of his fingers. Goosebumps ran up her spine as his brief touch and the gentle weight settled on her.

"I don't want to go inside yet." In that moment, she changed her mind about painting him in this setting. "I want to paint you like this, here in your garden at night. The man I see isn't the ambassador, inventor, astronomer, violinist, or obsessive book collector. You're a Renaissance Man."

"I'm not sure what you mean."

"Leonardo da Vinci was the original Renaissance Man: artist, sculptor, and so much more. You're like him. But you have something he didn't have. You can break a horse, dance a minuet, and play the violin."

Jefferson gave a husky shout of laughter. "I'm honored to be compared with da Vinci, but I fall far short of his accomplishments."

"Your accomplishments may not seem as great to you, but I believe history will see you differently than you see yourself."

"We will never know, will we?" He tipped his goblet and sipped.

Her mind snapped a picture of him, chin slightly tilted, flickering candlelight turning his hair crimson, his smile etching deep lines at the corners of his eyes. If she went without sleep for the next thirteen days, how many paintings could she complete? One that included every freckle on his face, or a manic thirteen.

She looked at the glass of lemon-flavored water. Lemon killed a few of the nasty bacteria—not all, but some. Oh, well. She swallowed a few gulps before returning to the wine. She swished it in her mouth. "This Chianti tastes as rich and varied as the Tuscan landscape."

He continued her imagery saying, "The sundrenched slopes and gently rolling hills allow the Sangiovese grapes to flourish to full potential."

"Your description sounds like a marketing pitch."

He rubbed his chin. "Your syntax often confuses me. Your thoughts must be in a mix of languages, and your words and phrases reflect that."

While listening to all the Founding Father audiobooks, she had tried to read a letter Jefferson wrote, and found the odd capitalization, abbreviations, and long sentences made it impossible to get past the first paragraph. He would find hers equally perplexing.

"A marketing pitch would be an advertisement to sell more wine. Your phrases—sundrenched slopes, gently rolling hills, flourish to full potential—all evoke pleasing imagery. If a buyer believes purchasing and savoring a certain wine will make him feel a particular way, then your advertisement has accomplished its goal."

"Marketing?"

"Look at it this way. When you went to the Hague to appeal to private Dutch bankers for a loan to pay the interest on another loan, a bit of juggling to restore America's credit, you were embarking on a marketing campaign. You successfully sold the bankers on the value of making an investment in America."

He looped one leg over the other and looked down his long nose at her. "Did you spend the afternoon reading my correspondence?"

"Of course not." *I read your biography.* "America's debt is common knowledge."

"It presses on my mind like a mountain." He stood, rubbing his forehead, as if all the worry was a weight pressing him down, a weight he couldn't shake. He paced slowly, back and forth.

She turned slightly in her chair and watched him pace, lofty and erect, with her heart thumping mildly against her chest, sensing the depth of his concern. She could ease it all by telling him his future. Although telling him he'd serve two terms as president might cause an instant heart attack. Instead, she brought up one of the men he was typically at odds with—Alexander Hamilton. They had profound differences in their political views and personalities. Jefferson was reserved and calculating. Hamilton was aggressive, direct, and ambitious.

"Hamilton will figure it out." She gave her words time to sink in and settle, unsure of how he would react. Jefferson stopped and faced her, his eyes bright and liquid blue in the candlelight, the mind behind the eyes quick and supple. She knew exactly how she would paint him—with shadow, light, and perspective. His eyes would give the illusion of following you, like the *Mona Lisa*, an optical illusion occurring only in art.

"Hamilton? He believes he's figured it out. He wants a national bank, but it would give the government too much power. He also wants the treasury to assume states' debts. The Southern states will never agree."

"Have you heard of compromise?"

"While Southerners will never agree to assume states' debts, Northerners will never agree to relocate the national capital to the South." He threw up his hands, exasperated, and said, "There *is* no compromise."

She steadied herself on the crutches, and moved closer to him, where she laid her hand on his arm, the linen of his shirt damp from the late evening air. "My grandmother explained this to me a long time ago. A compromise is the art of dividing a pie in such a way that all parties believe they're getting the biggest piece. Your job, Mr. Ambassador, is to figure out how to slice it."

The animation in his eyes said he found something she said humorous. "Mademoiselle Orsini, might you have a pie-slicing knife I could use?"

They walked toward the open French doors. "No, but I could paint one for you."

As they closed the doors behind them, she did a rapid calculation of the remaining hours she had before the brooch heated again. There wasn't enough time to paint everything she had in mind, and there was too much time to spend in Jefferson's presence for her to return home unaffected by his passion for art and wine and intellectual debate.

10

Richmond, VA—Kevin

WITHIN SECONDS OF Kevin's call for help, JL's room flooded with nurses and other staff looming over her, reviewing the monitor's printout, adjusting the monitor belt, checking the IV output. Within another minute the white-coated Dr. Winn hurried into the organized chaos.

The sights and sounds hit Kevin hard, like a wake-up call from his past, especially since the monitors painted a less than positive picture. JL's blood pressure sagged, and her heart rate bounced higher than normal.

"What's going on?" Dr. Winn asked, glancing around the room, quickly assessing her patient's condition.

Kevin kept his eyes on the monitor and JL while he said, "JL's bleeding picked up. The abruption must have worsened. You've got to section her now."

Dr. Winn studied the monitor, then examined JL while blood cascaded from between her legs and saturated the blue pad beneath her. "Mrs. Fraser, the abruption is worse. We've got to deliver your baby right now."

JL opened her eyes, letting out a soulful cry. She grimaced and squinted hard, trying to focus, but her eyes were cloudy and confused, and Kevin saw something else, something he'd only seen on her face once before—fear.

"We have to move quickly," Dr. Winn continued. "It'll seem like a crazy, three-ring circus, but we do this all the time. It should be okay." Dr. Winn squeezed JL's hand.

It should be okay. The words registered with Kevin, and he believed her, even though his son's heart rate had dropped significantly. He wanted to hold JL and tell her everything would be all right, but he couldn't lie to her, and there was a real possibility that it wouldn't be.

His heart lodged in his throat. Damn, he was scared, too. He shoved his shaking hands into the pockets of his jeans and backed out of the way.

Dr. Winn moved away from the bed, waving her arms. "Let's go." She held the door open, and four members of the nursing staff pushed the bed and IV pole through the doorway and out into the hall.

Kevin followed the entourage, but stopped in front of Dr. Winn, towering over her. "JL is scared. I have to go with her."

Dr. Winn lowered her voice so only Kevin could hear. "Remember you're in street clothes. Wait right here. I'll come and talk to you as soon as we're done."

His urge to protect JL washed over him like a whitecap hitting a granite coast. "You're not hearing me. My wife is terrified. I must stay with her. I can change in thirty seconds and be ready before you hit the operating room."

"Mr. Fraser." Dr. Winn gave him a forced smile. "I understand you have EMT training. Your experience should tell you this is an emergency, and the last thing we need is an interfering family member. I don't have time to argue. We'll take care of your wife. Please, stay here."

There were no further words between them, and Dr. Winn trotted after the bed as it flew down the squeaky-clean corridor toward swinging doors…straight into the obstetric floor's OR.

Kevin stepped forward before the intruding voice of his PTSD therapist shouted in his brain, *Put that damn Scottish temper aside. This is about JL and the baby. These people know what's best for them. Listen.* Kevin wanted to punch his therapist.

Now he knew what he had to do, and there was no time to waste. Thank God Charlotte reminded him JL's suite was stocked with extra patient gowns, hygiene items, and blue scrubs for the convenience of partners. He needed only moments to shed his street clothes and dress in hospital garb. He kept his ID card hanging on a lanyard around his neck, visible in case he was stopped and questioned.

He started down the empty corridor toward the swinging doors, his bootheels echoing loudly along the hollow hallway until he marched into the surgical suite with the confidence of someone authorized to be there.

The first room on the left was an unoccupied dressing room. He slapped on paper booties and a bonnet and tied a surgical mask around his nose and mouth. No one would recognize him, and he could walk freely through the unit and search for the room with the most activity.

An empty hospital bed was parked outside one of the operating rooms. The blue disposable underpad in the center of the bed had a large pool of blood with several small clots.

JL was behind that closed door. His heart surged up into his windpipe and lodged there, beating hard, trying to choke him. An explosion of adrenaline gave him a heightened awareness, along with stiffening his spine.

What was he going to do now? Barge in? Disrupt their preparation? Certainly not. Distract them and possibly cause an accident? God forbid. Then what? The truth was, he couldn't do any of those things. He could only stay outside and wait the way he was told to do.

He peered through the small window in the operating room door. *I love you, JL. I'm waiting here for you.*

He was dressed like the half dozen staff in the room. The anesthesiologist stood next to JL's head, Dr. Winn at her side, with two nurses opposite her. JL was covered with sterile drapes.

The anesthesiologist injected a series of medications into the IV lines, and within another couple of seconds she intubated JL. Thankfully the doctor had her back to Kevin, so he didn't have to watch the foot-long tube going down JL's throat. Knowing what was happening cramped his stomach. As soon as the tube was in place, the doctor hooked up the other end to the anesthesia machine.

Another woman entered from the back room, also wearing a surgical gown. She held her hands high, and one of the nurses helped her put on gloves, after which she folded her hands over her chest to keep them sterile.

As a former EMT, Kevin knew all the procedures, and that knowledge helped distance him emotionally from what was happening.

The woman who just entered glanced his way. *Charlotte.* He would have known her eyes anywhere. She'd saved his life, and now she would be there to save his wife and son. She walked over to the table and stood opposite Dr. Winn. Kevin was surprised the obstetrician agreed to let her participate, since she was related to JL. But, as he knew from experience, no one ever stood in Charlotte Mallory's way—not General Philip Sheridan, not Abraham Lincoln, not even Elliott Fraser.

Behind Charlotte, six others entered, one pushing an incubator. *Must be the NICU team.*

Kevin watched the anesthesiologist's motions closely. She would be the one to signal the surgeon when JL was successfully under anesthesia and the surgery could get underway. The nod came, and the surgical team moved quickly and efficiently. He checked the time. The baby should be out within ten minutes.

Hail Mary, full of grace, the Lord is with thee.

Kevin had never been religious, but he grew up in the Catholic church, and now, when he needed his faith most, he knew he could rely on it.

Blessed art thou among women…

With the ether screen at JL's chest level, Kevin couldn't see what the surgeon and nurses were doing.

…and blessed is the fruit of thy womb, Jesus.

He watched Charlotte for a sign, some indication of what was happening.

Holy Mary, Mother of God…

Charlotte occasionally glanced toward the anesthesiologist, checking the monitors.

…pray for us sinners…

From previous observations of C-sections, he would know from the motions of the surgical team when the baby was out.

Now and at the hour of our death.

He waited for a cry, a sign, a signal. Anything to tell him his son was alive.

And then a faint cry. So small, so quiet. Was it Lawrence?

Blane screamed when he was born, but Lawrence could only whimper. Then he cried out again, and in Kevin's heart it sounded like a sonic boom. His son was alive.

With her hands still folded, Charlotte gave him the okay sign.

His knees buckled, and he grabbed the doorknob to keep him upright. The baby was placed in Charlotte's arms. When that fact registered, Kevin pressed his face against the glass. For a brief second, she tipped the baby so Kevin could get a good look before she handed his son over to the NICU team.

As if in slow motion, he turned the doorknob, but his internal voice smacked him down. *Don't. There's too much at risk to interfere now.*

He stood on wobbly legs for another twenty-five minutes while they worked on JL, until several things happened simultaneously. The drapes were removed, the anesthesiologist turned off the medicine and removed the intubation tube, and Dr. Winn removed her gloves. It was over, and JL would be moved to recovery.

The adrenaline pumping through his veins shut off and fatigue set in. His shoulders slumped, and his legs shook the same way they did when he finished running marathons. He trudged back to JL's suite. He needed a few minutes to recover before he faced whatever came next.

Moving zombielike, he changed back into his street clothes, and was checking his phone messages when Dr. Winn entered the room. She squeezed his arm. The warmth and strength of her hand surprised him as much as steadied and reassured him.

She withdrew her hand. "The surgery went great. Your wife is still asleep. As soon as she wakes up in recovery, someone will come get you."

"And my son. How's my son?" His voice was much stronger than he expected—clear and pointed—like a gong summoning him to action.

"I don't know," she said, "but everything seemed fine when he was born. He was making crying noises and moving his arms and legs, so he didn't suffer from the abruption. Now he'll have to deal with the problems of prematurity. Someone from the NICU team should be here to take you up as soon as they've done their assessment and started treatment. In fact, Charlotte might be with him now. If so, she'll have more information for you."

He managed a smile, but it was short-lived. "Thank you, Dr. Winn. I'm sorry I acted like an ass earlier."

She returned his smile, but hers lasted much longer. "You behaved like a protective husband and father. Don't give it a second thought. I'm glad I could be here for your wife."

Having had surgery himself, and gone through several with Elliott, Kevin knew all about postoperative pain and wound care, but a C-section was different. On top of the pain from an incision, the patient also had to deal with postpartum concerns. "Are there any post-delivery issues I should know about?"

"There were no problems with the surgery," Dr. Winn said, "but there is a chance she'll need a transfusion later. We'll see how she does over the next few hours. In the meantime, feel free to call me if you have any questions. I'll be in the hospital a while longer and will be back for rounds at seven."

The doctor left, closing the door softly behind her. Kevin leaned against the wall, his legs refusing to hold him up a second longer, and he slid down the wall, coming to rest on the cold tile floor, to sit with his knees pressed against his forehead. And he cried. Just a little at first, from the corner of his left eye, a tear dripped past the bridge of his nose and into his new reality.

A cell phone rang. His phone or JL's? Both were on the bedside table. It didn't matter. There wasn't anyone he wanted to talk to right now. But if it was Elliott, he couldn't refuse his dad's call. Before he could push to his feet and reclaim his phone, the door opened, and a draft of cool air washed over him.

Then his father was there, squatting beside him, pulling him into his arms, tenderly patting his back. Elliott didn't speak. He just held Kevin and let him cry on his shoulder. When Kevin finally pulled back, Elliott handed him a monogrammed handkerchief. Kevin had thrown his bloodstained one away in the ambulance after the EMT applied a temporary bandage to his cut face.

"When ye're ready, tell me what happened." Elliott's voice was like the crunch of fine gravel.

Kevin climbed to his feet and stumbled into the bathroom, where he stood holding on to the edge of the sink, staring into the mirror. Who the hell was staring back? Whoever it was wore a damp, wrinkled polo shirt, had bloodshot eyes, and a fresh Band-Aid on his cheek covering the stitches Charlotte put in while he was in the ED.

He looked like a dead creature recently washed ashore. He splashed cold water on his face, knowing it wouldn't begin to repair the damage.

Goddamn it.

He hit the drywall with his fist. Why the hell were they here? They shouldn't be. This wasn't how they'd planned their weekend. Something in the cosmos had gone horribly wrong. Salty tears seeped into his bandage and stung the skin beneath.

Elliott walked through the open bathroom door and settled his arm on Kevin's shoulder. "Come on, lad. Let's sit down. Tell me what happened."

It was time for the analytical side of Kevin's brain to take control so he'd be ready for whatever came next. He eased out of the bathroom, dabbing at his wet face with rough paper towels.

"The abruption got worse. They had to do an emergency C-section. JL's okay. She's in recovery now. The baby whimpered when he was born and moved his arms and legs. The NICU staff rushed him away. I haven't heard anything else."

"Where's Charlotte?"

Kevin threw the wet paper towels into the trashcan. "Probably still with Lawrence in the NICU"

"I stopped by there, but the receptionist wouldn't tell me anything," Elliott said.

"If a smile or wink didn't work for you, there's no hope for me."

"To hell with a smile. I offered a bonus. A big one, including a year's supply of donuts. The receptionist didn't say a word. She just smiled at me until I gave up."

"You've lost your touch, old man." Kevin flopped down onto the sofa while Elliott inserted a pod into a Keurig coffee maker. "Fix me a cup, too."

"Large size?"

"Add a shot of whisky."

"Sorry, son. Don't have any. So what about Austin? Have ye called him?"

"JL didn't want to tell him. She's afraid it'll mess with his focus."

Elliott turned and stared at Kevin. "Last time she kept a secret from him, all hell broke loose. Is she sure she wants to do this? He'll be pissed as hell."

Kevin stared back, forcing himself not to overreact. "It's too late tonight." The cup filled with coffee, and Elliott handed it to Kevin, then fixed one for himself. "Besides, I can't call him without telling JL first. She'll see it as a betrayal. But as soon as I see her, I'll encourage her to call him, or let me call. That's all I can do."

Elliott sat down next to Kevin and sipped his coffee. "Austin is in Las Vegas. He's probably still in the gym."

Kevin raised a hand, gesturing his frustration. "Give it up, Elliott, or go home."

Elliott set his cup on the small table next to the sofa and pulled a sheet of paper out of his pants pocket. "Why don't ye start at the beginning so I'll have all the facts? Meredith will ask exactly what happened. If I don't have the answers, she'll call ye. And then she'll tell ye to call Austin, too."

Kevin counted to ten to keep from snapping at his father. Then counted to ten again.

"I talked to Charlotte once after we spoke, but it was before JL went to surgery. What happened to her?" Elliott asked.

Kevin's brain racked his last conversation with Elliott and replayed it. Then, as calmly as he could, he told Elliott everything that happened since.

Elliott sat back and drank his coffee while Kevin closed his eyes and rested for a few minutes. He had almost dozed off when the door opened with a *whoosh*. He jolted upright.

"Good. I'm glad you're both here," Charlotte said. "Did Dr. Winn come in to talk to you?"

Kevin nodded. "She told me JL tolerated the surgery well and was in recovery, but she didn't know anything about Lawrence. She said you were with him."

Charlotte pulled a chair up next to the sofa. Since he last saw her in the OR, she had changed into a fresh white coat over unwrinkled scrubs, brushed her hair, and put on lipstick. And she either had a twin who'd just come on duty after eight hours of uninterrupted sleep, or she'd taken a restorative drug. And if it was the latter, Kevin wanted one of those pills. The truth was, Charlotte Mallory was the epitome of a Southern lady and always, regardless of the circumstance, exuded grace, strength, and gentleness with the hint of fire. He found her composure comforting.

"I know you expect an honest report from me, without sugarcoating. So here it is. Lawrence is off to a good start for a twenty-eight-weeker. At delivery, he appeared to be in good shape, crying, making breathing motions, and moving his extremities. The NICU team took over right away, intubated him, got him stabilized, then moved him up to the unit."

Elliott referred to his sheet of paper. "How much did he weigh—"

"What were his Apgars?" Kevin asked over Elliott's question.

Charlotte looked from Kevin to Elliott, then back to Kevin. "Hard to say, since he was intubated right away. But probably seven or eight, which are good scores for being so premature."

"What—?" Kevin stopped and cleared his throat. "What are his chances?"

Charlotte didn't blanch. "A twenty-eight-weeker has about a ninety to ninety-five percent chance of survival."

"What about his weight?" Elliott asked again.

"A little over two pounds."

Kevin heaved himself up off the sofa and staggered over to the window perched high above the parking lot facing the heart of Richmond, as if he could find all the answers and solutions in the darkness of a city that had faced its own hardships and rebuilt from the ashes.

Elliott folded the piece of paper, returned it to his pocket, and rose to his feet, orator-style. "What problems are we facing? And is my grandson receiving the best treatment and care available?"

"I'm not a neonatologist," she replied calmly. "We have excellent physicians on staff, and they're with Lawrence now. Let's wait for their report."

"I want yer opinion." Elliott's voice lost its smoothness, and as usual, his tone made everyone around him tense.

Charlotte stood and gripped the back of her chair, her knuckles turning white.

Kevin didn't blame her for losing her patience with Elliott. He knew from experience that trying to control his father's demanding personality was pointless, at least for everyone except Meredith. If she'd been here, she would have told Elliott to stand down, and he would have done whatever she asked.

"I don't have an opinion. All I know are statistics. I don't know Lawrence's condition or the results of his labs. I can't tell you what you want to know."

"Then give me the statistics."

"There's a possibility he could have some level of learning disabilities or other developmental impairment. But again, this isn't my field of expertise. The folks in the NICU can answer all these questions."

Kevin's stomach lurched, and he barely made it to the bathroom before he threw up. Charlotte followed him, turned on the water, and handed him a cold washcloth. Kevin flushed the toilet and followed her out, wiping his face. She leaned against the counter, reached behind her, and grasped the edge while Kevin searched the closet for the hygiene kit. Finding it, he returned to the bathroom and brushed his teeth.

When he came back, he said, "Finish what you were going to say. I need to hear it all." Except for the one question he couldn't ask, and he hoped to God his father didn't either, because Kevin wasn't prepared for the answer.

Charlotte filled a cup with water from the sink in the room and drank deeply. "The severity of the disabilities or impairment can vary, and depend on many factors, including the need for and types of treatment received in the immediate neonatal period. The more intense the treatments, sometimes the greater the risk factors."

"But the odds aren't a hundred percent that he'll have disabilities or some impairment. Correct?" Kevin asked with a hopeful edge in his voice.

"About twenty percent will have no long-term problems," Charlotte said.

"So what ye're saying," Elliott said, "is Lawrence has a one in five chance that he won't have long-term problems, and the type of problems he could have depends on his specific needs during the immediate neonatal period."

"Elliott, again, these are only statistics," she said.

"What's his status right now?" Elliott asked.

"I don't know. The NICU will give Kevin a complete status report when he meets with them."

Kevin had heard enough. Whatever disability or impairment they might have to deal with, he could guarantee his son would be loved and cherished by the entire MacKlenna Clan, and the children would accept him with open arms and an abundance of patience. Whatever issues they had to deal with in the future, Lawrence would have the best treatment and care possible.

"When can I see him?"

"I don't know if they'll let you in yet. We can go up and see," Charlotte said. "The NICU is a family-centered unit." She pulled her phone out of her pocket and swiped with her finger. "I snapped some pictures."

Kevin accepted the phone in his shaking hand. Lawrence had a tube in his mouth and a bandage over his eyes. His skin was paper thin, and, young as he was, he looked old and wrinkly. And yet Kevin experienced such an outpouring of love for his tiny son, a frail imitation of the baby he'd expected.

When he gave his father the phone, Elliott sent the pictures to his own device. "Thanks." He handed it back to Charlotte. "How long will Lawrence be in the NICU?"

"Every day is going to be a challenge. He'll have good days and terrible days. We can hope for the best, but we're in for a long struggle. Even if things go well, it would be unusual to take him home for several months. Let's hope the family will all be together in Scotland for Christmas."

Elliott pulled Charlotte in for a hug. "Ye don't paint a pretty picture but, as always, I appreciate yer honesty."

"We've gone through a lot together, Elliott. We'll get through this, too. And watch your stress level. Your PSA will go up if you get overly stressed."

He smirked. "Don't tell Meredith."

Charlotte patted his back then hugged Kevin. "Come on. I'll show you where to go."

Kevin stopped in the doorway. "Call Meredith, but keep it on the Q.T. As soon as I have a complete picture, or as much as we can know right now, I'll schedule a conference call. And while you're sitting here by yourself, get down on your knees."

"Are ye asking me to pray for ye?"

"I'm asking you to pray for all of us, but especially Lawrence. The little guy will fight like hell. He's his mother's son. But he'll need a lot of help to get through the next several weeks."

Elliott's expression was stark with despair. "He's yer son too, lad."

Charlotte steered Kevin out of the room and down the corridor toward the bank of elevators.

"I want to see JL," he said, "but she'll expect me to see Lawrence first so I can tell her about him."

"How'd she and Elliott get to be so much alike?" Charlotte asked.

"I don't know, but sometimes she seems to have more of his genes than I do."

They drew abreast of the elevator, and Charlotte pushed the call button. A ping announced the arrival and the doors staggered open. "Are you kidding? You and Elliott are two peas in a pod. JL just has a few of his personality traits. Mostly his intuition and ability to see what others can't."

The doors closed behind them and she punched the number for the NICU floor. "For several years I thought David would take Elliott's place eventually, but it won't be him. The role of Keeper of the Stones will fall on JL's shoulders."

"Thank goodness we won't have to worry about it for a long time. By then we might discover James Cullen is the heir apparent." The door opened and they exited the elevator. The entrance to the NICU was to the right.

Charlotte's phone dinged with a text, and she checked the message. "I've got to go to ICU. The receptionist should let you in with the ID badge you have, since Lawrence was just born. You'll get a NICU badge in the morning. I'll be back as soon as I can." She returned to the elevator and disappeared.

He strode down the hallway like a warrior advancing toward enemy territory and entered the NICU's brightly colored reception area.

"May I help you?" a smiling young woman sitting behind the reception desk asked.

"I'm Kevin Fraser, and my newborn son was brought up here a

little bit ago. I want to see him." He wasn't going to be nice about this. "Not yet," or "Come back later," wouldn't be acceptable responses.

The woman typed on her keyboard. Then she looked up at Kevin. "May I see your badge?" Kevin removed it and handed it over. She held it up to the computer as if comparing the picture ID on the lanyard with the information on her screen. Apparently satisfied, she said, "Annette is your son's primary nurse on this shift. I'll let her know you're here." She made a call and announced Kevin. "She'll be out shortly."

Kevin replaced the lanyard around his neck. "Thank you." He moved over to the door to wait. Within five nerve-racking minutes the lock released with a loud, metallic click and a woman wearing pink and blue print scrubs pushed open the door.

"Mr. Fraser, I'm Annette, your son's primary nurse. Your son is still being assessed. If you'll follow me, I'll take you to Pod D."

The door closed behind him, followed by the click of the door relocking.

She led him through a brightly colored corridor. They passed Pod A, a large room with six stations, but only three incubators were hooked up. Near the entrance, a nurse was busy at a computer.

"Is the setup the same in each pod?"

"Each pod can accommodate six beds. Your son's pod has two other preemies, all about the same age."

Kevin had never intended to be a parent of a fragile infant, and was woefully unprepared for the journey. He knew his way around hospitals, but not this part, and the unfamiliarity terrified him. He needed to ease into it, but there wasn't time. He had to hit the ground running, and he was already several lengths behind.

They passed Pods B and C, and finally reached D. Four women, two in white coats and two in print scrubs similar to Annette's, were huddled around an incubator.

"Dr. Haggard is one of our neonatologists. On her right is respiratory therapist Susan Green, and beyond her are nurses Rita McGuire and Paula Lague. Everyone has a name tag, but you'll soon learn their names. If you want to have a seat, Dr. Haggard will give you a status report as soon as she's finished."

Kevin sat down and watched them work. Lawrence was in a plexiglass cabinet with a hinged hood mounted on a trolley with a warming light overhead. Kevin couldn't see his baby or what those attending to him were doing. The other two preemies were in enclosed incubators. When one of the nurses stepped aside, Kevin caught a glimpse of his son, who jerked and quivered, his skin thin and fragile. An ID card was inserted into the front of the incubator:

Baby Boy Fraser

Kevin's chest hurt all the way through to his spine. He covered his face with his hands, his elbows on his knees.

"Mr. Fraser."

Kevin glanced up. It was the woman Annette identified as Dr. Haggard. He pushed to his feet. "How's my son?"

She pulled a chair up and sat down, and he returned to his seat. "I'm Dr. Haggard, your son's neonatologist. I'm still waiting for some lab reports, but so far everything looks good. I know this is overwhelming, but all the machines and tubes track your son's heart rate, breathing rate, temperature, blood oxygen levels, and blood pressure. We're constantly monitoring his vital signs."

"He's on a ventilator," Kevin said.

"He was intubated immediately. An infant's lungs aren't fully developed at twenty-eight weeks, and we don't want him wasting precious calories trying to breathe on his own. Your wife's obstetrician ordered a course of betamethasone when she was admitted, which gave a boost to his lungs. The IV in his umbilical cord keeps him from being stuck repeatedly and provides us with an efficient way to inject medications. We're making everything as easy on him as possible."

She seemed to notice something out of the corner of her eye, but turned her attention back to Kevin. "It's going to take another hour or so to run all the initial tests to determine what we're dealing with. We are a Level III neonatal unit equipped with state-of-the-art technology to care for newborns with complex medical problems. Whatever your son needs, he'll get excellent care."

"Can I hold him?"

"Not yet. In about seventy-two hours, if he's doing well, you and Mrs. Fraser will be able to do kangaroo care. Are you familiar with that?"

"I was an EMT for a decade, but my experience with preemies is minimal. I do know what kangaroo care is. Unless there's some reason he can't be held, either his mother or I will hold him twenty-four hours a day."

Dr. Haggard sat back in her chair and looked at Kevin closely. "You'll be told this dozens of times, so I'll be first. We're here to take care of your son. You have to take care of you. You also have to set aside time for your other children, if you have them."

"We have a four-year-old."

"Did I understand correctly? Are you related to Dr. Mallory?"

"Distantly, but we're very close. JL and I live in Lexington, Kentucky. My Cessna crashed on landing today, and the seat belt pressure caused an abruption. Which obviously is why we're here."

"So the plan is to take him back to Kentucky?"

"Eventually, I guess, but not for a while. Blane, he's our other son, loves life at Charlotte's plantation, and he has cousins, grandparents, aunts and uncles there. It's the best place for him to be while JL and I are here with Lawrence, so we can stay in the area indefinitely."

Dr. Haggard's eyebrows lifted. "It could be several months."

Kevin's gut tightened, and stomach acid driven by fear heaved up his throat. He swallowed hard. "I can't think in terms of months. I have enough experience to know how tenuous Lawrence's situation is. I can only plan a day at a time."

"At least it sounds like you have options. Lots of parents don't. Financial pressure adds to the trauma. It's why I suggested you take care of yourself. We have a staff of neonatologists, nurse practitioners and nurses, respiratory therapists, nutritional therapists, and twenty-four-seven surgical coverage. We also work with pediatric specialists, lactation experts, and psychologists to ensure comprehensive, individualized care, and the business office is very accommodating."

"So you're telling me you've got it covered, right?"

"That's about it, Mr. Fraser. But never doubt that you are an integral part of your preemie's care team," Dr. Haggard said. "Your thoughts, feelings, and observations are critically important. Speak up. Ask questions. Voice your concerns. Share what's important to you. The NICU is a family-centered facility. Parents have twenty-four-hour visitation, and siblings three and older may visit any time after they've had a health screening."

It was almost two o'clock in the morning, and Kevin was finding it hard to concentrate on what she was saying. His mind was splintered between worrying about JL and worrying about his son.

"If you have any questions for me," Dr. Haggard said, "I'll be here until seven, and you can always leave a message. I'll get back to you as soon as possible. Annette will be your contact person for this shift. You'll get to know all the staff fairly quickly." She turned around to look at Lawrence's incubator. "It looks like they've finished. You can pull one of the recliners up next to your son and watch over him. Annette or another nurse will always be at the nurse's station, there in the corner. Whatever you need, just ask."

Kevin extended his hand. "Thank you. And on behalf of my father and I, whatever you need, just ask."

Catching the drift of his comment she said, "After an offer like that, I'm sure you'll be hearing from our Director of Philanthropy. Get some rest." Dr. Haggard returned to Lawrence's incubator, spoke to Annette, then left the pod.

The panel above the warming unit displayed Lawrence's vital signs. Kevin would have to do some research on preemies so he would know the ranges and what to expect if Lawrence went above or fell below them. Kevin caught his washed-out reflection in the sterile blue glow of the screen. Shocked, he jerked back, out of the way of the light.

A doll-sized blood pressure cuff was wrapped around Law-rence's tiny leg, no bigger than Kevin's index finger. Small sticky pads were stuck to his chest with leads to a cardiopulmonary monitor. An endotracheal tube was in his mouth. A pulse oximeter wrapped around his right foot. Bandages covered his eyes to protect them from the overhead warming lights, plus other cords and monitors.

If there had been anything in Kevin's stomach, he would have thrown up again. A few hours ago his son was happily sleeping inside JL's womb. Now he was stuck with needles, pinched and poked, and he couldn't even suck his thumb for comfort. How could Kevin tell JL their son had tubes in his nose, down his throat, and a mask covering most of his face? He looked like an alien, especially since he had no baby fat on him yet, so his skin was loose and wrinkly. Even his little ears were closed up like flower buds.

Annette came over and stood beside him. "You can touch him if you want."

"I do have a question." He had to dig down deep to find the courage to ask the one question he'd been unable to ask Charlotte, but he had to know. "Was…" He stopped and cleared his throat. "Was Lawrence deprived of oxygen prior to birth?" There, he got the words out.

"Your wife's abruption was severe, but not complete. We'll be doing additional tests, but so far it appears he was never without oxygen. He was intubated because his lungs are so immature."

Kevin almost keeled over with relief and an overwhelming im-pulse to drop to his knees in gratitude, all the while fresh tears poured down his face.

Annette handed him a tissue. "I know this is hard. But we're here for you and your wife. Whatever you need, just ask anyone on Lawrence's team."

There was so much to process. JL would never be able to handle it. Hell, he barely could himself.

Kenzie could. Kit could. Meredith, possibly, but Elliott was a no-way.

However long Lawrence needed to be here—six months, seven months, a year—Kevin would be at his side, stroking his little cheek, kissing the parts of him not covered by a piece of equipment, enjoying every minute of kangaroo care. Lawrence would never be alone.

But first Kevin needed information. He would hire instructors to teach him what he didn't know. He would read every book about micro-preemies he could find. He would become an expert on his son's care. He'd attend classes, talk to staff. He was more than Lawrence's father. He was his son's advocate, and he would fight every minute of every day for his fragile little boy who weighed less than a little girl's slipper.

"Do you want to hold his hand?" Annette asked.

"Yes." He set his phone on the chair.

After washing his hands, Annette showed him how to insert his hands through the portholes. "Would you mind taking our picture?"

He slipped his hand in and clasped Lawrence's tiny fingers while Annette took several photos. This was his son, and his heart swelled with love for him. He'd spent the past couple of months reading to Lawrence while JL slept, and he would continue to read to the little guy here in the NICU.

Kevin had thought he was prepared for the reality of a micro-preemie who might never walk or talk, but he wasn't. He was as helpless in this world of uncertainty and constant danger as his son, a babe so small that Kevin's wedding band would easily fit around his arm.

Annette showed Kevin the pictures. All the equipment attached to Lawrence looked even worse in the images.

And he looked sixty years old. Just like that, he'd aged. He looked as old as God.

11

Paris (1789)—Sophia

B EFORE RETIRING IN the early morning hours, Sophia asked Mr.
Petit to have someone wake her in time to enjoy breakfast with
the rest of the household. A gentle shake of her shoulder woke her
way too early. She opened one eye to see the sweet, heart-shaped
face of a young woman with big brown eyes and brown hair covered
by a white mobcap.

"Milady, it is time to wake up," she said in French. "I brought
hot water."

"Oui, merci." Sophia closed her eye and did a quick assessment of
her knee, lifting her leg slightly. The pain was probably a six now,
which was an improvement over yesterday.

When she asked Mr. Petit to have someone wake her, she must
have been under the influence. A chiding voice whispered in her
mind, *Of wine, or Thomas Jefferson?*

Wine, of course.

Their stroll in the moonlit garden, the late-night dinner, and the
ambiance had combined to create one of the loveliest evenings she'd
had in a long time. And their banter had encompassed a wide and
not-so-subtle range of topics.

It was rumored Jefferson had a very strong libido, and, while
neither of them did anything inappropriate, they had flirted

shamelessly. Her return ticket was stamped July 28, 1789, and she couldn't extend her trip a day or shorten it by an hour. If she wanted more evenings like last night, she'd better reconsider. It was the recipe for a heartbreaking disaster. She had fallen for Leonardo, and her heart spent weeks recovering from the loss. She couldn't go through it again.

"What's your name?" Sophia asked the young woman.

"Marguerite," she said shyly. "I was hired to be your chamber-maid and help you up and down the stairs."

Sophia laughed in surprise. "Really?" What an interesting way to eliminate the possibility of appearing downstairs again in her Tai Chi clothes. If Jefferson or Mr. Petit hired a chambermaid for her, Sophia would insist on paying the girl's salary.

Marguerite watched Sophia curiously while she performed several floor exercises that wouldn't irritate her knee, then stretched to relieve most of the tension that had started when she arrived, increased during the day, and blasted off the charts during her late-night dinner.

With the exercises done and feeling refreshed, Sophia gave herself up to Marguerite's tender ministrations. After bathing and dressing her, Marguerite coiffed and beribboned Sophia's wavy hair, and she had to admit being waited on was a huge relief. It would have been hard to manage a sponge bath on her own.

Sophia stood at the top of the stairs and visualized going down each step. "Would you please hold up my skirts so I don't trip on them?" she asked Marguerite. Sophia held onto the banister and used only one crutch while Marguerite carried the other. If Sophia lost her balance or tripped, she'd hurt herself, but at least she wouldn't fall all the way down.

The mouthwatering aromas of fresh-baked bread, coffee, and bacon wafted up the stairwell. She licked her lips, anticipating the taste of warm bread with jam. When they reached the bottom, Marguerite straightened Sophia's dress and fluffed her hair before pointing her toward the dining room.

Getting a little more agile, Sophia crutched past the French doors leading to the garden and hopped through the salon with Marguerite hovering anxiously nearby. Sophia stopped at the entrance to the dining room, and within five seconds had people, fixtures, and furnishings set in her mind, imagining the room as a painting.

Twenty crimson chairs were arrayed along a long mahogany table with five place settings, two candelabra, and a large center arrangement of white roses, irises, and trailing ivy. The same theme appeared in a bouquet on the marble-top sideboard.

The painting over the sideboard was possibly Joseph Wright's unfinished portrait of Washington, completed by John Trumbull during a visit to Paris. Houdon's bust of Voltaire sat atop a fluted marble column mounted on a massive pedestal. Both would be destroyed in the Library of Congress fire of 1851.

She never knew what extras she'd include in a painting, and using unique pieces added vitality and glamour to a portrait. The bust of Voltaire and the column would immortalize those works of art lost to history.

Jefferson stood next to the fireplace, his elbow on the mantel, his other hand at his hip, his attention focused on two animated teenage girls.

"Ah. There's Mademoiselle Orsini," he said, smiling.

The girls turned and acknowledged her with a slight bow, saying, "Mademoiselle," in unison.

"Papa said you were injured in front of our house and he had crutches made for you," the younger child said.

"Polly," Jefferson said. "It's polite to start with introductions. Mademoiselle, this is Maria. We call her Polly. And Martha. We call her Patsy."

"I'm pleased to meet you," Patsy said. "Papa says you're an artist and you're going to paint his garden."

Jefferson's oldest child was tall and gangly like him, with his elongated face, coloring, and red hair. Polly, by contrast, was petite with dark hair, and the prettier of the two.

Sophia crutched over to them. "He's commissioned me to paint his garden, but I'd like to have him in the painting. What do you think?"

"Why, it wouldn't be at all dignified!" Patsy said in a snarky tone.

Sophia had learned years ago to take snarky art critics in stride and let comments peel off easily without sticking to her. She leaned on the crutch shoulder rests and rearranged Polly's dark ringlets loosely on her shoulders. With the tip of her forefinger, she gently turned the child's head to the side. "You have a charming profile, and such luxurious hair. I would love to paint you."

Polly smiled, but Patsy's face clouded. Sophia didn't want to create any tension with the children which might add additional stress to Jefferson's life, so she quickly turned her attention to the disgruntled young lady.

"And you, sweetheart"—she used the same forefinger to study Patsy's profile—"have rich, thick hair like your father, and the same intelligent blue eyes. I would like to paint both of you—separately, together, and with your father. Would you like that?"

"What do you think, Papa?" Polly asked. "Would you like to have our portrait hanging in your cabinet?"

Jefferson's brows quirked as he glanced at Sophia with the same dissecting-a-bug look he'd given her before. "I can't think of anything I'd like more."

Patsy continued to hold her chin exactly as Sophia had positioned it. "We've never posed for a portrait. Papa has, of course, but no one has ever asked to paint us."

The throbbing intensified in Sophia's knee. She needed to sit. "As the children of Ambassador Jefferson, you should unquestionably sit for a portrait. Years from now people will wonder about you. As soon as I buy canvas and paint, we'll start."

Polly's face brightened. "Oh, what should we wear?"

"Hmm. Let me think," Sophia said.

Jefferson went to the table and pulled out a chair. "Why don't you sit, mademoiselle? I'm sure your knee is bothering you, and Mr. Petit has already positioned a stool under the table for your leg."

Sophia hobbled over to the chair and handed him the crutches.

"Thank you." She settled into the seat and rested her leg on the stool.

Patsy repeated her sister's question. "What should we wear, mademoiselle?"

Both girls sat opposite Sophia, with Jefferson at the head of the table. He picked up a copy of the *États-généraux* newspaper and perused the first page.

"Have you seen Vigée Le Brun's painting of the queen wearing a white muslin gown and straw hat?"

"I don't think we have, Papa. Have we?" Patsy asked.

"I heard it was a very controversial painting at the time. Madame Le Brun was asked to remove the painting from the Salon." He set down the newspaper, folded it precisely, and picked up his coffee cup.

"Oh, no. What happened?" Patsy asked.

A servant poured coffee into Sophia's cup. She spooned in sugar and added a dollop of cream. Stirring the contents, she said, "The painting was condemned as inappropriate for a public portrayal of royalty, which is crazy. The dress was gorgeous in its simplicity and elegance, and was made from very expensive cotton fabric."

"I've seen some of Madame Le Brun's paintings," Jefferson said. "She's quite talented. The incident you describe occurred prior to my arrival in Paris."

"Why did she paint her in such a dress?" Patsy asked. "It would be like you painting Papa in his garden. It's not appropriate for people in their positions."

Sophia sipped from her china cup, her skin prickling under the weight of someone's attention. She turned her head, right smack into Jefferson's watchful stare. If she needed to defend or justify an artist's interpretation of a portrait, she would without any qualms.

"Some believe Madame Le Brun was imagining the queen's desire not to be queen of France. Maybe not a wish to abdicate, but a desire to separate herself temporarily from the demands of the office."

"The queen might like to escape the demands of court, but I

don't believe she has any desire to be less than a queen." Jefferson set down his cup a little too hard, and it clinked against the saucer.

"Madame Le Brun's paintings are visually stunning. There's a delicacy to the way she handles fabrics, especially sheer fabrics like muslin." She turned away from him and addressed the girls. "You both would look elegant in similar dresses, with straw hats and copious ribbons. With about eight meters of fabric, I could make the dresses fairly quickly." It was the same style dress Sophia had intended to wear in her own portrait, and being reminded of her change in plans caused the briefest twinge of regret.

"Did Madame Le Brun remove the portrait?" Polly asked.

Another platter appeared, stacked high with bacon. "Yes, she did." Sophia forked two pieces onto her plate. "Madame Le Brun repeated the pose of the first painting, but outfitted the queen in a classic blue-grey silk dress. Her portraits are distinctive for their colors, which are bright and bold and perfectly chosen."

Polly spooned eggs onto her plate. "Can we see the painting, Papa?"

"I'm not sure where it is."

"Do you know, Mademoiselle Orsini?" Patsy asked.

It's in the National Gallery of Art, West Building, Ground Floor, Gallery 11.

Sophia wiped her mouth with the napkin. "We can visit Madame Le Brun's studio. Maybe she has it there. I heard she's going to Rome, so we'll need to go soon…if your father approves."

The sounds of boots on the hardwood floor and buckles clicking with every step reached the dining room seconds before the man wearing them. Sophia recognized the sound of William's stride from yesterday and glanced up expectantly.

He stopped short, his eyes wide. "Appears I'm late for breakfast. Please forgive me."

"Mademoiselle Orsini can't stand because of her knee," Patsy said, flashing a bright smile. "Papa insisted she sit, and we didn't wish to be rude."

"I see," William said. "And how is the mademoiselle's knee this morning?"

She hadn't put any weight on it yet and didn't dare try for another day or two. If she'd been at home, she'd lie on the couch all day. But a minor sprain wouldn't keep her from taking advantage of every second she had in Paris. She had thirteen days left to paint Jefferson and his daughters, and if she had any spare time, she'd sit for Jacques.

"It's not great, but tolerable. I can still manage a trip to the market for a few things."

Jefferson spooned a helping of grits onto his plate, pinging the silverware against the china. "Absolutely not."

Sophia swallowed her anger and exhaled calmly, trying to ensure her voice revealed nothing about her true state of mind, but doubted she could pull it off. Since her father threatened to disown her at seventeen, no one had ever used that tone with her. If she'd been able to walk, she would have left the table immediately, rude or not.

"Mr. Ambassador, you might be my host, but you are neither my father nor my husband. If—"

His jaw fell slack. He reached for his newspaper and flicked it back open. "As long as you're injured, you're my responsibility, and Parisians will be rioting again today." The coolness in both his tone and his furtive glance irritated her more than his words. "You can make a list of items you need, and William can see to them."

William heaped food onto his plate and attempted to defuse the tension by asking, "Did you remember Mademoiselle Bertin is calling on you this afternoon?"

"Mademoiselle Bertin?" Polly asked. "The queen's dressmaker is coming here? Can I meet her? What does she look like? Is she pretty?"

"I've seen a tool engraving of her by Jean-François Janinet," Sophia said. "And she's both enchanting and very talented. As the queen's *modiste*, she's credited with bringing haute couture to Paris."

"Haute couture," Polly said, imitating Sophia, not in a mocking way, just tasting the words on her tongue, and then she giggled. "Is she going to make clothes for you?"

"I lost my bags during yesterday's riot, and I need to replace my wardrobe. Marguerite intends to ask another lady's chambermaid if they have something suitable to sell. I can alter used dresses, add lace and ribbons, and the gowns will look brand new. I don't need much. Most of my time here will be spent painting, so all I really need is a simple dress and an apron."

"I met Marguerite this morning," Patsy said, folding her arms. "Papa hired her to tend to you while you're injured."

"I'm glad he did," Polly said. "Taking care of us and Mademoiselle Orsini, too, would have been too much work for Sally. Right, Papa?"

Jefferson exhaled, and his Adam's apple jumped when he swallowed. "Attending to Mademoiselle Orsini's special needs would have interfered with Sally's attention to her own responsibilities."

Patsy looked up suddenly, as if sensing an underlying purpose for Marguerite's employment. Then she quickly turned her attention back to Sophia. "How long will you require her services?" She managed a smile, but it was short-lived.

Sophia leaned back in her chair, signaling she was through with breakfast. "Not more than a couple of weeks. And, so everyone is clear about this, I'm paying Marguerite's salary, as well as other necessary expenses, including my art supplies." Although her statement was a public declaration, it was directed toward her host.

He gave her such a suspicious nod, she was tempted to return it with one of her own. One of her skills was the ability to solve delicate problems with bluntness, not nuance and finesse. At least with adults.

Relationships with teenagers oftentimes had to be massaged. She'd taught students with diva complexes and others who were understated flowers. As a teacher, she had to find a way to calm the divas while encouraging the shrinking violets to blossom. Not an easy feat.

As for the undercurrent at the table, she had to draw upon what she learned in Jon Meacham's audiobook. There were two unresolved relationships in the Jefferson household. William and Patsy and Jefferson and Sally Hemings. If Sophia remembered correctly, at the time of Jefferson's return from France Sally was rumored to have been pregnant with the first of their four surviving children. And Patsy was or would soon be brokenhearted over William's failure to propose marriage.

Sophia absolutely could not interfere. Situations had to evolve as history recorded them, which meant her disapproval had to be contained.

A servant removed Sophia's plate, and at her request refilled her coffee cup. Then she straightened her jacket, mentally fortifying herself for the impending conversation. She dared a glance at Jefferson. "I know you're concerned for my safety, Ambassador, but I intend to call on Monsieur David and Monsieur Watin, the color merchant, today. They were so kind to me yesterday. I know you've spoken to Monsieur David, but I still need to call on him."

He watched her in silence, and she was unsettled by his steely gaze.

"I'd like to visit the color merchant with you," Patsy said. "That is, if you don't mind."

"I'd enjoy the company," Sophia said. "We can discuss colors for your portrait, and Polly's, too. I think we should accessorize with blue to match your eyes."

Patsy frowned in much the same way as her father did. "Accessorize?"

"Add blue ribbons in your hair or pick a background with blue, or maybe a blue china cup or something. We'll have to look around. Or, you know what? You play the fortepiano. I could paint you there with a large flower arrangement in the background."

"And Papa with his violin?" Patsy asked.

"That would be perfect." Sophia smiled at Patsy. "After our visit to the color merchant, if the streets are safe enough, we could make a quick trip to the Palais Royal for ribbons and such."

"Papa said the shops there have very high prices," Polly said.

"Since I'm on crutches, it will be easier for me to shop away from the chaos and the noisy, dirty streets."

Jefferson scoffed. "It appears you're going to disregard my warning. If you insist, I'll escort you."

"I'm available to escort them," William said. "But I recommend going to the Palais Royal first and then to Monsieur David's atelier."

Patsy patted her father's arm. "I'm sure you're busy, Papa. Mr. Short can take us."

William's offer seemed to have the opposite of its intended effect on Jefferson. He squared his shoulders, a determined glint flashed in his eyes. "After what happened to the mademoiselle yesterday, extra caution is needed." An edge of impatience seeped into his tone.

"You intended to catch up with your correspondence this morning." William's glance flashed to Jefferson, and it appeared to an outsider—as Sophia was—to be an instance of William flexing his muscle at his boss.

The one-two word punch almost set Jefferson back on his heels. In profile, his strong, carved jaw was clenched tight and his eyes were fixed beneath a swath of ginger hair. "I'm charged with protecting Americans and making reports to America about the happenings overseas. To make my reports, I need to see firsthand how Parisians are reacting to yesterday's events."

"Can't you and Mr. Short both take us?" Polly asked.

The men could decide between themselves who was going and who was staying behind to work. Sophia finished her coffee and smiled at the girls. "Shall we get ready to go? Your father and Mr. Short can review their schedules to see who has available time."

"When will you be ready to leave?" Jefferson asked.

"I need to ice my knee first."

He pulled his watch out of his waistcoat pocket. "We'll leave at ten o'clock."

Mr. Petit entered the room and passed a note to Jefferson before addressing Sophia. "Is the mademoiselle ready for ice chips?"

Sophia was convinced Mr. Petit not only had eyes in the back of his head but ears fine-tuned as a bat's. "Do you mind bringing the ice bucket to the salon? I'll ice my knee there."

Jefferson read the note while tapping a rapid arpeggio on the table. In the silence of the room each tap had the intensity of a hammer blow. "I regret I cannot escort you this morning. General Lafayette will be here shortly."

"Mr. Short will protect us, Papa," Patsy said.

"I have every confidence he will." Jefferson stood and clasped William's shoulder. "Bring them back immediately if you encounter any violence." He then left the room, his shoulders stooped with the weight of responsibility.

12

Richmond, VA—JL

J L SLOWLY RETURNED to consciousness for the second or third time. Although her awakening could be the fifth, for all she knew, or could remember. And every time it had seemed surreal, more like coming out of a long-term, reversible coma.

Her heavy eyelids cracked open a sliver, not far, just enough to see her surroundings—cold, sterile, dark, and beeping. She had no sense of time. Her head rolled left to see a quietly beeping monitor, IV pole, curtained wall, then rolled right to see a chair and more curtains.

A small pillow and crumpled-up blanket lay abandoned on the seat of the recliner. Kevin would have tried to sleep, but did he? Her motto had always been to sleep whenever you could. If a crisis happened, you needed to be rested to deal with it effectively.

Somewhere beyond the curtains, thin wedges of bright fluorescent lighting—cold and inhospitable—filtered into her cubicle. The irony didn't escape her. Two or three disembodied voices, all speaking in low tones, either so they wouldn't wake her or to protect her from bad news, filtered in with the light.

One of the voices—the deep, smoky one—belonged to her husband. How long had it been since she first heard his voice in the Welcome Center hallway at Montgomery Winery? Seven years, two time-travel adventures, and the birth of their son. No. The births of their sons.

Her long-term memory was functioning, but she couldn't say the same for her short-term. The voices in the hall laughed out loud. What was so funny? What could Kevin possibly find to laugh about?

When she first heard his rich baritone all those years ago, her cousin—a hundred times removed—told her Kevin came with a warning label: "Heartbreaker. Proceed with caution."

It was a funny story, really, and they all chuckled about it now, but at the time JL threw caution to the wind, fell madly in love, and shamelessly jumped into bed with him, all within a few hours. Of course that led to the kidnapping of her oldest son and the entire MacKlenna clan, two deaths, a rogue cop, an explosion, the reveal of previously unknown fathers, two attempted murders, and Kevin's close call with death.

But those events were all in the past—part of her still-functioning long-term memory.

Funny, the things you think about when your brain is all mushy from an infusion of narcotics. She knew she had to be under the influence or else she'd be dealing with some serious pain. Pain. That agony was intact in her long-term memory too.

Her hand inched up the side of her leg to her hip, where it paused briefly as her fingers brushed the old scar. Moving on, her fingers roved over her belly—squishy, not hard. Her baby wasn't inside her.

Where is he?

Her worry now, her only concern, was for her baby. And no one would tell her anything about him. She patted the bed next to her hip, searching for the nurses' call button, but before she could press it, a nurse entered the cubicle, pushing the curtain aside to admit a bigger sliver of light.

"You're waking up again. How do you feel?" It was still too dark to see the woman's name tag or even her face clearly, until the nurse switched on the light above the bed.

JL blinked. *Laura.* Her name was Laura. "Like crap. And that's being polite."

Laura studied the monitor spitting out heart rate and temperature and God knows what else, probably how many ounces she'd peed. Laura repositioned the gadget, whatever it was called, on JL's finger.

"There's a handsome man out there who's been waiting for you to wake up," the nurse said.

JL glanced at the pillow and blanket in the chair. "Which means either Kevin or his father are out there. They look alike. Just ask my mother-in-law." If she'd been up to it, she would have laughed—her long-term memory was working again—remembering when Meredith walked up behind Kevin, wrapped her arms around him, and whispered a very naughty suggestion in his ear. When she discovered it was her stepson, not her husband, she nearly died of embarrassment.

"Did Kevin get any sleep?" JL asked.

"A little bit, I think."

"Good. Then he can take me to see our baby." But first JL would have to slip past Nurse Laura. She schooled her features and gave the nurse her most effective cop face. It was the tough-girl look she'd perfected after spending hours in front of a mirror, and had always gotten good results during the years she patrolled the streets of New York.

Laura's expression turned doleful. *The look* obviously didn't faze the nurse. If JL had lost her ability to intimidate, she was screwed. It was the only thing she had to balance Elliott's all-powerful presence with her pint-sized *grrrl* power. She'd always been petite, but it was more noticeable since the twins' recent growth spurt had the pair of ten-year-old hooligans towering over her statuesque five-two.

Laura moved around efficiently, checking the monitor, IV, and pulse-ox as if marking off items on her to-do list. Satisfied the IV was flowing smoothly, she said, "I'm going to inject Demerol into the line."

A coolness burned in JL's vein.

Laura lowered the bedsheet, checked the dressing, and pressed around JL's abdomen, her fingers moving adeptly, as if they were on a scavenger hunt. She studied the monitor again, pulled a piece of paper and pen from her pocket, and wrote down several numbers.

JL's squishy belly became a bone-crushing reminder that she'd been separated from Lawrence. "Where's my baby?"

"He's in the NICU, and the latest report says he's doing fine." Laura pulled the sheet back up, pocketed her note, then slathered sanitizer on her hands.

JL's nose twitched at the astringent smell of alcohol and iodine. She massaged her belly. It was so odd that her son was no longer in there. "When can I see my baby?"

"Dr. Winn usually makes rounds at seven, and she's the one who will need to sign orders releasing you to get up and move around."

There wasn't a window in the room, and JL's concept of time and place were totally screwed. As often as they flew cross-country and to Europe, they could be anywhere in any time zone.

"What time is it now?" she asked.

Laura raised her arm, checked her watch. "Five-thirty-six."

"AM or PM?"

"It's early morning."

A muscular orderly strolled by her cubicle pushing an empty wheelchair, and she wanted to scream *come back for me!* But he disappeared beyond the curtain. Unless he came back with the wheelchair, she'd never get out of here and find her baby.

"When can I hold my son?"

"Soon."

JL found the matter-of-factness in the nurse's tone sharp and annoying, even if it wasn't. The old JL—the one before Blane was born—wouldn't have put up with it. The current version was mellower unless she was riled. And she was moving quickly in the direction of riled.

Laura's tone conveyed a strange sense of foreboding, which rattled JL's messed-up brain. God, she wished they'd given her something other than a general anesthetic.

"Is there anything you need?"

JL glared at the woman as if she'd lost her mind. How could she have forgotten so quickly what JL needed? Was her short-term memory shot to hell, too? If so, JL needed a new nurse.

"I. Need. My. Husband. And. My. Baby." She repeated her needs slowly and definitively to trigger the nurse's memory. Hopefully, it would stick this time.

"Mr. Fraser is at the nurses' station. I'll tell him you're awake."

JL considered rolling her eyes, but the eye roll was a typical reaction of the old JL. "The nurses' station, huh?"—she couldn't resist, and rolled them anyway. "Better watch out. He has a thing for nurses."

"You must have been one," Laura said.

"Who, me? Be around blood and gore and guts?" She shivered. "No, I was a New York City detective."

Laura raised her brow in astonishment as she processed that tidbit.

Yeah, lady. So don't try to lie to me.

"You're so petite. I can't see you carrying a gun."

"I wore stilettoes, but I don't anymore."

"What? Wear stilettoes or carry a gun?"

So Nurse Laura had a sense of humor. Good for her. Humor would help her deal with obnoxious patients. And it complimented her unlined face, shiny brown hair worn in a messy bun, and big, heavily-lashed brown eyes that smiled easily at JL. How could anyone not like Nurse Laura?

"The gun." JL tried to say it flippantly, like it didn't matter. But honestly, she felt naked every time she left the house without a weapon. The truth was, though—if JL's long-term memory was still recalling the past correctly—she'd given up her guns to save her relationship. She could live without her Glock. She couldn't live without Kevin or her children. She yawned. She couldn't live without sleep, either. Her eyes drifted shut.

"I'll tell your husband you're awake. If you need anything, use your call button, okay?" Laura moved the device closer to JL's fingertips.

JL wrapped her hand around the plastic controls. If she needed anything? Really? Yes, she did. She needed her baby. Her droopy eyes snapped open again. "I want my baby."

In her sweet Tidewater accent, Laura said, patiently, "Dr. Winn will be here in a couple of hours. She'll tell you when you can get out of bed."

"I'm not asking to get out of bed. I just want someone to bring me my baby. What's so hard about that?" JL massaged her temples, trying to stave off a pounding headache.

Laura patted JL's arm and left the room just as Kevin walked in. "Hey, sweetheart. Does your head hurt?"

She looked up into his tired face to see his well-defined jaw was dusted with scruff. She pulled him down for a cuddle and a kiss. "I feel like I've been beat up and left on the mat. Where's our son?"

His dark eyes locked onto hers, and he grasped her hand, warm around her cold fingers. Tenderly he brushed her hair away from her face, tucking it behind her ear as if she was a child with a cut knee, not a woman who'd undergone emergency surgery.

"He's in the NICU. You can see him soon, but right now you can't get out of bed."

The tears stinging the backs of her eyes during her tough-girl impersonation finally broke through the dam and streamed down her face. She wiped her eyes with a corner of the sheet. "New mothers always get to be with their babies. Why won't they let me?"

Kevin anchored his elbows on the bed's siderail and leaned forward. "I've explained this at least five times, but you don't remember. It's okay, though. I'll repeat it a hundred times. You, sweetheart, are a stickler for obeying rules. Unlike the rest of us, gray is not in your color palette. Right now, the *rule* is you can't get out of bed. I can ask if they'll roll you up to the NICU."

"That's crazy. I can wait another hour. But if it comes and goes and I don't get to see Lawrence, then I'll insist they roll my bed up there."

Kevin pulled out a handkerchief and wiped her tears. She snatched the fancy linen, monogrammed with EBF, from him. "This is Elliott's. What happened to yours?"

"I left it in the ambulance."

Another memory tugged at her consciousness—airplane, Kevin's bleeding face. Shivering, she shook it away, wondering why she'd been longing for her short-term memory. On second thought, it could stay AWOL a while longer.

He tugged the handkerchief from between her fingers and dabbed softly at her cheeks. "I know you want to see him, babe, but you just had major surgery. You have a catheter and an IV. Dr. Winn has to order the removal of both, and she'll be here in a couple of hours. I promise you, you'll see him soon."

She sighed again, this time letting loose with a despairing one. "But I have to breastfeed him."

He held her face between his hands so she would narrow her focus to only him. "Lawrence is in the NICU. He's too small to breastfeed right now. But when you get to your room, you can start pumping your breasts."

"When can I see him? He's all alone."

"Shhh, babe. He's not alone. There's a whole team watching over him in the NICU, and I've been splitting my time between the two of you. I just got back." Kevin looked like hell. He was disheveled, and his eyes were red. He smoothed his thick, untidy hair back off his forehead, then rubbed his gray face. His knuckles lingered along his whiskered and bandaged cheek, before dropping away. "Do you want to see his pictures again?"

She blinked. "Again? But I haven't seen any pictures."

"You have, love. You just don't remember." He swiped his finger across his phone's screen and handed her the device. "Lawrence's primary nurse took this one of the two of us."

She gasped at the shocking, studio-quality picture of Kevin with the smallest baby she'd ever seen. He had a tube in his mouth, a nasal cannula, a blood pressure cuff around his ankle, an umbilical line, patches on his chest, and a blue knitted cap on his precious little head. Did he even have any hair? How could she ever touch him through all those cords?

The blue card on the front of the incubator said:

BABY BOY FRASER, 2.2 POUNDS, 14.8 INCHES.

Every inch of her skin broke out in a cold sweat. "Oh, my God. What have they done to him?" She dropped the phone, shaking her head. She was a cop. It was her responsibility to protect the weak and vulnerable. Why was she here when her precious, helpless baby was in a clear box?

"They're working to save his life. I'll take you to the NICU as soon as Dr. Winn says you can get up."

A tide of anger washed over her. Enough. She wasn't waiting any longer. She made a move to swing her legs over the side of the bed. The monitor beeped loudly, and the sudden movement sent shards of pain all the way through to her backbone. "Damn it!"

Kevin gently pushed her back down. "Babe, you can't get up. You have a catheter, an IV, and lots of stitches. You'll hurt yourself."

Laura rushed into the room, turned off the beeping noise, untangled the IV line, and checked the placement of the catheter to be sure JL hadn't dislodged any of the hospital's instruments of torture.

JL lit into him. She was tired of their patronizing attitudes. "Why won't anyone tell me where my baby is? I want Pops! I want Pete! They'll tell me the truth."

Arguing wore her out. Her eyelids drifted shut, and as sleep began to overtake her again, she heard Kevin whisper, "She was in a plane crash and had an emergency C-section. Our twenty-eight-week-old baby is in the NICU. Her family hasn't been allowed in to see her, and she can't remember anything from one minute to the next."

There's nothing wrong with my memory. I remember Kevin's voice...

Next time she woke up she'd call Pete. Her partner knew how to find lost people. He'd find her baby.

13

Paris (1789)—Sophia

HOPING TO AVOID the mob, Sophia, William, and the girls arrived at the Place de Louis XV, the largest public square in Paris, located between the Champs-Élysées and the Tuileries Gardens.

Instead, Jefferson's four-wheeled, convertible carriage brought them smack into the crowd.

An even larger mob than yesterday packed the square with fresh vigor. They stood shoulder to shoulder, and their hostile voices echoed the chants of *liberté* heralded by yesterday's violent horde.

The scene, the sounds, the swords and pitchforks raised in anger triggered Sophia's eidetic memories, her stomach tightened like a towel wrung dry, and she covered her ears, hoping to shut out the voices, but then quickly pulled her hands away. If the girls saw fear in her eyes and actions, they'd be scared too.

Instead, she imagined fields of summer grass, soft breezes, and crickets, lots of chirping crickets. It didn't work. The vividness of yesterday was indelibly imprinted on her brain, to hang forever in her mental art gallery.

"I don't recommend continuing on toward the Palais Royal…" William's voice trailed off as he stretched his neck, looking from one window to the other and back again. "I don't believe we're in danger, but I promised Mr. Jefferson we wouldn't take any risks."

Patsy and Polly sat on the rear-facing seat opposite Sophia and William. "Please close the top," Polly whispered. "I'm scared."

William immediately pulled up the front part of the soft folding cover, then the back part, and latched the two halves together in the center. Closing the top would make the heat in the carriage unbearable, but for Polly's peace of mind, Sophia would gladly suffer.

Polly leaned back, disquiet in her eyes. "They won't hurt us." Her sing-song voice turned the unspoken words—Will they?—into a question.

Patsy waved her hand dismissively. "We're Americans. Their problems aren't our fault."

"France is facing bankruptcy partly because of the enormous sums spent on the American Revolution," Sophia said, "and partly because of the famine caused by years of bad harvests."

"Well, if they don't hear us speak, they won't know we're Americans." Patsy fastidiously smoothed the printed cotton petticoat of her open-front dress. "From the way we're dressed, we could be French aristocrats."

"Aristocrats aren't very popular right now," Sophia said. "And the peasants have had enough. They're provoking a revolution over a long list of inequalities."

"You're well-informed, mademoiselle," Patsy said. "But Papa says all women in Paris are informed and discuss politics as well as any man. Women know their place in America and would never meddle in affairs of state."

Sophia scolded herself inwardly, *Stay out of it.* She glanced out at the rioters. She wasn't about to go out in that madness again. "There's nothing I need badly enough to risk another fall." She would rather be at home recuperating on her sofa, surrounded by her art and frescos. But she couldn't go home. Not yet. "Let's go to Monsieur David's atelier, then find Monsieur Watin."

"I concur," William said. "We're safe so long as we're in Mr. Jefferson's carriage. If we got out, it would be too easy to be jostled in the crowd and separated."

Polly visibly tensed. "Papa said the mob stole Mademoiselle Orsini's carriage and left her stranded. Then awful things happened." Her deep brown eyes welled with tears as she looked helplessly at Sophia. "I couldn't have been as brave as you were."

Sophia patted Polly's hand. "I wasn't brave. If I had been, I would have fought my way out instead of allowing myself to get sucked in." Jefferson deserved a tongue-lashing for oversharing with his daughters. It was nothing more than a thinly-veiled attempt to justify his invitation to Sophia to stay at the Hôtel de Langeac.

Poor Sophia. She had such a horrible experience. She needs to be with other Americans who can provide a safe place. Never mind the fact that she's an unmarried female artist and I'm an oversexed widower.

Even if Sophia confessed the story about losing her carriage wasn't true, she couldn't deny the horror of almost being set on fire. She shivered at the thought.

"William," she said softly. "Tell the coachman to take us back to the legation."

William raised his knuckles to rap on the back window to advise the coachman, but paused, holding his hand mid-air. "Would you like to see if we can go around the mob to reach Monsieur David's atelier before we turn back?"

Sophia placed her other hand on Polly's trembling shoulder, hoping to calm her. "His studio is a few blocks west of the Pont Neuf. But being out here is stressing us all. We should go back."

Polly shot Sophia an anxious glance. "I don't mind going there if his studio is away from…from"—she pointed out the window—"all the screaming."

"You're mistaken about the location, mademoiselle. Monsieur David is the most famous artist with an atelier at the Louvre," William said. "I've been there."

Her head snapped to the side, eyes wide. "But I went to his studio. If it wasn't his, then whose was it?"

"I couldn't say. Do you remember the address?" William asked.

"No, but I remember the location. Whoever the studio belongs to, the artist probably knows Monsieur Watin. At least I can purchase paints and canvases." She squeezed Polly's hand again. "What do you want to do, sweetie?"

"Get away from here. I'm afraid they'll take our carriage."

"Don't be silly," Patsy said. "William won't let anything happen to us. Mademoiselle Orsini didn't have anyone protecting her. We do. We should at least try to purchase art supplies before we return."

Polly nodded, seemingly at a loss for words, but she kept her hand tightly wrapped in Sophia's. For a dark instant, Sophia was back in the middle of the mob, being flung onto the mattress. She gulped down her distress and exhaled calmly, trying to make sure her voice would reveal nothing about her true state of mind.

"Take a right at the Hôtel de Ville, then a left at the next block," she said.

William relayed the directions to the coachman and the snap of the coachman's whip urged the horses forward, but the carriage barely crawled along the edge of the square.

When the mob realized the coachman wasn't going to yield the right of way to pedestrians, they finally moved aside, shaking their fists and shouting obscenities. Polly snatched her hand out of Sophia's grasp and covered her ears.

Why had Sophia insisted on a shopping expedition when she knew what was likely to happen? It was one thing to go out by herself, but why include the girls? "I'm sorry I suggested we go shopping."

Polly sniffed, "I wanted to. I just—"

"Didn't know how bad it would be." Sophia gave her a tight smile. "As soon as we get farther away, it won't seem as scary."

A block from the square the crowd thinned, and a breeze off the river eased the misery of the stifling heat. Although the streets were now passable, tension hung over Paris like a giant cloth baldachin, holding in the smoke, violence, and anger, letting it churn and gain momentum. Every day would be worse than the day before.

When the carriage passed the Hôtel de Ville, Sophia refused to glance out the window. But she didn't need to look to remember what happened. In her mind, her hand began to sketch the outlines of the scene. Then, as if in time-lapsed photography, the sketch added details until the governor lay butchered in the gutter in a pool of bright red blood.

The carriage bumped when it turned right, and the motion forced her forward. She automatically braced with her feet. Her knees absorbed the impact, and she gasped. "Jesus Christ!"

William drew a startled breath. "Mademoiselle Orsini, what's wrong?"

Four wide eyes stared at Sophia. Make it six. William gawked at her too. She couldn't speak, the pain radiating up and down her leg was too intense. Finally, she said, haltingly, "I...p-put pressure"— she sucked air between her teeth—"on my knee. Hurts."

If she'd been at home, she would have plunged her leg into an ice bath.

The pain was a throbbing heat coming at her in breaking waves. Several seconds ticked by. She focused on her other knee—the one that didn't hurt—and the three faces staring at her. Slowly her pain pulled back like the outgoing tide, taking a thin layer with it. Her knee didn't hurt less, but their worry hurt her more.

She made a frail attempt at a smile. "It's better now."

All three released audible sighs, but sharp concern lingered in their eyes.

"It must have been so horrible after all you went through yesterday to hurt your knee too," Polly said. "Is it better now?" The empathetic child turned her attention to Sophia instead of what was happening around her. The concern in her voice was enough to break Sophia's heart. The loss Polly had experienced in her short life—her mother's death, her sister's death, separation from an aunt she adored, and her father and older sister's long absences—would have turned most children into sulky, bad-tempered kids, but not Polly.

The pain switched from a screeching throb to a manageable one. "It was, sweetie. But the people weren't intentionally mean. They just got caught up in the moment. They've lived with tyranny for generations." Sophia cocked her head toward the window. "Listen to what they're shouting. Do you hear it?"

"Liberté," Polly said. "All people should be free. It's what Papa wrote in the Declaration of Independence—Life, liberty, and the pursuit of happiness."

"Except for the Negroes," Patsy said. "Papa should have included them."

"I agree," Sophia said. "So rather than wait for the law to change in America, we must continue to treat all people, regardless of color, with the dignity they deserve."

"What do you think will happen in Paris? Will the people return to their farms?" Polly asked. "Or will they stay and gather at the square every day?"

"After they get assurances, things will change, they'll go home. Then General Lafayette will lead his country through a long, bloody rebellion, just as he helped America through its war." Sophia glanced out the window to get her bearings. The shops looked vaguely familiar. "We're close," she said to William. The carriage continued down the cobblestone street. "There," she pointed. "That's it." She lifted her leg in anticipation of another jerky stop.

"Stop here," William shouted to the coachman. "I'll go inside and find out whose studio this is." He opened the door and alighted.

"I'll go with you, William." Patsy climbed out without waiting for him to answer.

Polly moved to the opposite side of the carriage to sit next to Sophia. "I'll wait here with the mademoiselle."

Sophia squeezed Polly's hand and forced herself to relax. By nature, she was not an anxious person, and she found being jittery both annoying and unproductive. But the startling events yesterday—arriving at the wrong time, discovering she was stuck there, and the injury to her knee—had thrown her off her game. Recovery would take longer than twenty-four hours.

The sun streamed through the carriage window like a spotlight shining on their interlaced fingers. Polly's small hands were smooth and silky, with a tiny scratch on one finger, and Sophia's were tanned with slightly swollen joints. For the last few years, she'd suffered through bouts of repetitive strain injury, and while Tai Chi helped with stretching and blood flow, she'd needed to modify her posture and how she held paintbrushes. Sitting in one position for several hours yesterday afternoon had irritated her right hand, and using crutches made it worse. Her fingers needed to stretch, but she didn't want to unclasp their hands.

"Polly," Sophia said. "I was thinking about what colors work best with your warm olive skin tone. And I think pink, purple, or green. What color ribbons do you have at home?"

Polly glanced up, as if studying the frame of the carriage top. "Red, blue, green, purple, and black. What color should I use?"

"Green or purple, maybe pink," Sophia said. "What's your favorite color?"

Before Polly could answer, William and Patsy returned with Monsieur Watin. Sophia's heart lifted, as if she'd reconnected with a lifelong friend. She'd learned several years ago in a victims' recovery class that a shared or similar bad experience bonded people who would never have connected otherwise.

The monsieur opened the carriage door, smiling warmly. "Mademoiselle Orsini, thank God you are safe." He reached for her hand and kissed the backs of her fingers. "Jacques and I were so distraught when we became separated. We searched the streets and even returned here, looking for you."

Sophia leaned forward. "I'm sorry I caused you distress. When I couldn't find you, I ran away."

"Jacques told me this morning that you reached the ambassador's house." Watin ran his hand slowly down the smooth wood of her crutches, smiling appreciatively. "I was sorry to hear about your accident. I hope it's not too serious."

"More annoying than painful. I'll recover in a few days."

"You were fortunate to find Ambassador Jefferson." He glanced at Polly. "I just met Martha. You must be Maria. I'm Léopold Watin, artist and color merchant."

"How lovely," Polly said, sounding exactly like Sophia. "Mademoiselle Orsini is going to paint our portraits."

"Well, the mademoiselle will need paint and canvases. Come." He handed the crutches to William. Then, without asking, he lifted Sophia out of the carriage and carried her inside the shop.

"So this is your color shop, too?" she asked, accepting the crutches from William.

"The front is my studio. The back is my workshop. I can provide every necessary item for painting and drawing. I will grind the colors to your specifications. I also have brushes, frames, stretchers, easels. Whatever you need."

"A one-stop shop. But I'm confused. I thought this was Monsieur David's studio. His painting of the Lavoisiers is here."

"D'Angiviller, director of the King's Buildings, issued an order prohibiting all artists from teaching female students in the Louvre. Jacques occasionally takes on a female student and works with her here. As for the painting, it will remain until it's safe to display at the Salon."

Sophia nodded slowly. "Now it makes sense."

He opened a door, swung it wide, and directed her with his outstretched hand. "Come into the back and we will discuss what you need."

She hobbled through the doorway into a room about half the size of her studio, feeling instantly at home. She crutched down one side lined with shelves loaded to overflowing with books, paper, charcoal, crayons, still life objects, paint splatter boards, and jars with paintbrushes, solvents and thinners. Two easels were set up in a corner holding blank canvases. The other side of the room was a work area, and the countertop was covered with artist tools and materials.

"What is this, mademoiselle?" Polly asked.

Sophia crutched over to her with Watin hovering at her side. "That's a chunk of lapis lazuli," Watin said.

"It's a semiprecious gem found primarily in the Middle East," Sophia added. "It's one of the most expensive sources for ultramarine pigment in the world. The signature hue is slightly greenish blue to violetish blue, medium to dark in tone."

"Are you going to paint with this color?" Polly asked.

Sophia picked up the chunk, brought it to her nose, and sniffed, getting a faint whiff of the sulfur content of the stone. "I couldn't paint without it."

Polly pointed to an object next to a powdered pigment. "And this?"

Sophia set the stone aside and picked up the object. "It's an animal-skin bladder. Painters store oil paints in them, then seal them with ivory tacks to prevent the paint from drying out."

"How clever," Polly said. "What other colors are you going to use?"

Sophia continued crutching her way around the shop, looking at items on the shelves. William leaned against the wall near the door, writing in a pocket-sized notebook. Even though he appeared engrossed in what he was doing, Sophia had a sense he hadn't missed one word of their conversation.

She answered Polly's question, saying, "For portraits, I'll use more flesh tones. Landscapes and your papa's garden will require a broader range of greens and browns." Some of the greens, such as Paris green, were highly toxic, and she'd have to wear a mask and keep the room well ventilated. "I won't be painting any *en camaieu*."

"A painting with only one color. Why would a painter do such a thing?" Patsy asked. "I learned to draw flowers and landscapes at the Abbaye Royale de Panthemont and we always used several colors."

"It's another form of art," Sophia said. "A painter might use two or three tints of the same color other than gray to create a mono-chromatic image. Jean-Baptiste Pillement has several *en camaieu* paintings. They're masterful, but it doesn't work for what I paint."

Watin sauntered over to his desk, opened a leatherbound book, and dipped a quill pen into an ink pot. "If you intend to paint portraits and landscapes, will your canvases need to be in a variety of sizes?"

Patsy picked up the lapis. "How do you make paint out of a rock?"

"The colors are ground up with fine nut or linseed oil. Within a couple of seconds, you'll have your paint color." She turned toward Watin. "I'll need a palette and an easel. No, make that two easels. I'll move back and forth between paintings."

Watin wrote in his journal. "How many canvases?"

"Several pure European linen three-quarters, half-length sizes. Whatever you have, all on stretchers."

"Linen is more expensive."

She picked up an H-shaped stretcher made of dark wood. "Cost doesn't matter. Get me the best you can, along with a complete chest of fifteen to twenty oil colors, fine Swiss crayons, charcoal, chalk, pencils, and drawing paper."

She glanced around the shop again. "Am I forgetting anything?" In Florence she had a supplier who came to her studio weekly, checked her stock, and resupplied as necessary. "Can I pay you to come by my studio every couple of days? I'll be painting from first light until the sun goes down and won't have time to keep up with my inventory. If I need a color and don't have it, I won't be a happy painter."

Watin gave her a blank nod, as if he didn't understand what she was asking. "You want me to visit your studio to see how much paint you have?"

"Or don't have, along with brushes, paper, chalk—everything. If it's not too much trouble."

"No one has ever asked me to do that, but I will. If," he added, grinning, "you'll let me see what you're painting."

"Sure. I let anyone who wants to see what I'm doing have a look, but I don't allow any comments. I don't want to hear anything that might distort or influence what I'm painting. As I get close to finishing, I'll ask the sitter what they think, but not before."

"I won't say anything." Watin ran his finger down the list he'd written in the journal. "Two easels—"

"Make it three," Sophia said.

Watin scratched through an item on his list. "And a palette. What about brushes?"

"Who makes your brushes?" she asked.

"A crafts guild in Nuremberg."

"Why there?" Polly asked.

Sophia picked up a paintbrush and examined it. "I don't know, but these are excellent brushes." She picked up another brush and smoothed the hairs over her palm. "Is this Russian sable?"

"I have less expensive brushes, but most of the ones I sell are sable."

"Do you have anything other than round and blunt brushes?"

"No, mademoiselle. I haven't heard of other shapes."

At home she used bristle brushes almost exclusively, in a variety of shapes: chiseled edge, flat, round, and fan-shaped for blending one wet color into another. Since Watin didn't have a variety of shapes, she'd trim the brushes to make do. "I'll take four dozen."

Watin's eyebrows shot up. "Four? Dozen?"

"I'll be working on at least three projects at the same time. When I need a clean brush, I don't want to wait for one." She set the brush down and fanned herself. The studio was as stifling as the carriage had been, and sweat trickled down between her breasts. Even the slight breeze coming off the river couldn't budge the heat from the morning sun, which streamed directly through the south-facing window. "How long will it take to get the order together?"

Watin tapped the tip of his pen against the page. "I'll prime the canvases this afternoon and deliver your order in the morning."

"Wonderful. That means I have today to set up a studio and help the girls decide what to wear, since we didn't get to the market to buy fabric for new dresses."

"If you think of something else, send word in the morning and I'll include it," he said.

She crutched over to Watin's desk and eased into a chair on the opposite side. Polly followed, took the crutches from Sophia, and leaned them against the wall. Sophia patted the arm of her chair. "You can sit here."

Patsy stood on the other side of the room next to William. "Where are you going to store all the painting supplies?"

"Good question. Your father didn't offer me a work space, and I didn't think to ask. All I require is a room with good light from the north."

"You could use the room across from his cabinet. He designed it to be his reading room, but he rarely uses it," Patsy said.

"I'll have to see if there's enough light from the windows."

"It has a door opening to a private garden. You could open it and have even more light," Polly suggested.

If the private garden was designed like the one she visited last night, it would be an alluring and intimate setting for a portrait. "It's up to your father. If I knew how much room I'll have, I'd order four easels instead of three." She wasn't sure she wanted to be that close to Jefferson and have him constantly looking over her shoulder. She pulled out her leather pouch. "This is a big order. I'll pay a deposit. How much do you want?"

"It's not necessary, mademoiselle. I can wait until you're paid."

"Ambassador Jefferson and I have an agreement. I'm painting in exchange for room and board. Oh, I almost forgot. I need to replace his ruled drawing paper. He probably uses it for architectural drawings, and I used several sheets."

Watin closed his notebook. "I know several Americans who would open their homes in Paris and Versailles and wouldn't require you to paint for your room and board. Women are always welcome."

Watin was truly an old soul concealed beneath classic good looks, brown eyes, and dark, wavy hair. Handsome, charming, and a Frenchman.

"The male-dominated art academies in Paris wouldn't be as welcoming," she said.

"A foreign woman wouldn't be a threat, and besides, you're passing through and wouldn't disrupt the established patronage circuits or meddle in the Academy's business. As engaging as you are, you'll be seen as a sparkling ornament."

Being a sparkling ornament wasn't high on her list of accomplishments. Matter of fact, it wasn't on her list at all. "If I lived anywhere else, I'd miss spending time with the Jefferson family." She played with Polly's curls, and the child smiled at her. "It's an amazing opportunity to paint them."

"Well," Watin said. "After you paint their portraits, if you decide you want to relocate, I can introduce you to other Americans who are well-connected to the Salons."

"I'm returning to America as soon as I can arrange transportation."

Polly drew a surprised breath. "Before we leave?"

Honey, I'm leaving the end of next week, and I can't change my ticket home.

"Maybe," Sophia said with a remorseful sigh. "But I'll finish your paintings before I leave. Don't worry."

"I'm not worried." Polly jumped up and rushed over to Patsy. "Will you wait with me in the carriage?"

"How much longer will you be, mademoiselle?" Patsy asked.

"I'm almost finished," Sophia said, unsure of what just happened.

William left with the girls, and Sophia reached for her crutches.

"Jacques wants you to sit for him."

Her eyes snapped back to Watin's. She owed Jacques her life, and hoped to plan time for him. If she didn't have to sleep, she might be able to get everything done. "I'll send him a note and explain. Maybe he can paint me painting."

Watin framed a space in the air with his hands. "I see you sitting in a relaxed pose at your easel, holding a brush to a partially finished work. Slightly used brushes at the ready, a palette cradled in your arm. A white turban in your hair, a dark, free-flowing dress with a white, ruffled collar of the same fabric as your turban. A wide red ribbon for a belt." He dropped his hands. *"Magnifique oeuvre d'art."*

She smiled and lightly touched his hand. "Very descriptive. I can see the painting, and anything Monsieur David painted would be brilliant."

"It's not my description," Watin said. "That's how Jacques described his painting of you."

"I'll write to him immediately and invite him to come for a visit. We'll talk and see what we can arrange." She stood and settled onto the crutches. "I guess we're done. Please bring your invoice tomorrow so I can pay you in full."

"Thank you for your business." Watin kissed one cheek and then the other. "When I see Jacques this evening, I'll tell him to expect a letter from you. And I'll see you again in the morning."

He escorted her to the front of the atelier. "Oh, I almost forgot." He hurried over to a table on the other side of the room. "You left this here yesterday. Jacques intended to have a wigmaker restore it for you."

"I have a lady's maid who seems to have a talent for arranging hair. I'm sure she can make it presentable again."

She left the shop and quickly settled into the carriage next to Polly, but the child wouldn't even look at her. "Polly," Sophia said softly. "We have a lot to do in the next few days. We'll have fun, and I'll need your help. And you know what?"

Polly looked up at her, a tear slipping down her cheek. Sophia wiped it away. "We can set an easel up for you, and I'll give you drawing lessons while I work. Would you like that?"

Polly sniffed and nodded. "Can I paint with a sable brush?"

Sophia chuckled. "You most certainly can."

Polly gave her a slight smile and sat up straighter. "Do you think I can be an artist too?"

"You, my dear, are Thomas Jefferson's daughter. You can do and be whatever you want. And so can Patsy."

Patsy's glance moved quickly to William and held his gaze for a long moment. Then she looked away and focused on something outside the carriage.

In the past five years, dozens of students had passed through Sophia's studio, and while she didn't always give her students what they wanted, she tried to always give them what they needed. And for these two motherless children, while she had a chance, she would give them time and attention, and try to boost their confidence. And God protect her heart, because there was no doubt when she returned home, a small part of them would go with her, as a small part of her would remain with them.

She leaned back in her seat and braced herself for the traumatic ride back to the Hôtel de Langeac. Within two blocks, they reached the mob—no longer contained within a few blocks of the square. Instead, the entire city seemed to swell with rioting peasants.

"Can we go around?" Sophia asked.

William knocked on the side of the carriage. "Take the Pont au Change and return to the legation by way of the south bank."

The coachman turned around but the bridge, lined with houses, was also packed with rioters. "We can't get through," he yelled.

William stuck his head out the window. "Turn around. We'll go north and circle back."

The horses nickered and danced nervously in their traces. In a panicky voice, the coachman yelled, "I can't go forward or backward. There are too many people."

The peasants bumped the carriage and made threatening gestures as they passed by. Sophia hopped over to the opposite bench seat, where she sat between the girls and wrapped her arms around them. "We'll be okay," she said. "They don't want to hurt us."

"But yesterday—" Polly said.

"Shh," Sophia said. "We'll get through this."

"There are so many rioters now." Patsy covered her ears. "The noise is deafening."

"Turn around," William demanded. "Go through the Marais district."

"I can't," the coachman yelled.

Sophia gave William a pleading look. His expression was one of fear and something else. Guilt at suggesting the bridge? It was gone before she could dissect it further.

The shouting, the people packed into such a narrow space, the stink from the city's main slaughterhouse located in the nearby Chatelet district, had her temples throbbing and her stomach churning.

She needed to protect the girls. The carriage couldn't withstand the onslaught of hundreds of people coming over the bridge. Would the bridge even support the weight of the structures and all the stomping feet? If she could walk, she'd suggest they get out and join the mob as it advanced on the square.

Wait. Maybe she couldn't get out, but the others could.

"William. Get out. Take the girls. Join the mob. As soon as you reach the Champs-Élysées, break away and hurry home."

"No, we're not leaving you behind," he said.

"You have a duty to protect them. Go. Now."

"No, mademoiselle. We won't leave you behind," Polly said, tears streaking down her face. "You can't even walk."

"I can if I have to. Please, go while you can. With any luck, the road will clear and I'll be home before you." She looked at William. "It's safer outside than in here. Please, take the girls now, and don't let go of their hands. The ambassador expects you to protect them. Not me."

William nodded. Then he pushed on the door but could only partially open it. He squeezed through and leapt to the ground. "Come, Patsy."

Patsy looked back at Sophia, and her expression nearly broke Sophia's heart. "I'll be okay. Go. Don't let go of his hand, and remember, if you get separated, run straight home."

Patsy climbed out, but Polly refused to leave. Remaining as calm as possible, Sophia said, "You have to go, darling. I'll see you soon." Sophia hugged her. "Remember, if you become separated, run home as fast as you can. You know how to get there. You can do this. And later I'll teach you how to paint. But now you need to do what I ask you to do."

Polly sniffed, "Yes, ma'am."

"Now, go."

William helped Polly down, and the three of them quickly disappeared into the crowd. The girls would be safe with William. If she handled this right, when they were all safely home, they could laugh about what happened and treat it as a huge adventure.

She eased her leg down and attempted to stand, but the pressure on her knee was excruciating. She had two choices. Remain in the carriage or try to keep up with the crowd while hobbling on crutches. In her heart she knew she couldn't manage it. She'd be knocked to the ground and stomped on.

The mob shook the carriage violently, trying to tip it over. Adrenaline crackled through her veins. She couldn't stop the carriage, but if she tucked and rolled, maybe she could minimize the damage and prevent a serious injury. It would be hell on her knee, though.

And then a more horrible fear flashed through her brain. She could fall off the bridge into the stinking Seine, and the layers of her clothing would quickly drag her to the bottom.

"Stop! Stop!" she yelled, her fingers holding fast to the window, the seat, anything she could grip, her knuckles turning white.

The horses screeched and reared, shaking the carriage, then tipping it far back, then slamming it forward, then tipping it back again. She had to let go of her crimp grip before it broke her fingers. And when she did, she slid off the bench seat and banged her head.

14

Richmond, VA—JL

AFTER BEING DISCONNECTED from all the hospital's torture devices—except the IV, in case she needed a transfusion—JL's doctor released her to her hospital suite and encouraged her to get out of bed, if only for a short walk to the bathroom. But she had more urgent things to do than a shuffle to brush her teeth. She was on her way to the NICU, and no one was going to stand in her way.

From her previous surgery, she was prepared for knife-stabbing pain when she tried to stand. She cranked the head of the bed—pushing the up arrow on the controls—as far as it would go, inch by agonizing inch, gritting her teeth.

Kevin emerged from the bathroom, soapy-scented and shaven, hair damp, dressed in a clean polo shirt and dark jeans instead of his regular khakis. The men in the family were so close in size they could easily wear each other's clothes. The jeans and shirt belonged to Braham. He always kept a change of clothes in Charlotte's office, and Kevin wasn't the first member of the family to dig into Braham's emergency bag.

She held her arms tightly to her belly. Her breathing was rapid and shallow, and a cold sweat coated her body. "I'm liking the idea of having my bed rolled to the NICU now."

"Too late. You have to get up and walk. Exercise opens your

lungs and pumps blood up from your legs to your heart, which in turn reduces the chance of getting pneumonia or blood clots. And you don't want either of those." Kevin helped her slowly swing her legs over the side of the bed. "Sit still a minute before you put your feet down."

"I've done this before. I know how to do it."

"Okay, babe," he said patiently. "But don't grit your teeth or hold your breath. It makes the pain worse."

"I know. I know. Don't bug me."

He held his hands up in surrender mode. "Just tell me what you need."

"I don't want to be a bad patient like Elliott."

Kevin chuckled. "You've got a long way to go, before you reach his status."

"I know you're trying to help me, but please, just let me do this at my own pace. I don't want to yell at you."

He pulled the wheelchair closer to the bed and locked the brakes. "That alone sets you apart from Elliott. He never cared. He yelled, cussed, and threw things."

She slowly rose up on shaky legs, Kevin standing close by with his arms outstretched. "It's your own fault." She growled at the pain, a little louder this time. "You enabled him."

"What can I say? He was my role model." Kevin helped her lower to the chair.

She was breathing heavily from the exertion. "What does that say about you? He was a drunken womanizer."

Kevin slid her feet into slippers before positioning first one foot and then the other on the foot rests. "Aw, shucks. Elliott wasn't that bad." Kevin looked up at her and grinned. "Besides, trying to control the behaviors of other people is a form of arrogance."

"And what does that say about Elliott? He tries to control everybody around him. God knows what he's going to do to the NICU staff. They might have to blacklist him from the hospital."

Kevin wheeled her out into the hallway. "Not this time. He'll sweet-talk them into doing whatever he wants by buying them off. If they need cameras for every baby, he'll buy cameras. If they want additional space, he'll make a large donation. If they need more personnel, he'll endow new faculty positions. Then when he asks for more access to his grandson, they'll be in his debt and have to find a way to give him what he wants."

"What am I supposed to do?" JL asked. "I can't fight him. If I don't want him there, he'll refuse to leave."

"The whole family is there for you. No one is coming up here until you're ready for company."

"But that doesn't include Elliott. I bet he's up there right now."

Kevin pushed the elevator call button, and when it arrived, he wheeled JL inside for the ride to the NICU floor. "I sent Elliott home."

JL glared over her shoulder. "See? What'd I tell you? He's been there with Lawrence before I've had a chance to see him."

"Only while I was with you. I knew you wouldn't want Lawrence to be up there without a family member to act as his advocate. If Elliott believes his grandson isn't getting the best possible care, he'll insist we fly Lawrence to Philadelphia, Boston, Cincinnati, or somewhere else."

"Which would be even more disruptive for Blane. At least in Virginia he gets to go to Uncle Matt's school and play with his cousins. He's happy here."

The elevator stopped, and Kevin wheeled her up to the parents' entrance to the NICU. He swiped his ID card under the reader, the lock clicked, and the door swung slowly open.

"Looks like you know your way around," JL said.

"Pod D will be our home away from home for a while."

"How long will he be here?"

"Probably till the end of the year."

Kevin wheeled her into the unit. Her heart lodged in her throat, and she licked her chapped lips. While she'd seen photos of Lawrence, she knew from experience pictures never truly prepared anyone for the reality of a serious situation.

Kevin pushed her down a long corridor until they reached Pod

D. As he wheeled her in, he massaged her shoulder. "It'll be okay, babe."

They were met immediately by a woman in scrubs who extended her hand to JL. "I'm Anne, your son's primary care nurse on this shift. I met your husband earlier. Lawrence is doing great, and I know you're anxious to see him." Anne had a sweet, trusting face with blue eyes, a long blonde ponytail, and a natural smile.

Another woman in scrubs approached them. "Mrs. Fraser, I'm Kelly Peterson, your son's respiratory therapist. Your little guy is doing well. We had an incident a little bit ago—"

Kevin's face blanched. "What happened?"

"His oxygen saturation dropped, and he started turning blue. We adjusted his endotracheal tube and he pinked right up. Dr. Fraser was here at the time. He immediately stood aside and watched over his grandson while we worked on him. He's a real prayer warrior, that one. You're lucky to have him."

"You know he's not a medical doctor, don't you?" JL said.

"He did mention his babies normally weigh a hundred pounds or more when they're born. I grew up on a farm, so I figured out right away that he was a veterinarian."

It was hard to think of Elliott as a prayer warrior. He was private about very few things. The entire family talked about his PSA results, his off-color language, the number of drinks he consumed, his intense love for his wife, and the number of cigars he smoked behind her back, but no one talked about his faith.

"By the way," Anne said, "I think your son definitely resembles his father and grandfather."

"Then he'll be another sexy Scotsman." She could already see Lawrence strutting behind his father, kilt swinging side to side, head high, deep-set brown eyes shining devilishly.

"Scotsman! Absolutely. And that only adds to his charm. Dr. Fraser is already a legend up here. We have an intern who's volunteered to be president of his fan club."

"Good grief," JL said.

Anne stopped next to an incubator. "Here's your little guy. You can slide your hands through the open portholes and touch him. If we don't have any more problems today, then the day after tomorrow you should be able to do kangaroo care. I'll help you manage all the tubes and cords."

"How long will I be able to hold him? A few minutes?"

"If he's doing okay, we try to limit it to four hours. We recommend you pump your breasts and use the restroom beforehand."

The sight of her newborn attached to all the tubes and cords shredded JL's insides. She pressed a hand against her chest to slow the terrified hammering of her heart.

Kevin knelt beside the wheelchair and gazed at her. "He's our miracle, babe. Our love will keep him alive. Give me your hand, and let's touch him together."

She raised her hand, but she was so scared it froze in midair. Kevin touched her wrist and guided her hand to the porthole, but she resisted. "I can't. I'll hurt him."

"No you won't." He sanitized their hands before inching hers into one porthole and his in the other. "Touch his hand. We'll hold his hand together."

"Look at his little foot. It was kicking me for months." JL smiled through her tears. "I have complained, haven't I? I'm sorry, little guy. I'd give anything if you were kicking me now. Can I touch the rest of him?"

"For right now, just his hand. We want him to learn that when someone holds his hand it's a soothing, caring touch. That the hand or finger is there to comfort him. Not to poke or tug on him."

"He's perfectly formed, isn't he?"

"Yes, he is. And we'll take him home one day to play with his brothers and his cousins."

"We'll take him to Austin's basketball games, too." Startled, she looked at Kevin. "Austin. I have to tell him."

"I know you didn't want me to call him, but I couldn't wait any longer. He had to know. I told him not to come home until the summer league is over, unless there was a serious need for him to be here."

JL nodded, understanding quite clearly what Kevin meant by *serious need*. "I couldn't have handled that conversation. Thank you for calling him."

JL relaxed her hand. Touching her baby wasn't nearly as scary as she'd imagined. She thought back—because her long-term memory was about ninety-nine percent functional at this point—to the nights she and Kevin made love under the down comforter at the Colorado ranch. She knew she was pregnant before they returned to MacKlenna Farm from their skiing holiday.

And hopefully Kevin was right. Their love would keep Lawrence alive.

Just as she was calming her fears, easing her anxiety, an alarm sounded, and Anne rushed to her side...

15

Paris (1789)—Sophia

WHAT SHOULD BE up was down.

Sophia had plowed into the soft fabric of the adjustable top and hit her head. It hurt almost worse than her knee. The two halves of the roof began to separate, and she could see daylight between the stretched seams. If the seams ripped open, she would be dumped out, trampled on, and pitched into the river.

None of those possibilities were survivable.

"Clear a path. Calm those horses," a man roared above the din. "You men… Get over there and get this carriage right-side-up. That's Ambassador Jefferson's carriage. Clear a path now!"

The horses whinnied and struggled as the carriage hung, teetering—neither falling nor standing upright. Sophia gritted her teeth and struggled to make out what was happening by sound alone, the best she could manage while she was upside down.

The quick thrust of her heartbeat banged violently in her eardrums. She was too terrified to believe her luck would last and she'd be rescued from the clutches of death a second time.

Why was this happening? Had she pissed off the brooch god? If he, she, or it was sending her a message saying she had abused her ownership of the brooch and was now suffering the consequences, then oh, man, the brooch god didn't have to worry about her.

She'd received the message loud and clear. Get her home safely, please, and she'd never use the brooch again.

"Calm those horses," the same man shouted, closer now.

A blur of mounted soldiers in white breeches and dark blue jackets flashed on one side of the carriage. Grunting, they forced the carriage back into its upright position. When it landed squarely on its four wheels, the carriage bounced once, twice, propelling Sophia up against the bench seat. Pain shot up her leg, she grabbed her knee and screamed.

The door flew open. A soldier with a chest full of medals and a silly powdered wig with rolls above the ears jumped aboard, swooped her up in his arms, and set her gently on the seat.

"Where are you hurt?" he asked.

Through clenched teeth she said, "It's my knee. There's nothing you can do."

He shouted out the window, "Calm those horses before they pull this carriage off the bridge." He leaned forward, staring at her, his elbows on his knees. "You're not Mademoiselle Jefferson. You must be..." His voice trailed off, but his gaze, if possible, grew more intense, a strange, vibrating stare, as if he were trying to bore straight through her eyeballs to the back of her head.

Sophia bit back threatening tears as pain radiated down her leg. "I'm Sophia Orsini. I'm...a guest."

He gave her a knowing look. "The artist?"

She tried to smile, but her mouth wouldn't obey. It was too busy gnawing on her lip to keep from screaming again. "Patsy... Polly... Mr. Short... They climbed out when the carriage got hung up...in the crowd. It was safer...to be on foot. The carriage was rocking...back and forth. The girls were so scared."

His tone shifted, taking on a sympathetic weight, but he didn't take his intense gaze from her. "Why'd you stay behind?"

"I can't walk." The pain was unbearable now, and she was afraid she might have torn her ACL, or worse. She needed ice and a pain reliever before she bit her lip in two. "The mob would have knocked me over."

"Do you know which way they went?"

"Toward the Place de la Concorde."

He squinted, a crease forming between his eyebrows. "I don't know that place. Where is it?"

"The Place—" She stopped and tried again, looking closely at her rescuer. "The Place de Louis XV. If they can get through the square, they're planning to walk home on the Champs-Élysées."

A soldier opened the door and looked inside. "General, the horses are under control, and we've cleared the path forward. What are your orders, sir?"

General?

Her pain synapses fogged up her brain and shrouded her mental portrait gallery with a thick, undulating fog. Who was this man?

"Turn the carriage around. Form an escort on both sides. Proceed toward the Champs-Élysées."

"Are you remaining inside, sir?" the soldier asked.

"For the moment, yes. Keep my mount close by and go slowly. We're looking for Ambassador Jefferson's daughters and Mr. Short."

"Yes, sir." The soldier closed the door and ordered the rioters to move aside so the carriage could make the turn.

The general sat back and looked at her. "Is your knee broken?"

"No, it's a bad MCL sprain, possibly impacting the ACL."

He came back at her with another squint and creased brow. "What is this…this…? MCL?"

She had no idea when the ligament was identified and first treated, and at this point she hurt too much to care. "A medial collateral ligament supports the knee along the inner side of the leg. It can be injured by a severe knee twist, which is what I did when I stepped in the pothole in front of the Hôtel de Langeac. Right now I need to ice and rest my knee and, most of all, stop reinjuring it."

"Are you a physician too?"

"No, but I've studied human anatomy, and I'm an athlete…" When he looked at her oddly, she said. "I like to be active, and I've had my share of injuries." She closed her eyes and breathed deeply through the pain. "I don't know what would have happened to me if you hadn't come along. I could be floating facedown in the Seine by now."

"We were on our way to Versailles when I recognized the ambassador's carriage. How did you come to be here?"

"We were coming back from Monsieur Watin's atelier and couldn't get turned around." She opened her eyes and studied the general's medals and red, white, and blue cockade. If she could think clearly, surely she would remember his name. "I'm so sorry to hold you up. I'm sure you have plenty to do today."

"It's my responsibility to see you safely back to the Hôtel de Langeac. Matter of fact, I just left there."

Ah, now she knew the identity of her rescuer—General Marie-Joseph Paul Yves Roch Gilbert du Motier, Marquis de Lafayette, known in America simply as Lafayette. Hanging upside down must have caused the confusion, because the general looked exactly like his portrait by Joseph-Désiré Court.

During her research trip to Paris in the spring, her tour guide had taken her to Cimetière Picpus, the only private cemetery in Paris. The cemetery was the final resting place of more than thirteen-hundred people, including members of Lafayette's family, who were guillotined and dumped there in a mass grave in 1794. He and his wife were buried nearby. Sophia knew very little about him other than he was a hero of the American and French Revolutions.

"I apologize for not recognizing you, General. It's such an honor to meet you, sir, and to personally thank you for your service to America."

He slightly tipped his tricorn. "It was my honor."

She liked the way his eyebrows lifted, liked their color, too, which was a few shades darker than his hair, slashing above his bright eyes.

"And may I say, mademoiselle," he continued, "you are as beautiful as the ambassador described."

Despite the pain, she managed a slight smile. "He was being kind."

"The ambassador mentioned you had a knee injury, and even

described the crutches you designed." Lafayette picked one up off the floor and ran his hand along the smooth wood. "I would like to show these to the physicians at the Les Invalides. There are dozens of men missing a leg who would receive immense benefit from having a pair."

"I'm sure Mr. Jefferson would give you a copy of his altered design to share with them."

The carriage lurched as it turned around, and she instinctively clutched the edge of the seat. The coachman drove faster now that he had a clear path, and the mounted soldiers rode next to them on both sides.

"I'm afraid we'll miss Polly and Patsy. I can't see much from these windows."

"We can pull the top back," Lafayette said.

She stared at the buttons holding his dark blue uniform jacket closed over his warlike chest. "We started out with it down, then ran into the mob, got scared, and closed it. With you here, though, the crowd doesn't frighten me."

Lafayette unlatched and lowered each side of the soft fabric that formed the roof of the carriage. The breeze swept over her, captured her hair, and lifted it lightly around her face. The coolness brought slight relief from the heat, but did nothing for the pain.

When they reached the Place de Louis XV, the carriage moved slowly along the edge of the crowd. A host of anxious faces turned toward them, and the din of jeering protestors died away as the carriage and escort passed by. This was as close as she'd ever come to a carriage ride through a European city with royalty. She was slightly tempted to do the queen's wave.

If she was considering waving to the madness, she needed to lie down and apply a cool cloth on her forehead. She clasped her hands and searched the crowd, soon realizing it would be impossible to find the girls in the throng of thousands. Lafayette frowned as he searched the plaza.

His worries went much deeper than finding two lost girls. Storming the Bastille was only the first in a series of clashes between the French people's revolutionary spirit and their leaders' monarchical ambitions. The general understood that. Was he thinking about what would happen when the king came to Paris, or were his thoughts further removed to say…next month, next year, a decade from now?

His black, leather-booted foot tapped against the floor, and he held his hands slightly apart, as if holding his reins. He obviously preferred to be on horseback. If she was an experienced equestrian without a knee injury, she'd rather be on a horse too. Being high above the crowd would allow him to see farther and assess the situation more quickly. And his well-trained horse, trotting alongside, didn't seem to be at all skittish despite the noise and congestion.

"General, would you be able to spot the girls more easily if you were on horseback? I'm sure they would be far more likely to see you."

His tight lips relaxed into a grin. "The ambassador would appreciate my careful watch over his guest."

"You can watch me just as easily on horseback. I'm fine. Really. And if it helps find the girls sooner, you should go."

"I'll have one of my men ride with you." He signaled the soldier who had conversed with him earlier.

"That's not necessary," she said. "Your escort is sufficient."

Lafayette spoke quickly to the soldier, who immediately relayed a message to the coachman. The carriage rolled to a stop, and he climbed out. As he closed the door he said, "I'll be close by."

The coachman turned onto the Champs-Élysées. Hundreds of rioters, or protestors, or just angry Frenchmen, were striding briskly down both sides of the boulevard toward the square. Polly must be almost hysterical being out in this chaos. Sophia couldn't return to the Hôtel de Langeac without her and Patsy.

I'm in a Paris state of…Hell.

As soon as they arrived at Jefferson's residence, she would send Lafayette and his men on their way, and she would wait in the carriage until William and the girls made it home.

They hadn't gone very far on the Champs-Élysées when a small voice yelled. "Mademoiselle. Wait!"

Sophia whipped around in the seat, turning toward the voice. "Stop!" The carriage rolled to a jerky stop. She stood on one foot, holding tightly to the side of the coach while she searched the tree-lined boulevard.

Lafayette rode up beside her. "What is it, mademoiselle?"

She hissed as a surge of pain ran up her leg. "I...heard Polly. They're close by...but I don't see them. Do you?" Oh, God. She had to find them. She cupped her hands to her mouth and yelled, "Polly! Patsy! Where are you?"

He turned around in the saddle and stood in his stirrups. He pointed. "There. I see them." The general trotted his horse through the traffic on the boulevard and executed a perfect emergency dismount when he neared the girls and Mr. Short.

Overwhelmed with relief, Sophia collapsed into the seat and buried her face in her hands. She'd survived another horrible day, and, thanks to William and General Lafayette, the girls would arrive home uninjured.

Her back and neck were stiff from the tension and being tossed around. She rubbed the hardened muscles at the top of her spine.

What would Jefferson say when he heard what had happened to them? He would blame her for endangering the welfare of his children. It had been a mistake to go shopping. Monsieur Watin was a successful color merchant, and William could easily have found him and delivered a message.

She'd made a complete muddle of things. Maybe she should ask Watin for a recommendation for alternate housing before Jefferson showed her the door.

Damn brooch.

Why had it dumped her here and now? She shoved her hand into her pocket and rubbed the pearl with her thumb.

But it remained cold as winter ice.

16

Richmond, VA—JL

JL'S HEART LODGED in her throat as her baby was surrounded by his medical team in an instant. She looked up at Kevin, standing behind her wheelchair, and in a pleading voice said, "Do something."

Kevin's head snapped up, and JL jerked when an instrument clanged to the tile floor.

"We have to let the medical professionals take care of him," he said. "I wish I could do something other than stay out of the way and pray, but…"

"What's wrong with him?" she asked, her voice breaking.

Kevin scratched his head, rubbed the base of his neck. "Probably his lungs, but it could be anything." He pulled JL's wheelchair back out of the way and held her hand. His hand was freezing—which was weird, because Kevin's body was like a furnace. In the winter, he ran in lightweight running tights. If he was cold now, it meant he was scared. Since he knew a hell of a lot more about medicine than she did, if he was scared, she was terrified. Claws of fear crawled through her, digging into her flesh as it crept up her spine.

She covered his hand with hers, sandwiching it in her shaky grip. A technician of some sort pushed a machine over to the incubator.

Anne moved away from the huddle to make room for the machine and came over to them. "Dr. Fox believes your son's lungs have collapsed. They're doing a chest X-ray to confirm the diagnosis."

"Will he have to have surgery?" JL was slipping into shock, numb with fear. She heard once that time was supposed to lengthen when a person was in shock, that the body shuts itself down. But she was experiencing just the opposite. Seconds raced by, pinprick sharp with unnecessary detail—other parents, murmuring voices around her, bubbling and gurgling machines, a small, helpless cry, Kevin's still-cold hand. She had to filter through it all, pitch extraneous details aside, and focus only on what was important—Lawrence.

Anne continued in a kind, soft voice that made JL's eyes prickle with tears. "This is not uncommon in preemies. If the X-ray confirms the diagnosis, treatment will be based on the severity of the symptoms."

JL reached for a tissue in the pocket of her robe, unfolded it, searching for a dry corner to wipe her eyes. "Why'd this happen to him? Hasn't he had enough trauma?"

"The tiny air sacs in Lawrence's lungs where oxygen and carbon dioxide are exchanged burst and cause air to escape. Preemies have very fragile lungs. As soon as Dr. Fox looks at the X-rays, she'll know better how to treat him."

JL rested her forehead in her hand. Didn't they know her brain was sluggish from drugs and pain and worry? "Everybody keeps giving me medical information, but my brain's too fuzzy to grasp all this."

Kevin massaged her shoulder with his free hand, the pressure tingling every nerve in her body. With their hands still clasped, she lifted her thumb to slide against his. His thumb, his hand, his body were a bulwark, a place of safety for her. Kevin was normally so unruffled, but all bets were off now.

Which scared the hell out of her.

"We don't want to be in the way," he said, his voice shaky as he sat still and stricken. His cheeks appeared hollow in the shadow of the lights, and his eyes were wide and desperate. Did hers look the same as his?

"For now you can stay right here. I'll keep you informed." Anne returned to the huddle, glanced back over her shoulder, and gave JL a tight smile lasting only a couple of seconds.

"I don't have the strength or a working brain to understand what's happening or what I need to do." She was a trained cop used to handling dangerous and life-threatening situations, able to act on a dime, read body language…but not today. She was out of her element.

Other women she knew who'd had C-sections never complained of being unable to function, to think, to respond. Charlotte. Where was Charlotte? She'd know what was wrong. Where was Pete? He'd get answers.

"I don't know what to do either," Kevin said. "We'll figure it out. We'll learn what we need to know."

"What's wrong with me? I feel like my body's been roused from a coma, but my brain is still asleep."

"You've been through hell. Things will get clearer as the drugs wear off." He kissed her and when he lifted his face, his eyes were soft.

The hustle and bustle, the white coats and blue- and pink-printed scrubs, the bubbling of Lawrence's oxygen, the low voices—calm yet serious—all blurred together.

Her own measured heartbeat thumped in her ear. But the other heartbeat she'd been aware of for months no longer fluttered unheard somewhere inside of her. The beat now pinged across the monitor over her son's head.

She broke out in a cold, shaking sweat. If this was her life now, knowing any minute her son could die, she would have to rely on others to get her through it. Regardless of what Kevin said, she didn't have the strength. If Lawrence died, how could she go on? Her head rested weightless against Kevin as he sat next to her, gripping her hand. She felt weak and lightheaded and her breathing was all wrong.

"I'm going to—"

Her eyes rolled back in her head, and that was the last she knew.

17

Paris (1789)—Sophia

WHEN SOPHIA, THE girls, and William arrived back at the Hôtel de Langeac, Jefferson wasn't there. Thank God. Sophia was in too much pain to deal with him right now. And if he demanded she leave the house, she would go, but she didn't know how she'd manage it physically.

Marguerite helped her climb the stairs to her room. Halfway up Sophia stopped. "Give me a minute." She broke out in a cold sweat. She was no stranger to injuries, but this was the worst ever. And having no competent medical care scared her, which intensified the pain.

They finally made it to her room, but by then she'd given up on trying not to cry, and tears poured down her face. "I…hardly ever cry, but…my knee feels like it's being hit…over and over with a hammer."

"Let me help you out of your dress. You'll be more comfortable."

Sophia didn't have the energy to care what happened. Somehow Marguerite stripped her down, sponged her off, and helped her into her Tai Chi shirt and trousers. On a one-to-ten scale, her pain was a fifteen, and she had a high threshold for pain. Finally clean and wearing unrestrictive clothing that allowed her to breathe easily, she crept into bed, groaning, hoping sleep would rescue her.

The muscles in her arms, neck, shoulders, and lower back were tense and tight. She needed a massage. She doubted Jefferson would know a masseur, but maybe Monsieur Watin knew a physician or scientist who understood the benefits of massage.

Or better yet, maybe she could teach Marguerite to identify trigger points and rub out the knots. She'd already proven to be resourceful and intelligent. She could probably do whatever Sophia asked her to do.

"If you'll fluff a few pillows behind my back and under my leg, I'll try to sleep for a few hours."

Marguerite lifted Sophia's leg, placed a pillow covered with towels beneath it, and packed ice around her knee. "Do you want me to stay with you?"

"That's not necessary, but will you check on me in a couple of hours and bring fresh ice and a cup of willow bark tea? The ice melts so quickly."

"Yes, milady. And I'll clean your dress while you sleep."

"Thank you. Being tossed around the carriage this morning got me pretty dirty. Let me empty my pockets first."

Sophia removed the pouches with her money, jewelry, and supplies and surrendered her traveling outfit to Marguerite's capable hands. Once she was satisfied Sophia was settled, Marguerite left and closed the door.

After stashing the pouches behind the pillows at her back, Sophia drifted off to sleep, worried about her knee and Jefferson's reaction to what happened during their morning outing.

A few hours later, Marguerite's sweet voice pulled Sophia out of a deep sleep. "Mademoiselle, do you wish to dine with the family?"

Sophia opened one eye, noticed the room had darkened and her leg still ached, and quickly closed it again. Rest, ice, and ibuprofen had done little to improve her condition. "I don't want to wake up. My knee hurts."

"What can I do?" Marguerite asked. "Do you want Monsieur Petit to send for the doctor?"

Sophia shook her head. "No doctor." After two days of being flung around like a beanbag, there wasn't an inch of skin without a red or purple bruise.

"I brought ice to repack your knee."

"Thank you. What time is it?"

"Six-thirty. Dinner isn't until nine, but I thought you'd want to bathe before you dress. If you don't intend to go downstairs, I'll bring food up to you."

"I can't get up. My entire body aches. Would you ask Monsieur Petit for a glass of red wine and some cheese and bread? I might want dinner later, but for now a light snack is sufficient."

It had been more than six hours since she'd had any ibuprofen, and the high level of pain concerned her. Could she have torn her MCL? Those injuries could respond well without surgery, but she would need to wear a brace, keep icing, and continue taking ibuprofen. After the pain and swelling subsided, she could begin rehab to restore strength and range of motion. Then later, when she returned home, she'd see an orthopedist.

While Marguerite packed ice around Sophia's knee, she said, "Miss Patsy and Miss Polly would like to see you when you feel up to a visit."

Honestly, what Sophia wanted to do was drink a couple of glasses of wine in the privacy of her room and go back to sleep, but she was curious to find out what Jefferson had to say. "The girls are welcome to come in anytime. What about Mademoiselle Bertin? Did I sleep through her visit?"

"The mademoiselle sent word saying the queen requested her appearance in Versailles. She said she would come another day."

"Oh good. I really need another dress." She would have to borrow an apron and be careful mixing paints. She couldn't afford to spill paint on her only dress.

Marguerite smiled. "I visited my friend, a lady's maid for the comtesse de Lameth. She had two dresses she was taking to the secondhand market to sell, and I brought them back to show Monsieur Petit. He said the asking price was reasonable, so he gave me money to buy them from the funds you deposited with Mr. Jefferson. After I clean and alter the gowns, they'll look wonderful on you. They'll match your eyes and blonde hair. The only problem is, you're bigger"—she patted her chest—"than the madame. But I can add lace and ribbons, and the dresses will fit you perfectly. Even the Comtesse will not recognize her old gowns."

"How did I get so lucky? You are a blessing."

"No, milady, you are the blessing. My prior employer was moving his family to his estate in Normandy and closing his Paris home. The entire staff was discharged."

"How horrible. What about family? Do you have any in Paris?"

"Everyone except my brother was killed three years ago in a fire."

Before Sophia returned to the future, she would secure a good position for Marguerite. And if possible, get her out of Paris. Thousands of people would lose their heads in the next few years, and the city was well on its way to becoming a terrifying place to live.

"Can you read?" Sophia asked.

Marguerite pressed a finger to her lips. "I've never told anyone, but my brother is a priest. He taught me to read and write, and I also studied mathematics, science, and languages. Besides French, I can speak English and Italian. If anyone knew he taught me, he would be severely disciplined."

"Your secret is safe with me."

Her big brown eyes lit up her face. "I borrowed books from my last employer's library late at night and returned them before the sun came up. But the glances I received from the monsieur led me to believe he knew I was borrowing them."

"I don't know your last employer, but Mr. Petit would certainly notice if you borrowed books from Mr. Jefferson. I'll bring books up here so you can read them. Will that help?"

"I've read one book by Voltaire and would like to read more."

"Voltaire? Impressive. I'm sure there's a volume or two on the shelves in Mr. Jefferson's cabinet. No library worthy of the name is complete without Voltaire. I'll see what I can find."

The door rattled with a timid knock. "Come in." An instant later it flung open and Patsy and Polly bounded in. "How's your knee, mademoiselle?" they asked in unison.

"If you don't need anything else, I'll go talk to Monsieur Petit while you visit with Miss Polly and Miss Patsy." Marguerite gathered up the bucket of melting ice and left the room.

"Mademoiselle, how do you feel?" Patsy asked.

Sophia patted the edge of the bed. "Sit here and tell me what I've missed."

Polly sat on the bed and Patsy pulled up a chair. "I was afraid Papa was going to terminate Mr. Short on the spot," Patsy said. "He said you never should have been left behind, and if that's how Mr. Short was going to protect those in his charge then he should look for other employment."

Patsy blew out an exasperated breath. "I stood up to Papa and told him Mr. Short had to make a decision quickly, and he concurred with your assessment that Polly and I had to be his top priority."

"And what did he say?"

Patsy sighed again. "He was terribly upset, but he finally had to agree that Mr. Short made the right decision under the circumstances. Then he blamed himself for allowing us to go out when he knew rioters still controlled the streets."

"The blame is mine," Sophia said. "I insisted on going out. I was wrong. Someone could have found Monsieur Watin and sent him a message to come to me, and none of this would have happened. I endangered all our lives."

Polly hugged Sophia. "Let's not talk about what happened. It makes my stomach hurt. Let's talk about what we're going to do tomorrow. But…I have a question."

"What is it?"

"What are you wearing?"

"Polly, how rude," Patsy said.

Polly picked at the bottom of Sophia's shirt, rubbing the red print fabric between her fingers. "I've never seen women's clothes like this before. You're wearing trousers."

"And they're very comfortable. I wear them to practice Tai Chi."

"Tai Chi?" Patsy asked. "What is that?"

"A graceful form of exercise to improve your quality of life and restore your energy. I've been practicing it for years. But to do it properly you need to be able to move freely, which isn't possible in my other clothing."

"Don't let Papa see you." Polly giggled. "He might faint." She rolled her head to the side, went limp, mouth open, playacting what her father would look like if he fainted.

Sophia couldn't stifle a twinkle of a laugh. "Well, last night I snuck downstairs to get a bite to eat and he caught me. He was…shocked. But he got over it when I told him walking with crutches is easier when dressed like this, and I also reminded him that he wouldn't want me to fall again, especially in the middle of the night."

Patsy fingered the shirtsleeve. "He wouldn't want you to fall again. But what do they feel like? The pants, I mean?"

"Very comfortable. I'll let you try them on."

"Oh, I almost forgot," Polly said. "Monsieur Watin sent over several packages, and Monsieur Petit carried them to Papa's reading room."

Having painting supplies to work with reenergize Sophia. "Already? What did he send?"

"We didn't open them," Patsy said, sounding mildly indignant. "They're your packages."

"Oh, I wouldn't have minded at all. You could have organized them. Did he send paper and charcoal? If he did, I could do some sketches. Do you want to go look?"

"Are you sure you don't mind?" Polly asked. When Sophia shook her head, Polly hurried out of the room.

Patsy walked over to the door and closed it. "Mademoiselle, may I ask you a question? I don't want to impose while you're bedridden, but I don't have anyone else to ask."

"Sounds serious. You can ask me anything, and I'll give you my best advice, although you don't have to take it."

Patsy returned to the chair. "If you give me advice, I'll certainly consider it."

"Okay, so what's up?"

"It's about Mr. Short." A pink tinge crawled up Patsy's neck to her cheeks. "What's your opinion of him?"

Sophia wasn't at all surprised by the question. Patsy's affection for Mr. Short was mentioned in Meacham's book. His fabulous audiobook narrator had a talent for reading with clarity, making it easy for her to remember so many small details. Jefferson didn't approve of Mr. Short's intentions and discouraged a marriage proposal. So how should Sophia handle this? There was only one way. With honesty.

"I think he's an honorable, intelligent man, and it's obvious you care for him."

Patsy nodded. "If I return to America with Papa, Mr. Short won't propose. He wants me to stay here."

"But you can't. Can you?"

Patsy knotted her hands together in her lap and stared at them for a long moment, obviously gathering her thoughts. Finally, she said, "Papa would be so disappointed if I stayed here. He depends on me."

"My opinion, for what it's worth, is that parents should never place limits on their children because of their own needs. When I was your age, I was very much in love with a young man. He was handsome and funny, and he loved me very much. The problem was my parents disapproved of him. They didn't believe he could meet their standards as a provider for their daughter."

"What happened?"

"They sent me to Italy to live with my grandmother, and she encouraged me to study art. I believe if I'd stayed in America, I wouldn't have become the painter I am today."

"What happened to the young man?"

"I don't know," Sophia said with a slight lift of her shoulders. "I never saw him again."

"How sad."

Sophia's heart snagged on the soft, wistful way Patsy said it. "I agree. It is very sad."

"Haven't you ever wanted to marry?"

"I've never met another man who measured up to him. If I ever do, I'd consider it."

"Mama made Papa promise he would never marry again."

A curious mix of emotions played in Patsy's eyes, and Sophia automatically reached for a pencil to draw the expression...but she didn't have one.

Often, when faced with a mysterious expression, its true meaning was more easily revealed in a drawing. In lieu of a pencil, she'd use a camera. In lieu of both, she pressed her brain's imaginary pause button and used her eyes to draw Patsy's face. Was Patsy seeing herself in her mother? Was she subconsciously wanting William to wait for her and not commit to another woman?

"What do you think of the request your mother made?"

"I don't have an opinion."

Buzz. Wrong answer.

"Sure you do," Sophia said. "Do you think your mother wanted him to spend the rest of his life alone?"

"He's not alone. He has us."

Buzz. Second wrong answer.

"By alone I meant without an adult companion. An adult of the opposite sex."

"You're not as old as Papa, and you don't have a companion."

Buzz. Too close to home.

"I'm not single because someone asked me to stay that way. I'm single by choice. And your Papa is still a young man," Sophia said. "He's handsome, intelligent, honorable, witty, and he deserves to be happy. You're old enough to remember your mother, right? You're not going to forget her, and you can share your memories of her with Polly. I think your mother didn't want her children to forget her. She didn't want another woman to take her place in your heart, in Polly's heart. If your father falls in love with someone else, it doesn't mean he didn't love your mother. In fact, it means he had such a wonderful marriage that he wants to recreate his happiness, which is a compliment to your mother. It's not dishonoring her."

Patsy had an unfocused gaze, seeming to look inside instead of outward. After a few moments she said, with some hesitation, "Do...do you like him? I noticed the way he looked at you this morning at breakfast. Like you were the only person in the room. Mr. Short has gazed at me like that before. It's why I noticed it."

Sophia knew where Patsy's thoughts were going, and she had to redirect them. "I do like him. But Patsy, I'm just here temporarily."

"But you're going back to America. Aren't you?"

Sophia hated lying, but she'd come this far with her story and had to continue with it. "I am, but I'm going back to New York City. I'm a painter and that's what I intend to continue doing when I return. My life's not in Virginia."

"Mr. Short said Papa will be offered a position in Mr. Washington's cabinet. If that happens, and he accepts, he'll live in New York City, too."

This was a double uh-oh moment. Sophia wasn't sure how to give Patsy a satisfactory answer. She couldn't tell her the truth, that she was returning to the twenty-first century, so it was time to dodge. "I thought this conversation was about you and Mr. Short."

"It started that way, but I'm curious about your feelings for Papa."

"Then let me ease your mind. There's a very real possibility that the government won't stay in New York City. So your father and I would only live in the same place a few months. And, more important, I'm almost forty years old—"

"You're forty? Impossible. I knew you were...older. But not that old."

"Thank you. I appreciate the compliment, but yes, I am *that* old, which means I'm too old to have children. If your father remarries, he will want a son. But why don't we talk about what you're going to do instead?"

But how could Sophia advise Patsy when she knew her future,

knew she would marry her third cousin Thomas Randolph and have eleven children—and William would not fight for her. Sophia's advice had to guide Patsy in the right direction.

"I think you and William have a special relationship, and it will probably last a very long time. But you belong in America. My advice is to tell William if he wants to marry you, he must fight for you now. Not in two weeks. Not next month. No one knows when your father's leave-of-absence papers will arrive, granting him permission to leave France. If William won't do as you ask, you have to let him go."

Tears slipped down Patsy's cheeks. She swiped them away with quick brushes of her finger, gritting her teeth. Sophia internalized Patsy's anguish, which forced her to grapple with old regrets and the harsh sting of abandonment.

Patsy sniffled. "He won't fight for me."

Sophia exhaled slowly, a tight knot of muscle squeezing her chest. How many nights had she cried herself to sleep because Pete hadn't fought for her? Nights? A decade's worth of nights. "Pete didn't fight for me either"—she barely got the words out—"and it hurt for a very long time."

She had to stay positive. If Patsy thought she would one day turn forty and be as full of regrets as Sophia, it wouldn't help her make the decisions she had to make now. "I know this doesn't ease your heartache, but you'll find a man to marry when you return home."

"You didn't find another man."

"You're right. I didn't. But I found my passion in art, and I'm very happy. I take several commissions every year, and I also teach young women how to paint. It's very fulfilling. Being a single woman is not your path, Patsy, but it is mine."

"I'll never love anyone else."

"Oh, sweetheart..." Sophia pulled Patsy in for a hug. "I know the feeling so well. But I believe you will."

The door blew open, and Polly made an elaborate entrance, grinning, her arms full of drawing paper and chalk stacked nearly to her chin. Patsy and Sophia pulled apart, and Polly glared at them.

Her eagerness faded, and she made a moue of doubt. "What are you talking about? What's wrong?"

"Nothing is wrong," Patsy said, avoiding eye contact with her sister. "We're talking about love and marriage."

Polly rolled her eyes and dumped her armload of supplies at the side of the bed. "There were paints and brushes in the packages too. But I didn't bring them. What are you going to draw?"

Sophia reached for a stack of paper. "I think I'll start with sketching the two of you."

"What do you want us to do? Sit straight in the chair?" Polly asked.

"Nooo," Sophia said, dragging out the word. "I want you to sit on the bed and tell me funny stories. I'll sketch while you talk. I want you to be animated and happy. I'm going to draw several sketches, so if you want to change places or walk around, go for it."

"Polly, you sit on the bed. I'll stay here in the chair," Patsy said.

Marguerite returned with a tray of grapes, slices of cheese, chunks of bread, a carafe of wine, and glasses. Sophia patted an empty spot on the bed between her and the girls. "Will you put the food here, Marguerite, and the wine on the table where I can reach it?"

Polly's big brown eyes opened wide in surprise. "Are we going to eat here?"

"We're having a picnic in bed. I want you to eat and talk and laugh while I sketch. Tell me about school. Tell me about places you've been in Paris."

Marguerite poured Sophia a glass of wine.

"Will you pour one for me, too?" Patsy asked.

Marguerite poured a second glass, then quietly left the room.

For the next hour or so, Patsy and Polly told stories about school, their friends, and visiting gardens and museums in Paris. They laughed until their sides hurt. Laughing was the best therapy for the emotional turmoil they'd experienced today, so Sophia kept encouraging them to tell just one more story while she sketched them making faces, tugging on their hair, and gently elbowing each other's arms, the kinds of things close sisters did to one another...

The kinds of things Sophia did with Lisa and her other girl-friends until she'd been forced to leave New York... The kinds of things she encouraged her students to do with their classmates.

Drawings were soon scattered all over the floor, and she could see in the chaos what expressions she'd captured in their eyes and mouths, and what was still missing, especially around the line of their jaws. When the sun set and the sky grew dark, Marguerite brought extra candles into the room, and the flickering flames added a warm, glowing atmosphere that Sophia was able to capture in the sketches.

The door partially opened, and a sudden electrical spark sizzled through the room. Her head shot up, and her eyes immediately found Jefferson's, which looked icy at first, but then quickly thawed. He lingered on the threshold, gazing at her as if locking her image in his mind, as she was locking in his.

"What's happening in here?" He canted his body around the door to get a full view of the room. "I've never heard so much laughter except at the theatre." He looked down at the sketches scattered on the floor. "Apparently another drawing frenzy has taken place at the legation."

Polly's prominent cheekbones lifted with a wide smile. "Come in, Papa. We're having a picnic and sharing stories while Mademoiselle Orsini draws pictures. Look at them." She spread her arms while her hands moved in mysterious circles, like an orchestra conductor. "They're everywhere, and I'm having so much fun."

He stroked his jaw absently. "I can tell. But this isn't the proper setting for entertaining."

Patsy gently touched Sophia's lower leg and in a soft, sympathetic voice said, "Papa, the mademoiselle can't walk. Where else should we be?"

"I'm sure the mademoiselle would prefer to rest," Jefferson said.

Polly cocked her head slightly. "She is resting, Papa. She hasn't moved an inch the entire time we've been here."

He ambled into the room and picked up an empty wine glass,

sniffed, set it down again. "Not only do you drink Chianti with dinner, but also as an *aperitif*."

"You've got this whole wine drinking thing wrong, Mr. Ambassador. Good wine is to be enjoyed all the time, but especially with food, even a simple meal like grapes and cheese."

"Would you like a glass, sir?" Marguerite asked.

Sophia looked up at him and, using only her eyes and eyebrows, repeated Marguerite's question.

He returned to his chin stroking, his go-to evaluation gesture. "It's not proper to be here. I'll be in my cabinet."

Patsy stood and sat on the end of the bed next to Polly, freeing up her chair. "This is your house, Papa. You make the rules. There's nothing improper here. This is a sitting room, and we're enjoying good conversation."

Sophia picked up her glass and saluted with it. "And adult beverages."

"So I see. Are you drinking out of two glasses, or is Patsy"—he looked down his nose at his daughter—"developing the habit of drinking wine with food?"

"It's quite good, Papa. Mademoiselle Orsini gave me a wine-tasting lesson. And it's true. The cheese and grapes bring out delicious flavors in the wine."

Jefferson gave Sophia a confused look that almost made her laugh.

"It appears you've conscripted another recruit," he said.

His reference to *another recruit* didn't go unnoticed. As a scientist, she was certain he would conduct several experiments on volunteers to discover if, in fact, wine enhanced the flavor of food.

"Look at the sketches, Papa. Aren't they wonderful?" Polly said.

Jefferson collected all the sketches, noticing a number at the top right-hand corner. He arranged them in numerical order and fanned them, eyes skimming each drawing. "I've never seen anything like this. They're moving pictures." He fanned the stack again and again, at different speeds, chuckling. "How'd you do it?"

After a glass and a half of wine without anything of substance to eat since breakfast, she wasn't sure she could explain. "Decades of drawing what I see. Why don't you sit and listen to your daughters' stories while I draw? They are compelling storytellers."

"Come on, Papa," Polly said. "Sit down, and we'll tell you about the mouse in Patsy's shoe."

Jefferson settled his large frame uncomfortably on the small ladies' chair. "A mouse?"

Patsy nodded. "In my shoe. I don't know who squealed louder. The mouse or me."

The mouse in Patsy's shoe story soon had Jefferson chuckling. But it wasn't until Polly told a story about a mouse who ate her French lesson that an unexpected, full-throttle laugh from Jefferson had them all howling except Sophia. She was focusing solely on her subjects, sketching him bowled over by his daughters' hijinks. They made such a racket that Monsieur Petit stopped and peeked into the room, as did Sally.

"Come in, Sally," Sophia said. "Pull up a chair and I'll draw you, too."

Sally fiddled with a silver heart looped on a ribbon tied around her neck. "I don't want to be in a picture."

"But I want you there," Polly said. "Sit by me."

Instead of sitting on the bed, Sally bent over to take her place on the floor, and as she did, her hands swept over her baby bump. Sophia shoved her moral outrage aside and added a bit of shading to emphasize the bump. She couldn't condone Jefferson's behavior with a sixteen-year-old enslaved woman, but neither could Sophia ignore it.

And that was the last sketch of the evening.

She enjoyed a satisfied, catlike stretch before setting the chalk aside and brushing her hands. "By my count I've done twenty drawings. You all look through them and decide which ones you want painted."

Polly and Sally gathered the remaining sketches and handed them to Jefferson. He thumbed through the stack until he came to the last one Sophia drew. His eyebrows flashed, and his gaze remained steady on the sketch until he raised his head and glared at her. "I'll consider all of these before I decide." He stood to leave. "We should let the mademoiselle rest. We've exhausted her."

Polly hugged Sophia. "Thank you. I don't remember when I've laughed so much."

Patsy hugged her too. "I don't have to remember, because I know I never have. Thank you, mademoiselle."

The girls, Sally, and Marguerite scurried out, giggling like the teenagers they were, leaving Jefferson with a glassy-eyed stare, shaking his head. "How'd you do that?"

Sophia smiled, remembering some of the young women who had studied painting with her, several with attitude issues. With the steady application of lots of attention, she never failed to bond with them. "I listen and provide a safe space where girls can be themselves without judgment. And your daughters are so sweet. I know you're proud of them."

She slid a linen napkin out from under the cutlery on the food tray and wiped the chalk residue off her fingers. Hours earlier Marguerite had washed dirt off her hands like a two-year-old child who had fallen in the mud.

Sophia's mind picked just that moment to torture her with the memory of her most recent near-death experience. She pushed the memory aside and a reminder slipped in behind it. She had yet to apologize to Jefferson for putting his daughters at risk, and he was due one.

She finished cleaning her hands and dropped the napkin onto the tray. "I'm sorry about this morning. I never should have taken the girls out, knowing the rioters were still on the streets. It wasn't smart. If you want me to leave, Monsieur Watin said he knows several Americans who would host me in their homes."

"I'm not asking you to leave. I should have insisted you wait until I was available, but I didn't. I share the blame. Patsy and Polly were distraught over what happened. They seem very attached to you. I had hoped you would be an influence on them, but after what I just witnessed, I can see the effect of your presence has far exceeded my expectations." His long fingers tapped the papers in his hand. "I do wonder, though, how you draw so quickly. It takes me hours to do one architectural drawing."

"I've been doing five-minute sketches since I was Patsy's age. Only a few ever get painted, but it's good practice. I draw freehand, and I don't have to rely on rulers or straight edges. They're not precise like your architectural drawings."

"Patsy and Polly look real enough to jump off this page." He held up one of the sketches, the paper drifting slightly in the breeze. "You've revealed Sally's condition with only a few chalk marks." His eyes deepened with something akin to regret, or maybe guilt.

"I draw what I see. But what you're looking at is an optical illusion. A trick of the eye. A visual manipulation. Sally's dress is cleverly shaded with darkened corners and shadows. You can see it two different ways. Look closely. Blink. Adjust the distance."

He stared at the sketch, blinked, moved the paper closer and farther away, and after a moment he inhaled sharply. "It's a flower design in the dress. It's not—"

"Art is in the eye of the beholder, Ambassador. You see what your mind tells you. You happened to see the swell of her belly before you saw the flower." She knew the baby was his, but there was no point letting him know his secret wasn't a secret.

"Is this a trick?"

"Sort of, but it's done with pen and ink, paint, chalk, whatever, and it teases the eye."

He glanced at the sketch again. "Now I see only the flower."

"You lose perspective."

Mr. Petit came to the door and handed Jefferson a message, which he immediately opened and read. "I'll respond shortly," he said to Mr. Petit, who nodded and left the room.

Jefferson shoved the note into his waistcoat pocket. "General Lafayette wants to use my house as a secret meeting place for him and six others who are attempting to forge a coalition. He believes it's the only way to prevent a total dissolution and civil war."

"So he's asking you to host a secret dinner that could compro-

mise you and change your involvement from spectator to participant. Are you sure it's what you want?"

"You're perceptive, mademoiselle. First you read my mail, and
now you read my mind."

"I didn't read your mail or your mind. I'm just"—What? A time
traveler? A scryer? She settled on "…politically adept, and looking at
this as an outsider. An ambassador is supposed to be a neutral party.
Right? Wouldn't the king see hosting a dinner as taking sides?"

"I can't decline Lafayette's request."

"It's only natural for you to be involved, if only as a facilitator.
Politics is your consuming passion, and Lafayette and his deputies
need to sort out their differences before the situation deteriorates.
But here's a thought to keep in mind: change happens when the
voices of the powerless intersect with the voices of the powerful."

"Who said that?"

"A historian named Jon Meacham."

"I haven't heard of him. What has he written?"

Your biography. "I heard him speak recently." She tucked the
pieces of chalk back into their box and set it aside, trying to decide
what to say next. "I know you're anxious about your vulnerable
republic, knowing any hour could bring devastating news."

For a long moment they existed in a vacuum—Thomas Jefferson and her, a woman from the future who knew his innermost
thoughts because he left a detailed historical record—staring at each
other, unable to breathe, and his eyebrow raised, giving her a
skeptical look.

"How do you know so much?"

For a moment, she couldn't think. Something messy had spilled
in her brain—a cup of coffee, a glass of wine—short-circuiting the
orderly hum of her logical thinking.

Even her palms were wet. And she was a dry-palms kind of
person, rarely stressed or uneasy. But after the past two days
everything was out of kilter, and while her knee pain continued, out
of kilter would be her new normal.

But what she wanted to know right now was, had she gone too

far? Had her knowledge of history pushed him to the edge? Was she swaggering into judgment of him without all the facts? No one knew for sure what his relationship with Sally was behind closed doors. And it was none of Sophia's business anyway.

He continued to stare, his eyes examining her, the odd clothes, the ice-wrapped knee, probably even the tenor of her thoughts. Now who was mind reading?

"You've come into my house to spy on me."

"I've been here less than forty-eight hours. And you invited me to stay, remember? In fact, I advised you against it. I'm not here to hurt you, betray you, or gossip about you. I'm only here to paint. As I've told you several times, when I paint, people talk. They love to gossip, and house servants talk to other servants. Whatever happens in one house is known in the neighbor's house."

"Did the new chambermaid Mr. Petit hired share such gossip with you?"

"No."

"If your listening skills are so attuned, you'd be an asset to any government, but now I'm leery of discussing anything of significance with you. And I regret informing you of General Lafayette's plans."

The air around them seemed to be crackling into pieces, preparing to shatter.

"Thomas, why would I want to betray my country or you? Why would I want to harm Patsy and Polly? I don't. When I finish my paintings, I'll leave. And that will be the end of it. But you need to know, secrets are impossible to keep."

He paced for a moment, then came to a dramatic stop in front of the window. The candlelight illuminated the glass in front of him and cast an odd glow about the fringes of his sandy colored hair. He was quiet for some time. When he spoke, he did so without turning. "It isn't clear to me or to Lafayette and his deputies whether progressive or reactionary forces will prevail in France. Since you know so much"—he turned slowly to face her—"is it clear to you, mademoiselle?"

The intensity in his penetrating eyes made her shiver. The information she'd gleaned from Meacham's book was, at least for her, either a blessing or a curse. "After the last two days, not much is clear. You'll only be here another few weeks. Your advice to Lafayette will go a long way toward progressive success. Whatever happens in France now will become its history. The part you play or don't play will be remembered. Host the dinner. Lafayette needs your advice. He needs to know he can count on you."

"Will you attend?"

"You just accused me of spying."

"Patsy is a suspicious sort, yet she has fallen under your spell. I know you're not a spy, but I also know you're more than a painter."

He was just as suspicious. So much so, she could almost reach out and grab a fistful of it, shake it up, and throw it out on the table like a handful of dice.

She needed to regroup and come at this from a different angle. The only way to make her time at the Hôtel de Langeac work was to mentally close all the Founding Father books and be as ignorant of the future as everyone else.

"Maybe it's time for us to secure a strategic alliance so you can be assured of my loyalty," she said.

Even from the other side of the room, the breath from his heavy sigh almost touched her face. "You are a woman of considerable strength, intellect, and talent, and, like my daughters, I have fallen under your spell. If you have bewitched them, then you have also bewitched me." He acknowledged his truth with a twitch of his lips and a lowering of the eyebrow that had been in a continuing state of skepticism since he first peered into the room.

"If we enter a strategic alliance," he continued, "may I request your presence at the dinner for the general? When I have a table full of guests speaking French, I struggle to understand them. I'd like you to sit next to me and translate."

"After tonight, I'll be painting every waking hour. However, if it's what you want, and if Lafayette agrees, I'll act as your translator. But Mr. Short's French is excellent, and he can translate quite ably for you."

"His French is considerably better than mine, but you have unique observational skills. When the meeting is over, I'd prefer to analyze the discussion with you."

Jefferson's deep-set eyes seemed to penetrate her soul, and although it was too intimate, she didn't break eye contact. "Thomas," she said softly, "I'm a painter, not an envoy. I'm leaving Paris soon. Don't push William aside. You need him. I'll be in my studio painting, and if you really want to hear my views, come talk to me after your company leaves."

A smile lifted one side of his mouth. It was a conspiratorial smile, a kind of wink. "Something tells me I won't have to tell you."

"Do you still think I'm here to spy on you?"

"No, Sophia. I believe you'll just read my mind."

18

Paris (1789)—Sophia

T HE NEXT MORNING Marguerite stood close by, wringing her
hands while Sophia navigated the stairs and hobbled toward
Jefferson's reading room. During Sophia's previous treks down the
hallway, the door had been closed. Now, standing on the threshold
and watching household servants roll up rugs and pack *objets d'art*,
she visualized how she would convert the room into a studio. The
natural light was perfect for painting. The best light to paint as the
Old Masters required using one light source placed above, in front
of, or to the right of the sitter.

Which means the easel has to go there... She pinpointed the spot.

The morning breeze—redolent of fresh flowers and damp
earth—blew into the room, stirring the dust collected under the rugs
and heavy furniture. Sophia blinked watery eyes and waved away the
slow drift of dust sliding over the bare wooden floor like snowflakes.

"I thought he'd give me a corner to work in"—she coughed
away the tickle in her throat—"not the entire room." She crutched
toward the open French doors.

"Monsieur Petit said the room wasn't going to be packed until
closer to the family's departure," Marguerite said. "But the ambassador ordered it done now so you can use it."

Sophia coughed again. She didn't want the household to be

disrupted because of her, but she appreciated Jefferson's willingness to let her use the room.

Now, how was she going to use the space as a background for the portraits?

She leaned on the crutches and considered her options. The white boiserie with flowery wallpaper inserts and a crystal vase of flowers sitting atop the mahogany fortepiano would highlight Patsy's formality and musicality. But Polly's personality required a more casual setting, something to show off her vivacious spirit.

Sophia's attention continued to rove over the architectural details of the room. The white background and the abundance of sunlight would soften Jefferson's portrait, making it distinctly different from other paintings of him. But before she could decide on a background, she had to determine the statement she intended to make. The background was almost as important as the subject.

Mather Brown painted a kit-cat style portrait of Jefferson wearing an elaborate wig and neck stock with a busy background, showing him less than half length. But Jefferson's disengaged, haughty expression wasn't the best way, in her opinion, to portray the founder of the modern democratic party.

Gilbert Stuart used a different approach and painted Jefferson with a blank background. When Sophia visited the National Portrait Gallery in Washington, DC, her impression of the painting was that Stuart intended to show the difference between the undisciplined past, as reflected in the Brown portrait, and an unwritten future, as expressed in his.

In her painting Sophia wanted to show, like John Trumbull did in his painting of Jefferson, the resolve and courage reflected in the tilt of his chin and the set of his mouth, and the intelligence conveyed by his clear eyes.

Her portrait needed to strike a balance among all Jefferson's portraitists, yet show the enigmatic man full of contradictions. He was a champion of individual liberties who owned slaves all his life. He was a fiscal conservative who lived deeply in debt. And he was an agrarian who thrived in big cities. Since he was so hard to pin down, she had to keep in mind what was most important to him.

He'd left instructions for his headstone to be inscribed with "Author of the Declaration of American Independence and the Statute of Virginia for religious freedom and Father of the University of Virginia." No mention of his years as ambassador to France, secretary of state, vice president, or president of the United States.

When she first looked for an audiobook about him, she found a review saying, "If Jefferson were a monument, he would be the sphinx. If he were a painting, he would be the *Mona Lisa*. If he were a character in a play, he would be Hamlet." She chuckled to herself, wondering if she could convey those three images in one painting.

Probably not. For her portrait, she wanted to focus on two concepts: father and freedom. But how could she express them? She had to pull back and see Jefferson as he was, and as he would be remembered…among other things, as one of the most elegant and fastidious men of the Enlightenment. So, what was it to be—this portrait of hers—to truly portray this enigmatic man? If those who knew him best considered him a puzzle, who was she to solve it?

Sophia's mind made a quick U-turn. Instead of considering the portrait, her statement, or the room's architectural details, her thoughts turned toward the subject—Jefferson's unbound hair and the ruddy skin of his sun-kissed cheeks.

"Sit over here, milady," Marguerite said. "Monsieur Petit had the sofa moved from the salon. He said you might be able to sit here while you paint. Do you think it'll work?"

"It depends on whether the easel's height is adjustable."

Sophia hobbled to the sofa, where she lowered herself to the cushion. Marguerite plumped pillows at her back and under her leg, fretting around her like a bumblebee, buzzing here, buzzing there. No one had ever waited on Sophia before, except her grandmother, who'd fed her comfort foods—bowls of *penne ai quattro formaggi* and gelato—while she cried out her broken heart.

She jerked her attention back to the room, back to the work going on her around her. It was too painful to remember the people who were no longer in her life.

All the grunts and groans of the men moving furniture reminded her of last month's art show and cocktail reception in Florence. She'd spent a hectic afternoon directing the hanging of her paintings. But this wasn't going to be an art show. This was a twelve-day painting frenzy, and at the end of it she hoped to have a portrait which would end up on display at the National Portrait Gallery or the Met in two hundred fifty years.

Seriously? Was that what she wanted? If she intended to go home and paint several more portraits of Jefferson, it would be insane to have any of her paintings at the Gallery or at the Met whose provenance would confirm it was painted by S.F. Orsini, an American painter who visited Jefferson in Paris.

An auction-house appraiser, art historian, or curator would compare her twenty-first century paintings of Jefferson to the eighteenth-century Orsini painting. Would the results be good or bad? She couldn't say. But it would be confusing. She'd never left a painting behind before. If she did this time, she could leave the painting unsigned and ask Jefferson not to mention her name in journals or correspondence, but an art historian would still find her name mentioned somewhere else.

Polly hurried into the room as fast as her skittering heels allowed, beaming. She reached for Sophia's hand and crushed her wrists with the force of her glee. "Monsieur Watin is here. I'm so excited. Papa is helping him carry your purchases." She then turned and skipped out of the studio as tiny dust motes circled her bouncing curls.

"She's so precious. I've never seen such a happy child," Sophia said to Marguerite, rubbing her wrists to get her blood circulating again. "I love her curls. I haven't seen her hair fixed that way before."

"I hope you don't mind," Marguerite said. "She asked me for help this morning while you were doing your exercises. She wanted to look perfect for you."

"For me?"

"In case you started her painting."

"How sweet. Thank you for styling her hair so elegantly." Sophia rested her elbow atop the back of the sofa and considered where she was going to paint the girls—inside, or out in the garden.

"What would you like me to do first?" Marguerite asked, pulling Sophia again from her deep well of thoughts.

"Fabric shopping, I think." They had already discussed clothing needs, and Marguerite said she could sew anything Sophia needed. "White linen for dresses for the girls and me, straw hats, ribbon, printed silk for two more pairs of trousers and shirts, and while you're looking around, find a fabric you like to make a dress for yourself."

Marguerite stared, shocked. After a few beats, her shock passed, and her tone was cautious when she said, "I don't need anything, milady. But you need new stockings."

Sophia pulled money out of her pocket. She wasn't going to push Marguerite this time, but if she didn't have another dress, Sophia would insist Marguerite buy fabric for herself. "If you need help, hire a seamstress to assist you. I need a quick turnaround."

Marguerite hid the money between her stomacher and stays. "I'll get a bucket of ice before I go."

"Mr. Petit will take care of it," Sophia said. "Be careful when you go out. It's dangerous. Better yet, ask Mr. Petit if the coachman can take you."

"I won't be alone. This is market day, and James is taking Sally and me with him."

James?

The name didn't click immediately, but then she remembered James Hemings was Sally's brother and Jefferson's chef. "Let me know when you return so I'll stop worrying."

Marguerite tugged on her lower lip with her teeth. "But why would you worry?"

"Because it's dangerous on the streets, and I don't want you to get hurt. I couldn't manage without you."

"I'll be safe enough. No one will bother us."

Marguerite was probably right. As a house servant, black or

white, she was unlikely to be accosted, but Sophia would have nightmares for some time after what happened to her on the streets of Paris. On the way out of the room, Marguerite passed Jefferson and Monsieur Watin on their way in.

Sophia smiled. "Monsieur Watin." She reached for her crutches to stand and welcome him, but he hurried to her before she could rise.

"*Non.* Don't get up." He kissed her cheeks. "I heard you had another dreadful day after you left my atelier. And now your injury is much worse."

Jefferson dropped packages onto the table and gazed at her, a glint in his eyes. "She should consult a physician, but she refuses."

"If it doesn't improve in a couple of days, I'll reconsider." Which was a big fat lie. Seeking medical attention, even if it would alleviate Jefferson's concern, was out of the question. She turned her attention back to Watin. "Did you hear General Lafayette rescued us?"

Watin carried his packages over to the long table where Jefferson had placed his. "The ambassador just told me what happened."

"Thanks to the general, we got home safely. And the girls are so eager to sit for their portraits. Were you able to get everything I ordered?"

"Everything has now been delivered."

"If you'll excuse me, I have a meeting at the Hôtel de Ville. If you need anything, ask Mr. Petit."

"Thank you, Ambassador," Sophia said. "I appreciate you giving up your reading room. We can start on your portrait later this afternoon if you have free time on your calendar."

"We'll discuss it when I return." Jefferson bowed slightly before heading toward the door, dodging packing crates. He paused there and turned back. "Mademoiselle, if you have an opening on *your* calendar, I'd like you to dine with me this evening."

She smiled and teasingly asked, "What's the wine du jour?"

"*Goutte d'Or de Meursault.*"

"A white wine from Burgundy."

He looked momentarily surprised, but then nodded, as though verifying something to himself. "You're familiar with this varietal as well?"

"It's a pale yellow chardonnay with a touch of fresh hazelnut and white peach. On the palate, the wine offers fresh almond aromas with a lively finish."

"And what would you pair with it?"

"Veal or freshwater pike."

He gave her the look again, the one that said he still doubted the whole food-pairing concept. "The dinner menu is rice soup, round of beef, turkey, loin of veal, fried eggs, fried beef, a pie of macaroni."

"And ice cream?" she asked.

"Always ice cream, mademoiselle." He laughed with an easy contentment, and his eyes were so blue, reflecting the color of his jacket, they verged on indigo. He slapped the doorframe as he strolled out.

Watin sat at the end of the sofa, tugging on his chin.

"What?" she asked. "You have something on your mind. What is it?"

"Nothing," he said, glancing around the room. "What can I do to help you? Where would you like to set up the easels?"

A breeze slipped in through the half-opened window behind her and ruffled the sketching paper Watin had stacked on the table. "You can help by telling me what's on your mind. I don't know you well at all, but I'm observant. You frowned at the ambassador. Why? What did you see or hear that caused you concern?"

An uncomfortable silence stretched between them while Watin continued to peruse the room. Finally, he said, "After what you've experienced in the past few days, I don't want to see you hurt again. Monsieur David and I feel responsible for you. The ambassador has been widowed for several years, and he seems discontent with his situation. He enjoys *la vie Parisien*, especially the company of intelligent, artistic women."

"You don't have to worry about me. I can take care of myself."

"Mademoiselle, you were nearly set on fire at the Bastille, then you stepped into a hole and wrenched your knee. Yesterday you almost fell into the Seine, and now you can't walk without assistance. It is our opinion, Monsieur David and I, that you require protection. And we do not wish to see your heart broken. The ambassador isn't a libertine, but he's lonely, and you are an *ingénue*."

"I assure you, I'm no *ingénue*, Monsieur Watin. I'm only interested in painting authentically, which requires an understanding of my subjects."

"And that can be acquired during an intimate dinner?" The pitch of his tone rose considerably, as did the lift of his brow.

"I'm not interested in painting windmills, or a checkerboard floor, or a tulip, or a guttering candle." She paused a moment to collect herself. Why was it necessary to explain? Because Watin now considered himself her protector.

"Some artists never need to leave home to paint," she said. "That's not me. I need to experience the world. If I can gain artistic insight while dining with Ambassador Jefferson, why would I not dine with him?"

Watin gave her an incredulous stare. "You *are* an *ingénue*. In Paris, an intimate dinner is not for an artist to gain insight, it's a prelude to more...intimacy. I assure you, the way the ambassador looks at you shows what's on his mind, and it's not art. I don't want you to be the mademoiselle du jour."

"Thank you for your concern, but you don't have to treat me like a Fabergé egg."

"What is a Fabergé egg?"

"A reference to something fragile." She patted his arm. "I have no intention of becoming the 'mademoiselle du jour.' And besides, I'm leaving at the end of next week."

Watin stared at her, wide-eyed. "Next week? Why? You purchased enough supplies to last three months."

She avoided his question about leaving and went straight to his statement about the supplies. "When I paint, I don't like to run out of anything. It makes me grumpy."

One of the workmen who had been moving furniture returned

carrying an easel. "Where does this go, monsieur?"

Watin jumped to his feet. "There, I think." He pointed to a spot near the French doors. "No, put it there." He paced the room, his expression dour, he turned in circles. "Ah," he sighed. "The green drapery needs to come down. It blocks too much light. Don't you think, mademoiselle?"

Like Watin, she needed a moment to recover from their conversation. Finally, she reached for the crutches and stood on her good leg. It was time for her to take charge. After all, it was her studio.

"I need all the natural light possible, but the panel on the far window needs to stay," she said.

"It would work with the mademoiselles' white linen dresses and straw hats."

"How'd you know about the white dresses?"

"Mademoiselle Polly mentioned it when I arrived. She wanted to know if I had her hat." Watin held his elbow in his palm while his finger tapped his cheek. "Mademoiselle Patsy is musically talented, poised, and particular."

"How do you know so much about the family?" Sophia asked.

"The ambassador and his daughters are well known in the salons of Paris."

"Oh." Although Sophia wanted to paint a natural portrait, she'd better stick with a traditional pose, or the painting might end up on a trash heap. "I see four items to work with: the open door to the garden, the green drapery panel, the upholstered walnut bergère chair, and the fortepiano with the crystal flower vase. I don't know yet if I'll include the white boiserie with the flowery wallpaper inserts. For Polly's portrait, I'm still thinking, but I'm leaning more toward a less formal setting."

"The garden, perhaps?" Watin asked.

The clack of boots against the hardwood floor announced Jefferson's return. She looked back over her shoulder. His expression was stern, the stack of sketches cradled in his right elbow. Obviously, he was on a mission, but a mission for what?

"I thought you went out," she said.

"William reminded me of a letter that needed to post today." He handed her the drawings. "Since you spent so much time drawing these, you might want to refer to them, but I expect you to give them back."

The constant flipping through the pages had smudged several of them, but they were only ideas to consider, not sketches to paint. "I'll be sure to return them without additional smudges."

Jefferson's eyebrow flashed at her before he turned his attention to Watin. "Allow me to show you out, sir."

"Oh, don't leave yet," she said to Watin, lightly touching his arm. "I need you to help me set up the easels."

Watin made a sweeping bow. "I am your most obedient servant, mademoiselle."

"As you wish," Jefferson said with a distinct tone of disapproval. He turned on his heel and strode from the room for the second time.

"Be careful out there," Sophia said to his back, then shrugged when he didn't respond.

Watin pointed at her sketches. "May I see those?" She placed them on the fortepiano, and he carefully turned each one, studying them closely. "Do you intend to paint all of these?"

"No. They're my five-minute sketches. When I'm not working on a painting, I'll go to a park or market and spend a couple of hours sketching. Half of those I did in Ambassador Jefferson's cabinet two days ago. The others are sketches of the girls I did last night."

He tapped his index finger on a sketch of Jefferson. "You can't paint this one. You'll breach propriety. It's a well-established fact that the only people who smile, in life and in art, are the poor, the lewd, the drunk, the innocent, and actors."

She laughed, pressing her fingers to her mouth. "So nature gave us lips to conceal our teeth and no one is supposed to smile? Seriously?"

Then she pointed to a sketch of the girls. "Look at the love and joy in their faces. What's wrong with showing such happiness?"

"Nothing is wrong with expressing love and joy, but not in a portrait. Portraits represent an ideal. They're crucial to preserving a person's visage. Portraits aren't to capture a moment"—he tapped his finger on Jefferson's sketch again—"like these. Portraits have permanence. If you paint the ambassador like this, you'll commit a permanent faux pas."

She knew Watin was speaking the truth, at least the eighteenth-century version of it, and Jefferson wouldn't approve of a smiling portrait anyway, but what about the girls? "You've given me something to think about. Now let's sit over here and settle our business. Do you have an invoice?"

As they were concluding, Polly and Patsy entered the studio. "This is so exciting," Patsy said. "Who are you going to paint first, mademoiselle?"

She glanced at the two smiling faces and knew she couldn't disappoint either one of them. "Well," Sophia said. "The first painting should be with both of you, perhaps in the garden. What do you think?"

The girls beamed. "Let's go outside and look around," Polly said.

As they hurried through the open doorway out into the garden, Watin asked, "Are you going to paint them sitting or standing?"

"There's a bench under the tree. One could sit on the bench and the other on the grass in front."

When a servant brought in another easel, Watin directed him to the garden. Sophia crutched to the door and watched while he positioned the easel, first in one location, then he moved it to another, checking the angle of the sun. She eased down the steps and hobbled over to him.

"You'll have the best light all day if you place the easel here." Watin waved to Patsy and Polly. "Come. Sit over here and let's see if this will work. You won't have the sun in your eyes, and neither will Mademoiselle Orsini." He positioned Patsy first, then placed Polly behind her with her hand on Patsy's shoulder. He turned to look at Sophia. "What do you think?"

"It's too formal. I want to see them more relaxed. Patsy, you sit on the bench and Polly, you sit on the grass and rest your hands together on Patsy's leg. Let's see how that looks." She turned to ask Watin what he thought, but he was gone.

Polly sat on the grass. "What about our white dresses?"

"Marguerite went to the market to get the fabric. First I'll sketch you on the canvas, but if I finish and the dresses aren't ready, I'll do individual drawings inside."

Watin returned carrying a canvas, and two workmen hauled out a chair and a stool. Watin directed the chair to be placed in front of the easel and the stool at an angle to support her leg. Satisfied with the placement, he set the canvas attached to a stretcher on the easel.

Sophia flicked her finger against the canvas, listening closely to the sound. "Good tension. Nice and taut with a smooth, fine-woven texture."

"This is so much fun," Polly said. "Do you want us to tell more stories?"

"I love your stories, sweetie. You can talk all you want, but once I place you, you can't move. We'll mark your places so when you take breaks, you'll be able to return to the exact spot."

"How else can I help you?" Watin's smile reached his eyes, matching the warmth of his voice.

"I was going to ask you to mix paint, but I don't need it yet. Would you have time to come by tomorrow?"

"I'll endeavor to be the best assistant you could possibly find."

"You have a business to run, but I will need help mixing paint."

"I'll see my customers early in the morning, then I'll come here. For now, while you sketch, I'll organize your studio."

She kissed his cheek. "Léopold, how'd I get so lucky to find you?"

"Monsieur David found you, and I lost you in the crowd." Watin pressed his hand against his chest. "But now here we are together."

An hour later she gave Polly and Patsy a break, and Mr. Petit came out to the garden leading servants carrying a tray with food and wine and a bucket of ice.

"I thought you and Monsieur Watin would appreciate refreshments," Mr. Petit said.

"Thank you. My knee is starting to throb." She smiled at Mr. Petit. "If I plan my time carefully, I'll be able to paint your portrait too."

"I'm honored. But Ambassador Jefferson would not approve of neglecting my duties to sit for you."

She pursed her lips. "Hmm. You're a valuable employee. If Mr. Jefferson doesn't return to Paris, he'll want you to come to America and manage Monticello. So we must have a sketch or a portrait of you."

Mr. Petit smiled, as if to placate her. "I'll station one of the servants nearby in the event you require anything else."

Watin had been inside during her conversation with Petit, and now he returned to the garden. "I've organized the paints, brushes, and sketching paper. Everything is within easy reach."

"Mr. Petit brought out refreshments. Are you ready for a glass of wine with some fruit and cheese?"

He glanced at the table next to the bench. "I don't believe I've worked hard enough for such a splendid reward."

"Mr. Petit takes good care of me." She crutched over to the bench, and while Watin poured wine, she stretched out her leg and wrapped her knee in ice.

"Why are you putting ice on your knee?"

She leaned back against the tree and squirmed until she found a comfortable position. "Blood flow to an injured area causes swelling. When you apply ice, it decreases blood flow and you have less swelling."

After examining her with a puzzled expression, he scratched the back of his head. "Another idea to go in the soup pot with smiling portrait subjects."

"Oh, ye of little faith. Ice really works, and smiling portraits will be popular one day."

He handed her a glass of wine and a plate of cheese and bread. "Not in this century, mademoiselle."

She gave a resigned laugh. "You're probably right."

Sophia was sipping wine when the girls returned. "May we see what you've done so far?" Patsy asked.

"You know the rule. You can look, but you can't comment on it yet."

"We promise," Polly said.

The girls stood at the easel and whispered to each other while Watin and Sophia talked about the Paris salon and the artists who were currently exhibiting.

"Hi, Papa." Polly waved. "Come see Mademoiselle Orsini's sketch of us."

Sophia's head shot up and her eyes met Jefferson's. If looks could kill... She struggled for a moment, wondering what to do, then offered him a sweet smile. He didn't smile back. Instead, he wheeled and closed the doors.

"What's wrong with Papa?" Polly's expression was pinched.

Sophia set her glass aside and reached for her crutches. "He must have had a difficult meeting. I'll go see what's wrong."

Watin set his wine glass down too and folded her hand between his. "Mademoiselle, it is best to wait until I'm gone. *Votre ambassadeur est jaloux.*"

"How ridiculous."

"When Madame Cosway was in Paris, the ambassador spent an unusual amount of time with her, but she was married to a coxcomb of a husband who bounced around the ballrooms, ogling ladies and flattering gentlemen who might give him commissions. You, my dear, are much like her, but without a husband. I am asking you again, please let me find other Americans to host you."

She shook her head. "There's nothing to worry about. My interest in the ambassador is strictly artistic." She couldn't tell Watin about Jefferson's affair with Sally, and, as charming as Jefferson was, she couldn't condone his behavior or exonerate him from abusing his power over a young girl with limited options.

"Remember, I'll only be here another week or so. Besides, the ambassador has a lot on his mind, and a painter is of little consequence."

Watin raised her hand and lightly touched her knuckles with his lips. "Until tomorrow, mademoiselle. But if you change your mind—"

"I won't," she said, "but thank you for your concern."

Watin reentered the house, and she kept her gaze on the empty doorway, hoping Jefferson would return, yet knowing he wouldn't. As tempted as she was to go to his cabinet, she couldn't. William would be there to discuss the meeting and write a report while Jefferson dictated. It wasn't her place. It wasn't her job. It wasn't even her time.

A thought emerged from the welter of emotions. Regardless of what she said to Watin, she didn't need a romantic dinner to study her subject. She already knew enough about Jefferson to paint his portrait.

A cold gust blew across her heart. If there had been any doubt before, she now knew where this had to end.

19

Richmond, VA—Pete

PETE PARKED HIS rental car in the Virginia Commonwealth University Hospital parking lot and made his way toward the entrance. Just before he reached the door his phone beeped with a What's App message. All the eighteen-and-above members of the MacKlenna clan were connected through the app, so news blasts arrived on everyone's device at the same time. Out of thirty-eight local time zones in use worldwide, members of the clan could be in half a dozen on any given day.

A message from Kevin read: *Lawrence's lungs collapsed. Procedure ongoing. JL fainted. She's anemic. Needed a blood transfusion. She's in her room. Meredith with her now. Elliott and I are in the NICU.*

"Jesus." Pete tapped in a status report: *Just arrived at hospital. Going to see JL.*

He followed the signs to the Birthing Center, and when he reached JL's room, he found Meredith massaging JL's feet. He squeezed Meredith's shoulder in a hello gesture. Since she was also at Charlotte's house for breakfast, they'd already shared the latest news from the Tuscany vineyards.

When JL laid eyes on him, she reached out, crying, "I'm so glad you're here." He wrapped her in a bone-crushing hug, stepped back, and thumbed away a tear on her cheek.

"Where else would I be, *ragazza tosta*?"

"I'm not such a tough chick right now. Lawrence had a crisis and I passed out."

"Whoa. Don't be so hard on yourself. You were in a plane crash, had emergency surgery, a blood transfusion, and your son is fighting for his life. You're handling it better than I would."

"Better than I would, too," Meredith said.

"So says the woman who went through chemo while pregnant. And, on top of that, lived with Elliott when he gave up pain pills and whisky. From what I hear, the second one was the toughest part of your ordeal," JL said.

"You make it sound a lot worse than it was. He had his bad moments, but he was, even then, sweet enough to fall in love with."

"My boys have no hope," JL said. "Kevin and I have mixed a Scottish temper with an Irish one."

Meredith covered JL's feet, chuckling, and put the lotion on the counter. "I've never seen O'Gradys act out the same way I've seen MacKlennas and Frasers misbehave. Let's hope Blane and Lawrence are more Irish than Scottish."

"I'm glad I'm just a good ol' Italian boy," Pete said.

"I am, too. You, Maria, Isabella, and Gabe have been welcome additions to the clan. We could use a few more." Meredith picked up her phone and purse. "If you'll stay with JL for a while, I'm going down to the cafeteria for a cup of coffee. I've asked for more pods for the coffee maker, but they haven't brought them up yet. Can I get you anything?"

"I'm coffee'd out. Take your time. I'm not going anywhere."

As soon as the door closed behind Meredith, Pete pulled a recliner closer to the bed, sat, and lifted the leg rest. Another What's App message came in. He read it quickly, smiled, and read it to JL. *Tube inserted into Lawrence's chest. Suction removing air. Will continue until all extra air removed. Crisis averted.*

Relief welled up in Pete's heart, but he tried not to let it show. His family went through a preemie birth with a cousin a few years back, and it hadn't ended well. He never mentioned it to JL. The birth coincided with the discovery of JL's first husband's infidelities, so it would have been piling on, and he'd never do that to her. Which was why he didn't plan to tell her about Sophia and her brooch.

"I just told Meredith I wasn't going anywhere, but I'll take you to the NICU if you want to go."

JL shook her head and turned slightly so she could see him better. "I passed out earlier. As soon as I came to, Kevin brought me down here. He'll need to rest soon. When he comes back, I'll go up there. Lawrence has two valiant knights guarding him right now."

"As patient advocates go, Elliott is a formidable one. He'll bulldoze his way through the hospital to get Lawrence everything he needs. I wouldn't be surprised if he decided to advocate for a larger hospital to treat Lawrence. Cincinnati Children's Hospital has a phenomenal reputation, plus it's close to Lexington."

"How do you know?"

"What? About Children's Hospital or Elliott?"

"Both, I guess."

Pete didn't say anything, but when the silence became uncomfortable, he yielded. "Just information I picked up along the way. As for Elliott"—Pete winked—"he'll want another wing in another hospital with his name on it."

"He doesn't care about a hospital wing in his name. He just wants the best treatment money can buy. It's his way of controlling the situation."

"Okay, but don't let him take control away from you. Kevin won't disagree with him, so you have to do what's best for you and your sons."

"I don't like what you're implying."

"We partnered for a decade, JL. And, I've known you since you started growing boobs. I know how your mind works. You don't handle sickness and medical emergencies well. You might relinquish control over Lawrence's medical care because you're so afraid he'll die. Then you'll wake up and won't like what's going on, but by then it will be so far out of your control you can't get it back. I don't want that to happen."

She pressed her fingertips against her temples, then pressed harder, clenching her jaw, then dropped her hands. "I don't either."

"Then stop thinking you're weak and can't make medical decisions. You're my *ragazza tosta,* and don't you forget it. And don't ask for the medical version for dummies either. Since you can figure out complex investigations, this should be a walk in the park. Stay on top of this, or Elliott will run over you."

"I didn't know you thought so little of him."

"Are you kidding? I worship at Elliott's feet. He's brilliant when it comes to business, but this is an emotional issue. Lawrence is his grandson. I've heard plenty of stories about his father, grandfather, and even his great-grandfather, not to be alarmed over what he'll do to protect his own. I don't want you to be a casualty."

She considered it, pursing her lips the way he'd seen her do hundreds of times, then slowly shook her head. "I don't have the energy right now."

"I'm calling bullshit on you. Six hours post-surgery from a gunshot that nearly killed you, you were dictating your report. You insisted on being included in wrapping up the investigation. So don't tell me you don't have the energy to manage your son's care.

"Sure, you're down right now, but I bet it's because you don't understand what's happening. Elliott doesn't either, but he's up there learning, talking to doctors and other staff. He's talking to parents of preemies, he's gathering information, and you should be educating yourself, too. Or he and Kevin will develop a rhythm and you'll be left out."

"How do you know all this? And Kevin wouldn't leave me out," she huffed. "You're wrong."

He lapsed into thought, then said, "Could be, but lucky for you, as I told you years ago, I'll always have your back."

"You've never sugarcoated anything. Kevin tries, but I call him out when he does." She straightened in the bed, grimacing. "Ouch."

"You okay?"

"Yeah. It just hurts to move, but as long as the pain is bearable, I don't want to take any more pain meds."

"Well, Kevin thinks he's protecting you, but it's the wrong way. I learned years ago not to leave you out in the cold, and if anyone does, they do so at their peril. When you gave up your guns to keep him, you surrendered more than your weapons. You lost your balls."

She pulled her lower lip through her teeth, but when he didn't take his eyes off her, she stopped. "Let's change the subject. My brain needs a break. How was Italy?"

The discussion was over, but Pete knew how her brain worked. He didn't feel bad about taking advantage of her weakened state to manipulate her. But somebody had to kick her in the ass, and since it had fallen at his feet dozens of times before, it naturally fell there again.

With two strong personalities like Kevin and Elliott, they'd leave her behind if she didn't step up. He could see it in her eyes now. She might be rubbing her butt from the swift kick, but she knew it was necessary. What happened next was up to her.

Pete laced his fingers behind his head. "The trip was too short. I left before Gabe and I could set up a schedule to update the security system and bring the new vineyard online."

"You didn't have to leave, but I can't say I'm sorry you did. We made a deal when we first partnered up. Always the truth. Always have each other's back. And that'll never change. So did you at least get to eat any good food?"

He chuckled. "With Maria cooking the best Italian food in the world, we don't have to leave MacKlenna Farm anymore. Oh, and by the way, she's cooking at the plantation right now. Amber's going to freeze-dry the meals so you can have gourmet Italian food whenever you're hungry."

"They're so sweet. Kevin said Elliott booked two suites at the hotel across the street, so we'll have a place to stay when they kick me out of here. It'll be nice to have healthy meals we can fix quickly."

After a beat he said, "I did go to Osteria Toscanella for dinner. Their food is on par with Maria's, but don't tell her I said so." He cranked the recliner back as far as it would go until he was almost horizontal. "Gabe was supposed to meet me there but got hung up at the winery over some dispute with a vendor."

"I love that street. Kevin and I have strolled across the Ponte Vecchio and walked the side streets to get the best gelato in Florence at the Gelateria Della Passera. It's not far from that restaurant. But there's also the coolest little shop named Il Papiro. They sell books, diaries, frames, and photo albums with covers of handmade, marbleized paper."

Pete avoided looking at JL for fear she'd read his mind and ask him if he found anything else interesting there. His eyes settled on his boots, their shine dulled by a layer of dust.

"What's so interesting about your boots?" she asked.

"My boots? Interesting?"

She gave him a rueful smile. "You've got something on your mind." Her tone shifted, becoming ever-so-slightly—for a *ragazza tosta*—coaxing and sympathetic.

He puffed his cheeks and blew out a long breath. "A woman." As much as he wanted to keep his own counsel, he also knew he had to tell JL about Sophia. After the lecture he just gave, how could he not?

"You don't have to say anything else. I know this year would have been your twentieth wedding anniversary. I'm so sorry."

Although surprised JL remembered, he kept his expression blank. "Don't worry about me. You've got enough on your mind."

"Of course, I'm going to worry. That's what friends do. And it's also what partners do." She lowered her bed and rested her arm over her belly as she reclined. "I can read your moods. Something else is going on with you. So fess up. What is it?"

"We'll talk about it later." He sat up and dry-washed his face before he fell asleep. "Tell me about Lawrence. Who does he look like?"

"He looks like Kevin, but you're not getting off the hook so easily. Connor will get it out of you, and if you tell him before you tell me, there'll be hell to pay."

He tilted his chin up to stare at the ceiling, boxed in by her demand. Any other time he'd tell her exactly what was going on but dumping his problems on her now wasn't fair. Not when she was coping with her son's tenacious hold on life.

He tried to back off. "It can wait until Lawrence is out of danger."

What did it matter if he waited five months before discussing it with the family? Wherever Sophia had time-traveled to was in the past. It wouldn't matter if he waited a month or five months to go after her. The diamond brooch would take him exactly where he needed to be. But what about Sophia's life in the present?

He considered Ivan Bianchi, Sophia's client. Ivan might go to the police if she didn't come back soon, and he'd hire a lawyer to get possession of his painting, which could get complicated and messy. Sort of like what happened to Amy Spalding Mallory when she went back to 1909 and left behind a boyfriend who ended up being charged with her murder.

An easy solution would be to call Gabe and help him break into Sophia's studio to grab the *Mona Lisa*. Then Pete could call Ivan and arrange a meeting to transfer the painting.

JL turned her head, squinted her eyes, and gave him an X-ray-eye look. "Lawrence might not be out of danger until Christmas. And I have a feeling whatever you're holding back won't wait that long."

"You're right. It won't, but you don't need to worry about it today. You need to focus your energy and attention on your son."

"What?" She emphasized the *t,* turning the word into a demand. She rolled her head back to face the ceiling and closed her eyes. "Now you're doing the same goddamned thing Kevin was doing to me, and you promised you wouldn't."

"Calm down. That's why I don't want to tell you. You'll just get—"

"Damn it, Pete. You know me. I function better when I have a problem to solve. I can't fix Lawrence. I can hold him, love him, talk to him, but I can't fix him. Give me a problem to mull over, to focus on so I won't cry the whole freaking day."

"You're not going to cry all day. Your hormones are screwed up right now, but they'll settle down. I'll tell you what's going on, but only if you agree to take charge of your baby's care before it's taken away from you and you're shut out as a decision-maker. You know those two stubborn Scots will do it, too. With the best of intentions, but they'll still do it."

She held up her right hand as if pledging to tell the truth. "So help me God. Now, tell me. Then you can wheel me to the NICU, and I'll send Elliott home."

That was exactly the pledge he wanted from her. "Sophia has a brooch."

JL's head jerked in his direction. "What? Damn. Say it ain't so, Joe."

"It's so. And this situation is different from the others, making it harder to figure out where she's gone."

"None of them have been easy, but David's always been able to narrow adventures down to year and location."

"This trip could be anywhere from the 1400s until now. Hell, she could have gone into the future for all I know."

"David will figure it out. He'll find a clue in her emails, books on a shelf. Maybe even the wine she drinks. There's a clue somewhere. What do you know so far?"

Pete lowered the chair and flipped through the pictures on his phone until he came to one showing the five portraits of Sophia. He handed the device to JL.

"She's gorgeous. The only picture you've ever shown me is the one from high school."

His brain froze for a moment, then quickly thawed. "But you met her."

"No. I didn't. You never brought her around. Since I lived in Pearl River and she was in the city, we ran in different crowds. By the time you and I were partners, she'd been out of your life for years, and mentioning her name was almost a hanging offense."

"You met… Uhhhh… It was around the time you went away to

the"—he made air quotes—"performing arts school."

"Well, no wonder I don't remember. That was when I was gone for six months to have Austin in secret." She stretched the pictures on his phone to study Sophia's face. "These paintings are extraordinary. Who painted them?"

"They're signed by Picasso, da Vinci, Donatello, Rubens, and Degas."

Her fingers, manipulating the picture on the phone, went rigid, her jaw dropped, and her head turned toward him in slow motion. "Leonardo? Like...da Vinci?"

"And Rubens, Picasso, Donatello, Degas."

"She's gone back *five* times!"

"Looks like it."

"Then...where's her soul mate?"

It was just like JL to zero in on the one question that had gnawed on him almost constantly since discovering Sophia had a brooch. He gave an uneasy roll of his shoulders. For over twenty years, he'd never stopped believing he was her soul mate. "As far as I can tell, she doesn't have one. Or, rather...she hasn't found another one."

"Did you tell Elliott?"

"We talked briefly during the flight over. He said he sensed a brooch was active, but he couldn't do anything about it until you and his grandson were out of danger."

"Then talk to David. Elliott might not approve an adventure, but at least you can put a plan in place."

"No can do. Elliott said it had to wait. If I go behind his back, he'll be pissed as hell."

Meredith entered the room with two cups of coffee and handed one to Pete. "I know you said you didn't want anything, but as red as your eyes are, I doubt you've had more than a couple of hours of sleep." She dropped her purse on the counter. "So did you tell JL?"

"Tell me what?" JL asked.

Meredith looked at Pete with her patented laser focus, and he almost melted under her intense scrutiny. Next to Elliott, she had the most highly developed sixth sense of anyone he'd ever met. Although JL's was highly tuned, it was only about ninety percent of theirs.

"Yeah, I told her. JL doesn't need to read tea leaves to discern what's going on around her. She's intuitive enough to figure it out."

"If Elliott doesn't want to deal with another brooch right now, fine," JL said. "But David needs to know about it. The family can wait for Elliott to pull the switch, but the trip needs to be on the table for discussion and planning."

Kevin entered the room and glanced from one person to the other until his eyes lingered on JL. "Planning what?"

"I'll tell you later. Right now, it's time to take me up to the NICU." JL pushed back the covers and eased her legs over the side of the bed.

Pete set his cup on the bedside table, lowered his chair, and pushed to his feet. "Crap, JL. Hold up a minute." He put his arm around her as she stood. Kevin pushed the wheelchair to the side of the bed, and together they eased her into the seat. Pete unhooked her IV and hung it on the pole attached to the chair.

"Are you sticking around?" she asked.

He yawned. "I'll be here, maybe catch a few winks while you're gone."

"Meredith, I'll send Elliott down. Would you two please go home and play with Blane? I know he's with his cousins, but he'll miss us eventually, and Elliott has a wonderful way of calming him down when Kevin and I are away."

Meredith hugged her. "I'll do whatever you want me to do."

"Take Elliott home. It'll make Charlotte happier too. She doesn't want another family member up here as a patient."

"I just talked to her downstairs," Meredith said. "She asked me to do the same thing. He's been up here for almost twenty-four hours."

"I'll send him right down," Kevin said as he wheeled JL from the room.

Meredith sank into a nearby chair, set her cup of coffee on a small table, and propped her flawless and ageless chin on her flawless and ageless fingers. "I don't know what you told JL, but whatever it was, it sparked a fire and empowered her. And she needed it…badly. When I left the room for coffee, she was as low as I've ever seen her, including the time she came home after she and Kevin broke their engagement."

Pete returned to the recliner. "JL needs to believe she's in control even if she isn't. She can't do much for Lawrence right now except be there, talk to him, touch him, but her mind will settle if she has a mystery to solve. It doesn't mean she'll worry less, but her brain will be able to switch gears, keep her balanced."

"Sorry, but she can't worry about her son and a brooch, too. She's liable to have a breakdown."

"Nah. You're wrong. Her brain needs an escape. My folks announced when I was a teenager that they weren't going to stay awake at night and worry about me when I was out with my friends. I thought they were weird. I knew everybody else's parents stayed up watching the clock until their kid came through the door. My mom said if anything happened to me, she'd need to be rested to handle the crisis. So she went right to sleep.

"That's how I see JL. When she's sitting in the NICU holding Lawrence for hours at a time, her brain will need somewhere to go. Like my mom went to sleep, JL will mentally escape the confines of the NICU."

"Frankly, it doesn't make much sense to me, but if you say so…" Meredith sipped her coffee. "Now tell me what you know."

There was a knock on the door and a woman in green scrubs peeked in. "I have the coffee pods you requested."

Pete swung out of the recliner and accepted the box. "Thanks." He set the pods on the counter and returned to the chair. "I assume you've heard of Sophia Orsini, the girl I married the night she graduated from high school."

"I've heard there was a girl who's never been replaced in your heart, but I'm not sure I ever knew her name."

"Right before Connor called me about the plane crash, I stumbled upon Sophia's art studio in Florence. Based on what I heard from a client of hers, I got suspicious, so I broke into her studio and upstairs apartment, where I found a hidden vault with five paintings of her." Pete handed Meredith his phone. "Those portraits are signed by da Vinci, Picasso, Donatello, Rubens, and Degas."

Meredith's jaw dropped. "That's impossible. They have to be forgeries."

"If so, why hide them in a vault secured by a state-of-the-art security system? Why not have them on display? The client I met commissioned her to paint the *Mona Lisa,* and Sophia left that painting sitting out in the middle of her studio. Granted, the alarm was on, but it wasn't locked in a hidden room like the others."

"If da Vinci really painted her portrait, it wouldn't have the age of a six-hundred-year-old painting because she brought it directly to the future. It would never pass as an original. A good copy, yes, but not an original da Vinci," Meredith said.

"Exactly. So back to my question. Why not display them?"

Meredith gazed off, looking far beyond the walls of the room, shaking her head. "If the paintings are originals, they have enormous value. They deserve to be well protected. I'd lock them up too. Then when I wanted to enjoy them, I'd go into my secret room with a glass of wine and relive my time with each artist."

He waited a beat or two to let the idea of the paintings sink in before he exploded his next little bombshell. "I found something else while I was searching her apartment."

Meredith emptied her coffee cup and pitched it into the trashcan. "Owning paintings by da Vinci and Rubens is quite enough. Nothing could be the cherry on top of that sundae."

"Well, there's whipped cream and a big, fat, red cherry. While searching Sophia's apartment"—he decided to skip the breaking into a safe part so she'd have deniability—"I found a wooden jewelry box lined with velvet and embroidered with four brooches: sapphire, emerald, diamond, and pearl."

"Seriously? We already knew the sapphire, emerald, and diamond came from Solicitor Digby. Now we know he also had possession of a fourth brooch. So how is Sophia connected to him?"

"Her grandfather was a Digby, which I just discovered. I don't know yet if he's *our* Mr. Digby, but her having possession of the jewelry box certainly points to that possibility."

"Kenzie needs to see the paintings. If Sophia is as clever as I think she is, there's a pattern there somewhere. Kenzie will spot it, and when she does, you'll have an idea of where Sophia has gone."

"There's one more thing," Pete said. "There's a parchment in the box written in Gaelic by James MacKlenna in 1625."

"What does it say?" Meredith asked.

"If my English/Gaelic dictionary is accurate, the gist is that MacKlenna gave a box of brooches to Seamus Digby to keep safe from the evil force."

"Elliott believes he can feel it sometimes. What else?"

"If the holder ever feels the force, he's instructed to give away a brooch to a trusted clan member to disperse the power."

Meredith hugged her elbows, running her hands over her upper arms. "This is giving me chills."

"Sophia is obviously a more experienced traveler than we are." Pete lowered the footrest and went over to the coffee pot. "You want another cup?"

"No. I've had enough." While Pete made coffee, she got up to gaze out the window. "We've got to find Sophia."

"If Kenzie can find a pattern in the portraits, we'll find her."

"Why don't you talk to Matt? He might know an appraiser who can answer questions about the paintings. Elliott has connections, but I'd rather not talk to him about this yet. The more information Kenzie has, the easier it might be to find a pattern or clue. You never know."

Pete stirred sugar into his cup. "I can't get involved in this, Meredith. Elliott told me to leave it alone until JL and Lawrence are out of danger."

She turned around and leaned against the windowsill. "I'll take care of Elliott. If you need authority to take the lead on this, I'll give it to you. It's now your job. Work it out, but keep me posted."

Pete dropped the stir stick in the trash and returned to the re-cliner. "No. Give it to David. If Elliott gets pissed, he won't fire David, but he might fire me."

"He can't. You own part of the company."

"He'll try. And besides, David is president of the corporation. We'll work together. But keep in mind, this might be expensive, time-consuming, and invasive. We'll be diving deep into that gray zone. He needs to take the lead."

"Why?"

"I'm too close to it. I don't want my feelings for Sophia to get in the way."

"Okay, if that's the way you want it, but I want Matt in on it too."

"No problem. I'll talk to David first and go from there."

"I have a question. Why aren't you giving her time to come home?"

Pete drummed his fingers on the chair's padded armrest for several moments. "For the past five years she's taken a two-week vacation every summer. She never tells anybody where she's going, only that she'll be back in two weeks. She's now two days past her return date. It's going to take us a couple of weeks to figure this out, gather a party of adventurers, and arrange for wardrobe, weapons, and money. That's four weeks. How much time needs to pass before we know for sure she's in trouble?"

"What about a soul mate? Has she ever brought anybody back with her?"

"She's not married and doesn't seem to have a significant other."

"She's time-traveled more than we have. Why didn't her brooch bring her back this time? It seems like the more we learn about the brooches, the more questions we have."

"I haven't seen or talked to Sophia in twenty years. All I remember about her art are silly caricatures she drew of her classmates, some futuristic paintings, and paint splatters with hidden messages. But, based on my limited investigation, she's spent her career painting like the Old Masters. So why go back to visit Picasso? The only thing I can figure is that she's still interested in modern art, artistic innovation, futuristic painting."

Meredith shrugged. "What's your point?"

"It's possible… I know it sounds crazy, but it's possible she's gone to the future to see the evolution of art a hundred or more years from now. She could return and start a new avant-garde art movement in the twenty-first century. Think about that."

Meredith gave a delicate shudder. "I'm not sure I want to. How could we ever prepare for a trip to the unknown?"

Pete shrugged. "It's what we do every time we travel. We don't know for sure where we're going or what life will be like. As an infant, Kit traveled more than a hundred and fifty years into the future. Why couldn't Sophia?"

Meredith's eyes seemed to plumb his. He held steady. He wanted an honest reaction, her first thoughts. Would it be doubt or possibility? Her eyes widened.

"We can't rule it out, can we?" she said.

The door flew open and Elliott stormed in. "My daughter-in-law just told me to go home. I was in the middle of a conference with the staff about Lawrence's treatment, asking if this was the best facility for his care. She wheeled in, interrupted the conference, and ordered me to go home. She said my health was in jeopardy. My health! There's not a goddamn thing wrong with my health."

His eyes flashed from Pete to Meredith. Then he leveled his fiercest glare on Pete. "This is a goddamn fucking conspiracy." To emphasize his statement, he made stabbing motions at the floor with his index finger. "Ye're trying to win Meredith's support to go back for yer lady love."

Elliott was showing all the warning signs of a volcanic eruption. "Let me tell ye right now, it's not going to happen. Not now. Maybe not this year." He whirled and slammed the door behind him on his way out.

"What the hell was that about?" Pete asked.

Meredith pushed to her feet and headed toward the door. "His tantrum doesn't change anything. Pull a plan together. I probably won't be much help right now, but I'll sign off on anything you or David need. Elliott turns seventy next month, and he's afraid the family will open the gate and shove him out to pasture. Plus, James Cullen will graduate early and go to law school, and I doubt he'll ever come back to live at MacKlenna Farm."

She shook her head. "JL's babies keep Elliott relevant. I don't know what happened in the NICU, but I doubt it was as horrible as he described." Meredith swung open the door. "I'll check in with you later."

Pete raked his fingers through his hair. "Aw, shit. What the hell did I just do?"

20

Paris (1789)—Sophia

A S THE SUN turned orange in the peaceful western sky, Sophia finished sketching the girls on canvas and dismissed them for the day. They hurried inside the Hôtel de Langeac with their heads together, laughing, reminding Sophia of her art students in Florence, except the two girls running off in tandem weren't sharing text messages and Instagram photos.

She stretched her arms over her head, chalk in hand, and smothered a yawn. If not for her bum knee, she'd run through a quick ten-minute Tai Chi routine. But she did have a bum knee, and her mind had already moved on to thinking about the elements in the portrait's background. Whatever she painted had to compliment, unify, and enhance the portrait.

The Grille de Chaillot, the customs gate at the corner of the Hôtel de Langeac facing the Champs-Élysées, was a possibility. The stone support columns in the gate were the same color and texture as the stone bench in the garden and would draw the elements together. Plus, the gate would always remind Jefferson of Paris.

Several times during the afternoon thoughts of him crept into her mind. Watin's comment about Jefferson's jealousy disturbed her. She didn't know whether it was true or not, but she wasn't going to dwell on it. Becoming emotionally involved violated her number one time-travel rule: Never, ever—again—fall for a man living in another century. After her time with Leonardo, it had taken months to regain balance in her life. And this time it wasn't just an irresistible man playing with her heart, but two charming young women as well.

She sat back, lifting her injured leg, pointing and flexing her foot, feeling the stretch while she studied the portrait's underdrawing. Tomorrow morning the girls would sit for her again, and she'd add the details of their faces. Then, as soon as Watin arrived, he'd apply a layer of varnish to keep the chalk from bleeding through the oil paint. When the varnish was dry, she'd paint over the underdrawing.

"I'd like to see the portrait," Jefferson said, interrupting her musings.

Her hand moved unconsciously to her neck to conceal the startled jump of her pulse, as she whipped her head around in Jefferson's direction. The late afternoon sun glinted off his red hair and sent her artistic heart rate soaring higher. She reached for a piece of chalk, desperate to capture his muscular physique filling the doorway and brimming with his unique brand of magnetism. His eyes creased deeply at the corners as he gazed at her.

"You surprised me. Are you in a better mood?" she asked glibly, both to lighten the moment and lower the sudden rise in her temperature. The seconds stretched out to occupy the silence between them. From the puzzled expression lingering around his eyes, she gathered her question must have confused him. She tried again without the glibness. "Last time you poked your head out the door, you all but growled at us."

He descended the low steps and crossed the garden toward her—all six-two of him. "Mademoiselle, I do *not* growl, and you will never see me ruffled." His swagger was all rough and tough and rugged, yet slow and deliberate. And after a struggle, she finally concluded that even if she broke his gait down frame by frame, it was unpaintable, because it was more than motion. It was the essence of Thomas Jefferson expressed in movement.

Now she doubted she could truly capture him on canvas. How could she paint him, because, as Maria Cosway wrote in her final letter to him, *Remembrance must be ever green?* Sophia mentally went through her color wheel. Green represented life, renewal, vitality, nature, ambition. He was surrounded by a green aura. Her sketch of him standing in the vineyard was the man she was beginning to know.

"You can look," she croaked out, then cleared her throat. "But you can't comment. That's the rule. I don't want your comments or opinions influencing my concept."

"I commented on your other sketches."

"Those were sketches. Paintings are different."

"Maybe my comments will improve the painting."

"That's rather egotistical, don't you think?"

"How so? You're painting my daughters. Who would know them better? You or me? I have pieces of their mother's jewelry I would like them to wear."

"Well, here's the thing," Sophia said. "Women have traditionally been painted while wearing expensive fabrics and stunning jewelry. Not because of their vanity, but because their portraits were painted for the male viewers. The women are passive, powerless objects subject to the controlling gaze of males. Husbands and fathers have wanted affirmation of their own status, which is borne out by the wife or daughter's clothing and jewelry.

"That's not what I paint. I want these portraits to empower Patsy and Polly. If they wore their mother's jewelry, you would notice that first. I want you to see them as loving, intelligent, and inquisitive young women."

He remained standing there, silently, blocking out the sunlight. She could barely see his expression, but there was something hesitant in the way he stood, arms folded, gazing down at her, something expectant, or perhaps it was simply indecision. He moved to stand alongside her. Now the sun flashed on his face, his strong jaw, the curve of his ear, the knot in his cravat, stark white against his ruddy neck.

The box of chalk slipped off her lap, landing at his feet. He picked it up and hesitated a moment before handing it to her, his warm fingers touching hers briefly before he drew them back. "No comments, then. But I have one question. Why don't they have faces?"

"I'll draw them tomorrow before Monsieur Watin varnishes the canvas. I want the girls to be fresh and bright-eyed before I sketch them."

He glanced around the small courtyard, too small for anyone to hide. "Speaking of the monsieur, where is he?"

She waved her hand, making light of the disappearance. "I sent him on his way. He has a business to run, and I kept him here too long."

Finally, she got an eyebrow twitch out of Jefferson.

"But what about you?" she asked. "You seemed rather irritated when you returned from your meeting. Did it not go well?"

He didn't answer right away. Instead, he picked up an errant piece of chalk almost completely hidden in blades of grass. "I was only there as an observer. Lafayette's Declaration of the Rights of Man and Citizen was the assembly's first order of business."

"Were any of your suggestions included?"

"It was impossible to identify a specific one, other than the provision to have an amending convention. But all in all"—he paused and tugged at his chin—"the whole outline of the assembly's priorities represent a superb structure to use going forward."

He sat on the bench and lounged against the tree trunk, again tugging at his chin. "During the next several weeks, members of the assembly will review the texts of the Declaration of Independence and charters from Virginia, Pennsylvania, Massachusetts, and Maryland."

She stopped what she was doing, picked up a piece of paper from the salon table situated next to the easel, and sketched him leaning against the tree, his fingers at his chin. As she sketched, she replayed his last statement. *Assembly will read charters…*

"So what are you saying?" she asked. "Now that the American experiment has passed the laboratory stage, it's worth studying?"

He squinted, his crow's feet on full display. "Mademoiselle, your political insight continues to astound me. You're as versed in American politics as you are in what's happening in France. How is this possible?"

"Women have brains, you know, but as of yet they haven't turned the world upside down and stripped men of the power to which they believe they're entitled." She cocked her head and studied his quizzical expression. "Haven't we had this conversation before?"

"Have we?"

"Yes, and while we're talking about Lafayette's 'Rights of Man and Citizen—'"

"Were we talking about Lafayette?" He rested his right foot on the bench and propped his wrist on his knee, his long fingers playing what could only be the fingerboard of an imaginary violin.

Was he teasing her? His eyes were shaded, so she couldn't tell. "We were talking about rights," she said. "And it's my opinion that women, as citizens of America, should also have the right to vote."

"Ah. You go too far, mademoiselle."

"You think the privilege of voting should extend only to men, some of whom are just plain idiots. If there's to be a vote, it should be fair, and extended to all adults subject to the government in question."

"Women are incapable of making political decisions. And if they were enfranchised, they might take it into their heads to run for office, an innovation for which the public is not prepared, nor am I."

Her mouth fell open. She wanted to scream or bop him over the head to beat some sense into him. "You don't have to look any further than your own daughter to see how silly that is. Patsy is intelligent, politically aware, and conversant on a multitude of topics. If she were given the right to vote, she would do so with an informed mind."

He tilted his head and gazed at her with intense focus. "Perhaps it would be acceptable in Paris, where women hunt pleasures in the streets and forget their nurseries. American women, on the other hand, are content with the tranquil amusements of domestic life. And they're too wise to wrinkle their foreheads with politics. They're content to soothe and calm the minds of their husbands when they return ruffled from political debate."

"*God forbid* that women ever extend themselves beyond the domestic line. You're a brilliant man, Ambassador. But your idyllic domestic ideal of American women contradicts your concept of life, liberty, and the pursuit of happiness. Women and people of color deserve equal rights. You think they don't have the brains to think critically, but it's only because they lack education. Reading expands one's mind. Granted, no amount of reading and learning will turn a person into a prolific writer like you and Hamilton, but education and reading can teach people to think critically and be good decision-makers."

"The obstacle to a good education is women's inordinate passion for novels. The result is a bloated imagination, sickly judgment, and disgust towards all aspects of the real business of life."

"So women shouldn't read books?"

"They should be taught to play the fortepiano, draw, dance, read, and such things as will make them worthy of the love of their friends. Along with the more mundane tasks of cooking, cleaning, and needlework. Above all, women should be taught to be industrious. Their entire regime of study should be to ready them for marriage. They have a single purpose in life, marriage and subordination to a husband. For the past five years, I've had to invest almost womanly attention to the details of the household. I find it perplexing, disgusting, and inconsistent with business. It's emasculating to attend to every facet of running the residence, no matter how small, to make sure there is no waste. Women are taught to do this, and they do it well."

"So the minister to France has been forced to do women's work." Her heart was now hammering in her rib cage. It was so easy to get angry at him. He was an eighteenth-century man, and he would never see a woman as an equal. His attitude was immovable and unchangeable. She turned back to her sketch and tried to work, telling herself it really didn't matter.

But it did.

She couldn't change history. She knew that. This wasn't her battle. Her causes were in the twenty-first century. She could participate in the Women's March and send money to save the whales, but she couldn't fight for Patsy and Polly's right to vote in the new democracy, and as frustrating as that was, it was the way it had to be. She couldn't judge Jefferson by the standards of her time. To lift him out of the context of his century and bring him into hers would be like trying to plant cut flowers.

She softened her tone and asked, "Do you ever wonder what people will think of this experiment in democracy in two hundred and fifty years?"

He pushed to his feet, grinning. "There is nothing foreordained about the American experiment. It has never been a set piece in a game of chess pitting an evil empire against a noble band of Americans. If the democracy survives twenty years, then the government should rewrite the constitution from scratch, and every twenty years thereafter."

"You're kidding. Aren't you? Look how long it's taking to get it ratified by thirteen states. Can you imagine if there were fifty?"

"Fifty?"

"At least. And getting that many states to ratify a new constitution would never happen." She set the sketch of him aside and returned to the portrait, but she was done with it for now. Her hand had a little shake to it anyway, and she'd only make a mess if she tinkered with it. "If legislators decided to rewrite the constitution, I hope, instead of giving the right to vote only to property-owning, taxpaying white males, they'll give it to women and people of color as well."

"Even if it's rewritten, Congress will never include women."

"Obviously, any forward-thinking conversation that includes women is a nonstarter for you, isn't it?"

"I'm wary of females influencing government, and I won't change."

Of course not!

She'd travelled to the fifteenth, sixteenth, seventeenth, nineteenth, and twentieth centuries, and now the eighteenth, and she'd never met such a womanizing misogynist. Trying to understand him was like viewing Monticello's architectural details through Virginia's early morning fog.

In a word, she would never understand him. Well, she used more than one word, but who was counting? She had to stop projecting contemporary values back into a different era.

"All right," she sighed. "I won't bring it up again."

He looked mildly shocked but pleased. "Mademoiselle, you're so assured of your position, you *will* make your point again. You're like a roof leaking in a rainstorm, a never-ending drip, drip, drip. That's a perfect example of why women should confine their comments to home and hearth."

She gave him an exaggerated exhale. "Mr. Jefferson, I doubt you will find in me the modesty, beauty, and soft disposition of other women of your acquaintance. So, tell me this… Why leave the issue for future politicians to resolve? There are thousands of women in America. Why wait until there are millions marching in the street, like Parisians demanding their rights?"

"If women can threaten a republican revolution in France, I fear what they might do in a country awakened to the rhetoric of equality."

"So if women are tied to home and hearth, they won't be a threat or march in the streets and demand their rights?" she said, her voice quivering. "Good luck with that."

"If I tried to include women's rights in the constitution, no one would sign it. It's more important to get a working document ratified than to spend years arguing. In Article V there's a process for amending the Constitution."

She mentally apologized to future suffragettes. *I tried.* "Now I know why you insisted that Lafayette include an amending convention in his Declaration of Rights."

Jefferson exhaled deeply before saying softly, and with an unusual amount of patience, "I am not without forethought, Sophia."

Their intense debate seemed to have exhausted them both. It was becoming a habit when they saw each other to debate first, wait for the tension to fizzle, then proceed with a normal conversation.

Had debating become foreplay?

Thankfully she had a ticket home in a few days. Leaving was a ten-foot wall standing between foreplay and the natural progression of physical attraction.

She changed the subject. "What else happened at the Estates General meeting? Anything you can share?" Her voice had returned to its ordinary timbre, not quivering at all now.

"General Lafayette was elected vice president of *L'Assemblee,* and he ordered the demolition of the Bastille."

"A wise move, I think. Don't you? I heard its destruction has been debated in government circles for over a decade."

"It's the symbol of the arbitrary detentions of the Old Regime, of the dreaded *lettres de cachet.* They should have demolished it years ago. Besides, it's also an enormous expense."

She brushed chalk residue off her hands. "I'm taking a risk here, but I value your judgment. I'll set aside my edict and ask if you have comments about the portrait."

He smiled. "When will you start painting?"

"A safe question, and I'll start painting tomorrow afternoon. While I wait for the varnish to dry, I'll move inside and sketch individual drawings of the girls. Although I might paint Polly outside." Sophia rested her cheek against her finger and thumb. "Not here in the garden. Maybe near the stables. If you're not out riding, I might include your horse. We'll see."

"I probably won't ride until later in the day. The king's coming to Paris tomorrow to meet with the Estates General."

"Will he come this way? I'd like to see him, but I don't want to go anywhere near the crowd again, and I don't think Patsy and Polly want to be out there either. We were all so scared."

As soon as Polly said the noise and crowd frightened her, Sophia should have insisted they all return to the legation immediately. Her failure to do so was a haunting reminder of a decision that could easily have gotten them killed. Life in the eighteenth century was more tenuous than in the twenty-first. For the next twelve days, she needed to keep the danger in mind and always take precautions.

"You'll be able to see the king and his entourage from the window in the salon. The streets will be overly crowded, and I don't want Patsy and Polly out there again." He looked directly at her. "Even with an escort."

"Then you expect trouble."

"The French love their monarch, but they're rioting for lower taxes and representation in government. In this heated environment, anything could happen. A mob is unpredictable."

"Lafayette can guarantee his safety. I watched the crowd willingly move aside for him yesterday. If they love their king, they love Lafayette just as much." She noticed a line in the portrait that bugged her, and she couldn't leave it alone. She erased it, but didn't like the new look either. "Has he said anything else about the dinner he wants you to host?"

"Nothing about the dinner, but he extended an invitation to join him in his box to see the opera *Richard Coeur de Lion*."

Instead of fixing the line, she picked up another sheet of paper and started a sketch of Polly with her head bent over the rose bush, sniffing the flowers. "Will the Marquise de La Fayette or his mistress be with him?"

Jefferson cleared his throat. "Did Patsy mention that situation to you?"

"How would Patsy know?"

"When she was away at school, she kept me apprised of the political tensions intruding into the convent's matriarchal family, which included reporting on marital infidelities."

Sophia hiked an eyebrow. "Interesting. But no, the information didn't come from her, and regardless of who accompanies Lafayette, you'll have a splendid time. After all the recent chaos and danger, a night at the theatre will be a pleasant diversion."

Jefferson strolled around the courtyard, scratching at a spot behind his ear. He stopped and cast his gaze at her, clearing his throat. "He also invited you."

The invitation caught her by surprise. Her hands dropped to her lap. "I can't go to the opera. If I fall again—"

"You won't fall," he said quickly. "Lafayette was concerned about your mobility. So he promised to have soldiers there to assist you in and out of the carriage and up and down the stairs. I'll be by your side, of course."

She shook her head. "I'd love to go, but I can't risk it. I'll stay here and paint. Why don't you take the girls? They'd love it."

"Polly is too young to appreciate the opera."

"She loves music as much as Patsy. There's nothing comparable to the Paris Opera in America. And besides, the girls may never get to Paris again. It'll be a wonderful memory for them."

Jefferson's stroll turned into a slow back and forth, his head down in thought. "Patsy will stay in Virginia, but Polly will return with me. She'll have other opportunities to see the opera."

"You're too valuable to America to return to Paris. You might prefer your natural passion of study and tranquility at Monticello, but planting a new world with the seeds of a just government is too remarkable a pursuit for you to choose your passion over the well-being of mankind. President Washington will want you in his cabinet. And you won't say no because politics provides a stage, and you'll never leave the drama. You're standing on the ramparts of history, Mr. Jefferson. What will you do to bend the world to your purposes?"

He planted his feet and folded his arms in a pose she was beginning to find annoying. "I don't know where your ideas come from. Pursuing my passion over laying my shoulder to the work of the day is not a choice to be made. I'll complete my commitment as ambassador and retire."

She slipped her foot off the stool and reached for her crutches. Until Jefferson received the new appointment from President Washington, he would continue to deny the obvious. "Enjoy your last few weeks in Paris with your daughters." She set the crutches under her arms. "I'm going inside. There's not enough light to continue working out here."

"I'll carry the portrait."

"Thank you, but Mr. Petit said he would have everything moved inside when I finished for the day." She hobbled toward the stairs, a little more agile with the crutches now. "On second thought, do you mind bringing the canvas? I'd hate for a strong breeze to come through the garden and knock it over. I haven't read a weather report in days."

"Where do you read weather reports?"

Oops. Did it again.

She made her way up the stairs while working through a possible answer. Conversing daily with Jefferson presented unique problems. During her other trips, conversations had always been about art, not this wide range of topics that constantly tripped her up.

"I met a man in Florence who for many years tracked the weather daily." She reached the door, and he moved quickly to open it. "He liked to make forecasts based on his records."

"What did he discover? This man...in Florence?"

The way he said, *this man,* he was obviously suspicious of her constant references to men in Florence. The crutches clicked rhythmically along the hardwood floor as she crossed the room to the sofa. "I don't know if there were patterns or not. I'm sure he projected his forecasts based on prior years' weather. I'm a painter, not a scientist. What do I know?"

"Did he write an almanac?"

"I guess so."

He held up the canvas. "Where do you want this?"

"On the easel."

Mr. Petit, right on cue, entered the room. "Mademoiselle, shall we bring the easel in from outside?"

The maître d'hôtel had to have spies all over the house to be so up-to-date on her comings and goings. "Thank you, yes, Mr. Petit. Have you seen Marguerite?"

"She's in the sewing room. Shall I fetch her?"

"No, don't bother her. I was just curious. What about Patsy and Polly?" Sophia reached the sofa and stretched out her leg.

"They're with Marguerite."

Sophia gazed over at Jefferson, who had taken a position in front of the easel, studying the portrait. When Mr. Petit brought in the chair and stool, Jefferson sat and leaned back. The delicate wood seemed too small for him. The room seemed too small for him. His shoulders strained against his jacket. He was too full of life and muscle to be contained by even the fine brown wool.

"The girls need time to dress if you're taking them to the opera," she said.

"The general will be disappointed."

"I hope you'll explain why I couldn't go out tonight."

He leaned forward in the chair, and after a few moments of exasperated silence he said, "Are you certain?"

"Yes."

"Then I'll ask Patsy."

If Jefferson was exasperated, so was she. Not since she'd been attacked years earlier had she been afraid to go out, but she was now. Down deep, her hesitation was about more than a fear of falling and additional injury.

She was afraid to go out with him, afraid to enjoy a night of music and companionship, and afraid of what he'd write in his journal. If he mentioned taking her to the opera, what would Jeffersonophiles think of her? Despite all their disagreements, she thoroughly enjoyed his company. He made her feel alive in a way she hadn't felt for years.

"I'd love to go, but I don't want to get caught in another crowd. I can't take the risk."

Mr. Petit reentered from the courtyard, carrying the tray of empty dishes. "Is there anything else I can get for you, mademoiselle?"

"Not that I can think of."

"Mr. Petit, would you ask Patsy to come to my reading room?" Jefferson waved his hand to encompass the room. "What *used* to be my reading room. Never mind. Ask her to meet me in the salon."

"Certainly. When dinner is prepared, mademoiselle, I'll set a table here for you. In the meantime, I'll have fresh ice brought out."

"I'll join the mademoiselle for dinner," Jefferson said, turning toward her. "I believe we discussed this earlier."

"We did. And you said the wine du jour was a *Goutte d'Or de Meursault.*" To Mr. Petit she said, "Mr. Jefferson and I will dine in the dining room." The studio was too small, too intimate for her to safely share a candlelight dinner with him.

Mr. Petit left the room, humming a little ditty she'd heard before, but she didn't know the title or the words. He had been so kind and thoughtful to her from the moment she entered the house, and she wanted to do something special for him before she left. A bonus, maybe.

"How much longer will you continue to ice your knee?" Jefferson asked.

"I'm forty-eight hours, plus some, from the original injury and twenty-four, plus some, from the second. I'll probably continue to ice for another twenty-four hours."

"Then what?"

"I'll start stretching without weight-bearing for another twenty-four. If the swelling continues to go down, I'll try to walk on it and see what happens."

He stood, uncertainty flickering in his eyes. "I'll go speak to Patsy now, and I'll see you at dinner." He walked out, leaving the door slightly ajar.

Except for the brief time between the girls leaving the courtyard and Jefferson arriving, she'd had almost no time alone, and she needed a quiet spell to regroup.

But when she tried to clear her mind, thoughts of Jefferson were always there, keeping her unsettled. She gathered the crutches and hobbled over to the table stacked with supplies. All she wanted was a sheet of paper and pencil. She had a sketch of him in mind.

"Sophia."

Her head shot up to find him standing in the doorway. Her cheeks warmed, as if he could read her mind and knew she'd been thinking of him.

"I just asked Patsy to attend the theatre tonight, but she and Polly are preparing for their portraits and don't want to go out." He walked over to stand directly beside her, so close she could feel the warmth of his body through his clothing and hers, and his scent wafted in the air. It was a pleasing fragrance, like soap and wood and leather and fresh air and flowers. The tip of his chin was within an inch of the crown of her head. "She and Polly said I should take you. You can't refuse me now."

"But I'll be on crutches."

"You can demonstrate them for Lafayette. Since he first saw them in the carriage, he's been very interested in learning how they work."

"He can stop by here, and I'll give him a demonstration." Her refusal was only half-hearted at this point. "I don't have anything to wear except what I have on."

"You could wear your Tai Chi pants and you'd still be the most beautiful woman there. Although I don't recommend you wear them. I'm afraid you'd cause a scandal. But to relieve your mind, Marguerite told me she just purchased a dress that needs only minor alterations to fit you perfectly."

Polly skipped into the room. "Mademoiselle. It's time to dress for the opera." She placed her hand on Sophia's back to hurry her along. "Wait until you see what Marguerite and her seamstress are making for you. You'll look so elegant and fashionable."

Jefferson folded his arms, smiling. "You have three hours."

As excited as Polly was, Sophia would rather risk another injury than disappoint her. "Would you ask Mr. Petit to send my dinner upstairs? I'll eat while I get ready."

While dining in her bedroom was cringeworthy, and her nonna wouldn't approve, in this situation it was necessary. She'd take little bites and pretend it was only a snack. Three hours wasn't enough time to finish the fitting, take a bath, get dressed, have her hair done up in an elaborate whorl, and then sit down to a meal. If she was going to survive the ordeal, she had to eat.

After three hours of tightening and stitching, several frustrated sighs, a few oohs and ahhs, and one big wow from her, the girls and Marguerite held Sophia's skirts as she descended the stairs and entered the salon.

"Stay right here," Patsy said. "I'm going to get Papa." She turned to go, but stopped and glanced over her shoulder. "He's going to be so surprised."

Shrouded in the yellow light of the candles and pale moonlight shining in through the salon's French doors, Sophia waited, a little wobbly, on one foot. She tugged on the sleeves of the chintz *robe à l'anglaise*, tight from the shoulder to the elbows and ending with flared lace.

A dainty pair of heels decorated with ribbons fit her feet perfectly, but she could only walk on one. Marguerite had also repaired her wig and adorned it with a few cleverly placed blue irises to complement her eyes' natural violet hue. For jewelry, she'd debated wearing the brooch, but in the end settled for the gold and platinum necklace with pearls and gemstones and matching earbobs. She pinned the brooch to the inside of her chemise. She didn't want to wear it, but she didn't want to leave it behind either.

"You can take the crutches, Marguerite," Polly said. "The mademoiselle can brace her hand on my shoulder for balance. Papa should see her without those ugly sticks." Her eyes sparkled as she bounced from foot to foot. "I can't wait to see his face."

Neither could Sophia. "Please stand still," she said. "I'm already a little shaky."

Mr. Petit came to the salon, holding his hands together at his chest. *"Vous êtes belle."*

She winked at him, and his smile curled up the corners of his mouth.

A minute later Jefferson entered the salon, his voice lifting into laughter, and then he stopped and stared at her hungrily. A little tic jumped at the side of his mouth. This might be a good time to feign an illness or faint theatrically and return to her room.

"You look…extraordinary."

So did he, handsomely dressed in a rich blue coat, lavishly embroidered silk waistcoat, and a crimped, double-pleated jabot. His black breeches stopped at the knee above white stockings, his black-heeled shoes were polished to a shine, and a square silver buckle gleamed in the candlelight. Thankfully, his hair was unpowdered, with his queue neatly tied with a ribbon.

"She's pretty, Papa, isn't she?" Patsy's voice was rich, her eyes sparkling.

Something vulnerable appeared in his expression, and time stopped for a moment, for just a heartbeat, and Sophia waited breathlessly for his answer.

"Of course she is," Polly said. "And we helped her dress. I wish I could draw so I would have a picture of the way she looks tonight."

A smile teased his eyes, which had widened into moons, as if he'd found something so marvelous he couldn't believe his good fortune. "An act of superb achievement." He cast his gaze about. "Where are your crutches, mademoiselle?"

Marguerite stepped out of the shadows. "Here they are, sir."

He took a single step in Sophia's direction, and his energy swept over her, prickling her skin, unnerving her for a moment.

"Your gown is the color of the red wine in a glass of *Clos de Vougeot.*"

His voice was as stirring as the way his eyes grazed the neckline of her decollete gown. The intimate touch of his eyes made every muscle tighten in breathless anticipation of losing herself in his labyrinthine character on a rose-scented summer evening in Paris.

21

Paris (1789)—Sophia

THE THEATRE DE Monsieur was located in the Salle des
Tuileries in the north wing of the Tuileries Palace. Even at this
late hour, the night was thick with the effigy-carrying mob chanting
"Vive le tiers etat." She flinched at every intersection, half believing
the mob would storm the street and attack their carriage with picks
and axes.

Why did she agree to come out into this madness? She hated
being afraid, but the events of the past two days had terrorized her,
and venturing out again, even with Jefferson at her side, had her
biting back the bitter tang of fear.

"You're safe with me, Sophia," he said.

"I didn't say anything."

"You didn't have to. Even when you're drawing you can argue
with me. I've brought up several topics since we departed the Hôtel
de Langeac, but you haven't engaged with me about women *or*
liberty. I can only surmise you're afraid of the crowds. But you don't
have to be. I won't let harm come to you."

"You can't control that mob." She closed her eyes, which made
it worse because she heard the screams and chants more clearly.

He tucked her arm around his, squeezing her hand. "Before you
arrived in Parris, I monitored a street battle between the mob and

the cavalry at the Place de Louis XV, and the cavalry was forced to quit the field to avoid being massacred. The people saw the withdrawal as a signal for universal insurrection. Now they're roaming all night through parts of the city without any attainable objective. We are in the midst of tumult and violence, but we are not in danger."

"Two days ago, that mob tried to kill me. No one is safe in Paris. Without full use of my leg, I'm defenseless. After tonight, I'm not leaving the Hôtel de Langeac again until it's time to leave France."

"Sophia, you are safe with me."

His confidence didn't ease her shaking. She pressed her hand to her chest, as if that could somehow absorb her stress—*poof, presto!*— and evaporate through the skin of her palm. She was not safe with him on any number of levels—especially when his eyes bored into her, or his warm hand brushed against hers, as it was doing now.

The coachman pulled to the end of a line of carriages discharging passengers near the marquee. Patrons crowded the sidewalk to enter the theatre for a night of entertainment while less fortunate men and women roamed the streets demanding food and liberty. Sophia's heart ached for the powerless and disenfranchised, which only added to the anxiety running rampant up and down her spine. She reclaimed her arm.

As soon as the carriage rolled to a stop, a soldier hustled to the door, opened it, and lowered the step. "Good evening, Mr. Jefferson, Mademoiselle Orsini. General Lafayette has charged us with seeing you safely to the general's box."

"Has he arrived?" Sophia asked.

"Yes, mademoiselle."

"How do you intend to manage this?" Jefferson climbed down, then turned back to her, extending his hand.

The man pointed to another soldier, who was standing next to an upholstered chair. "We intend to carry her, sir."

Jefferson's face pinched in concern.

Sophia quickly considered the chair, the two strapping soldiers, and the lively crowd. "Instead of using the chair, I'll use the crutches, but I'd like you two," she pointed at the soldiers, "to walk in front of us and clear a path. But don't push people aside. Just ask politely if they'll make room for the lady."

"Mademoiselle, are you sure? There are many steps to climb, and the floor of the theatre is already crowded."

"At least this crowd won't be angry. I can manage." Turning to Jefferson she went for levity, hoping to lighten her own mood. "You know, don't you, that as soon as people see me using these crutches, there'll be a demand for them. You'll need an assembly line to handle all the orders, and you'll make a fortune."

"What's an assembly line?"

He never let anything he didn't understand slip by without asking for an explanation. On previous trips, men had given her puzzled looks when they didn't understand her, and rarely, if ever, pursued an explanation. But not Jefferson. His quest for knowledge was endless, demanding, and at times annoying.

"I'll explain later."

"Allow me to carry you up the steps, mademoiselle," the soldier said.

It would at least keep her dress from picking up the yucky stuff in the street. "You have to promise not to drop me."

"You have no need to worry. I often carry my elderly mother, and I've never dropped her."

"Okay, let's go." With Jefferson standing nearby, arms outstretched, she stepped out on her good leg and eased into the soldier's arms. She held her breath as the soldier carried her up the steps and gently set her down.

Jefferson handed over the crutches. "When you're ready…"

She settled them under her arms, relieved she'd made it this far. Marguerite had reinforced the seams around the shoulders, the sleeves, and the sides of the dress, so if the soldiers kept the path clear and she didn't have to hurry, she might last the night without any ripped seams.

"Let's go. But if I wobble, please hold on to me." General Lafayette was in the house. With two of her rescuers at hand, surely she could handle the crowd. When the doors opened, her anxiety dipped but didn't fade completely. Ballet dancers floated around the stage while a heavily-wigged male singer was being lowered on a cloud. The scenery was—compared to twenty-first century theatre—on the level of an elementary school set design.

The horseshoe-shaped theatre had four grand tier private boxes immediately above the parterre, with four more on the second level. The entire interior was decorated in red—walls, velvet curtains, and flocked wallpaper. If not for the crutches, she would have blended in with the décor and never been noticed by anyone.

A time traveler should be invisible—her rules—leaving behind only fading footsteps, but the *thump, thump, swing, swing* of the crutches and the *swish* of her silk gown turned her into a spectacle as she crutched across the parterre. Out of curiosity, the crowd parted for her, as if she were following Moses through the Red Sea.

Women whispered behind open fans, and men cocked their heads in amusement. None of these people had ever seen a person walk—head high, weight fully on the handgrips—with the aid of two crutches, and she was determined to make her three-point gait as graceful as possible.

Jefferson, with his height, fair skin, and red hair, was recognized immediately with waves and nods. He might not have attained the nearly universal love and affection Benjamin Franklin enjoyed during his eight years as ambassador, but he managed to be an effective and competent representative of America, and he was well respected.

The orchestra was positioned in a semicircle in front of the stage. Each musician had a burning candle on their music stand, and several large crystal chandeliers with dozens of candles lit the center of the theatre. Sconces mounted on the walls and candelabra inside the boxes provided additional lighting.

With all the burning candles, the wooden structure could quickly go up in flames, trapping everyone inside. The thought of a fire immediately reminded her of the Bastille. She stopped and stared at Jefferson.

"What's wrong?" he asked.

"I just need a minute to locate the exits. Do you know where they are?"

"There may be one in the back, but the front entrance is the only one I'm aware of. Do you want to leave?"

"No. I mean…I don't know. But what if there's a fire?" A lump of dread pinched her throat. Why weren't these people worried? Didn't they know how easy it would be to die in a stampede? "All these people couldn't possibly get out through one exit." She shot a hard look to the right, to the left. "Why aren't there emergency exits?"

His nose wrinkled. "Emergency exits?"

This would never do. She couldn't stay here.

"Sophia, there's no need to worry. Lafayette wouldn't bring his best champagne if there was a possibility the theatre could go up in flames."

If Jefferson thought that would make her smile…he was right. She didn't disappoint, nor did she stop worrying. "Are you sure?"

"About the champagne?"

She managed to laugh. "Right. The champagne." She continued, swinging along behind the soldiers.

"His wine cellar is remarkable." Jefferson pointed ahead. "There he is now, leaning over the edge of the box. Do you see him?"

She looked in the direction he was pointing. "No, I don't. Is he wearing a uniform?"

"Not tonight. He has on a black coat. His box is the one closest to the stage."

"Oh, I see him now. Who's the woman?"

"The marquise," Jefferson said. "I thought Lafayette's aunt, Madame de Tessé, might be here as well. She's delightful, infinitely witty, and has been incredibly kind to Patsy."

"Lafayette has been a good friend to you."

"And to America. I was disoriented when I arrived here, but the disorientation produced clarity about myself and my native Virginia. I was constantly comparing the two—Europe and America. It was sometimes flattering, sometimes not. Europe might dazzle the traveler with its superior art, music, and architecture, but Americans are closer to nature, and thus to God."

She wasn't about to touch that pronouncement, even with the proverbial ten-foot pole. Jefferson was a deist who believed in one God, the creator, but he denied the occurrence of biblical miracles, the Virgin birth, and he'd literally cut the resurrection out of his supernatural-sanitized Bible.

She'd argue with him about the importance of rights for women and the enslaved from dawn to dusk, but never religion.

Sophia kept up her three-gait crutch, smiling her best *Mona Lisa* at the gawkers who cleared a wide path for her. Their expressions of curiosity and awe were both amusing and paintworthy.

"Mademoiselle Orsini," a man yelled.

She turned in the direction of the voice. Other than the Jefferson household, Lafayette, Watin, and David, she didn't know anyone else in Paris. Orsini was not an uncommon name in the eighteenth century. The man must be calling out to someone else. If she met another Orsini, what would she say?

"Mademoiselle Orsini," he yelled again.

Jefferson cast a glance around the theatre. "It's Monsieur David. He's up above. Do you see him?"

She looked toward the upper level of boxes and couldn't help grinning at the sight of his familiar face. All three of her rescuers were present, which somehow removed the heavy weight of worry from her mind.

"I could try to get up there. He's the most important painter in Paris. I should go to him," she said.

"The monsieur will find you during intermission. You'll be in the general's box, which always attracts a constant stream of visitors, Monsieur David among them."

"If you're rubbing shoulders with the rich and famous, you'll miss most of the opera. I'll tell you all about it on the way back to the Hôtel de Langeac." The melodrama in her tone was unbecoming, and she immediately regretted it.

"I won't abandon you, if that's what you mean to imply."

She relaxed her face and lightened her tone. "I know you won't."

He and Lafayette could flirt with every woman in the theatre, but from her study of the Founding Fathers, she'd learned the open display of French licentiousness appalled Jefferson. But even though French mores appalled him, the culture allowed him the freedom to pursue married women.

They arrived at the stairs leading to the rear of the private box. She assured the soldiers she could climb up unassisted, mainly because she didn't want to land on Lafayette's doorstep in a predicament similar to the one he found her in the day before. A girl had her pride.

The three stairs were narrow, with a short railing. She gave one crutch to Jefferson, who hovered again with arms outstretched, but she made it to the top without tumbling over. He reached in front of her and knocked on the door.

Lafayette opened it, making a sweeping bow. "Mademoiselle Orsini, welcome." He kissed her cheeks, shook hands with Jefferson. "Allow me to introduce my wife, Marie Adrienne Françoise de Noailles, Marquise de La Fayette."

Sophia didn't know whether to curtsy, shake the woman's hand, or just nod and smile. She went for a less than graceful curtsy-shake-nod-smile combination.

"I watched your progress through the parterre. Even with crutches, you move with grace and beauty," Lafayette said.

The heat in his stare was enough to bring a hot flush to her cheeks. The general was openly flirting with her. "Thank you, General," she managed to say.

"I must have a set."

"Of my grace and beauty?" she asked.

Lafayette looked puzzled, then he laughed. "Yes, by all means, mademoiselle."

She balanced on one foot, stacked the handles together, and gave them to him. "As soon as Mr. Jefferson applies for a patent, I'm sure he'll make a pair for you. But you can examine these."

"I only made a small adjustment to your design," Jefferson said.

"But your small adjustment makes them easier to mass market, and I'm not sure if a woman can apply for a patent in France or America."

"Come. Sit down, mademoiselle," the marquise said.

Clutching Jefferson's hand, she hopped the short distance to a chair next to the marquise, the strength in his muscled arm steadying her. As his thumb slipped over her knuckle, she blinked up at him, unsure of what the half smile on his chiseled face meant. He whispered, "When we can speak privately, I'll ask you to explain 'mass market' and 'assembly line.'"

"The concepts are related," she murmured.

Jefferson held her as she lowered to the seat.

"Ambassador," Lafayette said, "I don't know if you've met the comte de Mirabeau."

"Excuse me." Jefferson left her with the marquise and went to meet the newcomer.

The marquise waved her fan, and the candles in the candelabra behind her sputtered. Sophia kept an eye on the erratic flames. "You have obviously met with misfortune. What happened?" she asked. "My husband said you were in an accident but didn't elaborate."

Sophia opened the fan attached to her wrist by a ribbon, checked to make sure there wasn't an open flame behind her, and fanned herself vigorously. Navigating the parterre and climbing the stairs, all the while carrying an extra twenty pounds in clothes, had been an exhausting workout.

"I was so excited to meet the ambassador that I didn't watch where I was going and stepped into a hole. I went forward, but my knee went left, and I landed on Mr. Jefferson's chest and fell backwards. Only his quick reflexes kept me from landing in the dirt."

The marquise's eyes brightened. She tilted back her head, exposing the pale column of her neck to the candlelight, and laughed throatily, accelerating the speed of her fan. "The ambassador is so gallant. I feel confident that he swept you into his arms and carried you into the Hôtel de Langeac, where he is keeping you all to himself, depriving the rest of Paris of your beauty and charm." She paused and fanned herself while appraising Sophia with a speculative look. "I asked the marquis to demand your presence tonight so I could see you for myself."

"I wondered why Mr. Jefferson insisted I attend the opera tonight."

"The marquis can be very persistent," the marquise said, her eyes twinkling. "As can I. Now tell me, when will you be able to walk? I want to introduce you at Court so you will be admitted everywhere in Versailles. The Court genealogist will research your lineage to verify your nobility, but Monsieur David has already informed me that you are of the Gravina line of Orsinis. Since their line dates back to the son of Count Carlo of Bracciano in the mid-fourteen-hundreds, you will be admitted, and I will serve as your presenting lady for that very occasion."

What a terrifying thought. Sophia's lineage could be traced back to the old count, but the genealogist would never find a link to her. Fortunately, with all the upheaval in the city, the possibility of being presented at Court was slim to nonexistent. But just to be on the safe side, she added a few weeks to her expected recovery, and instead of two to four, she said, "It'll take six to twelve weeks before I can walk normally again."

"So long? *Mon Dieu.*" The marquise waved her fan dramatically. "Then the genealogist can proceed with verifying your lineage so there'll be no delay once you've recovered." She patted Sophia's lap. "And you're too enchanting to be hobbling into a room. You should be waltzing in on Mr. Jefferson's arm." She set her opera glasses on a shelf built into the short wall overlooking the parterre. "I watched you from the moment you entered the theatre. I don't know any woman who could have pulled off an entrance the way you did. Look at them down there." She waved her fan, encompassing the crowd below. "They're all abuzz about you. So tell me everything, before they've knitted a tale together that won't have a nit's worth of truth to it."

The marquise was too sweet to lie to, but Sophia had to tell the same story she'd told Jefferson. Short and sweet. "I'm an artist."

"I know."

"I've been living in Italy."

"I know that."

"I'm returning to America."

"I know that, too. I also know Mr. Jefferson has commissioned portraits of his daughters, and, since you are unable to walk, you're residing at the Hôtel de Langeac. I also know my husband came to your rescue yesterday."

"I was so frightened! I thought for sure the carriage was going to roll off the bridge into the Seine. If the general hadn't arrived when he did, I might be at the bottom of the river right now."

"How horrid." The marquise shivered. "The marquis said you were extraordinarily brave. After watching your entrance tonight, I agree. You have charmed the marquis, my dear, as you have me and Ambassador Jefferson."

Sophia didn't know how to respond, especially to the part about charming the ambassador. She knew she had piqued his curiosity. But charmed him?

Her eyes met his for a moment, and the room went still and the candles stopped sputtering. She studied his smooth, too-handsome face, searching for a clue to his thoughts, his intentions. She closed her fan and lowered it across her cheek. But when his eyes widened, she panicked.

She glanced at the marquise, whose brow was pinched with worry. Her red lips parted and then squeezed back into a tense line. Sophia whispered, "Did I just say something to Mr. Jefferson with my fan?"

The marquise nodded. "I love you."

Sophia rolled her eyes and groaned. "How do I say the signal was a mistake? Or I'm sorry?"

The marquise was trying her best to hold in a laugh, but the corners of her eyes creased with amusement. "Draw the closed fan slowly in front of your eyes."

She did just as the marquise described, only she didn't dare look at him. The last thing she wanted was to give the impression she had feelings for him. She liked him, enjoyed him, and she'd even had a fantasy or two about him. But love…? Heavens no.

"Mademoiselle Orsini," the marquise said, "if you don't gaze into his eyes, it won't have the proper meaning. It's all about the eyes, darling."

Sophia turned toward him and drew the fan in front of her eyes again, but this time she gazed at him. He nodded slightly. She didn't know what message she was sending or what he was receiving, but she decided to put the fan away before she accidentally propositioned him.

"Did I do it right?"

"Perfectly," the marquise said. "Of course, he'll wonder what you're apologizing for."

"Good grief."

The marquise trilled a laugh, up the scale and down. Then, smiling, she picked up the opera glasses and scanned the crowd. Watching her, Sophia had a vision of Jefferson standing on the bow of a sailing ship, telescope in hand, searching the sea…

She shivered, and the image shattered into thousands of pieces.

"When you finish painting the ambassador's daughters," the marquise said, "I want to commission you to paint my portrait." Once again, she set the glasses aside. "I'd like you to stay with us on the Rue de Bourbon if it's convenient."

Only once had she accepted a commission from a patron who had never seen her work. A man she met at an art exhibit wanted a small painting of his wife standing on the Ponte Vecchio. He'd been so pleased with the painting that he requested a formal portrait and had even flown Sophia to London to paint it. On top of the commission, he gave her a thank-you gift—a ticket to see *Hamilton*.

"You haven't even seen my work. You may decide I don't have talent."

"No, I haven't. But now that I've met you, and based on Monsieur David's observations, I have no doubt you are extraordinarily talented."

"Your blind faith is astounding."

The marquise's dark brown eyes softened. "Isn't that what faith is? Believing in what we cannot see."

"Then thank you for your faith in me. I'm leaving Paris in another week or so to sail to America, but if I have time before I leave, I'd love to paint your portrait."

"Surely not. You can't even walk. You *must* wait until Mr. Jefferson leaves Paris and travel with his party. I'll speak to him about those arrangements."

"He doesn't know when he'll be permitted to leave, and I need to go home."

Sophia didn't know much about Lafayette's wife other than she was a woman of extraordinary courage and was from one of the wealthiest families in France. Arguing with her was pointless. So she changed the subject. "Tell me about your children."

And so she did...

After an animated conversation about children and other Americans the marquise had entertained in her salon, she ended with a question Sophia couldn't answer. "How do you intend to paint Mr. Jefferson?" The marquise glanced over her shoulder. "As he is now, engrossed in the business of his country, or with symbols of his accomplishments?"

"An interesting question, indeed. I'd prefer to paint him surrounded by his passions—books, gardens, architecture, art, wine—but we haven't reached an understanding regarding pose and elements."

"Are you discussing my portrait?" Jefferson handed glasses of champagne to her and the marquise.

Sophia accepted the champagne flute. "I didn't know you were paying attention to us."

"You've had the full attention of my left ear, and the general the right." He pulled up a chair beside her. "The performance is about the start."

Lafayette sat down on the other side of his wife as the violins began to play.

"What do you know of the performance tonight?" she asked.

"A one-act *arlequinade,* or romantic farce in verse, entitled *Les Deux Billets* will be performed first, then the light opera *Richard Coeur de Lion.*"

Sophia tipped her glass, pinging it against his. "Thank you for insisting I come out with you, although it was very stressful getting here. Hopefully the trip home will be less so."

"It should be quieter. But if it's not, we'll circle around to avoid the mob."

She held the crystal up to appraise the color. "Clear, bright, pale yellow gold." She stuck her nose in the glass. "Yellow fruits, apricots, peaches, and dried fruit." Then she tried a sip. "Crisp. Apple. Dry. The acidity cuts right through to give the wine a great lift of freshness on the finish. I like it."

"What would you pair it with?"

"This is a balanced, food-friendly champagne." She sipped again. "I'd pair it with a simple grilled red meat without sauce, or crisp, cooked, and seasoned pan-fried vegetables." She held it up again. "Is this a Bollinger?"

He shook his head, and when he started to speak, she pressed her fingers against his lips. The previous owner of the Champagne House of Bollinger was Monsieur Dorsay's small Aÿ-Vineyard. "I'm mistaken. It's not a Bollinger. It's Monsieur Dorsay's Aÿ-Champagne. Right?"

He fixed her with a steely gaze. "How do you know?"

She couldn't tell him she'd dated a wine broker—a one-trick pony. All he ever talked about was wine, and while she finally tired of him and his cheating, she never tired of wine tastings. "I paint. I listen."

He hung his arm over the top of her chair, leaning closer. She inhaled deeply, picking up the musky scent of him just as the violins, graceful and elegant as swans on water, began to play. It was a head-spinning combination of delicious champagne, a handsome man, and violins.

She turned her attention to the stage as the violins turned urgent, then slowed to serene again, an astonishing transition as if the swans took flight. She emptied her glass and, without asking, the general refilled it, clinking the bottle against the flute.

"You and the marquise were talking as old friends," Jefferson said, also accepting a refill from the general.

"Conversations about children are timeless."

There was something shocking in his expression, in his eyes: an intensity of purpose hard and clean as polished steel. "I didn't know you had children."

"No, I've never—" She caught herself before saying she'd never been married. "My art has filled my life in place of marriage and children."

"I haven't seen an Orsini painting yet, but I find it impossible to imagine art to be more satisfying for a woman than serving her husband and giving him heirs."

She looked at him over the rim of her glass. Hadn't he heard anything she'd said about women's rights? If he'd been listening, he wouldn't have asked. Instead of repeating herself, she said, "If you must know, my parents didn't approve of my choice. Instead of marrying someone I didn't love, I became an artist."

"Do you regret it?"

"I've had a good life, Thomas. But when I see couples who love each other and have shared a lifetime together, I'm jealous. I know you had a good marriage. Usually men who've had a happy marriage end sadly want to remarry."

He sat back in his chair. "I promised Martha on her deathbed that I wouldn't remarry."

"I'm sure at the time it was the right thing to say. But you're a handsome, loving man, and you deserve a partner. You're in your mid-forties, and could live another forty years. Do you want to spend the rest of your life alone?"

"Do you?"

She smiled. "I'm not in my mid-forties yet."

Lafayette returned to his chair, and the opera began immediately, as if the performers had been waiting for him to take his seat. At intermission, Jefferson and Lafayette stood to talk with a constant flow of visitors. Sophia watched the people moving in and out of the box, looking for Monsieur David. If he couldn't come to her, she would go to him.

The marquise patted Sophia's arm to get her attention. "Look. There's Monsieur David."

The artist sidled up to their box, and, while standing on the floor, reached up, clasped the marquise's hand, and kissed her fingers. He then reached for Sophia's and kissed hers.

"Madonna, I heard about your accident. How is your knee?"

"Better."

"I spoke to Monsieur Watin this evening, and he told me everything. I'm jealous he's spent so much time with you. When will you sit for me? I know you intend to leave Paris soon. Will tomorrow be convenient?"

It would push back her other projects, but she couldn't say no. "I'm scheduled to start painting Mr. Jefferson's daughters in the morning. What time and where?"

"The general said carriages won't be allowed on the streets, and you're in no position to ride on horseback. I will come to the Hôtel de Langeac midafternoon." He kissed their hands again, and off he went.

"To meet Monsieur David, Ambassador Jefferson, and General Lafayette in two days is remarkable," the marquise said.

"And all three have come to my rescue." Sophia would rather have skipped the trauma, not met any of them, and proceeded with her plan to sit for Vigée Le Brun. She would have returned home with a portrait and no heartbreak. Now all bets were off.

"I didn't recognize the general tonight without his uniform, but he is just as handsome in his black coat."

"I'm fortunate that my husband stays fit when so many let themselves go, allowing marital contentment to expand them like big, round balloons. Even if Mr. Jefferson were married, I don't believe it would be the case with him. I heard he's a firm believer in physical exercise and walks four miles a day."

"It ensures bodily health and mental health, as well," Jefferson said.

"Oh, was your left ear listening again?" Sophia teased.

The orchestra began to warm up, and Jefferson returned to his chair. "You've had my full attention all evening."

She gave him a skeptical look. "I doubt that, but if I've had your left ear, that's sufficient." She fiddled with the gold and platinum necklace dangling at her décolletage.

"And why is that?"

"Because it's closest to your heart." Her fluttering fingers drew his eyes to her cleavage. She withdrew her hand immediately, and it joined the other, gripping her glass.

"Is it?" he asked, his gaze lifting. "I thought it was centered in your chest."

"It tilts left." Her face heated, and her blood rose under the sizzle of his attention. She raised her glass to her lips for a sip that turned into a gulp. "You missed Monsieur David, but you can see him tomorrow afternoon when he comes to the Hôtel de Langeac."

"I saw him during the intermission and asked him to stop by the box since you couldn't go to him. I look forward to welcoming him to the Hôtel de Langeac. But if you're going to sit for him, you'll have to postpone your departure. You've committed to painting Patsy, Polly, and the marquise—"

"And you," she said softly.

"If you sit for him, you won't have time to finish those paintings."

"It'll require several long days, but I believe I can manage."

Jefferson turned toward her, lounging on one hip, and hung his arm on the back of her chair. "I've consulted both Nathaniel Cutting, an American living in Le Havre, and Mr. Trumbull in London, to search for passage to America. The accommodations I've requested allow room for an additional passenger."

While considering a response, she slowly turned the stem of the crystal goblet. If she said yes he would include her in his plans. If she said no, he would continue to pressure her. "You're going to

Monticello. I'm going to New York City."

He was sitting in shadow, making it hard to see his full expression. "When we arrive in Norfolk, I'll hire a carriage to carry us to Richmond. We'll spend a few days at Mallory Plantation while I meet with legislators. Then we'll continue on to Monticello."

Mallory Plantation? It had to be the same estate owned by New York Times best-selling author Jack Mallory. She'd seen online pictures of his wedding, which was held in an expansive yard near a three-hundred-fifty-year-old willow oak on the banks of the James River. At the time she'd thought what a fabulous portrait it would have made, and even considered soliciting a commission.

Instead she listened to Mallory's audiobooks. The action and drama in his Civil War story pulled her to the edge of her seat and wouldn't let go, as his characters raced through Richmond the night it burned. His follow-up book about finding the Confederate gold was equally mesmerizing. The intensity of his vivid writing had her believing she was in the story, feeling the heat from the burning buildings. Now she wondered if he'd been there—on the streets of Richmond, at Ford's Theatre, and later in the cave where the treasure was found. Was Jack Mallory a time-traveler? She knew three other brooches existed. Someone had them. Why not him?

She tucked thoughts of Mallory into her mental file cabinet and considered Thomas's proposal, which was completely out of the question.

"I can't tour Virginia. I have to go to New York," she said.

"The first of the year, I'll take you there and stay to see you settled." His voice was the same—formal, yet soft and easy at the same time, rumbling naturally from his throat. She adored his voice, and she couldn't deny that listening to him, debating with him, even drinking wine together, made her dizzy with the newness of infatuation.

The actors appeared, and Sophia turned her attention to the action onstage, which saved her from giving him an answer or pondering the possibility of other travelers. She tried to concentrate but failed miserably, because different scenarios played and replayed in her mind. Could she stay longer? Could she travel to America with him?

No. Even if the brooch allowed it, what was the point? This wasn't her time or place. Like it or not, that's the way it was.

22

Richmond, VA—JL

J L SPOKE SOFTLY to Lawrence. "I'm going to hold your hand, sweetheart."

Most of the touching her preemie received was from the medical team, who pricked his foot, fed him, or adjusted his tubes, always tugging and pulling, stressing his tiny body. So for now, she and Kevin only held his hand or let him grasp their finger. JL's arms twitched with her desperation to hold her baby, but he was still too small, his skin too sensitive.

Lawrence had been through so much in the past four days. What would today bring? His lung event set him back, but since then he was doing well and had gained several grams.

JL had adapted to the cords, attachments, and quiet beeps, and was learning more about him every hour…the way he moved or cried out in his preemie whimper. Whenever an alarm sounded, her heart rate shot up like a puck in a game of strike-the-bell.

They'd met with Lawrence's health care team three times to discuss his treatment and prognosis. When JL repeatedly asked the same questions, Kevin became alarmed over her inability to concentrate, and, along with her constant headaches, he was concerned she might be suffering secondary trauma from the plane crash.

At his urging, Charlotte requested a neurological consult and a brain scan was ordered. The scans were clear but that didn't eliminate the possibility JL was suffering from PTSD. A psychiatric assessment was scheduled. JL agreed to meet with a psychiatrist, but since she refused all medications because she was breastfeeding, she was referred to a psychotherapist. The upshot was that she agreed, without arm twisting, to attend psychotherapy sessions and spend fewer hours at the hospital until she fully recovered from surgery.

That was the hardest part, but she agreed to the strict schedule because she knew firsthand how important her mental and physical health were to her family.

Kevin spent his mornings at the NICU and afternoons with Blane, either bringing him to the hospital for a visit or sitting in class with him. During the evenings Kevin floated back and forth between the NICU and JL at the hotel. Their hotel suite, thanks to Amber Kelly Grant, was stocked with gourmet freeze-dried food.

As for Blane, someone in the family often sent them pictures. In all the photos, he was either laughing or wearing the serious face he used when he read books assigned by Uncle Matt. The man was a godsend, a full-time grandfather and historian. All the MacKlenna men inspired the children, but Matt was gifted at challenging the kids to read, learn, and share.

Two of Matt's three grandkids were younger than Blane. After Matt added the children's edition of *The Three Musketeers* to their reading list, the boys decided they wanted to be musketeers. They constantly quoted the pledge: "All for one and one for all," but they twisted the words around and chanted: "All for all and one for one."

"Mommy!"

JL jerked, startling Lawrence, who whimpered at the sudden movement. She kept her hand wrapped around his, hoping to still him, but pulled her other hand out of the porthole and held a finger to her lips. "Shh. The babies are sleeping."

Blane's eyes and his O-mouth were huge as he tiptoed toward her. "Sorry, Mommy," he whispered. Then he turned to the other two moms in the room and apologized, still whispering, "I'm sorry."

Both women smiled.

JL slowly withdrew her other hand and sat back in the recliner. Blane shucked his backpack before climbing up into her lap. His hair and skin smelled of apple and amber and cedarwood.

"Did you shower with Daddy?"

Blane raised his arm and sniffed his shirt. "Do I smell like him? I used his new shampoo and soap."

She patted the top of his head. "And sculpturing gel."

"He has more bottles of stuff than you, Mommy." He sniffed her hair. "You smell different than we do."

"I smell like hospital and hotel. And those smells don't come out of a bottle."

"Next time I'll bring your shampoo so you'll smell like you're s'posed to." He sniffed her clothes. "Pew-eee. Hospital smell." He scooted around in her lap, his elbow digging into her belly.

She groaned.

"What's wrong? You got gas?"

"No, buddy. My stomach's sore."

He gently patted her belly. "It's all squishy in there. It used to be hard. What happened?"

"Lawrence isn't inside me anymore. Remember the book we read about how babies were born? He's in the incubator now."

Blane glanced over his shoulder at Lawrence, then looked back at JL's stomach, then back to the incubator. "The wrinkly doll in that box with all that stuff is my brother?" He curled his lip. "Will he iron out? Grandpa Elliott doesn't like wrinkles. I don't either."

"He doesn't have enough body fat yet, but he'll grow into his skin." JL wanted to laugh and cry, but she couldn't do either.

"Daddy told me if I wasn't quiet I couldn't come back to see you and the wrinkly guy. I like visiting Aunt Charlotte's hospital, but I'm not coming back up here until the laundry fixes him."

JL's lip quivered. "It's not kind to talk about the way Lawrence looks or the way anyone looks. You'll hurt their feelings. Lawrence is a preemie. He didn't stay inside me long enough to gain weight. But he will, and then he'll be handsome like you and your daddy."

Blane's expression turned downcast. "Is that a sure thing, or a maybe?"

"A sure thing," she said.

"Okay, I'll wait for him to get cute like me."

"We need to work on humility."

"What's 'umility? Like when it's hot and sticky outside?"

"No, that's humidity. Humility is having a truly grateful heart."

He clapped his hand over his chest. "I have a grateful heart. I'm grateful for you and Daddy, and Grandpa Elliott and Grandma Mere, and Pops and Maria." He glanced at the incubator. "And I'm thankful for my big brother and my little brother. That's grateful, right?"

She hugged him. "Right."

Blane reached for his MacKlenna green pack, unzipped it, and whipped out a stuffed white horse with black dots. "Grandpa Elliott took me shopping, and I found this horse. I paid for it with my own money. I named him Stormy, cuz Stormy went on a hard trip and came home skinny, like Lawrence. I want this Stormy to 'spire wee Lawrence to get strong and come home soon to play with me."

"It's a cute horse. An Appaloosa, right?"

"They didn't have a thor-bred like Grandpa Elliott's horses. I figured wee Lawrence didn't know the difference yet. I'll 'splain it all to him when he gets older. He's goin' to get older, right?"

JL wasn't sure how to answer him. Blane was too young to understand life and death. "He's older than he was yesterday but younger than he'll be tomorrow."

"I heard Aunt 'Lizabeth talking to Uncle Matt. She said when Lawrence has his first birthday, he won't really be one."

"Well…that's kinda complicated," JL said. "Preemies have a chronological age based on their actual birthday, and a corrected age based on when they should have been born."

Blane held his hand over JL's mouth. "Stop talking, Mommy. Too comp-e-cated." Blane pushed away from JL's embrace, climbed down, and stood next to the incubator. "I washed my hands, so I can touch him."

"Let's wipe them off, just in case Stormy has horse germs." She squirted hand sanitizer on her hands and wiped his between her own. "Now you can touch your brother, but you have to be gentle, remember? Just touch his hand."

"I won't make him cry. I'll touch just his finger. Uncle Matt showed me inca-bator babies on his Google machine."

"What's that?" JL asked.

Blane seemed to chew on the answer for a moment. "Well, see… I was eating Cheerios this morning in the big house kitchen. The TV was on, and Mornin' Joe said to use your neighbor's Google machine to get answers." Blane tilted his head. "I should tweet Mornin' Joe to let him know my iPad has google."

She couldn't hold back a smile. "What'd you learn on your Google machine?"

"Uncle Matt looked it up on his iPad. He said when I touch my brother I have to go like this"—Blane made short up and down motions with his hand—"because Lawrence has plugs to keep his blood from running out. You think blood is yucky, so I hope the plugs work."

"You're right. I don't like it."

"Daddy used to ride in an am-lance, so he 'splained it. The cords—" He stopped talking when Anne paused at Lawrence's incubator. Blane's face pinched with concern. He whispered, "Am I too loud?"

She squatted to be eye level with him. "No, you're fine. It's Blane, right?"

He cocked his head. "How'd you know my name?"

Anne pointed to a picture of him taped to the side of the incubator. "Your mommy taped a picture of you there. So what do you think of this little guy?"

"I think he's itty-bitty and wrinkly, and Grandpa Elliott doesn't like wrinkles." Blane picked up the horse. "This is Stormy. He'll teach the itty-bitty guy how to be big and strong. I want to put it in the inca-bator."

"We have to sanitize it first. Is that okay?" Anne asked.

"I know what that means! You're gonna take out the vi-lence and dirty words. Uncle Matt sometimes san-tizes his lectures for us kids. But I don't mind." He shoved the horse into Anne's hands. She wobbled and almost toppled over. He grabbed her shoulder. "Be careful there, sweetheart."

JL rolled her eyes and mouthed, "I'm sorry." Blane mimicked male family members' mannerisms and expressions. When he'd first repeated a four-letter word, they all promised to clean up their language. They still slipped and yelled *hell* this or *damn* that now and again, and Blane repeated every cussword.

Blane checked the timer on his watch. Kevin often set it to teach Blane the concept of time and how to count backwards from fifteen. The timer told him exactly how many minutes he had left to watch sports on TV or play a game on his iPad. Soccer was his passion— or, as they called it in Europe—football. He knew all the top European clubs and watched as many games as he could.

"I only have a few more minutes," Blane said. "Will ye show me how to touch the lad so I can be on my way?"

Anne stood, pressing her fist to her lips to smother a laugh. "Let's sanitize your hands and I'll show you."

"I did that already." Then he smacked his forehead. "I touched Stormy. He has horse germs." He turned toward JL. "Hit me again, ma'am."

JL squirted sanitizer on his hands. "Now do what Nurse Anne tells you, and you can touch his little fingers."

He stood next to the incubator, carefully following Anne's directions, slipped his arms through the portholes. He touched Lawrence's index finger. "My finger is bigger than his foot, Mommy. Hurry up, little guy, and get out of here so we can play."

Lawrence clasped Blane's finger. Blane's eyes were huge when he looked over at JL. "He grabbed my finger. He knows it's me. Oh, ye're a cutie, wee laddie. I think ye'll look just like me. Don't you think so, Mommy?"

"I think he will, buddy."

Blane slipped his hands out of the portholes. "That's all for today, wee laddie." He looked up at Anne, "Will you tell the doctors to take all that stuff off him, so I can hold him next time? Mommy told me I'll be able to hold the baby and read to him."

"All the stuff helps him eat and breathe," Anne said.

"Mommy said he'll get milk from her breasts like I did. He doesn't need all that other stuff," he said, waving his hand toward the incubator.

"Lawrence can't suck yet, so we put your mommy's milk in that tube in his belly."

"Oh." For an instant he looked confused, unsure of himself, then he quickly righted to what JL called his O'Grady goofy look.

"Where'd you leave Daddy?" JL asked.

Blane leaned to the right, leaned to the left. "We came in here together, but he's dis-ta-peared now. Guess he found"—Blane clicked his tongue—"a cute chick in the pod next door and stopped to make her 'quaintance."

"I'll see if your dad is out in the hallway," Anne said. "I'll let him know you're looking for him."

"How come you're talking like a cowboy? Who've you been hanging out with?" JL asked. "The twins?"

"Nobody 'cept Uncle Rick. We've been FaceTiming. He's coming to town tonight with Austin." Blane cut a glance toward the incubator. "Hey, I've got a big brother, and so does he. I'm a big brother now. Ain't that cool!" He lifted his shoulders and pressed down the front of his shirt. "Uncle Rick said he'd take me out for a ride on a Western saddle instead of a sissy hunt one. Daddy wants me to compete in eventing. But I want to be in a rodeo."

JL's heart burst to overflowing, pushing aside the fear and anxiety that had consumed her for days. She'd missed Blane's hugs, his stories, and most of all his bigger-than-life appreciation of the world. "Your daddy is such a good rider he almost went to the Olympics. Don't you want to ride like him?"

"Sure, Mommy. But I want...you know...to be out there on a branch."

After a puzzled moment, she said, "Oh, you mean you want to

branch out and not limit yourself to just one type of riding."

"That's what I said. To be out on a branch."

She hugged him. "You're too funny." She opened a bottle of water and took a long sip. "If you're going riding with Rick be careful. He's not the best rider in the family."

Blane snickered. "I've heard the story of how Noah outrode him when they were 'venturing in Colorado."

They'd never talked to Blane about the family's time-travel adventures, but it seemed someone had. She didn't want to talk about it now, so she changed the subject. "I'm glad he's taking you riding. Are you riding a pony?"

"Ain't no ponies at Mallory Planation."

"Please don't say ain't. It's not proper, even if you're using it to tease me."

He put his hand on his hip. "Well, shucks, ma'am. I'll do my best."

"So, cowboy, who's going riding? Just you and Rick?"

"No, ma'am. All the O'Grady dudes are going. They're going to teach me the things they taught Austin."

"Good grief. I didn't approve of half the things they taught Austin. Tell Uncle Rick I want to talk to him before he takes you out riding."

"Uncle Pete said he'd take care of me and make sure the O'Gradys don't teach me bad stuff."

She did an eyebrow-hike and watched him closely, half expecting him to jump on the Appaloosa and ride off into the sunset. "Uh...that's nice of Pete, but I don't trust him, either, when it comes to teaching my boys."

"But Uncle Pete's your partner, Mommy. You have to trust your partner. But don't worry. They're going to teach me family songs so I can sing with them. Uncle Connor said I could take your verses of 'Danny Boy.' What do ya think of that, sister?"

She chuckled. "I think you'll make a fine soprano."

His eyes narrowed, and his hand went to his throat. "Soprano? No can do. That's a girl's part. I'll tell the boys I don't want to sing a girl's part."

"I'm sure they'll let you do whatever you want. Would you like to sing softly to Lawrence?"

He flashed a look at his brother. "His ears work already? I didn't know that. Wait 'till I tell the O'Grady boys." Blane slapped his leg. "Man. They'll teach me hundreds of songs. I can sing to wee Lawrence till he comes home. But I don't know what's 'propriate to sing to a wee lad." He pursed his lips. "Molly Malone, I guess. She's got a statue in Dublin, you know. I've seen it. It's big. Turn on your phone and tape me."

JL pulled out her phone and pressed record. "Okay, I'm ready."

Blane cleared his throat then began to sing in a clear, high-pitched, perfectly tuned voice.

"In Dublin's fair city / Where the girls are so pretty / I first set my eyes on sweet Molly Malone / As she wheeled her wheelbarrow / Through the streets broad and narrow / Crying 'cockles and mussels, alive, alive, oh' / Alive, alive, oh / Alive, alive, oh / Crying 'cockles and mussels, alive, alive, oh.'"

Anne returned and clapped softly, as did the two moms who were doing kangaroo care with their preemies. JL had a hard knot deep in her throat, but she couldn't cry right now. Later she'd watch the video and cry her eyes out.

Blane crossed one arm over his waist and the other behind his back and executed a deep bow. "I've been singing that to wee Lawrence every night he's been in Mommy's ut-ur-us. Haven't I, Mommy?"

"You sure did, buddy." She gave his cheek an approving caress.

His watch beeped, and he tapped the stop button. "It's time to go." He looked up at Anne. "Can you take me to find my daddy?"

"Sure. I just saw him. He's right out in the hall talking to a couple of other dads."

"Do I get a goodbye hug?" JL asked.

"Sure, Mommy. I'll see you tomorrow." He kissed JL. Then he grabbed Anne's hand and towed her along to find Kevin.

They hadn't gone more than five feet when the heart monitor went *Beep! Beep! Beep!*

Anne dropped Blane's hand, turned back to the incubator. JL stood, unable to breathe. Lawrence was turning dusky blue. She pulled Blane aside and wrapped her arm around his shoulder.

Anne pushed the alarm cancel button then pressed the intercom to the entire unit. "D-3. Code down!"

Blane looked like a woodland deer. His eyes were huge as he swiveled his head, taking in the details of the NICU, the doctors and nurses gathering around Lawrence's incubator.

JL sat and pulled Blane into her lap, hugging him tightly.

"What's wrong, Mommy? What's wrong with wee Lawrence? Didn't he like my singing?" Blane's cheeks quivered, and fearful tears clustered at the corners of both eyes.

She didn't answer Blane right away, only sat there with him curled in her lap. He felt so good, so alive, so fragrant, an apple-scented bouquet of tender limbs tucked into her own. The precious bundle needed reassurance, or he'd be too scared to come up to see his brother again.

The room turned silent around her as her mind pulled back, distancing herself emotionally from the traumatic scene playing out in front of her. Kevin was with her when Lawrence had his last crisis, but he wasn't there now, and she had to stay strong for both her sons.

Finally, she said, "I don't know, buddy. The doctors and nurses will make him better. We just have to pray." She held a shaky hand to her forehead and shivered a little, the way she'd done lately after a long cry, when the fear fled, and she was left with nothing but the knowledge that, sooner or later, it would return and consume her again. A rush of trepidation overcame her, a premonition of something formidable, complicated. Something she didn't want to face.

"Okay, Mommy. I'll pray." He made a steeple with his hands, held them under his chin, closed his eyes. "God, this is Blane Fraser. Please help my brother. And, God, if you have time, will you take care of Mommy, too? Amen." He opened his eyes and gazed up at her, his shoulders squaring bravely. "When will we know?"

She couldn't take her eyes off Lawrence while he was being handled by a doctor. She couldn't read the name on her white coat, but JL didn't think she'd met the doctor before. "What, buddy?"

"When God will answer? Right now, or tonight?"

"Soon. I hope soon."

"I'll help while I wait on Him." He pushed her arms away and climbed down. "I'm not scared now, Mommy. Daddy takes care of me when I'm hurt. I'll take care of you and my brother."

As if he'd aged years, he moved to stand next to Anne and watched closely while she pricked Lawrence's heel with a lancet and squeezed blood into a tube while others checked connections and monitor readings. Blane grimaced, but didn't move away. Then he clasped his hands behind his back, stood straight in his MacKlenna Corporation khakis and polo shirt, feet set slightly apart, like a soldier standing sentry.

Kevin leaned over her chair, startling her. "What's going on?" he asked.

She shook her head, hoping a quick shake would relieve the sting in her eyeballs, and said in a tight voice, "Another event. He was fine, and then the alarm went off."

"What's Blane doing? Isn't he in the way?"

"I guess not," she said. In profile, Blane's long, curling lashes, the angle of his cheekbone in the slant of the NICU lighting, were indelibly imprinted in her brain. She wanted her little boy back. But he'd disappeared into the role of protective older brother, just like Austin did after Blane's birth.

"Jesus." Kevin made a move to go to Blane, but JL reached for his hand and squeezed it.

Blane, standing still in place, turned his head ever so slowly and mouthed. "I got this."

JL clutched a crumpled tissue to her chest and watched the faces of Lawrence's medical team for signs of worry or tension. They were there, but professionally held in check. A queasy feeling stirred the bottom of her belly. Her pulse fell into her fingertips thumping against Kevin's fingers. He glanced down at her, then knelt and pulled her into his arms.

"We have to keep praying. We won't give up," he whispered.

When she looked at him, she saw something like fear, or perhaps even desperation, in his eyes. Lawrence let out the sharp cry she'd learned was his "I hurt," cry, and JL shivered with a deep, convulsive shudder that challenged her faith.

Blane's little hand patted her shoulder, and her body slackened under his touch. "Don't cry, Mommy. God's taking care of him now."

23

Paris (1789)—Sophia

THE MORNING AFTER Sophia attended the opera with Jefferson, she awoke, determined to just do it—*fallo e basta*.

She had three portraits to paint and multiple sittings for Monsieur David. The fastest she'd ever painted one portrait was seventy-two hours. If she did nothing else for the next eleven days except sleep a few hours each night, she'd still have to break her seventy-two-hour record to paint three portraits. Without student questions, studio walk-ins, finances, marketing, shopping, phone interruptions, and preparing food, it was doable, although it might kill her.

The schedule meant no socializing or flirting with Jefferson, which had to stop anyway. She enjoyed it too much, and it would only lead to a broken heart—his, hers, or both. In the past few years he'd mourned the death of his wife, two daughters, and a relationship with Maria Cosway. And if Sophia's memory of the Meacham audiobook was correct, fear that Sally would remain in Paris to live in freedom instead of returning to her enslaved life at Monticello would be another potential loss to grieve.

Sophia didn't want to cause him more sorrow nor did she want to be an aphrodisiac for his grief. So she cloistered herself in her studio with paint and brushes, and sent regrets to dozens of invitations to attend salons, including Adrienne de La Fayette's. She also turned down Jefferson's private dinner invitations but had joined the family and Mr. Short for meals in the dining room.

Jefferson often came into the studio at night to talk. Sometimes he had something specific on his mind, and other times he just wanted a companion. On those occasions, she'd set down her brush and share a glass of wine with him.

Spending time with Patsy and Polly remained an important part of each day. While she worked, she answered their questions, gave advice, and taught Polly how to paint. Being with them was a balancing act. While she didn't encourage an attachment to her, she couldn't stop it from happening. Selfish, maybe. But she adored them.

Their portraits were among her very best work. The girls looked splendid in their chemise gowns of pure white muslin and straw hats. Patsy's copper ringlets draped her shoulders while Polly's dark hair was partially tied back in a blue ribbon.

Neither of them had wanted to smile. So Sophia used Leonardo's technique for creating *Mona Lisa* smiles for them, and she absolutely loved the results. When she gazed at their portraits, both girls smiled back mysteriously without actually smiling. And each portrait captured their essence. For Patsy—intelligence and inner calm. And for Polly—strong will and a joyful spirit.

Jefferson hadn't seen the girls' finished portraits. Nor had he seen his own, which wasn't one of her best. It was *the best* work she'd ever done. She wasn't sure he would like it, though, since it was so different from other portraits of him.

Which was why she considered taking it home with her. It would sell for at least half a million dollars. But this painting would never be sold. Following her death, all her unsold paintings would go to the Metropolitan Museum of Art, including the five in her secret collection, although the idea always distressed her. The appraisers and art historians would never be able to explain their existence. But the paintings had to be preserved. Sending them to the Met was the only way to ensure that would happen.

The historians would never understand her Jefferson portrait either. The paints and support—the canvas, wood, or paper—would date the painting. The realism style and the age would contradict it.

She looked down at her hand, at the faint glint of the brush held between her fingers. Had she ever felt like this before? That if she didn't paint, she might dissolve and become like a rain puddle out in the garden…that if she didn't paint, she might even stop breathing? Yes, she'd felt like this for decades. It was her absolute passion. And always, she looked at the world and the people in it as if preparing to celebrate them on canvas.

She set aside brush and oval-shaped wooden palette and studied the painting before her. It was everything she wanted it to be—a man full of contradictions, a man she'd come to care for, far more than she ever intended.

"Sophia."

She jerked, embarrassed to be caught so off guard by the man who consumed her thoughts. Swiveling on her high stool, she slowly faced Jefferson and tried to control the rapid thud of her heart.

The dying sun flooded unchecked through the watery glass of one unopened French door. The perfume of the gardens filled the air. He stood there, leaning against the doorjamb, the ribbons of bright green shrubbery winding in every direction behind him.

"What are you doing out there?" she asked.

He levered himself away from the door, and, with his elastic stride, entered the room. "The hallway door was closed. I didn't want to interrupt." He paused and glanced around the studio before continuing, "I wouldn't have said anything, but when you put down your brush, I took a chance, hoping you wouldn't mind a visitor."

She wiped sweat off her forehead with the back of her hand. "I don't mind. I could use a break."

He strolled over to the two portraits covered with sheets, his hands folded modestly behind his back. "Have you finished Patsy and Polly's portraits?"

"They're both signed."

"Does that mean your signature is the finishing touch?"

"My John Hancock always appears on the lower right-hand

corner."

He looked over his shoulder at her, his face shadowed and quizzical. "John Hancock?"

Oops. Another slap-my-forehead moment.

She gave him an innocent smile. "I heard after Hancock signed the Declaration of Independence with such a large, flamboyant signature, that his name became a synonym for signing your name. As in, 'Put your John Hancock here.'"

He shook his head, as if it would transform her nonsense into something comprehensible. "My name is not John Hancock. Why would I want to sign it as such?"

"It's an expression to add color to your language. Like adding a flock of bluebirds to a snowy winter *plein air* painting."

"What's that?"

"A style of painting outside, where you depict the effects of natural light and atmosphere unlike what you find in the studio."

"Who paints like that?"

No one until mid-nineteenth century Paris.

"I do, and I'll show you."

"I'll add that to the list of your expressions, opinions, predictions, and ideas such as assembly line and emergency exits that I keep in my journal."

"Sounds like a list of Orsinisms."

"What are those?"

"Never mind. But please, don't write them down. There's no reason to keep a list."

"I don't want to forget. Some actually have merit."

She skipped her hands down the limp fabric of her linen dress, as if ironing out the wrinkles could iron out her many time-traveling foibles. Her underarms prickled. There was no relief from the heat—inside, outside, or in the depths of his eyes. And no relief from the clock ticking down to her final minutes in Jefferson's time.

"Whether they do or not, whatever I've said has been for your ears only. Off the record. Not to be printed." The thought of having so many futuristic references in his journal sent her stomach churning like an out of control merry-go-round. "You can't write them down."

"Why on earth not?"

"Because historians will pore over your journals and correspondence, and they won't understand my comments when they're taken out of context. Do them all a favor. Erase all mention of me."

"No one will be sifting through my writings, and why would I want to erase mention of you?"

"To quote you, Mr. Jefferson, 'Why on earth not?' Don't you pore over everything written by Locke, Newton, and Bacon?" A gust of guilt, anxiety, and stress blew through her chest in a fury, stealing even the breath she needed to calm herself. The more she talked, the deeper the hole she dug. But she wanted him to understand his place in history and how confused historians would be by her presence.

"The man who wrote the Declaration of Independence and was ambassador to France will be of great interest to future generations. Scholars will study your work, just as you have studied scholars of the past. My predictions and opinions are irrelevant in the scheme of things."

"It's too late, Sophia," he said with a touch of his gaze, as if laying his hands on her face. "For the past thirteen days I've written down everything you've said. From your predictions, to your food and wine pairings, to your views on women, slavery, education, and voting. One day you might be proven right, and those same historians you mentioned will wonder why I was too stubborn to listen to such an enlightened artist."

She grinned. "Oh, that's easy, Mr. Jefferson. Because I'm an enlightened *female* artist."

He smiled. "Clever point, Mademoiselle."

"The French have"—*or will have*— "a wonderful fencing word for making your point. It's *touché.*"

He tried out the word. *"Touché."*

"Anyway, when you reach your twilight years and decide to define and defend your legacy, go back through your journal and delete everything I said."

"Unless death sneaks up on me and I have no time to prepare, I'll reread everything you told me and consider its relevance."

"I guess that's the best I can ask."

"You are a unique woman, and I attribute your uniqueness to living on the continent during your impressionable years. I'm not sure how you'll adjust to America after living abroad."

She got down off the high stool in front of his portrait, putting most of her weight on her good leg. "Are you suggesting I stay in Paris?"

"No," he said, a deep sigh electrifying his response. "However, you should be aware that opinionated women in America aren't appreciated as they are here in France."

"We've had this conversation before. While I'd like to stay in Paris and live in a city that respects me as a woman, artist, and citizen, I don't want to live through a rebellion. It's going to be too violent for me to stay here."

"This revolt is inspired by the American Revolution. I anticipate a similar result. There's hope France will become a liberal democracy along the lines of America, and the ideals of the republic will spread throughout the world."

Good luck with that.

She wasn't ready for him to see the portraits. But the discussion needed a new direction, and painting was usually a safe enough topic. Besides, his curious eyes kept circling the room and hovering around her.

"Do you want to see the girls' portraits?"

"My curiosity has never been so piqued. Neither Patsy nor Polly would tell me a thing about them."

"They wanted to keep the paintings a secret so they could surprise you."

"I'll act surprised."

Giving him a preview was selfish on her part, but she decided to unveil them for one reason. If he didn't like the portraits, his disappointment would crush the girls. This way, she could at least try to minimize the damage. Give him time to adjust before he viewed the paintings in his daughters' presence.

"In less than two weeks you've created three portraits. That's unheard of."

"In two weeks, you wrote the Declaration of Independence. That's unheard of."

"Seventeen days." His lashes swept guardedly down over his eyes, as if silently re-counting each day, and how long he spent away from his family.

She left her crutches against the wall, and, hobbling on the ball of her foot, limped over to the paintings. On a scale of one to ten, the pain level was about a four. Her knee was improving, but it would probably take another two to three weeks before she'd be able to walk without favoring the leg.

He watched her closely. "Why aren't you using the crutches?"

"It's easier to get around in here if I hobble."

"But it still pains you?"

"Not as much, but it's taking longer to heal than I thought it would."

Her fingers curled around the edge of the canvas as she stood beside him, just close enough to feel him without touching him. Then she slowly reached for the top corner of the sheet. "Are you ready?"

He raised his hands in front of his chest, palms out, and gave her an anxious smile. "Wait. First, tell me. Are you pleased?"

She pressed a hand to her breasts, as if she could contain her pleased heart, which was thumping louder and faster with excitement. She gazed at him, and with all the sincerity she could muster said, "It's some of the best work I've ever done."

He nodded, a signal to let go of the sheet. A quick tug, and it swirled, white and gauzy, shimmering down over the painting, revealing her masterpiece inch by inch until the sheet puddled on the floor beneath the easel. He stood there in stunned silence.

The ticking mantel clock was the only indication of time passing. She wasn't sure he was even breathing. There was no eye flicker or facial tick. Nothing. She gulped.

"Say something. Please."

"Your sense of color, perspective, and composition is extraordinary. Patsy's fingers appear to move over the keyboard." He leaned in and sniffed. "I expected to smell the sweetness of the roses arranged in the vase. You can almost feel the velvety petals, the music vibrating through the instrument."

"How does the painting make you feel emotionally?" she asked tentatively.

He cocked his head, as if puzzled by the question. He crossed one arm over his chest and held his elbow in the palm of his hand. His fingers teased the point of his chin. "The roses are such a lovely shade of yellow. Each petal is poised in dewy perfection, and in different stages of blooming, much like Patsy during her years in Paris."

He stepped back a few feet, gazed at the canvas, then moved closer again. Sunset was maybe a half hour away, and the daytime radiance was gone. He was viewing the portrait in subdued light, but it didn't detract from the painting.

"I've heard of a hybrid yellow rose growing in the Afghan Empire, but I've never seen one. Have you?"

She tipped her head toward the painting. "Unlike a horticulturist, I can make roses any color I want. They're captivating, aren't they?"

He pulled out a small notebook and pencil. "It's the color of lemons, but I've heard the yellow rose has an unpleasant odor."

"What a shame," Sophia said. "The color is superb."

He pointed with his pencil. "The sheet of music on the fortepiano is the *Overture to Mozart's Don Giovanni.*"

"What do you know of it?" she asked.

"The piece builds to a long, extended, controlled crescendo, and you listen with expectation." He paused a moment while he tucked away his notebook and pencil. "As I've watched Patsy the past few years, she, too, has been moving, growing in her role. She'll be ready to marry when she returns to Virginia."

Sophia rested her hand on his arm, on the warm cotton of his jacket. "But that's not how you feel. That's what you see and experience. What do you feel in your heart, in your soul? What emotions are stirred?"

He stepped back and she dropped her arm. But he continued staring at the painting. "Loss of her childhood, but a grand hope for her future."

He smiled at Sophia, and she warmed all the way through to her toes.

"Her face beams with intelligence and sensibilities. You can see it in her eyes. She's an animated storyteller, agreeable, and cordial, and beloved by everyone she meets."

Sophia tilted her head and looked up at him. Curls around her temples had slipped from her kerchief, and he pushed away those wisps of sweaty hair. Then he nudged her chin up with his thumb, and her lips parted with a sharp intake of breath. He lowered his head and kissed her right in the middle of her waiting mouth. He tasted like honeyed tea, the same heated honey purling through her veins. Warm ripples of surprise thinned the air in her lungs. When he pulled back slightly, his eyes lingered on her mouth a moment before he kissed her again.

The kisses happened so quickly, she thought her imagination had taken over. She took in the vulnerability in his eyes, the fear in his face, and all she wanted to do was hold him, reassure him—but she couldn't.

"We should"—she pointed over her shoulder in the direction of the painting—"get back to the um…painting."

"I didn't plan to do that."

"If you hadn't kissed me, I might have kissed you."

"That would have surprised me."

"Don't you think a woman who believes she should have the right to vote would also believe she could kiss a man too stubborn to kiss her?"

His smile carved a dimple into one cheek, and then he laughed, a full and unexpected sound. "How could I not?"

"Well, then, I'm glad that's settled," she said, smiling. "Let's finish with Patsy's painting, and then I'll show you Polly's."

He was standing right there, right there close beside her, softly breathing down the bridge of her nose with his ruddy lips, staring down to the marrow of her bones. After a moment he looked away, and then down at her again, quite calm and under control now, while she remained motionless, her thoughts rambling and intertwining like a vine, while the light glowed against his skin, casting him as a bronze god.

She murmured, blinked, and somehow unwound the spell. Because she had to. "Would you like to know about the sheet music? Why we decided to use Mozart?"

He pulled a gold watch key from a vest pocket and fiddled with the stem. Polly had told Sophia her papa carried a watch key with a braid of his late wife's hair. Was he reminding himself of his promise to his wife? Did he have a tinge of guilt about the kiss? Sophia let it slide for now and turned her attention back to Patsy's painting.

"Patsy selected the sheet music after I explained my vision for the portrait. Since Mozart wrote the piece in Prague while you were traveling around Europe, I thought it would be a nice reminder of your time here."

He plucked at his lips, thinking. "Patsy's smile is so mysterious. I wonder what's on her mind?" He glanced away, then turned back, as if to reassure himself the smile was still there. "When I turn away, her smile lingers in my mind. She's unforgettable." He glanced over to the other painting covered by a sheet. "If Patsy's painting is an example of your talent, you should be showing your paintings in the Salon."

"If I was staying in Paris, I would try to do that."

"I'd like to see Polly's."

Sophia removed the sheet, and the fluttering linen fell to the floor. Momentarily speechless, he braced his hands on the window-sill behind him and leaned against them. "Strong-willed, joyful nymph, dipping her toes in the lily pond." He smiled. "I feel both the coolness from the tips of the trees that line the edges of the portrait, as well as the heat of the sunlight touching her cheek. You can trace the bird-like bones of her shoulder blades through the linen of her dress. So fragile, yet her strong will comes through in her eyes."

"The fragility of her birdlike bones is in juxtaposition to her toes tickling the frogs in the lily pond," Sophia said. "Polly and I wandered around the garden and talked about my vision. She decided on the lily pond. I suggested dipping her toes in the water. She loved the idea."

Jefferson pushed off from the window and paced, going only about two or three paces in one direction, then reversed himself, all the while keeping his gaze on the portrait. "Her eyes watch me, no matter where I go in the room, as if by magic. If I stand in front of the painting, she's staring at me. If I move from side to side, the stare still seems direct."

"It's because she's painted gazing directly at the painter. It's sometimes called the *Mona Lisa* effect."

"That's da Vinci's masterpiece. It's hanging at the Palace of Versailles. When did you see it? You've refused to be presented at Court."

"I saw a copy in Madrid." *And please don't ask me about traveling to Spain.*

"Madrid? Did da Vinci paint the copy?"

"It's believed that it was painted by one of his assistants at the same time he painted the original."

She turned to hobble back to the easel holding his portrait, but he stopped her. His thumb slid over the curve of her cheek, the line of her jaw, stopping at her mouth. It seemed as if time had stopped for a moment, for just a heartbeat or longer. And then he kissed her again. This was no slow, gentle kiss. Their mouths opened immediately, and she gripped the back of his neck, pulling them together. A low moan like a growl rose from her throat as she pressed her body against his, luxuriating in the anticipation of what could come next.

But reality hit, and she slowly pulled away. "If you keep this up, you'll never see your painting."

"I can wait," he said.

She hobbled away, out of his reach. "Stay right there. I want you to see it from a distance." She grabbed the edges of the easel and slowly tugged it around. "Close your eyes. I'll tell you when to open them." She glanced back over her shoulder to be sure his eyes were closed. "Don't peek." The easel slid easily over the hardwood floor. "Okay. Open your eyes."

He did. And his eyes flashed, and he dropped onto the edge of the sofa. She'd had similar reactions from clients, but there was something in Jefferson's face she'd never seen before. She couldn't describe it or ascribe emotion to it.

"I wouldn't have approved this painting if you'd described it to me," he said.

A flash of defensive pride started to grow, but she stomped on it. "I painted the paradox that is Thomas Jefferson."

"You captured a moment, cut it out, and glued it there."

"I wanted to do realistic portraits, but to achieve that, I had to suspend the bounds of today's strictures of realism. Portraiture is a vanity business. The girls didn't want to be painted in casual poses, but I wanted to create paintings that would capture realism in the eighteenth century as well as the twenty-first century."

"Why?" he asked.

He casually crossed his leg at the knee, drawing her eyes to the muscle of his calf flexed in stark relief beneath its white silk stocking.

"Patsy and Polly are your surviving daughters," she said. "You are one of America's Founding Fathers. What you've done for America already, and what you'll continue to do over the course of your lifetime, will be remembered long after your daughters and their descendants pass away. When people in the future view this portrait, I want them to have a sense of the man I've come to know." She rubbed her finger along her bottom lip, reminding herself that the man she'd come to know was also the man she just kissed.

A knock on the door swiftly pulled her from thoughts of Thomas. It wasn't Patsy or Polly's low-level tap near the center of the wood. It was Mr. Petit's rap near the upper third of the door.

"Come in, Mr. Petit," she said.

He pushed the door open and entered the room. "The Marquis de Lafayette has arrived, sir."

How come I'm not surprised he knew Thomas was here with me?

"Thank you, Mr. Petit. Is he alone?" Thomas asked.

"Yes, sir. He said the others will arrive shortly."

"Ask him to come in here." Thomas turned back to his portrait.

A few moments later the Marquis entered the room smoothly. "So this is the *atelier du célèbre artiste Sophia Orsini.* On my last several visits to the Hôtel de Langeac, I've found the door mysteriously closed."

He accepted her hand, bowed slightly over it, and kissed her knuckles. When he released it, she glanced at the paint splatters, embarrassed that she'd been kissed by the charismatic Marquis de Lafayette with paint on her hand. It was almost as bad as being upside down in a carriage and not recognizing him.

"The marquise and I had hoped to entertain you, but alas, you have been cloistered here with the ambassador, and have deprived the rest of Paris of your beauty and talent."

Jefferson extended his arm toward his painting. "Lafayette, tell me what you think of this portrait."

He joined Jefferson in front of the easel and reached out to touch it. "This is *incroyable.* You're sitting inside this painting. I've seen you at your desk dozens of times, always exactly like this, lounging on one hip, fingering your watch key, pen in the other hand. A stack of books nearby. But instead of being in your cabinet, you're surrounded by your vineyards. There is a timeless quality about this portrait."

He paced back and forth in front of the easel. "We love portraits because they're human and emotional. They tell us about life rather than intellectual abstractions. Ambassador, this brilliant portrait is not art for art's sake. It's art for life's sake." Lafayette smiled at Sophia. "Please, accept my commission for a portrait of the marquise and myself."

"If I have time, I would love to paint both of you. Having a commission from General Lafayette would guarantee my future."

Mr. Petit returned to the door. "Your guests have arrived. They're in the salon."

Thomas collected her crutches. "Join us for dinner."

"Thank you, but I need to work. Your painting isn't finished, and I can't quit for the day until it's signed. I'd like to start painting the three of you, and"—she held out her hands—"I'm covered with paint."

To Lafayette, Thomas said, "I'd like to speak privately with Mademoiselle Orsini. I'll join you in a moment."

Lafayette lifted Sophia's hand to his lips again. "Your beauty will be a welcome addition at the table. The ambassador values your judgment. Your insights are perceptive, and your predictions would be illuminating."

"You have misunderstood the ambassador, sir. My opinions are not highly valued. They contradict many of his beliefs, especially concerning the role of women and voting rights."

"I do not have a habit of misunderstanding." Lafayette drew up into a tight soldier's stance. "*You*, mademoiselle, have misunderstood the ambassador. Now, if you'll excuse me, I'll go meet our guests. I'll tell them to expect an enchanting, intelligent woman with unusual insight."

Jefferson nodded to Thomas as he left the room, then moved to stand before the fireplace, one arm slung on the mantel, his expression rather mysterious. "If I've given you the impression that I don't value your opinions, it's the wrong one. I might not agree with you, but I respect your right to have them."

She returned to her stool and picked up a clean brush, something familiar to do with her hands, something easy, normal, and automatic, something to shake out the tingling in her fingers. "I've made comments to you that I never should have mentioned. I can't risk saying something that upsets one of those men. If they leave here angry, they'll talk to others about what happened here."

Thomas's brow creased, his large eyes narrowed into almond shapes with the corners tilting upward just a fraction—a look she'd sketched the night before.

"Lafayette assured me this meeting and the issues discussed would remain confidential."

"If word gets back to the king that you were involved, he would feel betrayed and it could damage the relationship between France and America."

"This meeting is too important, Sophia. I have to attend, and Lafayette has requested your attendance as well."

Oh, God. What was she getting into? She drew a massive breath into her lungs, knowing she couldn't refuse the invitation, nor could she advise them without hinting at the escalation of the violence to come. "Why'd you mention me to the general? I could have stayed here, worked, and talked to you afterwards."

"Because your insight would benefit Lafayette."

"I'm not dressed to attend dinner."

He cradled her face, and before she could react to this unexpected caress, before she could even bring her own hands up to him, he slipped the kerchief off her head and anchored his fingers in her hair. "It doesn't matter what you wear. The eye is drawn to you because of your intelligence and grace." He held her and pressed her against his chest. Then he kissed her, less gently than before, cupping the curve of her skull with his hand. "And your occasional stubbornness."

She backed away from him, from another imminent kiss, from the willing energy of his arms. This was her last night here, but she had to step aside. She switched tracks and let her brain turn to the one thing that would ground her—painting him, capturing his chiseled-jaw profile, the intensity of his eyes, the ruddiness of his complexion on canvas. Those details were preserved in the exact form, like candy in a glass jar. But the man, the gentleness of his hands, the softness of his kisses, would live only in her head and in her heart.

Only a few more hours, and this will all be a memory.

His brow wrinkled. "Have I overstepped, Sophia? I don't want to take advantage, but you are on my mind constantly."

"No, you haven't, but you have a houseful of guests. Can we continue this conversation later?" Later? When midnight arrived, the brooch would heat up and it would be time to go. She couldn't leave him without an explanation. He could handle the truth more easily than he could handle a simple disappearance.

"Yes, until later this evening." He drew her arm into his elbow.

She leaned on him. "I need to wash my hands and gather paper and chalk. I'll want to sketch the men at the table."

Minutes later, armed with the tools of her trade, she was escorted by Thomas into the dining room, and into history. She mentally wrote a rap song about the dinner meeting based on information from the audiobooks.

A group of Frenchmen / Looking for a solution / Discussed the revolution / And Thomas guided them / Toward a solution / For transforming a nation / From despotism to a…well…republic.

"Thank you for joining us," he whispered, absently rubbing the corner of his mouth with his thumb, drawing attention to the last place her lips had touched.

"You're welcome, but I don't suppose you'd consider serving wine with dinner."

"No, my dear. The meal will end in the American fashion, with wine served on a bare table."

Her pulse was off and running again, with each beat plucking a staccato rhythm against her skin. There was a good chance he might not thank her later.

A group of Frenchmen / Looking for a solution / Might not appreciate / A woman's interference.

24

Paris (1789)—Sophia

EIGHT MEN SWIVELED in unison when Thomas escorted Sophia into the dining room, a room already thick with tension. All but Lafayette, who was in uniform, were wearing lace cuffs, knee breeches, frockcoats, and big wigs—the flamboyant Macaroni style of dress. Their clothes reminded her of walking onto the set of *Hamilton* following the show, and a line of lyrics popped into her mind:

He knows nothing of loyalty / Smells like new money, dresses like fake royalty.

Dressing like fake royalty was preferable to dressing like a starving artist. How did she let herself get talked into this? With paint stains on her dress, and *oh, my God...* She caught her reflection in the mirror.

Too late now. So let's get this party over with quickly.

She would socialize, eat, and before the gathering got down to business in the *American fashion*, she would excuse herself. There was a painting to finish, and the clock was ticking toward the Cinderella hour—midnight. The brooch was in her pocket, and soon it would turn up the heat.

Leaving Thomas would be harder than it had been when she left sweet, talented Leonardo.

But leaving Pete had been a hundred times harder. *Oh, Pete.* The man was never far from her thoughts. Maybe this time, this year, when she returned home, she'd look him up. Even if he was happily married with a slew of kids, it was time to know for sure, and permanently let him go.

Thomas stood over her protectively while Lafayette introduced her to Pierre Samuel du Pont de Nemours; Antoine-Pierre-Joseph-Marie Barnave; Alexandre-Théodore-Victor, comte de Lameth; Henri François Lucretius d'Armand de Forest, Marquis de Blacons; Jean Joseph Mounier; Marie-Charles-César de Faÿ, comte de la Tour-Maubourg; and Pierre Nicolas d'Agoult.

They all kissed her hand and smiled flirtatiously.

"Excuse my appearance," she said, smoothing down the front of her dress. "I've been in my studio since early this morning. When the general extended an invitation to join you for dinner, I had only a moment to wash off the paint."

Monsieur du Pont clasped her hand again. "Even with paint, you would be the most extraordinary woman at my salon. I hope you'll accept an invitation to dine at your convenience."

"I'd be delighted. Thank you." She'd heard the monsieur's name mentioned in some context recently and wondered if he was the du Pont who emigrated to America and started the Du Pont dynasty. As for the other men, none of their names were familiar, except comte de Lameth.

Didn't Marguerite buy used dresses from the comtesse de Lameth's maid? Good thing Sophia wasn't wearing one of the secondhand gowns, although not even the comtesse would recognize them after Marguerite's skillful alterations.

The comte de Lameth slipped her hand out of du Pont's grasp, asking, "What do you paint, mademoiselle?"

From the outermost edge of her peripheral vision, she watched Thomas fall into his default stance—arms folded. "Portraits, landscapes, architecture. Whatever the client commissions."

Moving in closer, the comte de Lameth tugged her hand to his chest and gazed at her with what she'd call wicked eyes. "But you must have a preference."

"Well, sir"—she gave him a demure, slant-eyed smile—"I never tire of painting handsome Frenchmen."

He couldn't hold back a rumble of a laugh. While he continued his contagious laughing, she reclaimed her hand.

"If you need a recommendation," Lafayette said. "I've seen the mademoiselle's paintings, and I've offered her commissions to paint the marquise and myself."

"Then I must get in line this very evening," the comte de Lameth said.

If only she had time to paint Lafayette, or any of them. She would never have a painting hanging in the National Gallery unless she painted one in the eighteenth century. Thomas's painting had a chance, but not if she was whisked off to the future before it was finished. Outside, the sunset transformed the sky, pink and brilliantly gold, barely light enough to paint by, but here she was. Stuck. She couldn't spend her last night in the eighteenth century with the French nobility planning a revolution. She had to make her excuses and get back to work.

"Maybe the mademoiselle will give us a private showing before we leave tonight," the Marquis de Blacons said.

"The paintings belong to Mr. Jefferson," she said. "They're his to show."

"Of course you may see them." Thomas took her arm. "Shall we dine?"

He pulled a chair out for her, placing her to the right of his seat at the head of the table. Lafayette sat at the opposite end. Du Pont, Barnave and the comte de Lameth sat to Lafayette's right. Marquis de Blacons, Jean Joseph Mounier, comte de la Tour-Maubourg, and Pierre Nicolas d'Agoult sat to his left.

If Lafayette and the three men on the right held one position and the other four men held another, it would be a long road to reaching an agreement—if their jutting chins and narrow eyes were any indication. But it would probably depend on the issues they intended to debate or what compromise they hoped to reach.

As soon as the beef roast, mashed potatoes, and fresh vegetables from the garden were served, the Frenchmen began an earnest conversation about the uprising and disturbances in the streets. The men conversed rapidly in French, and while she could follow the conversation, she knew Thomas couldn't.

She whispered to him, "Do you want me to translate for you?"

"Do you mind?"

"Not at all, but what's the problem? What are they hoping to reach consensus about tonight?"

Jefferson put down his fork. "How much do you know about the veto power in the American constitution?"

She sipped her madeira before answering. "If I remember correctly, any bill passed by Congress and vetoed by the president requires a two-thirds vote in the senate to override it."

"Almost. I'm surprised you know that much. If you asked a citizen on the street, it's unlikely they would know. The bill is returned to the Chamber where the bill was initiated. If there's a two-thirds vote in that body, the bill then proceeds to the other Chamber."

"You didn't want it to be easy, did you?" The question was rhetorical, and he didn't respond. She continued whispering in English while the men at the other end of the table were shouting at each other in animated French. "Is this what the National Assembly hopes to accomplish? To establish veto power like that available in the American Constitution?"

"The crucial dispute is that half of the Assembly wants the king's power of the veto to remain absolute. The other half don't."

"What does Lafayette want?"

Thomas sighed. "A compromise that won't tear the country apart. The Assembly is debating three types of vetoes. An absolute veto would not be subject to an override by the Assembly. The suspensive veto could in some form be overridden, and the negative veto would deny the king any role in legislation."

Du Pont rose from the table, paced, then leaned over Lafayette's shoulder, pointing an angry finger at Pierre Nicolas d'Agoult. She quickly sketched him, extended finger and all. He was average in every detail: average height, average round features, probably average colored brown hair beneath his powdered wig.

When she got the scene sketched out, she asked, "Why don't they agree to the suspensive veto and go home? It sounds to me like a reasonable compromise."

Thomas picked at the corner of the sheet of paper she was drawing on. It wasn't to get her attention. It was, she suspected, a substitute for touching her hand or her face. "Lafayette has to find a way to make it palatable to the members who want the king to retain absolute power."

"Isn't the threat of total dissolution and civil war enough of an incentive?"

"They don't want to be threatened."

"No one does," she said.

"Lafayette is a well-informed politician and a good judge of men. He understands the ground of liberty is to be gained by inches, and that we must be content to secure what we can get from time to time," Thomas said.

"So the suspensive veto is sufficient for Lafayette?"

"We must press forward for what we can get. There will always be limits of politics, imperfections of government, and the realities of human nature."

She had to think about it for a moment. "Do you mean that because people and governments are so imperfect, we have to accept what we can get?"

"And work toward a compromise."

"We've already had this discussion, too," she said.

As the debate continued, she studied the men at the table, picking up on their individual idiosyncrasies, deciding how to sketch them. Who had the shortest temper, the most patience? Whose faces turned red while arguing? Who gestured? Who was the easiest to rile? Who was the easiest to placate? By the time dinner was finished, she had most of them figured out, and had already sketched several drawings.

The cloth was removed, the wine dispensed. She had intended to return to her studio after dinner, but unless they asked her to leave, she decided to stay for a while.

"What are we drinking?" she asked.

"Four Bordeaux wines: Lafite, Latour, Margaux, and Haut-Brion. Are you familiar with them?"

It continued to amaze her that the wines Thomas drank in 1789 were available in the twenty-first century, although they didn't taste the same. Matter of fact, a handblown, dark green glass bottle capped with a nubby seal of thick black wax, no label, but with the year 1787 and the words *Lafite* and the letters Th.J etched into the glass in a spindly hand was discovered behind a bricked-up cellar wall in Paris and auctioned in the 1980s for over a hundred thousand dollars. She never saw a picture of the auctioned bottle, but the one in his hand matched its description.

"The Lafite is known for its silky softness on the palate and its charming perfume," she said. "The Latour has a fuller body and a considerable aroma that begs for the softness of the Lafite. The Château Margaux is lighter and possesses all the delicate qualities of the Lafite, except it doesn't have as a high a flavor. And the Haut-Brion has more spirit and body, but it's rough when new. I'll start with the Lafite."

He filled her glass. "I hope someday you'll explain how your wine knowledge is so extensive."

She swirled, sniffed, sipped. There was more than a subtle difference between this and the varietal wines of the future, but this one was pretty good. "I like wine and make notes when I find a label I'm especially pleased with. But what about you? Your knowledge is more extensive than mine."

His eyes brightened in a definite lightbulb moment. "Tomorrow, let's travel to the vineyards of Châteauneuf-du-Pape between Orange and Avignon. Except for the tower, little remains of the castle. But there's a sweeping vista of the surrounding countryside with its vineyards, silver olive groves, and russet villages. You can paint, and we can sample the wines produced there."

"That's in the south of France, Thomas. It will take days to travel there. You can't leave Paris right now. Lafayette needs you." She reached under the table, and for only a moment, placed her hand on his knee, and the kneecap alone was so large her palm couldn't quite cover it. "And it would be improper, even by Parisian standards, for us to travel together."

He sat back in his chair, but then leaned forward again. "Then we'll go to the Château de Madrid. It borders the Bois de Boulogne. The rainbows of Marly were created by the famous hydraulic machine constructed during the time of Louis XIV to carry water from the Seine to the gardens of Versailles and Château Marly. From the terrace of the royal chateau at St. Germain you can see Paris. It would be a perfect place to paint. We'll bring your supplies and a picnic basket."

Her heart dropped into her stomach. What was she going to do? She couldn't vanish from his life while he planned an extraordinary outing. "Let's talk about it later."

While discussions continued, Sophia translated for Thomas and sketched the men as they huddled, paced, drank, yelled, and loomed threateningly over the table. Finally, as it neared the sixth hour of debate, Lafayette succeeded in developing a centralist coalition to support the suspensive veto.

With that issue resolved, they touched on whether the fundamental law of the French constitution could be revised, and if so how. Should it be changed at stated, periodic times, or as the need arose? If it was made difficult or impossible to alter, then the past would lay heavily over future generations.

"It should be difficult to alter, but possible," Sophia said in French.

The men turned toward her, their mouths, moments ago compressed in concentration, opened in surprise.

"I mentioned this to the ambassador recently. The American constitution required two-thirds of the states to amend the constitution. Currently there are thirteen states. It wouldn't be so difficult to get nine states to agree. But what if in a hundred years there are fifty states, and thirty-three states are needed to change the constitution? That wouldn't be easy to do. It could take years."

"Do you think they made the wrong decision?" Lafayette asked.

"Who am I to second-guess the brilliant men who wrote the document? With a few exceptions, I think they got it right."

Lafayette propped his elbows on the table, clasped his hands. "What didn't they get right?"

"They should have settled the slavery issue," she said. "I understand it was more important to get the document passed than deal with an issue that could have ripped the states apart. But a solution needs to be found in the next twenty to thirty years. And it's not going to get any easier. I also believe in a woman's right to vote. Both issues have been left for future generations to resolve."

There was an immediate reaction to her position that women be allowed to vote. The law permitted only the clergy, nobility, and the third estate (commoners) to vote.

"But there is at least a process in place to do that," Lafayette said.

"Mademoiselle Orsini," Monsieur du Pont said. "You have unusual insight into American politics as well as those of France. What are your predictions?"

"For France, or for America?"

"Both," Lafayette said.

She stood, pushed her chair to the table. "These are just predictions, gentlemen. Each of you could make your own. But here are mine, and then I must get back to my studio. For America, my prediction is that the framers created a document that will survive centuries with a few amendments. And slavery will tear the country apart, but will not destroy it."

She reached for her glass of wine and sipped. "As for France, your financial crisis has led to state bankruptcy, loss of confidence in the monarchy, and political destabilization. You are heading into a long civil war, where thousands will die, and none of you will be safe."

Every man quieted in stunned silence. "What's the answer, Mademoiselle?" the comte de la Tour-Maubourg asked in a shaky voice.

"Compromise. As you have done here. Feed the people. Don't put all the burden on their backs. Give the middle-class equal representation. This rebellion can sweep away the monarchy, the aristocracy, and the power of the church."

"The church has an important role in the life of all Frenchmen," Lafayette said.

"Separation of church and state is paraphrased in the First Amendment to the United States Constitution," Sophia said. "And the ambassador believes strongly in a wall of separation between them. I recommend you read the amendment."

"You paint a tragic picture, Mademoiselle. I'm reluctant to ask if there is anything else," Monsieur du Pont said.

She swirled the wine in her glass, watching the legs. Maybe she could pretend to be scrying. Her eyes were wide open, staring at the faraway window, and her heart was about to beat right out of her chest.

"One more thing, and this is strictly my opinion. Ask the king and queen to abdicate."

The Frenchmen's gasps sucked the air from the room.

"You asked for my predictions. You didn't say, 'Tell me only those I can stomach.' They are only predictions based on what I see. Won't you agree that the king is depicted as a weak man, and the people are unhappy with the queen over her excessive spending? France needs a strong monarchy or none at all."

She looked back at Thomas. "Wasn't it you, Mr. Jefferson, who said, 'We are not to be expected to be translated from despotism to liberty in a featherbed?'"

"He said it to me recently." Lafayette sighed, gripping the back of his neck, and shook his head. "But how could you know?"

"I hear things when I paint. But I'm now out of predictions and insights. Feel free to pitch them aside as the rantings of a crazy woman. I wish you the best as you go forth. But please, if you do nothing else, feed the starving people."

She reached in her pocket and wrapped her fingers around the brooch. "I'm sorry if I distressed you. But if you don't get this right, it could get very ugly in a couple of years."

The moon had come out long ago, a friendly half-moon, not too bright, but light enough to find her way home. She limped from the room as a buzz of voices rose to a fever pitch.

It was time to go home.

25

Richmond, VA—JL

J L AND KEVIN huddled on a sofa in the NICU's brightly painted waiting room with their sleeping child between them. Blane's head nestled in her lap, his feet in Kevin's. She replayed the latest emergency—a bowel perforation—and wondered how much more Lawrence's little body could endure.

All parents had been ushered out of the pod during Lawrence's surgery. Thank goodness the unit was fully equipped to handle emergencies instead of losing valuable time transporting preemies to the OR.

Kevin pocketed his phone. "It's been an hour. I'm going down to the pod to see what I can find out."

"Anne said it could take up to two hours. But I'm surprised none of the family is here. Did you send a group message?" JL repositioned herself to relieve the pressure of Blane's head without disturbing him. Between the soreness in her belly and the stiffness in her neck and shoulders, she was a mess. She rolled her head side to side, a signal Kevin picked up on immediately, and he reached over to massage up and down her neck, kneading the knots.

"I didn't tell them. I thought I'd wait…"

He let the sentence drop. JL knew what lay heavy on his mind, because it was a boulder pressing on hers. Would their tiny son pull through this emergency, too?

She skated her fingers along the back of Blane's hand, the smooth skin, the chubby fingers. But even in its smallness, he had a giant's hand compared to Lawrence's. And Austin's dwarfed them all. He could comfortably palm a basketball.

She leaned into the pressure of Kevin's thumbs. "I'm glad you didn't. I wouldn't want to sit here having to look into dozens of worried eyes. Yours are scary enough."

"Sorry. I don't mean—"

"It's okay, Kev. We're both scared shitless. I don't know... I don't know how I could get through it if we lost him."

"Shh..."

He pulled her to him and nuzzled the side of her face. His whiskers scratched, but she didn't care. At least she wasn't totally numb.

"Shh... He's a fighter. And he's got an incredible medical team. We have to trust them." Kevin's phone dinged with a message. He straightened and read it. "Meredith and Elliott are coming up to sit with Lawrence for a while."

"I complained about Elliott and smarted off, but since then he's stayed in his lane. No telling what he's doing when we're not here, but the staff hasn't complained about him."

"Excuse me."

JL glanced up to find a woman she'd seen earlier in the pod walking toward her with the grace of a dancer. Five-nine, one-twenty, blonde hair pulled up in a messy bun, wearing a chic summer cotton dress with strappy sandals. Without a doubt, her most striking feature was her denim-blue eyes. Unlike JL, she didn't have a post-partum baby bump. As a former cop, JL noticed things. And there was something about this woman that drew JL to her.

The man beside her was six-two, athletic, also blond and blue-eyed, wearing wrinkled khakis shorts and a polo-styled shirt with a Hampden Sydney College logo. They looked like two people who normally had everything in life figured out, but had been dealt a bad hand and didn't yet know how to cope. Not that JL and Kevin could claim they were masters.

"Hi," the woman said. "I don't want to impose, so I'll just take a minute. I'm Lisa Harrison. This is my husband Robert. Our daughter was born a few hours ago. We just got here and were asked to leave the pod because they were going to operate on your baby."

"Yeah, they kicked everybody out on our account. Sorry," JL said.

"Don't worry about it. Next time it could be us." Lisa dabbed at the corners of her eyes with a tissue. "I hope your baby will be okay."

JL pointed toward the modular chair next to the sofa. "Have a seat. I'm JL. This is my husband Kevin."

Robert set his backpack on the floor and sat in the chair next to Kevin. "We live in Farmville. We came up yesterday to visit our surrogate mother here in Richmond, and while we were there she went into labor eight weeks early. This is all so new to us. We don't know what to do next."

"Neither do we," JL said. "I've never known anyone who had a preemie. They don't teach you how to cope with the NICU in birthing classes."

Kevin stroked the back of JL's head. "JL had an emergency Cesarean four days ago."

"Seems like four months." JL shuddered. "Lawrence was born at twenty-eight weeks—"

"And we've had an emergency every day since then," Kevin added.

Robert wrung his hands. "They're doing an assessment on our daughter now. We don't have any information yet. Up to then it was a textbook pregnancy. Then this…"

"The staff is excellent," Kevin said. "As soon as they finish the assessment, you'll be brought in as members of the team, and they'll tell you everything. Keep you informed of all procedures. And there's always a nurse or other staff member available to answer your questions."

"We don't know what we're going to do. We only came here for the night. We haven't made any plans," Lisa said.

"We both teach at Hampden-Sydney College," Robert said. "We thought we'd have six more weeks to get the nursery finished and class schedules finalized so one of us would always be available to take care of Ruth. Now we don't know what's going to happen."

"Are you teaching this summer?" Kevin asked.

"Two classes. Tuesdays and Thursdays," Robert said. "I teach economics and business. Lisa's an artist and teaches fine arts. She can stay here, but I'll need to come and go."

"They told us in admissions that the NICU has a parents' room for overnight stays here on the floor," Lisa said. "The charge nurses decide each day who gets to use it based on who has the sickest baby. We've asked to be put on the list, but we won't know until later."

"If we don't get the room, I'll drive home tonight. Find some-one to cover my classes and pack clothes for us for a few days," Robert said. "Maybe Lisa can sleep in the chair next to Ruth's bed tonight."

"What about you guys? Do you live close by?" Lisa asked.

"We live in Kentucky. We have family in the area, but we got a room at the hotel across the street," Kevin said. "We both work remotely, so it's not a problem for us."

Robert grabbed a bottle of water out of the holder on the side of his backpack. "What do you do?"

"We work for a family-run company that breeds Thoroughbreds and makes wine," Kevin said.

"Do you travel a lot?" Robert asked.

"We do," JL said. "But it's not overnight travel. When we go somewhere, we stay for several weeks at a time."

Lisa glanced at her watch. "We could stay a few nights at the hotel, but it's not an option long term. We have good insurance, but if Ruth is here for several weeks, the bills are bound to mount up. Robert said he would work it out. All I need is a place to shower, and I'm fine with sleeping in a chair." She looked down at Blane. "Will your family keep your son?"

"Blane loves visiting his cousins. In fact he's happier in Richmond than he is at home. Kevin brought him up today for a visit and then alarms went off."

Robert's phone dinged with a text message. He read it, then put his phone back into his shirt pocket. "I was surprised they were doing surgery in the pod."

"When they told us what they were going to do, we were shocked," Kevin said. "But they have everything they need there, and it was too risky to take time to transport him to the OR. It inconvenienced the parents in the pod, but the babies are their priorities. Not us."

JL nudged him. "Look. There's Anne. They must be finished. You go talk to her."

Robert stood. "I hope you get good news."

Lisa patted JL's arm. "We'll talk later."

Robert and Lisa reclaimed the sofa where they'd been sitting. Lisa opened a book and Robert got out his phone.

Anne pulled a chair up in front of Kevin and JL. "It went well. Gas-containing cysts invaded the intestinal wall and led to a perforation. We irrigated and aspirated the site to minimize the peritonitis and sewed him up. He tolerated the surgery well, and he's medicated right now."

"Can we see him?" Kevin asked.

"Yes." Anne smiled down at sleeping Blane. "But you might want to take him home first. We need to keep the pod quiet and avoid stressing Lawrence."

"You said I should be able to do kangaroo care later today," JL said in a hopeful voice.

"Not today. We'll see how he is tomorrow," Anne said. "The surgeon is in the pod dictating surgical notes. She said she'd be there to answer your questions."

JL squeezed Kevin's hand. "Go talk to the doctor. Then you can take Blane to the plantation."

Kevin tapped keys on his phone. "Elliott will be here in two hours. I'm texting him to come earlier and bring Meredith, and she can take Blane back with her. I don't want to leave right now."

"Okay," JL said, "but you go with Anne to see Lawrence and talk to the doctor. You'll know what questions to ask. Come back when you can, then I'll go in there until Elliott and Meredith get here."

"You need to rest," Kevin said.

"I can make it until I get back to the room. As soon as Meredith leaves with Blane, we'll go to the hotel. For now, I'll close my eyes and rest while he's still asleep."

Kevin slipped out from under Blane's feet. "I'll be back in a few minutes. Text me if you need anything." He kissed JL and Blane, then hurried from the room. Anne spoke briefly with Robert and Lisa, and they jumped up and followed her out.

JL closed her eyes and leaned back against the wall. She had just dozed off when someone kissed the top of her head.

"You look done in, *ragazza tosta*."

She slowly opened her eyes. "Where'd you come from?"

Pete picked up Blane's feet and sat next to her. "The parking lot. I didn't expect to find you in the waiting room. What's going on?"

"Lawrence had a perforated bowel. They operated on him, and they said he did okay. Kevin just went in to see him."

"Why didn't you send a message? I would have come sooner."

"We thought we'd hear from the surgeon before anyone could get here."

"You look like you're barely holding up. Why don't I take you and Blane to the hotel?"

"Kevin sent Elliott a text to come up early and bring Meredith, so she can take Blane back to the plantation."

Pete pulled his phone from his pants' pocket. "That's crazy. I'm already here. I'll take Blane." He tapped the keys on his phone, and a few seconds later, it dinged with a reply. "It's Elliott: *'I'm coming up there. Meredith will stay here to take care of Blane tonight.'* Good. That'll give you and Kevin time to rest."

"Why are you here in the middle of the afternoon?"

"I had a meeting with the Virginia Wine Marketing Office to talk about a joint promotion project between wineries in Virginia and Tuscany."

"Why you?"

He shrugged. "We all play multiple roles in MacCorp. But I'll put my foot down if Meredith ever asks me to go house-hunting."

"Worked out okay for Connor," JL said.

"Yeah, well... He just got lucky."

Blane rolled over. He pushed on her belly, and she sucked air through her teeth. "Damn. That hurt."

"Switch places with me. Or better yet, I'll sit in the chair and hold him so you can stretch out. You've got to be uncomfortable with a gut full of stitches."

"He'll be okay without a pillow now." She lifted Blane's head and scooted out from under him. Pete arranged a chair so she could sit and put her feet up on the sofa. "You know what I think?"

He pulled up another chair. "Most of the time I have no idea."

She smirked. "Ha. Ha. I think Meredith just wanted to give you something to do while you wait to talk to David about Sophia and the brooch. I don't think you should wait any longer."

"I'd be surprised if David doesn't already know. Have you ever known Elliott to keep a secret from him?" Pete asked.

"I've never known Elliott to keep a secret, period, except for Kevin's true parentage," she said.

"You're probably right, but David is Elliott's alter ego. He's never kept a secret from McBain. Never. Ever."

"David didn't know about Kevin."

"Elliott might not have confessed that he was Kevin's father, but David knew the truth."

Blane opened his eyes. Looked curiously at Pete, then at JL. Yawning, he sat up. "Hi, Uncle Pete. Did you come to see wee Lawrence?"

Pete held out his arms. "Come here and give me a hug."

Blane rolled off the sofa and climbed up into Pete's lap. "Wee Lawrence is having an op-ration. He's a sick laddie."

"I heard, but they're done now, I think."

Blane jerked around toward JL, his eyes wide. "Is it true, Mommy? Wee Lawrence is okay now?"

JL smiled, hoping she could hide her worry from him. "Your daddy is with him, and he should have news for us any minute now."

"Hey, partner," Pete said. "Why don't you go back to the plantation with me? I bet Uncle Matt has homework for you."

Blane scooted down. "Oh no." He slapped his forehead. "I forgot about schoolwork. I have to go to the pan-tation, Mommy, or I'll be up till…till…" He looked at his watch. "Forever." He tugged on Pete's hand. "Let's go, Uncle Pete."

Pete was a gem, a true friend, and had come to her rescue so many times. "You sure you don't mind?"

"'Course not. This little guy is like my own kid. Aren't you, Blane?"

"No, I'm not your kid. You're my uncle. Let's go."

"Kiss JL goodbye."

"She's not JL. She's Mommy. Why do you call her JL anyway? It's a silly name. Her name is Jenny Lynn O'Grady Fraser."

Pete chucked him lightly under the chin. "Which is why I call her JL. Who'd want a name like Jenny Lynn?"

"Not me. I like being Blane Fraser." He gave her a sloppy kiss on her lips. "Bye, Mommy. Uncle Pete can help me take a bath tonight." Blane leaned in and whispered. "He's got a penis like me and Daddy and Grandpa Elliott. I seen it. It's bigger than Grandpa Elliott's."

Pete straightened and grinned. "God, I love that kid."

JL tried to swallow a laugh, but when it threatened to burst out, she had to cover her mouth with her palm. When she got herself under control she said, "Blane, it's not polite to talk about people's pieces and parts."

"But everybody knows us guys have penises." He held his hands out to his sides and pumped them up and down. "What's the big deal?"

"Pete can explain it to you on the way back to the plantation.

Give me another kiss."

Blane kissed her again. "Come on, Uncle Pete. Can we stop by Target on the way home?" He dug into his pocket and pulled out a few bills. "I still have money. I can buy wee Lawrence another present."

"What'd you have in mind?" Pete asked.

"Oh, I don't know. He can't do much yet." Blane looked down at the money. "Maybe I'll get a new Xbox game."

"Did you get the money out of the bank to buy a present for Lawrence?" JL asked.

Blane nodded, with a deep, gusty sigh. "Guess that means I have to spend it on him or put it back in the bank. But Mommy. Can't I take a'vance on my div-dends?"

"You can, but only if it's an emergency, and you still have to donate a portion of it to your charity."

He smacked his lips and looked at the ceiling as if deep in thought. "I don't really need anything." He gave her the bills. "Will you put this in the account?"

"Sure, but what if you have expenses when you go horseback riding with your uncles?"

"If I do..." He looked up at Pete with a serious face. "If I need money, will you float me an interest-free loan? I'm good for it."

Pete patted his shoulder. "Sure thing, buddy. Let's haul out of here."

"You mean haul ass?"

"Blane Allen Fraser!" JL said. "Watch your language."

"I'll try to, Mommy. But Daddy said I needed to haul ass this mornin' or we'd never get to the hospital."

JL rolled her eyes. If Blane repeated comments she'd made lately, it'd be worse.

Pete winked at her. "Text if you need anything." He and Blane clasped hands and headed toward the door just as Lisa returned. JL had noticed she left her book on the sofa.

"Oh, my God! Pete Parrino?" she said. "Is it really you?"

"Lisa!" Pete dropped Blane's hand and pulled Lisa in for a hug.

"I haven't seen you in decades."

"I know," she said. "How are you?"

"Been better. Been worse."

Blane stuck out his hand. "I'm Blane Fraser."

Lisa leaned over. "I know who you are. I was talking to your parents while you were sleeping."

"Do you have a wrinkly baby like wee Lawrence?"

"I do. Her name is Ruth."

Blane turned around. "Mommy, wee Lawrence has a friend now in the NICU. But it's a girl!"

"I know. I met Lisa a while ago." JL joined them. "I've known you most of my life, Pete. Partnered with you for a decade. Heard more stories than I can recall, but you never mentioned anyone named Lisa."

"Lisa and Sophia were best friends in high school."

"Small world," JL said.

"Do you know Sophia?" Lisa asked.

"Only what Pete told me."

"I saw her several years ago, while I was in Florence doing research for a Renaissance class I was scheduled to teach. We spent a week going to museums in Florence and Rome."

Robert walked in. "Excuse me. Lisa, Ruth's medical team wants to meet with us now. Come down when you're ready."

"Oh, okay. I'll be right there." She hugged Pete again. "Are you here in Richmond? I'd love to catch up."

He pulled out a business card and handed it to her. "I'll be here for another week or so."

"He's staying at Aunt Charlotte's pan-tation, too." Blane grabbed Pete's hand and tugged him along. "Nice to meet you, ma'am. I hope your Ruthie-pie doesn't need an op-ration like wee Lawrence."

"Ruthie-pie?" JL asked. "Where'd that come from?"

Blane tapped his head. "Out of here, Mommy. Did it sound like Grandpa Elliott?"

JL shook her head, sighing. "When you get back to the plantation be sure to do your homework."

"Nice to meet you, Miss Lisa." Blane glanced up and studied her face. "Lisa? You have half of *Mona Lisa's* name."

A laugh warmed Pete's voice, and he said teasingly, "Ask her what her first name is."

Lisa shook her head and waved away the question. "No. No. No. Please don't."

Blane tugged on Pete's hand again. "She doesn't want me to ask, so let's just haul ass."

"Blane Allen," JL snapped.

He tried to wink, but he didn't have enough eye control and ended up blinking both eyes. "I'm just teasing ye, Mommy."

"Yeah, I can tell."

"Let's get out of here before you end up in time out," Pete said as he hurried Blane to the door.

Watching them disappear Lisa said, "What a heartbreaker."

"Pete or Blane? They're two peas in a pod."

"Speaking of pod, I've got to go."

"I'll walk with you. Kevin was going to come back for me, but he'll text if he can't find me. Let me get my gear." JL gathered up her purse, sweater, and bottle of water while Lisa picked up her book. "What are you reading?"

Lisa showed JL the cover. "I grabbed this out of my studio so I'd have something to read during the ride. I could leave it here and nobody would take it." They walked out of the waiting room and into the corridor.

"What's it about?" JL asked because the cop in her wanted to know, plus her spidey senses were floating off the chart. This meeting wasn't random. A brooch was at work. How? Why? Which one? She didn't know, but given time, she'd figure it out.

"It's about an eighteenth-century artist named Maria Cosway. She had an affair with Thomas Jefferson while he was ambassador to France."

"The only reason I know Jefferson was in France is because I saw a Broadway musical and memorized the lyrics *Thomas Jefferson's coming home. He's been in Paris for so long."*

"*Hamilton!* Wasn't it awesome? I started taking dance lessons when I was three, just so I could dance on Broadway. By the time I reached high school age, I was more interested in painting and sculpting. Dance fell to the wayside."

JL linked arms with Lisa. "Well sister, we've got a lot more in common than preemies in the NICU."

"I can't believe you know Pete. What happened between him and Sophia was criminal. I know Sophia never got over him."

"Pete never got over her."

"So what's keeping them apart now?"

"Oh," JL said. "Just time."

26

Paris (1789)—Sophia

SOPHIA CRUTCHED BACK to her studio, quietly closed the door, and leaned against it, her heart pounding.

If she had a key, she'd lock it to keep Thomas out. Of what? The room or her heart? It was too late to lock her heart. He'd already found his way in.

How insane. She couldn't fall in love with a man from the past. And she couldn't fall in love with this man—a Founding Father, a man she disagreed with on fundamental principles, a man who'd impregnated an enslaved woman.

It's a different time. I can't judge him by twenty-first century standards.

It was crazy, though. Thank God she was leaving. But she couldn't up and leave without an explanation. And she couldn't tell him the truth.

Could she answer a few of his most confounding questions? No. Could she tell him how future generations would immortalize him despite his contradictions: a slave owner who believed in the fundamental right to life, liberty, and the pursuit of happiness? Maybe.

"Erggg." She wasn't cut out for this time-traveling life. No. Wait a minute. That wasn't true. The brooch screwed up the date for some reason. On her other adventures, it had always taken her where she wanted to go. If she'd followed the plan and sought out Vigée Le Brun when she first arrived, even though she appeared three years later, the adventure would have gone swimmingly. The Bastille would still have been stormed, and her involvement in the event wouldn't have changed, but Monsieur David would have directed her to Le Brun's atelier instead of suggesting she seek out the American ambassador.

Next year she would stick to the plan. What could happen in 1900 Vienna? Two weeks with Gustav Klimt and the dizzying Viennese Waltz would have her world turning upside down. She smiled, imagining the art, the dresses, and the dancing. Then she groaned. Another adventure? No way.

The clock on the mantel chimed the half hour. She had ninety minutes to finish Jefferson's painting and write farewell notes before the brooch heated.

After mixing paint, she returned to the canvas. As she sat on her stool critiquing the portrait again, she had to agree with her previous assessment. It was her very best work. The portrait was a tangible vision of who Thomas was—both sides of him—his intelligence and his passion. While his literary skills had poetically pitted the contradictory parts against each other in his famous "Head and Heart" letter, she had accomplished the same on canvas.

She chuckled, thinking of a comment she had read about his famous missive. Thomas had said in a four-thousand-word letter to Maria Cosway what Alfred, Lord Tennyson had said in fourteen words sixty years later: *Tis better to have loved and lost than never to have loved at all.* Sophia wasn't sure if she agreed or not.

But what would become of this painting? Would it hang at Monticello? Would Thomas give it away? Would he store it in a closet, to be ruined by moisture and mold? It would break her heart if it was destroyed. When she returned home, she'd research the painting. If it didn't exist, she'd paint it again, and the second one would probably surpass the first one, although it would never be considered a life painting. She'd have more time to make it perfect, to make his lips…perfect.

Her heart resettled its rhythm into her painting pace. She dipped the brush into the paint and added highlights to his brow bone, upper and lower lids, and cheekbones, to show the direction of the sunlight falling on his face. Then she added a dot of white on the lower lids where they met the irises, giving the eyes a touch of moisture, bringing them to life. She groaned as the virile man steamed up the painting. Now that she was looking at him, she realized she'd never be able to recreate this portrait. There would never be any doubt that it was a life painting. She'd captured the powerful connection between subject and artist. But it was a transferrable emotion. Anyone looking at the painting would believe Thomas was looking at them with the same desire.

When she glanced at the clock, she gasped. An hour had passed. In thirty minutes the brooch would heat and the door to the future would open.

She signed her name on the front of the painting, dated it, and added the location—Hôtel de Langeac, Paris on the back. But the A in Paris was capitalized instead of the P. No one would think anything about it, at least not for another hundred years.

Satisfied with her work, she moved the easels to set the three paintings side by side, with Thomas in the middle. It was an impressive collection, and would stand as a centerpiece for an art show in any venue in twenty-first century Paris.

If only she had a camera. She formed a rectangle with her fingers, looked through a pretend viewfinder, and squeezed her finger. "Click. Click." She had individual sketches, and they would have to do.

A light knock on the door startled her. Her hands dropped, her fingers still in the shape of a camera. She flicked her fingers, dissolving the image.

"Come in."

Thomas partially opened the door but kept his hand on the knob as he idled in the doorway. "Am I intruding?"

She glanced at the clock—eleven-forty-five. "No. Come in." She smiled when a bottle of Lafite magically appeared. "You brought wine." *Our last glass together.* "How sweet." She stretched to look behind him. "Where's Lafayette?"

"He went to a salon." Thomas set the glasses on the worktable, poured wine into one, and handed it to her.

She took a quick sip then set the glass aside. The paintbrushes needed to be cleaned and the paints stored away. Hopefully, Polly would continue to paint, and Sophia wanted to leave the studio clean and organized. "Why didn't Lafayette invite you to go with him?"

"He assumed I had other plans."

"Oh. Well, how did the meeting end?"

He filled his glass and sipped. "They came to a logical accord, agreeing that the king should have a suspensive veto, and that there will be no hereditary legislators. France will be governed by a constitutional king and one legislative body, the latter elected by the people. The liberal party will present a solid front to the aristocrats and control the Revolution."

"As long as it's controllable," she said, cleaning the brushes.

"I'm concerned, though, about the possibility that my position has been violated. In the morning I intend to confess to the Minister of Foreign Affairs and explain the circumstances."

"I wouldn't worry," she said. "He'll probably be pleased to learn the men had the benefit of your moderating influence."

"I know too well the duties I owe to the king, to France, and to the United States, to meddle with the internal affairs of the country." Thomas carried his wine across the room, where he stood in front of the paintings.

"You are a rare talent, Sophia. My daughters are alive in these portraits. They look like they could step out of them. I'm dazzled by their evocative poses and expressions." He sipped his wine, studying the paintings. "The shadows of male portraitists have obscured female contemporaries, but you are the exception."

She dried the brushes then inserted them in a canvas sleeve with individual pockets. "I don't believe gender plays a role in the ability to create a compelling painting. As for being an exception, it's not me. It's Vigée Le Brun. She's the much-needed chink in the chain of male painters who have built the canon of figurative painting."

"I disagree."

"Well, as they say, 'Art is in the eye of the beholder.'"

"If art is in the eye of the beholder, then everyone will have their own interpretation."

"Exactly," she said. "My goal with every portrait is to create an inspiring figurative painting that speaks to the present and offers glimpses into the future." She watched Thomas move about the room, studying the portraits from different angles and distances.

He circled around the back of the portraits. "You made quite an impression tonight."

"I said more than I intended."

"You answered their questions."

She carried her glass to the sofa, where she leaned back and stretched out her legs. Comfortable at last, after a long day of sitting on her stool. "The next few years will be difficult ones in France. You're returning to America just in time."

"What will it be like when I return?"

The flat-out tell-me-the-future question surprised the heck out of her. "Are you asking me to consult my Tarot cards to foretell your future in America, or France?"

"You speak with such authority that I believe you truly do know the future."

"I have no genuine supernatural prophetic abilities." She swirled the glass before taking another sip.

"Then what *do* you have?" he asked.

"An active imagination. I see things and interpret their mean-ings—all completely subjective, by the way. France's problems didn't occur overnight, and won't be solved overnight. The situation will get worse before it gets better, and it doesn't take a seer to predict that."

He set his glass down and clasped his hands behind his back. He'd let his guard down, and his expression was soft, and for a minute he just gazed out the window into the darkness.

"What's on your mind, Thomas? I know it's not my lack of

prophetic abilities."

He turned, and there was a curious mixture of yearning and desire in his eyes. "I'm a man of honor, and my behavior, I hope, has never been circumspect. But earlier this evening my actions were abominable."

"I don't remember you doing or saying anything abominable."

He paced for a minute, ten paces in one direction, and ten paces back. "When I invited you to stay at the Hôtel de Langeac you were concerned for my reputation. Not your own. I assured you other artists had resided here and that it was appropriate to open my home to Americans. But I failed to protect you from my advances. And for that, you have my deepest apologies."

He picked up his glass and took a substantial swallow. "Lafayette asked if I'd taken advantage of you. When I didn't answer, he asked me to extend an invitation to you to be his guest during the remainder of your visit in Paris."

"Hmmm. I guess since he saved my life, he believes he should protect my honor as well. How gallant. He needn't worry. You and I are both single adults. What we do in private is no one's business."

"Our behavior wouldn't be condoned in Virginia."

"Lucky for us, we're not in Virginia. The way I see it, you're delighted by my openness and my ability to move around the world freely. You find my witty repartee interesting, but I'm not the type of woman you want in your domestic realm."

"You're not like the French women at all." He removed his jacket, hung it over the back of a chair, and sat next to her. "Patsy and Polly are very fond of you. Having you as a companion during our trip to America would ease the adjustment they'll have to make."

"And might create a scandal."

"There would be nothing untoward if you accompanied Patsy and Polly. When we reach Norfolk, I'll arrange a carriage to carry the three of you to Monticello, and I'll ride ahead on horseback."

"But I'm going to New York City."

He clasped his hands and circled his thumbs. "Come to Monticello. When my neighbors see these paintings, they'll be as impressed as I am, and they'll commission portraits of their family members. You'll have enough work to last through spring. In six months, when it's time for me to return to Paris, Polly and I will travel with you to New York."

There was no reason to argue with him. She wasn't going to America, and this discussion was upsetting them both. "Let's talk about it later."

Thomas lounged in the chair and glanced longingly around the room. "When I return, I won't use this room."

"Oh, but the light is perfect in here, and when you open the French doors the garden comes inside. Why not return it to its original purpose?"

"Your studio has become the center of life at the Hôtel de Langeac. The echoes of your laughter, Polly's giggling, and Patsy's humorous stories will live on long after you're gone. I couldn't bear the loneliness of its emptiness."

She twirled the stem of the wine glass, watching the wine swirl inside the bowl. "I kept shushing the girls. I was afraid we were disturbing you."

"My concentration was interrupted, but I didn't mind. I often laid down my pen and listened to the conversation. Patsy and Polly not only learned art history from you, but botany, science, astronomy, mathematics, literature, and poetry as well, all under the guise of painting. I couldn't understand why they would have an interest in astronomy."

"If you make education relatable, even the boring topics become interesting," she said. "Not everyone wants to study astronomy. But if you explain how light changes in the studio over the course of the year based on the position of the sun, then students become aware of how light and the changing seasons impact art. Everyone has a thirst for knowledge, Thomas. Even women. Even African Am… Everyone."

He straightened his back. "I appreciate what you've taught them, but Patsy and Polly mustn't neglect learning the skills they need to run a household."

"God forbid they learn multiplication tables." She picked up several sheets of paper and chalk from a basket on the floor and sketched him sitting there in his neatly tied stock and embroidered silk waistcoat with pearl buttons.

He refilled her glass then his own. "Since you've finished these paintings, I'd consider it a personal favor if you'd paint the marquise's portrait next."

"I'll send her a note tomorrow."

He leaned forward, holding the bowl of the glass between his hands. "It's not only the echoes I'll miss, Sophia. I can't imagine being here without you, without your off-key whistling."

Her face heated. "I don't whistle off-key," she said defensively.

He laughed, and the musical quality of his voice reminded her there was nothing musical about her own. She could paint the embodiment of music using fingers positioned on instruments and joy-filled faces. But making actual music eluded her, and she'd been told enough times to believe it.

"You whistle and sing off-key, but it's not horrible." He let his smile show in his voice, softening his critique.

"Oh, you're cruel. When have you heard me sing?" She sipped her wine, smiling at him above the rim. When she lowered the glass, he slipped it gently out of her hand, and set it on the table.

His smile grew. "Yesterday you were singing a little ditty about Jack and Diane—two American kids growing up in the heartland. Where is that? The heartland?"

"It was just a ditty. It didn't mean anything." She swallowed, hoping to conceal the flutter in her voice.

He moved effortlessly from the chair to the edge of the sofa, and his nearness accelerated the racing of her heart. He cupped a hand round her cheek, softly tracing her cheekbones, her jaw, her forehead with his thumb. "I apologized for my earlier behavior, and I apologize for what I'm about to do now."

He eased her head back and kissed her. This was no slow, gentle kiss. Their mouths opened immediately. A low moan like a growl rose from her throat as she pressed her body against his. It didn't

Katherine Lowry Logan

take much for one kiss to slide into the next, for the familiar pressure of his hands, first upon her shoulders, then sliding down her back, reducing their resolve to shambles.

She wrapped her arms around his neck, pulling him in tight, seeking the warmth of his mouth to quell her hunger. He drew her into a world where his touch and the pressure of his body filled her mind, spirit—all of her. A world of no thoughts, no words.

His fingers curled into her hair, taking hold, pulling her head gently back. He freed her mouth and began a slow descent down her neck to the hollow where her throat met her collarbone, and then another kiss, an inch farther down, and then another, right at the neckline of her dress. His hand lay upon her thigh, gathering the soft linen of her skirt between his fingers, his thumb crawling upward, exposing her skin.

He pressed her backwards onto the pillows as she furiously untied his stock.

Suddenly a haze of panic clouded her vision.

Was this what she wanted?

Yes.

Then a resounding *no* plowed through her brain like a bouncing pinball. She pressed her hands on his chest. She couldn't do this and then disappear from his life. It wasn't fair to either of them.

"This...isn't right. We...can't do this," she said.

His moan vibrated against her, a husky sound of need.

But he didn't need to be told a second time. He sat up, lowered her skirts, and straightened his own clothes before plowing his fingers through his beribboned hair.

"Thoughts of you consume my waking hours and haunt my sleep."

She had a pretty good idea what those thoughts were, because hers were probably similar. But he didn't need to know. Besides, they weren't in love with each other. Attracted? Yes. And in the eighteenth century, it was more than enough.

But not for her. She had the whole kit and kaboodle once before, and a partial kit and kaboodle a couple of other times, but this situation was different. She wouldn't give in to short-term pleasure with long-term consequences.

Heaving a deep sigh, she rose from the sofa and limped over to the open French doors, blotting at the sweat trickling between her breasts.

She tried soothing her rising panic with thoughts of home—massage, hot shower, air conditioning. But it didn't work.

The warm, rose-scented breeze washed over her as she glanced up into a night sky so bright it looked wet. But blocks away the mild roar and flickering torches of the rioters were a constant reminder of the violence building in the city, and how the brooch had screwed up her holiday.

Thomas's slow steps toward her were marked by the old wooden boards creaking. She could feel the weight of him standing beside her, close enough to detect the whispering of the fine linen of his shirt as he breathed, close enough to feel her small stature compared to his. She wove her fingers with his and tipped her head back against the doorframe. Leaves hissed in the breeze, creating random patterns of shifting shapes against the inky sky.

"I can't keep my hands or my thoughts off you. If you hadn't stopped me, I would have taken you right there. And I'm not in the habit of deflowering virgins on a silk upholstered sofa."

She wasn't about to correct his assumption. "You're attracted to artistic, intelligent women. That combination of qualities is your Achilles heel."

"Achilles heel?" he asked.

"The one weakness you can't resist."

"Then *you* are my Achilles heel, because I can't resist you." His tone was as intimate as a caress, a brush of his hand down her cheek and neck.

The clock struck twelve, and she jerked. She'd been expecting the hour, but was surprised when it arrived so quickly. Through the linen of her dress, the breeze turned cold on her skin.

This was the moment she'd been waiting for. Then why was she ambivalent? Because there were so many goodbyes to say. Not just long goodbyes, but forever ones.

And she had no portrait to take home to add to her collection. Monsieur David had pleaded with her to let him exhibit his portrait of her at the Salon when it was finished. He was far enough along now to finish it without her present.

Thomas pulled her to him and took her mouth again. All resistance fled, burned away by the heat of his touch, leaving her weak and wanting. His mouth roamed at will, no longer gentle as he devoured her, ravenous against the smooth curve of her throat, the soft flesh of her ear. With a guttural groan, he jerked her even closer with powerful arms, consuming her mouth with a kiss surely driven by the sheer will to ravish.

She broke the kiss and rested her forehead on his chest. His heart pounded against her cheek.

"You are one of the truly greatest men God will ever put on this earth." She slipped her hand into her pocket as the seconds ticked past the witching hour. "You'll be remembered through the ages for everything you've accomplished"—She used her fingernail to flick open the brooch—"and will accomplish in your lifetime. People listen to you because you are the master of the science of human rights."

Perspiration dampened the back of her neck, and she had the strangest sensation that she was observing herself from the other side of the room. "I'll never forget the day I tripped and fell into your arms."

"I'm sorry you were hurt, but the injury kept you here with me, with Patsy and Polly."

She rubbed the brooch between the fabric of her skirts and her palm. "When you look at your portrait, I hope you'll remember our conversations about women and voting and freedom."

"When I look at these portraits, I'll think of you. But why are you talking like this? You sound like you're leaving tonight. You must be tired. I'll call Marguerite to help you to your room."

She had only a few minutes left to tell him what she wanted him to know. She rubbed the brooch harder, her breathing more and more erratic. "Don't be a contradiction, Thomas. If you believe in freedom, free all those who are enslaved. If you believe in education, teach all who desire to learn. If you believe in the pursuit of happiness, let those around you freely pursue a joyful life."

Her entire body was primed, ready for what was to come. When she came through the fog two weeks ago, the pearl was hotter than it had been on previous trips, and she had tossed it back and forth. But now...

It was stone...cold.

Fear rang in her bones as she rubbed the stone harder and shook uncontrollably.

"Sophia." He backed up a little to look down into her face. "What's wrong? Are you sick?"

"I have to go." She pushed past him, shambling away as if sleepwalking through the garden, putting distance between them to face the delinquent brooch wizards alone. *"Chan ann le tìm no àite a bhios sinn a' tomhais an' gaol ach 's ann le neart anama."*

"Sophia!" Thomas rushed after her. "Come back inside. It's late. And you don't have your crutches."

He reached for her arm, but she yanked it away. Her stomach did flips of fear—crippling, paralyzing fear.

"I can't...I can't breathe." A jolt of dread shook her so hard she could scarcely move. She limped toward the gate leading out onto the Champs-Élysées. "Heat up. Please heat up," she mumbled.

This time he reached for both of her arms and held her in place. "You're shaking. Tell me what's wrong." There was a new tone in his voice. Not just concern. Fear.

He sounded so far away. Everything around her was fading. *"Chan ann le tìm no àite a bhios sinn a' tomhais an' gaol ach 's ann le neart anama."* The blackness was coming for her. *"Chan ann le tìm no àite a bhios sinn a' tomhais an' gaol ach 's ann le neart anama."* But the brooch wasn't heating. She held it between her hands and blew on it. But it didn't get any warmer.

"What are you saying?" he asked. "I don't know what you're saying." He swooped her up into his arms and rushed back into the studio, where he placed her gently on the sofa. "The blood's drained from your face, and you're shaking like a person with palsy. What in God's name happened? What language are you speaking?"

She squeezed her eyes shut, pulled herself back from the unknown blackness, focused her energy on the brooch to ground herself in the here and now, but the shaking worsened. "When was the B-Bas…tille stormed? What was…the date?"

"Fourteenth of July."

"What's…t-today?"

"The twenty-eighth."

Confirmation held the sting of a knife cut. "Fourteen…days. Two weeks…ago."

"A fortnight," he said.

She wasn't wrong about the date. The brooch had always worked at midnight at the end of the fourteenth day.

This time it wasn't working. It delivered her to the wrong year, and now she was stranded in the eighteenth century. And no one knew where she was. Even if they knew, they'd have no way to come after her.

Absolute terror shook her to her core. Thomas pushed the sofa closer to the fireplace, lit the laid fire, grabbed his jacket, and covered her with it. "My God, Sophia. What's wrong?"

When she didn't respond, he threw open the door and yelled for Mr. Petit. "Get the doctor. Sophia is having a spasm." He poured wine into a glass, lifted her head. Somehow she was able to drink a few sips, but she couldn't stop shaking. It was worse than the post-anesthesia shaking she had following previous surgeries.

"I'm scared." A tear trickled down her cheek.

He wiped it away with his fingertip. "I'll protect you."

"I want to go home."

"I'll take you there."

"I want to go to *my* home."

"I'll take you wherever you want to go."

"You can't!" She rolled over onto her side, curled into a ball.

In her mind she was seventeen again and being ripped from

Pete's arms.

She covered her mouth with her hands while chanting, *"Chan ann le tìm no àite a bhios sinn a' tomhais an' gaol ach 's ann le neart anama. Chan ann le tìm no àite a bhios sinn a' tomhais an' gaol ach 's ann le neart anama. Chan ann le tìm no àite a bhios sinn a' tomhais an' gaol ach 's ann le neart anama."*

No matter how many times she chanted the incantation, there was no fog, no smell of peat, no hot brooch. Only the crackling of the fire and Thomas's strong arms.

27

Paris (1789)—Sophia

FOR FOUR DAYS Sophia was almost comatose. She either sat in the garden, barely speaking, or she rested in her room. She ate very little and slept even less.

Thomas told everyone her frantic pace the last two weeks had exhausted her, and the doctor had prescribed bedrest. He allowed the girls short visits once a day, and Marguerite stood vigil to make sure everyone obeyed his edict. The brooch stayed pinned to Sophia's dress, close to her skin so she would know immediately if it heated.

So far, it hadn't.

What was she going to do? She spent hours mindlessly gazing off at nothing, hopelessly lost in time.

Thomas's temporary leave still hadn't arrived, and he was waiting to hear from John Trumbull about booking a ship to depart from the Isle of Wight. It was assumed she would travel with them. She had yet to say yes or no. Staying in Paris wasn't an option. Returning to Florence as an Orsini would get complicated. Going to America was the wrong direction. Maybe London would be a good compromise.

Early on the fifth day, while sitting in the garden, Marguerite placed sketching paper and chalk in her lap. "Mademoiselle, everyone is concerned about your health. Please, won't you sketch today?"

Sophia recalled a memory of her grandmother setting a college catalogue in her lap after she'd grieved for an entire month over losing Pete. "You have a life to live. Start living it today," her nonna had said. Marguerite was telling her the same thing.

She still had a life to live. Her mind couldn't remain stalled in neutral forever. A plan for her future had to be made, and what better way to start the planning process than with a mild workout? Maybe afterwards she'd feel like sketching.

"Will you get my Tai Chi clothes? I'll do a short workout, then sketch for a while."

Marguerite's face lit up. "I have them in the studio. If you'll come inside, I'll help you undress."

Fifteen minutes later Sophia was immersed in an intense workout, ignoring the minor knee pain. Each posture flowed into the next without pause, ensuring that her body was in constant motion, promoting serenity in gentle movements. She hadn't set out to go through her entire repertoire of rhythmic patterns and positions, but once she started, she continued, searching for the inner calm she desperately needed.

After a final deflect, parry, and punch, she pivoted around, scooped down, stood up, brought her feet together, and bowed. When she looked up, Thomas was standing in the middle of the open French doors, his arms folded, the sun hitting him full on the face. She was disheveled and sweaty, but from his awed expression, he didn't seem to care. She swiped sweat off her brow.

"Good morning, Ambassador."

He stepped out into the garden. "That was the most alluring series of movements I've ever seen—part heron, part ballerina."

Her unbound breasts went rigid under his heated gaze. "How long were you standing there?"

"Marguerite told me you were exercising. I came to see for myself and was so enthralled I couldn't leave. I stood in the shadows so I wouldn't disturb you."

"I'm glad I did a short routine, or you could have been there for hours."

He pulled on the gold chain dangling from his waistcoat pocket and checked the time on his watch. "Two and a half to be exact. But I could have stood in the shadows for twice as long. Come inside. Mr. Petit fixed a pitcher of lemonade. He thought you'd be thirsty."

"Would he mind bringing it out here?"

"I'm sure he wouldn't. But I'll do the honors." Thomas tucked the watch back into his pocket, went inside, and came out carrying a silver tray. He set it on the table next to the bench and filled their glasses. "If Tai Chi was developed for self-defense, at that turtle pace, every practitioner would be killed instantly."

She wrapped a linen towel around her shoulders and dabbed at the sweat on her neck and cheeks. "Tai Chi loosely translated means Supreme Ultimate Skill. Its history comes from the legend of the snake and crane. After witnessing a fight between them, Tai Chi was created."

"I can see the snake and crane in your movements, but the crane would have been bitten on the leg and killed."

She shook her finger back and forth. "Not so fast, Grasshopper. Let me show you." She dropped her towel on the bench, bowed, and then proceeded to perform a two-minute demonstration at combat speed. She finished, bowed again. "Now do I have a believer?"

He stared in open-mouthed disbelief. "You must teach me."

"I take it that's a yes." She picked up her towel again and wiped off additional sweat. "If you want to learn, you'll need a pair of loose-fitting pants and shirt so you can move freely. Marguerite can make them for you. If you want, we can start in the morning at sunrise." She sat down, closed her eyes, and concentrated on nothing except her breathing—in, out, in, out.

Thomas joined her on the bench and sat quietly until she opened her eyes. Then he handed her a glass of lemonade. "Why did you call me a grasshopper?"

"It's a reference to a novice." She drank deeply, then wiped her mouth with the bend of her finger. "The snake and crane are a perfect exhibition of the principles of adapting to change and the ability to blend soft and hard, strength and yielding. The crane can swoop down from a tree with its wings fully spread and use its hard beak to initiate an attack. The snake uses its deceptive coiling movements to evade danger and then lashes out with its tail. They could eventually tire themselves out and call it a draw."

He refilled her glass. "Debates with you are often like a battle between a snake and crane. But with us it's usually a draw."

"Hmm. I'm not sure how to take that. At least I'm not the loser." She finished her second glass of lemonade. "Now that I'm somewhat recovered, I owe you an apology. It's been very stressful since I arrived in Paris. With what happened at the Bastille, then my knee injury, and the painting frenzy, it created a perfect storm." She untied her hair and ran her fingers through it to let the sweat dry. How could she explain how horrendous it had been to discover she couldn't go home again? She couldn't. Even now she found it impossible to believe. "I snapped. I have no other explanation."

"It happened so quickly, I knew I had caused it."

"It wasn't anything you did."

"Since you've been here you've worked day and night. You haven't slept and have barely taken time to eat. The doctor said you should recover after sufficient rest." He set his glass aside and laced his fingers with hers. "You have overtaxed yourself, but I'm at fault. I apologized once for my behavior, then proceeded to transgress again."

"An unmarried man kissing an unmarried woman isn't a transgression. Unless the kiss was forced. Then it would be wrong. A few kisses didn't cause a mild breakdown. It was a combination of exhaustion, fatigue, and the knee injury."

And total anguish at the possibility of being stranded in the eighteenth century.

He fixed her with his intense gaze. "Are you sure?"

She set her glass down, placed her hand over his, sandwiching it between hers, and squeezed. "Can we put it behind us and not talk about it again?"

"I will, if you'll answer one question."

She reclaimed her hands and retied her ponytail. "I'll try." At least he didn't ask her to answer truthfully.

"What language were you speaking?"

"Gaelic. It's a Gaelic…blessing. I'm not sure of the translation." She had to tell him something, so she fell back on the ancient Irish prayer. "A literal translation is 'May you succeed on the road,' or 'bon voyage,' or 'May the wind be ever at your back.' I learned it as a child and I fall back on it…" She rolled her hand around. "Sort of like a mantra."

Mr. Petit came to the door. "The Duke of Dorset is in the salon. Shall I ask him to return later?"

"No, I need to speak with him. I'll be right there."

Thomas stood and gazed down at Sophia, and a jolt of electricity sizzled through her, spilling from the roots of her hair clear down to the tips of her toes.

"We have an invitation to attend Lafayette's salon tonight," he said.

Heat had returned to her cheeks, and it had nothing to do with exercise or the warm August morning. "Why don't you go without me? The General will ask when I can start on their portraits, and I'm not sure yet."

"I'll pass along your regrets. Until later, then."

After Thomas left, she stretched out on the sofa Mr. Petit had moved out to the garden earlier. What was she going to do?

She closed her eyes and slipped back into meditative breathing, searching for clarity. She mentally traveled back to the day her grandmother gave her the brooch. Then later, when she discovered the letter from James MacKlenna. With the help of a Gaelic dictionary, she'd translated it. Weeks after that, she time-traveled for the first time—accidentally. Talk about frightening. But once she met Leonardo, nothing else mattered until the brooch warmed up again.

But that wasn't the case this time. Going home mattered. Recovering her life mattered. Making peace with Pete's ghost mattered.

The pearl had taken her back and forth five times, but the sixth time it screwed up. Why?

She snapped her fingers repeatedly as she attempted to draw something from memory. The answers were clanging around in her brain, trying to sort themselves out.

She shivered, feeling all goosebumpy. "Come on. Come on. I know you're in there." If only she had someone to brainstorm with. Together they could solve her dilemma. What if she told Thomas? Would he believe her? He'd have to. She knew everything about him…at least everything Meacham—in *The Soul of America*—thought the reader needed to know.

A lightbulb exploded in her brain.

Kapow! Thwack! Zam! Digby!

What about him? *Think. Think.* What did she know about her grandfather and his family? Digbys were around in 1625, and they were still around in the twenty-first century. That meant only one thing—they had to exist now—in 1789.

She paced back and forth in the garden. Her heart was beating so fast it might just burst through her chest wall and take off on its own Digby search. Here a Digby, there a Digby, everywhere a Digby.

But where was the beginning of the Yellow Brick Road?

The beginning was in Scotland. Right? Of course. So all she had to do was get there, ask around, find a Digby. Simple. Once she found one, she could flash her brooch and watch for some sign of recognition, then trade her pearl for another one.

Was she crazy? But what were her options? Live in the eighteenth century for the rest of her life? No. That wasn't an option at all.

She had a lot to learn about Scotland in the eighteenth century. Thomas might have some helpful books, but what she really needed was firsthand knowledge from someone who had spent time there. Someone who knew the country well.

She snapped her fingers. *Bingo!* The perfect candidate was visiting Thomas at that very moment—Britain's Ambassador to France, the Duke of Dorset.

She rushed into the studio and dressed. But her hair was still damp and her face flushed. There was an important guest in the house, and she should respect Thomas's position enough to look respectable. She would sneak upstairs and let Marguerite help her change and dress her hair. If she looked and smelled like a scullery maid, His Grace would ignore her. Thank goodness Thomas closed his door when he met with diplomats.

She opened the door to the hallway and froze. The Duke was sitting in Thomas's cabinet, looking suddenly flustered. He coughed lightly and looked inquiringly at her. Then he pushed to his feet, his heeled shoes clacking against the floorboards. "Mademoiselle, I had so hoped to see you." The rapt eagerness with which the Duke kissed her hand and topped it off with a smile, didn't reach his calculating eyes taking in everything about her appearance. Self-consciously, she patted the bun at the base of her neck, which she'd hastily pinned up, missing several strands of damp hair.

"Mr. Jefferson was just telling me you haven't been feeling well." The Duke made a sweeping gesture with his arm. "You're not using those dreadful crutches. Your leg must have improved. You're much too lovely to be using them."

"It's better, thank you."

"Then I hope you'll consider accepting a commission to paint my portrait."

"I'm flattered, Your Grace. I have Monsieur David's sitting to finish, then General Lafayette and the marquise to paint. If there's time, I'd be honored to accept your commission."

"Then I'll impress upon General Lafayette to make himself immediately available to you."

She turned back toward the door. "If you'll excuse me, I need to make myself presentable, but I would like a few minutes of your time before you leave."

"We're finished, Mademoiselle Orsini." Thomas removed a stack of books from a chair and pulled it up close to her. "Please, have a seat."

She patted her hair, hopeless as it was. "I'm really not presentable. Continue with your meeting and I'll return shortly."

The Duke gazed at her, one eyebrow slightly raised as he scrutinized her face. "Mademoiselle, you could wear sackcloth and ashes and you would still be exquisite. Sit down and tell me your concerns."

She fiddled with her hands. This wasn't a conversation she wanted to have with Thomas present, but it looked like she was stuck. "I was told many years ago about distant relatives in the Scottish Highlands. I was wondering how difficult it would be to find them."

The Duke laced his fingers over his ivory silk waistcoat with embroidery on the collar and pockets. "What's the family name?"

"Actually, there are two. Digby and MacKlenna."

"Those families were involved in the Jacobite rising of '45. After Culloden the British dismantled the ancient clan structure. Carrying weapons was forbidden. Highland dress was outlawed. Even playing bagpipes was banned. Survivors were imprisoned and eventually transported to America. Twenty years later the Highland Clearances resulted in massive emigration. It's likely your relatives, if they survived, are in America."

There could be no mistaking a sudden jump of Thomas's eyebrows. "I have acquaintances with those surnames. Seamus Digby practices law in Richmond. James MacKlenna was given a land grant after the late war and settled in Kentucky. They might be your kin or know what became of them. Both men serve as representatives in the Virginia House of Delegates."

"Why does Mr. MacKlenna serve in the Virginia House if he lives in Kentucky?"

"Kentucky isn't a state yet. It doesn't have a seat of government."

"Oh, I thought it was one of the early states."

"Mr. Hamilton pushed the bicameral Congress to admit Kentucky and Vermont to balance the additional northern and southern representation, but Congress was too busy writing new laws, appointing federal judgeships, and deciding on departments in the executive branch. It's hoped both will be admitted next year."

She leaned back in the chair, the rails and spindles made small creaking sounds. Could it possibly be so simple? She slowed her breathing to force calm into her shaking hands as her fluttering heart beat wildly against her stays.

This James MacKlenna wasn't the same man who wrote the letter in the brooch box, but he could be… What? A five- or six-times great-grandson. Sophia found that no matter where she traveled in the twenty-first century, everyone on the planet was now connected by three and a half degrees of separation.

In 1789, it appeared the degree of separation was one.

"We'll be spending a few days in Richmond before we travel on to Monticello," Thomas said. "The House of Delegates will be in session, so I can arrange introductions to both gentlemen."

"Would they agree to meet with me?" she asked.

"You have the advantage there, mademoiselle. Offer to paint their portraits and you'll have their undivided attention."

"I commend you, Ambassador," she said. "It's a brilliant plan."

The tangible intensity as Thomas gazed at her was the most evocative look he'd ever given her. A glow rose in his face. Whether it was calculated or not, he now knew she had a strong reason to stay in Virginia, which had been his goal all along. If she remained in Richmond to paint their portraits, the weather would be too bad to travel north until the snow melted. But if either Mr. Digby or Mr. MacKlenna could help her, the weather wouldn't make any difference.

"When I return to Britain," the Duke interjected, "I'll be happy to inquire if there are any Digbys or MacKlennas in the Highlands."

"How very kind. Thank you, Your Grace." She stood, surprised to find her trembling limbs would hold her erect. "I'll leave you to conclude your business."

She returned to her studio, closed the door, and leaned against it. With a Digby and a MacKlenna in America, there was hope she'd find her way back home. When the door to the future finally opened, if it ever did, how sad would she be to leave? A question she couldn't answer for sure, but if she had to guess, she'd bet her heart would be badly cracked.

28

Richmond, VA—JL

TWENTY-FOUR HOURS AFTER Lawrence's surgery, JL was enjoying kangaroo care with him. Holding her sweet baby against her chest—skin to skin—was the most wonderful sensation in the world, and the benefits for her son were too numerous to count.

Finally, she was truly able to bond with him.

It was extraordinary to hug Kevin and hold Blane—absolutely to the moon and back—amazing. But snuggling with Lawrence was different. There had been horrifying moments when she was afraid she'd never be able to hold him, feel his warmth and, yes, his fragility and his strength.

Kevin snugged his chair next to her recliner, stroking her head while Lawrence gripped Kevin's index finger, creating a circle of love. "He settled as soon as his cheek touched your skin. Did you notice? I swear he almost sighed." Kevin leaned closer and said, in a voice as intimate as a touch, "I know how he feels. I'm jealous."

JL kissed her baby's head. "Don't worry, Lawrence. Daddy's not taking your place. You can stay right where you are."

Lawrence made a small grunting sound, opened his eyes, then closed them, as if saying, "Okay."

"He knows where he is by your scent, your voice, the rhythm of your heart," Kevin said softly.

"That's what Anne said, but I'm not convinced yet. He's so tiny. He feels as light as one of Blane's stuffed animals."

"He'll gain weight. A few ounces every day. Which reminds me, be sure to leave your nursing pads in the incubator so he'll smell you when you're away."

"What a clever idea."

She shivered as a chill tingled along her shoulders and arms, and down her back. Her hormones were out of whack, and the air conditioning was set lower than she was used to. "I need a blanket. It's July and I'm freezing. I don't know why Lisa doesn't freeze to death wearing those short sundresses."

"Her hormones aren't screwed up like yours, but it is chilly in here. And I have just the thing." He dug into his duffle bag and pulled out a Kentucky blue crocheted blanket with a white UK in the center. "Maria just finished this."

"I'm surprised it's not maroon and gold for the Cavaliers." JL sighed as instant warmth bathed her legs, her hips, her belly.

Kevin tucked the blanket under JL's feet, which were decked out in pink non-skid hospital socks. "Don't expect her to switch loyalties until Isabella finds out where she matches. Maria said Isabella's first choice was the University of Kentucky College of Medicine. If she can do her residency in pediatrics there, she'll be thrilled."

"That'd be perfect," JL said. "With this family's herd of kids, having a pediatrician in the family would be awesome." JL pulled the blanket up a little higher to capture Lawrence in the blanket's additional warmth. "Will you take a picture to show Maria we're using her gift?"

Kevin pulled out his phone. "Smile." He snapped several pictures of JL, then squatted beside her chair and took a few selfies of the three of them.

Elsewhere in the room white coats and patterned-print scrubs surrounded Ruth's incubator. From JL's position she couldn't see what they were doing. *I hope she's okay.*

"I do too," Kevin said.

JL glared at him. "I didn't realize I said that out loud."

"You didn't, babe."

It still freaked her out that she and Kevin could read each other's minds. If they were in the bathroom at the same time getting ready for bed, or in the morning before work, they often had head conversations.

"Before long most of our conversing will be through mental telepathy," she said.

"As long as the physical contact doesn't stop, I can handle that form of communication."

JL was warm and toasty, snuggling with her baby, and for a few moments she closed her eyes and knew God was in His Heaven and all was right with the world.

Kevin traced his finger down her cheek, the side of her neck. "What are you thinking?"

She smiled. "That right now is a perfect moment, but perfect moments don't last very long."

"Ditch the cynicism. You're too beautiful to have permanent creases in your forehead."

"I think I'll stay a cynic and just get Dysport injections like everyone else. Besides, I can't ditch the trait. It's a counterweight to your eternal optimism. It's easier to find middle ground when we start at opposite poles."

"If you think I'm the eternal optimist, have a longer conversation with Robert Harrison. As worried as Lisa is about the hospital bill, Robert is just the opposite. He had an appointment at the patient accounting office today and had absolute confidence he could work out a payment plan without wiping out his portfolio. He said convincing Lisa everything would be fine was more challenging than dealing with the hospital."

"I haven't seen her in a couple of hours." JL sighed. "I feel like we're all riding on the same perpetual Ferris wheel. Every hour one of our cars comes to the bottom, but none of us can get off. This situation is fraught with stress. At least we don't have money or childcare issues. Our situation is probably unique up here. We need to find a way to help as many parents as we can."

"Elliott's setting up a fund to subsidize one room per pod in the hotel while he's negotiating a deal to buy it. His plan is to convert it into efficiency apartments just for NICU parents. That should help. And for parents who can't stay in Richmond, he's buying cameras so they can watch their preemies around the clock."

"When he does something extraordinary like that, I feel so guilty for getting mad at him, but sometimes I can't help it. He can be so controlling. But as for putting his name on a hotel, I can't see it," JL said. "A new wing, yes. An endowed chair, yes. But not a hotel."

"When it's finished, he'll donate it to the hospital. He'll get a plaque on the wall and a huge tax write-off."

"That will help, but only if he manages the selections so the Harrisons get a room every night."

"He'll figure it out."

"I'm sure he will. I noticed he even stuck his nose into Rick's selection of a catering company for the winery's reopening event."

"Don't read your emails, JL. They'll only stress you out more."

"Honestly, I need a distraction from constantly worrying about Lawrence. And right now, I don't have any responsibility for solving the company's problems, but I need to know what's going on. You know how I am."

"Elliott got involved because Meredith wasn't happy about using someone from Kenzie's PTSD support group for the biggest event the winery has ever had. She wanted an established business, but Rick assured her the new company could pull it off, and it was important to Rick to award the contract to a veteran-owned business."

"Good for him for standing up to her."

Kevin clicked keys on his phone. "If looks have anything to do with competence, then this woman has it in spades. She's exotic. Tall, lanky brunette with big brown eyes. Her name is Billie Malone."

JL looked at the picture on the website. "Billie looks like a frigging model. She's gorgeous. But she doesn't look like a Billie

Malone."

"Her name is Wilhelmina Penelope Malone."

Despite JL's stress she laughed. "Who would do that to a child? It's worse than Jenny Lynn. Bless her heart. I'd go by Billie, too."

"According to the About Me section on her website, the Army Rangers shortened her name to Billie."

JL laughed again, and then cooed to Lawrence, apologizing for disturbing him. "Meredith might intimidate a lot of women, but she'll never intimidate an Army Ranger with a name like Billie Malone."

"She never intimidated you."

"That's because when I met her I was wearing an NYPD badge and had a gun in my hand." Lawrence squirmed again, and this time pooped in his diaper. "Oh, precious baby. Do you feel better?" She glanced up at Kevin. "I don't think Lawrence liked the part about me carrying a gun."

"I don't either." Kevin glanced around and spotted Anne working on Ruth. "When Anne finishes, I'll tell her Lawrence needs changing."

"If he's going back in the incubator, the respiratory therapist has to manage all the cords and connections. Which means once they take him, I won't get him back." JL wasn't ready to let him go, but he needed to be changed.

She and Kevin were both watching Anne move efficiently around Ruth's incubator. "I heard something interesting about Robert today."

"Must have come from Charlotte. I can't imagine anyone else talking to you about him."

"You're right," Kevin said. "You know how she is about history, especially Virginia's. She said Robert's ancestor was a general in the Revolutionary War and Speaker of the Virginia House of Delegates when Thomas Jefferson was governor."

"I didn't know Jefferson was a governor. I thought he was just one of those Founding Fathers they made president."

Anne came over and knelt next to JL's chair to get a better look at Lawrence. "Is he doing okay?"

"He needs to be changed."

"As soon as his respiratory therapist gets here, we'll take care of him." Anne returned to her desk while JL closed her eyes and rested, enjoying the last few minutes holding her son.

"I just got a text from Elliott," Kevin said. "Kit is on her way here to stay with Lawrence, and Elliott will be here in a couple of hours."

"Is Cullen coming with her?"

"Probably. They go everywhere together."

The respiratory therapist came over and, working together, she and Anne managed all the cords and tubes with only a few whimpers from Lawrence. JL shivered, missing the featherlike weight and warmth of him on her chest. Once he was back inside the incubator, JL changed his diaper.

One day you'll pull up your big-boy pants and run off to find your brother.

The incubator's lid closed, severing the mystical oneness with her baby. They were now separated by sheets of plexiglass. A tension headache erupted, bouncing hard between her temples.

She returned to the recliner and slipped on her shoes. "I need to get something to eat and try to pump my breasts. Let's go to the hotel and fix one of Amber's meals."

"I'll do whatever you want." Kevin repacked the blanket, zipped up his duffel bag, and slung it over his shoulder. "Where's your jacket?"

"If you don't have it, I must have left it in the moms' room."

He unzipped the bag again and dug through it. "It's not here."

"I'll go look. Will you call Kit and find out when she'll get here? I don't want to leave until she's in the building." JL gathered up her purse, bottle of water, and ambled out of the pod. As soon as she rounded the corner, she bumped into Lisa, who was wiping her nose. "Whoa." JL grabbed Lisa's arm to steady herself. "Hey, are you okay?"

Lisa shuddered. "Yeah. I guess."

"You don't look it."

Lisa stared at her for a second or two. Then her eyes traveled to some indeterminate spot behind JL and grew distant, as if looking at some past event miles away or days earlier, or…hell, maybe just five minutes ago. Lisa leaned her head and shoulder against the yellow wall, fisted her hands, and sort of gave in to the moment, sighing, shaking her head, twitching her body, the kinds of things a stressed-out person does when they don't know what else to do.

JL stood by, tense with concern that Lisa and Robert might have received bad news and Lisa was trying to process what she'd just been told. JL wasn't fully functioning, and at times she doubted she was even chugging along at fifty percent, but whatever she had to give, she would.

"What's going on?" JL asked. "I have connections, and I know people who know people. If I can't move a stubborn mountain, I know engineers who can."

"You've got enough on your own plate worrying about Lawrence. You don't need my junk too."

"Look. I'm a cop—retired, but I'm still a cop. We aren't needed when life is good. People need us when life has gone to shit. Doesn't matter how much I have on my plate, I always have room for more."

Lisa's eyes softened. "I just received a call from our birth mother. She was going to pump her breasts for a few weeks to help Ruthie get a good start, but now she's not going to do that. She's been rooming with a friend from school this summer, and now she's decided to move to California and start graduate school. Robert wants to get our lawyer involved, but I don't want to spend more money on her or legal fees. Every penny is earmarked for Ruth's care."

"Can the NICU get donor breast milk?"

"There's a milk bank in Norfolk, but it's not covered by our insurance. Robert told me we could use some of our savings to pay expenses, and he ordered me"—she made air quotes—"to stop worrying."

"If Kevin told me to stop worrying, it would go in one ear and out the other. You can't tell someone to stop worrying."

"The problem is, we have different views about money. He grew up in an affluent family in Charlottesville. I grew up in a working-class family in New York City. I know what it's like to live paycheck to paycheck. And besides, I'm a natural worrier. I saved every penny I could to pay for a surrogate, and now I'm afraid we won't be able to pay Ruth's expenses."

"They won't hold Ruth hostage until the hospital bill is paid. The business office will work with you."

"I know they will, but I'm obsessive, and can't stop worrying."

"Then go see my psychotherapist. She's in the building and insurance pays for the sessions."

"Give me her number and I'll call and make an appointment." Lisa patted her chest. "I don't deal well with things I can't control. When I was seventeen, I went on spring break with friends. One day, while we were at the beach, someone broke into our room and stole my food money. My girlfriends were all on tight budgets. No one could float me a loan. We were all eating fast food and skipping meals. I had to get a job stocking shelves so I could eat."

"Sounds like you handled it with panache. You knew what you had to do and did it. You took control."

"It's gotten all warped in my head. When I don't have money of my own, I feel out of control." Lisa ran her hands over her hair and pulled it together in a ponytail she then looped over her shoulder. "I mean, Robert has this covered, but having my own secret stash is insurance for me. I know it's not logical—"

"Logical?" JL gave Lisa a reassuring squeeze on her arm. "Putting our babies in Plexiglas boxes isn't normal or logical. Hey, here's a thought. Why don't you sell one of your sculptures and keep the money in your secret stash? Bet it will make you feel better."

"I don't have time right now to look for exhibitions to take my art."

"Kevin's father has connections in the art world. He can make a few calls and sell whatever you want."

"I couldn't impose."

"I'll impose for you. Send me photos and descriptions of your sculptures, and he'll take it from there."

Lisa's shoulders slumped as tension seemed to seep out of her. After a minute she said, "I have four pieces ready to sell. There's a market for my work, but I just can't deal with it right now."

"If those sell, you'll have plenty in your secret stash. Right?"

Lisa let loose with one of those half laughs that pop out when you really want to cry, or you find yourself so overcome with relief that you can't do anything else.

"I know I'm crazy. Robert just rolls his eyes. But I can't help it."

"We all have our little idiosyncrasies."

"Now you know mine, what's yours?"

JL raised one shoulder in a half shrug. "I'm a hard-ass cynic."

"I don't believe that for a minute."

"Trust me. I wouldn't have survived the streets of New York without a healthy dose of cynicism." JL's cell phone beeped with a text message. She looked at the screen. "Blane sent me a beating heart emoji."

"He's so cute."

"He's a handful," JL said.

"So where are you going now?" Lisa asked.

JL pointed over her shoulder. "I was going to the moms' room to look for my jacket."

"Oh, okay. I'll see you in the pod," Lisa said. "And, JL, thank you. I'll send the photos and information."

JL watched Lisa walk away. She knew what it was like to live paycheck to paycheck, and when emergencies popped up, she used to run out of money long before the week was up.

Neither she nor Lisa had any idea if their preemies would have long-term medical issues, and if they did, what out-of-pocket expenses they'd have. But JL would never have to worry about money. And once Lisa sold her art, she might not have to worry either.

JL searched the moms' room and found her jacket, swung it over her shoulder, and returned to the pod. Kit MacKlenna Montgomery had arrived and was standing over Lawrence's incubator with Kevin. Kit was a decade older than Kevin was now, because of the years she spent living in the past, but you couldn't tell. Her green eyes were still as bright as they'd been in her family pictures, her hair was the same shade of blonde, and her petite figure was still trim and muscular.

JL went over to Kit and gave her a hug. "Thanks for sitting with him. Where's Cullen?"

"He and Braham assigned a scene from Romeo and Juliet to read and discuss. The kids decided they wanted to act it out instead. So they put their creative hats on, designed a set for the performance space in the library, divvied up parts, and sent out email invitations for a performance at seven o'clock."

"Oh... I'm sorry to miss it. Does Blane have a part?"

"Everyone who wanted a part got one, but only a few have a speaking role. Blane is a tree."

JL grinned at Kevin. "Ah. A tree. How cute. I'm sure he's thrilled just to be part of the action. Do we have time to get to the plantation?"

"If you want to go, it would be good for you. And a wonderful surprise for Blane."

The decision tugged on JL's heart. If she went to the plantation, it would take longer to get back if there was an emergency. This was one of those situations the NICU staff warned her about. She had two other sons. They needed her too.

"Okay. I'll go," she said before she could change her mind.

"If you want to see the performance, Kit, I'll stay," Kevin said.

"Heavens, no. Been there, done that. The first time I reenacted a scene from Romeo and Juliet was on the Wyoming prairie. Adam Barrett played the role of Tybalt, and I played dual roles: Romeo and Mercutio. While we were sword fighting, we were interrupted by a mother's heart-wrenching scream. I can still hear it." Kit shivered. "I've never acted in a Shakespearean role since." She glanced at Lawrence and ran her hand along the top of the incubator. "It was an amazing trip, but full of hardship and heartache."

"You met Cullen," JL said.

"You wouldn't believe all the excuses Elliott made for you," Kevin said. "He spread a rumor that you were living in Scotland in seclusion. I had no idea what was going on."

"He was furious because I went off without him." Kit shivered again. "So, how's Lawrence been today?"

"No emergencies. We're taking it hour by hour, though," JL said.

Kevin picked up his duffel bag and slung the strap over his shoulder. "JL did kangaroo care for a few hours."

"I'm sure it was wonderful to hold him. Now, you two run along. I'll text Kenzie and tell her you're coming."

Kevin swept his arm around JL's waist and steered her toward the entrance to the pod. "You heard Kit. Let's go."

JL didn't get two feet away when she noticed Lisa sliding her hands in the portholes of Ruth's incubator. "That's Lisa Harrison," JL said to Kit. "She's a sweetheart. She's also an artist, and Pete knew her when she was in high school. It's such a small world."

"If there's any down time, I'll speak to her. Now enjoy the play, and don't worry about this little guy. I'll watch over him."

JL stood in the entrance to the pod and watched Kit sanitize her hands before slipping them through the portholes. If anyone could handle things here, Kit could. JL squeezed Kevin's hand, and together they drifted out of the NICU, leaving part of their hearts behind.

29

Paris (1789)—Sophia

THOMAS'S LEAVE OF absence from President Washington arrived on August 26, 1789, but it was another month before he was able to tie up loose ends and prepare for departure.

Except for Sophia, who knew what was happening from a historical context, probably no one in France was more acutely aware of the gathering storm than Thomas. His intimacy with Lafayette and his access to the ministry and diplomatic corps, put him in a favorable position to learn exactly what was going on. As far as she was concerned, it was past time to get out of the city, out of the country, and off the continent.

Sophia often went with him to assembly meetings to sketch the people in attendance. At her suggestion, he included the sketches in his letters to John Jay. It was a marketing strategy for her, because if she couldn't go home again she would need to grow her business. Including her sketches in his correspondence was a perfect way to promote her art.

Watin had restocked her supplies over the past few days, and she'd packed them in black leather traveling trunks. Her paintings were crated or rolled and her sketching materials boxed. There wasn't anything left to do as she walked through her studio except check items off her list and lock all the trunk lids. Even though she used the room for only a few short weeks, the space vibrated with memories.

While being stuck in Paris was stressful, something amazing had taken place in her studio, something so unique it could never, ever be recreated. She had become, in the truest sense of the term, an Old Master. She could now check off the three requirements: (1) a painter of skill, (2) who painted in Europe, and (3) before 1800.

While she was already a painter of skill, Jacques David's two-month master class on eighteenth-century art had propelled her talent into another dimension. She chuckled at the thought. She was already in another dimension. She didn't have to be propelled anywhere.

How art historians would eventually evaluate her paintings of Thomas, the girls, Mr. Petit, Sally and James Hemings, Lafayette and the marquise, she could only guess. If she made it home again, it would be mind-boggling to read the reviews.

She stood at the French doors, shaking slightly at the thought of how her art would be remembered. But what about her? What would she remember about her time in Paris? What would she hold forever close to her heart?

That was easy. Time spent with Thomas. They had visited Parisian gardens, fountains, pavilions, and shady paths, shopped at the Palais Royal, visited museums and toured the countryside, dined at the marquise's salon, and attended the opera. They laughed, flirted, drank wine, and longed for something impossible.

Reality was hitting her now with a severe case of stomach jitters, and she fidgeted with her hair ribbon, her apron strings, and even a broken fingernail.

Her mind was a storm of what-ifs.

Crossing the Atlantic in the eighteenth century wasn't safe. What if the ship sprang a leak, a big leak? What if they were attacked by Barbary pirates? It happened to ships in the 1780s. Wasn't there a Barbary War? She couldn't remember when it happened.

Large bodies of water made her anxious. She wasn't a strong swimmer, which was why she'd never entered a triathlon. Ha. Ha.

Bad joke. Not only wasn't she a strong swimmer, but she was the slowest runner she knew. Bicycling was her strong suit.

I wonder when bicycles were invented. Maybe Thomas can make me one. "I'd enjoy riding a wooden bicycle more than a horse."

Marguerite laughed softly. "Are you talking to yourself, milady? I don't know what a wooden bicycle is, but I know how much you dislike your riding lessons."

Sophia whirled to find her maid swishing through the empty room carrying a leather satchel the size of a small briefcase. She enjoyed Marguerite's laughter and its unfettered energy. It was often contagious, but today she had too much on her mind.

"Yes I am, and finding myself an awful bore. What's in the satchel?"

"I found this at a shop at the Palais Royal. It will hold sketching paper, pencils, and chalk, so you'll have what you need when you want to sketch during the journey."

"How clever." Sophia accepted the satchel, untied the straps, and peeked inside, pleased to see Marguerite had already packed it. "Did you pick up the last of your dress order while you were out?"

"Yes, milady. They're all packed, but Mr. Petit questioned me about the purchases because he knows I could have made everything I bought."

Sophia retied the laces and handed the briefcase back to her. "He's right. I hated paying such exorbitant prices, but we ran out of time. What'd you tell him?"

"That I'd be managing your household and studio when we arrive in America and you want me to look...*pratique.*"

"Yes, businesslike, exactly. What'd he say?"

"He said you are an unusual woman, very fair and thoughtful, and he'd never question any decision you made." Marguerite smiled. "I think the monsieur will miss you."

"I'll definitely miss him." Sophia had become rather attached to the maître d'hôtel, and she couldn't believe Thomas was leaving him behind. But somebody had to stay and pack up the rest of the belongings when Thomas finally realized he wouldn't be returning to

France.

As for Marguerite, Sophia had debated for about five minutes whether to take her to America. Marguerite could have a prosperous future if she emigrated. So after consulting with Marguerite's brother, Sophia made Marguerite an offer. If she would accompany her to America and help Sophia get her home and studio established, then Sophia would help her open a dress shop, and she could become America's Rose Bertin.

Sophia locked the last of the trunks and gave Marguerite the keys. "Have the other trunks been loaded in the wagon?"

"Yes, milady, and they're coming for the ones in here shortly."

"Where are Mr. Jefferson's daughters?"

Marguerite slipped the keys into a pocket inside the satchel. "The mademoiselles are saying farewell to their schoolmates."

"Oh, I forgot they were stopping by. What about Mr. Jefferson?"

"He went to call on Monsieur Houdon to pick up his plaster busts."

Hands on her hips, Sophia tapped her fingers. "Hmmm. I hope Monsieur Houdon prepared them for shipping."

Thomas had taken Sophia to Jean-Antoine Houdon's studio, and she'd been honored to meet the preeminent sculptor of the French Enlightenment. When he discovered she'd been studying with Jacques David, he invited her to spend a day at his studio. One of his terra-cotta, patinated busts of Thomas would one day be on display at the Met in New York City, and two others in Philadelphia and Paris. And a marble bust made from the plaster original would one day be on exhibit at the Museum of Fine Arts in Boston. To see the busts in the sculptor's studio had been an awe-inspiring experience. And, not to overdramatize, but she did pinch herself while she was there.

If Thomas ordered twelve and only three of the plaster busts survived to be exhibited in the future, did it mean the others hadn't survived the trip to America? Or were they destroyed years later?

"I thought Mr. Jefferson wanted to get an early start this morning. Was he going anywhere else?" Sophia asked.

"He had an appointment with General Lafayette."

Sophia's mental art trivia catalogue flipped open, giving her a start. If Thomas was going to see Lafayette after leaving Houdon's studio, did that mean he was delivering a bust to Lafayette as a farewell gift? The provenance of the Jefferson bust at the Met dated back to 1934, when it first appeared on the art market. The bust was traced back to Lafayette's daughter. Coincidence?

Envisioning the presentation of the bust to Lafayette and their farewell made her heart ache. The men wouldn't see each other again until a brilliant fall day in 1824, two years before Thomas died. Thirty-five years.

If Sophia went thirty-five years without seeing someone she cared about so much, she wouldn't recognize them. She hadn't seen Pete in twenty, but she knew without a doubt her heart would recognize him even if her eyes did not.

"I guess we're finished, then," Sophia finally said. "You can tell the men to come get the trunks."

"I'll go get them now."

"I'll be out in the garden." Sophia wanted a few minutes alone to say goodbye to her studio and the garden where she and Thomas spent so much time. The sound of her thumping crutches still echoed in the room. And there was another echoing sound that couldn't be ignored—their soft moans. She shivered, shaking her head as she strolled around the small garden, remembering every moment with him—and General Lafayette, too.

While she was painting the general he often reminisced about Thomas's time in Paris, especially the early years, when Parisians saw the reticent, red-haired American Ambassador as some variation of a country bumpkin, a man out of his league when pitted against the seasoned diplomats of Europe.

Sophia couldn't imagine him as a country bumpkin. To her he was a Renaissance Man, and an incredible kisser.

They still disagreed on three major issues—women's rights, slavery, and religion. Although they agreed to disagree, the issues remained points of contention. While their differences didn't cool their ardor on moonlit strolls in the garden, the issues were a ball and chain around her ankle, and kept her from stepping over the sizzling, invisible line. A physical relationship would have been condoned in France, but, God forbid, if she had sex with him and ended up pregnant, what would she do?

One illegitimate Jefferson child at a time was more than enough.

As she gazed around the garden, she could see Thomas doing Tai Chi with her every morning. Her knee had healed, and, after some coaxing, he agreed to try a few movements, quickly discovering he had an aptitude for the powerful, graceful form of exercise.

For the past three weeks they started every day with an hour routine that usually spilled into the next. The exercise delayed the start of his schedule of letter-writing, which normally began at sunrise and continued until one or two o'clock. So either he would add an hour or write fewer letters. Instead of twenty thousand letters in his lifetime, his enjoyment of Tai Chi might reduce the number of letters to eighteen thousand.

History could blame the unwritten ones on her.

The carte blanche she and Thomas had in Paris to travel around the city together, or sit in the garden late at night drinking wine, or dance the waltz she taught him while humming off-key, couldn't continue once they left Paris.

And their relationship would change dramatically as soon as they set sail. Even though he cursed France's mores, he enjoyed the freedoms it allowed. So did she.

Biting back a tear, she reentered the studio.

Lafayette's signed portrait was still there. She wrote a brief note to him and attached it to the back of the painting next to the date and location. He was sending a courier later today to pick it up. Her painting of the marquise was delivered the prior week. They were hosting a salon tonight to showcase both portraits and had wanted to exhibit them while Sophia was still in Paris, but then she would have had to turn down dozens of commissions, so Lafayette agreed to postpone the exhibition until after she left. Having an exhibition with portraits of Thomas and Lafayette would have been the highlight of her career.

Her last conversation with Lafayette was cryptic. She warned him to be careful, but she didn't come right out and tell him his future. How could she? He wouldn't have believed that before the revolutionary storms subsided, he would be charged with treason, flee the madness, and languish more than five years in an Austrian dungeon.

As she stood in front of his painting now, goose bumps prickled the back of her exposed neck. The maturity in her art was a result of Jacques David's instructions, but the visceral energy had come from experiencing eighteenth-century painting through his emotions, through his world view. Now she was a twenty-first century painter with an eighteenth-century perspective.

She circled around the room for the last time and turned back to gaze on a space that would be razed in the nineteenth century. So much had happened within the walls of the Hôtel de Langeac.

She yawned, recalling the last bottle of wine she and Thomas shared the night before. She stayed up late, listening to him wax philosophical about the revolutionary nature of the rights of man in Europe. By two o'clock she was so exhausted, it was hard to act as an affectionate check on his episodic flights of philosophy.

That was the role James Madison played with dexterity. But the Founding Father was in New York City, where she would soon be as well. With a proper introduction and a recommendation from Thomas, perhaps Madison would commission his portrait.

She was leaving the studio for the last time when Thomas met her in the hallway. He tugged her back inside the room and closed the door behind them. "I couldn't leave here without kissing you one last time."

She gazed up into his eyes. "We're not saying goodbye." *Yet.*

"We'll have no privacy on the ship, and once we arrive in Virginia I'll be set upon with correspondence and meetings."

And with luck I'll find a way home.

"We'll still have our quiet walks at night," she said. "We're old enough to be grandparents. If we don't flaunt it, surely your friends and associates will be glad you have a companion. Don't you think?"

A breeze danced over them, and he gathered her close, molding her body to his, and she closed her eyes against the images of their moonlight walks flickering through her mind like a silent film. She brushed her lips across his face, feeling the contours of cheekbone and chin and brow, of the sensitive skin below his ear and along his jaw, seeking to know him to his bone and blood, to the brilliant mind that challenged her every heartbeat.

"My friends will be pleased for us when they see how happy we are," he said.

She glided her hands along his chest to feel his heart pounding beneath his coat, his shirt, his skin. If she could only stop worrying about the upcoming trip and what might happen when they arrived in America, she could fully enjoy the time they had left.

"Marry me," he mumbled against the skin of her neck.

Shock went straight to her heart, and she froze, temporarily unable to move or speak or even breathe.

He nibbled gently at her ear, whispering, "I adore you. Patsy and Polly adore you. Marry me, Sophia."

She took a breath, a sharp inhale, but she couldn't find her voice. She tried to force calm into her shaking body and curb her fluttering heart where it beat against her corset lining like a panicked moth against a pane of glass.

She pulled away from him, and her shock found its voice. "You don't know what you're asking. Patsy and Polly remember the promise you made to their mother. If you tell them you intend to remarry, they'll be devastated."

He gazed at her with intensity and focus, and it would be so easy to lose herself in his raw and powerful need. But she couldn't. Not with so much uncertainty swirling about them.

"The children will accept my decision. Besides, Patsy will soon marry and have a home of her own. I want to tell them I've asked you."

Until she met with Mr. Digby and Mr. MacKlenna, she couldn't make any decisions. And even then, she would never give up hope that her brooch would work again.

"Don't mention it to them, please," she said. "We have much to talk about before we could ever consider marriage." Her mind was working furiously but going nowhere, like a broken engine.

"What's left to talk about? We've covered every conceivable topic during our late-night walks. There isn't anything I don't know about you that could change my mind."

Well, Mr. Jefferson, I'm from the twenty-first century.

"The ship's captain can marry us," he said.

"You might have been thinking about this, but I haven't. I need time to catch up to you."

"Do you love someone else? Is that why you won't agree to marry me?"

"No, that's not it." She fiddled with the chain to the watch key containing a braid of his late wife's hair. "We'll discuss this when we get to Virginia."

He held out his hand. "I'm shaking with need for you."

"I'm shaking as well." Her desire was as intense as his, but this trip had messed up her cycle, and she wouldn't risk going home pregnant with Thomas Jefferson's baby. "I've known you for a little over two months, and I care for you, but I can't marry you."

His warm breath tickled her cheek. "I don't understand why you're refusing me. I know we have our disagreements, but those can be resolved—"

"Women's rights and the end to slavery can be resolved? Seriously?"

"Not immediately." He paused, then said, "I will wait until we arrive in Virginia. We can marry in Richmond."

Surprise was hardly the word she would use. It was more like bowled over. "We'll talk about next steps after I meet with Mr. Digby and Mr. MacKlenna. And until then we have expectations to discuss. I'm an artist, Thomas, and I intend to continue painting."

"If you would like to paint family members, it can be arranged, but you'll be so busy at Monticello you won't have much time."

"That is exactly what we need to talk about, because I won't give up painting to manage Monticello, especially when you're likely to accept a position in Washington's cabinet and live in the capital."

"I'm going to Monticello for a few months before returning to Paris to finish this assignment."

She straightened her hair and pressed down the front of her dress, not because they needed it, but because her fingers itched, and she didn't have a pencil or paintbrush to hold. "The men need to get in here to load these trunks. Let's talk tonight over a glass of wine." She opened the door and escaped out into the hallway.

"I don't like confrontation and disagreements," he said.

"I know you don't. And I know stress makes you physically ill and brings on a migraine. I don't want that to happen, but we have a way of pressing each other's hot buttons and tempers flare"—she snapped her fingers—"just like that."

He squinted. "Hot buttons?"

"Issues of concern. You must come to terms with what kind of woman you really want, regardless of where you live. Do you want an American Angel, a domestically-oriented helpmate who believes her place is in the home attending the needs of her husband and children? Or do you want a European Amazon, a woman out in society, engaged in political thought?"

"I want a woman who knows her place, and allows a man to take the lead and make important decisions affecting their lives. Not a politically and socially assertive Amazon seeking self-fulfillment and challenging men in exclusively male domains."

She shot him an irritated glance. "Then, Mr. Jefferson, you don't want me. If I ever marry...*again*...I expect my husband to be my partner and confidante."

He stared at her as if she'd grown a second head. "As soon as you arrive at Monticello, you'll—"

"Thomas," she interrupted gently. "An angel cannot be an Amazon, and an Amazon can't change into an angel."

"You grew up in America. You might temporarily believe you're an Amazon, but you're not. Once you return, you'll remember your place again. Our discussions over wine are always enlightening. I look forward to continuing this debate." He lifted her hand and kissed it, and then sauntered away, whistling.

Sophia rarely used profanity, but the only thought she had was, "I'll be damned." Thomas Jefferson, Founding Father and future President of the United States, had asked her to marry him, expecting her to turn into a sweet, domestic angel and be at his beck and call.

Was she crazy, or was he?

She was a lot of things, but crazy wasn't one of them. She belonged in the twenty-first century, where a woman could be whatever she wanted to be—angel or Amazon or anywhere else along the spectrum. She followed him down the hallway. But she didn't whistle.

It was September 25, 1789, and she was returning to America.

30

Normandy, France (1789)—Sophia

THERE WAS NOTHING easy or comfortable about traveling in the eighteenth century, and Sophia dreaded what was to come.

They traveled by carriage over heavily rutted roads that often left her bruised. God only knew what her body would look like after several days of a cross-country trip to the coast in a carriage without springs.

Traveling back in time had only taken Sophia a few whirlwind seconds, but going from Paris to Norfolk without planes, trains, and automobiles would take several weeks. And, depending on weather delays, it could take months.

Waiting in airports for delayed flights drove her nuts. How was she going to handle waiting for the weather to clear so a ship could sail? Probably not well. But then again, she'd be with Thomas. If they didn't argue, and he didn't pressure her for an answer, it might be… What? Enjoyable? What could possibly be enjoyable about sailing the high seas in a wooden boat? She didn't even like cruise ships.

But since it was the only way she could meet MacKlenna and Digby, she'd suck it up. The option to strike out on her own and go to Scotland to search for MacKlennas and Digbys was still available. She considered the option at least once a day, but always rolled back around to the one big question: Where did she ultimately want to end up if she had to stay for a while, like a year or two or longer? Not on the continent. And not in the UK.

Her knowledge of American history between the end of the Founding Fathers' era and the start of World War II was rather thin, but she didn't think there was a war in America until the 1800s. She couldn't say the same for Europe.

If Mr. MacKlenna or Mr. Digby didn't have a brooch able to open the time portal, maybe they'd have some insight into the stone's peculiarities, like why it worked one day and not the next. It was almost like Barbara Eden of *I Dream of Jeannie* was inside the stone, one minute happily granting wishes, then getting ticked off and ignoring all human requests.

Sophia emerged from the Hôtel de Langeac to find Mr. Petit overseeing the loading of trunks from her studio into the last of six full wagons. The maître d'hôtel would travel with them as far as Le Havre, where he would supervise offloading the baggage, then he'd return with the vehicles and horses to Paris.

Thomas assisted Sophia into the carriage, where she joined Marguerite, Patsy, Polly, and Sally. Their carriage was the first vehicle in the small caravan. At least as the first vehicle in the caravan, they wouldn't be eating dust or mud splatter.

"Will you be riding ahead or alongside us?" Sophia asked him, taking her seat next to Marguerite.

"James and I will be close by if you need anything."

She sat back and gazed one last time at the Hôtel de Langeac, wondering if anyone would have the forethought to save the painting in the dome when the mansion was razed.

"Do you know the distance to Le Havre?" Polly asked. "I don't remember much of my trip here, but it seemed as if we rode in a carriage for a month."

Sophia patted Polly's knee. "It's a hundred forty miles and will take four days."

Patsy grimaced. "Is it really that far?"

"I'm afraid so," Sophia said, "but I know a few car games to play."

Patsy gave her a questioning look. "Car?"

"Did I say car? I meant carriage. The first game is called I Spy. I'll look out the window and find something interesting. Then I'll tell you what letter it starts with."

"In English or French?" Patsy asked.

"Let's use English. Okay. Ready? I spy something with my own eyes, and it starts with the letter…G."

"Gate," Polly said.

"Yes!" Sophia clapped. "That was an easy one. Now it's your turn."

Thomas presented his two passports, one from the king and the other from Lafayette, at the gate. The documents allowed the American Minister, his family, servants, baggage, and carriages to leave France. Technically, she wasn't family or a servant, but she doubted anyone would stop them.

The I Spy game continued while they rode out of Paris and crossed the Seine, and they were laughing so hard, Thomas rode up and looked in Sophia's window. "What's so funny?"

"Mademoiselle's game, Papa. It's so much fun. Do you want to play?"

He turned in his saddle and smiled at Sophia. "No, Polly. I'd rather listen to the laughter."

Sophia couldn't take her eyes off him. He was a bold, fearless rider, and the master of his horse. When he sat in a chair, he lounged, but on horseback he sat squarely in his seat with good hand position. She might not know much about horseback riding, but she knew what looked good. And he did.

"It's your turn, Mademoiselle," Polly said.

Sophia turned back to the girls. "Okay, but I have a request. Since we're leaving Paris, and since I'm an American, would you all please call me Sophia?"

"Oh, no, Mademoiselle. We can't call you by your Christian name," Polly said. "Papa wouldn't approve."

"Then how about Miss Sophia?"

Patsy and Polly looked at each other, nodded. "Unless Papa disagrees, we'd like to call you Miss Sophia," Patsy said.

Sophia squeezed Marguerite's hand. "That goes for you, too, sweetie."

"Oh, no, I couldn't."

"You and Sally may both call me Miss Sophia. I won't answer to anything else. So there. Now, back to the game. I spy something with my own eyes, and it starts with the letter...B."

Thomas led the entourage from Paris, and as the day progressed they traveled through Normandy's rolling hills and green country-side, passing churches and small villages. According to Patsy, this was the same path they followed when she and her father first arrived in France. Sophia once drove through Normandy from Paris, and had toured the American Museum and the five D-Day beaches, but they were traveling north of the famous World War II sites.

On the first night they lodged at an ancient Norman town along the Seine with the spectacular Collegiate Church Notre-Dame at its heart.

As Thomas assisted her from the carriage she said, "There's a famous painting in that church, the *Melun Diptych*, painted by the French court painter Jean Fouquet. I'd love to see it."

"I was told the church needed money and the panels were sold a decade ago," Thomas said. "One panel went to Germany and the other to Antwerp."

She already knew the panels had been sold and where they were. She just didn't know the date of the sale other than the eighteenth century. "What a shame. I would have loved to see them together."

"If you want to visit the church, we can see where the panels hung for three hundred years."

She let out an exaggerated sigh. "I guess I could solemnly stare at the empty space and leave a bouquet of flowers."

He smoothed a nonexistent mustache, but he couldn't hide his teasing smile. "The paintings weren't stolen, darling. They were sold."

"Stolen or sold, the diptych isn't there anymore and the panels are separated, which is even more tragic."

"If you decide you want to go after dinner, I'll escort you."

But after dinner Sophia was too tired to go sightseeing, and there was no reason to stand looking at an empty wall unless she wanted time alone with Thomas. And while the thought was enticing, a bath was calling her name.

The next day the party proceeded to Bolbec, a thriving market town in the arrondissement of Le Havre. Since it was a wine-growing region, Thomas couldn't pass through without inspecting the vineyards. Sophia sent him on his way while she shopped with the girls. She found a pair of toile cushions with a charming print of a man in a blue suit and striped stockings with a bird in his hand and a dog by his side. Since there were two more days of riding in the carriage, her butt and back would thank her. Marguerite found several pieces of linen that would make elegant gowns, so Sophia bought enough for four, and Marguerite assured her she would have the new dresses made before they arrived in Virginia. Sewing would give Marguerite and Sally something to do on the ship, but what about Patsy and Polly?

The question answered itself when they found a bookstore where Sophia purchased three leatherbound journals. After the wind had carried off a sketch of Thomas on horseback, she realized drawing on loose paper while traveling was a bad idea. This would keep her notes and sketches safely attached.

Due to packing and last-minute visits with schoolmates, Polly had missed her painting lessons, so she could use a journal for her sketches and trip notes. Patsy wasn't interested in keeping a journal or drawing, so instead she selected the book *Cecilia* by Frances Burney. Sophia wasn't familiar with the author or title, and hoped it was appropriate reading for a young American woman. Thomas would let Sophia know if it wasn't.

Two days later they arrived in Le Havre. In the twenty-first century the city was designated as a UNESCO World Heritage Site. Most of it was destroyed during World War II, but it later became a symbol of reconstructed European cities. She'd visited the new city and hoped there would be time to tour the original before they boarded a ship to cross the Channel.

The carriage stopped in front of the Hôtel L'Aigle D'or. "Looks like we're here, girls. Gather your things."

"Miss Sophia, tonight will you help me with the sketch I was working on? I tried to draw Papa on his horse, but the animal looks more like a dog."

Patsy made a noise somewhere between a laugh and a hiccup. "I'm not sure even Miss Sophia can help you turn a dog into a horse."

Grinning, Sophia said, "I wouldn't be so sure, Patsy." Sophia glanced at the drawing. "Maybe it can be a pony instead."

Polly gave her sister a so-there face.

"Papa would *never* ride a pony," Patsy said smartly.

Sophia eyed the sketch again. "Maybe the picture could be a satire."

"Of what?" Patsy asked.

Sophia didn't do satirical paintings. "Maybe the pony could represent his view that all men are created equal."

"I don't understand," Patsy said.

"I don't either. But your papa is waiting for us. Shall we go?" Sophia didn't have an end game in mind when she mentioned the idea of a satire. But if Thomas was sitting atop his views on equality, then the disproportionate size of the beast of burden certainly could be satirical. Or it could represent him riding, Pope-like, on a donkey in a show of humility.

"Miss Sophia," Polly said. "I have an idea. The pony could represent our young republic, and Papa is riding the animal, guiding the country in the right direction."

"That's perfect, Polly. Your papa will like that very much." Sophia almost felt guilty for her interpretation, but wasn't that what art was all about? A viewer should always be free to search for multiple meanings within the context of the painting.

Thomas opened the carriage door. "What will I like?"

Polly hopped out. "My latest sketch, Papa. I'll show it to you this evening."

He gazed into Sophia's eyes while reflexively whisking away a bead of sweat trickling down his temple. The emotion she saw in his eyes shook her to her core and beyond, if that was possible. Before she fell into his arms and kissed him passionately, she gathered her pillows and journal and, accepting his hand, climbed down from the carriage.

"I've booked two rooms here," he said. "Would you join me for dinner?"

"Shouldn't we all dine together?"

"Patsy and Polly will dine early. From the look of those dark clouds, we might be here a couple of days, and I'd like you to explore the city with me. I'll get a recommendation for a place to dine tonight."

They entered a stunning courtyard encircled by stone walls and heavy oak doors. The girls had gathered around a nearby flower garden with a pond and were thankfully too far away to hear.

"If there are any vacancies, I'd like my own room," Sophia said.

Thomas stared up at the sky, grimacing. "That's an extravagant expense."

"I'll pay for it, of course."

"In a few weeks we'll be married. By law your property will come under my control—"

She jerked at his archaic assertion, but instead of running as far from him as possible, she stood her ground and looked him squarely in the eye. "First, I haven't agreed to marry you. And second, even if I do, my property will remain my own. I'll be happy to share my resources with you, but, Thomas, you're in debt, and I can't live that way."

His voice sounded almost normal, but an angry flush covered his ruddy face. "As soon as I'm reimbursed for my expenses and—"

"As soon as you're reimbursed, you'll spend the money on improvements to Monticello or another order of wine. You inherited debt from your father-in-law—"

He stared in open-mouthed shock and disbelief. "My finances

are none of your concern. And may I ask how you know about my father-in-law's estate?"

"Uh... I told you weeks ago that people talk, and I listen." Heat rose up her neck to her chin to her cheeks. "I'm sorry. I had no right..."

His finances weren't her concern, but she needed to put a stop to any thoughts he might have of using her money, her painting income, to offset his debts. Sadly, the sage of Monticello would die heavily in debt. If he didn't already have two marks against him—his views on women's rights and slavery—his financial situation alone should be enough of a red flag to keep her far away from him.

"Paying my bills has always been a priority for me," she said. "Other than necessities, I don't buy anything until what I owe is paid off." She put several livres in his hand. "This is for my room and board and passage to America."

He stared at his hand, unsure of what to do with the money. "I can't take this."

"I'm not your responsibility, Thomas. And if you won't take it, I'll strike my own deal with the captain of the ship."

"Mr. Trumbull has made all the arrangements. Mr. Lawrence will take my Draft on Grand for one hundred guineas to cover the cost of the ship and the ship's stores."

"I don't know what that means. Is that a check? A bank draft? Surely he'll accept livres. All of France does."

"Sophia, don't involve yourself in my finances."

"I won't, just as long as you don't involve yourself in mine."

"Until we're married, I won't," he said, without a flicker of doubt in his eyes.

"Which means you'll let me pay my expenses." She wrapped her hand over his, closing his fingers over the money. "Now, shall we go see about our rooms?"

It was storming when they went to dinner later. While sitting at the table after the meal drinking a local wine, Thomas gave her a soft look. "You're staring," she said.

"No, Sophia. I'm gazing." He looked away, but a moment later, he was staring again, and it made her heart squeeze. "If we were sitting in the garden at the Hôtel de Langeac, I'd kiss you."

She leaned forward with her forearms on the table. "If we were in your garden alone, I'd kiss you back."

"The weather might keep us here several days. We could find a few private moments."

For a long time all they could do was stare, or, as he had said earlier, gaze. In the extended silence, the butterflies in her stomach began to feel like frantic birds, and all she could think about was how much she wished they were alone, yet how glad she was that they weren't. She had no idea how this story was going to end, but couldn't imagine closing the book without at least one night together, whatever that would entail. The thought of a final chapter for them was scary.

He touched her forehead with a lingering stroke of his fingertip, and the touch loosened something in her all the way through her diaphragm and down between her legs.

"The furrows in your brow deepen when you concentrate, especially while you paint, but you're not painting now. What's on your mind?"

She squirmed in her chair as she cleared her throat. "I'm sure my thoughts are not far from yours. But Thomas, I'm not a young girl now, and I won't act against my self-interest or allow others to impose theirs."

"'The art of life is the art of avoiding pain, and he is the best pilot who steers clearest of the rocks and shoals.'"

She lifted her glass. "Your epigram has been my motto since I was seventeen. But sometimes we can't avoid the rocks and shoals no matter how far or fast we turn the wheel."

He gave her a small, wistful smile. "I haven't seen the philosophical side of you. I'm not sure what to make of it."

"Make of it what you will, sir, because I'm not sure either." The melancholy in her voice surprised her. But it was typical when haunting memories of Pete and their forced separation came to mind.

She changed the subject. "There are places I'd like to see and sketch here in Le Havre, even in the rain. But what of you? Is there any business you can conduct? I heard you mention something to Mr. Cutting when you returned from your tour this afternoon about cargoes from America returning with empty holds. Why is that? Surely there is something France can export, even with a rebellion brewing."

"Ships unload their cargo and have nothing to take back except salt, but salt can only be bought at a mercantile price at places on the Loire and Garonne."

"But they're on the Biscay side of France, hundreds of miles away."

"I posted a letter to comte de Montmorin, hoping to get a concession from the farmers-general to allow American vessels to load with salt at Honfleur, opposite Le Havre, paying only mercantile rates."

"If you can accomplish that, it would be a wonderful way to end your diplomatic career in France."

"'Tis not an end yet, my dear. I'll return in several months to complete it."

"Thomas, you have to be prepared for President Washington's offer to serve in his cabinet."

He was frowning now, his gaze turned inward. He wore that look, she had learned, when he was listening to whatever inner voice drove him to rehearse different scenarios in order to respond appropriately.

"I've said before, I'll finish the job I have, then retire."

Sophia sighed and pressed her hand over his, holding the stem of the wineglass. "Be prepared. You're too valuable to the president to be left behind in France or the mountains of Virginia."

"We shall see, my dear. We shall see."

31

Richmond, VA—Kit MacKlenna Montgomery

K IT WATCHED JL and Kevin leave the pod, his arm around her, JL leaning against him. He was more than a foot taller, and while they were both physically fit, Kevin dwarfed her in size and presence. But JL had the heart and courage of a bear, and when she was pissed off, the growl of one too.

Of all the girls Kevin had dated when he and Kit were in high school, none of them were like JL. He'd dated the country club girls, the beauty pageant winners, girls more interested in the social scene, clothes, and shopping. He always had a knockout blonde on his arm or next to him in whatever expensive sports car his parents bought for him. He avoided career-minded, tough girls, and maybe that's why he and Kit had become best friends and not boy-friend/girlfriend all those years ago. She was drawn to him for the same reason she loved her godfather Elliott—his heart for people and animals—although she was unaware at the time that they were father and son.

The years she and Kevin worked as EMTs at the same Lexing-ton fire station had cemented their friendship. While it took a while to reestablish their relationship after she and Cullen returned to live in the future, she and Kevin had found their way back. Now a day didn't go by when they didn't text or call.

It had taken her a while to warm up to JL, to break through her hard-ass exterior, but once Kit did, she and JL became fast friends. How could they not? They both loved Kevin. And while JL didn't worship at Elliott's feet the way Kit did, JL did have a healthy respect for him—when they weren't squabbling.

JL could be an odd bird, but the oddest thing was her unusual friendship with Jack Mallory. The former Southern playboy and the former NYPD detective had forged an unexplainable and unbreakable bond. You just had to shrug and accept the closeness without trying to analyze it.

The brooches had brought an amazing group of people together and cemented the connections with love and a bit of magic. Kit and Cullen were the first, and their love had started the dominos falling with amazing precision. Braham and Charlotte found each other in the middle of a war, and so did David and Kenzie. Then Jack and Amy, Daniel and Amber, Connor and Olivia.

Who would be next? Whose lives would be turned upside down by a brooch? If no more showed up in Kit's lifetime, it would be just fine with her.

Since Lawrence's birth, Kit's memories of babies had played on a constant loop in her mind. The Shakespeare reenactment brought a sad memory front and center, and now, gazing down at Lawrence, Kit's mind floated back almost four decades.

She and Cullen were married on a hot day in June of 1852 at Chimney Rock, Nebraska, and had ridden off to spend their wedding night at a hot spring. They returned to the wagon train the next evening.

"It's quiet as a hog's tit," Adam Barrett had said as they rode back into camp.

But the peace and quiet hadn't lasted. Kit found Adam's mother Sarah laboring on a cot inside her tent. Kit hadn't even known her friend was pregnant with her sixth child. She'd been so pissed when she found out, especially at John, Sarah's husband. The wagon train was still nine hundred miles from Oregon, and the hardships they'd experienced so far were minimal compared to the ones that lay ahead.

Kit stroked Lawrence's hand, remembering the night in vivid detail, remembering the pain, remembering the sadness. Sarah had only been twenty-four weeks pregnant. And Kit knew when she found her friend that if Sarah had the baby, it wouldn't survive the night.

The moment Sarah realized what was about to happen—that her baby would die—broke Kit's heart. Sarah had been so brave. She knew both the pain of childbirth and the pain of losing a child, and now she had to endure both again.

Amid muffled groans, Sarah pushed her tiny baby out into the world. He was so small, smaller than Lawrence. Kit lightly touched the tip of Lawrence's nose, remembering so clearly the undeveloped features of Sarah's baby. Kit had cleaned the infant, felt the beat of his heart, a heart that beat for only a few minutes. She glanced up at the monitor tracking Lawrence's heartbeat.

If I'd brought Sarah and the baby forward in time, could I have saved him? The question had haunted her through the years, and now even more so.

Lawrence squeezed her finger, and she smiled down at him.

She had longed to save Sarah's baby, but at the same time knew heroic efforts would only delay the inevitable. And she had given her word to Cullen that she wouldn't use the brooch to take Sarah and the baby to the future.

But what if she had?

Could modern medicine have saved him? And if so, what physical disabilities would he have had? His dependence on modern medicine would likely have required them all to stay in the future.

Kit's attention returned to the cardiopulmonary monitor, and she studied the numbers, all within normal parameters. Without the machines, no one would know if Lawrence's heart slowed or his temperature dropped.

When Sarah's baby was born, she'd wept over him, sprinkled his forehead with her liquid love, and named him Gabriel. While she and her husband sang their baby into Heaven, Kit left them to find

Cullen and cry for the baby she'd elected not to save. Tears had streamed down Kit's face then as well as now. She swiped them away, still wishing she had done more.

Someone came up behind her, and strong arms with large, familiar hands encircled her. She placed her hands over Cullen's, the backs of which were sparsely peppered with dark, graying hair, and she leaned into him.

"I was worried about ye, lass," Cullen whispered near her ear. "I couldn't stay away."

"I'm okay. You should have stayed to watch the show."

"Braham had it under control, and my bride's state of mind was more important. I didn't want ye to be up here by yerself."

"I've been up here before by myself."

"Aye, ye have. But only for an hour while Elliott met with the Director of Philanthropy." Cullen nuzzled her ear, breathing warm air on her neck. "Lawrence is so small. Was Gabriel this size?"

"What made you think of him after all these years?"

"He's been on my mind as much as he's been on yers. I was just too much of a coward to mention it."

She patted Cullen's hands. "Me too. But I should have known he was on your mind too." She drew in Cullen's scent of strength and purpose, absorbing the radiant warmth of his love, so intoxicated by it that she snuggled up as close as she could. She didn't want to lose a single precious moment of him.

It was exactly what she did, exactly how she had felt that night on the prairie. "Gabriel was smaller than Lawrence. Four weeks makes a huge difference in their development."

"Smaller?" Cullen asked. "Then I could have held him in my hand." He kissed Kit's cheek. "I shouldn't have made ye promise not to take Sarah to the future. Now that I've heard what's being done for Lawrence, the same could have been done for Gabriel. I should have encouraged ye to save his life instead of thinking of myself and exacting a promise from ye."

"You made the right decision, and I've never blamed you," she said.

"But I've blamed myself, especially now that I can see what's possible."

"Look how small and helpless Lawrence is. Look at all the cords and tubes. You've heard about all the struggles JL and Kevin have endured since Lawrence was born. How in the world could Sarah, John, and the other children have handled it, plus adapt to the twenty-first century?"

"Adapting isn't so hard. Look at how Braham and I adjusted, and Maria and Isabella, Patrick, Gabe, Noah, Daniel, and Emily. John and his family could have managed as well."

"If we had all come back, Braham would have come too. And his presence would have screwed up everything that's happened since. He might not have met Charlotte, and I might not have found my father. And it would have turned the Barretts' lives upside down, all with no guarantee Gabriel would have survived."

"We should have given him a chance."

"Lawrence will be in the NICU for several months, and we still don't know if he'll have long-term health issues. It wouldn't have been right to put the Barretts through such agony. If I had it all to do over, now that I know what I know, I'd make the same choice."

Kit sanitized her hands again and slipped them back inside the incubator to hold Lawrence's hand. "My decision that night was also based on my belief the ruby brooch wasn't meant to be a revolving door. I knew so little about the stone then. Later I even thought that once the ruby, sapphire, and emerald were together, a permanent door would open. We now know it's not true. We need twelve brooches to fill the slots around the door in the cave. Then we won't need one brooch to come and go. We'll have the combined power of twelve stones to open the door. And who knows? There could be more than twelve brooches."

"Do ye think there are?"

She shrugged. "I don't know. And no one knows if the door will open to the past or the future. Who in their right mind would ever want to go through to the other side? Not me."

"Traveling into the future isn't so bad. I did it."

"But you had family here. If we go into the future, we won't know anyone. We've always had the benefit of knowing the history of the time we visited, but this would be a complete unknown. I hope the rest of the brooches don't show up until I'm long gone or have returned to the nineteenth century."

"So ye haven't heard the rumor." There was something in Cullen's expression, maybe in his eyes, that shocked her. There was an intensity of purpose as hard as polished steel, shot through with something akin to fear or deep concern.

"I've heard several lately. Which one are you referring to?"

"Another brooch is active."

Kit gasped and jerked her hand. Lawrence twitched in response. She added slight pressure to her touch to settle him. "To quote JL, 'Say it ain't so, Joe.' How do you know?"

"Pete confided in me. Elliott knows, but he doesn't want to deal with it right now because of Lawrence. Meredith and JL both told Pete to talk to David and plan a rescue. But he hasn't."

"Pete told JL? Recently? Like since Lawrence was born? How could he be so insensitive?"

"JL knew something was wrong and kept pressuring him until he confessed. She told him not to wait. She doesn't want anyone in the family to postpone business or personal matters because of Lawrence. Including going on an adventure to rescue Pete's old flame."

"Since I haven't heard about it, I assume it's staying a closely guarded secret for now. What do you know about the woman or where she went?"

"Her name is Sophia Orsini. She's an artist."

"Oh. I've heard of her. She's incredible. Several art critics have compared her paintings to the Old Masters. I wouldn't go that far, but she is a brilliant painter."

Cullen pointed across the pod with his chin. "The woman over there, Lisa something, is a friend of Sophia's."

"Who told you that?" She studied the woman. "Oh, never mind, I know. Charlotte tells Braham everything, and Braham tells you everything."

"Do ye want to hear the rest of the rumor or not?"

"Go ahead."

"Sophia and Pete eloped the night she graduated from high school. Her parents were so distraught they had the marriage annulled and shipped her off to Italy to live with her grandmother. They haven't seen each other in twenty years."

"How sad," Kit said.

"Sort of like ye returning to the future when ye thought I was dead."

"That *was* sad."

"The rest of the rumor is that Sophia is a Digby."

Kit gasped. "So we'll finally find out who he is."

"We might. She also has a letter about the brooches written by James MacKlenna in 1625. I haven't seen it yet, and don't know the contents. But get this…"

Kit was in no hurry to get this or that. "You sound like the twins." She fixed her eyes on her husband and waited for the moment of the big reveal.

He held up his hand, palm flat. "Sophia has made five trips back in time."

"And now she can't get home. See? What'd I tell you? Her brooch ran out of tickets. She's stranded, and someone has to make a dangerous trip back to God knows where to get her. There's probably a war going on. Like World War I or Vietnam or Korea. God knows."

"Ye sound like JL."

"She's a woman after my own heart. But I'll never be so cynical. Well, except when it comes to believing there are a limited number of rides for each brooch."

"Then we may never go home," Cullen said.

"I know you're only staying because I'm not ready."

"I'm not ready either," he said. "If we had to stay permanently, I wouldn't object. It would be hell to lose Braham again."

"I miss our children and grandchildren," she said, "but as we get

The Pearl Brooch

older the medical benefits become almost as important. Between my brain tumor and your heart attack, I'd be hesitant to leave behind this level of medical care. And I wouldn't want to leave Emily until she's settled in a career."

"The lass has been a true joy, even though we don't see her often enough."

Kit looked up at him. "But you text her three or four times a day."

"I'd text more, but I know she's busy with class and studying, and I don't want to be a nuisance."

"It doesn't stop you from texting me every thirty minutes when I'm working in my studio."

The corners of his mouth twitched. "At home, yer studio was in the house. Now I have to take the golf cart to the other side of the farm to watch ye paint."

"To harass me, you mean."

He grinned. "Ye do have a mighty fine sofa in yer studio." The heat from his thoughts was palpable, and her cheeks flamed.

"You said the same thing about the desk chair, the carpet, and the worktable."

Cullen's eyes twinkled. "They're all fine as well."

Kit stroked Lawrence's finger, thinking back to Gabriel and the decisions they made that night so long ago. "So much has happened recently. The plane crash, JL's emergency surgery, Lawrence's struggle, Meredith's grand reopening at the winery, and now a new brooch. It's a lot of stress. But I think the Barrett family would have had quadruple the stress if we'd brought them all to the twenty-first century to save Gabriel." Kit withdrew her hands from the portholes and turned to wrap her arms around her husband's waist.

"Based on the babies and parents I've seen up here, I wouldn't have wanted to force John and Sarah to go through that. It would have shaken even Sarah's faith. But it doesn't relieve the guilt I've carried for years," she said. "Charlotte made the decision to bring us here to save our lives. We made the decision not to bring Gabriel to the future, and he died."

They both looked down at Lawrence as he slept. "It's time we let go of the guilt and enjoy this child," Kit said. "Not as a substitute for the one we lost in '52—"

"But as a gift," Cullen said, "who will connect us to those we left behind and may never see again."

32

The Clermont (1789)—Sophia

T HE STORM IN Le Havre continued through the next day and the next. Sophia and Thomas ate out every evening, usually by themselves, while the girls sat in a covered section of the courtyard with Marguerite and Sally and listened to Patsy read her book. Sophia didn't mention Washington's offer again.

As dead set as Thomas was against a government position other than the one he currently held, she knew he would eventually accept Washington's offer. In fact, she looked forward to the moment when his mind would change, or the proverbial light bulb would turn on.

They were delayed in Le Havre for a total of ten days. By the time they were finally able to board Captain Wright's vessel to sail across the Channel, they had been away from Paris for two weeks and hadn't even left France. Although they were moving faster than the Allies did following D-Day, it was much too slow for Sophia.

She boarded the ship expecting to reach England in a few hours since the Eurostar from Paris to London made the trip in a little over two hours. The Dover to Calais ferry took ninety minutes. How long would an eighteenth-century sailing ship take?

Twenty-six miserable hours. And she'd never been so sick.

The choppy, bumpy water defied belief. When the GIs crossed

the Channel on D-Day, the soldiers threw up in their helmets. Although she vomited in a chamber pot, not a helmet, she knew exactly how they felt…or would feel in 1944.

Marguerite tried to care for her, but the poor thing ended up sicker than Sophia, if that was possible. "If the water is like this when we sail to America, I'll die," Marguerite groaned as she hung her head over the chamber pot.

Sophia handed her maid a wet cloth. "It won't be like this. The Channel has a reputation for being an unpredictably rough journey."

The unfortunate weather didn't even end when they reached the Customs House at Cowes, a small town on the Isle of Wight off the coast of England. No one was surprised when weather delayed them again. While they waited, Sophia and the girls went sightseeing around the island, where they peeked into the deep well at Carisbrooke Castle and stared out the window in the ruins where the imprisoned Charles I tried to escape through the bars, getting embarrassingly stuck between his chest and shoulders.

After ten days the weather cleared, and they finally set sail for America on the *Clermont,* a fully-rigged ship. They were the only passengers on what looked like a tall-ship replica of *The Bounty,* a wooden ship used in the movie *Pirates of the Caribbean: Dead Man's Chest,* which Sophia had watched three times on Netflix.

The ship had two large, identical staterooms below the quarterdeck, one port side, the other starboard. Thomas claimed the one port side. Patsy, Polly, Sally, Sophia, and Marguerite shared the other, and James would sleep on a hammock with the ship's crew. When it came to women, there was nothing fair about life in the eighteenth century. Thomas should have been a gentleman and given up his room, but hey…he was who he was, and where else could he sleep? The girls double-bunked, made do with what they had, and spent as little time as possible in the cabin.

They all agreed with Trumbull's assessment of the ship, though. It was a floating version of the Hôtel de Langeac—sans the appropriate number of bedrooms—with a very nice quarterdeck for exercising and viewing the Atlantic. Frankly, Sophia preferred to view the ocean from thirty-five thousand feet.

The first five days on board the *Clermont* were as miserable as the Channel crossing. Sophia apologized profusely to Marguerite and promised smoother sailing ahead.

The weather cleared and, with the benefit of favorable winds and fine autumn weather, Captain Colley decided to lay a straighter course than the more circuitous route originally planned. And finally the skies during the day were blue and warm, and the evenings full of stars.

One morning she carried her easel on deck to try out the bracing system Thomas created to keep the easel from moving. The breeze was cool, and the brine reached deep inside the wrinkles of her brain, laying its fingertips on certain memories of Pete at the Jersey Shore. The last month of her senior year in high school they had spent every weekend at the beach, enjoying the sun and surf while planning their elopement. It had all been perfectly planned, perfectly executed…and perfectly disastrous.

She set her face into the wind, hoping the sea spray would wash away painful memories, but even a gale-force wind would find the task impossible. He was always with her, even though she knew it was unlikely she'd ever see him again.

She locked the easel in place. The movement of the ship made painting impossible, but she could sketch the underdrawing for a painting of Thomas, who happened to be standing on the quarter-deck, the sleeves of his white shirt rippling in the wind, his hair pulled back and tied with a ribbon, his large hands gripping the helm's handles, a sly smile on his face.

His profoundly sexual nature was visible in his eyes, around his mouth, and in the way he gripped the handles with his long fingers. This was a painting she could recreate without any notes, without any sketches. Just like the one of him standing in the vineyard holding a handful of soil. What was it about his hands, with their dusting of thick, auburn hair, that she found so enticing? They were gentle when he touched her face, expressive when he talked, easy when he held his horse's reins, strong when he pressed her against him, and graceful when they were quiet and still. Houdon should have sculpted not only his bust, but his hands as well.

Captain Colley, tall and spindly, watched over her shoulder while she worked. The curling tips of his sun-bleached hair hung loose at his nape, and squint lines at the corners of his eyes could only be earned by a lifetime spent at sea.

"I'd like to purchase the painting," he said.

"You may have it. But tell Mr. Jefferson you commissioned it, and this is what you asked for. He likes composed, ordered portraits. He believes free-flowing paintings of him are unflattering."

The captain's eyes moved from the painting to Thomas. "There's nothing unflattering about a man standing at the helm of a ship. I'll tell him the painting will hang in my house, so no one else will see it."

"Then he'll wonder why you want it."

Captain Colley's mouth twitched. "Mr. Jefferson is a most unusual man. He knows as much about the sea as a sailor, and as much about the ocean tides as the moon."

"He also knows as much about wine as any vintner in France, so I'm not surprised." She glanced at Thomas again. His black-booted feet were well balanced on the deck, and his black waistcoat and wide black belt gave him the look of a swashbuckler that she found intensely erotic.

"Where do you live?" Sophia asked, to escape her thoughts of Thomas.

The captain gazed out over the sea with a tender expression on his weatherworn face, as if he was longing to be in two places at once, unsure of where his home truly was.

"I'm from Norfolk, but I built a house in Amagansett on the South Shore of Long Island. When I'm not sailing, it's where I live now."

Memories of staying at her high school friends' summer homes in Amagansett tickled her, and she smiled. She and her best friend, Lisa, were the only ones in their crowd who didn't have a summer home on Long Island. Good God, she hadn't seen Lisa in years.

How was it possible? When she got home, she'd call her. If—

The thought of not going home again cut another jagged, painful wound in her heart. How many would she have by the time this adventure ended?

If she was stuck here permanently, would she continue to believe every day held the possibility of the brooch coming alive again, or would she give up hope? She closed her fist around a piece of blue chalk, knowing deep in her gut that she'd never give up, then bit back her worries and began to sketch the sky. Both clouds and sky had some of the softest edges she found in nature, and she loved painting them, but only sketching was possible on a swaying ship.

"Are you going home after you drop us off in Norfolk?" A little gust of salt wind came off the ocean, and she grabbed and held on to the canvas.

"I'm going to Charleston first, then New York. Is there a reason you asked?"

She lowered her hand and looked up at him again. "My plan is to go to New York, but I won't be ready to leave for two to three weeks."

"Do you have family there?"

"Not any longer. No relatives at all." Her grandmother had died hoping Sophia would reconcile with her parents, but they died tragically before she contacted them. Death had robbed her of the chance.

No, wait, that wasn't true at all. Reconciliation had been sucked into the vortex of her unresolved anger, where it still swirled round and round and round.

"Will the painting be finished by the time you go to New York?"

"What?" She shook away the guilt and thought about the captain's question. "Finished? The painting? Well, it could be."

"Then I'll stop on my way back from Charleston. If you'd like to sail on the *Clermont* again, I could take you to New York."

"Marvelous," she said. "Then next time I'll paint *you* at the helm." Sailors, she had discovered, were a stoic lot. They didn't emote. Painting the captain would be a challenge.

He grasped her free hand and held it longer than necessary. Instead of releasing it after a moment, his grip tightened, not uncomfortably, just snug. His hand was callused and warm, much larger than she thought, the skin so rough it seemed to scratch her skin.

"I believe we've reached an agreement, Miss Orsini." He finally let go of her hand.

She glanced in Thomas's direction. His eyes were narrowed into the sun. His skin was darker now, a smooth golden tan from spending days entirely on the deck of the ship.

"Would you mind keeping this between us?" she asked.

"Certainly." He turned to go, scratching the side of his face, but stopped. "Miss Orsini, I might be able to assist you further. I have a sister-in-law in New York City who's a recent widow and has a house near the harbor, but she'll be forced to sell it if she doesn't take in boarders. There's room to accommodate you and a studio, and I think you would get on well together. I could write on your behalf, if there's interest."

"That's kind of you, captain."

"You're a kind person, Miss Orsini."

When the captain returned to his post and relieved Thomas of the responsibility of steering the ship, she shuddered with relief, deep and absolute. She had transportation to New York and a place to live. But it was only her backup plan. She had to believe MacKlenna or Digby had a working brooch. If they didn't, she would continue to believe the brooch was temporarily malfunctioning, and in that scenario, she would need a place to live.

Transportation to New York—check. A place to live and paint—check. Thomas working in the city as secretary of state—check.

I'll make a brand new start of it / In old New York.

33

Norfolk, VA (1789)—Sophia

TWENTY-THREE DAYS OF swift sailing and perfect weather brought the ship to a dense fog off the coast of Virginia. For three days, the thick November mist clung to the shore, making it impossible for Sophia to get even a glimpse of land. It didn't matter really that she couldn't see, but Captain Colley couldn't either.

Finally, with the aid of a strong headwind, he escaped into the Chesapeake Bay at the same moment another vessel was speeding out of port. The two ships barely avoided a head-on collision, but the outgoing ship grazed the *Clermont*, taking off part of her rigging.

Sophia was huddled on deck with Patsy and Polly when the ropes, cables, and chains came crashing down. Both girls screamed, but Sophia's scream froze in her throat. The tension and fear drawing her nerves tight as a bowstring knotted even tighter while the ropes dangled like menacing snakes above their heads. The deck's ghostly creaking had her lungs straining and struggling for her next breath.

Most frightening of all, though, were the waves pounding the port side of the ship, each one a siren's call, *Come to me.*

Sophia frantically searched the fog-shrouded deck for Thomas. His height and air of control identified him, standing head and shoulders above the sailors. He was pointing into the fog, shouting, but she couldn't hear what he said.

"Can we go below?" Polly asked in a shaky voice. "I'm afraid one of those loose ropes will fall on my head."

Sophia didn't want to leave the deck. If another ship sideswiped them or collided head-on, they could be trapped below. "I'm not sure it would be any safer there."

Patsy took charge, grabbed Sophia and Polly's hands, and dragged them down the stairs. Inside the cabin, Marguerite and Sally were huddled in a corner of one of the berths, eyes wide with fright. Polly jumped in with them.

"Are we going to drown?" Sally whispered, as if saying it out loud would cause it to happen.

Sophia climbed in next to Polly and wrapped her arms around the shivering child. "Not today," Sophia said. "But it was pretty scary up top. We're pulling up alongside the dock now, though, so if the ship goes down, we'll be rescued easily enough."

"You're never afraid, Miss Sophia. Like when we left you in the carriage on the bridge, you weren't scared."

"Well, that's not quite true. I'm afraid of water I can't walk across."

The girls laughed. "We've been sailing over deep water for weeks," Patsy said. "You never acted scared."

"Now you know why I was always drawing. My studious face looks the same as my terrified one."

They laughed again, and the fear gripping the girls evaporated while the tightness in their faces relaxed.

Thomas ducked his head and entered the cabin, hauling his mahogany traveling writing box, the size of an attaché case, under his arm. The box was quite ingenious, really, and Sophia had used it often during the trip. She hadn't been at all surprised when he told her he designed it and had it build by a cabinetmaker in Philadelphia. At her request, he agreed to post a letter to the cabinetmaker to commission a smaller one. Hers would have a shoulder strap and a latch to hold the box shut. If he wasn't improving upon something, she was. What a pair they made.

"Gather whatever you want to take with you. It's time to disembark," he said.

Polly climbed out of the berth first. "Papa, did you know Miss Sophia is afraid of water she can't walk across?"

Thomas propped his free hand on his hip and looked askance. "Why, Polly, I would be afraid if she could."

"Oh, Papa. She means walking through shallow water. Not walking over deep water like Jesus Christ."

"Thank you, Polly, for the explanation. However, I don't believe Jesus of Nazareth walked on water, either." He nodded at Sophia. "I'll meet you all topside."

Thomas was a devout theist. He believed in a benevolent creator to whom humans owed praise, but he didn't believe Jesus was born of a virgin, multiplied the loaves and fishes, or was raised from the dead. He was brilliant and intellectually curious, and he preferred to make his own judgments, even in matters of religion.

After one religious discussion when he said he was a real Christian, a disciple of the doctrines of Jesus, and called Christ's teachings the most sublime and benevolent code of morals which had ever been offered to man, she relaxed.

But when he continued with a dismissal of the Trinity, she knew she could never discuss religion with him again. She was a product of Catholic schools, regularly attended confession, and rarely missed Sunday Mass, even while traveling. Her faith was the bedrock of her core convictions. Without it, she didn't have the foundation to fight for anything. Their differing views on religion created a barrier between them.

"Come on, girls. Let's not keep him waiting." Sophia collected the two leather satchels and double-checked to make sure she had the velvet bags with her pearls and diamonds and personal items from home. The contents of which were dwindling fast.

Marguerite gathered her sewing basket. "Sally, will you carry Miss Sophia's new pillows?"

Sally tucked a pillow under each arm. "Will our belongings be safe here? All the gifts I bought for my family and my pretty dresses are in my trunk. If I lose them, I won't have any mementoes of my days in Paris."

Sophia glanced at Sally's trunk, which was constructed of the same thick leather as all the others. "It's too heavy for us to carry. But if you want to choose a few special things, you could bring those with you."

Sally stared at the trunk, tapping her foot. "I'll leave everything in there for now."

"Patsy and Polly, grab your books and journals and anything else that's not packed away," Sophia said.

With arms loaded, they left their cabin. Sophia glanced over her shoulder, and the hairs on the back of her neck stood on end. What she was leaving behind was irreplaceable—a trunk full of rolled-up paintings and sketches, along with others crated in the hold.

When she reached the deck, she asked Thomas, "Would you send two men to our cabin and have them bring up our trunks? I don't want to leave them behind."

"When they unload the cargo, they'll get them," he said.

"Please," she pleaded. "It would ease our minds. My paintings are in there, along with Sally's gifts for her family. They're irreplaceable."

Instead of arguing, he caught the captain's attention and requested the trunks in the girls' cabin be removed immediately from the ship. The captain appeared annoyed, but complied with the request, and within minutes their trunks were stacked on the dock.

"Thank you," Sophia said.

"I'll have them sent to the inn," Thomas said.

"I hope there's a nice Inn in Norfolk where we can wait while Papa arranges a carriage to take us home," Patsy said.

Sophia sniffed the air. The wharf had its own particular tang, different from Le Havre and Isle of Wight…or maybe it was simply her imagination creating an olfactory difference between Europe and America.

She wobbled as she climbed down the gang plank. Recovering her land legs might take a while. When she reached the dock and could see better through the fog, she nearly wept. "What happened to Norfolk?"

"Is this a town?" Marguerite asked.

"The British governor had it burned the second year of the war, but they're rebuilding," Jefferson said. "This is a busy port."

"Papa, the Treaty of Paris was signed six years ago. What have they been doing since then?" Patsy asked.

"This place is nothing more than a village of shanties," Sophia said.

"Where are we going to stay tonight, Papa?" Polly asked. "In a tent?"

"We'll find something more suitable than a tent," Thomas said. "Norfolk is part of Virginia, and Virginians will open their doors for us." With his free hand he tugged on his waistcoat and straightened his cravat. "Come along."

Sophia chuckled. They had all complained about the city except Thomas, who saw the goodness of Virginians over the inadequacies of Norfolk. They followed him through the muddy street to the only hotel in town to discover there was no room at the inn.

But when word passed through Hotel Lindsay that Thomas Jefferson had just arrived, several patrons insisted on vacating their rooms. Thomas sat at one of the long oak tables and drank ale with them while the girls went upstairs with their trunks to settle in.

Marguerite hung the new dresses on pegs in one of the bedrooms. "How long will we be here?"

"Hopefully just overnight," Sophia said. "Although I doubt Norfolk has a livery, so I'm not sure where we'll find transportation."

"If Mr. Jefferson is right about Virginians, then maybe they'll open their stables, too."

"You're very astute, Marguerite," Sophia said. "And if you ask him, it's probably what he would say."

A pounding on the door preceded Patsy's panicked voice, crying from the hallway, "The ship's on fire."

Sophia yanked open the door. "The *Clermont?*" The news gripped

Sophia's gut, as tight and relentless as a vise. Her framed paintings were in the belly of the ship.

"Look." Patsy pointed out the window, but all Sophia could see were flashes of fire in the fog.

"Come on. Let's hurry. They'll need help with the bucket brigade." Sophia locked the door before hurrying after the girls, who were already flying out the inn's front door.

By the time they reached the dock, fast-moving flames were spreading through the cabins and smoke belched from cracks in the walls and open windows. A bucket brigade had already formed, and men were heaving buckets of water onto the fire.

"It's no use," the captain yelled. "It's moving too fast."

"We can't quit," Jefferson hollered back, filling another bucket with water from the bay. There were only about a dozen men on the line, and to douse the flames they would need a dozen more.

"All of Papa's papers are in his trunks. He'll be devastated," Patsy said.

"Thank you, Miss Sophia, for having our trunks removed," Sally said.

Sophia hugged her. "I just had a feeling. I hope Mr. Jefferson's papers survive."

She was fighting back tears, though, over the possible loss of his books and papers and her paintings and supplies in the hold.

But Sally and her brother had left France, where they had a legal right to claim freedom on their own terms only to return to slavery in Virginia. If Sally had lost her trunk, she would never be able to share her mementoes with her mother or hold them to remember her adventures. Even if Sophia lost every painting she ever painted, she would never lose as much as Sally.

"Sally," Sophia said, wiping her cheeks. "Go back to the hotel. This smoke is not good for you and your baby."

Sobbing, Sally said, "I'll wait at the end of the dock. The wind's blowing in the opposite direction."

"Come on, Sally. I'll go with you," Polly said.

Dozens of men ran toward the ship, but it appeared the fire was too far out of control to extinguish. Thomas trudged away, his head hanging, and Sophia's heart broke for him, too. Five years of papers, a portion of his book collection, and crates of wine and furnishings were all lost.

The men fought the fire tenaciously and saved the ship, but the cabins had been heavily burned. When it was safe, Thomas and Captain Colley boarded to survey the damage. Sophia and Patsy waited on the dock, hugging each other and coughing from the smoke in the air.

Twenty minutes later, Jefferson joined them on the dock. His flushed face was coated with a sheen of sweat, his clothes dusted with ash, his neckcloth a dark gray. "As far as I can tell"—he coughed—"our trunks didn't burn. They all survived the fire intact."

Sophia was flabbergasted. "The flames were shooting out the windows of our cabins. And you're saying nothing burned? How's that possible?"

He wiped his brow with a handkerchief, already a dirty gray. "Everything in the cabins burned—furniture, bedcovers, lamps, wall hangings."

"Except the trunks?" Patsy asked. "Your papers are safe, Papa?"

"Yes. Captain Colley will have my trunks delivered to the inn. The fire didn't reach the belly of the ship, so all the crates are safe as well."

"Patsy, go tell Polly and Sally the good news."

"Here comes the captain," Thomas said. "He's one lucky soul."

"Miss Orsini. May I speak with you?"

"Go on," she said to Thomas. "I'll meet you at the inn."

"Are you sure?" There was a distinct note of disapproval in his voice. "I'll stay with you, just the same."

She glanced back at the captain, who had been stopped by a sailor, and then she turned to Thomas, summoning a casual smile. "Captain Colley commissioned a painting. He wants to discuss details. I'll be along shortly."

"You didn't mention that. I'll negotiate for you. How much do you hope to get for the painting?"

She hugged her elbows with her palms to keep from swatting him. "I'm quite capable of negotiating this. I'll meet you at the inn as soon as I finish with the captain."

His brows slanted down like an angry hawk, and they glared at each other over a bristling silence. Finally she said, "Thomas. I'm an artist. I paint, and I sell my paintings. I've been negotiating with patrons for years. I know the value of my work. I know how much I want for a painting, and what I'm willing to accept."

"I'll listen and offer—"

She gave up on the thought of swatting him and instead pressed both hands on his chest. "I'll take care of this, and I'll meet you at the inn when I'm finished." Instead of waiting for additional protests, she squared her shoulders and left him scowling.

Sweat dribbled down Captain Colley's leathery cheeks, and he pushed his disheveled hair away from his face. "I won't be going to Charleston now. It will take at least a month to make repairs, so I'll miss picking up the shipment in South Carolina. Instead I'll head straight to New York. If you need to sail sooner, I can—"

"No," she interrupted. "I can wait, and I'll certainly have the painting completed by then."

"I'll send a message when the ship is ready to sail. Where will you be?"

"I don't know yet. As soon as I reach my destination, probably Richmond, I'll write and let you know. When you're ready to leave, you can send a message to me. Will that work for you?"

"It should, yes, and I've already penned a letter to my sister-in-law and should have a response before we leave Norfolk."

"Thank you for agreeing to take me. I hope the damage isn't extensive."

"It could have been much worse."

Sophia glanced around shantytown, wondering again why the town wasn't more developed, since it was a major shipping hub. "It looks like there's a shortage of building materials. Will you have trouble getting what you need?"

"There's an abundance of raw materials for ship construction around Norfolk. We won't have a problem."

"They must use all the materials for ships instead of building a center city."

"The shipwrights stay busy. There's an impressive shipbuilding and repair depot nearby. You've been living in France where buildings are centuries old, but old around here is a handful of years."

"Well, it's obvious I have a lot to get used to. I'll see you in a few weeks," she said.

By the time she finished with the captain, Thomas was nowhere to be seen. If he asked how much the captain agreed to pay for the painting, what would she say? A free trip to New York? No, it would spark an argument she wasn't ready to have. But he was going to New York after Christmas. He just didn't know it yet.

Boisterous voices spilled out of the inn's open windows. A celebration was in progress. When she entered and spotted Thomas in the middle of the throng of men with raised glasses, she knew the cause of the good cheer.

Patsy and Polly were seated at a nearby table. "What's going on?" Sophia asked.

"The mayor, the recorder, and aldermen from the borough of Norfolk are here to formally greet Papa, congratulating him on his safe arrival, thanking him for his eminent services to the trade of his State, and fervently wishing him happiness and continued success in the important station to which he has been called by a grateful country." Patsy handed Sophia a week-old copy of the *Virginia Gazette.* "There's an article in the paper saying President Washington nominated Papa for secretary of state, and the Senate confirmed him."

"What did he say?" Sophia asked.

"That service to his country was the first wish of his heart."

Sophia sat down next to her. "So the politicians are here to greet a high official of the new government, not merely a diplomat."

"You knew he'd be offered this position, didn't you?" Patsy asked in an accusatory tone.

"Your papa is too valuable to be left in Paris right now. President Washington needs him in New York."

"But he's needed at Monticello. He's given the government five years. He should be allowed to go home and take care of his farm," Patsy said.

Sophia put her arm around the girl's shoulders, half expecting her to sluff off the embrace, but she didn't. "I'm sure he feels the same way."

Patsy pushed her teacup aside and then shrugged off Sophia's arm. "Then why would he agree to take the job?"

"He hasn't yet."

"But he will, won't he, Miss Sophia?" Polly asked. "He'll go to New York. I'll go back to Eppington and stay with my aunt and uncle. It will be like when Momma died. I won't see him again for years."

"But weren't you happy at Eppington?" Sophia asked, her heart breaking for Polly.

"Yes, but that was before we were all together in Paris. Now I want us all to be together at Monticello."

Sophia could identify with the feeling of wanting to be all together as a family. It was what she'd hoped for after she and Pete married, that her parents would accept the marriage, and they could all be happy. But her idealism had been shattered, her heart broken, her life ruined.

She managed to climb out of the ruins and become a very successful painter, but at what cost? She lost Pete. She lost her parents. And here she was...about to lose it all again. No, not all. As long as she could paint, she'd always have something left.

She slapped her hands on the tabletop and stood. "This melancholy will ruin our day. We have so much to be thankful for. The ship didn't sink in the Atlantic. It didn't burn down in the Chesapeake Bay, and because of the graciousness of a few Virginians, we have rooms for the night. Let's go upstairs. This celebration will continue for a while, and from the looks on your faces, this isn't going to cheer you up."

"Papa doesn't look happy either," Patsy said.

Sophia linked arms with the girls. "I don't imagine he is. He wanted to finish his assignment in France and retire to Monticello."

"Then why doesn't he do it?" Polly demanded.

"Because he's a patriot and believes it's his duty to serve at the pleasure of the president."

Patsy shook her head, her eyes glossy. "Poor Papa."

"Well," Sophia shrugged. "At least he'll get his face on Mount Rushmore."

Polly glanced up, and Sophia noticed, not for the first time, that Polly seemed even more fragile than normal, with dark circles under her eyes. The trip had exhausted the poor little thing. She needed to get home and rest in the warm embrace of her extended family.

"What's Mount Rushmore?" Polly asked.

Sophia glanced back at Thomas, who was accepting a glass of ale from one of the politicians. "Oh, it's sort of a museum," she said distractedly.

Thomas looked uncomfortable as he swallowed a bite of food from a tray on the bar, then he sipped from his glass, and smiled with effort, and a fragility that must be tugging at his insides. He had his heart set on returning to Paris, but instead he was heading from a boiling pot in France to one almost as hot in New York City. The fight with Hamilton over America's debt wouldn't be easily resolved, and his tenure as the nation's chief diplomat wouldn't be memorable enough for him to list it as an accomplishment on his tombstone.

Sophia couldn't worry about him right now, though, or even America. Her focus was on what Mr. MacKlenna or Mr. Digby could do for her. If they couldn't do anything, then she and Thomas would both go to New York City. He would continue to pressure her to marry him, and she'd continue to resist. Eventually the capital would move to Philadelphia, and he'd go too.

And that would be the end of it.

If the time portal didn't open within a year, she'd have to go to Scotland, which meant crossing the Atlantic again. What a dreadful thought. But she had no choice. The brooches came from there, the magic was conjured there, so the answers had to be there.

But first, while she still had good light, she had a painting to finish.

34

Mallory Plantation—JL

J L AND KEVIN opened the front door of the Mallory Plantation mansion, home to Jack and Amy, and passed through the quiet entry hall.

JL saluted the portrait of General Mallory hanging over the fake fireplace. Jack's ancestor fought in the Civil War and, according to Jack, the painting had been hanging in the same spot since that war ended.

Also, according to Mallory family lore, the painting replaced a portrait of the first General Mallory painted after the Revolutionary War. That general now hung in the dining room along with a portrait of his wife. Jack loved those two paintings, and believed they'd been painted by a visionary who understood not only the subjects, but Mallory Plantation as well.

But JL thought Jack's portrait should be the one hanging in the entryway. Amy thought so too, and had interviewed several portraitists, but hadn't been impressed with any of their visions for the portrait. Until she found someone who understood the Mallorys and their connection to the Commonwealth of Virginia and the land they'd owned for four hundred years, Jack's portrait wouldn't be painted.

JL padded slowly through the house toward the back door, following the sounds of laughing children. The heat wave had broken, and it was an unusually cool evening for July in Virginia. The windows stood wide open while the punkah-style ceiling fans swung in unison. The temperature had prompted the adults in charge of the Shakespearean production to change the venue to the willow oak instead of the small performance space in the library.

She and Kevin paused when they walked out onto the back portico holding hands, taking in the action.

A dozen or more tiki torches defined a semicircle area between the house and the willow oak, and lawn chairs were set up between the torches and the tree. Sheets were strung from one branch to another, creating a backdrop for the grassy stage. The boys' costumes consisted of black pants, white shirts, red capes, and funny-shaped hats with feathers. The girls wore long cotton dresses with ribbons and bows in their hair, and multicolored capes swung behind them as they ran away from the boys who wielded plastic swords. The prop department might have gone a bit overboard giving this rambunctious crew plastic weapons. JL counted thirteen kids ranging in age from three to sixteen.

The men in the family were standing away from the stage on the far side of the tiki torches. From the aromas wafting downwind, they were all smoking cigars and drinking whisky.

Kevin kissed her. "I'm going to talk to the guys."

JL tried to laugh, remembering a time when things were simpler, when it took so little to make her laugh. But now she lived in fear that her phone would ring, and it would bring bad news.

"Enjoy your cigar," she managed to say.

"Mommy!" Blane left the group of kids and charged toward her wielding his sword, but Kevin caught him and swung him up over his shoulders. "You're not supposed to be here."

Kevin twirled a giggling Blane through the air. "Why not?"

"Pops said your job is to be with the wee lad who's sleeping in the inc...abator."

"Aunt Kit's with him so we can watch your performance. What time does the show start?"

Blane pointed with his sword. "Soon as the uncles finish their cigars." Then he pointed in the other direction. "And the aunts are running lights from up there."

JL moved off the porch and looked up to see the upper portico ablaze with candles. She counted eight women in rocking chairs. "Is that what they call rocking and drinking these days? Running lights?"

"Heck no, Mommy. That's theatre talk for turning spotlights on and off."

"JL, come up here," Amy yelled. "We have a cushioned lounge chair and a pitcher of virgin piña coladas."

"Who's up there? I can't see," JL yelled back.

The women sounded off. "Meredith here."

"Kenzie."

"Charlotte."

"Amber."

"Olivia."

"Maria."

"Elizabeth."

"It sounds like the wives' club is holding court. As soon as I get a hug from Blane and talk to Jack, I'll come up. Save me a drink. I need those carbs."

"Charlotte is explaining the pros and cons of using Dysport or Botox to prevent frown lines and wrinkles on our foreheads," Amy called down.

"I need to hear about that," JL yelled back. "Mine are getting worse every year."

"Can you get up the stairs?" Amy asked. "We'll come down if you can't."

"I thought you guys were running lights."

"Kenzie is. We're only here for moral support," Amber said.

"Okay, bring down the pitcher. I don't want to climb up and then have to come back down for the show."

"Give your mom an easy hug, and I'll go chat with the uncles," Kevin said.

"Are you going to smoke a cigar? The twins can't wait to get old enough to smoke Uncle Braham's 'spensive cigars. Robbie said one cigar cost five hundred dollars. Talk about something going up in smoke. That's crazy. Don't you think so, Daddy? Henry says when you get old enough to smoke Uncle Braham's cigars, it's a sign."

"Of what?" Kevin asked.

"That you're a MacKlenna Man."

"Is that like being a Marlboro Man?" JL asked, teasingly.

"Who's that?" Blane asked.

She made a face. "A smoker, and I don't want you to ever start. Got it? And Trainer Ted yells at the uncles when he hears they've been smoking."

"I don't want Trainer Ted to yell at me. I always do my exercises. I want to be a good runner like Daddy, so I can do the Kentucky Derby Festible Marathon when I'm sixteen."

"Festi…val," Kevin said. "As fast as you are now, I bet you'll be able to do it before you're sixteen." Kevin set Blane on the ground, and he ran straight to JL. "Slow down and be careful with that sword. Even plastic swords can hurt people."

Blane put on the brakes before he plowed into her and dropped his sword. "I'm glad you're here, Mommy. I've got a big part in the play. I'm one of the sailors who deliver a letter from Hamlet to Horatoe."

"I think that's Horatio," JL said.

He waved his hands around his head. "Whatever." Then he leaned in and whispered. "I was going to be a tree, but I talked it over with Uncle Matt, and he found another part for me."

JL eased into one of the chairs lined up facing the tree and hugged him. "You're such a big boy. Are you getting along okay without me?"

"I'm grown up. I can even disagree with the director. It's easier for me to…you know…get along without my mommy and daddy. The wee lad needs your 'tention more than me."

She struggled to speak over the lump in her throat. "You're…you're killing me, buddy." She squeezed him. "You're so sweet. Lawrence really does need me right now."

"I thought you were going to call him Lance. Us boys think Lance is a better name than Lawrence. But don't tell Pops. We know it's his name too, but we don't have to call him Lawrence because we call him Pops. So we're calling the wee lad Lance. Got it?"

"I certainly do. Now give me a hug. I want to go talk to Jack."

Blane gave her a hot, sweaty hug, his damp hair tickling her cheek. He smelled like a little boy who'd played in the dirt and eaten hot dogs with ketchup. "I love you, baby boy."

"I'm *not* a baby boy. The wee lad is your baby boy now." He kissed her cheek again and started to run off.

"Hey, Blane, don't forget…"

He fisted his hands on his hips, jutting out his elbows. "Make my bed, eat my vegetables, and never, ever lie to the FBI." He then gave her a thumbs up. "You can count on me."

She pulled on his cape.

"Hey, don't tug on Superman's cape," he said.

"Don't pull the mask off the old Lone Ranger either," she replied.

Blane giggled as he picked up his sword. "That's funny."

His cape lifted behind him as he ran off, and her eyes misted. It took a moment to compose herself. God, she loved that little guy. And she loved her littlest one, too.

As soon as she imagined Lawrence in the incubator, her milk let down. She folded her arms and squeezed her breasts, but they leaked anyway. Another hour and she'd have to pump. While thinking about Lawrence, she slipped her phone out of the side stash pocket in her leggings and sent Kit a text: *How's he doing?*

When Kit didn't respond right away, JL pocketed her phone and went to join the smokers, staying upwind from them. If she got cigar smoke in her hair, she'd have to wash it before she returned to the hospital.

Pete gave her a hug. "It's good to see you out of the hospital. Do you want me to get you a chair?"

"No, I want to talk to that thug standing next to you."

Pete glanced left to right. "Are you talking about your brother or

Mallory?"

"It's a tossup."

Connor pulled her in for a hug. "How do you feel, sis?"

"Good enough to be here."

"Guess that means she's talking about me." Jack wrapped his arm around her shoulders. "Whatever it is, I didn't do it." He kissed the top of her head. "What's up, kiddo?"

"Where's Elliott?" she asked, before breaking away from Jack to give hugs to David, Braham, Daniel, and her other brother, Shane.

"He's helping Matt and Pops behind the curtain," Connor said.

"I thought Jeff and Julie were coming up," she said.

"Too many kids' activities," Connor said. "And he's got a trial in Federal District Court."

Braham handed Kevin a cigar. "This is an E.P. Carrillo Encore Majestic, named Cigar of the Year by *Cigar Aficionado*. All Nicaraguan tobacco from three major growing regions."

"Sounds good." Kevin passed the cigar under his nose to take in the aroma. "Smells sweet. Do I have to listen to a long spiel before I can light up?"

"Aye," Braham said. "Writing reviews in *Cigar Aficionado* and making recommendations is the only way I can justify buying such expensive smokes." He pointed with the cigar held loosely between two fingers. "This is a medium-bodied cigar with enough flavor to appeal to those who smoke more than a fair amount, but also appeals to those who don't smoke as much."

"Can I light it now?"

"Hang on, I'm almost done," Braham said. "Ye'll taste the vanilla oak. Just look at this burn." He rolled the cigar between his fingers to show Kevin. "It's razor-sharp. Holds the ash. Well-constructed."

"Are you done now?" Kevin asked.

"Aye. Enjoy." Braham put his cigar between his teeth, struck a match, and held the light while Kevin rotated the foot of the cigar above the flame, drawing in smoke.

JL never tired of watching the delicate dance, and sometimes wished she could smoke one too, but they made her gag. It was one of the manliest activities they could do. And these men knew how to smoke one and make it look sexy as hell. They'd all earned a man card that simply couldn't be revoked.

She linked arms with Jack. "Walk with me. I want to talk to you about something."

Connor puffed on his cigar, blowing rings and watching them merge with others hovering nearby. "What's so important that you can't tell the rest of us?"

"I'll tell you later, nosy," she said.

She and Jack ambled down to the permanent pier he had constructed to dock the boats he and Braham bought when the kids wanted to learn how to bass fish. It had become one of Blane's favorite activities.

Not to be outdone, Amy and Charlotte bought a customized catamaran houseboat. The girls had planned to spend most of the weekend on the water, but the plane crash cancelled those plans.

JL and Jack sat in the Adirondack chairs parked there and Jack puffed on his cigar.

"How's Lawrence today?" he asked.

She waved away the smoke. "Since I texted you two hours ago, nothing has changed."

Jack smiled. "Has it been that long?"

"You couldn't tell it by me. Some days seem like they last thirty hours, and others seem like only six. I'm always tired, and I live in constant fear that one of the buttons on Lawrence's incubator will go off."

"You've got a lot of family who will cover for you, so you can get out of the hospital, spend time with Blane, take a nap, get drunk—"

"You know I can't drink right now."

"Then go get one of those pedi things. Whatever you want. We're here."

"I know, but I worry when I'm not with him almost as much as I worry when I am." She grabbed Jack's glass and sniffed the whisky instead of drinking it. "I smell cherry, fresh fruit"—she smacked her lips, imagining the flavor—"pineapple, fudge, vanilla, honey."

"And Seville oranges," Jack said.

She handed it back and smacked her lips again. "Damn, it smells smooth. What is it?"

"Glenlivet—a fifty-year-old single malt scotch whisky."

"Sounds expensive."

"Braham only serves the best with his cigars."

They sat in silence for a moment, listening to the waves lapping against the pier and the sides of the boats. "Have you ever thought about how the family gets stronger with each new set of soul mates?" she asked.

"As a matter of fact, I was jotting down a few notes the other day, tossing around story ideas about soul mates, but it hit too close to home. I need more information about the history of the brooches."

"To write about them and tell the world?" JL was aghast. "The evil force will find us for sure."

"Relax. You're way too stressed. I don't want to write what's real. But you know how active my imagination is. I might inadvertently write the truth without knowing it."

"Stay on the safe side and throw those notes away."

"I already did."

"Good." JL stared up at the stars. "You know, since Amber and Olivia came along, a steel-strong camaraderie has formed in the family. I feel like together we could fight evil all around the world. I know we can't really, but it feels like it. Am I making any sense?"

"We were just friends who had Elliott in common until you O'Gradys came along. Y'all filled out the clan. Then when the Kellys came in, man... Now we're more than a family. I don't think we could fight evil around the world, but we might be able to solve world hunger."

"I love the story about Kit finding Braham meditating at the Kansas River...or was it the North Platte? Some river along the Oregon trail. She asked him if he was trying to solve the problem of world hunger."

"It's a good story."

She shifted to get more comfortable, but without a cushion in the chair it wasn't going to happen. "Back to the family and fighting evil... I call it soul mate power. That's what we have. Wish I could, but I can't explain it any better."

"I like it," Jack said. "But you didn't drag me down here to discuss soul mate power. What's up?"

"Did Pete mention Sophia to you?"

"Not recently. Why?"

"She's gone missing."

Jack blew out a mouthful of smoke. "Like the police are looking for her kind of missing or brooch missing?"

JL gave him a hard look, her heart pounding a bit. "Brooch missing."

"Damn. It's been four years since the last one. I was hoping the kids would all be grown before the next one showed up." Jack tipped back his glass and emptied it. "Pete's been so quiet lately. I wondered what was going on with him. Figured it had to be woman trouble. Guys don't like friends to pry. When we're ready to talk we will, but otherwise—"

"Pete was ready to talk, but Elliott told him to keep it to himself," JL said.

"Elliott can't keep that kind of information from us. We're all owners of the company and have a stake in the brooches."

"He knows, but he's the Keeper. Which means he can make that kind of decision based on what he feels is best for the brooches and the family. He believes searching for Sophia will cheat Lawrence out of the attention he deserves."

Jack rolled his cigar and flicked the ash into the river. "I don't believe that. Do you?"

"I don't believe it's the reason he told Pete to hold off," JL said. "It doesn't make any sense. If a rescue mission is organized, and the travelers use the diamond brooch, they'll only be gone a few minutes. I think he's using Lawrence as an excuse, and his real fear is growing old and being pushed aside."

"Elliott's smart enough to know when it's time to relinquish control," Jack said.

"I'm convinced it's the debate he's having with himself. He's afraid he won't know."

"Set Elliott's issues aside. What's your other concern?" Jack puffed his cigar.

"I want you to go with Pete to find Sophia."

"Why me?"

"Come on, Jack. You've pouted over Connor and Rick's Colorado adventure for four years. You're dying to go on another one."

"I'm not sure how Amy would feel about another trip. Any ideas where Sophia went?"

"Pete has a few clues, but it will take Kenzie's unique talent for recognizing patterns to figure out where. But," JL leaned forward. "You'll love this…"

"Okay. What is it?"

"Sophia has already made five trips to the past."

Jack yanked the cigar out of his mouth. "Jesus Christ! Then she's more experienced than the rest of us." He studied the cigar for a moment before pulling a short draw and blowing out puffs of smoke. "So, she's gone back and forth five times, and on the sixth trip she doesn't return. Sounds like to me either the purpose of her brooch isn't about finding a soul mate, or she's injured, possibly dead."

"I considered those possibilities, but I don't believe she's dead. She might be injured or incapacitated, but if she has possession of the brooch she could still come home."

"Or, like Kit, Charlotte, and Amber, she found her soul mate in the past."

"Yeah, but they all came home, and besides, I believe Pete is her soul mate."

"Are you sure?"

"God, no, but he thinks so or he wouldn't still be single." JL pulled out her phone to see if she'd missed a response from Kit. Nothing so far. "We've had lots of bad stuff happen during adventures, but nobody's gotten seriously hurt."

"If you don't consider getting hanged a serious injury or—"

"None of us will ever get over Carolina Rose's death." JL's phone beeped with a text message. It was from Kit: *All fine. Enjoy the play.* "Kit says everything is fine at the hospital."

"Good. So what do you want to do about Pete?" Jack asked.

JL sent Kit a short text: *Play hasn't started yet. Be back in a couple of hours.* She put her phone away. "According to the bylaws of the company, Elliott has to be notified first if someone wants to call a meeting. He doesn't have to agree, he just needs to be told."

"You want me to notify him so he'll get pissed at me instead of you?"

"He won't get pissed at you. He'd get pissed at Kevin or David or me. But not you. Something changed between you two after Carolina Rose died. If there's something you want that's within his means to give you, he will."

Jack sighed. "I'll tell him tonight that I intend to schedule a meeting for tomorrow afternoon at one o'clock. He'll ask me if I'm doing this because I want to go on another adventure."

"Do you?"

"Like I said, it depends on where Sophia has gone." Jack flicked the ash over the water. "Amy would like to be a guide like Kenzie was for Amber, but she's done with the violence. It has to be a time period without a war or major societal upheaval."

"Good luck with that. I don't think you can find a decade without one or the other." JL pushed to her feet, grimacing at the pull on her incision. "Schedule the meeting. If I'm available tomorrow, I'll call in, but don't wait for me."

"What about Kevin?"

"It depends on what's going on with Lawrence. If I'm doing kangaroo care, we might call in. It's a wait-and-see kind of thing."

Jack stood and hugged her to his side as they headed back toward the tree where the spotlight was now directed on the hanging sheets. "What about Rick? Do you think he'll want to go on another trip?"

"Rick flew in, visited Lawrence and me in the hospital, then returned to California to finish his work on the reopening celebration. Blane said he's coming back to take him horseback riding. I haven't talked to him. I think going on an adventure is a distraction he doesn't need right now. His focus is on doing a perfect job for Meredith. That's a high bar," JL said. "Everybody wants to do a perfect job for Meredith, but it only happens when she does the job herself."

"Yeah. He's figured that out."

JL looked up at Jack. Moonlight fell into his blue eyes and glinted off his perfectly styled blond hair. "You're the best friend a girl could have. But don't tell Pete. He'd be jealous."

"Don't tell Amy. She already is."

JL smacked him in the arm. "She is not. We almost died together in the belly of that ship. We're BFFs."

Jack clamped the cigar between his teeth at a jaunty angle. "If you say so, kiddo. Now, let's go enjoy some Shakespeare under the willow oak."

35

Mallory Plantation (1789)—Sophia

O N NOVEMBER 29, Thomas wrapped his hands around Sophia's waist and swung her up onto the bench seat of a borrowed buckboard. The wagon belonged to one of the kind Virginians living in Norfolk who volunteered to carry Jefferson's party and baggage as far as Mallory Plantation in Charles City County, located several days' ride from Norfolk. Thomas said the weather was unusually cool, but it wasn't cold enough to snow or freeze the creeks they had to cross.

The only positive so far was the surrounding beauty, even though the weather delays in France and England had brought them to Virginia too late to enjoy the fall foliage when it would have been an artist's heaven. She knew from previous visits to the Washington, DC area that the countryside in October was a blanket of burnt orange, crimson, gold, the green of pines, and the deep jewel tones of the oaks. But now the wind and cool temperatures had brought down the leaves, and the fading colors covered the ground and crunched beneath the wagon wheels. When they neared plantations and towns, the delicious scent of hickory fires drifted in the air.

There was still beauty in the landscape this time of year, when the colorful face of autumn had passed and the season hadn't turned to winter. The naked trees let her artist's eye see the bone structure of the forests, the loneliness of it all, and the attempt to hide secrets in the underbrush until spring. As tempting as it was to remain in Virginia until winter loosened its grip and pastel colors popped up in the meadows, she didn't think she could stay that long.

If her foreseeable future was living in the eighteenth century, then she was going to New York, the center of business and government, at least for a few more months. After the Residence Act, which would be passed by Congress in July 1790, the government, including Thomas, would relocate to Philadelphia until the government moved to the new Federal District—in what would become Washington, DC—in 1800. Since Sophia had to earn a living as an artist, what better place to be than New York City? When the government relocated next year, she'd have to decide which city provided more opportunities to grow her business—where bankers lived or where politicians lived?

While debating the pros and cons of living in New York, Philadelphia, or Virginia, she forgot about the cold. But as her choices became more confusing, the cold reality returned. Shivering, she clutched a thick wool blanket more tightly around her shoulders. If she was this cold, Polly might be even colder. Sophia had insisted she dress in several layers of skirts, and Patsy, Marguerite, and Sally were snuggled with Polly under heavy blankets in the back of a wagon. Hopefully it was enough to keep her from becoming chilled.

Thomas had mentioned Polly's constitution was on the sickly side like her late mother's, but she hadn't been sick since Sophia met her. If there was anything she could do to save the eleven-year-old from dying in her mid-twenties, Sophia would do her best.

When the wagons lined up at the start of the day, Sophia insisted her wagon be placed behind the one with the girls that James was driving, so she could keep an eye on them. They had yet to send out a distress call, but she still watched them with her hawklike vision.

With Thomas riding ahead on horseback, the party journeyed in the slow, easy, social manner of the time, stopping at every friend's house on or near the road. At the speed they were traveling, it would take forever and a day to get to Mallory Plantation.

At every home they visited, Sophia sketched the family with Thomas and left the drawing as a thank-you gift. When folks saw her sketches, many commissioned paintings. People understood the importance of preserving their likeness for generations to come. If she decided to stay in Virginia until spring, she had enough work to keep her busy. And the money she made would cover the cost of opening a studio and setting up a home for her and Marguerite when they reached New York, without having to sell more jewels.

Thomas wrote to both Mr. MacKlenna and Mr. Digby, asking them to come to Mallory Plantation, but he didn't mention Sophia or a reason for the request.

As the miles fell away, her anxiety skyrocketed, and she fidgeted so much the buckboard driver asked if he needed to stop the wagon. From then on, she just let the butterflies in her stomach flitter here and there while her mind wandered to her students and the things she'd miss if she never returned.

On the tenth day of travel, the wagons rumbled down a long drive with fading emerald green lawns rolling out on every side of a Flemish-bond brick three-story Georgian manse with a double portico. Sophia had seen the pictures in Jack Mallory's wedding publicity shoot, but the touched-up photographs couldn't compare with seeing the plantation firsthand. She couldn't wait to stroll around the premises and sketch the property as it looked now, especially the willow oak in the backyard. The tree was about a hundred fifty years old now, which was half the age of the tree in the photograph.

A man, quite familiar-looking, tall and striking with blue eyes and a head of thick gray hair curling into his forehead walked out under the portico just as Thomas dismounted and the wagons pulled to a stop. While a servant led his horse away, he moved quickly to Sophia's wagon, and swung her through the air to solid ground. She experienced a sensation of weightlessness and the world disappearing around her, and then his hands were gone.

"Mr. Jefferson, welcome to Mallory Plantation." The general spoke in a warm Tidewater accent, sounding like Thomas, although

Mr. Mallory's voice was much deeper.

"It's nice to be back, General," Thomas said.

Sophia had dissected Thomas's accent from the moment she first heard him speak, and it had taken until now to completely nail it down. In place of New England's rapid, metallic whine, Virginia's speech was a soft, slow, melodious drawl that came from the nose, not the throat. Thomas's, and, she assumed the Mallorys would do the same, adding syllables where New Englanders subtracted them. Vowel sounds were prolonged, embellished and softened as in ha-lf for half, ke-er for care, puriddy for pretty, fuust for first, and the *pièce de résistance* wah-a-tah-mill-i-an for watermelon. She often asked Thomas to name his favorite fruit just to hear him say it, and then she'd imitate him and laugh.

He escorted her up three wide stone steps to shake hands with the general, who could easily pass for Jack Mallory's older brother. "Allow me to introduce Miss Orsini from New York. She's returning from an extended stay in Italy."

The general gave her a look more suited for reprimanding an orderly than querying a woman standing on his portico. "Is your family still in New York or Italy?"

"They're deceased," she said. "I've been studying art in Italy, and met Mr. Jefferson while visiting Paris. He volunteered to escort me home."

The general gave Thomas a similarly curious glance. "Then you knew about the offer from President Washington before you left the continent?"

"I read it in the newspaper as soon as I docked in Norfolk. Honestly, I was surprised."

Patsy, Polly, and Marguerite joined them on the porch.

"So these are the comely Jefferson daughters I've heard so much about from Mr. and Mrs. Eppes," the general said.

"These are my daughters," Thomas said, resting one hand on Patsy's shoulder, the other on Polly's. "And this," he nodded toward Marguerite, "is Mademoiselle Bonnard from Paris. She's Miss Orsini's companion and *couturière*."

Marguerite curtsied. "*Bonjour.*"

"A Frenchwoman. How delightful. Do you speak English?"

"But of course, *Général* Mallory. I also speak Italian."

The general then gazed at Sophia. "Where in Italy did you study?"

"I was in Florence for twenty years."

The general smiled down at her, his bright eyes squinting in the sunlight. "Ah, so the prodigal returns."

With a nonchalant beauty queen wave, Sophia said, "That's me."

"What do you paint?" he asked.

"I have a preference for portraits, but I'll paint whatever the client commissions—buildings, landscapes, copies of the Old Masters."

"Mrs. Mallory will be delighted to hear she has a French *couturière* and a portraitist visiting Mallory plantation."

A petite woman, a perfect ballerina size, with high cheekbones, blue eyes, and wearing a brocade silk gown embroidered with insects and flowers, waltzed out onto the portico.

Her honeyed hair glinted in the sun. Sophia would paint her near a window to show the glint in her hair, the blue in her eyes, and her alabaster skin.

"Did I hear…French *couturière*, darling?" The woman spoke with the same Tidewater accent, turning the word darling into dah-lin.

"Yes, you did," he said, then added, "I believe you've met Mr. Jefferson."

"Of course. We attended the ceremony when you were sworn in as governor of Virginia."

Thomas bowed over her hand. "Delightful to see you again, Mrs. Mallory. Allow me to introduce Miss Orsini."

"Miss Orsini is an artist," the general said.

Mrs. Mallory set her hands on her hips. "Splendid. Do you have paintings to exhibit? I'd love to see them. Portraitists so rarely come to Virginia, and if they do, they stay in Richmond, and we don't hear about them until they're gone."

"I painted several of Mr. Jefferson and his daughters while in

Paris, which we have with us. With his permission, I'll gladly show them to you."

"I invite you to gaze upon all of them," Thomas said. "Shakespeare said 'the eyes are the windows to the soul.' The artist who captures the eyes and the personality of the sitter is a rare breed. Miss Orsini is that and more. Once you see her portraits, you'll immediately commission your own."

Sophia lowered her head to hide her flushed cheeks. Her sketches had earned commissions for portraits at their previous stops without Thomas's interference, but he was blatantly promoting her now. Why?

"You are indeed impressed by Miss Orsini's talent," Mrs. Mallory smiled warmly at Sophia.

The general slapped Thomas's shoulder. "A delegation from the legislature is coming to welcome you home. They'll be joining us for luncheon at two o'clock."

"I'm sure the ladies will want to change out of their traveling dresses and rest before company arrives," Mrs. Mallory said.

If Thomas's letters to MacKlenna and Digby were received, and if the men were available to travel, then they were likely members of this delegation. Two distinct emotions immediately warred inside her: terror and an almost nauseating excitement. It was possible she might be able to go home today, although highly unlikely. If MacKlenna and Digby had brooches, they wouldn't carry them around. The jewelry was either at their homes here in America or, God forbid, in Scotland.

All the wrangling in her mind was unsettling. If she was given the chance to go home today, how could she vanish? *Poof!* What explanation could she give Thomas?

And what about her? The thought of leaving was heartwrenching, but she didn't belong here. She had her students, her business, her friends, her life. And she was very much afraid that sooner or later she would royally screw up and change the course of history.

"Shall we go inside?" Mrs. Mallory suggested. "Your traveling trunks will be brought to your rooms."

The general opened the door, and Mrs. Mallory swept through it gracefully, making a dramatic entrance into her own home. There was no way in the world Jack Mallory's bride would enter a house with such a flourish. She wouldn't even enter a stadium broadcasting box so dramatically. What would this Mrs. Mallory think of the current one? Sophia chuckled to herself. It would be fun to meet her. And didn't Jack have a sister? Wasn't she a doctor or something? Now that would be an even funnier comparison. She probably wasn't a Southern belle—a steel magnolia—at all.

"I can stay with Sally in the servants' quarters," Marguerite whispered to Sophia.

Sophia shook her head to clear thoughts of people who occupied this mansion in the future, and said in a confidential voice. "You're my companion. Not a servant. You'll stay with me."

Behind her the general said, "After you've refreshed yourself, Mr. Jefferson, come to my office. I have correspondence from President Washington addressed to you."

"I won't be long," Thomas said. "Oh, by the by, do you know if Mr. MacKlenna or Mr. Digby are members of the delegation?"

"I know they are both attending Assembly meetings, but Mr. Henry selected the participants. I don't know who he invited."

"I haven't heard anything about Mr. Henry in a good while," Thomas said.

The general clasped him on the shoulder. "Mr. Henry intends to retire from public service next year and practice law. We are trying to dissuade him, of course."

"If he can resist President Washington's arm-twisting, he might be able to."

Sophia turned and looked up at Thomas, sensing he was thinking of Washington's *fait accompli*—appointing him secretary of state and having Senate approval before he even returned to America. Thomas seemed to force his features to relax, as if hoping to erase the traces of his growing annoyance over the appointment. She had learned to recognize the signs in his jaw, his neck, the intensity of his eyes, signs he tried now to hide.

He followed the general farther into the large foyer with its fabulous carved walnut, square-rigged, flying staircase. The staircase was included in the article accompanying Jack Mallory's photo shoot. Since Thomas seemed to ignore the architectural wonder rising three stories without any visible means of support, he must have studied it on previous visits, because it would normally be too intriguing for him to pass up.

"I'll send up your trunks," the general said. "Come to my study when you're ready. I'll gather your mail."

Thomas pursed his lips. "Mail? I was expecting only correspondence from the president."

"There are several pieces posted from New York, along with one letter from Mrs. Eppes."

Sophia turned her attention away from Thomas and the general and followed the girls up the stairs to the second floor. The only other interior shot of the house in Jack and Amy's photo shoot was in the dining room. Amy, following a Mallory tradition of brides etching their initials in the window panes with their engagement rings, etched hers while a grinning Jack gazed at his bride. It was incredibly romantic.

Amy looked more like a Vogue model than an ESPN baseball analyst and former Olympic athlete, and Jack and Amy's portrait would look amazing hanging over the fake fireplace in the entry that currently featured a poorly painted portrait of an ancestor. When it came to art, Sophia was as critical of other artists as she was of herself.

The second floor of the mansion mirrored the first, with a large hall and four bedrooms. Mrs. Mallory showed them to a room facing the James River which had a door leading out to the upper portico.

"The room is fabulous," Sophia said. "And the view of the river and the willow oak is extraordinary. And the bright, natural light is perfect for painting."

"Maybe this evening you can display your art while Miss Jefferson entertains us on the fortepiano. And it would be enchanting to hear Mr. Jefferson play his violin again," Mrs. Mallory said.

"I would like that very much," Patsy said. "But Papa doesn't play his violin often since his wrist injury. I'll ask him."

"I didn't hear about his injury. It must not be his writing hand. He's still a prolific correspondent," Mrs. Mallory said.

"Unfortunately, it was, but he makes do," Patsy said.

"I don't want to embarrass him," Mrs. Mallory said. "You'll know best whether to ask him or not." She glanced around the room, as if taking an inventory of what needed to be done. "I'll have hot water sent up. You'll have time before luncheon to wash and change out of your traveling clothes."

She swished out of the room as eloquently as she had swished through the front door. Sophia rolled her eyes at Marguerite, who covered her mouth and giggled. "Your traveling dress is more elegant than her gown."

"Then she'll love your ideas for new ones."

Polly plopped down on one of the two canopied beds curtained with damask drapes. "Which bed do you want, Miss Sophia?"

"You know me, sweetie. I'm so tired by the time my head hits the pillow, I don't care where I sleep."

Polly giggled. "Patsy, Sally, and I will sleep here, and you and Marguerite can have the other. This bed looks like it's a little larger."

Sophia tickled Polly, and they rolled together over the counterpane. "If you need a larger bed, you may have it."

Polly laughed, begging. "Please don't tickle me."

Sophia sat and hugged Polly to her side. Her forehead and neck were warm. "You're catching a cold. Why don't I have a lunch tray sent up for you? Then you can stay in bed and rest. Okay?"

"Sally and I will stay with her," Marguerite said. "I prefer not to eat with the delegation. Whoever they are."

"Nonsense. If you don't feel comfortable, you need to get over it, because from now on you'll find yourself in all sorts of social situations. You're charming and your French air gives you a certain appeal that American men find fascinating. If you don't want to talk to anyone, say something in French, and smile. And that's also my advice to Patsy. If you don't like a man's attention, speak to him in French. But don't say anything ugly. He might understand you."

The girls laughed. "Miss Sophia, you say the smartest things. I wish I was more like you," Polly said.

Sophia wagged her finger back and forth like the pendulum of a metronome. "No you don't, silly. You want to be yourself. You're sweet and lovable, smart and witty, and I adore you." She attacked Polly again with lots of tickles.

Polly wiggled around, trying to scoot out of reach while laughing hysterically. "Stop. Stop."

As soon as Sophia stopped, they heard the jangling of harnesses and clomping of horses' hooves, and they darted out into the hallway to stand by the window. Carriages and men on horseback were coming down the drive. She returned to the bedroom. "Looks like company has arrived. I need to change."

Their trunks and pitchers of hot water were brought to the room, and within minutes they had stripped down to their chemises to wash. Marguerite helped her into a clean gown and dressed her hair.

"You look *exquise*," Marguerite said.

"Papa won't be able to take his eyes off you, Miss Sophia," Polly said, so lamblike in her innocence.

"Your father will be so busy talking with his friends, he won't even notice I'm in the room." Sophia checked her appearance one last time. "Come downstairs when you're ready," she said to Marguerite and Patsy.

On the way down, Sophia pinned the pearl brooch to the bodice of her light blue taffeta gown. It was the first time the jewelry had been out of her pocket since its miscalculation on July 14. As she made the turn to climb down the last flight of the flying stairs, Thomas and the general came through the front door behind several men who then entered the parlor. Instead of following them, Thomas and the general continued toward the rear of the house.

When Thomas saw her, he said, "I'm going to read President Washington's letter. I won't be long."

The taffeta dress rustled around her ankles as she reached the bottom stair. "Is there any doubt what it says?"

"I'm sure he's cordially inviting me to accept the place on his cabinet. I hope he gives me the choice to return to Paris if I prefer to do so."

"I believe the president expects you to accept," the general said.

"Have you decided what to tell him?" Sophia asked.

"I have the response dictated in my head," he said. "*Dear President Washington, I prefer to remain in the office I hold, the duties I know and feel equal to rather than undertake a place more difficult. But,*" Thomas added dryly, "*it's not for me to choose my post. As president, you must marshal us for the public good. If, after learning my preference is to return to France, you still believe it is best to transfer me to New York, my inclination must be no obstacle to your plan. Signed Th. Jefferson.*"

"Sounds like the perfect response." He was taking the news much better than she'd expected. "Looks like we'll both be going to New York City."

Mrs. Mallory emerged from the dining room and signaled to her husband. "Luncheon is served. Would you inform our guests?"

"I'll deal with the correspondence later. Let's enjoy the meal," Thomas said.

Sophia approached Mrs. Mallory. "Polly doesn't feel well. She won't be joining us. Could you have a luncheon tray sent up for her and her maid?"

Mrs. Mallory touched Sophia's arm in an obvious show of concern. "Should I send for the doctor?"

Sophia patted her hand. "Not yet. I think what she needs right now, is rest. If she doesn't feel better tomorrow, Mr. Jefferson might want the doctor to check on her."

Thomas cupped Sophia's elbow and guided her into the dining room. "Does she have a fever?"

"She's warm, but if she stays in bed and out of the cold, she should feel better tomorrow."

"Thank you for making those arrangements." Then he leaned in and whispered, "Consider yourself well kissed."

She smiled. "I thought it would be less distracting if I just took charge."

Thomas stationed her at his side to welcome each member of the delegation as they entered the dining room. She tried to move away, but he held onto her arm. "I want to introduce you. Please stay."

Was it a command or a request? Since he said please, she considered it a request, although his tone made it sound like a command. This was his day to be recognized and celebrated, so she would be careful not to complicate it...yet.

The first to enter was a handsome man just shy of Thomas's height with a commanding presence. His hair was dark and curling. His features were classical, but more Greek than Roman. His deep-set hazel eyes were shaded, bright, piercing, and very expressive, and her fingers itched to sketch him, whoever he was.

"Mr. Henry, may I present Miss Orsini from New York?"

The man acknowledged her presence with a nod. "My pleasure."

Sophia searched his face again, and then recognized him from an oil on canvas by Lawrence Sully owned by the Mead Art Museum of Amherst College. "I'm sorry, Mr. Henry. I didn't recognize you at first. It's an honor to meet you, sir, and to thank you for your rousing speeches."

"You're too kind, Miss Orsini," Patrick Henry said.

Thomas continued the introductions as the men entered the room and moved toward the table. So far, no MacKlenna or Digby. By the time the last two men entered the room her hopes had faded.

The first of the two men was several inches shorter than Thomas, and on the lanky side, with a dark complexion and wavy blond hair.

"Mr. MacKlenna, thank you for coming."

"Yer letter was serendipitous, Mr. Jefferson. Before yer invitation arrived, I was already elected to join the delegation to welcome ye home."

Thomas nodded. "Indeed it was. I was writing on behalf of Miss Sophia Frances Orsini from New York." He turned to Sophia. "May

I introduce Mr. James MacKlenna? He was awarded a land grant of four hundred acres in what will become the new state of Kentucky. And we will lose a valuable member of the Virginia Assembly."

"At least if I'm elected to the Kentucky legislature, I won't have so far to travel." Mr. MacKlenna held her hand, bowed slightly, and when his head came up, his eyes fastened on her brooch.

"When do you think it will happen?" she asked, more to fill the air than caring when Kentucky gained statehood.

"I hope soon." Mr. MacKlenna's eyes remained fixed on her jewelry until he finally stood aside for the last man entering the room.

It wasn't until the man shook hands with Thomas that she pulled her gaze away from Mr. MacKlenna. The man's nose was too big, his brows too rigid. His lips, though, were full, which softened him a little. If she painted him, she would soften his brows and nose as well. She didn't do it often, but sometimes the sitter's portrait needed tweaks.

"Seamus, it's good to see you," Thomas said.

Sophia flinched at the man's name. It was the same as her grandfather's.

"Was my letter to you also serendipitous?" Thomas asked.

"When I learned of the delegation, I informed Mr. Henry of yer request. He invited me to accompany the group." Seamus clasped Sophia's hand between his large ones, and, without waiting for an introduction, he said, "Miss Orsini, I'm Seamus Digby. That is an unusual piece of Celtic jewelry. I wonder if ye might allow me to examine it more closely after lunch?"

"Certainly," she said, as graciously as possible, but barely able to contain her excitement. Both men recognized her brooch. She could almost smell the paint in her Florence studio.

Thomas guided her toward an empty chair, placing her between him and Patrick Henry.

Just then Marguerite entered the room carrying the leather satchel. Mrs. Mallory indicated a place between MacKlenna and Digby on the opposite side of the table, but before Marguerite sat down, she walked around and handed the satchel to Sophia.

"I thought you'd want to sketch the delegation."

"You're so thoughtful. Thank you. Where is Patsy?"

"She wanted to stay with Polly, but I think she's very tired and preferred to rest."

"Please let Mrs. Mallory know she won't be joining us."

On the way back to her seat, Marguerite whispered to Mrs. Mallory who then instructed a servant to remove the extra place setting.

"Is Patsy also ill," Thomas whispered.

"The trip has exhausted them. They didn't feel up to dressing and socializing this afternoon. Mrs. Mallory asked Patsy if she would play the fortepiano tonight. Maybe they'll feel better later."

Thomas squeezed her hand and smiled. Across the table, Mr. MacKlenna also smiled. She nodded smartly before turning her attention to gathering supplies from her satchel. Mr. MacKlenna obviously knew why she wanted to talk to him, but his smile said so much more. Like he knew something she didn't. Well, that would all change as soon as she had five minutes alone with him.

She removed several sheets of paper and pencils and placed them on the table next to her plate.

"Do you intend to draw during luncheon?" Mr. Henry asked.

"While we were in Paris, I attended several meetings of the assembly with Mr. Jefferson so I could sketch pictures of the speakers. He included them in his correspondence to Mr. Jay and Mr. Madison."

Recognition flitted across Mr. Henry's face, then his smiled widened. "So you're the artist?" He leaned forward, glanced at Thomas, shook his head, then leaned back again. "Mr. Jefferson kept your identity a secret from Mr. Jay. I heard he asked Mr. Jefferson the identity of S.F. Orsini, and Mr. Jefferson replied, 'An artist in residence.' We, of course, assumed you to be a male artist."

"As you can see, I am not."

He regarded her for a moment, and then something curious, almost serpentine, glimmered behind his carefully veiled eyes. Then, in a snap, the glimmer disappeared, replaced by a dreamy detachment he must habitually wear, since it suited his face so naturally.

"How did you become his artist in residence?" Mr. Henry asked.

"It's a long story," she said.

"I'd like to hear it."

"Just as long as you don't use it in one of your famous oratories."

"Famous? I'm not sure they should be called 'famous.'"

"'Give me liberty or give me death' will be remembered long after you're gone." He gave a modest shrug, and she continued. "I arrived in Paris the day the citizens stormed the Bastille." Now his eyes widened with curiosity. "After escaping a dangerous situation, I ran down the Champs-Élysées and found myself at the Hôtel de Langeac."

"Mr. Jefferson's residence." By his inflection, Mr. Henry was aware of the occupants of the Hôtel de Langeac.

"When I saw the ambassador, I hurried toward him, stepped into a hole, twisted my knee, and fell *splat*"—she clapped her hands lightly but still drew Thomas's attention. He leaned forward in his seat—"against his chest, bounced back, and, if not for his quick reflexes, I would have fallen to the ground."

Mr. Henry's lips twitched. "How gallant of our Mr. Jefferson."

Thomas smiled and sat back. Although he was conversing with General Mallory and another delegate, she could tell from the angle of his chin that he was listening to her. With his left ear, no doubt.

"Very much so," she smiled. "Then he swooped me up and carried me into his home. He felt responsible for my injury and insisted, since I made no housing arrangements in advance, that I would be his artist in residence while I healed. The real reason he invited me to stay at the Hôtel de Langeac, though, was his hope that I'd be an influence on his daughters, to help them acclimate to living in America again. France is different in so many ways from America, especially Virginia."

"Do you speak French?" Mr. Henry asked.

"Yes, both French and Italian, but I don't speak Virginian."

The lines of his face curved into a contagious smile. "No, you don't. Your accent is different from any I've heard. But tell me this, Miss Orsini. How talented an artist are you?"

"I paint like an Old Master with a modernist twist. I use more depth, dimension, and color than traditional artists, and the emotion is more expansive."

"I'm not sure what that means—"

Thomas cleared his throat, and Sophia pressed her fist against her mouth to cover her smile. She knew exactly what he was thinking... *Read a book, Mr. Henry, and you'd understand.*

"I have painted several portraits of Mr. Jefferson and his daughters." She lowered her voice. "If you can keep this between us, if you'll allow me to paint your portrait, I won't charge you."

"If the painting is as good as you believe it will be," Mr. Henry said, "when others see it, they'll want you to paint them as well."

She grinned. "Starving artists need to be creative in how they advertise their talent."

"I doubt you're starving, Miss Orsini. Mr. Jefferson is well known for his lavish table and excellent wines."

"Why, Mr. Henry, didn't you accuse the ambassador of being unfaithful to good old-fashioned roast beef in favor of French cuisine?"

He scratched his neck, the tips of his ears pinking. "I might have said something similar. But tell me, did you ever have any old-fashioned roast beef while in Paris?"

"Not only roast beef, but fried chicken, country ham, a variety of peas, beans, greens, and wah-a-tah-mill-i-an." She shook her head. "I couldn't bear to eat grits, though."

Mr. Henry roared with laughter while glancing over at Jefferson. "I apologize, sir, for accusing you of being unfaithful to Southern cuisine."

Thomas smiled at Sophia. "Did Miss Orsini mention she couldn't stomach grits?"

"Yes, sir. She most certainly did." Whatever differences the two men had in the past that had caused Thomas to describe Mr. Henry as his nemesis, their joking didn't convey enmity at all.

Throughout lunch Thomas brought himself up to date on the political situation. "North Carolina has accepted the new Constitution, I heard."

"Rhode Island has rejected it again," the general said. "The amendments Mr. Madison designed to meet the major objections in our ratifying convention to provide for the protection of individual rights has been ratified by the House of Delegates."

"But not by the Senate," Mr. MacKlenna added.

"They'll be adopted," Mr. Digby said. "And they'll cut the ground out from under the feet of the antifederalists."

Everyone at the table looked at Mr. Henry. "Ye've been in the minority so often, I'm surprised ye haven't quit the Assembly in disgust," Mr. MacKlenna said.

"As the only antifederalist at this table, I feel safe in telling you I am quitting. This is my final year," Mr. Henry said. "It's time I return to private practice while I still maintain my popularity."

"You can't do that!" the general said. "Who would we argue with?"

The general's comment brought a round of laughter from everyone at the table. But there was still an undercurrent of tension Sophia didn't understand.

"Tell us about France, Mr. Jefferson. What do you think will happen to the monarchy?" Mr. Henry asked.

Thomas's eyes fixed on Sophia with pensive admiration. "The queen isn't popular, but I don't think the populace wants to eliminate their king. I will admit, though, Miss Orsini has spent more years in Europe than I have. Through her clients, acquaintances, and travels, she's acquired a deeper understanding of the mood sweeping the continent."

The men looked at her. Their faces showed doubt warring with puzzlement. She was in America, not France, and women here didn't discuss politics. So why had Thomas thrown the question to her? To prove he could change one of his positions?

"The monarchy hasn't been a good steward of the country's finances. They spent a lot of money in America in hopes of reclaiming the holdings they lost to Britain, but famines and mismanagement have almost ruined the country. It will take years before France is solvent again. I predict Frenchmen will act exactly as the colonists did here in America, and will throw out the monarchy in a long and bloody revolution."

That drew a loud buzz as the men discussed it among themselves.

"How often do your predictions come true?" the general asked.

"Often enough that they're taken seriously."

The men went silent. "Will France be stronger after the revolution?" Mr. MacKlenna asked.

"I'm not sure how to answer," she said. "If you're asking if France will be a thriving nation in two hundred years, I predict it will be, but not as strong as America."

"How could ye possibly know such a thing?" Mr. Digby asked.

"It's a prediction, sir. But I also predict that in the same time frame, no democracy in the world will ever match what has been created here in America. The founding documents are brilliant. And, with a few exceptions, they will stand as written."

Both Mr. MacKlenna and Mr. Digby were now strangely silent while the others talked among themselves.

She clinked her knife against her crystal goblet to gather everyone's attention. "I've spent the past twenty years in Europe. As a painter, I've met kings, queens, a pope, the aristocracy, and generals. When people sit for a portrait, they talk, they predict, and I listen. I'm well-informed, well-read, and highly educated, and I make predictions based on what I hear, what I discern, and what history tells me."

She paused, set down the knife, and let her shortened curriculum vitae speak for itself. Then she concluded with, "May I suggest we finish this delightful meal, clear the table, and linger over conversation and wine. Mr. Jefferson has some wonderful Normandy wines to share." She hid her shaking hands in her lap, and didn't dare look at Thomas, but she could feel his eyes. His hand found hers and squeezed it warmly.

Only then did she take a deep breath.

As soon as the table was cleared and the wine served, Mr. Henry stood, "To the late Minister Plenipotentiary, we bring you both welcome and congratulations from both houses of the General Assembly."

The delegation applauded, and while the speeches continued and the wine flowed, Sophia sketched the men at the table. After two hours and dozens of sketches, she excused herself. Her hand was cramping, and she needed to stretch and take in some fresh air.

Following her nose, she found the exit to the back portico, where she could get a closer look at the willow oak and the James River. Whoever had the forethought to plant a tree with such grand stature should know the tree had become a lasting monument to him or her. Although the yellow and russet-red leaves piled on the ground, the scene was majestic and begged to be painted.

"Would ye walk with me along the river?"

Startled, she whipped around to see Mr. MacKlenna standing there holding her cape. He placed it around her shoulders. She buttoned it and pulled the hood up over her head. The wind off the river was rustling the leaves as they proceeded down a stone path toward the edge of the water. They stood there watching the waves ripple against the shore.

"Ye're not from here, are ye, Miss Orsini?"

She shook her head. "No, I'm not."

He wrapped her arm around the crook of his elbow and directed her toward the narrow path running parallel to the river. "Tell me about yer brooch, lass. How is it ye came by it?"

"It came from my grandfather, Seamus Digby."

Mr. MacKlenna inhaled sharply. After a moment he said, "Please continue."

"It came in a wooden jewelry box with a letter from James MacKlenna written in Gaelic in the year 1625. I assume James MacKlenna was your ancestor."

"Aye," Mr. MacKlenna said.

"He was the Keeper of the brooches," Sophia continued. "According to the letter, in 1625 the Keeper's identity was in danger. He feared an evil force would find the brooches. To keep them safe, he dispersed them among his clan. My grandfather's ancestor was given a box with four identical brooches, except the stone in the middle of each brooch was different. One had a sapphire, another an emerald, the third had a diamond. And"—she touched her brooch—"this one. I know I'm not supposed to talk about the brooches because of the evil force, but I need help. This brooch brought me here, but it won't take me home."

Mr. MacKlenna stopped, gazed off, and said, "'The stone will take ye to a world unknown, through amber light to a time not yer own, to the one of yer heart, and the truth ye'll be shown.'"

"That might apply to other stones, but not mine. It hasn't brought me to the one of my heart, and I've learned no truths. I came to the wrong time, Mr. MacKlenna, and I want to go home. I was hoping either you or Mr. Digby would have a brooch you could trade with me. One that works."

"Ye're not supposed to go home, lass," Mr. MacKlenna said.

"That's crazy," she said. "The brooch has taken me home five previous times. Why not now?"

He held her hand between his own. They were warm, almost hot. He gazed deeply into her eyes, as if searching her soul...for what, she didn't know.

Maybe he was deciding whether to give her another brooch. Her spirits lifted. Her hopes soared.

Was there something she could say to prove her worthiness? She was a good person. She loved and cared for others. She would never intentionally hurt a person or an animal. She would turn her heart inside out so he could search it thoroughly.

Then his eyes flickered. He'd made a decision. Surely he would help her.

His hands cooled. "When the stones combine their energy, there's a mighty force that seeks out good and destroys all that isn't. In the hands of evil, the power of the stones could destroy the world."

She gasped. "Then take mine. I don't want it to be used for evil."

He stroked the top of her hand. "Ye must keep yer brooch. To give it up now will interfere with all yer stone has done and will do."

"But it doesn't work." Tears pooled in her eyes. "And I want to go home."

"Yer destiny is not in the future."

"Of course, it is. That's where I belong." She pulled her hand out of his grasp and dabbed at her eyes with a handkerchief tucked into her sleeve.

Mr. MacKlenna reclaimed her hand. "Lass, yer destiny is here, in this time and place. The singular purpose of each stone is to bring soul mates together."

"What? Like a love potion?"

"Soul mates create family. There is strength within a family, and that strength protects the Keeper. *Chan ann le tìm no àite a bhios sinn a' tomhais an' gaol ach 's ann le neart anama.* Love is not limited by time or space, but the capacity of the soul," he said. "The soul is where love resides. Soul mates increase the love and make it indestructible. It's the only way to defeat the evil force."

"Soul mates should also share core beliefs, faith, and values. I want to go home, Mr. MacKlenna. Will you please trade brooches with me?"

"I can't, lass. Yer destiny is here. Another brooch will not help ye. It won't take ye home. Ye're meant to be here."

Her knees buckled, and she leaned against him for support. "I don't believe it. I'll talk to Mr. Digby. Maybe he'll trade a brooch."

"Mr. Digby canna help ye now."

"This is crazy. It can't be true. There's no soul mate waiting for me in this time."

"Ye're wrong. Yer soul mate is here."

"I don't believe you."

He turned her gently to see Thomas walking toward her. "There's yer soul mate, lass. Love him well. For it's certain, he's in love with ye."

36

Mallory Plantation—Pete

P ETE ENTERED JACK'S house a half hour before the meeting with a laptop in his backpack, a slide projector screen under one arm, a projector under the other.

After Elliott sent him a text late last night to let him know he agreed to a family conference at one o'clock today, Pete spent the rest of the night pulling together a PowerPoint presentation featuring Sophia and her art. It would have been easier if the meeting was held at the resource center and he didn't have to lug equipment into Jack's almost three-hundred-year-old mansion, but the kids were in the resource center working on a project with one of their tutors.

After setting up the equipment in the dining room and moving a speakerphone from a side table to the dining room table, he poured a cup of coffee from the usual carafe on the sideboard, settled in his seat, and waited for everyone else to arrive.

He tried to look relaxed, but truthfully, he was sweating like he'd run a 5-K in sixteen-fifty, and he hadn't run a race that fast in almost twenty years.

He didn't know how this meeting was going to play out, but regardless of the support he received or didn't, he was going after Sophia. He failed her twenty years ago, and he wouldn't let her down again.

By one o'clock the adult family members were either sitting at the table or had called in to participate remotely. Elliott poured a cup of coffee and took his seat at the head of the table, then marked his territory, carefully arranging his cup, laptop, and phone.

His right hand had an unusual tremor. Pete was immediately alarmed and considered canceling the meeting, but everyone was either there or on the phone, and postponing would only confuse and stress everyone, and it might even exacerbate Elliott's tremor.

Elliott knocked on the table. "This meeting of the MacKlenna Adventure Company is called to order. Meredith, call the roll."

Sitting at his side, watching him closely, she flipped open a notepad with a long list of names. "Just say aye or remote when I call your name. Kit and Cullen."

"Aye, aye."

"David and Kenzie."

"Aye, aye."

"Kevin and JL."

"Both remote. We're in the NICU, so we're putting our phones on mute. If you ask us a question, don't expect an answer right away," JL whispered.

"Matt and Elizabeth."

"Aye, aye."

"Pops and Maria."

"Aye, aye."

"Jeff and Julie."

"Both remote," Jeff said.

"Shane."

"Remote. Sorry guys, but I had to be in Colorado this afternoon."

"Gabe."

"Remote."

"Rick."

"Remote."

"Braham and Charlotte."

"Aye, remote."

"Jack and Amy."

"Aye, aye."

"Daniel and Amber."

"Aye, aye."

"Connor and Olivia."

"Aye, aye."

"I have eighteen present and eight attending remotely," Meredith said. "None of the children, even those college age or older, were notified of the meeting."

"I have to break off in fifteen minutes," Charlotte said. "If you have any medical issues, bring them up early or I'll have to get back to you later."

"I think wee Lawrence is the only medical concern we have right now," Pops said.

"And he's doing great today," JL whispered. "It's Kevin's turn to do kangaroo care, and I have to pee."

A wild laugh sparked from Connor. "TMI, sis."

Elliott knocked on the table again. "Some of us don't have all afternoon to sit here. Let's move it along. Ye might already know why we're here. If ye don't—"

"Elliott, if you don't mind, I'll take it from here." Pete stood, hitting the table with his hip, sloshing his coffee. Kit grabbed a napkin and wiped up the spot. "Thanks."

Elliott gritted his teeth before leaning back and crossing his arms.

"The day of Kevin and JL's plane crash I was in Florence. Gabe and I were supposed to meet for dinner, but he couldn't make it. I had left the restaurant and was strolling down Via Toscanella when, farther up the street, I saw a man rattling a locked security gate installed at an art studio. I didn't know what he was up to, so I stopped and asked."

"Did you flash your badge, too?" Shane asked.

"No, but I told him I was a former NYPD detective. Turns out he was rattling the gate because he was pissed. He had commissioned a painting, and the artist was supposed to deliver it to him that day. But she wasn't answering her phone, and she obviously wasn't at her studio. While talking to him, I discovered the artist was someone I hadn't seen in almost twenty years."

"Small world, Pete," Connor said. "Sophia?"

Pete nodded.

"Shit," Connor said.

"I'm missing something," Kenzie said. "Who is she?"

"The love of his life," Connor said.

Pete glared at him.

"Whoa, touchy," Connor said.

"Leave him alone," Pops said. "Everybody knows what happened, but they're being discreet and respectful."

"How come I'm the only one who doesn't know the story?" Kenzie said. "I'm sorry, Pete."

David squeezed her hand. "It's a guy thing, babe. I'll fill ye in later."

Pete gave Kenzie a slight nod and continued, "I learned from the client that Sophia takes a two-week vacation every year, but this year she was late returning. The client and I exchanged contact information, and after he left I broke into her studio."

"Because she was a few hours late returning from a holiday? Sounds like an invasion of her privacy to me," Kenzie said.

"The client told me Sophia didn't keep her paintings in her studio or in her apartment on the second floor, but the security system was unusually sophisticated for a building without valuable art. So I searched the studio and the upstairs apartment and discovered why it was protected like the New York Fed's gold vault."

Kenzie put her elbows on the table and leaned forward. "Sounds like your nose was twitching. I know you wouldn't break into a woman's apartment without cause. McBain, on the other hand, would do it in a heartbeat. But I believe I know where this is going."

"And you'd be right," Pete continued. "In the living room, I discovered a fake wall. It took a while to find the point of entry, but I finally got the door open. Inside was a narrow room with these…"

He clicked the share button on his laptop and a photograph of Sophia's five portraits was projected on the portable screen.

"She's captivating," Kenzie said.

"Yes, she is." Pete's heart rate shot up just seeing the paintings. He had looked at them dozens of times, but seeing Sophia on the large screen tore him up.

"The painting the client wanted to pick up was a copy of the *Mona Lisa*. He didn't tell me how much he paid her to paint the copy, but he said her paintings sold between two and three hundred thousand euros."

David whistled. "She must be good."

"Are those self-portraits?" Kenzie asked.

"No." Pete walked over to the screen, and using a pointer, said, "This portrait is signed by Leonardo da Vinci."

"A forgery?" David asked.

"I don't know." Pete pointed to the second one. "This portrait is signed by Picasso, this one by Donatello, this one by Rubens, and this one by Degas."

Kit joined Pete in front of the screen and examined the portraits closely. "If these are forgeries, and I assume they are, they're extraordinary. An artist must be extremely talented to paint like both da Vinci and Picasso. Their inspirations were different, medium was different, canvas was different. But some will tell you they have a great deal in common. But still..." Kit backed away, but remained standing, chewing on her lower lip, while she continued to stare at the paintings.

Pete returned to his laptop and flipped to the next slide in his presentation. "I found this box in a small safe under her desk."

David immediately went over to the screen and stood to the side next to Kit. "Anything inside?"

"Yes and no." Pete switched to the next slide showing the inside of the box, and everyone around the table shoved to their feet.

"Jesus Christ!" Amy said. "My diamond was in there."

"Charlotte's sapphire, too," Braham said.

"And my emerald," Kenzie said.

"Is this woman related to Mr. Digby?" David asked.

"Good question," Pete said. "Her late grandfather was Seamus Digby, a solicitor in Edinburgh."

There was stunned silence, and everyone dropped back into their chairs.

"I'll be damned," David said. "The fourth brooch in the box appears to have been a pearl. Do ye think yer friend used it to go back somewhere?"

Kit returned to her seat, visibly shaken. "If this artist has a brooch, then she's gone back five times, and those portraits are real. She's actually met da Vinci, Picasso…Rubens. And sat for them."

"Six times," Pete said. "But this adventure hasn't ended well for her. She's always come back in exactly two weeks. She's now a week late."

"Where do ye think she's gone?" David asked.

Pete shook his head. "I don't know. I found emails about a spring research trip to Paris. But there's no information about artists or time periods or anything like that."

Kenzie opened her laptop and typed. "Da Vinci was from the sixteenth century. Donatello from the fifteenth. Rubens from the seventeenth. Picasso from the twentieth century. Degas from the nineteenth. Looks like she's missing an eighteenth-century artist. Any ideas?"

"First thing that jumps out to me is they're all men. Weren't there any female painters?" David asked.

"There weren't any remarkable female painters in America until the nineteenth century," Kit said. "But there were several famous ones in Europe in the eighteenth century."

"Wait a minute," JL whispered over the speaker phone. "I don't remember her name, but there was an eighteenth-century painter who had an affair with Thomas Jefferson."

"Where'd you hear that?" Pete asked.

"From Lisa Harrison."

"Who's she?" Kenzie asked. "Where have I been that I've missed so much?"

David smiled at her. "Ye've been busy, babe."

"Lisa and Robert Harrison have a preemie in the NICU," JL said. "She knows Pete and Sophia from her high school days in the city. Anyway, she was reading a book the other day about a female artist. Lisa's not here right now or I'd ask her."

"I'll google it." Kenzie typed on her laptop. "The woman was Maria Cosway and the affair happened in 1786 in Paris."

"When was the French Revolution?" Kit asked.

"1789," Jack said.

"It started then, but it lasted ten years," Matt said. "Jefferson left Paris a few months after the storming of the Bastille and returned to America to become Secretary of State."

"He met his second wife while he was in Paris. Wasn't she an artist?" Jack asked.

"She was an American, and returned with him," Matt said. "They married after the government moved from New York to Philadelphia in 1790." He paused and glanced at Pete. "Her name was Sophia Frances Orsini and she signed her paintings S.F. Orsini."

Pete slammed his fist on the table. "That's impossible! My Sophia's name is Sophia Frances Orsini, and she signs her art S.F. Orsini. Are you telling me—?"

He couldn't speak past the knot in his throat. He cleared his throat again and again. Then in a hoarse voice asked, "Are you telling me Sophia went back in time and married Thomas Jefferson?"

"I'm looking at a picture of Jefferson's wife," Kenzie said. "And she could be the twin of the woman in those paintings."

"I don't think she's a twin, Kenz," David said. "I believe Pete's Sophia and Jefferson's Sophia are one and the same."

Elliott abruptly knocked on the table. "We have another Mallory Conundrum here. This meeting is adjourned and will reconvene at seven o'clock. Bring me solutions." He gathered his laptop and phone, then he and Meredith left the room.

Everyone else stayed seated, too stunned to speak. Pete poured a whisky at the sideboard, tossed it back, and poured another. Sophia married Thomas Jefferson. How was that possible? He downed a second drink before returning to his chair, carrying a third.

"What's the Mallory Conundrum?" Elizabeth asked. "I don't understand what's happening, and I don't like it when that happens." She pushed back from the table. "I'm going to talk to Meredith."

"Cullen and I are scheduled to take the kids fishing," Braham said. "We have to go, but we'll discuss the situation and bring our thoughts to the meeting at seven."

"Amber and I have to get to the studio," Daniel said. "We have a cooking show to tape. We'll be back tonight."

"We're signing off," JL whispered. "Lawrence needs our attention. We'll call back when we can. Are you coming up here, Pops?"

"Maria and I will be there in an hour," he said.

"Looks like most of us have other things to do right now," Olivia said. "Connor can stay, but I have a doctor's appointment."

"No, I'm going with you," Connor said.

Kenzie eyed them suspiciously. "Do you two have news? You weren't drinking last night, Olivia. What's up?"

"We don't know for sure. If we have an announcement, we'll make it tonight."

Matt kissed his daughter's cheek. "I hope you get good news."

"Me too, Dad."

The others who had called in remotely clicked off with promises to call back in at seven, leaving Pete, Matt, Kit, Jack and Amy, and David and Kenzie at the table.

Jack refilled his teacup and spooned in some sugar, then leaned against the sideboard sipping the brew. "If Pete's Sophia married Thomas Jefferson, we can't go get her. We could screw up two hundred years of American history."

"Possibly world history," Matt said.

"Maybe *she* screwed up history and we need to reverse it," Kenzie said. "I changed history when I went back to 1944, but it was only my family history. Sophia would have known what happened in the world for the next two hundred years. She could have tweaked something. There could have been a war she helped Jefferson steer clear of. She could have given him a piece of information, like how to find South Pass. How did Jefferson know that? He told Lewis and Clark exactly where to go to get through the Rockies."

"Maybe we would have gotten into another war with Britain in the early 1800s if not for some incredible diplomacy by Jefferson based on information from Sophia," Matt said.

"Elliott was right. This is the Mallory Conundrum," Jack said. "It happened to me. Talk about a screwup. When I went back in time without Charlotte and was hanged for conspiring to kill Lincoln, I changed our family's history. When Charlotte and David went back to rescue me, they stopped the hanging, and our family history stayed the way it was before my execution. But it was too late for Charlotte, because she grew up knowing a Mallory had participated in the conspiracy. It's a conundrum."

"It sure as hell is," Kenzie said. "When I changed my family history, I came back to a father I didn't know. He had suffered from being the son of a traitor. But after I saved my grandfather, his history was rewritten, and he was a hero. I still have trouble believing my father is as warm and loving as he is now."

"Charlotte carried her history back in time with her, like we all do when we travel. When she saved me," Jack said, "she kept my history from changing, like I said. The Mallorys weren't persecuted, the plantation house wasn't burned, the property wasn't confiscated, even though it was the history she knew. It was hard for her to accept that the Mallorys were an honored and revered Virginia family."

"As far as Charlotte knew, the Jack Mallory who conspired to kill Lincoln was reviled as a villain in the American psyche," David said.

Pete shivered. He didn't know where this discussion was going, and he didn't like it at all. Without JL and the rest of the O'Gradys at his side, he was adrift with people he hadn't grown up with and didn't know as well.

But he had to ask. "What if Sophia went back in time, told Jefferson about the Civil War, and convinced him when he became president to enact legislation to free all enslaved people? We would know a world where that war never happened and the racial division in our country didn't exist. Would we want to undo that?"

"But the war did happen, so we know she didn't influence him," Kenzie said. "God knows we studied it enough at West Point."

"But what if she had? We never would have been taught about the Civil War in high school because it never would have happened. When we find Sophia and she asks if she changed anything, we'll have to compare histories."

"This is giving me a headache," Kenzie said. "Matt, Jack, and I were history majors, so we know Thomas Jefferson married Sophia Frances Orsini, a brilliant artist. But most people, even if they know who the third president was, probably don't know his wife's name."

"I didn't," Pete said. "I mean, I've heard of Martha Washington, Jackie Kennedy, and then the ones in the last couple of decades, but other than those women, I couldn't give you any other names."

"Here's a question for the other two historians in the family," Kenzie said. "When Sophia was First Lady, she officially named the building the White House, and the term became a metonym for the president and his advisors. If she never becomes First Lady, what's the White House called?"

Jack let out an exasperated sigh. "We can't answer any of those questions until we find her."

"That's why Elliott didn't want to have a meeting," Pete said. "He used Lawrence as an excuse, but it wasn't the entire reason. He knew about the conundrum. He knew it all. I don't know how, but he did."

"I know Sophia was torn from yer arms as a young woman, and it broke her heart as well as yers," Elliott said from the doorway. He moved farther into the room. "I won't allow this family to break her heart again. Once is enough. Once is enough for ye, too, Pete."

"What about Jefferson?" Kenzie asked. "His heart was broken when he lost his first wife. If he's in love with Sophia, taking her away from him will break his heart again. Do we have a right to do that? And maybe they are soul mates. Maybe Sophia stayed because it's where she wants to be."

"And maybe she doesn't," Pete said. "Maybe she married him because it was the best option available to her in 1790. Maybe she wanted to come home but couldn't. I agree with Elliott. This time she has to be given a choice. She's not in love with me. In all these years, she never called or wrote, and in all honesty, I didn't write or call her either, but she does have a life here and a very successful career."

"None of us want to hurt the lass or the president, but we have to know for sure if she's there by choice," David said.

"Tread softly." Elliott turned to leave but wavered slightly and grabbed the door frame.

David rushed to his side. "Do ye need help?"

"No," Elliott said. "The doc changed my meds, and I'm a little wobbly. I'm going back to Charlotte's house to lie down."

"Elliott, wait," Pete said. "I have to know when you found out about Sophia and me."

"I had ye thoroughly vetted, as I've done with all of ye. It's my job as Keeper to protect the stones. I'll do whatever is necessary to protect them and the family."

"When did you know Sophia married Thomas Jefferson?"

"About ten minutes after ye told me she'd disappeared." Elliott pointed at the two portraits at opposite ends of the dining room. "These are S.F. Orsini paintings. Sophia has been in this room in another time." He went over to the window and tapped it. "She was married here and etched her initials on this windowpane. We're all connected, Pete. Be careful what ye change. It could have a direct impact on all of us."

And with that, Elliott left them again.

Amy went to the window and ran her finger over the etching in the pane. "Jack, there's an SFO etched in the glass next to my initials. I remember noticing them at the time and having one of those someone-is-walking-over-my-grave sensations. Those of us who don't go on this adventure can stand here and watch Sophia's initials disappear."

"Or not." Jack stood behind Amy, wrapping his arms around her and gently rubbing her small baby bump. "I was so proud that day. It meant—and still means—so much to me to have someone who loves me and wants to be a part of the Mallory tradition."

She turned in his arms and kissed him. "Thank you for wanting me."

David cleared his throat. "Either get a room or come back to the meeting."

Jack sat down in the chair Elliott had vacated and pulled Amy onto his lap. "You have our full attention."

"I recommend a small party of adventurers go back for Sophia," David said. "I want Jack and Matt on the team because they're historians. They'll be able to debrief Sophia. It'll be imperative for her history and our history to be compared—"

"I'm going too," Pete said. "You're not leaving me out."

"Okay," David said. "But Jack and Matt must compare histories, figure out what changed. If Sophia altered the future in a significant way, she can't come home."

Can't come home.

Shivers chased over Pete's skin, and he had to sit down. Leaving Sophia behind was unacceptable. He didn't give a damn about history. "I won't leave her there."

"Based on what Matt and Jack discover, ye might have to."

"That's bullshit," Pete said. "If Sophia changed history, then by leaving, history will revert back to what it should have been."

"I agree with Pete," Jack said. "I'm not going to make a value judgment about what is best for history. I firmly believe we don't have the right to change anything. Sophia needs to come home."

"Hold on a minute, Jackson," Kit said. "I spent three decades living in the nineteenth century, and, while I didn't enjoy every minute, I never regretted my decision. If Sophia wants to stay, you have to trust that she'll do what's best for the country."

"You're willing to give her the option to decide what's best, but not me?" Pete asked.

"This is about love," Kenzie said. "We're arguing about the wrong thing. The brooches bring soul mates together. If Thomas Jefferson is Sophia's soul mate, we need to butt out. Period."

"S.F. Orsini has an incredible body of work. Not everyone knew she was Thomas Jefferson's wife," Matt said. "She made Jefferson very wealthy and allowed him to free all his slaves. Matter of fact, a painting was just found in a house in Long Island. It'll be auctioned off, and the owner will make a fortune. Her paintings are worth millions."

"Oh, God. What a frigging mess," Kenzie said.

Jack stroked his hands up and down Amy's arms. "This must be like it was when Charlotte discovered what happened to me."

"Ye only changed yer family's history. If ye'd stopped the assassination, then we would have had a serious problem," David said.

"Jack, why don't we go over to the resource center and review Jefferson's history," Matt said. "We can pinpoint major events. Maybe we can identify areas that could have changed because of Sophia's influence."

"If Sophia doesn't marry Thomas Jefferson, and returns to the future, all her paintings will vanish. Can you imagine what a loss that would be to the art world?" Kenzie said.

"A huge loss," Kit said. "We can't be responsible for that."

"Most of her paintings are from the early nineteenth century. The world would lose a major portion of her body of work, but the ones she painted in France and when she first arrived in America would still exist," Matt said.

"Sophia Orsini Jefferson lived until her nineties. She was a prolific artist. We're talking about hundreds of paintings, not just a handful. The loss would be comparable to losing da Vinci's 'Medusa Shield' or Lindos' 'Colossus of Rhodes' or Gustave Courbet's 'The Stone Breakers.' We just can't do it," Kit said.

"Should we even tell her about her body of work?" Jack asked.

"No, we can't. If she stays, she'll know her future. We can't tell her," Pete said. "Do you want to know how long you'll live? What day you'll die? I don't. God, that would be awful. And besides, we still don't know for sure whether the twenty-first century Sophia and the eighteenth-century Sophia are the same person. It's possible they only resemble each other."

"There's been an interesting controversy surrounding an Orsini painting of Jefferson in Paris," Matt said. "Pete, see if you can find a picture of the painting titled 'Jefferson in Paris' by S.F. Orsini and pull it up on the screen."

A minute later the portrait appeared. "Now see if you can find a picture of the back where the artist signed the location of the painting and the date." A moment later, a second picture appeared on the screen. Matt went over and pointed to the word Paris. "Look at the A. What does it look like?"

"The Eiffel Tower," Kenzie said. "What's your point?"

"How could S.F. Orsini in 1789 paint an A resembling the Eiffel Tower when the tower wouldn't be built for another one hundred years?"

Pete slumped as all his hopes squashed together in his chest. "Sophia went to Paris with her grandmother the summer before her junior year in high school. She sent me a postcard with three words: I love Paris. The A in Paris was the Eiffel Tower."

He poured another whisky at the sideboard. Was this his third or fourth? Didn't matter. He wasn't driving.

Then he went to examine the window with Sophia's initials etched in the glass. He skimmed the tip of his finger around the S, the F, and the O.

Did you think of your first wedding when you carved your initials? Did you love him as much as you loved me?

"Here's some food for thought," Kenzie said.

Pete turned to face her, barely holding on to rational thought, desperately needing a life raft of hope.

"If the travelers have a choice when to arrive in the past, they could choose to arrive in Paris in 1789 before Sophia meets Jefferson. Before she falls in love. Before she marries him. Before she changes history."

The square sail on his little life raft billowed in the wind. "That's exactly what we should do, Kenzie. Go back to Paris and find her before she meets Jefferson. That's the answer."

"No, it's not!" Kit swung her arm and knocked over her coffee cup. She grabbed a handful of napkins and soaked up the spill. "You can't do that to her."

"Why not?" Pete asked.

"We know she met Thomas Jefferson, married him, and, from all reports had a very happy life. She's also listed as one of the top ten Renaissance to Neoclassical painters. You can't take that away from her without her knowledge. It would be criminal. She has to make an informed decision. Which means *telling* her everything."

"If we do, and she decides to stay, she'll know her future. Which isn't fair either," Pete said. "Do you want her to stay, fall in love, then go home? That's bullshit. There will be broken hearts all around."

"The travelers should go back to the point before Sophia meets Jefferson. It's the only logical choice," Jack said.

"The early paintings Sophia did of Jefferson are some of her best work. As an artist, although my talent pales in comparison to hers," Kit said, "if I lost an opportunity to paint Jefferson, Washington, Madison, Hamilton, and the rest, I'd be pissed."

Pete slammed his laptop shut and the large screen went blank. "If Sophia has a choice, she won't stay."

"Ye haven't seen her in twenty years, Pete. People change. She's not the same woman ye knew," David said. "She was a high school student. Now she's almost forty years old. If ye're not prepared to walk away and leave her there, then ye don't need to go on this mission."

Pete jumped to his feet. "I won't leave her behind!" His tone was sharp, cutting through the thickening air.

Calmly, David said, "Ye might not have a choice."

Pete came around the table and poked his finger against David's chest. "You'll give Sophia a choice, but not me?"

David glared at Pete, at his pointed finger. He leaned into the pressure of Pete's finger. "To choose what?"

Pete punched his finger into the rock-solid, muscular chest. "To stay behind, goddamn it!"

Jack set Amy aside and stood, pointing at Pete, and shouted over their raised voices, "You're not staying behind!"

There was a palpable, almost physical dislocation of air and space, a tremor that promised violence between the two men of similar height and weight, but Pete backed down.

Because that's what men did when they challenged David McBain. There was something in his eyes. Something in his stance. Something in his voice. You knew he would kill you.

But it had never stopped Pete or any of the men in the family from challenging David and initiating a fight. A fight they knew they couldn't win. David earned his mental toughness in special ops. Pete and the O'Gradys earned theirs in the Marines. They all were tough as steel and could be mean as junkyard dogs. They could kill without second-guessing, love with unfathomable passion, and protect the innocent against injustice, even if they had to sacrifice their own lives.

But McBain? He was all that and more.

Silence descended on the room, except for the heavy breathing.

Kenzie pushed between the two men. "At ease." She turned her back on Pete and kissed David as if no one else was in the room. It didn't do a damn thing for Pete, but David laughed.

"The clan needs to vote on this. We can't make an arbitrary decision when it impacts all of us," David said. "We have to put it up for a vote."

"Fine," Pete said, hitting the whisky again...because it's what men did when they backed down from a fight with McBain. "But what exactly do you want to vote on?"

"Do the travelers go back to Paris in 1789 before Sophia meets Jefferson and bring her home? Or do they go to New York City in the spring of 1790 before Sophia marries him?" Kenzie asked.

"The only fair way to ask that question is to have equally persuasive people argue the two positions," Kit said.

"I'll argue for going back to Paris before Sophia meets Jefferson," Pete said.

"You're too emotionally involved," Kenzie said.

"I suggest Braham and Cullen," Amy said. "They're both lawyers. They're both from the past."

"No, not Braham," Pete said. "He wanted to change history by saving Lincoln's life."

"Then who?" David asked.

"Get Jeff up here. He's never time-traveled. Never been backed into the position of changing history or fighting for the love of his life. He could be a dispassionate advocate for one side or the other," Amy said. "Let Cullen and Jeff argue both sides and then the family can vote."

"I call bullshit," Pete said. "Humans can't make this decision."

"Then who's going to make it?" Kenzie asked. "Do you want to play rock, paper, scissors, or flip a coin?"

"We could, but I suggest the brooch will make the decision for us." Pete said. "If we all focus on Sophia and not a specific time period, the stone will take us where we need to go. If it's Paris before she meets Jefferson, then so be it. If it's moments before she marries him, then so be it. If we put the question to a vote, we'll pit those who vote for love up against those who vote for reason, and everybody will get pissed off. It's not worth it."

"So we'll leave it up to the brooch," Kenzie said. "I hope you can live with that, Pete."

"I'll have to," he said.

Matt looked from David to Pete and back again. "You two had me worried. I thought for sure we were going to have a cultural battle."

"Are you kidding? Italians are part of Scottish culture," Kenzie said.

"In every wee town and village there's an Italian somewhere," David said. "We've been trying for almost two centuries to combine the best of Scottish directness with Italian warmth, courtesy, and generosity of spirit."

"Sorry, but I didn't see directness or generosity of spirit in that exchange," Matt said. "I only saw a former Marine and a former soldier ready to beat the crap out of each other."

David slapped Pete on the back. "We can fight, but Pete knows I've got his back."

"And I've got his," Pete said.

"Can we get back to business?" Jack asked. "Costumes will basically be the same whether we go to Paris or New York City, so that's easy enough. But now we have to decide who's going." He pulled Amy into his arms. "I want to go."

"I thought you would. If I wasn't pregnant, I'd go with you. You won't get into trouble, will you?"

He kissed her. "My troublemaking days are over. I'm just old, boring Jack now. But I'd like to take Patrick."

"He'd love to go, I bet, but you'll have Lincoln and Noah crying foul."

"The rule is kids can go if a parent goes," Jack said.

"I'd like to go," Matt said. "And if Noah wants to go and his parents agree, I'd like to take him. His chronological age is only fourteen, but he has a much older mindset. And since he's just shy of six feet, he looks older."

"If Noah and Patrick go, Lincoln will go nuts."

"If Braham and Charlotte agree, I'll be responsible for him," Jack said. "He is my nephew."

"There's no way in hell I'll be left out of this rescue," Pete said.

"Then we have three adults and three teenagers," David said. "I'm putting Jack in charge."

Jack was nibbling on Amy's neck, and his head shot up. "Me? Are you serious?"

"The Mallorys are connected to this story. Ye've got the experience. Ye can handle it, but ye might have to use a different last name."

"I could use my mother's maiden name. She was a Pendleton... Wait... No, that won't work. There was a Pendleton in the Virginia legislature with Jefferson. If it comes up, I'll just say I'm distantly related to the folks at Mallory Plantation."

"Just tell them you're the family black sheep and were disowned years ago," Amy said.

Matt sat back and clasped his hands over his stomach. "Do you realize who'll be in New York City in early 1790?"

An ecstatic smile spread over Jack's face, reaching his eyes, widening them. Pete hadn't seen him do that since his wedding day. "I could have an orgasm just thinking about it."

David rolled his eyes. "Don't let me regret my decision."

"Just messing with you." Then to Matt he said, "All the Founding Fathers in one place. It boggles my mind to think of meeting George Washington, John Adams, Alexander Hamilton, John Jay, and the rest. I'll be a kid in a candy store."

"Okay, I'm regretting it now," David said.

"The thought of meeting them is overwhelming." Matt pushed away from the table. "I need to prepare."

"Hold up," David said. "When can ye be ready to go?"

Jack got out his phone and pulled up his calendar. "It will take our costumers three, maybe four days to make two outfits apiece. We'll need to go to Lexington to get the brooches and weapons for Pete, and gold and a few diamonds to sell. Five days max."

"Five days should give us enough time to do a thorough review of Jefferson's life, the Compromise of 1790, historical events of the nineteenth and twentieth centuries. Can you think of anything else?" Matt asked.

"Why don't we head over to the library and hit the books for a couple of hours, then draw up a plan to present at tonight's meeting."

"What do you want me to do?" Pete asked.

"Ye'll need to go to Lexington to pick up the brooches, weapons, and gold," David said.

"I'll go through Sophia's catalogue and order reprints of all her paintings," Kit said. "You'll want to take those with you. If she returns, those paintings will disappear. She might want to recreate them later."

"You're brilliant," Kenzie said. "But I wouldn't give them to her yet. I'd wait a few months for the experience to soak in and give her time to recover from the emotional upheaval in her life. If she walks away from Jefferson when she has strong feelings for him, she won't want to see the paintings for a while."

"I'd like to have jpegs," Pete said. "If they're on my laptop and I take them with me, they won't disappear."

"Which reminds me, we should print out every mention of her we can find. The library at Monticello will be full of articles. I'll go there tomorrow and talk to the docents. They always have the best stories," Kenzie said.

"I'll expect everyone to report on their assignments at tonight's meeting. Matt, be sure to clear Noah's participation with Amber and Daniel. The same for Lincoln. They'll need to attend the meeting. Anything else?"

"Not that I can think of," Pete said.

"Then let's get to work," David said. "And remember, we're not going to discuss the dilemma. We're leaving it up to the brooch. It will take ye where ye need to go."

37

Mallory Plantation—Pete

PETE HEADED FOR the exit at the conclusion of the seven o'clock meeting. Everyone signed off on the plan to send him, Matt, Jack, and three hyper-excited teenage boys on a mission to rescue Sophia.

Well, everyone except a pissed-off set of twins who cornered their father like two growling lion cubs. A recent growth spurt had added several inches to their already imposing preteen height.

"It's not fair, Dad," Henry said, fists at his waist, elbows jutting out.

"Not fair at all." Robbie's jutting elbows abutted his brother's and created a formidable barrier in front of David.

Pete stopped to watch the confrontation. David always had control over the twins. Although he occasionally let them think their roles were reversed.

"We know how to ride, shoot, and hunt better than Patrick, Noah, or Lincoln. You can't do this to us." Henry slapped his forehead. "We'll never live it down."

Robbie grabbed his brother's hand to stop him from beating on himself. "We're not better than Lincoln."

Henry glared at him. "Shhh. Our skills are close. And besides, his dad rode with the Union Cavalry. They were the best riders ever."

Pete leaned against a bookshelf, chuckling. The twins were smart, athletic, and had a sense of humor and a memory for jokes second only to their mother. It wasn't that Pete didn't want responsibility for them because they wouldn't obey. That wasn't it at all. They were always obedient. Pete just couldn't be responsible for them on this adventure. As soon as he had the chance to talk to them, he'd try to explain his position.

Robbie turned toward his brother, scrunching his face. "Nah, they weren't. American Indians were better riders than anybody."

"Better than jockeys?" Henry demanded. "Their average speed in the Kentucky Derby is thirty-five miles an hour."

"Thirty-seven. Just ask Uncle Elliott," Robbie said.

"I can't ride as fast as a jockey," Henry said.

Robbie tugged on his chin. "Me neither, but we can hunt better than Lincoln."

David remained standing, legs spread, arms folded, his expression one that would have cowed most men. The boys appeared to have forgotten he was even there.

"Lincoln can snare a rabbit with a string a lot quicker than we can," Henry said. "And don't forget he shot down that light fixture in San Francisco."

Robbie chuckled. "Man, he set the place on fire, too."

"He was just doing what Uncle Braham told him to do."

"I could have shot it down and not caused a fire."

Henry shoved Robbie. "Liar. The light fixture was full of burning candles. Didn't matter who shot it down, the place was going up in flames."

"Don't hit yer brother," David said.

"Lincoln's a lot older than we are," Robbie continued as if David hadn't spoken. "No wonder he can ride, shoot, and hunt better than we can, but we've got Noah and Patrick beat."

David grabbed Robbie to keep him from giving Henry a payback shove. "Listen up. We're not having a contest to see who can ride and shoot the best. The single criterion here is who are ye bringing to the dance? And ye two don't have partners. Plus, ye're not old enough."

"You're making up rules, just like you did when we were little and couldn't go into the security center until we were six," Robbie said, shaking loose of David's grip.

If there was a betting pool on how this comedy act was going to shake out, Pete would bet on David. If Pete ever had kids, how would he handle this kind of thing? He wasn't sure, but he certainly wouldn't go to the family priest for advice. The priest's heart might have been in the right place all those years ago, but his advice was based on what was best for Sophia's parents, not on what was best for her or Pete.

David would have advised Pete to run after the woman he loved. And if he had, they would have a houseful of children by now. The woman he remembered wanted a dozen. From the research he'd done between meetings, he sadly learned she never had children with Jefferson, probably a huge disappointment for her.

"Age doesn't matter either," Robbie said. "Don't you remember Lincoln went back to rescue his dad when he was a lot younger than we are now?"

"And he saved everybody," Henry added. "See, Dad? Us kids can do adult-sized acts of courage."

Pete laughed. David didn't.

"Okay, lads. Here's the deal. Get permission from Pete, Matt, and Jack. If one of them is willing to accept responsibility for ye, then ye can go. But either ye both go, or neither of ye go. I won't have one left behind grumbling about it for the next year. Got it?"

"Do we have to get all three to agree, or just one to take responsibility?" Robbie asked.

Pete laughed again. *Gotta love 'em.*

David never broke character, but as soon as the boys were out of the room, he'd crack up. "Ye each need a person to take responsibility for ye."

"Not fair," Henry said. "We're a set. A pair. We go together."

"That's right," Robbie said. "You just said both of us go or nobody goes. It's only fair if one person takes responsibility for both of us."

"I told ye the terms. Grumbling about it won't help. Take it or leave it," David said.

Robbie grabbed Henry's arm, pulling him aside. "Uncle Matt and Uncle Jack are our best bet. Forget Uncle Pete. He's a definite no."

"Okay, you talk to Uncle Matt. I'll find Uncle Jack," Henry said.

Kenzie jumped up out of her chair. "Whoa. Just a minute. You can't make that deal. They're not going without you, McBain."

David kissed her cheek. "Don't worry, Kenz. No one wants responsibility for them."

The boys slung their arms around each other's shoulders. They were mirror images of each other, with matching University of Kentucky basketball T-shirts and long shorts, and curly red hair they attempted to tame with hair products. Their faces glowed with something akin to defiant determination.

"Dinna be so sure, Da," Robbie said in his best imitation of his dad's Scottish accent. "Watch and learn."

Kenzie mouthed, "Watch and learn?"

The boys turned as a single unit but ran off in different directions.

"Uncle Jack!" Henry yelled.

"Uncle Matt!" Robbie yelled.

When Pete heard one of his catch phrases—watch and learn—thrown back at the twins' parents, he pushed open the door and escaped the building. He knew now how the standoff was going to end. Matt had quoted Churchill at the conclusion of the meeting, "Study history, study history. In history lies all the secrets of statecraft."

Neither Matt nor Jack would agree to take the twins, and David would need all the secrets of statecraft to negotiate world peace in the McBain household when the twins had to face the reality that they were never going on an adventure without their father.

Pete went outside to clear his head, walking without a destination in mind, eventually finding himself at the dock with a front row seat to the gold and blue sunset as dusk lowered a curtain over the James River.

He wasn't a painter like Kit and Sophia, or a historian like Matt and Jack, but he read and wrote poetry, not only for the rhyme and rhythm and the vivid imagery, but for the story and love language. How many poems had he written to Sophia over the past two decades? Hundreds. How many had he sent her? Zero. Volumes of his poems were tucked away in locked boxes in his Colonial-style two-story house on MacKlenna Farm, but no one had ever read them or even knew of his passion.

He meandered almost to the end of the dock, listening to waves lap against the pillars and the sides of the bass fishing boats and the pontoon. If he had the keys, he'd take one out for a night run on the river. Instead, he climbed aboard the pontoon and punched in the security code to switch off the alarm. He might even sleep out there tonight.

"Pete," Charlotte yelled. "Wait."

Charlotte wasn't alone. She brought reinforcements—Amber, Kenzie, and Amy—a quartet of brooch ladies. They had all been stranded in the past: Kenzie and Amy in the twentieth century, and Amber and Charlotte in the nineteenth. Amber and Charlotte had both fallen in love with men from that time, men who had agreed to live in the future, but their situations were completely different from Sophia's. Thomas Jefferson could never come to the twenty-first century. Talk about screwing up history.

Pete didn't know much about the third president. The one thing he did know, he didn't like at all. The man had slept with his wife. Okay, maybe legally Sophia wasn't his wife anymore, but still...

"We want to talk to you," Kenzie said.

Pete headed straight for the liquor cabinet. "Sorry, but I'm all talked out."

Kenzie followed behind him. "We've come to encourage you."

He pulled out a bottle of whisky. "You want a drink?"

"Sure. Give me a short-pour."

"That's all you want? You've got to go back and face your sons."

Kenzie grabbed two glasses from the cabinet. "I'm not going back until David sends me an all-clear text."

"Smart girl." He poured whisky into the glasses. "Amy can't drink, but Charlotte, you and Amber can. After all, it is your liquor."

"Sure," Amber said. "Give one to Charlotte, too. She's got the night off—no work, no call. The drink will help keep her from going back to town to check on patients when she doesn't have to."

Kenzie opened the refrigerator. "Amy and Carlton Jackson Mallory VI want an orange juice."

"He'll be the ninth," Amy said. "It's so perfect, very baseball-ish."

Kenzie stared at Charlotte. "Seriously, did she say baseball-ish?"

"I'm going back through family records to be sure," Charlotte said. "I was going to look when Margaret Ann was born, but never did."

"Trust me, he's the ninth," Amy said. "Jack's not usually wrong when it comes to numbers. Matter of fact, he's rarely wrong about anything. It's so annoying. He knew I was pregnant before I did."

Amber accepted her drink. "How'd he know?"

"He said I tasted different."

"Stop!" Pete said. "I'm a guy. Have a little respect."

Laughing, they carried their drinks to the open deck and settled in on the sofas, tucking their feet under their hips. Four intelligent, talented, wealthy, sensuous women whose husbands doted on them. And for the time being, Pete had them all to himself—a harem. What a lucky son of a bitch he was.

He put his feet up on an ottoman and leaned back. "Okay, what brings you ladies out here? And keep it clean." He sipped the rich-flavored Balvenie, sighing at the honeyed sweetness, a real classic. And because Amy's comment had twisted his thinking, he remembered his wedding night and how sweet Sophia had tasted.

"We all have stories of going back in time and being abandoned by a brooch," Amy said. "But we don't regret the way things happened."

"Well, I don't regret the way things ended, but being abandoned in the middle of a Civil War battle was terrifying," Charlotte said.

"I was a soldier, dropped into the middle of a London air raid, with no backup and no way to protect myself. I was terrified too. It was awful," Kenzie said. "I never stopped wanting to go home."

"If Olivia, Connor, and Rick hadn't come after me," Amber said, "I would've died."

Amy shivered. "JL and I almost died, too. And I had a boyfriend and a job I loved. I wanted to go home, and was convinced I could find a way, but Jack came along before I could start looking."

"So what's the point?" Pete asked. "I've heard all your stories. Sophia's situation was different. She found her soul mate and decided to marry him and remain in the eighteenth century."

"It wasn't her first choice," Charlotte said.

"Maybe, maybe not. From what I know now, she was a beloved First Lady, a wonderful mother to Jefferson's daughters, a cherished grandmother to his grandchildren, and a prolific and extraordinary artist. She led a very full life."

"But we don't believe it was what she wanted," Kenzie said.

Charlotte sipped her drink. "Kit met Cullen in the past, and they remained there until they got sick and had to come to the future."

"But that was where Kit was meant to be," Kenzie said. "She was living in the future by mistake. Not the other way around."

Pete took a long drink of the whisky, tasting the gentle spice with a little vanilla. He needed a cigar. Hell, he needed a lot more than a drink and a smoke. "The brooches don't make mistakes."

"It sure seems like it when you get dumped somewhere and can't go home," Kenzie said.

"The brooches force you to turn challenges into opportunities. They teach you to move from self-pity to a place of compassion for others. You don't have to give up, or even be afraid to start in the first place. You learn that if it doesn't kill you, whatever it is will make you stronger. Each of you remained resilient through failure and persistent through obstacles. I know. I've read all your reports, all your comments, all your trials and tribulations. I know your stories. And this time it's different."

"No it's not, Pete. Sophia has a successful career in Italy," Amy said. "I can't believe she doesn't think about her art and her studio every day. I can't believe she doesn't close her eyes, click her heels, and say, 'There's no place like home.' I can't believe she wants to stay there and abandon her life in the twenty-first century. It just doesn't make sense."

"Pete, stop and think where you were the past five years during Sophia's summer holidays," Kenzie said. "You might have been in Italy at the time, but you were never close enough to discover she was missing and go after her. The brooch kept trying until you were in the right place at the right time."

Amy gasped. "I think you're on to something. There was no point in abandoning Sophia in the past if no one was going to rescue her. Pete had to be in the right place too. Just like Jack and David were in the right place to come after us."

Charlotte's jaw dropped. "Oh, my God. I think you're right."

"Makes sense to me, too." Amber's phone beeped with a text message. "I've got to go. Daniel wants to go out with Braham, and Mom and Dad are eating a late dinner with Elliott and Meredith."

"Where are the guys going?" Kenzie asked.

"They're probably coming down here," Charlotte said. "There's an inlet about a half mile up the river. Braham, Cullen, and Daniel love to go there at night and fish. They say it's the only place quiet enough to believe they're back in the nineteenth century."

"Is that where they want to be?"

"I think they just like to reminisce," Charlotte said. "You know, reminisce about 'the good ol' days.'"

"Daniel couldn't give up the internet and hot showers," Amber said. "And Noah and I would refuse to go back, and you couldn't peel wee Heather off Dad's lap. Daniel has permanently relocated to the twenty-first century."

Charlotte finished her drink and washed her glass in the sink. "Let the brooch guide you, Pete, and when you find Sophia, tell her how you feel."

Kenzie added her glass to the soapy water. "Don't dick around.

If she's at all confused about whether to go home or not, your feelings have to be part of her deliberation."

Pete let out a heavy sigh and refilled his glass. "If we're relying on the brooch to take us where we need to go, we might show up after she's married."

"Not gonna happen," Amber said, adding her empty glass to the mix. "It's just not consistent with what we know about the brooches. I wish I could go after Sophia. Kenzie was so wonderful when she and David and Rick came after me and explained how the brooches worked. But what was so cool was giving me time in the past to do what I wanted to do, until I got so sick Rick had to take me home." Amber hugged Kenzie. "And now you're my BFF."

"I thought *I* was," Amy said with a fake pout.

"We are the brooch ladies," Charlotte said. "There isn't another closer or more loving group in the world. We share a common experience, and we're all happier, our lives have more meaning, and we all have greater life satisfaction because of what we've been through."

"I thought it was because we all married really hot guys and have fantastic sex," Kenzie said.

Charlotte grinned. "Well, that too."

"Aaagh! Too much information." Pete said. "It's time to hustle you guys off the boat."

"What's the hurry?" Amber asked.

Kenzie pointed down the dock. "Those sexy men coming this way. Can't you smell the cigars?"

"I'm leaving," Amy said. "The smell makes me sick."

Charlotte hugged Pete. "Don't let anything we said discourage you. We're all praying for you and Sophia, and we can't wait to meet her."

Kenzie, Amy, and Amber hugged and kissed him, too, and the brooch ladies departed the pontoon just as the guys arrived.

"We softened him up for you," Amy said.

Jack pulled her into his arms. "Don't leave."

She waved away the cigar smoke. "Get that thing away from

me."

"Oh, sorry." Jack handed the cigar to Braham. "Hold this a minute." Braham held it while Jack hugged and kissed his wife.

David twirled Kenzie around, then pulled her toward him in one fast, fluid move, ending in a perfectly executed dip. "Stay with me."

"How could I say no to you?"

He lifted her up for a kiss.

"But I'm tired. I'm going to go take a long bath while Granny Alice puts the girls to bed. What happened with the boys?"

"God, Kenz. Talk about ruining a mood."

"I didn't ruin anything. You're here with Daniel, Jack, and Braham to drink whisky and give Pete a pep talk. So what happened?"

"Jack promised them an adventure before summer ends."

"What did they say?"

David twirled Kenzie again. "They want to go to Tibet."

She spun back into his arms then spun out. "Oh Jesus. I hope you nipped that in the bud."

"I told them the monastery was closed to visitors in the summer," Jack said.

She swished her hips then came back to David for another dip. "And they believed you?"

They did until Blane told them to check their Google machines to see if I was telling the truth. What the hell is that all about?" Jack asked.

"Blane was eating breakfast in the kitchen the day after the plane crash, and Morning Joe was on the TV." Kenzie popped up out of the dip and kissed David. "Joe Scarborough told his audience if they heard something and didn't know if it was true or not, to go to their neighbor's house and check their Google machine. Blane thought it was so funny he started calling his iPad a Google machine. Since then, every time he looks sad, I ask about his Google machine and he laughs. Works every time. But he's a smart kid. It won't last much longer."

"What about the trip?" Charlotte asked.

"They found out I was telling the truth. So next month we're all going camping and whitewater rafting in Colorado."

Pete moved away from the group of soul mates and returned to the liquor cabinet and the one thing that could keep him warm tonight. Steeping in self-pity didn't become him, but he'd become an expert at spinning thoughts and words to avoid feeling the pain of his emotional isolation. And now it was staring him in the face.

He'd been such an idiot. Why hadn't he gone after Sophia twenty years ago? He could be standing on the dock hugging his wife, just like the other guys. Why hadn't he turned challenges into opportunities? Why hadn't he been persistent through the obstacles Sophia's parents stacked in their way? And his parents, too. Why had he given up?

Because he'd been so damn scared Sophia would tell him her parents were right and he wasn't good enough for her. It had been easier to accept defeat than to be persistent. And now he was too late.

How in the hell could he ever compete with Thomas Jefferson? The only white house he could offer Sophia was a colonial-style home on a horse farm, while Jefferson could give her the most important white house in the world.

What a dumb-ass he'd been.

38

Mallory Plantation—Pete

FIVE DAYS LATER the entire clan gathered on the back lawn near the willow oak, ready to send Pete, Jack, Matt, and three teenage boys back in time to rescue Sophia. JL and Kevin—sans Lawrence, who remained in the NICU under the watchful eye of his medical team—were also there to enjoy the send-off and their two hours of desperately needed couple time.

A picnic spread was laid out on portable tables, overflowing with Kentucky hot brown sliders, chicken salad sandwiches, macaroni salad, potato salad, tuna salad with green apples and eggs, pimento cheese stuffed deviled eggs, fried chicken, hamburgers and hot dogs on the grill, and pies, cookies, and brownies for dessert.

For the Italians there were aged and soft cheeses, prosciutto, salami, olives, carrots and celery, melon, figs and pears, Italian bread and focaccia, gelato, chocolate and pistachio biscotti, and sweet corn panna cotta with fresh blueberry compote.

And lots of wine, Southern sweet tea, pink lemonade, and beer.

Badminton and volleyball nets were set up, along with cornhole and croquet. Phones were tucked into pockets for emergency use only, and there were no iPads or laptops. Jeff and Julie and their kids, Gabe, Shane, Rick, Austin, and the three college kids, had all flown in to celebrate wee Lawrence's three-week birthday and

Sophia's return to the twenty-first century. If the diamond brooch worked as expected, the travelers would all return within minutes of leaving.

Amy wanted to watch the initials on the window disappear, but she didn't want to miss Jack and Patrick leaving and returning, so she decided to stay in the backyard. Jack took a picture of the etchings to take with him so the image wouldn't be lost when history reverted to what it had been. None of them had doubts about the outcome, at least that they'd admit to. The result of the adventure would be as it should be.

Matt had filled a leather trunk with his favorite Jefferson books and rolled-up prints of Sophia's art. He wanted to keep the books with the revised history to do a deep dive into the minutiae of Jefferson's life and American history to find out what changed and why.

Amy held her four-year-old daughter and hugged Jack and Patrick goodbye. Jack lifted his little blonde-headed Margaret Ann out of Amy's arms, then swung her high in the air until she giggled. Then he gave her a big kiss on her cheek.

"Is Daddy's little girl going to be good for Mommy?"

"We're playing baseball," Margaret Ann said. "I'm going to use my Christy Maf…son glove Mommy had made. It's funny-looking."

"Mathewson didn't care what it looked like," Jack said. "He was a helluva pitcher."

Margaret Ann pushed against him to get down. "Bye, Daddy. Bye, Pat-Pat." She ran off screaming for the youngest O'Gradys—cousins wee Heather and Betsy, and the youngest McBains, Laurie Wallis and twins Alicyn and Rebecca.

"Come back, lass," Elliott called after her. "We're going to take a clan picture."

Margaret Ann made a U-turn and hurried back to stand by her parents and brother.

There was a calling of the clans: McCabes, McBains, Montgomerys, Frasers, Grants. Then came the Irish O'Gradys and Mallorys, and the Italian Riccis, one Moretti, and one Parrino.

Following group pictures, the travelers lined up for several small group ones. Phones were allowed briefly. While everybody else was wearing shorts, T-shirts, and summer dresses, the travelers wore tight breeches, leggings, embroidered and brocaded waistcoats, white linen stocks, and three-cornered hats.

"We look like damn American flags," Pete groused. "This wig itches, and how the hell am I supposed to convince Sophia, while I'm wearing this getup, that I'm the man she married twenty years ago?"

"She'll recognize you. You've aged some. We all have, but you've only added a couple of pounds. You still have all your hair, and only a few wrinkles at the corners of your eyes." JL hugged Pete and kissed his cheek. "Here are my last words of wisdom. Don't you dare let her get away from you again. Got that?"

Pete saluted, his eyes watering. "I don't have a good feeling about this."

JL's eyes watered too. She tightened Pete's stock and straightened it. "Listen here, partner. When we were out on surveillance, you *never* had a good feeling about what we were doing. So forget about the hairs on the back of your neck, or your spidey senses, or whatever is acting up right now. Forget them. They aren't worth shit."

Blane, standing beside her, gasped. "Moo-ooom! You said a bad word."

"I know," JL said. "But sometimes it's all Pete understands."

"Do you know what shit means?" Blane asked.

"Shh," JL said. "You're not supposed to use that word."

"Then how the hell is Uncle Pete supposed to understand me?" Blane asked, waving his arms.

"You're not supposed to use that word either."

"Then how is anybody supposed to understand me? Pops says hell and Grandpa Elliott says hell and shit and fu—"

JL slapped her hand over his mouth. "Don't you dare say it."

He peeled her hand away. "I was going to say funny words. What the hell did you think I was going to say?"

JL turned around and yelled, "Kevin Fraser, come get your son."

Kevin sauntered toward her, trying hard to keep a smile from popping out. "Come on, Blane. Let's play soccer."

Blane turned to run off, but stopped and hugged Pete around the waist. Then he shook his finger, and lowering his voice said, "Hey, let's be careful out there."

"Okay, Sergeant," Pete said, giving him a smart salute.

Blane giggled and ran toward his dad. "I said it just like Sergeant Esterhaus." Excitedly, Blane jerked his fist up and down. "Just like him!"

JL glared at Pete. "He's too young for that show."

He shrugged. "Blane comes from a family of cops. What can I say?"

"One day you'll have kids of your own and it'll be payback time." Then she hugged Pete again. "Look, I hope this works out, because I won't be able to deal with what comes next if it doesn't."

"What do you think comes next?"

"You'll find someone on the rebound, marry quickly, and you'll never be happy."

Pete shook his head. "No, I won't, and that's a shitty picture."

"I'm just telling you like it is. After all, I'm the biggest optimist in this family," JL said.

"Bullshit," Jack said.

JL gave Jack a hug, too. "Take care of him, will you? Don't let him get his heart broken again."

Jack hugged her back. "I'll do what I can. Take care of my family."

"Sure will. I won't let them out of my sight." She looked over at Amy and winked.

Matt moved away from his teary-eyed wife and joined the others under the tree. "Let's get this show on the road."

"Wait." Robbie and Henry streaked across the lawn, cloth sacks flopping in their hands. "We've got something for you." The twins skidded to a stop in front of the three teenagers and handed them each a knapsack. "We filled these with candy bars and chips and gum and stuff. You know, in case you're there for a day. You'll get hungry. Back then they didn't have good stuff to eat," Robbie said.

"We were going to put a six-pack of Cokes in there, but we figured they'd explode in the vortex."

"Wouldn't that be cool, Robbie?" Henry said.

The twins looked at each other like they were reconsidering their decision not to include soft drinks. Then they shrugged. "If they're going to explode, we want to be there. Right?" Robbie asked.

David squeezed his sons' shoulders. "That's a sign of true sportsmanship, lads. I'm proud of ye."

"We know you wanted to go," Lincoln said. "We'll bring back pictures, but we won't talk about the adventure unless you want to hear what happened."

Robbie and Henry ducked their heads and dug divots in the ground with the heels of their sneakers. After a moment, Robbie's head popped up, then Henry's. "We want to hear everything. Especially the stuff the uncles don't know about. Got it? So have fun for us," Robbie said.

"And if you see George Washington, ask him if the cherry tree story is true," Henry said.

"That's a good one Henry. I'll do it," Noah said.

David smiled at Kenzie, who was wiping her eyes. She mouthed, "Love you, McBain."

Pete joined Matt and Jack under the tree next to their leather trunks and portmanteaus. Matt looked a little sickly. "You okay, man?" Pete asked.

"I've heard about all the twisting and turning. I've never liked roller coasters."

"It goes fast, but you won't be the first one to get sick."

Matt gave Pete a hopeful look. "Did you get sick the first time?"

"No one knows. So let's keep it between us."

"Thanks. Even if it's not true, I feel better."

"Hey, man." Pete winked. "I wouldn't lie to you."

Elliott gave Pete the sapphire brooch. "Here's your backup."

Pete tried pinning it to the inside of his waistcoat pocket, but his hand shook. He was like a new rookie officer feeling like he belonged anywhere but where he was. After piercing his finger twice, he got it pinned, then tugged on it just to be sure.

Elliott gave the diamond brooch to Jack. "Don't throw it out any windows."

"I've got too much to come back to. I won't screw around."

Elliott then shook hands with the men, and each one pulled him in for a man hug and slap on the back. When he let go of Pete, Elliott said, "It'll work out. It may not be easy, but it will eventually work out."

"Are you giving me Obi-Wan Kenobi advice?" Pete asked.

"It's the only kind I've got." Then, seemingly as an afterthought, Elliott said. "If ye have to tell Jefferson the truth, tell him anything but the date of his death. No man wants that information."

"And don't screw with the slavery issue," Braham added. "If the states settle the issue early in the nineteenth century, there won't be a Civil War. If there's no war, I'll never meet Charlotte. Remember, ye've messed over yer sister once before, Jack. Don't do it again."

"But you can do a lot for women's suffrage, so feel free to interfere on behalf of women everywhere," Kenzie said. "We might be accepted as cadets into West Point sooner than 1976."

"I won't touch slavery but will advocate for women. Anything else?" Jack asked.

"Term limits would be good," Charlotte said.

"If they institute term limits, Mom and Dad wouldn't spend half a century in the Senate," Jack said.

Charlotte gave her brother an odd look. "So? My parents were schoolteachers."

"Goddamn it. Let's get out of here," Jack said. "Charlotte will never let me forget my screwup."

Charlotte laughed. "I forgave you years ago, but I don't mind letting you feel unforgiven occasionally. It keeps you humble."

"I'll make sure Dad doesn't mess up," Patrick said. "I don't want to be back on the streets of New York City in 1909."

"The ripple effect could send me back to 1878 Colorado," Noah said.

"Geez. I'd never be born," Lincoln said. "Maybe we should reconsider this trip."

The boys looked at each other, lips pursed, foreheads scrunched, heads shaking.

Lincoln, carrying a suitcase, stepped out of line. "I'm not going."

Patrick picked up his bag. "If you're not going, I'm not either."

"I'm not going to be the only kid on this trip. I'm out of here. Sorry, Grandpa," Noah said, grabbing his bag.

"Wait a minute," Robbie said. "You can't change *our* history. We can go now." He snatched the goody bag from Lincoln's hand. "I'll need this. It's packed with my favorite junk I'm not allowed to eat except on trips."

Henry marched over to stand next to his brother, squaring his shoulders, and grabbed the bags from Noah and Patrick. "Yeah. That's right. You can't mess up our history."

Matt leaned over, propping his hands on his knees, bringing himself eye level with the McBain twins. "What event did we talk about last month? There was a big anniversary."

The twins looked at each other. "D-Day?" Robbie asked.

"Yeah, it was D-Day when all those brave men stormed the beaches in Normandy. I remember," Henry said. "What's that got to do with us?"

"I was there," Kenzie said. "Or would have been if your dad hadn't rescued me."

"I rescued her for the second time in only a few hours," David added. "If yer mother had stayed put—"

"What?" Kenzie sounded scandalized...if you ignored the grin toying with the corners of her mouth. "Don't you mean if you hadn't lied to me?"

David kissed her. "Water under the bridge, Kenz. This has been litigated over and over."

"You're right." She looked down at her sons. "If World War II doesn't happen... If D-Day doesn't happen, your dad and I won't meet. You could be a ripple effect too."

The boys gasped, their mouths forming amazed circles. "Say it ain't so, Kenz."

"'Fraid it is. Do you still want to go?" she asked.

They shook their heads. Then Robbie said. "Sure. I want to go." Then he giggled, grabbed Henry's hand, and the twins ran off to join the other kids on the volleyball court. "Have a good time," they yelled.

The three teenagers shucked their coats and picked up paper plates at the table. "We'll grab a couple of burgers and be right here when you come back," Lincoln said.

Charlotte, Amber, and Amy immediately gathered for a group hug, bouncing around like they'd won a tournament. When they finally moved apart, they physically deflated with relief. Some of their relief rubbed off on Pete. The situation he, Matt, and Jack were heading into would take a great deal of massaging, and having three impatient teenagers around would have caused more tension. And he was already tense enough.

Jack made a circling motion with his hand. "Gather around and let's get out of here."

The three men formed a circle around their luggage and linked arms. Jack opened the brooch, and all together they recited the chant: *"Chan ann le tìm no àite a bhios sinn a' tomhais an' gaol ach 's ann le neart anama."*

The air was heavy with the fragrance of peat. A thick fog rose from the ground in a strong blast of air, swirling and creeping up into the willow oak.

Blane waved his arms and turned in a circle. "Where'd they go, Mommy?"

"They'll be right back. Hang on a minute."

It was the last thing Pete knew until a sour smell nearly gagged him. His stomach churned, but he couldn't take deep breaths to settle it because of the smell. When the fog cleared so did the stink. He had no idea where he was, or where Matt and Jack were, but thankfully his senses weren't on high alert. There appeared to be no immediate danger.

Damn. Where the hell was he? France or America. God, he hoped it was France. Was the nearby water the Hudson River or the Seine?

He walked down an incline toward a small, private beach and studied the shoreline on the opposite side. His stomach roiled again. Say it ain't so, Joe.

39

New York City (1790)—Pete

PETE'S JACKET FLAPPED open in the breeze stirred up by the river. It was definitely the Hudson not the Seine. The air was warm, but not hot and muggy. The trees surrounding the private beach were in full leaf, and late spring flowers painted the slope in vibrant colors. It could be early June.

What did that mean for Sophia? Matt mentioned Jefferson had been involved in a big event in June, but Pete hadn't been paying attention. His only thought was Sophia, finding her, apologizing, and confessing his love. In that order. He couldn't think about her possible feelings for Jefferson. Whatever they were, she had to let them go and come home. Period. He knew what was best for her.

He was operating under the assumption it was 1790…but was it? They had newspapers, right? All he had to do was find one.

He'd spent a couple of decades as a detective in this city. He knew how to find information and locate people. He was in his element. Although early New York in no way resembled the city he knew so well, he did know a few historical facts about the city, like Evacuation Day, the day the British left New York at the end of the war. In hindsight, he should have read a history book in preparation for this trip. Honestly, though, the only history he was interested in was his own, and he was here to change it, to rewrite the mistakes of his youth.

But first he had to find Matt and Jack.

When they went back for Amy, they all landed in Central Park, but were scattered all over the eight hundred forty-acre park. The brooch had dropped them like pick-up sticks that time. And it looked like the brooch did it again.

There had been a reason for separating them in the park. JL was mistaken for a prostitute and arrested, but she got a lead on Amy's whereabouts while in jail. So, if there was a reason now, Pete had to be open to all possibilities, even one that might send him off course.

He slung his knapsack over his shoulder and proceeded up the slope at the opposite end of the beach, finding himself at the New York Harbor. The only people around were the men who worked there, and they didn't even give him a passing nod.

He walked along a row of red brick townhomes and reached an old fort in the process of being razed. The demolition crew was dumping the debris into the river for landfill. If this was the tip of Manhattan, he was watching the destruction of Fort Amsterdam. The construction of the fort in the 1600s marked the official founding of New York City. Now the Alexander Hamilton U.S. Custom House stood there. He could thank one of his teachers in elementary school for that tidbit. Or was it in middle school? He couldn't remember. Until college, he'd lacked focus. Then the Marines finally straightened him out.

Was it possible Sophia's parents had been right to do what they did? No. Never in a million years. Even if they were still living, he wouldn't let them off the hook. And he'd never once been tempted to light a candle for them.

He turned away from New York Harbor, teeming with sailing ships, and headed toward town until he reached a teardrop-shaped park enclosed by a cast-iron fence with sawn-off finials—another historic landmark. The landmarks still standing could be counted on one hand. Maybe two, but not many more.

He'd reached Bowling Green Park, the first public park in New York City. There was no Charging Bull. No Fearless Girl. But even in the twenty-first century, she wasn't there now. The symbol of female empowerment had been moved to stand in front of the Stock Exchange. He liked her much better facing down a charging bull.

He pictured Sophia as Fearless Girl. How many men with archaic values had she argued with while living in the past? He'd argued with the mayor and city council members over relocating the bronze sculpture. Their reasoning that in her new location she would inspire more companies to hire women—Fearless Girl's original purpose—didn't fly with him.

He couldn't imagine the feisty woman he knew would put up with harassment and discrimination. Didn't men in the eighteenth century believe women belonged at home with the children? If anything, that alone convinced him Sophia wouldn't stay here if she had a chance to leave.

Finding landmarks calmed and somehow settled him with a sense of belonging. This was his city. And he loved it. In this time, the park was at the center of the fashionable residential area. If he hung around, everyone of importance would pass through here. There weren't any benches like there were in the future, so he paced back and forth, watching and waiting.

Men strolled in and out of the park and talked among themselves. Pete was good with faces, and so far he hadn't recognized any of the men whose pictures Matt showed him. Jefferson's face was imprinted on his brain forever. If he came around, Pete would recognize him. He wasn't sure what he would do. He couldn't demand to know where to find Sophia, but he could tail Jefferson. Sooner or later he'd lead Pete directly to her.

After an unsuccessful hour he decided to change locations. Maybe the government people were all in court, or legislating, or whatever they did during the day. If so, they'd be meeting in Federal Hall, a few blocks away.

He looked around, but none of the surrounding buildings were familiar, and while the layout of the streets was similar, it wasn't what he was used to. As leader of this rescue, Jack made two crucial mistakes: not making plans for a meet-up place, and not bringing maps of the early city. Which didn't bode well. Pete had been on enough adventures, he should have thought of it himself.

He wasn't worried about Matt and Jack finding their way. They knew the people and the history. And having time alone to search for Sophia was okay with Pete. All he had to do was find Jefferson, and he'd find her.

He followed the crowd, making his way to Murray's Wharf at the foot of Wall Street on the East River. From there he followed Wall Street, discreetly checking out every woman who went by.

Would he recognize Sophia in colonial dress and hat? Of course he would. It wouldn't matter what she wore. He'd know her anywhere. His heart would know her.

He continued up Wall Street, a muddy thoroughfare with cobblestone sidewalks and two- and three-story brick buildings lining both sides. Federal Hall stood at the end, facing him and towering above the other buildings. Carts, carriages, and men on horseback clomped and creaked as they passed by.

Pete couldn't remember ever seeing a picture of the first rendition of Federal Hall, and the reality was a bit of a surprise. There was no wide, steep staircase. No monument of Washington. No groups of international tourists or sidewalk vendors selling hot pretzels.

The building ahead of him was a two-story Queen Anne-style building with bilateral symmetry, rows of painted sash windows set flush with the brickwork, stone quoins emphasizing corners, central triangular pediment set against a hipped roof, a tower, and a recessed balcony.

JL had laughed at him early in their partnership when he described architectural styles of buildings as they drove down the streets of the city. He'd taken an elective in college on NYC architecture and never forgot it.

History only impressed him when it concerned his city. And ahead of him was the actual building where George Washington took the oath of office, where the Bill of Rights was adopted, where the first Congress met. If this building had been saved instead of razed in the early 1800s, it would not only be the most historical building in America, but also the most valuable. How could anyone put a price on the place where it all began?

He reached the front of Federal Hall and dodged the flow of traffic to find a spot to surveil the people coming and going.

"Pete!"

He turned to see Jack and Matt standing near the side of a building, Matt's trunk and a suitcase stacked between them.

"Where have you been?" Pete asked.

"We arrived a few blocks from here," Jack said. "We figured Federal Hall would be the best place to find Jefferson."

"Yeah, I was a little slow in figuring that out. What's the date? Do you know?"

Matt opened a newspaper with the masthead *United States Gazette*. "We bought this from a newsboy, then we hired him to help with our luggage. If it's today's edition, it's June 20, 1790."

Jack pulled a map from his pocket. "We got a lead on a boardinghouse located on King Street. According to this map, it's close by. We should go there and drop off our bags."

Pete looked at the map over Jack's shoulder. "That's too far away. We need something within a block or two. I saw a boardinghouse down the street, and two men were leaving with luggage. Either they were checking out or looking for rooms and there was no vacancy. I'll check it out. Stay put."

"Wait." Jack dug into his pocket. "I just traded a nugget at a bank a block from here, and I have a handful of money. I don't know how much you'll need."

Matt picked up two suitcases. "Take these with you. Jack and I can handle the trunk."

Pete pocketed a few coins, then carrying the suitcases, returned to the building with the sign he'd seen earlier, pushed open the door, and entered a busy establishment that looked respectable enough, which meant there were no drunken sailors falling on the hardwood floor. After two years in Afghanistan, he could sleep anywhere.

Ten minutes later he was back to report his success to Matt and Jack. "We got two rooms. I don't know what shape they're in, but for an extra coin I got clean linens and a promise of a bath."

"Works for me. Let's drop off the trunk and come back here," Jack said.

"Maybe one of us should stay. Keep an eye out for Jefferson," Pete said.

"Probably not a bad idea. Matt and I will go drop this off and meet you back here. If you're gone, we'll assume you're following Jefferson or Sophia. There's a tavern over there." Jack pointed. "See it? We'll go there and listen to local gossip. We'll either be at the boardinghouse or the tavern. If we go anywhere else, we'll leave a message with the landlady."

"Sounds like a plan." Pete settled in to wait, hoping it wouldn't be long. But even if it was an hour, two hours, or longer, it was nothing compared to the twenty years he'd already waited.

40

New York City (1790)—Sophia

SOPHIA SAT IN the balcony of Federal Hall watching Congress argue over the topic of the day while sketching speakers from Southern states arguing against assuming states' debts, or as it was more notably called: the assumption issue.

Hamilton wanted the federal Treasury to take over and pay off the debt the states incurred during the war. The Treasury would issue bonds that rich people could buy, giving them a tangible stake in the success of the government. Thomas didn't like the idea because it would grant too much power in the national government. Nobody had a better idea. They just didn't like Hamilton's. So the argument continued.

For the past several weeks she'd been making daily treks to Federal Hall to sketch the government at work. Then she sold the sketches to the *United States Gazette*. It was part of her marketing plan to interest New Yorkers in her work.

To date she'd received two commissions: John Jay and John Adams, but she had Jefferson to thank for those. If she could snag George Washington, she'd paint him for free, but she hadn't gotten a commitment from him yet. The next time she saw him, she'd lay out her vision for his portrait. It was so brilliant, he couldn't refuse her.

While members of Congress took a break, she flipped back through pages of her journal where she'd copied sketches of every painting she'd done, including the ones in Paris. The commissions she'd been offered while traveling to Mallory Plantation from Norfolk had come to fruition, and those paintings kept her busy until early March.

When she finished the sailing portrait of Thomas in early January, she sent it to Captain Colley along with a message that she was staying in Virginia until spring. He'd returned a thank-you letter along with a note from his sister-in-law inviting Sophia and her companion to rent the lower floor of her home.

Sophia had made a tidy sum, and so had Marguerite, who designed Parisian gowns for Mrs. Mallory and her friends. She and Marguerite had enough money to open a studio and workshop in New York. She also sent Monsieur Watin a shopping list in January. He had agreed to send supplies upon request and draw down on the funds she deposited with him until she found a reliable color merchant in America. Everything had been waiting for Sophia when she arrived at Mrs. Colley's house.

She turned another page and found a sketch of Patsy in her Marguerite-original bronze silk wedding gown. She married her third cousin, Thomas Mann Randolph Jr., in February at Monticello. It was a splendid wedding, and Thomas wanted to make it a double wedding, but Sophia refused, saying it was Patsy's special day, and she deserved all the attention.

After he settled Polly at Eppington with her aunt and uncle, Sophia and Thomas left for New York City, promising to return for a long visit in the fall. If she and Thomas married, Polly would come live with them.

The trip to New York was hell. They encountered eighteen inches of snow, and Thomas and James Hemings were forced to give up their horses in Alexandria. They crowded into Sophia's carriage and rode the rest of the way with her and Marguerite.

Every time he asked her to marry him, she said, "Not yet." And Marguerite asked her daily what she was waiting for.

She and Thomas still had issues to resolve. Ownership of her painting income, a softening of his views on her rights as a woman, and an understanding that they would always live in the same city. She was not going to be abandoned at Monticello to take care of his home and hearth. As soon as he agreed to her terms, she'd marry him. They would have to agree to disagree when it came to religion, but she was a practicing Catholic and would insist on a church wedding. A justice of the peace did the ceremony the first time, and look how well that turned out.

The arrangements at Mrs. Colley's house at 6 State Street on the southern tip of Manhattan were perfect. Their leased premises consisted of two bedrooms, a combination studio/sewing room, and a receiving room. The house was one of several in a long row of mansions with an unobstructed view of New York Harbor. She'd painted a picture of the view and it hung in the studio window as an advertisement.

Shortly after they arrived in the city, John and Abigail Adams hosted a small dinner party to celebrate Thomas's forty-seventh birthday. Sophia presented him with a painting of his beloved horse Caractacus, a direct descendant of the Godolphin Arabian, one of the three stallions that founded the modern Thoroughbred. Of all the paintings she'd done to date, it was his favorite.

The assembly hall quieted, and Thomas moved to the podium.

He hadn't mentioned making a presentation today.

She snapped her journal shut and picked up paper and pencil to sketch him. When she sketched him at work, she added a hidden picture in the folds of his coat, usually the face of his antagonist de jour. So far no one had noticed.

Thomas's antagonist today was Alexander Hamilton. Actually, he was every day, but this afternoon the animosity so thickened the air in the chamber that it reached the balcony and engulfed her in its sticky quagmire. Their quarrels over assumption and the location of the national capital had grown so vitriolic, it wasn't far-fetched to wonder and worry if the union might break up over the issues. She knew it wouldn't, of course, but no one else did.

During his five years as a diplomat Thomas was largely removed from American politics. But now, as a senior cabinet officer, he was exposed to the voracious attention of the New York political class, and it was taking him a while to acclimate.

Sophia did what she could to encourage him, but at other times sent him to visit with John Adams. Thomas's dependence on his old friend was obvious and touching. Their friendship would later be tested, but in the sunset of their lives they would reconcile and die within hours of each other on July 4, 1826—the 50th anniversary of Independence Day.

When Thomas finished his speech, she gathered up her supplies and hurried to meet him on the first floor. He grinned when he saw her, and she bussed his cheeks. "You were brilliant."

"And you, my dear, are biased."

"Maybe, but only two other people down there will get their faces on currency notes."

"I don't know where you get some of your ideas." He glanced down the hallway, distractedly. "I need to find John Jay, but first I'm going to walk you home. And we have a dinner engagement."

Every night they either had an invitation or Thomas hosted his own dinner party. "Where are we going?"

"The president has invited us to dine with them."

Her face flushed. Why had Washington invited them to dinner tonight? They dined together only a few evenings ago.

Thomas looked askance. "What'd you do? I've seen that look before."

She stepped back to give him room to explode, although he rarely got angry at anyone. His motto was: *When angry, count to ten before you speak. If very angry, count to one hundred.*

"What did you do, dear?" he asked again.

She'd never drawn a sketch of President Washington in her hidden pictures, and the one of him in today's paper might have been noticed. It was time to confess, and she wasn't at all sure how Thomas would react.

"The sketch of you in today's paper has a...well... It has a hidden picture in the folds of your coat."

Thomas folded his arms and glared down at her. "I know."

"You do?"

"There's nothing you do that I'm not aware of."

She was incensed. "Are you spying on me?"

"Absolutely not," he said calmly. "But I have adversaries who take great delight in advising me of your peccadillos."

"Peccadillos? What kind of word is that? Do you mean picadillo? That's a Latin American dish. I guess your adversaries consider me a little spicy."

His mouth turned up just a little, but she could see him laughing at her at the back of his eyes. "I don't know the word picadillo. But peccadillo is a petty sin or trifling fault."

She blinked, unable to hide her shock. "A sin? You're calling my art sinful?"

He dropped all pretense of controlling his laugh, and his delighted guffaw echoed throughout the hall. There was a private joke she wasn't privy to in there somewhere, and it made her mad.

When she realized others were staring at them, she grabbed his arm and hauled him toward the door. "Let's get out of here, and please stop laughing at me, or I'll tell you exactly what I think of you in Italian." When they stepped outside onto the sidewalk she said, "Now tell me what's so funny."

"My dear, the city's abuzz with talk of your hidden pictures. The newspaper has doubled its subscriptions. Everyone wants to be the first to discover who you're satirizing in the day's paper."

"How come I didn't know? How come the publisher didn't tell me? And if he's gained so many new subscriptions, my sketches have more value. Tomorrow I'll tell him I've raised my prices. He can pay more, or I'll take my business elsewhere."

"I don't know why you didn't know," Thomas said, looking quite amused. "It appears you're the last person in New York City. And I agree. You should be paid more."

"Thank you for agreeing, and how long have you known?"

"Darling, I spotted it immediately in the first sketch you sold.

Since I discovered your first hidden picture last summer, I look at every sketch and painting for something out of place or an object that shouldn't be there."

"I didn't know that either." It was unlike her to be so imbecilic. She was always the first to know about anything new in the art market. She didn't paint to the market, but she was always aware of what was selling. Until now… She was off her game.

"Being the subject of one of your hidden pictures has become a badge of honor. Those you haven't satirized feel unworthy and have fallen into fits of depression. I was even offered a bribe to put in a good word on a particular congressman's behalf. Then a senator from Pennsylvania picked an argument with me where it would draw your attention, hoping it would get his likeness in one of your sketches."

She was stunned. "Are you serious?"

"You've brought entertainment to the city, darling. I've heard there are wagers made daily as to whom your next victim will be." Thomas led her down Wall Street through thick pedestrian traffic. "I heard President Washington was flattered this morning when he found his own visage in your drawing."

"Was he really flattered? Or did he act flattered to save face? I need to know if I'm going to be chastised at dinner."

"He's not angry. He's hoping to entertain an announcement from me."

"So you've decided to run for president in '93? If so, it's too early. John Adams should go next."

"Ha. I'll never run for that office. When I finish my term as Secretary of State, I intend to take my bride home to Monticello." He held her gaze, his own slowly taking on a wry amusement.

She batted her eyelashes in mock innocence. "I haven't met your bride. Is she someone I know?"

He stopped and glanced heavenward, as if praying for divine intervention. He must have gotten some, because he gazed down at her and said very softly, "I want you to be my wife. I don't want to wait another week, another day, another hour. Only this morning, I received a letter from Polly. The first line asked, 'Has Miss Sophia agreed to marry you?' I can't write her back and tell her no."

Sophia fixed him with a direct look. "Please don't use your children to pressure me into doing something I'm not ready to do."

He inhaled, straightening as air filled his lungs, adding another half foot to his already towering height. She might never see his face again if she gave him another reason to inhale so deeply out of exasperation with her.

"If I must agree to your two conditions before you'll say yes, then I will. All your painting income will belong to you, and you'll never be alone at Monticello. When I'm away doing the work of the government, you'll always be with me."

There was one more condition she hadn't mentioned before. It might be a deal-breaker, but she had to protect her interests at a time when women had none. She intensified her look and stiffened her spine, but it didn't make her any taller.

"I want your agreement in writing."

His face twisted into an expression of pure shock and incomprehension. "You what?" He leaned over slightly, looking down, an intimidating stance that didn't work with her.

"You're a lawyer," she said. "You can draft a document that will stand up in court. I'm serious, Thomas. Money falls through your fingers like sand. I'll help you turn Monticello into the magnificent plantation you envision. I'll help you build the finest wine collection in America, but we won't go bankrupt doing it."

His face slowly reddened. "Let's get out of this crowd. There are too many ears." He turned her away from Federal Hall and they continued their stroll down Wall Street.

Out of her periphery, she spotted three men watching her, but she turned so quickly she didn't have time to study them. A vision of their surprised faces remained behind her eyes. They looked odd, out of place. Newcomers, probably.

The vision remained, haunting her. What was it about them? Something familiar. They must have reminded her of…home. She shook the thought away as she did every time it popped up and lingered in her heart—her students, her career, her secret art.

When she and Thomas reached the wharf, he directed her away from the clamor and rush of dockworkers off-loading sailing ships and toward an unattended stack of crates lashed together by ropes.

"I'll draw up a document and sign it in front of witnesses. Tell me now what other demands you intend to place on me. I will meet every term, every condition, but only today. I will not negotiate with you again."

She didn't like ultimatums. Who did? In the twenty-first century, she would walk away from his take-it-or-leave-it position. She had options. She could walk away now, but she didn't want to. If Mr. MacKlenna was right, this was exactly where she was supposed to be. She loved Thomas. She couldn't say she was *in* love with him, but she did love him, and cared a great deal about him. And Lord knows she wanted him. But was it enough?

"If I don't protect my interests now, I'll never have another chance."

"Have I ever done anything to give you the impression that I would dishonor you in any way?"

"No, you haven't. But conditions change, people change, values change. What's important this year loses its importance the next. And sometimes we choose not to fight for what we believed in only months earlier."

"I won't change in how I feel about you. If it were possible, I would give you the moon and use the stars for wrapping paper." He cupped her cheek and gazed into her eyes. "I love you, my darling. Marry me."

How could she possibly say no? He agreed not to abandon her at Monticello, and he agreed her income was her own, but would he object to her working?

"Thomas, if we're married, will you insist I close my studio, stop going to Federal Hall to sketch, stop seeking commissions?"

"As a married woman, you cannot go to Federal Hall to work. You cannot sell your sketches to the newspaper. I will allow you to seek commissions to paint women and children and landscapes, but certainly no men. You will be the wife of the secretary of state. You'll be held to a different standard."

Tears burned at the back of her eyes. "You asked what other demands I had. You just listed them. I have to work. You just told me how much my sketches are enjoyed, and in the next breath you yanked it away. You want to stifle my creativity. Don't you understand that I would wither and die without my art? Just as you would wither and die if you couldn't write. You can't do that to me."

"But you'll put me in an untenable situation where I'll be open to attack from my adversaries."

"I wouldn't do that to you, and I wouldn't do it to me either."

She glanced past Thomas and saw the three men she'd seen earlier. They were loitering, watching her…but not in a creepy way, not like stalkers. It was more like they wanted her attention. She pinched the bridge of her nose, squinting her eyes as she tried to synch her memory with her eyesight.

"I can't think right now. We'll have to finish this discussion later." A tension headache, with a dull, non-throbbing pain in her scalp gathered strength. Further negotiations were out of the question.

"If we don't finish it right now, I won't have time to draft our agreement."

She stroked the side of her head. "There is no agreement without those additional terms."

"Sophia be reasonable. Women in Virginia don't do what you're proposing."

"We're not in Virginia. We're in New York City. And I don't want to argue with you right now."

"What does that mean?"

"It means…those are my conditions."

She glanced at the men again. They weren't huddled with faces averted. They stood facing her, like an attacking army. Men of equal stature with equal determination in their eyes. Her gaze moved in slow motion back to Thomas's tight face. What was happening? And then… *Wham!* Her memories collided with the present.

Peter Francis Parrino.

How was it possible, after all this time, that he was here? In 1790 New York City? Was he a figment of her imagination? She blinked. But nothing changed.

"My head is splitting. I need to lie down," she said.

Thomas grasped her hand, gripped it tightly within the crook of his arm, and they continued down State Street toward Mrs. Colley's house. If her breathing was hard, his was harder.

"I have to consider what you're asking and the ramifications. Your demand conforms with your prior pronouncements about women and their roles in society. I should not be surprised. Yet, I cannot agree—"

"Well—"

"Shh," he said. "I cannot agree without contemplation."

She stopped and looked up at him. "Then you're going to consider it?"

After twenty years, Pete picked this moment to drop back into her life—a pivotal moment. How could life get more complicated?

"I will consider it, Sophia. There is no guarantee I will take your position. In the meantime, you should also think about what you're asking of me, of societal norms, and your expectations."

"If you're asking for my bottom line—"

He rested a finger on her lips, his eyes widened for a moment, then narrowed in calculation. "I want to marry you. We will negotiate. Neither of us will get everything we want, but hopefully we will both get satisfaction."

She licked her lips. Her mouth was almost too dry to speak. She squeaked out, "I will reconsider my position, but I make no guarantee anything will change. What time will you pick me up?"

"Nine o'clock. And if there are any other issues, you must present them when I see you next or they will not be considered."

His willingness to even consider her position spoke powerfully of his love for her. But if she gave in to him, she'd never be happily married.

Happiness wasn't guaranteed. But if a marriage didn't start out on equal terms, it had nowhere to go but down and out. She and Pete had not been on equal terms all those years ago. He was a few years older, lived on his own, and planned to enter the police academy. She had just graduated from high school. She was living at home and had no set direction.

Nowhere to go but down and out.

"Jefferson!"

They both turned in the direction of the shouting voice. John Jay stood on the opposite corner, waving his hat to draw Thomas's attention.

"John and I have missed each other twice today."

"You mentioned you were looking for him. Go ahead. I'm only a block from home."

He turned his face back to her, lifting his chin so the sun glimmered like water along his jaw and cheekbone. She would never forget the way he looked right now, caught between pressing his case further with her and dealing with urgent government business, totally unaware of the disaster looming behind him.

He kissed her cheek softly. "I'll call on you at nine, darling." He jogged over to John Jay, dodging carts and wagons until he reached the corner. He waved at her, then he and the first Chief Justice of the United States went back up Wall Street. She stood still a moment to collect herself, then she turned to face her ghost.

"You're twenty years too late, Pete." This was bizarre, beyond bizarre, meeting like this.

"I know, and I'm sorry. But I'm here now to take you home."

Something—a weird ripple, like a pebble thrown into still water went through her, and for an instant she thought she'd never breathe again. But she did.

"I'm not going home."

He raised one eyebrow, plainly unconvinced. "Of course you are."

All she could do was shake her head. He lifted her chin higher with the tip of his finger, forcing her to look directly at him. His eyes were warm, and the color of storm clouds. They flickered and instantly changed to dark green, the color that signals to storm watchers to prepare for the worst.

"I'm not going anywhere with you. Eight months ago it might have been different, but not now. I learned the truth from Mr. MacKlenna and have accepted my destiny."

"Are you talking about the James MacKlenna who owns a farm in Kentucky?"

She looked at the man who asked the question. His eyes, his smile, were lifted straight off the pages of a magazine. She could hardly wrap her mind around Pete's presence, but pair it with Jack Mallory's, and her non-throbbing headache turned into a pounding one.

"You're Jack Mallory. How in the world you and Pete hooked up and landed on the street I was walking down in 1790 New York City has to be Aesop's best fable."

"It's an interesting story," Jack said. "His former NYPD partner has an amethyst brooch, and my sister has a sapphire."

"I didn't know there was an amethyst." She rubbed her head. "There's probably a brooch with every gemstone out there. They should all be carried up Kilimanjaro and pitched into one of its three volcanic cones. I'll even volunteer for the mission." She squeezed the bridge of her nose, but it didn't help the pain.

Pete opened his knapsack, pulled out a small wooden box, looked inside, and handed her two ibuprofens. He returned the box and withdrew a canteen. "It's Evian."

She swallowed the pills and guzzled the water. "Thank you." Instead of handing it back, she took another long gulp. Safe water was hard to come by in the city. "I met Mr. MacKlenna last fall, and, yes, he has a farm in Kentucky. But he's a member of the Virginia legislature, and was part of the delegation to welcome Thomas back to America. We met at Mallory Plantation."

"We know you were there," Jack said. "Your portraits of the general and his wife are hanging in my dining room."

"Still? How nice. They're kind and generous people." She was talking to Jack but didn't take her eyes off Pete. The green she'd seen in his irises turned back to brown. The sun had played a trick on her, or the light was reflecting off his jacket. She returned the canteen.

"What else did MacKlenna tell you?" Pete asked in a calm voice, but the twitch in his jaw outed him. His calm was fake, just like his love for her had been.

She stiffened and crossed her arms, hands locked tight on her elbows. "MacKlenna is a descendant of the original Keeper. Do you know about the keeper?"

He nodded. "Yes."

"You probably know more than I do then. Anyway, we had a long talk about the brooches, the magic, the purpose. Do you know where the diamond and emerald brooches are?"

He nodded again.

"You definitely know more than I do. The stones bring soul mates together. Did you know that too?"

Pete nodded a third time. "Jefferson isn't your soul mate."

His flat statement stomped on her last, best nerve. Her head was splitting, the afternoon sun was beating down on her, her stomach was growling, and the man she once loved was lying to her again.

"Then who is? Certainly not you. You could have been, but you chose not to be. You lost all claim to me. Go home. There's nothing for you here." She turned to go, but he reached for her arm.

"This isn't where you belong. Let's get out of here."

Her arm burned where he touched her, all the way through to her skin, his hand leaving a permanent imprint. But he was too late. Why hadn't he come decades ago?

Her heart rate galloped while she remembered the buckets of tears, days without eating because every tiny bite made her sick at her stomach. Pain like she'd never known before wracked her body and kept her awake night after night.

And he had done nothing to help her.

"You...asshole!" The vehemence in her voice reflected her residual pain. "You can't sweep into my life after all this time and make demands. I told you, you have no right. If you need it explained further, ask your buddy Mallory. He's a lawyer. And if you need further evidence that you're not in *my* picture"—she jabbed her finger against her chest—"Thomas and I are getting married. Go away, Pete. And leave me the hell alone."

"If that's the way you want it, then tell me this... Tell me you don't still have feelings for me. Tell me you don't still love me."

She looked at him hard, and it broke her heart in places never broken before, and, in a voice that didn't belong to her, she said, "I don't love you. I stopped a long time ago."

With as much dignity as she could manage, she walked home. She didn't dare look over her shoulder. If they followed, so be it. They could find her easily enough. Tonight, if she and Thomas could come to an agreement about her final conditions, she would agree to marry him.

She didn't give a damn about Peter Francis Parrino—

Or her studio—

Or her students—

Or her career—

Or her secret portraits—

Or ever going home.

41

New York City (1790)—Sophia

SOPHIA SAT IN her studio attempting to paint a portrait of Thomas standing outside Federal Hall with George Washington and John Adams. The first, second, and third presidents—the only portrait of the three men together. She painted the light moving across the building, changing colors and shapes while chasing candlelight flickering in the windows, deepening colors on the horizon, and street lanterns lit just before dark.

The Last Light of Wall Street. That was the title. She would donate it to Federal Hall and hoped it would survive the decades…the centuries. But no artist throughout history ever had any guarantees. Would Leonardo have painted the *Mona Lisa* differently if he had known she would someday be considered the greatest portrait of all time?

No, he would have painted her the same way. *Mona Lisa* was perfection from the beginning—a complex figure very much like a complicated human.

Sophia moved away from the canvas and cleaned the brushes. She couldn't paint anymore today. What a laugh. All she'd done since returning from the encounter on the street was paint a flickering candle. How ironic was that?

Thick tears tumbled down her cheeks. They flowed from a broken place within her, a badly mended break that was permanently misaligned, leaving a gap where her resolve to live happily in the eighteenth century resided until now.

Until Pete's appearance turned the gap into a maelstrom spewing out all her doubts and insecurities.

Why now? Why not July 14 when she almost died at the Bastille? That was when she needed him. She didn't want him here. Her work had never been more challenging, people more enthralling, and Thomas more loving.

She replayed that last thought…*Thomas more loving.* In her heart she knew he would meet her halfway. It might mean Marguerite would have to accompany her to Federal Hall so she wouldn't be the only woman there. But he would find a way to compromise. He wanted her that much. And in all honesty, she wanted him.

She hadn't slept with him yet. Fear of an unwanted pregnancy kept her from surrendering. So she fantasized about him and sketched them in various sexual positions. The drawings weren't pornographic. They were erotic.

Well, maybe borderline pornographic.

And Thomas found them on her desk.

Let's be clear. She didn't leave them in a conspicuous spot. They were in a stack of sketches from the morning's session at Federal Hall that she had yet to organize, to throw out the ones that weren't any good, to set aside the drawings to take to the newspaper, or file those she wanted to keep for future reference.

When she caught him holding the drawings, wide-eyed, pink-faced and speechless, she went on the offensive. "You're not looking at anything your mind hasn't already conjured up. Are you?"

His mouth moved like a fish, but no words came forth. Eventually he found his voice, although only a whisper. "You pulled these directly from my imagination." His ears pinked, and his cheeks pinked even darker.

She hugged him. "They're my fantasies as well."

His eyes darkened, and she knew exactly where the conversation was heading. His pulse beat visibly in a vein at the side of his neck.

"How can they be yours? Even in Europe, female artists don't paint nude males. You couldn't have drawn these without extensive training. Look at these lines, the musculature. I see in these sketches the true sensual majesty of the classical nude. How did you learn?"

At The Florence Academy of Art she worked from life under natural north light, in the tradition of the masters. She didn't idly copy both female and male nude subjects, but learned to translate nature in a way that was both anatomically accurate and artistically appealing. She understood the male body, and she knew Thomas's even though she'd never seen him undressed.

Her interest in the male physique, though, began much earlier. And now his question—how did she learn?—churned the water, stirred up her past, and forced a confession.

"I heard once that a realist embraces honesty of emotions and the essential beauty of sexual truth. But, set that aside..."

She was stalling, and the small hairs began to prickle on the back of her neck. Confessions always came with a price. What would hers cost her? Thomas believed she was a virgin.

"I was married once, for twenty-four hours. My parents had the marriage annulled and sent me to live with my grandmother in Italy."

He cocked his head and gave her a queer look that went straight through her. She couldn't read it. Did he feel sorry for her? Was he confused? Disappointed?

"How old were you?"

"Seventeen."

"And the marriage was consummated?" His voice was almost conversational, but his feathery brows arched high in question.

"Yes, it was." She would never tell him that she and Pete had consummated their marriage months before the ceremony. Many times.

He rolled up the sketches, tucked them into the inside jacket pocket, and so ended the conversation.

After the sexy picture episode, Thomas was more relaxed around her, and she was more comfortable with him. It was as if they'd had their first clumsy night together and gotten it out of the way. The sketches told him everything he needed to know about her, and if he did exactly as she'd drawn, they would have the most fantastic sex either of them had ever had. And he knew it. She could tell by the angle of his chin.

And now Pete had come to ruin her life, exactly the way he ruined it before when he failed to stand up for her. It all seemed so tied together somehow. One man married her and easily gave her up, and another man wanted her desperately and was willing to go to unusual lengths to have her in his bed.

She organized her painting supplies and washed her hands. Painting was done for the day. Fortunately her head no longer hurt. She'd used her last ibuprofen weeks ago and was grateful to have some from Pete to ease the pain. As if a pill could ease what had transpired.

Could anything?

Maybe if he had said, "I love you. I made a mistake letting you go. I've regretted it all my life. I've traveled over two hundred years to make you mine again." Maybe that would have impressed her.

Enough to go home with him?

No. Her life was here, with Thomas, and even if Pete had thrown himself prostrate on the ground and confessed his undying love, it wouldn't have mattered.

"Miss Sophia."

She spun toward Marguerite who was standing at the open door. "Yes, ma'am. What's up?"

Marguerite snickered behind her hand. Sophia's questions often didn't translate in any of the languages Marguerite knew. So she just laughed.

"There's a gentleman named Matthew Kelly at the door. He'd like an appointment with you."

"I don't feel like meeting with anyone right now. Ask him to come back tomorrow."

"If you refused to see him, he wanted me to give this book to you, but he asked that you not read past the marker."

"What a strange request." Sophia accepted the book and opened it to the marked page. There was a drawing of her and Thomas at his first inauguration. Her initials were on the bottom corner, and the caption beneath it said the drawing was the property of the Thomas Jefferson Foundation—Founded in 1923 for its dual mission of preservation and education.

She rubbed a knuckle beneath her nose, trying to express in words what she felt. Mr. Kelly must be the man who was with Pete and Jack. If he was the only one standing at the door, maybe she could get through a conversation with him.

"Is he by himself?"

"Yes, but he said if you want the others present, he would arrange it."

"Tell him I have a few minutes to meet with him, and only him, before my next appointment."

"I didn't know you were expecting anyone else this afternoon," Marguerite said.

"I'm not, sweetie. I'm just telling him that."

Sophia remained standing, and received Mr. Kelly graciously, as if he'd come to commission a painting. With the flat of her hand, she gestured toward an empty chair. "Please have a seat. I apologize for my rudeness earlier. It wasn't directed at you." Matt remained standing until she seated herself. "Where are your cohorts?"

"Jack hauled Pete off to Fraunces Tavern to calm him down."

"Getting drunk will only make him meaner." She scratched her forehead, ashamed of herself. The Pete she once knew would never hurt anyone except a bully who deserved it. "I'm sorry. I didn't mean that. It was cruel and untrue. So what can I do for you? And how did you get mixed up with those two?"

"We have sort of a family connection," Matt said.

"You sound more like a Midwesterner than a New Yorker or a Virginian."

"Colorado, but my wife and I built a house on five acres at Mallory Plantation."

"That ties you to Jack, but how did you all meet Pete?"

Matt sat back in the wing chair. "Pete's partner at the NYPD, JL O'Grady, was the one with the amethyst brooch."

"I knew several O'Gradys: Connor, Patrick, Shane, Jeff, and they had a sister. Are they related to this JL?"

"JL stands for Jenny Lynn. When she joined the NYPD, she shortened her name. But yes, you've got the right family."

"Where'd her brooch take her?"

"Hers was broken. It carried her to California for a weekend in the Napa wine country where she fell in love with Kevin, son of Elliott Fraser. Elliott is the Keeper. As for me, I'm a lawyer, historian, and teacher."

"How nice for Pete. He has two attorneys who can straighten him out." When Matt grimaced, she apologized. Again. "Please continue."

"My daughter found my wife's family brooch, an amber, and she traveled back to 1878."

"Amethyst and amber. I wonder what other two brooches were in that box. But what brings you here, Mr. Kelly? Not, here at my house, but here in 1790. Why'd you come?"

He leaned forward and pointed at the book in her lap. "When we discovered where you were and that you married Thomas Jefferson, we needed to find out what history you changed."

"So I really do marry him." Having confirmation of the marriage was…what? Surprising? Shocking? Exciting? A tingling sensation raced down her spine all the way to her toes and back up again. *Mrs. Thomas Jefferson, First Lady Sophia Jefferson. Please welcome the First Lady…*

It was a little bit of all three, but mostly exciting. "Why do you think my marriage changed history, or will change history?"

"We don't know whether it did. We only know that if not for your brooch, you wouldn't be here. You wouldn't play a part in Jefferson's story. So what was his life like before you?"

"If I'm not here, then he'll continue his relationship with Sally Hemings, his late wife's enslaved half-sister. It lasted decades and produced six children."

Matt slapped his chest and started breathing so hard he was going to hyperventilate if he didn't get control of himself. Sophia reached for his hands and placed them over his mouth. "Breathe through your nose. In and out." She hurried to the decanter on her desk and poured him a whisky. "Here, drink this."

Matt drank slowly, and after a couple of minutes his composure returned to normal. "My goodness. I haven't had a shock like that since I heard my daughters traveled through time. Thomas Jefferson has been on a pedestal for two centuries for his exemplary behavior in his personal life and in government. His management of Monticello is the standard for how to operate an enterprise upholding strict conservationism and fiscal responsibility."

Sophia refilled Matt's glass. "In the history books I read, he died bankrupt and all his slaves except Sally Hemings and her children were sold to pay his debts. The Hemings's children were freed either when they turned twenty-one or released in Jefferson's 1826 will. Patsy Jefferson Randolph allowed Sally to leave Monticello shortly after her father's death."

Matt upended his glass again. "I've always wondered if there had been a glossing over of his faults, but I've read ninety-nine percent of what's been written about him, and he was never faulted. His positions were argued vigorously, but never his character or his passion for his country. I find this news impossible to reconcile."

"He is the same man, Mr. Kelly. He just needs a financial planner. He's brilliant, a prolific writer, and passionate about what he believes. And he's lonely. Thomas is happiest when he has someone to love and is loved in return. He didn't have a happy childhood, and he's spent most of his life trying to recreate the emotional attachments he didn't have as a child and young adult. The man in my history deserves your loyalty."

"But this enslaved woman, I can't justify that."

"Sally was the only woman he cared for who didn't, wouldn't, or couldn't leave him, short of death. His wife and two daughters died, and Maria Cosway wouldn't divorce her husband and run off to America with him. In my history, Sally was always there in the lonely hours."

"Very little attention is given to his first wife, or even Cosway. But volumes have been written containing your sketches and anecdotes about your love affair and marriage. It's listed as one of the ten great romances that shaped the world, like Ferdinand and Isabella."

"*Santo cielo!*" She shivered briefly despite the heat. "I don't want that kind of responsibility. Would you?"

"Not at all." Matt finished the whisky and set the glass aside, declining Sophia's offer of a refill. "It's why I study history instead of making it. I considered politics at one time, but decided it wasn't for me."

"Being half of a perfect romance isn't for me."

"As long as you stay here, that's what you will become."

She glanced at the clock on the mantel. She needed to bring the conversation to a close. Before she dressed for dinner, she wanted to rest for an hour. "What else can I tell you? I'd like to get done with this so you can return home. I'm sure your family is anxious to have you home again."

"The nice thing about traveling with the diamond brooch is you return only moments after you leave. None of our other brooches have that property. What about yours?"

"Two weeks. The brooch always returned me two weeks to the day, except this time. It's refused to heat up again."

"We don't know why your brooch worked five times and then refused to work again. Some believe it was because Pete wasn't in the right place to rescue you before."

She burst out laughing, and a flood of emotion came pouring out. Tears streamed down her face and she laughed and laughed. Finally she got herself under control and wiped her face. "I'm sorry. That was priceless and a very interesting interpretation, but it's hogwash."

"We didn't have much to go on," Matt said.

"Then how exactly did you find me?"

"Detective work. We had photos of your five paintings from the fifteenth, sixteenth, seventeenth, nineteenth, and twentieth centuries. So we started with the eighteenth century, since you didn't have a painting from the seventeen hundreds. We considered the idea of a female artist. Maria Cosway came to our attention, and she was a straight shot to Thomas Jefferson. Once we got to him, we got to you."

Something didn't sound right. She did an instant replay. *Five paintings.* "How did you find my paintings? They were in a secured location that was guaranteed to be unbreakable."

"Oh!" Matt glanced down at the carpet, avoiding eye contact.

"Mr. Kelly. How'd you find my paintings?"

He looked up, sheepishly. "You'll need to talk to Pete. He found them."

"The only way Pete could have found them was to search my apartment. How did he get past security? It's a state-of-the-art system."

"You'll have to ask him."

"No, I'm asking you, and if you want more information from me," she did a come-hither motion with her hand, "you have to give me something in return." She stood. "Feel free to call on me again when you're ready."

He stood and motioned for her to sit. "He didn't know you were in Florence. He'd finished dinner at a restaurant up the street and saw a man trying to break into your studio. He stopped and talked to him and discovered he was your client. Pete made the connection, and, based on comments your client made, he became alarmed. So he entered your apartment, searched it, found the paintings, and the box the brooches were in."

She was aghast. "I've never felt so violated." She poured herself a glass of whisky and drank the whole thing. "I'll ask you again. How'd he get past my security system?"

Matt shrugged. "That's what he does. He designs and maintains security systems at all MacKlenna Corporation properties around the world. He's an expert."

Her body felt like a balloon with a slow leak. "I can't believe it.

Of all the nerve."

"He had our partner in Tuscany contact your client and make arrangements for him to pick up his *Mona Lisa*. Pete didn't want him calling the police and reporting your disappearance."

"I guess I should thank him, then. My attorney has instructions to liquidate all my assets after a year. An agreement with my accountant to pay all my bills kicks in after a month. But I've never had an emergency contact. I appreciate Pete taking care of Ivan. He would have made a lot of noise and gotten the police involved."

"I heard Ivan was very appreciative."

Sophia shook her head, thinking about her client panicking over his *Mona Lisa*. "Okay, Mr. Kelly. Ask your questions."

"This is a big one. Is there a Civil War in your history?"

"Civil War, World War I, World War II, the Korean War, the Vietnam War, Iraq, Afghanistan."

"Same here," Matt said.

"There was another war against England in 1812, I think. I don't know much about it, except it was a pointless war that nobody won. The White House was burned. The only other time in American history when a foreign power occupied the United States capital," she said. "Was that in your history?"

"There was no war. The disagreement was over trade and expansion," Matt said. "Thomas Jefferson hated the English, but he was able to negotiate a peace treaty. He did a masterful job, understood what was at stake, and agreed to meet with both Napoleon and King George. It was America's first shuttle diplomacy. Brilliant. It's been used as the model for American diplomacy ever since."

She wandered over to the window and stood there, gazing out over the river as the sun began its downward slope over New Jersey. "It sounds like America is in better shape because of my presence here."

"We don't know for sure. We'll need to look more closely."

"Tell me about Mr. Jefferson's children. What does history say happened to them?"

"I'm sorry to say, but his younger daughter, Polly, died in her mid-twenties. She wasn't in good health."

"Oh, no." Pain gripped Sophia's belly. "I was hoping I could do something to extend her life."

Matt joined her at the window. "You're not God, Sophia. You can't choose who lives and dies. History has been written once. It's not for you to rewrite it."

"History has been written twice, and I *did* rewrite it, Mr. Kelly."

"Touché."

They stood there quietly, watching seagulls dip and rise above the churning gray water and sailing ships, breathing in the herbal essences of the flowers growing on the slope of what she considered her own private beach. She loved being near the river more now than during her childhood, which was spent not far from here.

"What happened with the women's movement?" she asked. "Did they get voting rights before the Nineteenth Amendment?"

"No."

"Did Thomas die before his eighty-third birthday?"

"No."

"I feel like I'm swimming in the present yet submerged in the past. Everything that's different is better for Thomas. He won't be condemned because of his relationship with Sally Hemings. He'll avert a second war with England. He'll die leaving behind a well-managed plantation. Why wouldn't I want this altered history for him?"

"Because it's altered. I like the altered version too, but it's not the way it should be. Wouldn't it be nice if we could all live an altered life that's factored out our crap, leaving only the good stuff?" Matt asked, with a hint of a nervous laugh.

"If I marry Thomas, I'll become a First Lady. What do the history books say about me?"

"You'll become a beloved First Lady, a cherished grandmother to Jefferson's grandchildren, and a prolific and extraordinary artist whose paintings are exhibited in museums all around the world. You are considered the only female Old Master."

"Me?" she gasped. "Me?"

"You," Matt said. "Although there are some who say you don't qualify because you don't meet all three criteria. You are a painter of skill, who painted in Europe, before 1800. But they argue the body of your work was produced in America after 1800."

"What kind of paintings? Landscapes or portraits?"

"Portraits of every famous person in the late eighteenth and early part of the nineteenth century."

She chuckled. Thomas would give her what she wanted.

"As long as they consider the paintings I did in Paris, it's good enough for me. The paintings of Thomas and Lafayette are among my best work."

"Which is why it's hard to deny you the honor."

She turned to face him, the white curtains, blowing in the breeze, flapped against her. "There's no downside to my being here."

Matt squeezed her hands. "If you stay, Sophia, make sure it's for the right reason."

She squeezed his in return. "Painting immortality is a pretty good reason, Mr. Kelly."

"I find it frightening," he said.

"Surprisingly, after spending time with Leonardo, Picasso, Donatello, Rubens, Degas, and Jacques-Louis David, I don't. To attain that status is an artist's dream."

"But is it your dream as a woman?"

"What an odd question, Mr. Kelly. I'm not sure I can separate the two."

"I have daughters. They both have careers, but having children was always part of their plan."

"Plans often go awry. I grew up jealous of my friends who had siblings to play with on snowy days when school was closed. I only had my dolls. I swore when I grew up, I'd have a houseful of children."

"My wife and I have three grandchildren and another one on the way. They are such a joy."

Sophia studied Matt's face and stature, guessing his age to be early sixties. His skin had a leathery texture from spending hours in the sun and wind, but he had a rugged Robert Redford look about him. She would paint Mr. Kelly in a rustic setting, surrounded by books—old books, weathered like his face, a little frayed at the edges—with startlingly green eyes gazing out on the world with quenchless curiosity.

"You probably already know I'm thirty-seven. When I turned thirty, I realized my art was my life and that I probably would never marry and have children. I made two significant decisions and opened a studio to bring kids into my life. I've loved every minute of it. But I am curious. Do Thomas and I have children?"

He looked at her closely, probably trying to decide if she could handle the truth.

"If you're wondering if I can handle the disappointment, I can," she said.

"No, you never have children."

Her face twitched, and she suppressed the urge to cry. "Hurts more than I thought it would."

Matt propped one hip on the edge of her desk. "We argued about what to tell you. Our inclination was to go to Paris and intercept you before you met Jefferson. But Kit MacKlenna Montgomery disagreed."

"Is she related to James MacKlenna?"

"His great-granddaughter, I believe, but that's a long story." Matt paused before continuing. "Kit believed you should be told about your art and marriage to Jefferson. She said you should have all the facts before you decide what to do. Now that you know about the success of your paintings and your marriage, the decision is more difficult."

"What do you think I should do?"

Matt did a finger rat-a-tat-tat on the desk. "I believe you've significantly altered American history. From what I know so far, it's worked out to America's and Mr. Jefferson's benefit, but we've got to dive a lot deeper to know for sure. You stopped one war from happening. People lived who should have died. But what else has changed? We don't know yet."

"I'm not a student of American history, so I don't know how much help I can be. But I can't think about it anymore today. I'm caught in the middle of two radically conflicting desires. What I ultimately decide to do can't be based on what's best for me, can it?"

"I'm afraid not, Sophia. When my daughter traveled back in time, she was concerned about changing the outcome of a railroad war. You hold a war with England in your hands."

42

New York City (1790)—Sophia

SOPHIA RELAXED ON a quilt in Bowling Green Park, sketching the president's house across the street. Sitting on the ground wearing stays wasn't so bad, but getting up without assistance was nearly impossible. She usually imposed on someone she knew to help her up, but so far today she hadn't seen any of the regular park walkers.

She and Thomas had a wonderful evening dining with the president and Mrs. Washington the night before. The president complimented her on the hidden picture and agreed to sit for her. She was ecstatic, and the look of pride on Thomas's face touched her immensely.

On the way to her house following dinner he said, "When I came to pick you up this evening, I was prepared to tell you I was still considering your conditions but was not as averse to them as I'd been originally. After Mr. Washington agreed to sit for you as soon as he finished sitting for John Trumbull, I saw your face and I knew I could never deny you anything."

She kissed him. "Thank you. I hope I never do anything to cause you to regret your decisions."

"My policy has been and always will be that I'll offer no public response to personal attacks, but I will respond to you, if your actions cause public embarrassment."

"I would expect no less, sir." She kissed his cheek. "To change the subject, tell me your impressions of the president. Just between us."

"He's often distant and aloof, incapable of fear, meeting personal dangers with the calmest unconcern. Perhaps the strongest feature in his character is prudence, because he never acts until every circumstance, every consideration is weighed in a rational, mature manner. I'm less impressed with his intellectual gifts. His mind is great and powerful, but without being of the very first order. His penetration is strong, though not so acute as that of Newton, Bacon, or Locke. His temper is naturally irritable, and one must always be careful around him."

"How...interesting." She would take Thomas's insights into consideration as she planned Washington's portrait. "What's his opinion of you?"

"You'll have to ask him."

"I will," she said. "I'll let you know what he says."

Thomas kissed her hand that he was holding. If the day hadn't been so traumatic, she would have invited him in for a glass of wine, but when her past collided with her present, she had to settle one before she could live happily in the other. And so far, there'd been no settling.

The president's house sat on the corner, and from her vantage point she could see everyone who went in and out. Alexander Hamilton appeared a few minutes ago, but he hadn't gone inside. He just paced back and forth on the sidewalk. Washington and Hamilton's strong partnership would last well over two decades, so it was unusual for Hamilton to be outside pacing instead of inside discussing a problem with the president directly.

Hamilton looked like he hadn't slept in days. His hair was disheveled, standing on end, as if he'd been ripping it out. His clothes were rumpled, his gait awkward. He prided himself on always appearing dapper and polished, but today he was dejected and haggard, almost as if he'd been caught having an affair. But that wouldn't happen until next summer, and would be one of America's first sex scandals.

Sophia was so engrossed in Alexander's strange behavior and how to interpret it in a drawing, that she didn't notice when someone sat down next to her until he cleared his throat. She jerked in surprised.

"Pete! You scared me."

"I'm not sure you would have heard a gunshot, you were so into what you're doing."

"I would have noticed that."

He pointed with his chin. "Who's the man?"

"Alexander Hamilton. He's in bad shape today. He's trying to start America's bank, and he doesn't have the votes to get his debt plan through Congress."

"So that's Hamilton." There was a slight lift in Pete's voice. Since he was a former NYPD detective, it would take a lot to impress him. Obviously the first secretary of treasury did.

Pete's deep brown eyes conveyed focused interest. "I saw the musical *Hamilton* a few months ago in London. If the history in the show was accurate, then I guess the secretary is concerned about his banking plan."

"He's hinted he'll have to resign if it fails. Of course we know it won't."

"The pressure is on. The big dinner with Jefferson must be soon. Wouldn't you like to be in the room?"

She dropped a couple of off-key bars of "In the Room Where It Happens."

Pete twisted his finger in his ear. "You still can't carry a tune."

She laughed and gave him a playful shove on the chest. "I still love music, though, and I sing and rap in my studio when I'm by myself."

She had a flashback to the CDs he made for her in high school with their favorite music: "Truly Madly Deeply" by Savage Garden, "I'll Be" by Edwin McCain, "Iris" by Goo Goo Dolls, "A little More Time" NSYNC, "I Don't Want to Miss a Thing" by Aerosmith,

"Always Be My Baby" by Mariah Carey, "I Think I'm in Love With You" by Jessica Simpson, "Nothing Compares to You" by Sinéad O'Connor, "My Heart Will Go On" by Celine Dion.

Where were those CDs now? She left them in New York when she was sent to Italy, and she hadn't found them in her parents' house when she cleaned it out following their deaths. There were still some boxes of her clothes and schoolbooks she hadn't gone through yet.

Her parents tried to scrub Pete out of her life, and they might have succeeded—if they'd done a heart transplant.

A small smile played around Pete's face as if he, too, remembered the CDs.

"So when were you in London?" she asked, hoping to pull both their trains of thought into neutral territory.

"I'm in and out of there every few weeks."

"We could have passed each other at Heathrow and not even known it." Before she finished the sentence, she wished she could reel it back in. There was no way she could pass by Pete and not know him. But then she remembered yesterday. She'd walked right by him and hadn't recognized him.

"Trust me, Soph-darling. If I'd been anywhere near you, my antenna would have sparked."

She let the comment and his pet name for her go without a verbal response and moved the conversation back to Hamilton. Unfortunately, she couldn't do anything about the tingling sensation up her back hanging on like a slow, dying light in the sky. "If you're curious, the meeting is happening tonight. Thomas invited Alexander and James Madison to dine with him."

"Wouldn't you like to be in the room?"

"I'm always in the room," she said. "Thomas journals everything that happens in his life, and these days he adds my sketches to fill out his reporting. So it's not a matter of whether I'll attend his meetings, but how much paper to bring with me."

"It's weird to hear you call him Thomas, but I guess if you're going to marry the guy you should call him by his first name."

"It was a while before I could separate the man from the histori-cal character—" She quit talking when she spotted Thomas exiting Washington's residence. The two men had a confidential and cordial relationship. She wasn't surprised to see him there, but he must have gone inside before she arrived at the park. Hamilton was just reaching the door with his back-and-forth pacing, and the two men collided.

"Is that Jefferson?" Pete asked.

"Yep. America's third president. The sage of Monticello."

"Will he get mad if he sees me with you?"

"No, but I'd rather not have to explain who you are."

"Does he know you were married before?"

She nodded. "He knows."

Jefferson and Hamilton talked for a few minutes, then Jefferson sauntered off without appearing to notice her.

"Why didn't he see you? I would have."

"He probably did, but his mind is on the myriad of problems the government has right now."

"Will he care?"

"He was jealous of my color merchant in Paris, but he got over it. He does have a weird envy of Mr. Washington, though. As for other men, he's so used to seeing me with male clients that he rarely comments these days. But he'll be curious about you and wonder how I know someone he doesn't."

Pete picked up the stack of sketches and looked through them, glancing up at her in obvious appreciation. "I saw your *Mona Lisa*. It was extraordinary. You have incredible talent." He flipped to the next sketch and the next without saying a word, but his jaw clenched tighter and tighter with each flip. It was easy to read between the lines. He was wondering the same thing she had often wondered. If they had stayed married, would she have pursued her art?

He cleared his throat and set down the drawings. "Do you keep up with all of Jefferson's business?"

"Most of it. One day, I suppose, I'll be the first White House photographer, but instead of taking photographs, I'll sketch meetings and events."

Pete looked crestfallen. "It sounds like you've made the decision to stay."

She set the drawing she'd been working on and the pencils aside and turned to face him. "When I arrived in Paris, the city was insane. There were thousands of people in the streets, and I was swooped up into the middle of the hostilities. It was July 14. The day they stormed the Bastille. I was this close"—she held her thumb and index finger an inch apart—"to being set on fire in a horrible case of mistaken identity, and I've never been so scared.

"I was rescued by Jacques-Louis David, who's considered the preeminent painter of the era. He was also very political, and a player in the revolution. When I told him I had just arrived and lost my possessions in the riot, he suggested I go see the American Ambassador. I did."

"Did this David guy just let you go? Couldn't he take you there?"

"We went to watch a beheading first."

"Tell me it ain't so."

"Unfortunately, it is so, or was. We were hoping no harm would come to the man, but the crowd smelled blood. In the commotion, we got separated. When I couldn't find him, I ran away.

"I ended up on the Champs-Élysées. That's where I met Thomas. I ran toward him to get off the street, stepped into a pothole, wrenched my knee, and couldn't walk for a month. He felt so guilty he insisted I stay at his home, the Hôtel de Langeac. I thought I would only be there for my annual two-week holiday. But my brooch never heated up. I was stuck in the eighteenth century."

"You aren't stuck now. You can go home." His tone was pleading, and it tugged at her heart.

She glanced away and bit the inside of her cheek to keep from crying. "Funny, how the thing you thought you wanted most loses its importance when you discover you can't have it. Once I accepted my fate, I found something I didn't expect."

"And ended up in America," Pete said.

"I thought if I went to Scotland, I might find a MacKlenna or a Digby who would trade brooches with me. I mentioned their names to Thomas, and he said Mr. MacKlenna and Mr. Digby were Virginia legislators and would be in Richmond when he arrived back in America. I figured it was safer on the other side of the pond while a revolution was taking place on the continent."

Her mouth was dry, and she licked her lips. Pete offered her his canteen, and she took a long draw, smacking her lips at the sweet taste.

"What happened when you met MacKlenna?" he asked.

"He smashed my last, best dream when he told me I couldn't switch brooches because the one I had brought me to my soul mate."

"And you believed him?"

"Who was I to contradict the Keeper's descendant, especially after he told me I couldn't get another brooch?"

"Do you love him?"

"I assume you're asking about Thomas, not Mr. MacKlenna." She gave Pete a wry smile. "I do love him."

Pete remained stoic, but a tick at the corner of his eye told her he was anything but.

This had to be as uncomfortable and painful for him as it was for her, but she needed to make him understand she was where she was supposed to be. Almost everything she ever wanted was here. She glanced at his left-hand ring finger. There was no tan line indicating a ring had ever been there.

"Thomas is an incredible man," she said. "Most of the time I think I'm starstruck and maybe I am, but the man is brilliant, with a wonderful sense of humor. He's passionate about life, art, and wine, and has an unrelenting curiosity. I enjoy every minute I'm with him, even though I get furious with his archaic views on women, but even those views are softening."

"If you want to be starstruck, come home with me, and I'll take you to the Montgomery Winery reopening event next month. The most famous people in the arts, entertainment, and politics will be there."

"I had cocktails with George and Amal Clooney at a Venice art show six months ago, and I did a painting for them. But that's not what I meant by starstruck. When I'm around men like Washington, Adams, Hamilton, Jay, even Burr, I feel like I'm in the presence of greatness. It's weird, because I know how great they are, but they don't. They're just ordinary men doing extraordinary work. And I get to witness it and document it."

"This isn't a role to play. This is your life, Soph-darling. You're not here to draw pictures of them in meetings and dinner parties. That's not what's important. History nerds don't care about the small stuff."

"You're wrong, Pete. We do," a man said from behind them.

Sophia glanced up to find Jack and Matt standing over Pete's shoulder. She had spent several hours with them that morning comparing histories. Almost all the changes they identified were to America's and Thomas's benefit, which helped solidify her decision to remain in the past.

"We care a great deal," Matt said. "A record of those details rarely exists outside of the materials Sophia left behind."

Pete looked up, growling. "Thanks. I was working a different angle, trying to convince her it didn't matter." He looked at Sophia and shrugged. "I want you to go home. Not because I want to pick up where we left off—"

"Left off? Peter Francis, we didn't leave off anything. We were physically torn asunder."

It was an electric moment, and nobody moved until Jack raised his eyebrows theatrically. "Peter Francis? Sounds like a Pope's name."

"How'd you two get the same middle name?" Matt asked.

Sophia struggled to control her temper. "It's not the same. It's spelled a different way."

Pete climbed to his feet, his eyes had the shocked, uncomprehending look of a man who had just been sucker-punched in the gut. "Father Francis was our priest. He retired a decade ago, thank God.

He can't give out more lousy advice to young, brokenhearted parishioners."

"What'd he tell you?" Sophia asked.

"Nothing." Pete gave her a facial shrug, lips downturned. "Nothing I should have listened to anyway."

Jack pointed across the street. "Who's that man? He looks familiar."

"Alexander Hamilton," Pete said. "Can't you tell? He's screwed up like the rest of us. Looks like he's been on a ten-day drunk."

"Let's take a walk." Matt slapped his hand on Pete's shoulder, but he twisted his body, and Matt's hand fell away.

Sophia made a move to stand. "Let me help you." Jack helped her up, then gathered her papers and portfolio and folded her quilt. "May I escort you home?"

"Thanks, but why don't you and Matt go over and talk to Alexander? You can give him advice he won't get anywhere else."

"Do you think we should?" Matt asked.

"I think you're the only two people in the world right now who can talk him off the ledge. You know how it turns out. Give him some confidence. Let him know Thomas and James Madison are ready to compromise."

"Aren't you helping the enemy?" Pete asked.

"No. It's part of the deal, and not a secret around here. It just needs someone to take the initiative to put the terms on the table and make a commitment. It should happen at dinner tonight with Thomas, Madison, and Hamilton, but if Hamilton is meeting with those two Virginians, he needs an edge. Give it to him."

Matt and Jack were bursting with the same kind of excitement she would have if she'd ever been awarded The Hugo Boss Prize—$100,000 and a solo exhibition at the Guggenheim Museum in New York.

"Where will you be?" Jack asked.

Sophia looked at Pete. They had to get things settled or neither one of them could ever move on completely. "Pete and I are going for a walk down by the river. There's a private beach," she pointed, "in that direction. When you finish with Hamilton, come find us."

Pete slipped her portfolio into his backpack and strapped the quilt to the carabiners and quickdraws. When the pack was settled on his shoulders, she looped her hand around his arm and they strolled off in one direction while Matt and Jack headed toward Hamilton.

"That may not have been the smartest idea," Pete said.

"Why not?"

"Jack has a history of going rogue. Is there anything he can tell Hamilton that will change history?"

"He could tell him not to have an affair and not to participate in a duel with Burr. I don't know what would happen if Hamilton doesn't die in 1804. He might be president instead of someone else. He's such a brilliant man, and he could accomplish so much more."

She watched the three men exchange introductions and had a moment's panic. Was it possible to screw up a conversation and make a radical change to history? No, Mallory would be sensitive to the possibility. And if he wasn't, surely Matt would be careful.

"Let's go take off our shoes and splash in the water."

He hugged her hand to his chest. "This is killing me, Soph-darling."

She gazed up into his glimmering eyes. "It brings up a lot of pain we don't need to carry any longer."

"Should we just chuck it in the river?"

"Great idea."

They crossed the street and climbed down the other side of a grassy knoll dotted with flowers. The area would one day be part of Castle Clinton National Monument and The Battery, but today no one was there. No one was ever there. It had become her own private beach, easily accessible from the back door of Mrs. Colley's house. She could go in and out without anybody seeing her.

Playing in the waves was an unheard-of activity. People didn't swim because they were afraid of drowning.

When they reached the sand near the lapping waves, the air was sweet, and a warm breeze was gently blowing through the nearby trees. The bank was alive with nesting ducks taking advantage of the shade provided by some tall reeds. Pete dropped his backpack and spread out the quilt. She immediately plopped down and pulled off her shoes.

"This is where I came through the fog. I was hoping it was Paris so I could find you before you met Jefferson." He pointed toward the tops of the townhomes visible from the beach. "The brooch dropped me almost at your backdoor."

"How ironic. Twenty years ago, we were separated at the backdoor to my parents' house."

"Your parents shouldn't have done what they did to us," he said. "It didn't screw you up, but it did me."

"It didn't screw me up? Did you really just say that?" She threw her shoe at him. He was quick enough to dodge the bullet, and it flew past him. She spoke with more vehemence than she intended, putting her anger out there to be dealt with. "The hell it didn't. Why else do you think I'm close to forty, unmarried, and childless."

He picked up her shoe and dropped it on the quilt. "I am too, Soph-darling."

"Don't call me that again! Your term of endearment is no longer endearing." She removed her other shoe, and he crouched to avoid the second missile coming his way.

"Sorry. I didn't mean to offend you. It's just how I feel."

"It doesn't offend me. It's just outdated, and I don't want to hear it."

"Well, tell me how you really feel, Soph—"

She glared, daring him to say it again. When he didn't, she dropped the shoe.

He knelt beside her and undid her garters. "I've always dreamed one day I'd remove my bride's garter at our wedding reception." He rolled down her stockings, folded them, and placed them inside her shoes.

"You removed my pantyhose. That has to count for something."

"I wanted the whole garter toss to the groomsmen deal. Jack did it at his wedding."

"Who caught it?"

Pete chuckled. "I did."

"It's not too late," she said. "You can still do it."

"I'd have to find someone I love more than I love you."

"Don't do that, please. If you'd loved me, really loved me, you would have come after me."

He propped his elbows on his knees and held his head. "Father Francis told me to let you go. He said your parents knew what was best for you, and that I couldn't support you and take care of a family. He said you were better off without me. He also said your parents told you the very same thing. As the weeks went by and you never wrote or called, I got it in my head you believed the lies. When I thought of calling you, I was too afraid you'd tell me never to contact you again."

He scrubbed his face. "The only way I could see through the pain was to join the Marines. When I got out, I was accepted into the police academy and finished college at night. The years melted away. I hooked up with MacKlenna Corporation and now spend more time in airplanes than I do at home. I'm more than able to support a wife, but I can't find one who comes close to you."

Tears pushed into her eyes. "You didn't contact me because you were afraid? Impossible! The man I knew was invincible, not afraid of anyone, and you got it in your head to be afraid of me. That's crap!"

She wanted to jump up and kick sand or water at him, but damn it, she couldn't do it gracefully. She pulled to her knees and pushed up using his shoulder.

"Where are you going?"

"To kick water at you." She lifted her skirts and ran.

"Wait." He yanked off his shoes and stockings and ran after her, and they splashed and laughed as they plowed through the gentle waves. She scooped handfuls at him, and he scooped water at her. Then she ran away, laughing as he chased her.

When he caught her, they held hands and walked back splashing through the shallow water. Her hand felt so natural in his. "How's your family?"

"We lost Dad two years ago."

"I'm sorry. He was a great dad. He was a better dad to me than my own."

"He loved you, that's for sure. But even he told me I had to respect your parents' wishes. Mom told me eloping was irresponsible of both of us."

"What about your brothers and sisters?"

"They're all still in the city. Mom stays busy. I get home every few weeks for a night or so, and I've taken her with me when I visit the company's vineyards in Tuscany. She loves it there and wants me to buy a house so she can go more often. The Frasers have told her she's welcome to stay in the main house whenever she wants to go, but she feels like she's imposing."

"Are you going to buy a place?"

"Probably. I have an agent looking for a small vineyard. If something comes along, I'll buy it."

"Another irony in this saga. I leave Italy, and you move there."

"You don't have to leave."

She gave him a bittersweet smile. "We'll never see each other after today. Let's not argue or pressure me to change my mind. Let's just walk in the water and remember those days when we were young and in love. Let's make this last memory the one we'll cherish most."

"The memory I'll always cherish is the first time we had sex."

"We were so hot for each other, and so stupid."

"Hey, speak for yourself, sweetheart. I knew what I was doing."

She scooped another handful of water at him. "Really? I guess that's why you had a smile and I had tears."

He splashed water on her. "It wasn't so bad."

She gave him a fake smile. "Maybe not for you..." Then she brightened. "The next time, though, was awesome."

He clasped her hand again, and they swung their arms back and forth while they continued walking through the waves. The bottom of her skirt was soaked, her bodice drenched, and her hair was tumbling around her shoulders.

He swung their arms up so he could kiss her hand. "I couldn't wait to see you again. I sat in class and counted the seconds."

"We were so young."

"I always thought we'd have a thousand nights and a houseful of children."

"A thousand nights sounds like forever when you're seventeen. I thought we'd have a houseful of kids, too. Now I know I never will."

"You can. Come home with—"

She placed her hand over his mouth. "Please don't say it."

He removed her hand, and without asking, kissed her. She didn't know if it was the sand beneath her feet, the lapping waves, the choking call of the seagulls, but the years simply drifted away. She was no longer an ancient soul, but seventeen again, French kissing the love of her life, experiencing the sexy rush of adrenaline and butterflies in her belly. One of life's sweetest, simplest, most honest pleasures. And just like when she was a teenager, she didn't want it to end. Nothing else mattered. Only that moment in time.

He bracketed her hips with his strong hands and pulled her down into the sand and surf and claimed her mouth again in a kiss so deeply passionate, so uniquely him, so heartfelt, and so memorable that she cried, but she couldn't stop kissing him.

Finally, she rolled off and sat there in the shallow water, weeping.

"I'm sorry. I keep saying it, but I really am," Pete said.

She gazed at him, noting the little changes around his eyes, the gray streaks at his temples. He still looked the same—handsome and sexy—and he laughed the same. But it was different now. It had to be. They sat in silence for the longest time, holding hands, not speaking, just sharing the moment.

"I'm so lucky to have had time with you all those years ago. I am who I am today because I was well-loved as a young woman. It's my wish for you to find your soul mate as I have found mine."

Tears glistened in his eyes, and when he spoke again his voice sounded hoarse and scratchy. "I'll never stop loving you."

She had a sudden constriction in her throat, a burning sensation, a spasm of her abdominal muscles. "It's time to let go and move on. Deep down I always believed we'd have another chance, and it's kept me chained to the past. I don't blame you anymore for not coming after me. And I hope you don't blame me for not reaching out to you."

Just then an image came to mind, and she knew how she wanted to paint him—here on the beach, his pants covered with sand, the sun reflecting off the water, a single set of footprints beside him, a comforting smile on his face. She would title it *Forgiven.*

And she also knew it would take time and emotional distance before she could even sketch the portrait in her journal.

"I've never stopped believing we'd have another chance, either. But, Soph, why didn't you call me? Just to let me know how you were doing?"

"When my parents told me you'd made a mistake and didn't want a wife, I believed them."

"They did a number on you."

"They did a number on both of us, and I've never forgiven them. Maybe it's time I did."

He squeezed her hand. "We should have trusted the love we confessed to each other on our wedding night."

"We were just too young."

They continued to sit there, letting the waves roll over them. The sun dip below the horizon, casting lengthening shadows over the city. She would have to leave soon to get ready for the dinner at Thomas's house.

"Pete! Sophia!" They turned to see Matt and Jack jogging through the sand, waving. The Second Coming couldn't have put a more delighted expression on their faces. They simply glowed.

Pete helped her up out of the water. "Did you set Alexander straight?" she asked.

Jack frowned at her. "You're soaking wet. How are you going to explain your appearance?"

"There's nobody to explain to, and it won't be the first time I've gone home like this."

Now Pete frowned at her. "I'm not sure I want to hear about that."

"I fell in. I was walking backwards and tripped. Ruined a dozen sketches of the river. Fortunately, my townhome backs up to that slope, and I can come and go without anyone seeing me."

"Your lips are red and swollen. How are you going to explain that?" Jack asked. "I don't want Jefferson challenging Pete to a duel."

She rubbed her finger over her lips. "That won't happen. I'll put a cold compress on them later. So tell us. What did you say to Hamilton?"

"There's no historical record of the meeting at 57 Maiden Lane when Jefferson, Madison, and Hamilton met to hammer out the Compromise of 1790, but we just wrote the script for a play," Jack said. "When Hamilton left us, he was primed for the dinner on Maiden Lane."

"You're primed too," she said. "You're glowing."

"Must be the ale," Jack said.

"Jack secretly taped the entire conversation, which continued over ale at Fraunces Tavern. We just now left him. He had to go home to dress for dinner."

"We told him Madison would support assumption—or at least not oppose it—if something was granted in exchange," Jack said. "It would be a bitter pill for Southern states unless something was done to soothe them."

"Was Hamilton at a loss?" Sophia asked.

"Yes. So we suggested—"

"You suggested—" Matt said.

"Okay, I suggested," Jack said, "that Philadelphia should be a temporary capital for a period of ten years, followed by a permanent move to the Potomac site, and if Madison seemed to hesitate, to work out a favorable treatment for Virginia in a final debt settlement with the central government."

Matt consulted a piece of paper he pulled from his pocket. "Hamilton said he would exert his utmost efforts to get the Pennsylvania congressional delegation to accept Philadelphia as the provisional capital and a Potomac site as its permanent successor."

"We explained to Hamilton, the quintessential New Yorker, that he would be bargaining away the city's chance to be another London or Paris, the political as well as financial and cultural capital of the country, and his compromise on this testified to the transcendent value he placed on assumption," Jack said.

Matt consulted his paper again. "I told him the decision would not sit well with many New Yorkers, and they would see it as high-handed. But in the end it would work out, and eventually New York City would be the financial capital of the world, and every global business would have a presence here."

"You two are so wound up you're about to explode," Sophia said.

Jack tossed his hat in the air and caught it. "I've never been in such a creative state. I've got to start writing." He tossed his hat again. This time the wind carried it toward the water. He ran after it and plucked it from the sand a second before an incoming wave soaked it. "I've got to sit down with pen and paper."

Sophia laughed at him. "What did you think of Hamilton?"

Jack brushed the sand off his hat. "Personally, I think he's very boyish, but beneath the military bearing is an almost androgynous quality."

"During the conversation, he went from abject despair to inexpressible elation at the possibility of winning final backing for his funding scheme," Matt said.

Jack tossed his hat again, but this time Pete snatched it out of the air. "Stop it! It's not a damn boomerang. And you smell like ale, but you act like you took a handful of uppers. Do your trance thing and get yourself under control." He dropped Jack's hat on the quilt. "Do it now."

"I'm not sure I want to. I like this feeling."

"But you're driving me nuts. I've never seen you like this."

"It's not my hyperactivity that's bothering you, but if it will make you feel better, I'll do it." Jack closed his eyes and took several deep breaths.

Pete and Matt watched him expectantly. Nobody moved for several minutes. Then, Jack slowly opened his eyes and there was a calmness about him.

"Did you see anything?" Pete asked.

Jack shook his head. "Nothing that makes sense. Sophia was standing under the willow oak at Mallory Plantation weeping."

Pete's eyebrows drew together. "Was she hurt?"

"She didn't appear to be physically injured."

"Mr. MacKlenna and I were standing near the willow oak when he told me I couldn't switch brooches," Sophia said. "I was teary eyed, but I wasn't weeping. How did you learn to do that?"

"I spent two years at a Tibetan Monastery studying an esoteric meditative discipline. It saved my sanity when I was in prison for conspiring to kill Lincoln."

"I take it since you're here now, you got out. So tell me, were you in Richmond the night of the fire? I read your book, and the description was terrifying."

"My sister, her husband, and I were all there. It was hell."

"So your trances take you either to the future or the past," Sophia said. "If you saw me at Mallory Plantation it was in the past."

"I've gone to the future before, but it's rare. I can't go into a trance to see where the stock market is going to close."

Pete removed Sophia's portfolio and pencils from his knapsack and handed them to her. "If we could back up a hundred years, I want to know why your trance took you to Mallory Plantation."

Jack shrugged. "Maybe because everybody is there waiting for us."

Sophia opened her portfolio and pulled out a sketch of Hamilton pacing in front of George Washington's house. "Here. This is the only sketch of Hamilton in utter despair." She pulled out another one. "Here's one of James Madison dining with Thomas at his house on Maiden Lane. You now have a drawing of the dining room."

Jack stared at the pictures. "Are you sure?"

"Of what? That the drawing is Thomas's dining room?"

He smiled. "No, are you sure you want to give them away? I can take a picture of this."

"You can have them. I'll sketch several at the dinner tonight."

Matt studied her for a moment. "Did you and Pete get your issues resolved?"

She gazed at Pete. "I think so. We're good now, right?"

He rubbed the little bump in her right earlobe. "Sure. We're good."

She and Pete sat on the quilt and put their stockings and shoes back on.

"I have something for you." He dug in his knapsack again. "This is from the entire family." He placed a small leather pouch in her hand.

She lifted her hand up and down, feeling the heaviness of the pouch. "What is this?"

Jack reclaimed his hat and set it back on his head. "A few gold nuggets. If you never sell another painting, you could live at the Ritz for the rest of your life."

"I can't take this. Thank you. But no." She tried to hand it back, but all three men refused to accept it.

"Here's the thing," Jack said. "Braham McCabe married my sister. He was a Union major and a special agent for Abraham Lincoln. After the war, he was one of the men who built the transcontinental railroad. He sold all his stock, traded the cash in for gold, buried it, and came forward in time. Nobody knows the value of the nuggets in his vault. Billions probably. A few years ago, we found the Confederate gold and the treasure hidden with it. Made us a lot of money. We can afford it. So consider it your dowry."

"But don't give it away," Pete said. "The money is for you. We don't ever want you to be without. And if you ever need us, send a message—"

"I won't," she said. "My life is here."

Matt looked at Jack. "Then I guess our job is done. We should go."

"Let's get our gear and head out." Jack helped Sophia to her feet while Pete shook out the quilt and folded it.

Matt hugged her. "I'm sorry you're not going with us."

"I enjoyed our visits, Matt. Thank you for being so understanding."

Jack hugged her next. "Thank you from the bottom of my heart for encouraging us to meet with Hamilton. I interviewed John Wilkes Booth, but believe me, this was the most remarkable experience I've ever had, outside of my wedding and the birth of my daughter. I'll never forget it, and I'll never forget you."

"I saw your wedding pictures in a magazine. I would have loved to paint you and your wife. After meeting your grandsire and his wife, I know exactly how I would paint you."

"Amy has interviewed several artists but has yet to find someone whose vision she likes. It may never be painted."

"Well, keep looking."

Pete was last to get a hug. "I'm glad we had this time together. May your life be like good wine…"

"Tasty, sharp, and clear," she said.

"And like good wine, may it improve…"

"With every passing year," she said, finishing the Italian blessings she'd repeated many times. "I didn't know you'd grow up to be a poet."

"I didn't know you'd grow up to be Mrs. Thomas Jefferson."

"Who would have thought it?" She smiled at Pete. "Thanks for coming after me, and please tell Kit MacKlenna Montgomery she made the right call."

"Goodbye, Sophia," they said in unison.

She left them standing on the beach because she didn't want to watch them walk away. She didn't want to see Pete vanish before her eyes. She'd had an afternoon with him to relive their youth and young love, and she would never forget it.

But finally she could let him go.

At the last possible moment she turned and looked back, but no one was there, only footprints in the sand. And she thought of the last song on the wedding CD Pete gave her—"My Heart Will Go On" by Céline Dion:

Love can touch us one time / And last for a lifetime…

43

New York City (1790)—Sophia

CONGRESS SPENT JULY and August hammering out the details of the Residence Act and the Funding Act of 1790. The compromise brokered by Madison, Hamilton, and Thomas would one day be regarded as one of the most important bargains in American history. And Sophia was there where it happened.

She had two dozen sketches of the men yelling and hand-wringing, and at the end she posed them in a Jimmy Carter, Anwar Sadat, Menachem Begin look-alike handclasp for posterity. She would one day paint the final sketch with two hidden pictures. The compromise would have happened with or without Jack Mallory and Matt Kelly, but it gave them a story to tell, and a connection to the Founding Fathers. She smiled every time she thought of those two time-travelers and their childlike glee.

Sophia had an artist friend whose daughter worked at the New York Federal Reserve Bank located on Maiden Lane, opposite the street from where Thomas's house stood when the compromise was brokered. On the top floor of the bank building there's a circular conference room, and important decisions that saved the country were made there during the 2008 financial crisis—the room where it happened.

The irony was not lost on Sophia.

She spent the summer painting full-length portraits of Washington, Hamilton, and Adams. She wanted hers to compliment John Trumbull's paintings, while also being distinctly different. She met with the artist over tea, and they spent hours talking about art and painters he knew, painters she'd studied. They also discussed in depth the importance of painting accurate depictions of events and characters, and where and when it was appropriate to take artistic license for the benefit of the painting.

By September she and Thomas had packed their belongings for the move to Philadelphia, where Thomas had rented a four-story brick house at 274 High Street with plenty of room for Polly and a small studio. Once they moved there, she might rent a shop so she'd have more room to accommodate a few students.

A Parisian milliner who owned a shop on Broadway had been courting Marguerite for the past three months, and Marguerite's dressmaking business was thriving, bringing fashion and haute couture to New York. She'd even hired two seamstresses to keep up with the work, and she didn't want to leave the city. Marguerite spent all of August making Sophia's trousseau, and already had orders for similar gowns.

Sophia didn't want to leave without her, but Sophia, of all people, would never stand in the way of love.

Together she and Thomas had designed a betrothal ring using one large pearl and several diamonds. It was the most exquisite ring she'd ever seen, and she fell into his arms when he slipped it on her finger. They would have made love that night, but Thomas said he would prefer to wait since they were so close to their wedding.

Sophia purchased a coach and had it modified to accommodate their needs. Then at the last minute, invited Thomas to go see it, and as she'd suspected, he made several alterations. The carriage maker had to work nonstop to complete the job by the day of departure.

John Adams had already advised her to let Thomas select the team to pull the carriage, which was excellent advice. She'd discovered a sort of Doctor Jekyll and Mr. Hyde when it came to Thomas and horses. He was always polite, soft-spoken, and not given to confrontation, but on horseback a change came over him, and he would fly into a fit of rage and even abuse a disobedient horse.

The first time she saw him do it she was livid. The second time she yelled at him that horses weren't just chattel, and the third time she told him if he ever abused a horse again, she'd walk out of his life forever. She knew she was judging him by her standards and century, and the idea of animals' rights would have puzzled him, but it was never too early to start a social change movement.

On August 12, Congress met for the last time in Federal Hall. And she was there to sketch it all. Two weeks later, on August 30, Washington stepped onto a barge moored at Macomb's Wharf on the Hudson and left Manhattan, never to return.

Abigail Adams was not happy about moving to Philadelphia—it just wasn't Broadway, And Sophia, a born and raised New Yorker, had to agree.

Passage of the funding and assumption bills restored millions of dollars in worthless certificates of indebtedness to face value, and an influx of wealth bathed New York speculators in prosperity. Investors eagerly bid up the price of the new three- and six-percent federal securities, dreaming of fortunes to come.

Sophia even considered jumping into the speculative market but was afraid her relationship to Thomas would cause her investments to be highly scrutinized and considered by some to be insider trading. Of course it wouldn't be, but she had agreed not to do anything to embarrass him, even if it would make him a multimillionaire.

New York City's future seemed secure, federal capital or not. This separation of powers—government and finance—had no parallel in the Western world. London, Paris, Amsterdam, Berlin, Vienna, Rome, Madrid, Lisbon were capitals in the fullest sense. Those cities were hubs of politics, business, and culture.

Although no longer the capital city, New York's destiny was to be the city of capital.

44

Mallory Plantation (1790)—Sophia

SOPHIA AND THOMAS rode out of New York City in high spirits. He and James Hemings rode on horseback while she had the carriage to herself. She missed Marguerite already, but presented the most positive, cheerful face she could when they said goodbye. Sophia had taught her all she could about being a modern woman and managing a business, and her door would remain open if Marguerite decided later to move to Philadelphia.

Sophia thought back to the day she and Marguerite and the girls left Paris, and how much fun they had playing I Spy. This trip would be so lonely, but she would see Patsy and Polly at Mallory Plantation, and the three of them would plan Sophia and their father's wedding.

Thomas had already written General Mallory to let him know they'd be stopping by on their way to Monticello, and Sophia penned a short postscript to let him know she had a personal request she hoped he would consider. Thomas also wrote to Mr. MacKlenna and Mr. Digby, advising them they would be at Mallory Plantation, and that Sophia would like to visit with them again.

During the ride to Virginia she spent the time organizing hundreds of sketches, looking for the few she would paint.

'Inside my journal / My best work shines / Page after page of the most

sublime / Sketch after sketch / Eyes go blind / Five, six, seven, eight / Nine / Loses herself / One shot one shot / Once in a lifetime / Never let go / In a Philadelphia state of mind."

She would be so embarrassed if anyone ever read her songs or, for that matter, heard her spitting fire. She had a former student to thank for introducing her to rap. She smiled thinking about him. He just completed his second year at The Florence Academy of Art and had a bright future ahead of him. Her smile quickly turned to a frown at the thought of her other students. Students she'd never see again.

I can't think about them now. If not now, when?

She shook her head and turned her attention back to organizing her sketches.

She double-checked to be sure the sketches she intended to paint were duplicated in her journal. In her time, she would have scanned them into a computer as her backup, but now her journal was all she had. Losing it would be like a computer crash, so the journal was never out of her sight.

Marguerite made several small, elegant cross-body bags for her out of different fabrics, matching or coordinating with her dresses, and sized to fit her pencils and ever-expanding journal. The bags had even become a fashion statement. All the ladies in New York had begun carrying them. And soon the fashion would show up in Philadelphia.

As they drove up to Mallory Plantation ten days after leaving New York, she had the strangest sensation that she was coming home. She couldn't explain it, describe it, or understand it. It was just simply a total body experience. And she thought about Jack and Matt and, most of all, Pete.

Was there a way to leave a message? Maybe a painting of the willow oak with hidden pictures, but it had to be interesting enough to survive the two centuries between now and when Jack and Amy occupied the house, between now and when Matt and his family would build a house nearby, and between now and when Pete would come for a visit.

Thoughts of her time-traveling visitors flew away with a pair of osprey gliding over the mansion toward the river. She laughed when Thomas opened the carriage door and swept her into his arms.

"You are beaming, my darling. I hope one day you'll be as happy to be at Monticello."

She whispered. "I'd kiss you if it wouldn't be so scandalous."

"I don't care," he said, and kissed her lightly on the lips.

General and Mrs. Mallory met them on the porch. "We're so pleased to welcome the future Mrs. Jefferson and her betrothed." The general kissed both her cheeks and shook Thomas's hand.

Mrs. Mallory hugged her. "I'm so happy to see you again. Mr. Jefferson already informed me Miss Bonnard is remaining in New York. I am heartbroken."

"She made my trousseau and sent patterns along. If there's anything you like, your seamstress will be able to make the gowns for you." Sophia and Mrs. Mallory locked arms and entered the mansion talking about fabrics.

"Mr. MacKlenna and Mr. Digby will be here for supper. They said Miss Orsini wanted to visit with them," the general said. "And Polly and Patsy both sent messages that they would be at Monticello preparing for the wedding and couldn't wait to see you both."

"I'm disappointed, but there's no reason for them to make the trip just to turn around and go back," Sophia said. "I can't wait to see them." She glanced up at Thomas. "Did you know?"

"No, but I'm not surprised. They wanted to decorate the house and prepare the food as a surprise. They couldn't get it all done if they met us here."

"I'm thrilled to know Mr. MacKlenna and Mr. Digby are coming. We didn't have time to talk about family connections, and I want to trace the Digby family line to discover where it connects with the MacKlennas."

"I didn't know it did," the general said.

Sophia waved her arm. "It's waaay back."

"Our connection to the MacKlennas also goes way back," the general said. "Michael Mallory, the founder of Mallory Plantation, came to America from Ulster in 1613. He married Mr. MacKlenna's two-times great-aunt."

"So if I can find how the Digbys are related, we'll be kissin' cousins," Sophia said with a laugh.

"We're all related somehow, sweetie," Mrs. Mallory said. "Now let's go upstairs and get you settled. I'll send my maid in to assist you."

As Sophia followed Mrs. Mallory up the stairs she said, "Later I'd like to present my request to the general."

"He's been so curious," Mrs. Mallory said. "Mr. Jefferson didn't give any hints in his subsequent correspondence, so the general has been unusually gleeful, convinced it has something to do with your art. He's even suggested to me privately that it might be a full-length painting to hang at the House of Delegates in Richmond."

"Oh, dear," Sophia said. "It's nothing so grand, but if he has his heart set on a full-length portrait, I'd be honored to paint one."

Two hours later, Sophia joined them in the drawing room, wearing a blue silk brocade gown. When Thomas saw her, his eyes lit up. "Marguerite has outdone herself with your gown. You look like an angel."

"Wonderful," Sophia said. "Maybe the general will find it more difficult to say no to my request if he also thinks I look angelic."

The general stood. "I agree with Mr. Jefferson. But Miss Orsini, my dear, I would be hard pressed to deny you anything in my power to give you. You have become like a daughter to me."

She dabbed at the corner of her eye. "I thought…" She stopped and started again. "I thought we had developed a special bond during our painting sessions, and I certainly look upon you as a father image." She smiled at Thomas. "Which is why I'd like to ask you to give me away at my wedding."

The general's jaw dropped, and when he recovered from the shock, he hugged her. "My dear, I would be so honored."

Thomas stood back, plucking at his chin in thought, his eyes twinkling. "Excellent. I will expect a sizable dowry from the bride's father."

The general laughed outright. Then he stopped and gave Thomas a sober look. "I will provide twenty-five acres toward her dowry."

"No. No. No," Sophia said. "Giving me away is all I want."

Mrs. Mallory patted her arm. "Now, now. Don't be hasty. I've known my husband for fifty years. I suspect he's hoping you'll build a home here so he'll have you nearby in his doddering old age."

"I don't need land to build a house. I'll just stay here in the mansion, and I promise to come once a year. We'll sit under the willow oak, watch it grow, and I'll sketch both of you. And we'll drink wine and talk late into the night."

The general slapped Thomas on the shoulder. "If land is out of the question, I'm sure we can settle up with a payment of…let's see. Ah, a crate of wine, perhaps? Since your last visit, I've ordered everything you suggested, and it has only just arrived."

Jefferson laughed. "A crate of wine it is!"

"Now that we've settled that matter…" The general dusted his hands together. "Miss Orsini must participate in a Mallory family tradition."

"Please call me Sophia. Miss Orsini is so formal."

He smiled. "Sophia it shall be. Now come with me to the dining room."

Sophia followed him there, where he stopped in front of one of the windows and examined her betrothal ring. "I insist we open a bottle of wine for this special occasion. I'm sure the groom hasn't traveled this far without a few bottles of his favorite wine crated among his luggage."

"General, you know him so well," Sophia said.

"I'm not sure what the occasion is, but if it involves my bride, I'll certainly provide the wine for a celebration." Thomas stroked his finger along the line of Sophia's chin. "Do you have a preference, my dear?"

"Humm. The Lafite? What do you think? We've enjoyed it at several important events, so perhaps it should be part of this one, too."

"Excellent choice." Thomas went out to the hall to speak with the butler. When he returned, he said, "James will be instructed to find a bottle of the Lafite. Now we can continue. I'm anxious to discover this tradition you've been invited to participate in."

Sophia didn't have to wonder. She already knew.

"And your brooch is striking," the general said. "I noticed it last time ye wore it but failed to mention how beautiful it is. The design is very similar to your ring."

"Did Mr. Jefferson design both?" Mrs. Mallory asked.

Sophia placed her palm over the brooch. "No this is a—"

Her breath caught. The world stopped turning on its axis, and instead flopped upside down, taking her with it. Panic doused her with uncertainty and fear, and her heart rate galloped far ahead of her present reality. She stood there staring, futilely wishing it wasn't happening.

But it was. The brooch was warm.

"A what, dear?" Mrs. Mallory asked, her eyebrows arched.

"A what?" Sophia repeated, unable to remember what she'd been talking about.

"The brooch? You said it was a…"

"Oh. Family heirloom. I'm sorry. I must be more tired than I thought. It was a gift from my grandparents."

"It compliments your ring beautifully," Thomas said.

"Under your watchful eye"—Sophia paused and faintly smiled— "the jeweler exceeded all expectations."

"This family tradition involves yer ring," the general said. "It was begun by my four-times great-grandmother. She was convinced the diamond in her betrothal ring was paste. If she could prove it wasn't genuine, she could call off the marriage she didn't want. If she couldn't etch her initials in the glass, it would prove the stone wasn't real."

Sophia already knew what happened, but she asked because it was the proper thing to do. "Was the diamond real?"

The general laughed. "Yes, and the marriage proceeded. Since then, all Mallory brides have inscribed their initials on the window-pane. Now that you are part of our family, I would like you to participate in this tradition."

So this was where Amy Spalding would inscribe her initials. Sophia tried to remember where Amy would scratch hers. If Sophia inscribed hers close to where Amy's would be, there would always be a connection of sorts between them.

Sophia stood in front of the window, her heart continuing to race. This was an important moment, not only for her and Thomas, but for Jack and Amy.

"If you'll take off your ring, darling, it'll be easier to manage. I'll help you." Thomas pulled her hand from over her heart. "Your hand is very warm. Are you ill? Your face is flushed."

"No," she said. "Just excited."

Thomas removed her ring and placed it in her palm. She almost dropped it, but her training kicked in and she focused on what she was doing. Satisfied, she slipped her ring back on her finger.

The butler came to the dining room. "Mr. MacKlenna and Mr. Digby have arrived. Shall I show them in?"

"Yes," the general said. "They can join us in the drawing room."

"I'll bring the wine there," the butler said.

They returned to the drawing room and greeted their guests. The conversation quickly turned to the Funding and Residency Acts, and continued throughout supper.

When dinner ended, Sophia said, "While the conversation continues, I wonder if I might borrow Mr. MacKlenna for a few minutes?"

Mr. MacKlenna pulled out her chair as the general and Thomas also stood. "Shall we walk along the river? It's a delightful fall evening."

"Let me grab my shawl and I'll be right with you." Sophia returned to her room for her cross-body bag and shawl, then met Mr. MacKlenna at the door. As soon as they were far enough away that they couldn't be heard she said, "The brooch is alive again. Why now?"

He didn't say anything for a long moment, then finally said, "I don't know."

Sophia was aghast. "What do you mean you don't know? You're the expert. You're the one who convinced me I was here to marry my soul mate. Now the brooch wants to take me home. Why now?"

"I don't know," he repeated. There was no ambiguity, no hemming and hawing, no uncertainty. He simply didn't know.

She set her lips, making it obvious how angry she was, but she didn't raise her voice. In the evening quietness, a raised voice would easily be overheard. "What do you know? Anything?"

He exhaled heavily and turned to face her. "Legend says an ancient tribe once lived in Caledonia. They made the brooches from black rocks that had fallen from the sky and gemstones they acquired from trading with Vikings. After many centuries, a small group of survivors traveled south to the Highlands and intermarried with Clan MacKlenna. When the leader of the clan discovered the brooches possessed unusual powers, he took precautions to protect them from the outside world. He became known as the Keeper. When the Keeper uncovered a threat to the brooches' security, he appointed twelve guardians to protect them. No one but the Keeper knew how many brooches there were, or the identities of those chosen to guard them. The knowledge has been passed down through generations of MacKlennas."

"You have the knowledge, then?" Sophia asked.

He shook his head. "I was not in line to become a Keeper."

"Do you know about the unusual power?" she asked.

"Only that the knowledge is of the future."

Sophia turned away from him and continued walking. "This doesn't make any sense."

Mr. MacKlenna waited a moment before he caught up with her. "Don't ye have knowledge of the future, lass?"

"Yes, but I come from—"

"Exactly," he said.

"I don't understand. You explain one part by confusing me with another. I thought you told me I was here to marry my soul mate."

He tucked her hand around his arm and they continued along the shore. The sun was setting, and the panoply of trees—beech, dogwood, hickory, maple, and oak—were exploding in hues from bright, gleaming yellow to the deepest scarlets.

"Since the first Caledonian married a Highlander, a marriage of soul mates has taken place, joining knowledge of the past with knowledge of the future."

She had never in her life been so confused, except for the day her parents put her on a plane to Italy. "Now I have a chance to go home."

"Ye've always had it, Sophia."

"No, I haven't!" she said sharply between clenched teeth. "The brooch was dead to me."

He tapped her forehead with his fingertip. "Maybe ye don't understand it here but do ye understand it here?" he tapped the pearl in the brooch. "What does yer heart tell ye?"

"It tells me... It tells me I love Thomas, and I would never hurt him."

"But would ye give up yer life in the future because ye don't want to break a man's heart? Now ye know ye can go home, what do ye want?"

They reached a fencerow marking the property line and turned around to go back. "Friends came for me, but I didn't go. Doesn't that answer your question?"

He patted her hand in the crook of his elbow. "No. Because ye believed this was where ye were supposed to be."

She glared at him. "Because you told me it was"

"Lass, the brooches are made from rock not of this world. We have no control over them. For centuries we have tried to understand the power, but we know only a portion of what's to be learned."

"Tell me what to do," she pleaded.

"I canna tell ye. Ye have to do what's in yer heart."

"You can't leave me like this, without some advice, some direction. You can't leave me out in the cold."

He turned to look at her and held her hands. "My advice, lass, is to tell Mr. Jefferson where ye're from. Yer answer will come from him."

She snatched her hands away and swallowed a sob. "I know you're the Keeper and you have all the answers to my questions. But you won't tell me because you've taken some secret clan blood oath.

"I've spent two decades studying faces and expressions, and I can see behind yours. You will go to your death with what you know, so I won't ask again. You gave me the only advice you could, and I will accept it. I don't know how Thomas will handle the news. It might make sense to him, or it might destroy his love for me."

"But ye have to tell him."

Sophia glanced toward the house. Thomas and Mr. Digby were coming toward them through the twilight. "Oh, one more thing. Now I know why you haven't let me talk to Mr. Digby. You're afraid his blood oath isn't as strong as yours."

She whirled on her heel and hurried to meet Thomas. He pulled her shawl up on her shoulders. "Did you and Mr. MacKlenna have a productive conversation?"

She looked at Mr. MacKlenna. "Oh, sure. He told me everything I wanted to know."

Mr. MacKlenna and Mr. Digby nodded at them and strolled off back toward the house.

"You look angry," Thomas said.

"Maybe a little, but mostly just confused."

"Tell me. Perhaps I can help you straighten it out." He guided her toward a stone bench beneath the willow oak.

"I'm not sure it's possible. It's very convoluted."

"You've told me many convoluted things. I can listen to another one."

Oh, God. How could she do this to him? She'd been lying to him for more than a year. Once trust is lost, it's almost impossible to reclaim.

He'd never again believe another word she said. Their relationship would never be the same. *He* would never be the same. He'd look at her with contempt, and it would break her heart.

She loved him, and she loved what they had together. The small chill in her heart expanded until it chilled her through and through.

He pulled her into his arms. "You're shivering. We should go inside."

"It's not the temperature. Kiss me." The kiss was delicious and impatient at the same time. It wasn't a devouring kiss, but, while it was languid, it was driven by a need to possess him, to be part of him, now and always. She clung to him, wanting to rip off his clothes and make love in a way she never had before. Rough and certain and demanding.

When they broke apart, he wrapped his arm around her and held her close. "Tell me, Sophia. Your mind is restless. We've been together every day for fourteen months and I've never seen you this distressed, not even when your knee was injured."

She pulled away from him and sat up straight, touching her warm brooch. "Here it is. I'm…I'm not from here, Thomas."

"I know, darling. You're from New York."

"Yes, but I'm not from this time. I'm from the future. From the twenty-first century."

He looked completely blank for a moment, as if not grasping what she'd said. Then it struck him, and blood rushed to his face.

"Think back. To our early conversations. To my predictions. To my unusual knowledge. To my strange statements."

"It's rare for a woman to know what you know, but—"

"Thomas, it's rare for *anyone* to know what I know, because I'm not from here. I'm from another time."

"This is impossible. Is Mr. MacKlenna responsible for this craziness?"

"He knows I'm not from here."

Thomas pushed to his feet and paced. "I don't know why you're saying this and discrediting a valuable member of the Virginia Assembly."

"Would you be still and just listen to me for a minute.? Then I'll answer all your questions."

"Answer this and then I'll listen, because if you can solve this problem, I'll believe anything you say. Why can't I grow grape vines at Monticello?"

"I told you I wasn't from here, and you want to know why you can't grow grapes? I'll tell you. Trying to cultivate *Vitis vinifera*, the classic European wine species, is virtually impossible until many years in the future. You can't control black rot and destructive pests such as phylloxera. Monticello will eventually find success in the twentieth century, when your European varieties are grafted on hardy, pest-resistant native rootstock."

Thomas dropped back onto the stone bench. "How could you possibly know that?"

"Do you know how many times you've asked me that very question? I lost count the first week I was in Paris."

"Still. How do you know?"

"In the twenty-first century, I dated a man who was a wine broker. He taught me everything I know about wine, including wines at Monticello."

"What does dating mean?"

"I had a relationship with him."

"Did he bed you?"

She closed her eyes and grimaced. "Thomas—"

"Did he?"

"I've never told anyone, but he cheated on me. I broke up with him and haven't seen him since. And that's all I'm going to say about it."

"You said you would answer all my questions. That's one of them."

"Don't you want to know about the moon? How many amendments there are to the constitution? How many states make up America in the twenty-first century?"

He leaned back against the tree and crossed his arms. "Am I limited?"

"Limited? What kind of question is that?"

He looked down his nose at her.

"No, you're not limited."

"Then I want to know."

By not telling him, she was making a much bigger deal of it. "Yes, I slept with him."

"But you wouldn't with me. Why?"

"I don't have any birth control."

"What is that?"

"To keep from becoming…enceinte. In my time there are multiple ways, which allows more sexual freedom."

"I already do not like your time."

"You would be fascinated by the science, the medicine, the technology. You wouldn't sleep for days."

He leaned forward and pressed his elbows on his knees. "How did you get here? By ship?"

She fluttered her hand through the air like a dancing firefly. "Through space. Through a vortex. Through a door that opened and ushered me in."

"Let's walk," he said.

He didn't touch her this time. He kept a small distance between them as they strolled along the shore, the same path she had taken with Mr. MacKlenna.

"When my grandmother died," Sophia said, "she gave me this brooch. I only discovered its unusual qualities later. Inside the pearl is a Gaelic inscription. When you recite the words, a fog engulfs you, and carries you to another time.

"I arrived in Paris the day the mob stormed the Bastille, but my plan had been to arrive in 1786 and commission Vigée Le Brun to paint my portrait. Instead I arrived in 1789. I needed help, and Mr. Watin and Mr. David suggested I find you."

"Sound advice."

"I thought I would only be in Paris for two weeks."

"Why?"

"That was the length of my previous trips. But this trip was screwed up from the beginning."

"Where else have you gone?"

"I spent two weeks with da Vinci, two weeks with Pablo Picasso. The same with Donatello, Peter Paul Rubens, and Edgar Degas."

"I haven't heard of Edgar Degas or Pablo Picasso."

"Picasso is from the twentieth century and Degas is from the nineteenth."

"Enough of this. I don't believe Jesus Christ turned water into wine. How could I possibly believe you can travel through the centuries? You need to drop this notion immediately and never speak of it again."

She had to get through to him and there was only way—shock him. "You'll be the third president of the United States and the greatest man to ever hold the office. In 1969, men will land on the moon and take a giant step for mankind. Doctors will operate on brains and put artificial hearts into bodies. By the twentieth century, people in New York can talk to people in London and in China on a little box they hold in their hands. Hundreds of people will fly in one airplane from New York to London or Paris or Rome in a matter of hours.

"In my time, there are forty-eight contiguous states from here to the Pacific Ocean three thousand miles away, plus Alaska and Hawaii. There are twenty-seven amendments to the constitution. The first ten are the Bill of Rights. Don't ask me what the others are, except I do know the nineteenth amendment will give women the right to vote."

He strode away from her, stood near the water, and rubbed his head. "I don't believe any of this."

"Are you getting a headache?"

"Yes."

She dug into her pocket and pulled out an ibuprofen Pete had given her. "Can you swallow this without water? It will help with your headache." He swallowed it without asking what he was taking. She reached into her pocket again and this time pulled out a piece a paper. "Look at this."

He tilted it to see the page in the dying light.

"What does the caption say?" she asked.

"'The Inauguration of Thomas Jefferson, Property of the Thomas Jefferson Foundation—Founded in 1923 for its dual mission of preservation and education.' Where'd you get this?"

"In June, three men from my time came to New York to get me. They believed I was stuck here."

"And they wanted to take you back?"

"Yes, but I wouldn't go."

"Why?" he asked. "If you're from another time as you claim, why didn't you go?"

His indifference was painful.

"Because I love you and plan to marry you."

"I saw you sitting on your quilt in Bowling Green Park one afternoon. A man was sitting with you. I didn't know him, and you never mentioned him. I thought it was odd, but we were both so busy it slipped my mind."

Telling him about Pete was pointless and would add more confusion, not clarity. "The first time I met Mr. MacKlenna, he told me I was here because you're my soul mate. I believed him. It's why I didn't leave."

"Do you still?"

"I love you, Thomas. And I want to marry you. I came from almost two hundred forty years from now. A lot has changed during those years. Virginia has over two hundred wineries. A drug called penicillin was invented that cures infections. Clean water, sanitation, and hygiene can eliminate millions of deaths from diseases every year."

"You're serious."

"I am. Bloodletting is dangerous, and it kills people. It's an insane practice. Don't ever let anyone do it to you. They'll do it to George Washington, and it will hasten his death."

He glanced up at the moon, and his profile thrilled her as an artist and as a woman, just as much as it had the first moment she saw him.

"If I ask you what will happen tomorrow, will you know?"

"Probably not, unless it's an important day in your life worth marking for historians." She sat down on the bank and watched him. His face was losing its tension. His curiosity was winning over his doubt.

"In Paris you knew what would happen the night Lafayette came to dinner. You knew what would happen the night I met with Madison and Hamilton. You knew we would reach an agreement."

She nodded.

He made a sharp turn and faced her. "You know the day I'll die."

It was a rhetorical question.

He trotted back up the bank and paced some more, then stopped abruptly. "Sophia, I couldn't face a day knowing you have all the answers. I don't want to know why I decide to run for president. You'll take away the wonder, the worry, the stress. What's left for me to do?"

He paced again, stopped, and faced her. "What happens to Alexander Hamilton?"

"That's an odd thing to ask," she said.

It was as if his mind was racing through so many questions, he just tossed one out to see where it would go. She pulled her knees up and wrapped her arms around her legs.

"I can't tell you. Once it gets in your head, you'll never forget it. There is one thing, though," she added, "and this applies to both you and Hamilton. There is a journalist named James T. Callender who will not be a friend to either of you. There's an old saying, 'Keep your friends close, and your enemies closer.' He's one of those you should keep as close as you can, or he'll cause you a great deal of trouble."

"Callender? I'll keep it in mind."

"There's one more thing, and this is very important. Stay true to your friendship with John and Abigail Adams. Even if you strongly, vehemently disagree with each other, always and forever remain friends. It's not worth losing them over political differences. The country will survive your differences, and, in fact, will survive a lot more than Adams and Jefferson disagreements. But the loss of friendship leaves a forever hole."

Thomas pulled her to her feet. "Sophia, I love you, but I can't live with knowing you already know everything that will happen to me and to this country. I would never need to make another decision. All I'd have to do is ask you what happens next. You know the day I'll die. Every morning I would wake up and wonder, is it today? Is this my last day on earth? I wouldn't have to wonder. I could ask you, 'Am I going to die today?' Who in their right mind would want that? I don't."

"What are you saying? You don't want me now because I know your future?"

He pulled her into his arms and kissed the top of her head. His arms were tense, his breathing heavy. "Would you want me if I knew the day you would die?"

Prickling sensations surrounded her eyeballs until tears poured out in a flood of sorrow and anguish and other emotions she couldn't identify. "I wouldn't care. It wouldn't matter. It would save us a lot of trouble. We could spend my last day on earth doing the things we love. And I could die in your arms."

"I don't want to know the day you die, or the day I'll die."

The knot of pain in her chest was excruciating. "Then I won't tell you."

"But I'll see it in your eyes. You'll be grieving my death before it arrives."

"No, I won't. I promise."

He held her at arm's length. "You couldn't keep that promise."

She didn't know about his heart, but hers was shattering into a thousand pieces. "I can try."

"My dearest Sophia." He pulled her in for another hug. "You have brought such joy to my life. I will never forget you."

She wept on his jacket. "I can't leave you. Please don't send me away."

"I'll miss you always, but you must return to where you belong."

"I belong here with you."

"No you don't. Not now."

"We just need more time to talk about this. We can work it out. It doesn't have to end."

Mr. MacKlenna appeared at her side. "Come, lass. It's time for ye to go."

"I won't go. I won't leave him." She grabbed Thomas's arm. The pain in her chest was thundering like an approaching freight train heading toward a cataclysmic explosion, just like in the movies. *Boom!*

"Sophia," Mr. MacKlenna pulled her hand off Thomas and said sternly, "Ye're not supposed to be here. Ye must go home." He unpinned her brooch and opened the pearl. "Speak the words, lass, and return to yer time." He kissed her cheek. "Be brave, Sophia. Now, go."

Crying too hard to speak, she could only gasp, "I love you."

When she didn't move, they walked away from her.

"Thomas, wait! Tell the girls..." Tears poured down her face, her mouth opened in a silent scream. How could this be happening? "Tell them...I love them. Tell them how much I was looking forward...to our reunion. Tell them... Oh, God, don't do this. Please."

"I'll tell them, Sophia. I'll tell them everything."

"Tell them how much I treasured every letter, every drawing they sent me."

"I'll tell...them."

"Tell them I wanted to be a grandmother to their children."

Thomas was so choked up he could barely speak. He took a step toward her, but Mr. Digby held him back. "I...will...tell them."

"Tell Polly not to stop painting. To find another teacher."

Thomas wiped tears away with the heels of his hands. "Sophia, I love you." He made a move toward her again, but both Mr. MacKlenna and Mr. Digby held him back.

They left her standing alone on the bank of the James River, silhouetted by the moon.

Then came deep baritone voices chanting in Gaelic: *"Chan ann le tìm no àite a bhios sinn a' tomhais an' gaol ach 's ann le neart anama."*

45

Mallory Plantation—Jack

T HE ENTIRE MACKLENNA Clan was waiting patiently around the willow oak when Jack, Matt, and Pete came through the fog. There was a collective gasp when Sophia's absence was noticed.

Robbie elbowed his way through the adults to stand in front of Pete. "Where's the girl?"

Henry followed him. "Yeah. You're supposed to get the girl. What happened?"

Pete tousled Henry's hair, causing a minor crisis. "The girl didn't want to come home."

Henry turned to face Robbie. "Stand still so I can fix my hair." He used his brother as a mirror to repair his spikes, but Robbie's barely-contained laugh almost ruined their comic routine.

Satisfied the damage was fixed, Henry turned back to Pete. "You wore the wrong outfit. If you'd worn Viking clothes you could have stolen her."

Robbie bumped Henry's shoulder. "You don't steal people, stupid. You kidnap them."

Henry put his face right smack in front of Robbie's. "Hey. Who you calling stupid?"

"Sorry, bro. I didn't mean it."

Henry turned back to Pete. "That's what you should have done.

Kidnapped her. Get the right clothes and try again."

"Uncle Pete," Blane said. "Viking clothes might be wet like the ones you're wearing. They were sailors. Next time wear cowboy clothes. Cowboys always get the girl. Just ask Uncle Rick. Come on Robbie, let's go play soccer."

Robbie put his arm around Blane's shoulders. "I'm glad we didn't go on such a dud mission, aren't you?"

Blane dropped the soccer ball he was holding and kicked it. "Yeah. I don't like to wear wet, smelly clothes, 'xcept when I play soccer."

They all ran off, chasing the ball.

Amy put her arms around Jack and kissed him lightly. "Where did you go? Paris or New York?"

"We arrived in New York City in June 1790 and found Sophia within two hours."

"You've only been gone"—Meredith looked at her watch—"two minutes. How long were you in the past?"

"About twenty-four hours," Jack said.

"Well, great. So you found her after she fell in love with Jefferson. So what happened when she saw you?" JL asked.

Matt slapped Jack on the back. "We spent the afternoon with Alexander Hamilton, talking about his financial plan and how he could reach a compromise with James Madison and Thomas Jefferson."

"Two Virginians and an immigrant. Isn't that a line from the musical?" Braham asked.

Charlotte winked at him.

"It was the most phenomenal afternoon," Matt said.

JL put her hands on her hips and glared at him. "We don't give a damn about Hamilton. We want to know about Sophia. What happened to her?"

"You don't have to be mean," Kevin said, wrapping his arms around JL.

"Sorry," she said. "But we've been sitting here waiting for you to bring her home."

Pete's nostrils flared. "What? All of two minutes. What an inconvenience."

"Why'd you let her get away—again?" JL's mouth twitched as if she was struggling to hold back tears.

Jack pointed his finger at her. "Get off his back, JL. Pete didn't let her do anything. Sophia made her decision without our influence."

"Why would anyone want to live in 1790? It doesn't make any sense."

Kevin whispered in her ear. She looked up at him and nodded. Then she stepped out of his embrace and eased into the nearest Adirondack chair. "Tell us what happened," she asked in a much calmer voice.

David and Braham rearranged the rest of the chairs, letting the women sit in a semicircle in front of the time-travelers. David gestured toward the grassy area in front of the chair. "Pete, you have the floor."

"Sophia met James MacKlenna and Seamus Digby here at Mallory Plantation. MacKlenna told her the brooches carry people to their soul mates, and that Thomas Jefferson was hers."

"Who is Mr. MacKlenna? I mean how is he related to me?" Kit asked.

"If it was 1790, then James MacKlenna would have been your great-grandfather," Meredith said. "He started MacKlenna Farm, then returned to Scotland, where he died. His son James, Sean and Jamilyn's father, came over and ran the operation."

"The son was my grandfather. We were at his bedside when he died at MacKlenna Farm," Kit said.

"So how did MacKlenna know Jefferson was Sophia's soul mate?" Kenzie asked. "Did he just pick an eighteenth-century single Founding Father out of the air and said, 'This man is the love of your life?' Because it sounds insane. We all know Pete's her soul mate."

Pete grabbed a beer from a cooler and took a long drink. "Jefferson is, not me. Sophia told me she was going to marry him."

"How do you know she wasn't forced to say it?" JL asked.

"Come on, JL. I'm a cop, remember? She wasn't under duress. We spent the afternoon at the beach talking and finding closure."

JL came up out of her chair, slowly, but she made her point. "What the hell? You've mourned her loss for twenty years. Damn it! You have one afternoon together and find closure. Come on. You can't bullshit a bullshitter, Parrino. I know you, and I know you couldn't have walked away...unless..." JL took a deep breath and blew it out, then returned to her seat and crossed her arms.

"Finish it. Go on. Finish what you were going to say."

"Unless she told you she was in love with someone else and it was over between you two. Like over...forever."

Pete took another long pull on his beer. "That's what she said. Then we reached a place where we could both move on."

JL shook her head. "If you can do that, I'll be happy for you."

"I'm good. This is the end of it. Now, I'm going over to Charlotte's, change my clothes, and when I come back, I'm getting stinking drunk." He grabbed another beer, dodged the children, and hurriedly left the backyard.

Connor snagged a couple of beers from the cooler. "I'm going with him. I saw him like this a few times when he came back from Afghanistan. He's about to break down. He shouldn't be alone. If he's in a mood to talk, we'll talk. If not, we'll just sit on the porch and drink beer." Connor hustled after Pete, and they disappeared through the tree line.

"We all need to give him some space." Jack reached for Amy's hand. "I'm going inside to change. Walk with me."

Amy circled her arm around him. "Are you okay?"

"I wish it had worked out differently for Pete. Sophia is amazing. She's got a piece of all of you. Kit's spunk, Meredith's business acumen, Kenzie's perception, Charlotte's singular focus, your natural ease with people, Amber's ability to turn society on its ears and still be adored, and Olivia's prissiness."

"Well, I'm glad to know what you think of us gals."

Jack kissed her. "I adore each of you."

"I think you fell in love. Should I be jealous of a woman who's been dead two hundred years?"

"She could walk into the backyard right this minute, and you'd know instantly you had a new BFF. She's that kind of gal."

"I'm sorry I won't meet her, then. We could all use another good friend."

Jack snugged his arm around her waist and together they walked toward the house. "There was something else going on, but I couldn't put my finger on it. Once I settle down to write my report, it'll come to me. It hasn't all clicked into place yet. Something was missing. I might have noticed it if Matt and I hadn't been so absorbed with Alexander Hamilton. We have enough material for a book or a screenplay."

"You're going to write a play? Very impressive. Do you think you'll open on Broadway?" Amy laughed. "I wouldn't put it past you, Mallory." She kissed him, and he rubbed her baby bump. "I'm going back to chat with the girls while you change. The kids have been waiting for you so the family can have a real baseball game."

"They don't have to wait for me. Austin can play with them."

"Yes, they do have to wait. And you know you love it."

He kissed her nose. "Where's my glove?"

"Patrick has it. Hurry up."

"Okay, but I don't want you near the field."

"I'm near the field four times a week."

"Yeah, but you're in the press box. Not down there where men get hit in the head and other painful places." He patted her ass as she turned and went in the opposite direction.

Jack kicked off his shoes when he entered the house and stopped at the kitchen. The breeze from the punkah ceiling fan blew on his sticky neck, cooling him off. Could he stand there long enough to miss the game? Nope. Wasn't possible. The kids would track him down, and if he wasn't there, Amy might step in. If she got hit by a ball, he'd never forgive himself.

He scrounged around the kitchen. "There's no tea? Come on." He checked the pantry. It was his own fault. He made the most recent trip to the grocery store.

Instead of tea, he poured a cup of coffee and sipped the dark brew while wandering through the house. A child's cry stopped him in his tracks. He went immediately to the dining room and looked out the window to see who was crying. It wasn't a blood-curling scream, so nobody was bleeding or dying. Charlotte was already there with a Band-Aid and a sucker, always a crowd-pleaser, and the crying stopped immediately.

From what he could see, it was a McBain girl twin. Three years old and Jack still couldn't tell them apart. He remained standing at the window, waiting to see who would cry next. When one Ninja got a Band-Aid, another soon suffered a minor injury.

Looking out over the crowd of people—of family—he wondered how he got to be so blessed. There were two dozen people out there who had stuck with him during his jackass days and waited for him to grow up. Now he had a fantastic wife, two kids, and another one on the way. He was one lucky son of a bitch.

As he stood there watching the action out on the lawn, he caught a flash of light from his periphery. He jerked. "What the hell?"

He scanned the floor, the ceiling, to his right, to his left. Nothing. He knew something significant just happened. He closed his eyes, relaxed, and fell into another trance. He saw a man wearing a leather apron making repairs to the window. Jack opened his eyes and skimmed his hands over the glass. He reached Amy's initials and traced them with his fingertip then moved to Sophia's—

But they weren't there.

"Damn it."

He rushed into his office, climbed the library ladder, opened the glass door, and pulled down the first General Mallory's daily journal. Jack carried the large ledger book to his desk, pushed papers and books aside, and opened the frayed cover.

He couldn't read the small, slanted script without his glasses. Where were they? He moved papers. Nothing. He checked his jacket hanging on the coat rack. Nothing. He stomped back to his desk and found them next to his computer.

Now he could read. He thumbed through the pages until he reached the summer of 1790. Using his finger as a guide, he scanned down the page, moving quickly through the summer months.

Congress ended the session, boxed up, and moved to Philadelphia the end of August. Jefferson would have gone to Monticello first.

Jack's finger continued to guide his eyes down the page.

Which would have put Jefferson at Mallory Plantation in early September.

Which was where Jack found what he was looking for. The general made an entry the second week in September saying he'd been asked to give Sophia Orsini away in marriage to Thomas Jefferson. The next entry reported her etching her initials in the window. And the next one knocked Jack's legs out from under him. He dropped into his chair. The general recorded:

Sophia Orsini, bride of Thomas Jefferson, fell into the James River, was dragged under and carried away by a fast-running current. Thomas Jefferson, James MacKlenna, and Seamus Digby witnessed the accident. Several attempts were made to rescue her, to no avail. Her body was never recovered.

"Holy Christ."

He continued reading: *Four days after the service, a glassmaker was called to remove Sophia Orsini's initials. It was believed they would bring bad luck to future Mallory brides.*

Jack sat back in his chair, gripped his hands together over his midsection, and considered what this meant for Pete. Short of calling her studio, there was no way to know if she truly died, or it meant she'd returned home.

"Where are you?" Jack asked the missing woman.

Elliott strolled into the office. "Who are ye looking for?"

Jack hesitated, not sure he wanted anyone to know what he just discovered.

"Who?" Elliott repeated.

Jack went over to the door and closed it. "This has to stay on the Q.T. until we figure out what it means."

"Shoot." Elliott sat in one of the wingbacks in front of the desk.

Instead of returning to his desk chair, Jack sat in a matching wingback next to Elliott. "I don't know where Sophia is. Her initials disappeared from the window. I searched General Mallory's journal and found an entry describing her drowning in the James River. Following her service, the initials were removed. It was considered bad luck to keep them."

"Goddamn it," Elliott said. "Can ye go back to get her before it happens?"

"Maybe." Jack stretched out his long legs and tapped on the leather arms of the chair. "Two bits of information make this suspicious. First, James MacKlenna and Seamus Digby were witnesses to the accidental drowning. And second, her body was never recovered."

"It wouldn't be unheard of for a woman's clothing to drag her under the water and sweep her away. But having a MacKlenna and a Digby as witnesses, I agree, makes the drowning suspicious. Why don't ye call her?"

"If she's home and wants to see Pete, she'll call him. If she doesn't, I don't want Pete to know. At least not today."

"Why not? The lad feels like crap."

"Sophia needs her space to recover. If she and Pete are going to have a future, she needs time to settle the past before she moves into the future. When she's ready, she'll let us know."

"If ye weren't the one saying this, I might not believe it, but after what ye went through with Carolina Rose, who am I to second guess ye? But ye're opening yerself up for another problem."

Jack spread his hands. "What am I not seeing?"

Elliott crossed his legs and fingered the knife-edged pleat in his khakis. "When Kit, Cullen, and Braham were on the Oregon Trail, Braham received a letter from his father. The letter informed him that the lawyer in San Francisco who had hired Braham and Cullen to practice in his law firm had lost his daughter in a tragic accident. The reason it mattered was because Cullen planned to marry her. If Braham revealed the news to Cullen, he was certain Cullen would leave the wagon train and hurry to California to comfort the man who would have been his father-in-law. Braham reasoned that if

Cullen left the wagon train, he and Kit would never have a future. So Braham didn't reveal the tragedy."

"Okay, so what?" Jack said.

"Cullen was so angry that Braham, feeling guilty, left the wagon train. Soon after, Cullen was attacked, thrown off a cliff, and presumed dead. Kit returned to the future. If Braham had stayed on the wagon train, the attack wouldn't have happened, or if it had, Kit wouldn't have given up and gone home."

"What's your point? We know Kit and Cullen eventually found each other."

"If ye intend to keep this a secret from Pete, ye have to be aware ye might make a bigger mess of the situation. Lies of omission never work out. Just ask David and Kenzie. David's lie of omission nearly got Kenzie killed."

"It's not our decision, Elliott. And revealing what we know or don't know isn't going to get anyone killed."

"Ye're probably right. Why not let Gabe keep an eye out for her? He can find some excuse to talk to her. If she just got home after five weeks, she'll need to go out for groceries. Gabe is an enterprising sort. He'll figure it out, but we need eyes on her before we say anything to anyone else."

"Pete told me if things didn't work out with Sophia, he was going to Australia to work on a project with Shane. What do we do then?" Jack asked.

"Stay in touch with Shane. If Pete starts dating someone and it looks like it could get serious, we'll need to bring him home. He doesn't need to marry someone on the rebound."

"You want to break up a potential relationship because you hope Pete and Sophia will get together now when they obviously couldn't work it out before. That doesn't make much sense."

"None of this does. We work with what we have. Right now, we don't have anything. Let's wait for Gabe's report. If she is home, and she doesn't call ye or Matt or Pete, then ye'll have to go see her."

"Amy can't make the trip. Sitting so long while pregnant will drive her nuts."

"Then don't tell her why ye're going."

"Of course I'll tell her," Jack said.

"Amy will tell JL. JL will tell Kit. Kit will tell Maria. And on and on and on until everyone knows but Pete. Not gonna happen. So keep it to yerself."

"You'll tell Meredith."

"I'll make ye a deal. Neither one of us will tell our brides. We'll both catch hell, but we can blame it on the other guy."

Jack considered the ramifications. Amy might understand. He wasn't so sure about Meredith. "Okay. Deal. But if you tell Meredith and force me to lie to Amy, it will really piss me off."

"Consider it payback."

"For what?"

"Do ye want me to list all yer sins, or just the top three?"

Jack reached for his coffee cup, sipped, and made a face. "This is barely drinkable, hot or cold. I don't know why you don't drink tea."

"It's a sissy drink."

"It's eleven o'clock in Italy," Jack said. "I'll call Gabe. He'll still be up. I'll explain the situation, make sure he understands this is strictly confidential, and get him over there tonight to see if there's any movement, lights, anything. You do know, don't you, that David could break into her security system and we'd know immediately."

"Absolutely not," Elliott said. "Pete's already violated her privacy once. We're not going to do it again unless it's an emergency. And we're not there."

"Elliott!" Meredith called from the hallway.

"In here. Jack and I are catching up."

Meredith pushed open the door and waltzed in. "Jack, you're wanted on the baseball field, and I'm taking JL to the hospital. Everything is fine with Lawrence, but she's ready to go. Kevin's had too many beers and can't drive."

"Is she pissed?"

Meredith shook her head. "I think she encouraged it. Charlotte locked up the keys to the boats. Nobody needs to be out on the water tonight. One of those drunk Scotsmen might fall into the river and drown and no one will ever find his body."

Jack set his cup aside, removed his glasses, and cleaned them with his handkerchief, avoiding Meredith's penetrating gaze.

Elliott turned to look directly at his wife. "I'll drive Kevin to the hotel later. Are ye driving JL's rental car?"

"That makes the most sense. Don't you think?"

Elliott stood and pulled his wife into his arms. "I think everything ye do makes sense." He kissed her. "I'll be up there in a couple of hours."

Meredith gave Jack a hard look. "I don't believe for a moment that you two are catching up. Something is going on, and you think you can keep it to yourselves. You two are the worst ones in the family about keeping a secret. I'll find out, and so will Amy."

At the door, Meredith stopped and turned. "By the way, the early American look you've got going on with that costume is the best time-traveling look you've ever had. You're quite a macaroni, Jack Mallory." She laughed and whirled out of the room.

"Good luck with keeping this to yourself," Jack muttered.

46

Florence, Italy—Sophia

W HEN THE FOG lifted, Sophia was standing in her dark living room sobbing.

Too brokenhearted to stand, she dropped to her knees while a fresh surge of tears flowed down her face.

Hail Mary, full of grace, the Lord is with thee.

She tried swiping them away with shaking fingers, but they came too fast, too thick, too many.

Blessed art thou amongst women…

Bereft of Thomas's arms, she clutched her own around her and collapsed into a ball of flesh and blood and heartache.

…and blessed is the fruit of thy womb, Jesus.

The rest of her life had been planned out in her mind. She and Thomas would have spent the next ten years in Philadelphia while he served as secretary of state and vice president. Then eight years in Washington while he served as president, followed by retirement at Monticello surrounded by Polly and Patsy's children. She would have had a front row seat to paint American political life as the country entered the nineteenth century.

It was all gone now. Thomas was gone. The girls were gone.

Her mind painted a block of ice slammed by a pick, over and over and over, chips flying dart-like in all directions, puncturing walls and ceilings and floors. Her soul was shattered.

Now what? Teach art. Paint. Watch the world from the sidelines. She had depended on her two-week holiday each year to keep her inspired. Now the brooch was unstable, she could never trust it again. Her inspiration was shattered.

He shouldn't have let MacKlenna and Digby send her away. Why had Thomas allowed it? If she'd had more time to talk to him, he wouldn't have been afraid of her. They could have found a solution.

"Oh. God!" She pounded the floor. "If only I'd had more time. If only…"

Sleep rescued her from the agony, but it didn't come easily, and didn't last long enough. And worse, it was filled with angry voices and twisting and turning that wrung out her insides until they were on the outside, leaving her heart dangling by an artery over an abyss. Then dead bodies everywhere. Severed heads. A burning mattress. Cannon fire. Sailing ships. Sickness. Rain. Rain. Rain.

You can't stay here. I don't want to know when I die.

"Stop!"

She awoke screaming, her body aching from sleeping on the hardwood floor. "Make it all go away. I can't bear it."

She dragged herself to the shower and stayed there, unable to find any joy in the shampoo and soap and hot, hot water. Only when she was left with icy water did she shut off the faucet, wrap one towel around her body, another around her head, and fall into bed, wet and shivering.

Sun shining in her eyes woke her up. She closed the blinds, rolled over, and went back to sleep. The next time she woke there was total darkness. She ignored the rumbling in her stomach and fell asleep again. The next time she woke, sunlight seeped through the gaps between the slats in the blinds. Her stomach wouldn't let her sleep another minute. She had to eat. How long had it been? Days? Centuries?

Did it even matter?

After slipping on running shorts and a T-shirt, she padded to the kitchen. There was nothing in the refrigerator. She knew there wouldn't be, because she tossed everything out before she left on her holiday. She looked anyway, then slammed the door on the cold, empty space.

She walked in circles around the kitchen, then checked the refrigerator again. Maybe something was hidden in a drawer, on the door, or even in plain sight. Nothing except an open box of baking soda. She'd done a clean sweep. Then just for the heck of it, she closed the door and opened it one more time. Three times was a charm. Right?

Not in this case, sister. Try the freezer.

It was packed with nutritious meals. But she hated frozen food. Even good frozen food was bad. The meals were always a last resort for when she painted late into the night and nothing close by was open for takeout.

She popped a lasagna dish into the microwave and set the timer according to the instructions on the package, as if cooking it correctly would improve the taste. Good luck with that.

She needed a drink. Anything but wine. She'd never drink wine again without thinking of Thomas and wondering how he was doing. Which was dumb, because now he'd been dead for over two hundred years.

While the microwave ticked away, she set the table and sat watching the timer count down to zero. When it was done, she forced herself to eat every bite.

It wasn't easy. Matter of fact, it was hell. For the past several months, she and Thomas had enjoyed dinner out almost every night, or they ate alone at his house.

Alone. The word took on a new, gut-wrenching meaning tonight.

She cleaned the dishes, threw away evidence of her frozen food sin, and went back to bed. When she woke hours later, she ventured down to the studio. *Mona Lisa* was gone thanks to…Pete. Her stomach spasmed at the thought of him. She couldn't have him in her head right now. To him, she was dead. And that was the way it had to be.

Junk mail and flyers shoved through the mail slot were piled on the floor. She scooped them up and returned to her bedroom. With her journal in one hand, the mail in the other, she crawled back into bed.

She turned each journal page slowly, and each sketch triggered a fresh batch of tears. How many days could she go on like this? She needed to go to the market for fruit, milk, eggs, and cheese. But she didn't want to go out. She didn't even have the energy to dress.

Before tossing the junk mail in the trash, she flipped through it just to be sure there was nothing important. A hot pink flyer caught her eye. It was a new delivery service. All she had to do was place an order online, pay for it with a credit card, and then send the service the pickup information. Sounded fishy. They could run off with her stuff.

She booted up her computer to check their website and read several reviews. Looked legit. She could try it once. It wouldn't be a huge loss if they never showed up with her order. But if they did, then they could also pick up her painting supplies. She was low on everything.

With a bit of ambivalence, she filled out the information on the website and placed the orders. A few minutes later she received a confirmation number and an estimated time of delivery.

"Not bad."

If this was a legitimate company, she'd never have to go out again. Never have to dress. Or shower. Never have to talk to anyone. All she had to do was breathe.

No. Wait. She had students starting the middle of August. And she was in no condition to inspire anyone. Inspiring herself was going to be a challenge. But could she cancel an entire semester?

She sent an email to an artist friend who also graduated from The Florence Academy of Art. A lie came easily, and she told him she contracted a blood disease while on holiday and spent two weeks in the hospital. Now she was home recovering but was too weak to teach this fall. Could he handle her eight students?

A few minutes later, she received a reply. Yes, he could. Then she sent out a group email and lied to her students and parents. And yes, even lied to Emma and Greta. With that guilt-inducing task completed, she sent her accountant a note with instructions to continue managing her finances until further notice.

There was also an email from Lukas. He was in Naples. His mother was seriously ill, and he wouldn't be back in Florence for three or four months, possibly longer. She sent a return email saying she would light a candle for his mother.

With business out of the way, she could hibernate until art classes started up again in January. Maybe by then her soul would find its way back into her body.

But there was one more thing she had to do. She opened the safe, removed the box, and returned the brooch to its spot on the tapestry. Then she removed her betrothal ring and placed it next to the brooch. She closed the box and clutched it to her breasts as tears tracked down her face. After a few tearful minutes, she returned the box to the safe.

She crawled back into bed with her journal. If she was going to spend the next several months painting in seclusion, what was she going to paint? Did she even want to?

She flipped pages and put a check mark in the lower right corner of every sketch she *wanted* to paint. Then she went back through the checks and double-checked the ones she *had* to paint. Then lastly she triple-checked the ones she *would* paint.

Thirty-six paintings in all. A third of them were of Thomas, five were Thomas and the girls, both in Paris and arriving in America. The rest were of Washington, Adams, Madison, Jay, Hamilton, Burr, Trumbull, New York City in 1790, Federal Hall, the docks, sailing ships, the Mallorys, and two paintings of the famous dinner meeting. But those two she'd keep for herself.

In the studio, she set up three easels. She would switch from one painting to another as inspiration moved her.

It was midafternoon when someone knocked at her back door. *Right on time.*

She was barely presentable—long painter's coat, rolled-up khakis, T-shirt, long hair in a ponytail, and paint-splattered canvas shoes—but the delivery guy wouldn't care, and she didn't either.

She almost smiled when she saw him—Italian, fantastic bone structure, tall, muscular, mid-thirties, a hundred-watt smile, and deep brown eyes that told a story. She immediately knew he was an old soul, and he reminded her of Watin. She could trust this guy.

"Miss Orsini, I'm Gabriele."

"Come in. Just set the packages on the shelf."

He turned and looked at her, shaking his head. "If they go upstairs, that's where I'll take them."

She didn't want a stranger in her living space. "This is fine."

He didn't insist, simply set the packages down where she indicated. "Your street is on my route, so I'll be doing most of your deliveries. I also run errands if you need something dropped off. Or," he glanced around, "if you need heavy equipment or furniture moved, I'll do whatever the customer requires."

"I don't have anything right now, but it's good to know." She moved toward the door. "Until next time, Gabriele. Thank you." The message was clear. It was time for him to go.

Now she had food and paint, she didn't need anything else.

For the next three days, she barely slept. On the fourth day, she needed more paint. She filled out the form and placed the order. Four hours later he showed up at her back door with the paint, a smile, and a daisy.

"Thank you," she said, sniffing the flower.

"I thought it might make you smile."

Several days later she needed canvas, fruit, and fresh bread. She considered going out and getting what she needed, but it required dressing, and if she saw one of her students it could get very awkward. So she placed an order, and a few hours later, Gabriele stood at her back door.

"Do you mind bringing the box of paint into the studio?"

"Not a bit." He followed her in and stopped at a portrait of Thomas and the girls. "Who are these people?"

"Thomas Jefferson and his daughters Patsy and Polly."

"Thomas Jefferson? The third president of the United States?"

She nodded.

"It looks like they were right here sitting for you. This painting is amazing. The colors, the detail. It's in France, right?"

"Yes, how did you know?"

"I recognized the gate. I've seen something similar in Paris."

"Well, you're very observant."

He smiled and sort of ducked his head. "I try to be. So can I take this fruit upstairs? Or do you plan to eat it now?"

"It's for later," she said. "But you can go ahead and leave it on the counter in the kitchen."

She returned to her painting. When Gabriele came back down, he was tucking his phone into his pocket. "Do you have another pickup?" she asked.

"*Sì.* Down the street. What would I do without a phone?" He stopped in front of another painting. "Who's this guy?"

"Alexander Hamilton."

"The dude on the American ten-dollar bill who died in a duel?"

She tried to laugh, but it didn't come out that way. It was more of a snort. "You either know your American history or your American money."

"Little bit of both. Goodbye, Miss Orsini. I'll let myself out."

"Gabriele." He stopped and looked back at her.

"Call me Sophia. It looks like we'll be seeing each other regularly. Actually, you're the only person I do see."

"Anytime, Sophia." He gave her his killer smile again and left through the back door.

As the weeks passed, the weather changed, the finished paintings filled up more and more space, and she and Gabriele spent more time together, eating lunch at the corner restaurant, sharing gelato in the afternoon, or going to Sunday Mass. He told her about his girlfriend and his interest in wine. He never asked her personal questions, and all she offered about herself was her passion for painting.

One day during the second week in December, he came in and found her on the floor crying beneath a painting of her and Pete sitting at a large table surrounded by a group of smiling people.

Gabriele sat down next to her and put his arm around her. "Madonna, what happened? Are you hurt? Talk to me?"

She swiped at her tear-streaked face. "You're the only person I've talked to in months." Her voice cracked as she continued crying. "I've put everyone off. I missed my American Thanksgiving. Christmas is around the corner, and I miss my family. I miss the people…I love."

Gabriele pointed at the painting. "Are those the people in the painting?"

"Yes," she said, taking in big gasps of air, her chest heaving as she sobbed.

"I haven't seen this one before. When did you paint it?"

"Just…now," she said between gasps.

He chuckled. "You're good, but not that good."

"I-I started it yesterday and j-just finished."

"Which means you haven't eaten or slept in twenty-four hours."

"T-thirty s-six."

He grabbed a box of tissues off the worktable and used one to dry her face. "You know that's not good for you."

"I-I know. But this picture flashed in my mind, and I-I had to paint it. I j-just now signed it."

He brushed her hair back off her face and tucked it behind her ears. "So did you drop to the floor in exhaustion?"

"N-No. I looked at it and saw what I'd painted."

He smiled. "I thought you normally looked at what you painted."

She smacked his arm. "This was different." She grabbed a tissue from the box and wiped her face. "I was in a painter's zone. It's never happened to me before. My hand developed a mind of its own, and I wasn't really aware of what I was painting. Then my hand just quit. The brush dropped to the floor. I stepped back and got a good look. When I saw what I'd painted, I collapsed."

"It's incredible. The lighting in the vineyard is amazing. The pasta, cheese, vegetables, and bread on the table look real enough to eat. The grapes look juicy, and I can taste the wine in the glasses. I guess since you're in a wedding gown, it's your wedding feast. So who's the lucky groom? It certainly isn't the redheaded fellow you've been painting for months. Whoever it is, I'm jealous."

"It's the wedding feast I never had. The one I always wanted. The two people on my left are my parents. They're dead now."

"You look exactly like your mother, Madonna. She's stunning."

"People often asked me if we were sisters. I loved her so much. We were always together. Something happened to her when I was born, and she could never have more children. So she doted on me. I always confided in her. She had such high expectations for me to go to college and graduate school and be successful in a career I loved." Sophia blew her nose. "I disappointed her."

"How could anybody be disappointed in you? You're talented, loving, and *bellissimo* inside and out. If your mother was alive today, she'd be so proud of you."

"I shouldn't have pressured Pete—he's the guy in the painting. I pressured him to elope, and everything went to hell from there. I just wanted to be with him. I couldn't stand it. It was like that from the first day I met him."

She wiped her face, and sniffled. "We were so much alike—our dreams, goals, the very core of who we were as individuals and as a couple. We grew up in the same Italian Catholic neighborhood in the city. I didn't care about anything but him."

"How old were you?"

"Sixteen when we met. Just turned seventeen when we had sex for the first time. It was almost a spiritual experience, like we were joining souls and becoming one being. I've never had a feeling like it since." She smiled at Gabriele. "Sounds crazy, doesn't it?"

"No, it sounds like you were very much in love. So what about this guy? Where is he now?"

"I'm not sure. But he never remarried, and he still loves me, or he did a few months ago. And I'm still in love with him. I never truly stopped."

"Then why are you sitting here on the floor? Call him. There's a wedding feast waiting to happen."

"He thinks I'm dead."

A laugh rumbled through Gabriele. "Then he'll have the surprise of a lifetime when he hears your voice." He pulled his phone from his pocket. "Here, you can use my phone."

She waved it away. "No, not right now. And I don't know how to reach him anyway. After the holidays, I'll track him down. Maybe we can meet in London. He said he was in and out of there every few weeks. The city would be neutral territory. Or maybe we could meet in Scotland. I want to go by my late grandfather's law office anyway, so that might be a good place to meet."

"Don't wait. *L'amore chiama.*"

"If love is calling, I know I shouldn't wait, but I will. I need a week at a spa and several weeks at the gym, and my hair needs to be cut and colored, and my nails—"

"A man in love doesn't care about any of those things."

"Maybe not, but I do. He hasn't seen me...I mean, seen me undressed...in twenty years."

"Men don't care. He'll want you just as you are."

Sophia's heart lifted. "I'm glad you said that. But I'm still going to do it my way. A month or two won't make any difference."

"If you need any help, I know a great personal trainer who'll be glad to get you in shape."

"I might need him." She stood, picked up the brush, and placed it on the work table. "I don't know what I would have done without you these past few months. But now that you've listened to me and dried my tears, what can I do for you? Do you want me to paint your portrait or your girlfriend's?"

"Leave a good review. That's enough."

"I've already written five."

His eyes twinkled. "Madonna, a business can never have too many good reviews."

"I know I'm just a customer, but you've been a good friend to me since the first day you came to my door."

"It's been an honor and a pleasure to come here and watch your paintings and you come alive." He studied her for a moment and then said, "May I give you a hug? I think you need one."

She didn't wait for him but threw her arms around his neck. "God, do I. Thank you, Gabriele." She lingered in his arms, it felt so good to be held. Then she straightened and followed him to the back door. "Until next time."

He kissed her cheeks. "You're amazing. And I can't wait to see how different your life will be this time next year."

She smiled. "I can't either."

47

Florence, Italy—Sophia

T WO DAYS LATER, Gabriele knocked on Sophia's back door right
on time with her delivery. When she opened it, she gasped,
"Jack Mallory!"

He wrapped her in his arms and swung her around. "I'm so glad
you're not dead."

When he set her down, she looked at him, then Gabriele, then
back at Jack. She was flabbergasted. "How long have you known I
was here?"

Jack scratched his nose, stared at the floor, glanced around the
room, all the while Gabriele leaned against the work bench with his
arms folded, smiling.

Jack scratched the back of his neck. "Well, it's like this. Your
initials disappeared from the dining room window shortly after we
returned. I looked in General Mallory's journal and discovered you'd
drowned. If the entry hadn't mentioned Mr. MacKlenna and Mr.
Digby, I might have believed it, but with those two as witnesses, it
didn't smell right. There was no way to find out if you'd come back
without calling and I didn't want to do that. I figured if you wanted
us to know you'd reach out."

Her head jerked, and she glared at Gabriele. "You know him?
You tricked me? How could you? We're friends." She dropped onto

an extra painting stool in the storeroom, and her shoulders slumped. "I'm speechless." Gabriele started to move toward her, but she held up her hand, palm out. "You have some explaining to do."

"Don't blame Gabe," Jack said.

She shot Jack a look, her nostrils flaring. "Shhh!"

Gabriele crossed his arms, uncrossed them, put his hands on his hips, dropped them to his sides, then finally gave up and shoved his hands into his pockets. "It's like this, Madonna. I emigrated from Italy a few years before I met Jack's wife in New York City in the year 1909."

Sophia's jaw dropped. "You're a—"

"Traveler? Yes, I am. We had quite an adventure. At the end of it, Jack asked me if I wanted to go home with them. I said yes. After a couple of years getting acclimated, Elliott Fraser sent me here to manage the company's vineyards in Tuscany, and I love it. I've never been happier."

"So you don't really work for a delivery service?"

Gabriele shook his head. "When Jack called and described the situation, he said to use my imagination and find a way to check in on you regularly. But I didn't want to impose. It was best to let you take the lead and decide how much interaction you wanted."

She gave Jack a hard look. "So why are you here now? I've been back for months."

"Gabe said it was time to let you know we knew you were back, and it was time to let Pete know you're here."

She gasped, her heart pounding. "You told him?"

Shock jumped in Jack's eyes. "No! The news has to come from you, not me."

"Then if it's up to me, I'm not ready."

"We're not here to push you, only to press Pete's case in his absence." Jack walked to the door leading to the studio. "And while you're thinking about it, can I take a look in there?"

She shrugged. "Sure. Why not?" She followed him into the studio.

"Holy shit!" Jack walked around the room, studying all the paintings. "Gabe said you were in a painting frenzy. I asked for pictures, but he wouldn't send any. He said nobody could see them until you were ready. They're amazing. Are you having an exhibition?"

"I'd like to, but I decided to finish the collection before I send out inquiries. I'd like to do something in America."

Jack's eyes twinkled. "I have an idea that will stand the art world on its head." He continued looking at the paintings. "I can't say anything yet but hold off on sending out inquiries. You won't need to. I got this under control."

She looked at him curiously, her head to one side. "Give me a hint?"

"Nope, but first there's a trip I'd like to arrange. Are you available next week?"

"I guess," she said.

"Good, pack warm clothes. Gabe will make all the arrangements and have a plane here to get you. He'll travel with you, too."

"I don't want to cause a problem with his girlfriend."

Jack waved his hand. "If Gabe ever settles down with one woman—hell, I'll even give him two women—it would shock the entire family."

Sophia frowned at Gabe. "So I guess we'll spend our travel time finding out what else you lied about."

"I figured if you believed I had a girlfriend you wouldn't feel pressured or threatened."

"Gabriele, I learned within a week that you are completely full of it. But I love you anyway."

His chest rose and fell in a long sigh. "I was afraid you'd hate me when you learned the truth."

She shook her head. "I could never hate you. Get mad, yes, but never hate you."

The relief in his voice sounded real when he said, "Lying to you was the hardest thing I've ever done. But I did it for Pete, and now he owes me." Gabriele winked at her. "Payback's hell."

"You need to get back to the winery," Jack said. "According to Meredith, you no longer have an excuse to delay the reports you owe her."

Gabriele snapped his fingers. "Damn." He and Jack did a fist bump. "Catch you later, bro. You too, Madonna."

Jack made a face. "Wait. What's this Madonna crap?"

"I'm a nineteenth-century Italian, remember?"

"So it wouldn't be appropriate if I called her that?"

Gabriele rolled his eyes. "*Ciao, caro.*"

Sophia kissed his cheeks. "Call me tomorrow."

After Gabriele left, Sophia said, "Come upstairs. I'll open a bottle of wine and show you my art collection."

"I'll have to get Elliott on the phone. He told me if I got to see a da Vinci, he better be on the phone to enjoy the experience vicariously."

She squeezed his hand. "When did you last see Pete?"

"He left for Australia shortly after we returned. I've seen him on video conference calls, but I haven't talked to him. Elliott, Gabe, and I are the only ones who know you came back, and none of us have told him."

She led the way to the kitchen and picked out a perfect wine to drink while viewing a one-of-a-kind art collection. "Pete would know the truth if he googled Jefferson."

"Maybe. But he's not the type to rub salt in an open wound. He won't look." She presented the bottle, label side up, for Jack's approval. "Excellent choice. A Montgomery Winery chardonnay. Meredith would be pleased."

"My local shop ordered this for me, and it's been selling out since the owner first stocked a couple of bottles." Sophia opened it and poured two glasses. "Here's to da Vinci." They clinked glasses. "Are you going to call Elliott?"

"Damn." Jack punched in a number on his phone and put it on speaker, but the call went to voicemail. "You missed it, Elliott. I'm about to see a da Vinci."

Sophia sipped her wine. "Should we wait?"

"Hell no. He lost out. So…open Sesame."

She pushed the lever to open the wall. The lights came on, revealing the paintings.

"I'm speechless."

"I'm sure that's a first." They walked toward the collection in a surreal stillness.

"Where did the sixth one come from?"

She picked up the remote and punched a button to activate the audio system. The sounds of a Mozart symphony quickly filled the room. "I'm surprised your spy didn't tell you when it arrived. I went crazy and cried all afternoon."

"Gabe never mentioned anything about you, really. Only updates about your health and the circles under your eyes. He thought any other information was too intrusive. I wanted to beat the shit out of him a few times, but this was his gig. I couldn't interfere."

"He's a good man. I can't wait to hear his story."

"Enough about Gabe. Tell me about the painting."

"It took a while to track it down. It's by Jacques-Louis David, and he painted it while I was in Paris. The owner didn't want to sell it until I told him the sitter was an ancestor of mine who died during the revolution, and I added a little incentive. I offered him a painting of Jefferson and Lafayette as a bonus. When he looked up the prices of my paintings, he decided he was getting a fantastic deal. So he sold it. I would have paid twice what it was worth."

"Now you have the painting you went back to get."

She stood in front of the painting, fondly recalling those summer afternoons at the Hôtel de Langeac. "Yes, I have the painting, and so much more." She stood on tiptoes and kissed his cheek. "So much more."

48

Fraser Castle, Scotland—Pete

PETE WALKED OUT of Fraser Castle zipping up his down parka, shivering.

He could be in Sydney, where it was eighty degrees. But no. Elliott wanted him in cold Scotland for a week of face-to-face planning sessions. After sending his stallions to New South Wales for more than three decades, Elliott recently decided if his horses were going to stand their Southern Hemisphere seasons near Sydney, he no longer wanted to lease an equine facility. He wanted MacCorp to own it. This was Shane's project, but every stallion there had a full book, and with so many mares coming in, it was impossible for Shane to leave right now.

But here he was, freezing his damn balls off. Might as well freeze 'em. They weren't doing him any good. He couldn't remember the last time he had sex. It was long before he discovered Sophia was missing. Since then he'd had no desire for anyone else. Even his therapist told him not to rush into a relationship. It would happen when the time was right. On the flight over, he thought he was getting close. If he met someone at a bar or cafe, he'd ask her out. Or maybe one of McBain's "sisters" had a sister. According to family lore, he used to have one in every city in Scotland.

Pete's phone beeped with a text message: *Meet me in the barn. E.*

What the hell was Elliott doing out there? He no longer kept riding horses on the property since the kids all wanted to go ATVing. So now the stalls were filled with all-terrain vehicles of varying sizes and speeds.

Pete stepped inside the barn. "Elliott!"

"Down here, lad," Elliott said, his voice echoing off the walls of the stone barn.

Pete followed the voice toward the far end, where he found a groom hitching two bay Clydesdales to a red sleigh with a bundled-up four year old in the driver's seat.

"Hi, Uncle Pete."

"Hi, buddy. Where are your parents?"

"Daddy and I were reading *The Wonky Donkey* to wee Lawrence—hee haw—but he had to jump on a con-frence call."

"Wee Lawrence?" Pete asked.

"No silly. Daddy did. Wee Lawrence can't talk, but he wants to eat all…day…long. Daddy and I can't feed him because…you know…we don't have"—Blane patted his chest—"the right 'quipment. So now I'm out here helping Grandpa Elliott."

Pete laughed at Blane's fast-talking charm. "I'm sure you're a big help with wee Lawrence." Pete glanced at Elliott. "So what's up?"

"Well, it's like this." Elliott followed behind the sleigh as the groom drove it out of the stall and out the back door. "Meredith and I have been out cross-country skiing every day this week about this time of day."

"Me too," Blane said. "I went skiing yesterday. But I got tired and Grandpa Elliott had to bring me back. You have to have strong legs to ski. Trainer Ted said he'd help me get stronger."

Pete chucked Blane under the chin. "You sure you want that kind of punishment? Trainer Ted can be mean."

"He's not really mean, Uncle Pete. He just wants you to follow his plan. If you don't …well, he yells. That's why I always do what he tells me."

"I'll have to remember that advice." He looked at Elliott again. "So, finish your story. It's colder than hell out here."

"Hell's not cold, Uncle Pete. It's hot. You know, hotter than hell."

"Okay. It's cold enough to freeze my ass off. How's that?"

"Well, that's cold." Blane rubbed his butt. "I've got ski pants on. My ass isn't cold."

Elliott chuckled. "Lad, I have to remind ye to watch yer language." Then to Pete he said, "Every time we've been out skiing, we've seen this woman walking by herself around Loch Lomond—"

"I didn't see her," Blane said.

"That's because ye got tired and had to come home," Elliott said. "Meredith even saw her at a café in town, and she wasn't wearing a ring."

"Okay. So what?"

"She's in her late thirties, athletic. A real looker. The kind of lass ye want to take home to mom. The warm and natural kind. Ye know what I mean? Meredith thought ye should go meet her and invite her to dinner."

"Everybody will be here tonight, Uncle Pete."

"If this lass can tolerate a castle full of screaming babies and toddlers, ye might find yerself an interesting woman worth taking out a second time." Elliott held out the reins. "Give it a go, lad. It might turn out to be something. Might not. But at least ye put yerself out there. And the next time will be easier."

Pete looked at the reins and shook his head. "I'm not driving that. Horses hate me. I'll take one of the ATVs."

"Nope. It has to be the sleigh. Grandma Mere said you need to make the right…" Blane glanced up as if searching for a word.

"Impression," Elliott said. "She's the marketing and branding expert, so she should know."

"If I was marketing or branding something, I'd take her advice," Pete said.

Elliott held out the reins. "If ye don't do this Meredith's way, I'll catch hell. And if I catch hell, so will ye. Do us both a favor and take the damn sleigh."

Pete looked at the Clydesdales' docks and tails. "This better be worth it." He yanked the reins out of Elliott's hands. "Hop out, Blane, and somebody tell me how the hell you drive this thing."

Blane didn't move. "Go cluck-cluck or kiss-kiss and snap the reins. It's easy, Uncle Pete. Even I can drive it. To stop, pull back and say whoa."

Elliott rested his hand on Pete's shoulder. "I took Meredith for a ride shortly after I met her. She was putty in my hands. But if ye ever tell her I told ye, ye're fired."

"You can't fire me. I own part of MacCorp."

"I'm Chairman of the Board of MacKlenna Corporation until the day I die. I can make yer life miserable."

Pete lifted Blane out of the sleigh, set him down next to Elliott, and climbed in, shifting slightly to find a comfortable position on the hard leather seat. "You already have, old man. I could be in sunny Sydney right now."

"Don't ye dare call me old."

Blane shook his finger at Pete. "Don't call Grandpa Elliott old. He doesn't like it. But all grandpas and grandmas are old. It goes with the job."

Elliott looked down at his grandson and grimaced. "So ye're calling me old too?"

Blane clasped Elliott's hand and smiled up at him. "Just calling it like I see it, Grandpa."

Elliott grinned like an idiot.

The groom returned with a pile of wool blankets and stacked them on the seat next to Pete. Then Elliott handed him a flask. "Take this, but don't drink it all before ye meet her. A sip or two for courage won't hurt. But if ye drink too much out in the cold, yer dick won't work right and ye'll be pissed as hell."

"Sometimes Elliott, your charm overwhelms me."

Elliott barked a laugh. "I've thanked the Lord every day since ye and the O'Gradys stormed into my life. Now get yer ass out of here."

"Wait." Blane ran across the barn and grabbed a cowboy hat sitting atop a hay bale. "Here, wear Uncle Matt's cowboy hat."

Pete pulled the well-worn hat down low over his forehead. "I got the jeans, boots, and now the hat."

Blane smiled. "This time you'll bring back the girl."

Pete trembled, every muscle tensed, his whole body in the grip of some powerful emotion, a combination of sadness and regret that he'd failed twice. "I didn't do so good last time, did I?"

Blane tried to wink at him and instead blinked both eyes. "Everybody needs a second chance. Right, Grandpa?"

Elliott swooped Blane into his arms and kissed his cherry-colored cheek. "Aye, even an old grandpa."

Pete rolled his eyes. "What are these two monsters called?"

"Highlander Spirit and Winter Jubilee," Elliott said.

"Those sound like racehorse names."

"Yeah, but that's a hell of a lot better than Fred and Ginger."

Blane patted Highlander Spirit's withers. "Take Pete to find the girl."

Laughing, Pete drove the sleigh away from the castle and into the winter forest, deeply breathing in the chilly, pine-scented air, listening to the gray-spotted woodpeckers, catching glimpses of red deer, until the world seemed reduced to its essentials.

He wasn't ready to admit he was glad he flew twenty-one hours to get here, but he did love the Highlands—the people, the mountains, the traditions. It was like nowhere else in the world.

When he reached Loch Lomond, the beauty was simply stunning. The turquoise blue water rippled crystal clear. His neck itched, and he scratched it, but it didn't go away. His radar was pinging. Not to warn him of danger, but something else…something he couldn't put his finger on.

He scanned the horizon. Not another soul within miles. He was soaking up God's country all by himself.

"Crap." No mystery woman. He must've missed her. And he'd gotten himself all worked up to meet someone. Maybe he'd go into town later and ask around. Stop by the café, the bookstore. Maybe he could find her.

"Cluck. Cluck." He snapped the reins and drove the sleigh along the path skirting the loch. If he followed it, eventually he'd be on the path back to the castle. After sucking in airplane air for so long, the fresh air lifted his spirits.

He was driving straight into the morning sun, so he pulled his hat lower to shade his eyes. He squinted. Someone was coming his way, but he couldn't tell if it was a man or a woman.

As he got closer, his radar exploded. *Impossible. It can't be.*

He pulled back on the reins. "Whoa." And he sat there as a silent tear streaked down his face.

Damn you, Elliott. How could you keep this a secret?

If he didn't do something to control his emotions, he'd start blubbering like an idiot. He tied off the reins and jumped out.

"Are you the girl Elliott sent me to find?" God, she looked incredible, poured into a red snowsuit with a white beanie, her long hair gathered and draped over one shoulder.

"Probably." She glanced around. "I don't see anyone else."

How was he going to play this? If he touched her, she might dissolve as his images of her had throughout the years. And if she was real, he'd strip her in the snow and make love until they both froze to death.

No. Too drastic. Play for the laugh and go from there.

He scooped up a handful of snow, formed a perfect, ice-hard snowball, and drew back his arm.

"Don't you dare, Peter Francis Parrino." Sophia took off running, screaming, "Don't you dare throw that. I *hate* snowball fights."

God, he loved her, but damn it, he was going to throw it anyway. She should have called him. It hit her smack in the middle of her back. She scooped up a handful of snow and made her own ball.

"You're gonna pay for that." She ran toward him and threw it, hitting him in the chest.

He tossed his hat on top of the pile of blankets, laughing. "Excellent example of a girly throw, Soph. I taught you to hurl better than that." He picked up more snow to make another ball and so did she.

She threw hers first and ran away. "Don't hit me. Don't hit me.

You throw too hard."

"You didn't think so when we had snowball fights in Central Park."

"I was younger then."

Instead of throwing the snowball, he tackled her, and she giggled like a school girl as they rolled downhill, the air crackling all around them with sexual energy, hot enough to melt all the snow surrounding Loch Lomond. Her beanie came off and her hair entangled him as they rolled and rolled, finally coming to rest near the sleigh.

He captured her mouth, and the kiss he gave her was a promise of unleashed passion. Suddenly his fingers were in her hair, gripping strands of it. He was pulling her closer and closer still while small wanting sounds vibrated up from deep within her throat, driving him insane. He instantly went hard against her. If he didn't stop, he'd lose himself right there in the snow like a horny teenager.

Her face was mere inches from his, and every memory of her, the slight part of her lips when she was turned on, the pink in her cheeks, the glaze over her eyes, the tautness of her chin, were dead on. He stroked his thumb along her jawline and down to the collar of her snowsuit. He unzipped it to kiss her neck, and he couldn't stop himself. He kept tugging the zipper lower and lower. And all he found was skin.

But he stopped.

Because there were things he needed to know first. He rolled off, tucked his arm under his head, and lay beside her in the snow. "When did you come back, and why?"

She turned to look at him. "I told Thomas I was from the future."

"That was brave."

"I had to. My brooch heated up."

Pete almost wept at that news, because it meant she wasn't supposed to be there.

"I asked Mr. MacKlenna what I should do. He said to tell Thomas where I was from. I did, and Thomas told me he couldn't live with someone who knew the future, who knew the date of his death. He said he would never have to solve another problem because I already knew what was going to happen."

Pete rolled over on his side and stroked the line of her jaw and down her neck again, gazing into her eyes. "The important part was, your brooch heated up. Jefferson wasn't your soul mate."

She cupped his face. "The brooch knew my heart better than I did. In hindsight, I was so caught up in the idea of being considered an Old Master, a First Lady, the wife of Thomas Jefferson, and a grandmother. It was all heady stuff. But it wasn't heart stuff. You've always had my heart, Pete. Always."

Everything was wild and fresh and eroding his balance. Thank God he was already on the ground, because he knew his legs wouldn't support him. And then she was kissing him back, her mouth both pliant and demanding. Desperate for more, he changed the angle of the kiss, then nipped restlessly at her bottom lip just to hear her low, throaty moans.

He reached inside her jacket to touch her, caress her—.

"You don't have anything on under this. You'll freeze your ass." He had to get her out of the cold. And if he didn't get himself out of the cold, he'd shrink to nothing.

"I didn't think I'd need anything on under this."

She arched her head to one side, inviting his lips to slide down the column of her throat, an invitation he accepted.

"I haven't been out here long enough to get cold. Gabriele dropped me just a few yards from where you first saw me."

"Gabriele?"

"You know…the guy who broke into my apartment and stole the *Mona Lisa*."

"He didn't steal it."

She moaned. "I know. I'm just giving you a hard time."

"I'm hard enough."

She moaned louder. "I love it when you talk naughty like that." Her eyes were liquid with desire, her lips full and reddened.

He kissed her softly, without the urgency pulsing through him. "You haven't changed a bit."

"Not with you. You complete my circle. You always have."

He kissed her forehead, her eyelids, then covered her mouth with his, caressing her lips lightly with his tongue. The experience of her body beneath him simply filled his mind—a place of no thoughts, no words. He didn't break the kiss until he pulled away and began a slow descent with his tongue and lips down the column of her throat.

"I couldn't have made it through the last few months without him."

Pete forgot who they were talking about. "Without who?"

"Whom. Gabriele."

"I'm kissing your neck and you're talking about another man. How many times did he hit on you?"

"He never did. He was always a perfect gentleman. I thought he was just a delivery guy who was extra nice. Turned out he was your friend who only wanted to take care of me in your absence. Matter of fact, the sleigh ride was his idea."

Pete stared at her, puzzled. "That's weird. He knows horses don't like me."

"You'll have to ask him."

"Gabe's a hell of a good friend. I'm glad he was there for you. In fact, I can't wait to hear this story. But how'd you know I was on my way down here?"

"Elliott sent a text as soon as you drove off. He planned it all down to the second, even your air travel."

"Son of a bitch."

"Well, they tricked me, too. Got me on an airplane under false pretenses. I was going to wait a few more weeks before I called you."

"I'm glad they tricked you, then." He couldn't take his eyes off her and her creamy skin.

"Are you just going to stare at me, or are you going to kiss me some more? It's a little drafty."

"I want to make a meal of you, and I want you to make a meal of me, but right now I'm not going to kiss you again until I have you naked in a bed." He pulled her to her feet. "Where's Gabe? He can take the sleigh and I'll take his car."

She pointed up ahead. "He had an errand to run, but said he'd be right back and would meet us around the bend."

"You know what this means, don't you?"

"I have a pretty good idea."

"Where's your hotel?"

"Jack made the reservation. I don't know where."

"I'll tell Gabe to cancel Jack's reservation, and I'll make a different one for us. I don't want anyone to know where we are."

"We have to go to dinner tonight. Elliott made me promise we'd show up. We don't have to stay all evening, but they want us there. And I can't wait to meet all the kids."

"The kids go with the parents, so you'll have to put up with them, too."

"I've met them all."

"When?"

"Last night. We had dinner at Louise and Evelyn's B&B in Edinburgh. Gabriele and I had rooms there, but everyone else came back to the castle."

"While I was in the air, you all were celebrating."

She kissed him, and their passion was so explosive, so well matched. She grabbed the lapels of his jacket and kissed him again with rising urgency, and he responded, disregarding their surroundings and the immediate world until one of the horses snorted and forced him to remember where they were.

"Just tell me Maria is planning a big Italian dinner tonight."

She pulled back, her eyes widening. "You're thinking of food while I'm standing here with my jacket open, exposing myself?"

He slowly zipped up her snowsuit, barely resisting the urge to do just the opposite. "If I don't think of food or something else, I might embarrass myself."

She looked down at the bulge in his jeans and cocked her head slightly. "Am I imagining things or are you…bigger?"

"Let's stick to food."

Sophia laughed. "Maria said she has to cook a few Scottish dishes, but she's preparing all your favorites."

"Great sex. Delicious food and wine. And more great sex." He picked up her beanie and tugged it onto her head. "Damn. You look exactly like the picture I've carried in my mind all these years." He swooped her up into his arms and kissed her. He could barely pull his mouth away long enough to set her down on the sleigh's bench and cover her with layers of wool blankets.

He pulled the flask from his jacket pocket. "How about a nip of whisky?"

She reached for it. "Carrying a flask is a bold personal statement."

"I always thought it showed practical forethought with a flair for the dramatic."

She sipped and shivered, wheezing. "Wow. Potent."

He kissed her forehead and cheeks, chin and lips, savoring the taste of whisky in her mouth. "God you taste good." He placed Matt's hat back on his head, adjusting it until he had its brim at just the right angle, then he slipped in beside her and gathered the reins. "If I don't get you in bed within the next fifteen minutes, we're going to try out this bench seat."

She bounced up and down. "I'd prefer a bed, but if you want to give this a go, I'm game."

"You always were. But nope. Not this time. I'm going to act responsibly for both of us. We can wait a few more minutes. After all, we've waited twenty years."

"Well, I can't wait. I'm in a hurry. Give me the reins. I want to drive."

"You hate horses."

She slid the reins out of his hands. "I'm still not completely fond of them, but I'm better than I was." He put his arm around her, and they rode off into the sunset.

Well, the sun wasn't setting, and to be honest he couldn't care less. She turned to look at him and he captured her mouth in a sensuous kiss that held years of pent-up desire and longing—a kiss meant to last forever.

She pulled back on the reins. "I thought you were in a hurry."

Her mouth was soft and warm, and she leaned into him eagerly. He didn't want to stop, but he wanted her too much to continue. "Give me the damn reins." He snapped them, and Highlander Spirit and Winter Jubilee trotted off through the snow.

Sophia removed her beanie and tossed it into the air, laughing. "What could be better than driving away in a Norman Rockwell painting?"

"Driving away with me, Soph. What was lost has been found again."

49

New York City (Fourteen Months Later)—Elliott

ELLIOTT STOOD AT the back of the Hayes Theater on 44th Street in New York City. He'd spent the first forty-five minutes of Jack and Matt's three-men, one-act play, *Dinner on Maiden Lane,* sitting next to Meredith in their box holding her hand, but he was too damn nervous to sit still for the remainder of the play.

There'd been five preview shows to work out the kinks, and finally officially opened tonight. You would have thought he was the playwright or director, not the producer. He had money in the game, so it was a tax write-off for him, but Jack had skin in the game. If the play flopped, it could hurt his brand and book sales.

Jack had spotted several theatre critics and was now backstage biting his nails. He was a hell of a lot more sensitive about his reputation than Elliott, who'd been known for years as an arrogant son of a bitch.

Sophia scooted in beside him and stood there rubbing her barely noticeable baby bump. It had taken her and Pete three fertility cycles using her frozen eggs to get pregnant, but now they had a healthy fetus and five more months to go.

The baby wasn't her worry tonight, though. Following the play, two hundred and fifty people—art critics and serious collectors— were also invited to a private champagne exhibition entitled *Thomas*

Jefferson and The Beginning of the Republic. The collection consisted of thirty-six paintings from the sketches she'd drawn during her time in the past, and Lisa's sculptures of Jefferson, Washington, Adams, Hamilton, Madison, and John Jay.

Sophia was also the set designer for the production. Who better to design the room where it happened than one of the people who were there? When the curtain first opened, there had been a collective gasp at the sight of the elegant set design. Sophia had every piece made to replicate Thomas's fixtures, furnishings, draperies, and wallpaper. The set was as authentic as it could be.

"Where's Pete?" Elliott asked.

"He went next door. Said he wanted to check a few details. He's more nervous than I am."

Elliott knew exactly why Pete went next door. It was a surprise for Sophia. Tonight was the culmination of months of hard work and dedication, and Pete had something special for her.

Elliott was so proud of all of them.

As soon as the curtain dropped, critics' reviews would post on the website "New York Stage Review" at the same time reviews would post at traditional media outlets, so they wouldn't have to stay up all night waiting for the news.

The director, David Tillman, joined them at the back of the house. "We have a hit," he said.

"How do ye know?" Elliott asked.

"I've been watching the audience. They're mesmerized. No one is fidgeting or checking their watches. Everyone will want to know the same thing I asked Jack and Matt. 'It's so real. Where'd the material come from?' You're going to get the same questions when the art critics see the exhibition. The paintings are phenomenal. And to open the play and exhibition the same night is brilliant. Look, I've got to go. I'll see you next door." David disappeared into the darkness.

Tillman wasn't fooling Elliott. The man was as nervous as everybody else. This business was a crapshoot. Just like horse racing. You think you have a winner, but you never know until critics post their reviews, or a horse crosses the finish line.

"Let's go up to the box and get out of the crowd. I don't want ye knocked over in the rush to exit the theatre."

Elliott escorted Sophia up the stairs, and they reached the box just as the final lines were delivered. The curtain closed and opened again to thunderous applause. When theatregoers leapt to their feet, Elliott knew Tillman was right. They had a hit.

The MacKlenna Clan, except for the kids who stayed home, and Robert and Lisa Harrison, filtered out through the back entrance and entered through the rear of Sardi's next door.

Waiters were already circulating, serving hors d'oeuvres and champagne in the upstairs special events room, which was packed with works of art, patrons, and large vases of fresh flowers. A string quartet playing Beethoven could be heard over the chatter and laughter.

"Come here a minute," Elliott said to Sophia. He escorted her into a small room where a painting covered by a sheet stood on an easel with a single light shining above it.

"What's this?" she asked.

Pete came in behind her. "This is for you, Soph. Matt found it, Elliott made all the arrangements, and I bought it. I figured tonight was the best time to give it to you."

"A painting?" She clapped. "What a wonderful surprise. Let me see it."

Elliott removed the sheet, and the white silk shimmied to the floor.

Sophia's hands went to her face, covering her mouth, as she sucked in a deep, shuddering breath. She wobbled, but Pete held her steady. "Where did Matt find this?" She walked up close to the painting and touched the frame. "What a wonderful gift." She kissed Pete. "Thank you. I started this when I was on the *Clermont* during our journey to America."

She gazed fondly at the painting. "I finished it at Mallory Plantation during the winter of 1789 and sent it to Captain Colley, the captain of the *Clermont,* as a thank-you gift."

Matt and Elizabeth waltzed into the room. Elliott had never seen the lawyer/historian float on air, but that's what he was doing. "It's an absolutely riveting, psychologically absorbing painting, Sophia," Matt said.

"How'd you find it? Of all the paintings I did, this was the one I never thought would survive."

"A couple of years ago I read an article in *The New York Times* about the renovation of a house in Amagansett. They discovered a closet behind a built-in bookcase, and the painting was in there with pieces of early American furniture. Pete bought it at a private auction, had it restored, and here it is."

"Thank you all so much. This is so amazing. I guess it will give the art critics another example of how I paint just like the eighteenth-century Sophia Orsini."

Jack entered the room holding Amy's hand. "Sophia, you need to get out there. The art critics are asking for you." Then he whispered, "You've got your story down, right?"

"Several nights of vivid dreams after seeing *Hamilton: An American Musical.*"

"Okay, good luck," Jack said.

Sophia gave Matt and Elliott a hug and, holding Pete's hand, walked out to meet her critics.

Meredith kissed Elliott. "The night's a huge success. The play, the art, Lance and Ruth taking their first steps. It's a night for the history books."

"I have to say, tonight almost beats winning the Triple Crown."

"Nothing beats that. Come on. The photographer is waiting for you."

He hand-pressed the front of his tuxedo jacket. "How do I look?"

"Like a Scottish studmuffin. Your legs are as sexy as ever."

"It's because these kilt hose cover the scars."

They walked out into the exhibition space. He was one of nine—Kevin, David, Cullen, Braham, Daniel, James Cullen, Lincoln, and Noah—wearing formal Scottish attire. It seemed appropriate on a night like this for the men to be kilted. Without the Celtic brooches, none of this would have been possible. Not the play. Not the art. And especially not the brides, all wearing dresses made from Fraser, Montgomery, McCabe, McBain, Grant, or Digby plaids.

Jack came over with his iPad, grinning hugely. "Read this."

Elliott put on his glasses. "'The high school American history class field trip is about to become a thing of the past. When high schoolers—or theatre patrons of any age—cast their eyes and ears on Jack Mallory and Matt Kelly's amazing, multilayered one-act play *Dinner on Maiden Lane,* you can bet your two-dollar bills that Hamilton, Madison, and Jefferson become more than historical characters to them. Mallory and Kelly, teaming with director David Tillman, have a connection to this material bordering on supernatural possession...'" Elliott glanced up and removed his glasses. "Ye've got yerself a hit. Congratulations."

Beaming, Jack said, "We sure do!" Before taking the iPad to share the review with the others, he hugged Elliott. "Thanks for everything. And I mean—everything."

Meredith kissed Elliott on the lips. "Congratulations. You were ahead of the curve on this one. I thought a small local theatre would work best. But not you. You were convinced the play deserved to start at the top. All I can say is, thank goodness we bought Amy's house on Riverside Drive. If we'd had to stay in hotels, we would have spent more on housing than on the production."

Elliott wrapped his arm around her and held her close. "We've had a good run this year. It's been a joy to watch Lance and Ruth grow and thrive, and I'm not the only one still amazed at how they hit all motor, language, and social and emotional milestones. And Amy and Olivia had healthy babies. Rick did a super job with the winery reopening, and sales are almost back to what they were before the fire. Pete and Sophia had their church wedding. Amber's business is skyrocketing. The kids are excelling, and I'm about to retire."

"Promises, promises. You say that once a month," Meredith said.

"Maybe, but so do ye."

"Rick's in a position to take over the winery, but let's talk about it later. Tonight is for the kids. Look at them. They're all so happy."

"Because they're all drunk. Didn't ye hear all the bitching this afternoon?"

"I was there, remember? They all want to take the company in different directions. I thought David and Braham were going to punch each other out."

"Look at them now. True Scotsmen."

Meredith looked over at the two men toasting each other. "Got to love 'em."

At midnight, waiters served Glenmorangie, and pipers marched into the room playing "Scotland the Brave," and there wasn't a dry eye in the place. By the end of the musical program all the sculptures were sold, and there was only one painting without a sold sign—a two-hundred-year-old portrait of Thomas Jefferson standing at the helm of the *Clermont*.

When the room thinned to only family members, Meredith said, "Let's go home, Elliott. It's been a long day, and this crew will be here celebrating till dawn."

Elliott sent a text to his driver to pick them up in the alley. A few minutes later, he and Meredith said good night and left through the rear door. Before it closed, he looked back at all the couples hugging and laughing.

"Good night, lads and lassies. May God hold all of you and all the wee ones at home in the palm of his hand."

THE END

ABOUT THE AUTHOR

Katherine graduated from Rowan University in New Jersey, where she earned a BA in Psychology with a minor in Criminal Justice. Following college, she returned to Central Kentucky, where she worked as a real estate and tax paralegal.

Katherine is a marathoner and lives in Lexington, Kentucky. When she's not running or writing romance, she's enjoying her five grandchildren: Charlotte Lyle, Lincoln Thomas, James Cullen, Henry Patrick, and Meredith Lyle, and a dog named Ripley.

Please stop by and visit Katherine on her social media sites or drop her an email. She loves to hear from readers.

Website
www.katherinellogan.com

Facebook
facebook.com/katherine.l.logan

Twitter
twitter.com/KathyLLogan

I'm A Runner (Runner's World Magazine Interview)
www.runnersworld.com/celebrity-runners/im-a-runner-katherine-lowry-logan

Email:
KatherineLLogan@gmail.com

Family trees are available on Katherine's website
www.katherinellogan.com/books/the-celtic-brooch-family-trees

*   *   *

THE CELTIC BROOCH SERIES

THE RUBY BROOCH (Book 1)
Kitherina MacKlenna and Cullen Montgomery's love story

THE LAST MACKLENNA (Book 2 – not a time travel story)
Meredith Montgomery and Elliott Fraser's love story

THE SAPPHIRE BROOCH (Book 3)
Charlotte Mallory and Braham McCabe's love story

THE EMERALD BROOCH (Book 4)
Kenzie Wallis-Manning and David McBain's love story

THE BROKEN BROOCH (Book 5 – not a time travel story)
JL O'Grady and Kevin Allen's love story

THE THREE BROOCHES (Book 6)
A reunion with Kit and Cullen Montgomery

THE DIAMOND BROOCH (Book 7)
Jack Mallory and Amy Spalding's love story

THE AMBER BROOCH (Book 8)
Amber Kelly and Daniel Grant's love story
Olivia Kelly and Connor O'Grady's love story

THE PEARL BROOCH (Book 9)
Sophia Orsini and Pete Parrino's love story

There are many more Brooch Books to come! Shane, Rick, and Gabe need to find their soul mates, and there's another generation ready for their own adventures!

If you would like to receive notification of future releases
sign up today at KatherineLLogan.com or
send an email to KatherineLLogan@gmail.com and put
"New Release" in the subject line

*   *   *

Thank you for reading THE PEARL BROOCH.
I hope you enjoyed reading this story as much as I enjoyed writing it.
Reviews help other readers find books.
I appreciate all reviews, whether positive or negative.

AUTHOR NOTES

In March 2016 I saw *Hamilton: An American Musical* on Broadway.

The music is simply brilliant. I listen to the songs when I work, run, and drive my car. When my granddaughter, Meredith, gets in the car with me, if the album isn't playing, she turns it on. Hamilton's story is so much more than his duel with Aaron Burr, which is the only thing I remember from high school history classes.

Once the music was in my head, I knew I wanted to write a story that included the Founding Fathers, but I was already committed to writing The Pearl Brooch, a story about an Italian painter. While researching female artists, I stumbled upon Maria Cosway, an Italian-English musician, society hostess, and portraitist. Her dear friend was Angelica Schuyler Church, Alexander Hamilton's sister-in-law.

Wow! A connection to the Founding Fathers.

Then I discovered Cosway was rumored to be the love of Thomas Jefferson's life. The more I read about Jefferson, the more interested I became, and decided to focus on him instead of Hamilton. The day I referred to Jefferson as Thomas, I knew I had a story to tell.

Keeping all the balls in the air was indeed a challenge. And finding a way to tell a love story without the hero and heroine showing up on the same page until the end was a huge obstacle to overcome. If I wrote the story the way it was demanding, it would throw out the blueprint I've used in the other books—girl goes missing, hero goes to rescue her, and all sorts of bad stuff happens until they find their happily ever after. In this story a rescue wasn't even necessary.

The deeper I dug into Sophia's backstory and passion for art, the more I grew to love her. I think Sophia had repressed her emotions for so long that she was able to continue putting her art before her own true happiness. The idea of being considered the only female Old Master was too compelling for her to walk away from.

The Brooch books always surprise me. I never know where my muse is going to take me or what it intends to reveal. Each one is a wonderful journey. The revelations about the brooch history and Mr. Digby were as much a surprise to me as they probably were to you.

I traveled to Florence in May 2018. One of the tours I scheduled was a wine and dinner tour which included dinner at the Osteria Toscanella. After the meal, we walked down the cobblestone street past the Studio d'Arte Toscanella. I backed up, went in, and introduced myself to the owner/artist Lukas Brändli. The next morning, I had a three-hour art lesson with Lukas.

Originally from Switzerland, Lukas moved to Florence in 2003 seeking a classical artistic education at The Florence Academy of Art. He paints and exhibits in Switzerland, France, and Italy. In 2014 he opened Studio d'Arte Toscanella.

When I returned home, I sent him an email and asked if I could put his studio on the cover. He happily agreed and created a picture. I was a little slow to understand his concept, but while gazing at the picture one day, I slapped my forehead, just like Blane. The bicycle mirrors the brooch.

And that's not the only mirror.

There are three overarching ones: JL and Sophia's storylines of fear and holding on to hope, Sophia's forced separation from Pete and later from Jefferson, and her travel by ship to America mirrored her flight to Italy as a seventeen-year-old.

My deep dive into Jefferson's life—America's first foodie and wine connoisseur—revealed a man full of contradictions, but I couldn't help being swept into his orbit. He inherited debt, spent a great deal of money on Monticello, and died in debt. His positions on religion and women are well documented, and I (or Sophia) enjoyed debating with him.

For more information on Jefferson, check out the Th Jefferson Monticello website.

The events on Bastille Day are close to what actually happened. The real rescuer of the woman almost set on fire was Aubin Bonnemer, but for story purposes I changed it to artist Jacques-Louis David, who was an active participant in the revolution. He has a very interesting history. Mr. Watin is a creation of my imagination.

The Hôtel de Langeac was demolished in 1842. There's a plaque on the corner of the Champs-Élysées and the rue de Berri to mark its location. If you're in Paris, see if you can find it and send me a picture!

Mr. Petit was encouraged to come to America, and he served as Jefferson's *maître d'hôtel* in Philadelphia until Mr. Petit returned to France in 1794.

The trip from Paris to Norfolk was documented by Jefferson and others he met along the way. The fire on the *Clermont* did happen and none of their belongings were destroyed. I removed the girls' luggage for ease of explanation.

I talked to several women who had preemies and JL's experiences were a compilation of what they went through. MacKenzie Hicks, who was the inspiration for our beloved Kenzie McBain, is a NICU nurse at Cincinnati Children's Hospital. She was a fantastic resource.

When I was in Paris last summer, I met Sherrin Hersch from New York City, who was visiting Paris with her granddaughter. I sent Sherrin my French dialogue for corrections. The mistakes, if any, are my own!

I am deeply indebted to Dr. Ken Muse, retired Chief of Endocrinology at the University of Kentucky. Ken has walked me through all the medical disasters in the Brooch books and always comes up with an interesting little plot twist.

I couldn't have made it through this book without the help, guidance, and assistance of my fantastic Editor Faith Freewoman and my Virtual Assistant/Story Development Consultant Annette Glahn, along with three awesome beta readers: Robin Davis Epstein, Marjorie Lague, and Paula Retelsdorf.

What's next for the clan? I'm tossing around a contemporary romance set in Napa with Rick and Wilhelmina Penelope Malone, as well as a long historical with Shane and the opal brooch possibly set in Australia. My sweet spot seems to be America in the 19th century so we'll see where the topaz takes us. And we might be back in Italy for Gabe's story. But one thing is for sure, there will be more than twelve brooches. I can't wait to tell Robbie and Henry's stories. Can you imagine them as thirty-year-olds? I can't!

Nor can I imagine writing a book outside the MacKlenna world, so as long as you keep reading, I'll keep writing!

Blessings to all, *Katherine*

40527221R00345

Made in the USA
Middletown, DE
27 March 2019